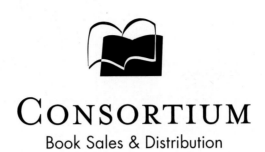

CONSORTIUM
Book Sales & Distribution

Where **Independent Publishers** Live

Fall / Winter 2007–2008

Congratulations to all our award winners!

2007 ALA Notable Book

Firmin
*Adventures of a
Metropolitan Lowlife*
Sam Savage
Illustrated by
Michael Mikolowski
Coffee House Press
TP $14.95
978-1-56689-181-3 CUSA

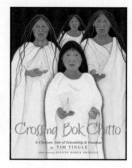

**2007 ALA Notable Book
for Middle Readers**

Crossing Bok Chitto
Tim Tingle
Illustrated by
Jeanne Rorex Bridges
Cinco Puntos Press
TC $17.95
978-0-938317-77-7 CUSA

2006 *New York Times* 100 Notable Books

Gate of the Sun
Elias Khoury
Translated by
Humphrey Davies
Archipelago Books
TC $26.00
978-0-9763950-2-7 CUSA

Old Filth
Jane Gardam
Europa Editions
TP $14.95
978-1-933372-13-6 USA

2007 Miriam Bass Award: Melville House
Congratulations to Valerie Merians and Dennis Loy Johnson, winners of the
2007 Miriam Bass Award for Creativity in Independent Publishing.

Valerie Merians and Dennis Loy Johnson

Recent Award Winners

2007 Pulitzer Prize for Drama

Rabbit Hole
A Play
David Lindsay-Abaire

"An intensely emotional examination of grief, laced with wit, insightfulness, compassion and searing honesty . . . an uncommonly affecting and absorbing play."—*Variety*

"The sad, sweet release of *Rabbit Hole* lies precisely in the access it allows to the pain of others. . . . This anatomy of grief [taps] a reservoir of feelings common to anyone who has experienced the vacuum left by a death in the family."—*The New York Times*

A story of loss, heartbreak, and forgiveness—told through daily moments and emotional hurdles—as a family moves on after the accidental death of their four-year-old. With a critically acclaimed Broadway premiere, featuring Cynthia Nixon and Tyne Daly, *Rabbit Hole* has been hailed as an artistic breakthrough for the highly regarded David Lindsay-Abaire. A drama of what comes after tragedy, it captures "the awkward-ness and pain of thinking people faced with an unthinkable sit-uation—and eventually, their capacity for survival" (*USA Today*).

David Lindsay-Abaire is the author of *Fuddy Meers*, *Kimberly Akimbo*, *A Devil Inside*, and *Wonder of the World*. His plays have been produced at theaters throughout the United States and around the world, including Manhattan Theatre Club, Minetta Lane Theatre, Soho Rep, Woolly Mammoth Theatre Company, South Coast Repertory, and the Arts Theatre on London's West End. He is currently working on the Broadway-bound musicals *High Fidelity* and *Shrek*.

Rabbit Hole
A Play
David Lindsay-Abaire
Theatre Communications Group
TP $13.95 | 978-1-55936-290-0 USA

Recent Award Winners

Table of Contents

Visit **www.cbsd.com** for the latest news and a searchable list of all our titles, complete with up-to-date stock information.

To-Do List
Illustrated by Maya Waldman

To-Do List inspires young and old not to take life too seriously. The "tasks" on Maya's to-do list range from the everyday—buy milk, be less messy, go on vacation, make friends, and no fighting—to the exceptional—dance like an octopus, hug flowers, star gaze, smile giant, eat sweets, and count clouds.

Each "task" is adorned with an ink drawing that has been painstakingly hand-rendered in astonishing detail. Soon enough, your own to-do list will include enjoying the novelties found on every page.

Maya Waldman is an illustrator of all things tiny and precise. She is currently spending a year in the Marshall Islands teaching children, swimming in a lagoon, lazing about in a hammock, and eating coconuts. When Maya isn't traveling, she lives in San Francisco.

I bet "speak pineapple" and "climb ice cream cones" aren't on your to-do list!

Children's Fiction
October
7 x 5 | 48 pp
40 B&W illustrations
TC US $12.95 | CAN $15.50
978-0-9741319-5-5 CUSA

Marketing Plans

Co-op available
Advance reader copies

Author Events

San Francisco, CA

Mad Tausig vs the Interplanetary Puzzling Peace Patrol
A Fiendishly Fun Puzzle and Mystery Book for Kids
Ben Tausig
Illustrated by Goopymart

Children's Fiction / Games
6 x 9 | 80 pp
40 B&W illustrations
TP US $7.95 | CAN $9.50
978-0-9741319-4-8 CUSA

Give Me That!
Usa Tanaka

Children's Fiction
9 x 10 | 32 pp
22 Color illustrations
TC US $15.95 | CAN $19.50
978-0-9741319-0-0 CUSA

Lola & Fred
Illustrated by Christoph Heuer

Children's Fiction
8⅜ x 11⅞ | 42 pp
39 Color illustrations
TC US $15.95 | CAN $19.50
978-0-9741319-8-6 CUSA

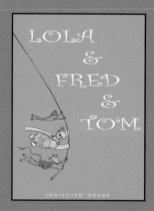

Lola & Fred & Tom
Illustrated by Christoph Heuer

Children's Fiction
8½ x 11⅞ | 48 pp
44 Color illustrations
TC US $15.95 | CAN $19.50
978-0-9741319-9-3 CUSA

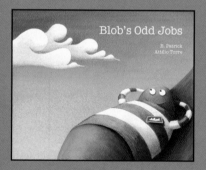

Blob's Odd Jobs
B. Patrick
Illustrated by Attilio Torre

Children's Fiction
10 x 8 | 48 pp
23 Color illustrations
TC US $16.95 | CAN $20.50
978-0-9741319-3-1 CUSA

Is That Funny?
B. Patrick with Leo D. Schotz
Illustrated by L.J. Ruell

Children's Fiction
9⅞ x 8½ | 32 pp
27 Color illustrations
TC US $15.95 | CAN $19.50
978-0-9741319-6-2 CUSA

A&C Black
London, England

A&C Black was formed in 1807 and for over two hundred years has developed a successful and authoritative collection of books encompassing a range of subject areas.

In drama, A&C Black has recently acquired Methuen Drama, which, in addition to its own practical theater list and the New Mermaids series, now makes them one of the United Kingdom's leading drama publishers.

In reference, A&C Black is most famous for publishing *Who's Who* and *Whitaker's Almanac,* both distinguished works of reference known worldwide. A&C Black also incorporates Peter Collins Publishing, which includes subject dictionaries and language titles that are used by students, translators, and professionals around the world.

In business, A&C Black leads the way with a number of key titles and series aimed at business professionals and students alike.

In sports, A&C Black has a range of titles aimed at coaches and players. They are well-known for their martial arts titles and Complete Guide series.

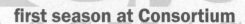

first season at Consortium

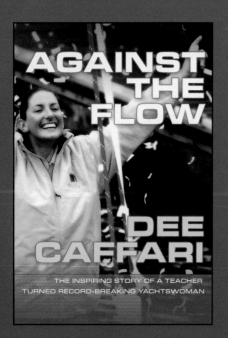

Sports & Recreation /
Biography & Autobiography
September
A Paperback Original
A&C Black
6⅛ x 9¼ | 208 pp
15 Color photographs
TP $16.95
978-0-7136-8533-6 USA

Marketing Plans

Co-op available
15,000-copy print run
Book Sense mailing
National advertising:
Adventure Sports Magazine • The Atlantic
Monthly • Condé Nast Traveler • Earth
First! Journal • Feminist Studies • Frontiers
Newsmagazine • National Geographic
Adventure • The Women's
Review of Books

Against the Flow
The Inspiring Story of a Teacher Turned Record-Breaking Yachtswoman
Dee Caffari

"Dee has inspired the imagination of a worldwide audience. She has joined only four men who have achieved this feat. Other women may follow, but she will always remain the first."—Sir Chay Blyth

This is the inspirational story of an ordinary woman who gave up her career to learn how to sail and become the first woman to circumnavigate the world against the prevailing winds and currents.

Her story is an adventure in the truest sense of the word. It is about physical hardship in terrible conditions, overcoming solitude, sleep deprivation, the worry of crucial equipment failing, thirty-four days of gales, twelve-meter waves, cyclones, and a lightning strike. It is also about a woman who stepped outside her safe zone and gave up a good job and financial security, all because she wanted to sail. She dared to dream, and her courage resulted in a place in the history books alongside a handful of men.

Includes a foreword by James Cracknell, the double Olympic Gold-winning rower.

After an early career as a high school physical education teacher, Dee Caffari realized that her destiny was a life on the water. She gave up her job and worked with Mike Golding Yacht Racing, completing a number of offshore races. During the 2004–2005 Global Challenge Race, Caffari successfully skippered eighteen amateur yachtsmen around the world. In the same seventy-two-foot yacht, *Aviva*, she completed her record-breaking circumnavigation, finishing it on May 18, 2006.

More people have walked on the moon than have successfully completed a westabout circumnavigation.

A&C Black

How Coaching Works
The Essential Guide to the History and Practice of Effective Coaching
Andrea Lages and Joseph O'Connor

HOW COACHING WORKS

THE ESSENTIAL GUIDE TO THE HISTORY
AND PRACTICE OF EFFECTIVE COACHING

Andrea Lages
Joseph O'Connor

This book draws together the themes and principles of coaching, revealing the ideas that work at the root of all successful coaching techniques. It is a must-have for practicing coaches, students, and anyone interested in this increasingly popular subject.

Coaching is very big business. Over the last decade it has become one of the most popular approaches to personal and business development. However, most coaching books tend to focus on just one method, and just one of five main areas: executive coaching (for senior business people), business coaching (for companies to improve results), life coaching (for people who want a better sense of fulfillment and well-being), sports coaching (for individual athletes), and team coaching (for teams in sport or business).

Pragmatic and informative, *How Coaching Works* is the first book to explain the key concepts that underpin *all* of these different areas. It also explores how different ideas have blended together to give rise to what we know as coaching today, and singles out what works.

The book is written by two of the world's leading experts in this field. **Joseph O'Connor** and **Andrea Lages** are co-founders of the International Coaching Community, a community of over one thousand coaches from thirty-one countries. They are experienced coaches and have worked in life, business, and executive coaching. O'Connor is a leading consultant on coaching, training, and neuro-linguistic programming (NLP). He has published twelve best-selling titles, including *Introducing NLP* and *Coaching with NLP*. His work has been translated into eighteen languages.

Coaching—life, executive, business, sports, and team— is the new big business.

Business & Economics /
Organizational Development
January
A Paperback Original
A&C Black
5⅛ x 7¾ | 256 pp
TP $19.95
978-0-7136-8261-8 USA

Marketing Plans

Co-op available
Book Sense mailing
National advertising:
Business Ethics • Newsweek •
Seattle Post-Intelligencer

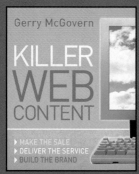

Writing / Business & Economics
September
A Paperback Original
A&C Black
6¾ x 9⅜ | 224 pp
25 Color photographs and charts
TP $24.95
978-0-7136-7704-1 USA

On the Internet, if you're not read, you're dead!

Killer Web Content
Make the Sale, Deliver the Service, Build the Brand
Gerry McGovern

"Genius! Gerry McGovern gets it! If you read one book on managing a website, this is it. A must read for any web manager in any organization, large or small, government or private."—Bev Godwin, director of FirstGov.gov

Written by an internationally acclaimed specialist in this field, *Killer Web Content* provides the strategies and practical techniques you need to get the very best out of your web content. The book helps readers to: provide their website's visitors with the right content at the right time, make sure their website has the best possible chance of getting into the first page of search results, and understand the benefits of blogs, RSS, and e-mail newsletters.

Gerry McGovern (www.gerrymcgovern.com) is a managing partner at a consultancy that focuses on maximizing value from web content.

Marketing Plans
Co-op available • Advance reader copies • Book Sense mailing National advertising: Blue Collar Review • Business Ethics • GreenMoney Journal • The Journal of Popular Culture • Newsweek • NiaOnline.com • North American Review • Perspectives on Anarchist Theory • Publishers Weekly • Sentence • subTerrain Magazine • U.S. News & World Report • The Village Voice • The Writer Magazine • The Writer's Chronicle

---

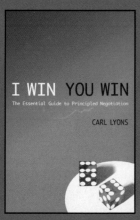

Business & Economics / Management
October
A Paperback Original
A&C Black
4½ x 7 | 224 pp
TP $14.95
978-0-7136-7705-8 USA

Negotiation is an essential skill in all areas of life.

I Win, You Win
The Essential Guide to Principled Negotiation
Carl Lyons

Negotiation is an essential skill in all areas of life. It is a series of maneuvers that we move through in order to get the best possible deal for ourselves, our company, or our organization. How far we will go to achieve our goals is where the rub lies. Full of useful exercises, case studies, and accessible advice, this book will help readers achieve their goals by showing them how to prepare effectively, build rapport, communicate openly, and enhance trust in their business.

Carl Lyons is a life coach and organizational training consultant. He spent ten years working for ICI in a variety of senior roles before setting up his own company, ReCreate. During his time at ICI, Lyons trained executives in the techniques of ethical negotiation. His first book, *Skilful Living*, was published in 2004.

Marketing Plans
National advertising: Business Ethics • GreenMoney Journal • The Journal of Popular Culture

A&C Black

Can I Change Your Mind?
The Craft and Art of Persuasive Writing
Lindsay Camp

"This is a cunning, masterly, and hugely readable book. You'll learn at least as much from how he writes as from what he writes about—and that's saying a great deal." —Jeremy Bullmore, columnist for *Campaign, Management Today,* and the *Guardian*

We all need the ability to argue a case effectively in writing. Drawing on his long experience as a leading copywriter, Lindsay Camp shows how it's done—whether the end product is a glossy magazine ad, a new business proposal, a page for the company website, or just a hasty e-mail to your boss.

Lindsay Camp has been a freelance writer for over twenty years. He began his career at J Walter Thompson, one of the United Kingdom's largest advertising agencies. He has been invited three times to judge the "Writing for Design" category in the D&AD Global Awards, the advertising and design industry's Oscars.

Business & Economics / Writing
October
A Paperback Original
A&C Black
5⅛ x 7¾ | 224 pp
TP $14.95
978-0-7136-7849-9 USA

This book will help get you the results you need, whatever you want to say.

Smoke and Mirrors
How to Bend Facts and Figures to Your Advantage
Nicholas Strange

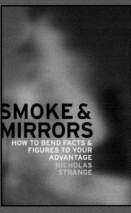

Smoke and Mirrors takes a comprehensive and entertaining look at how charts, graphs, and diagrams can be used to massage a message in business, research, or government without fibbing outright. Using real examples, it describes fifty-seven different techniques of presenting information in a way that supports your angle. Each technique is given a PDQ (potential deceit quotient) as well as an STD (sore thumb discount).

Droll and informative, *Smoke and Mirrors* is a perfect companion for anyone who produces charts and graphs at work, anyone who has them thrust upon them, and anyone who wants to read between the lines.

Nicholas Strange is an independent management consultant. A graduate of the London School of Economics and INSEAD in Fontainebleau, he began his career at McKinsey before becoming director of Ingersoll Engineers, with an international responsibility for graphics and other consultant training.

Business & Economics /
Organizational Development
September
A Paperback Original
A&C Black
6 x 9¼ | 208 pp
TP $19.95
978-0-7136-7924-3 USA

The company report may never look the same again.

Business &
Economics /
Management
September
A Paperback Original
A&C Black
Business on a
Shoestring
4¾ x 6¾ | 208 pp
TP $12.95
978-0-7136-7541-2
USA

Boosting Sales
Bob Gorton

The Business on a Shoestring series helps small business owners grow their business imaginatively, effectively, and without spending a fortune. Aimed at entrepreneurs with vision and commitment but not a lot of cash, each book is packed with ideas that really work, real-life examples, step-by-step advice, and sources of further information.

Boosting Sales will help you make the most of every sales opportunity. With it, you will learn how to look at your current sales and work out where you want to go next, talk to and nurture your existing customers, look for new customers, and respond promptly to prospects.

Business &
Economics /
Management
September
A Paperback Original
A&C Black
Business on a
Shoestring
4¾ x 6¾ | 208 pp
TP $12.95
978-0-7136-7546-7
USA

Marketing and PR
Nick Wilde and Phil Holden

Marketing and PR are essential if you want to spread the good word about your business. You may have the best products and services available, but if no one knows about them, you won't benefit. This book includes: the idea of "promote or die!", knowing your market, creating a marketing plan, investigating niche marketing, writing great marketing copy, getting your press releases noticed, investigating piggyback marketing deals, and getting the best from permission-based e-mail marketing.

Business &
Economics /
Management
September
A Paperback Original
A&C Black
Business on a
Shoestring
4¾ x 6¾ | 208 pp
TP $12.95
978-0-7136-7706-5
USA

Cash Management
Tony Dalton

Understanding your cash flow is vital. *Cash Management* helps you to keep track of how much money you're making (or not). Chapters include: understanding cash flow, knowing where the money is, the rules of credit management, reducing debtor days, influencing non-paying or slow-paying customers, and managing stock.

Business &
Economics /
Management
September
A Paperback Original
A&C Black
Business on a
Shoestring
4¾ x 6¾ | 208 pp
TP $12.95
978-0-7136-7547-4
USA

Surviving a Downturn
Jeremy Kourdi

All businesses go through hardships, but their reaction can make the difference between survival and failure. Realistic but inspiring, this book covers: realizing there's a problem, focusing on what you do best: your core business, spending sensibly, being paid on time, cutting down on inefficiency, steadying the ship and maintaining staff morale, working at external relationships (the bank, customers, suppliers), working out survival tactics (and ways to stick to them), and not letting things slip.

A&C Black Business on a Shoestring Series

Working Ethically
A&C Black

Business &
Economics /
Management
February
A Paperback Original
A&C Black
Business on a
Shoestring
4¾ x 6¾ | 208 pp
TP $12.95
978-0-7136-7548-1
USA

There has never been more interest in working ethically, and many small business owners are leading the way in finding positive solutions that benefit them and their community. This book covers key issues to help you do the same by offering invaluable advice on: creating an ethical strategy for your business, finding suppliers who share your aims, banking ethically, buying positively, respecting and protecting the environment, and contributing to your local community.

Delighting Your Customers
Avril Owton

Business &
Economics /
Management
February
A Paperback Original
A&C Black
Business on a
Shoestring
4¾ x 6¾ | 208 pp
TP $12.95
978-0-7136-7542-9
USA

Your relationship with your customers is probably one of the most important you'll ever have. No business can survive without them, and reaching customers is a big challenge for small companies. This book offers you advice on key issues such as: understanding your customers, creating a customer service strategy, hiring the right people, setting up and implementing complaint processes, and adding a personal touch.

Making an Impact Online
Antoin O Lachtnain

Business &
Economics /
Management
February
A Paperback Original
A&C Black
Business on a
Shoestring
4¾ x 6¾ | 208 pp
TP $12.95
978-0-7136-7545-0
USA

Having an online presence is essential for most businesses these days. Don't think that a small budget means that you can't compete with larger organizations; if your site is laid out well and your content is compelling, you can! This book offers advice on: choosing the right domain name, smartening up a basic website, search engine listings and optimization, instant messaging, and e-spotting.

Excellent Employment
Ann Andrews

Business &
Economics
September
A Paperback Original
A&C Black
Business on a
Shoestring
4¾ x 6¾ | 208 pp
TP $12.95
978-0-7136-8210-6
USA

Recruiting the right people to help your company flourish and grow can be a real headache for small business owners. The process can be expensive and time-consuming, but this book will guide you through the minefield with information on: defining the job properly, drawing up a job description, advertising in the right places, drawing up a shortlist, interviewing dos and don'ts, and inducting new employees.

A&C Black Business on a Shoestring Series

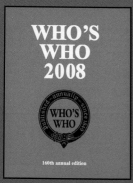

Who's Who 2008
160th annual edition
A&C Black

Reference / Biography & Autobiography
December
A&C Black
7⅞ x 10⅝ | 2,650 pp
TC $325.00
978-0-7136-8555-8 USA

Britain's most famous reference book—a biographical record of the great and the good.

"The famous red covers of *Who's Who* are exclusive and only the enduringly notable get into them. After a week with the new *Who's Who* (and though it's heavy to pick up), 'you can't put it down' best describes my feeling."—Matthew Parris, *The Times* (London)

"As a journalist I'd be lost without *Who's Who*."—Michael Crick

"*Who's Who* is a mirror in which society glimpses a reflection of its own achievement." —*The Times* (London)

This is the 160th annual edition of the internationally respected and renowned source book of information on people of influence and interest in every area of public life. It is the first *auto*biographical reference book in the world and, after 160 years, still the most accurate and reliable resource for information supplied and checked by the entrants themselves.

Who's Who 2008 & Online Voucher
A&C Black

Reference / Biography & Autobiography
December
A&C Black
7⅞ x 10⅝ | 2,650 pp
TC $500.00
978-0-7136-8550-3
USA

The electronic edition of *Who's Who* enables readers to search the database in a very different way than the print volume, and includes access to the eleven-volume resource, *Who Was Who*, dating back to 1897.

Writers' & Artists' Yearbook 2008
Completely Revised and Updated Every Year, 101st Edition
Foreword by Alexander McCall-Smith

Writing / Reference
October
A&C Black
5¾ x 8¼ | 832 pp
TP $34.95
978-0-7136-8371-4
USA

The best-selling yearbook for writers and artists, this is a comprehensive, up-to-date directory of media contacts that contains a wealth of practical advice and information on a huge range of topics including copyright, finance, submitting a manuscript, e-publishing, prizes, and awards. Features include hundreds of new contacts and updated listings, as well as new articles by Alexander McCall-Smith, Claire Tomalin, Jane Green, Isabella Pereira, and others.

A&C Black

Children's Writers' & Artists' Yearbook 2008
Foreword by Jacqueline Wilson

Writing / Reference
October
A&C Black
5¾ x 8¼ | 400 pp
TP $29.95
978-0-7136-8370-7
USA

This is the comprehensive guide to markets in all areas of children's writing. It contains a wealth of practical advice and information by well-known children's media experts, as well as a comprehensive directory of children's publishers. Features include new articles by Jacqueline Wilson, Lauren Child, Rosemary Canter, Stephen Briggs, and others.

Actors' Yearbook 2008
The essential resource for anyone wanting to work as an actor
Edited by Simon Dunmore and Andrew Piper

Film & TV /
Performing Arts
November
A&C Black
5¾ x 8¼ | 400 pp
TP $29.95
978-0-7136-8471-1
USA

"The wide range of information and contacts should be a huge help to those undertaking their new journey."—Dame Judi Dench

Actors' Yearbook is a comprehensive reference guide to acting for television, film, and theater. It lists contacts and addresses for all sections of the acting world, from agents to production companies, and articles provide a valuable insight to the profession.

Filmmakers' Yearbook 2008
By filmmakers for filmmakers— essential contacts and advice
Edited by Tricia Tuttle

Film & TV / Reference
November
A&C Black
5¾ x 8¼ | 304 pp
TP $29.95
978-0-7136-8470-4
USA

"A reservoir of information."—Anthony Minghella

"The essential new 'black book' to the film industry."—www.shootingpeople.org

Compiled by industry experts, this essential guide offers well-researched, in-depth contact information and practical advice from leading filmmakers to help you get your film made and successfully released.

Musicians' & Songwriters' Yearbook 2008
The essential resource for anyone working in the music industry
Edited by Jonathan Little and Katie Chatburn

Music /
Performing Arts
November
A&C Black
5¾ x 8¼ | 304 pp
TP $29.95
978-0-7136-8472-8
USA

The essential "black book" to the music industry, this authoritative reference lists contact names and vital information to enable you to produce, sell, and perform your music.

Writing / Poetry
November
A&C Black
5¾ x 8¼ | 352 pp
TP $29.95
978-0-7136-8469-8
USA

Poetry Writers' Yearbook 2008
Edited by Gordon Kerr and Hilary Lissenden

Writing poetry is more popular than ever, and there has never been a greater opportunity to find an outlet for your work. *Poetry Writers' Yearbook* gives detailed listings of publishing companies, events, and competitions where your voice can be heard.

This edition includes a foreword by Simon Armitage and contributions from established poets George Szirtes, Andrew Motion, Colette Bryce, and Carol Ann Duffy.

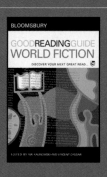

Literature & Essay /
Literary Criticism
September
A Paperback Original
A&C Black
5⅛ x 7¾ | 496 pp
TP $14.95
978-0-7136-7587-0
USA

Bloomsbury Good Reading Guide
Edited by Nick Rennison

This book features hundreds of authors and thousands of titles, with navigation features to lead you through a rich journey of some of the best literature to grace our shelves.

Literature & Essay /
Reference
March
A Paperback Original
A&C Black
5⅛ x 7¾ | 448 pp
TP $19.95
978-0-7136-7999-1
USA

Bloomsbury Good Reading Guide to World Fiction
Edited by Nik Kalinowski and Vincent Cassar

Reading, like traveling, takes you on a journey of discovery into new places, cultures, and ways of living. This book is a literary exploration of global proportions, a rich survey of the finest novels set or written in other countries.

Literature & Essay
September
A Paperback Original
A&C Black
4⅛ x 5¾ | 320 pp
TP $9.95
978-0-7136-7583-2
USA

100 Must-Read Classic Novels
Edited by Nick Rennison

This book is a rich selection of writing that has influenced the twentieth century and beyond. With one hundred of the best titles fully reviewed and a further five hundred recommended, you'll quickly set out on a journey of discovery. The book also allows you to browse by theme and includes "a reader's fast-guide to the classics," past award winners, and book club recommendations.

A&C Black

100 Must-Read Crime Novels
Edited by Richard Shephard and Nick Rennison

Literature & Essay
September
A Paperback Original
A&C Black
4⅛ x 5¾ | 320 pp
TP $9.95
978-0-7136-7584-9
USA

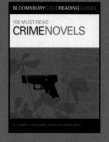

Want to become a crime novel buff, or expand your reading in your favorite genre? This is a good place to start! From the publishers of the popular *Bloomsbury Good Reading Guides,* this book contains a rich selection of some of the best crime novels ever published.

100 Must-Read Science Fiction Novels
Edited by Stephen E. Andrews and Nick Rennison

Literature & Essay
September
A Paperback Original
A&C Black
4⅛ x 5¾ | 320 pp
TP $9.95
978-0-7136-7585-6
USA

This book is arranged by author and includes some thematic entries and special categories, such as science fiction film adaptations, science fiction in rock music, and Philip K. Dick in the mass media. It also includes a history of science fiction and a new definition of the genre, plus lists of award-winners and book club recommendations. Includes a foreword by Christopher Priest, the multiple-award-winning science fiction author (with a major film adaptation of his book, *The Prestige,* released in 2006).

Is There a Book in You?
Alison Baverstock

Writing / Reference
January
A Paperback Original
A&C Black
5 x 7¾ | 256 pp
TP $12.95
978-0-7136-7932-8
USA

Many people feel they might have a book in them—but how do you know whether you have what it takes to be a writer, whether your writing is any good, what you should write about, and whether you should dedicate proper time to begin your dream? This book asks pertinent questions of you via a questionnaire, with each chapter providing a background to the relevant point in the questionnaire. It's also packed with advice from experienced writers, including P.D. James, Philip Pullman, Jacqueline Wilson, Margaret Drabble, Katie Fforde, and more.

Wobbly Bits and Other Euphemisms
Over 3,000 ways to avoid speaking your mind
John Ayto

Reference / Language Arts
October
A Paperback Original
A&C Black
5 x 8 | 352 pp
TP $16.95
978-0-7136-7840-6
USA

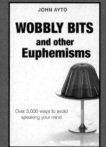

Wobbly Bits and Other Euphemisms is the essential guide to polite conversation. Covering everything from the politically incorrect to the seriously taboo, this humorous book offers over three thousand ways to avoid speaking your mind! Subjects covered include crime, sins, sex, the body and its parts, clothing and nakedness, bodily functions and secretions, illness and injury, old age and death, work, poverty, government and politics, warfare, and race.

A&C Black

Writing / Technology
& Industrial Arts
November
A Paperback Original
A&C Black
5⅝ x 8½ | 192 pp
TP $19.95
978-0-7136-7761-4
USA

Writing for Video Games
Steve Ince

Video games are a lucrative market for scriptwriters, but writing for video games is complex and very different from traditional media such as television or film. This practical guide shows how you can adapt your writing skills to this exciting medium. Written by an award-winning games writer, the book provides a realistic picture of how companies work, how the writer fits into the development process, and the skills required: storytelling; developing interactive narrative, characters, and viewpoints; dialogue comedy; and professional practice.

Sports & Recreation /
Psychology &
Psychiatry
September
A Paperback Original
A&C Black
6⅛ x 9¼ | 240 pp
30 Color photographs
and illustrations
TP $39.95
978-0-7136-8186-4
USA

Coaching Knowledges
Understanding the Dynamics of Sport Performance
Jim Denison

In this book teachers, lecturers, and coaches from Bath University's "Team Bath" coaching and teaching faculty look at how various "knowledges" influence every coach's daily practices. The first section is written by sports scholars who have or are still coaching, while section two is written by coach educators who are active elite coaches. The final section features three in-depth interviews with three master international coaches.

Sports & Recreation /
Science
September
A Paperback Original
A&C Black
6⅛ x 9¼ | 192 pp
50 Color photographs
and B&W illustrations
TP $34.95
978-0-7136-7871-0
USA

Sports Biomechanics
The Basics: Optimising Human Performance
Anthony Blazevich

For coaches, athletes, and students of biomechanics, *Sports Biomechanics* answers real-world questions in sports using easily comprehensible language and clear and concise diagrams. Each chapter is devoted to answering questions in a single area of sports biomechanics with the scientific underpinnings of sports performance clearly explained.

Sports & Recreation /
Health & Fitness
September
A Paperback Original
A&C Black
6⅛ x 9¼ | 416 pp
200 B&W illustrations
TP $39.95
978-0-7136-8278-6
USA

Sports Training Principles
Frank W. Dick

Written by world-renowned coach and president of the European Athletics Coaches Association, Frank W. Dick, *Sports Training Principles* is the ultimate reference on training theory and practice for all coaches responsible for developing athletes to fulfill their performance potential. It covers: anatomy and basic biomechanics; energy production systems; psychology, learning procedures, and technical training; performance components (strength, speed, endurance, and mobility); training cycles; periodization; adaptation to external loading; and coaching methods.

A&C Black

Closer
Patrick Marber

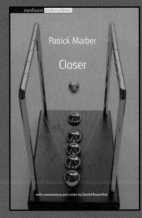

"Love and sex are like politics: it's not what you say that matters, still less what you mean, but what you do. Patrick Marber understands this perfectly, and in *Closer* he has written one of the best plays of sexual politics in the language: It is right up there with Williams' *Streetcar,* Mamet's *Oleanna,* Albee's *Virginia Woolf,* Pinter's *Old Times,* and Hare's *Skylight."—The Sunday Times*

This student edition comes complete with a full introduction, plot synopsis, commentary, discussion of the film adaptation, bibliography, and questions for study. It is the perfect edition for anyone studying the play at school or college.

Patrick Marber also co-wrote the screenplay for *Asylum* (2005), directed by David Mackenzie, and was the sole screenwriter for the film *Notes on a Scandal* (2006), for which he earned an Academy Award nomination for Best Adapted Screenplay.

Marketing Plans
Co-op available • Advance reader copies

Drama
September
A Paperback Original
Methuen Drama
5⅛ x 7¾ | 224 pp
TP US $14.95 | CAN $18.00
978-0-7136-8329-5 CUSA

Patrick Marber's searing follow-up to *Dealer's Choice* establishes him as a leading playwright.

93.2 FM
Levi David Addai

"This is a must-see new play, not only for young people but for everyone. Levi has his finger on the pulse—a writer to watch out for."—Choice FM

Coach and Bossman are a dynamic duo tearing up the airwaves at Borough FM. Together they have become radio heroes, but someone's getting above their station, putting Borough FM in the shade. There's a storm brewing, and the live phone-ins might not be able to provide all the answers. United they may stand, but divided . . .

93.2 FM is a sharp comedy about friendship, dreams, and the conflict awakened by ambition. It's about achieving your goals and what may or may not be compromised along the way.

The play premiered at the Royal Court Theatre, London, in September 2006.

Drama
September
A Paperback Original
Methuen Drama
5⅛ x 7¾ | 96 pp
TP US $14.95 | CAN $18.00
978-0-7136-8437-7 CUSA

A sharp look at contemporary music culture.

Drama
February
A Paperback Original
Methuen Drama
5⅜ x 8½ | 320 pp
TP US $34.95 | CAN $42.00
978-0-7136-7758-4 CUSA

Marketing Plans

Co-op available
Advance reader copies

Acting on Impulse:
The Stanislavski Approach
A practical workbook for actors
John Gillett

"I'd recommend this book to anyone wanting an introduction to Stanislavksi or Chekhov or acting in general."—Matt Peover, trainer and theater director, London Academy of Music and Dramatic Art

"Contains all the important things that need to be said about learning to act . . . in an extremely logical and sensible manner."—Simon Dunmore, editor of *Actor's Yearbook*

An inspiring and technically thorough practical book for actors that sets down a systematic and coherent process for organic (from the "inside-out"/experienced emotion) acting. The author offers a step-by-step, Stanislavski-based approach to text, role, and performance to be used in everyday work and gathers together in one volume the essential tools that serve to re-create human experience. John Gillett builds on his experience of teaching at a drama school level as well as his thirty years of acting. For acting students and professional actors who have become mystified and frustrated with trying to understand Stanislavski's approach, this book is an accessible guide to inspire a truly real and audience-captivating performance.

Contains all the important things that need to be said about learning to act.

A&C Black

At the Sharp End

Uncovering the work of five leading dramatists: David Edgar, Tim Etchells, David Greig, Tanika Gupta, and Mark Ravenhill

Peter Billingham

At the Sharp End is a critical examination of five leading dramatists who have made an indelible mark on today's theater. Peter Billingham introduces the work of David Edgar, Tim Etchells, David Greig, Tanika Gupta, and Mark Ravenhill.

Drama
February
A Paperback Original
Methuen Drama
5⅜ x 8½ | 176 pp
TP US $15.95
CAN $19.50
978-0-7136-8507-7
CUSA

Days of Significance

Roy Williams

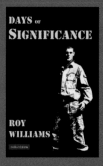

Days of Significance is the new work by Roy Williams commissioned by the Royal Shakespeare Company and staged at the Swan Theatre in January 2007.

Drama
September
A Paperback Original
Methuen Drama
5⅛ x 7¾ | 96 pp
TP US $14.95
CAN $18.00
978-0-7136-8328-8
CUSA

Eden's Empire

James Graham

Fifty years ago, Britain propelled itself into a disastrous war in the Middle East. Condemned by the United Nations, the prime minister was left fighting for his political life against a party disillusioned and a public betrayed.

Drama
September
A Paperback Original
Methuen Drama
5⅛ x 7¾ | 112 pp
TP US $14.95
CAN $18.00
978-0-7136-8378-3
CUSA

Mother Courage and Her Children

Bertolt Brecht

Translated by Michael Hofmann

A new translation by Michael Hofmann is published to coincide with the United Kingdom's national tour by English Touring Theatre.

Drama
September
A Paperback Original
Methuen Drama
5⅛ x 7¾ | 128 pp
TP US $14.95
CAN $18.00
978-0-7136-8466-7
CUSA

A&C Black

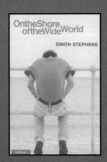

Drama
September
A Paperback Original
Methuen Drama
5 x 8 | 144 pp
TP US $14.95
CAN $18.00
978-0-413-77517-7
CUSA

On the Shore of the Wide World
Simon Stephens

Set over the course of nine months, *On the Shore of the Wide World* is an epic play about love, family, Roy Keane, and the size of the galaxy.

Drama / Reference
November
A Paperback Original
Methuen Drama
7⅜ x 9¾ | 256 pp
TP US $34.95
CAN $42.00
978-0-7136-7757-7
CUSA

Performance Lighting Design
How to light for the stage, concerts, exhibitions and live events
Nick Moran

New technologies have made lighting more prominent in live performances of all kinds—not just stage theater—and in many courses lighting has been subsumed into "performance lighting."

Drama
September
A Paperback Original
Methuen Drama
5⅛ x 7¾ | 112 pp
TP US $14.95
CAN $18.00
978-0-7136-8398-1
CUSA

pool (no water) & Citizenship
Mark Ravenhill

Two exhilarating plays by the author of *Shopping and F***ing: pool (no water)* is a shocking play about the fragility of friendship and the jealousy inspired by success; *Citizenship* is a work for young people.

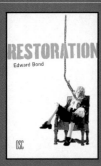

Drama
September
A Paperback Original
Methuen Drama
5⅛ x 7¾ | 96 pp
TP US $14.95
CAN $18.00
978-0-7136-8330-1
CUSA

Restoration
Edward Bond

A new edition with program notes of Edward Bond's play set in eighteenth-century England, published to tie in with the tour by Oxford Stage Company.

A&C Black

Rise and Fall of the City of Mahagonny

Bertolt Brecht

Translated by Steve Giles

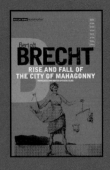

Drama
November
A Paperback Original
Methuen Drama
5⅛ x 7¾ | 176 pp
TP US $18.95
CAN $23.00
978-0-7136-8674-6
CUSA

Bertolt Brecht's operatic play produced with Elisabeth Hauptmann, Caspar Neher, and Kurt Weill was first staged in 1930. Translated and with commentary by Steve Giles, this critical edition is the first English translation of the approved Versuche text of 1930–1931.

Yerma

Federico García Lorca

Translated by Gwynne Edwards

Drama
September
A Paperback Original
Methuen Drama
5⅛ x 7¾ | 208 pp
TP US $14.95
CAN $18.00
978-0-7136-8326-4
CUSA

Yerma (meaning "barren") is one of three tragic plays about peasants and rural life that make up Federico García Lorca's "rural trilogy." It is possibly Lorca's harshest play following a woman's Herculean struggle against the curse of infertility.

Arden of Faversham, 2nd Edition

Edited by Martin White

Drama
November
Methuen Drama
New Mermaids
5 x 7¾ | 128 pp
TP US $14.95
CAN $18.00
978-0-7136-7765-2
CUSA

This "lamentable and true tragedy," as it is announced on its title page, dramatizes a domestic murder of the sort that nowadays scandalizes and thrills the readers of tabloid newspapers. As the introduction to this edition shows, sexual and material covetousness is the central theme running through the play, which is commonly rated "unquestionably the best of all Elizabethan domestic tragedies."

Bartholmew Fair, 2nd Edition

Ben Jonson

Edited by G.R. Hibbard

Introduction by Alexander Leggatt

Drama
September
A Paperback Original
Methuen Drama
New Mermaids
5⅛ x 7¾ | 192 pp
TP US $14.95
CAN $18.00
978-0-7136-7427-9
CUSA

This edition has been updated with a new introduction that examines *Bartholmew Fair* as a reading text, as a text for performance, and as a play that questions theater itself. There is a lively and comprehensively researched account of the play's historical, social, and theatrical context. Alexander Leggatt has also updated the commentary and further reading section.

The Alchemist
Ben Jonson
Edited by Elizabeth Cook

Drama
Available Now
Methuen Drama
New Mermaids
5⅛ x 7¾ | 192 pp
TP US $14.95
CAN $18.00
978-0-7136-7104-9
CUSA

Notes on the lexical, semantic, and theatrical aspects of the text are presented alongside this Elizabethan comedy.

The Changeling
Thomas Middleton and William Rowley
Edited by Joost Daalder

Drama
Available Now
Methuen Drama
New Mermaids
5⅛ x 7¾ | 176 pp
TP US $14.95
CAN $18.00
978-0-7136-6884-1
CUSA

The Changeling is a popular Renaissance tragedy in which the relationship between money, sex, and power is explored. Frequently performed and studied in university courses, it is a key text in the New Mermaids series.

Dr Faustus
Christopher Marlowe
Edited by Roma Gill

Drama
Available Now
Methuen Drama
New Mermaids
5⅛ x 7¾ | 144 pp
TP US $14.95
CAN $18.00
978-0-7136-6790-5
CUSA

Christopher Marlowe's play has two different recognized texts, with most editions based on the B text. Due to recent arguments for the authenticity of A, this edition is based on the A text. It includes a discussion of biographical, dramatic, and theatrical aspects of the play.

The Importance of Being Earnest
Oscar Wilde
Edited by Russell Jackson

Drama
Available Now
Methuen Drama
New Mermaids
5⅛ x 7¾ | 176 pp
TP US $14.95
CAN $18.00
978-0-7136-3040-4
CUSA

"Comes as close to perfection as any comedy I can think of."—*Daily Telegraph*

Oscar Wilde's "trivial play for serious people" is a sparkling comedy of manners. This hilariously absurd satire pits sincerity against style, barbed witticisms against ostentatious elegance. Wilde's brilliantly constructed plot and famous dialogue enrich the appeal of his celebrated characters, as he turns accepted ideas inside out and situations upside down in this, his masterpiece.

A&C Black New Mermaids Series

The School for Scandal
Richard Brinsley Sheridan
Article by David Crane

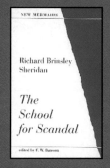

Drama
Available Now
Methuen Drama
New Mermaids
5⅛ x 7¾ | 208 pp
TP US $14.95
CAN $18.00
978-0-7136-6290-0
CUSA

This is an updated edition of Richard Brinsley Sheridan's play, *The School for Scandal*. It also contains an article written by David Crane on the play's original staging, arguing that knowledge of staging and performance requirements is important to an understanding of the play itself.

Tamburlaine
Christopher Marlowe
Edited by Anthony B. Dawson

Drama
Available Now
Methuen Drama
New Mermaids
5⅛ x 7¾ | 174 pp
TP US $14.95
CAN $18.00
978-0-7136-6814-8
CUSA

Tamburlaine is Christopher Marlowe's story of a Scythian shepherd who, through using his brutality, lust for power, and charm, becomes a mighty conqueror and the king of Persia.

'Tis Pity She's a Whore
John Ford
Edited by Martin Wiggins

Drama
Available Now
Methuen Drama
New Mermaids
5⅛ x 7¾ | 174 pp
TP US $14.95
CAN $18.00
978-0-7136-5060-0
CUSA

John Ford's savage play of incestuous love retains its power to shock even contemporary audiences, and yet it is also a moving and restrained exploration of the tragic consequences of forbidden relationships.

Detailed commentary notes are included alongside the play text for easy reference. There is also a list of further reading suggestions included to aid research.

Volpone
Ben Jonson
Edited by Robert N. Watson

Drama
Available Now
Methuen Drama
New Mermaids
5⅛ x 7¾ | 174 pp
TP US $14.95
CAN $18.00
978-0-7136-5433-2
CUSA

Volpone is part of the New Mermaids series of modern-spelling, fully annotated editions of English plays. Each volume includes a critical introduction, biography of the author, discussions of dates and sources, textual details, a bibliography, and information about the staging of the play.

All for Love
John Dryden

Drama
Available Now
Methuen Drama
New Mermaids
5⅛ x 7¾ | 160 pp
TP US $14.95 | CAN $18.00
978-0-7136-7105-6 CUSA

The Critic
Richard Brinsley Sheridan
Edited by David Crane

Drama
Available Now
Methuen Drama
New Mermaids
5⅛ x 7¾ | 112 pp
TP US $14.95 | CAN $18.00
978-0-7136-3188-3 CUSA

Epicoene
Ben Jonson

Drama
Available Now
Methuen Drama
New Mermaids
5⅛ x 7¾ | 224 pp
TP US $14.95 | CAN $18.00
978-0-7136-6668-7 CUSA

Bartholmew Fair
Ben Johnson

Drama
Available Now
Methuen Drama
New Mermaids
5 x 7¾ | 224 pp
TP US $14.95 | CAN $18.00
978-0-7136-3531-7 CUSA

Duchess of Malfi
John Webster

Drama
Available Now
Methuen Drama
New Mermaids
5⅛ x 7¾ | 184 pp
TP US $14.95 | CAN $18.00
978-0-7136-6791-2 CUSA

Every Man in His Humour
Ben Jonson

Drama
Available Now
Methuen Drama
New Mermaids
5⅛ x 7¾ | 154 pp
TP US $14.95 | CAN $18.00
978-0-7136-4397-8 CUSA

The Beaux Strategem
George Farquhar

Drama
Available Now
Methuen Drama
New Mermaids
5⅛ x 7¾ | 192 pp
TP US $14.95 | CAN $18.00
978-0-7136-7000-4 CUSA

The Dutch Courtesan
John Marston

Drama
Available Now
Methuen Drama
New Mermaids
5⅛ x 7¾ | 120 pp
TP US $14.95 | CAN $18.00
978-0-7136-4475-3 CUSA

Gammer Gurton's Needle
Charles Whitworth

Drama
Available Now
Methuen Drama
New Mermaids
5⅛ x 7¾ | 112 pp
TP US $14.95 | CAN $18.00
978-0-7136-4497-5 CUSA

A Chaste Maid in Cheapside
Thomas Middleton

Drama
Available Now
Methuen Drama
New Mermaids
5⅛ x 7¾ | 144 pp
TP US $14.95 | CAN $18.00
978-0-7136-5068-6 CUSA

Eastward Ho!
George Chapman, Ben Jonson, and John Marston

Drama
Available Now
Methuen Drama
New Mermaids
5⅛ x 7¾ | 120 pp
TP US $14.95 | CAN $18.00
978-0-7136-3983-4 CUSA

An Ideal Husband
Oscar Wilde

Drama
Available Now
Methuen Drama
New Mermaids
5⅛ x 7¾ | 208 pp
TP US $14.95 | CAN $18.00
978-0-7136-6687-8 CUSA

The Country Wife
William Wycherley

Drama
Available Now
Methuen Drama
New Mermaids
5⅛ x 7¾ | 192 pp
TP US $14.95 | CAN $18.00
978-0-7136-6688-5 CUSA

Edward The Second
Christopher Marlowe

Drama
Available Now
Methuen Drama
New Mermaids
5⅛ x 7¾ | 176 pp
TP US $14.95 | CAN $18.00
978-0-7136-6669-4 CUSA

The Jew of Malta
Christopher Marlowe

Drama
Available Now
Methuen Drama
New Mermaids
5⅛ x 7¾ | 160 pp
TP US $14.95 | CAN $18.00
978-0-7136-6670-0 CUSA

The Knight of the Burning Pestle
Francis Beaumont

Drama
Available Now
Methuen Drama
New Mermaids
5⅛ x 7¾ | 120 pp
TP US $14.95 | CAN $18.00
978-0-7136-5069-3 CUSA

Man of Mode
George Etherege

Drama
Available Now
Methuen Drama
New Mermaids
5⅛ x 7¾ | 208 pp
TP US $14.95 | CAN $18.00
978-0-7136-6689-2 CUSA

The Relapse
Sir John Vanbrugh

Drama
Available Now
Methuen Drama
New Mermaids
5⅛ x 7¾ | 130 pp
TP US $14.95 | CAN $18.00
978-0-7136-2887-6 CUSA

Lady Windemere's Fan
Oscar Wilde

Drama
Available Now
Methuen Drama
New Mermaids
5⅛ x 7¾ | 102 pp
TP US $14.95 | CAN $18.00
978-0-7136-6667-0 CUSA

Marriage A La Mode
John Dryden

Drama
Available Now
Methuen Drama
New Mermaids
5⅛ x 7¾ | 120 pp
TP US $14.95 | CAN $18.00
978-0-7136-6666-3 CUSA

The Revenger's Tragedy
Cyril Tourneur
Edited by Brian Gibbons

Drama
Available Now
Methuen Drama
New Mermaids
5⅛ x 7¾ | 112 pp
TP US $14.95 | CAN $18.00
978-0-7136-6664-9 CUSA

Late Medieval Morality Plays
Edited by G.A. Lester

Drama
Available Now
Methuen Drama
New Mermaids
5⅛ x 7¾ | 160 pp
TP US $14.95 | CAN $18.00
978-0-7136-6661-8 CUSA

The Playboy of the Western World
John M. Synge

Drama
Available Now
Methuen Drama
New Mermaids
5⅛ x 7¾ | 138 pp
TP US $14.95 | CAN $18.00
978-0-7136-4322-0 CUSA

The Rivals
Richard Brinsley Sheridan
Edited by Tiffany Stern

Drama
Available Now
Methuen Drama
New Mermaids
5⅛ x 7¾ | 192 pp
TP US $14.95 | CAN $18.00
978-0-7136-6765-3 CUSA

Love for Love
William Congreve
Edited by Malcolm Kensall

Drama
Available Now
Methuen Drama
New Mermaids
5⅛ x 7¾ | 160 pp
TP US $14.95 | CAN $18.00
978-0-7136-4323-7 CUSA

The Provoked Wife
Sir John Vanbrugh

Drama
Available Now
Methuen Drama
New Mermaids
5⅛ x 7¾ | 128 pp
TP US $14.95 | CAN $18.00
978-0-7136-6665-6 CUSA

The Roaring Girl
Thomas Middleton with Thomas Dekker
Edited by Elizabeth Cook

Drama
Available Now
Methuen Drama
New Mermaids
5⅛ x 7¾ | 192 pp
TP US $14.95 | CAN $18.00
978-0-7136-6813-1 CUSA

The Malcontent
John Marston

Drama
Available Now
Methuen Drama
New Mermaids
5⅛ x 7¾ | 176 pp
TP US $14.95 | CAN $18.00
978-0-7136-4288-9 CUSA

The Recruiting Officer
George Farquhar

Drama
Available Now
Methuen Drama
New Mermaids
5⅛ x 7¾ | 192 pp
TP US $14.95 | CAN $18.00
978-0-7136-3349-8 CUSA

The Rover
Aphra Behn

Drama
Available Now
Methuen Drama
New Mermaids
5⅛ x 7¾ | 128 pp
TP US $14.95 | CAN $18.00
978-0-7136-6671-7 CUSA

She Stoops to Conquer
Oliver Goldsmith

Drama
Available Now
Methuen Drama
New Mermaids
5⅛ x 7¾ | 104 pp
TP US $14.95 | CAN $18.00
978-0-7136-6794-3 CUSA

The White Devil
John Webster

Drama
Available Now
Methuen Drama
New Mermaids
5⅛ x 7¾ | 192 pp
TP US $14.95 | CAN $18.00
978-0-7136-6793-6 CUSA

Woman Killed with Kindness
Thomas Heywood

Drama
Available Now
Methuen Drama
New Mermaids
5⅛ x 7¾ | 128 pp
TP US $14.95 | CAN $18.00
978-0-7136-6690-8 CUSA

The Shoemakers Holiday
Thomas Dekker
Edited by Anthony Parr

Drama
Available Now
Methuen Drama
New Mermaids
5⅛ x 7¾ | 144 pp
TP US $14.95 | CAN $18.00
978-0-7136-6660-1 CUSA

The Witch
Thomas Middleton

Drama
Available Now
Methuen Drama
New Mermaids
5⅛ x 7¾ | 160 pp
TP US $14.95 | CAN $18.00
978-0-7136-3945-2 CUSA

A Woman of No Importance
Oscar Wilde

Drama
Available Now
Methuen Drama
New Mermaids
5⅛ x 7¾ | 176 pp
TP US $14.95 | CAN $18.00
978-0-7136-7351-7 CUSA

The Spanish Tragedy
Thomas Kyd

Drama
Available Now
Methuen Drama
New Mermaids
5⅛ x 7¾ | 140 pp
TP US $14.95 | CAN $18.00
978-0-7136-6792-9 CUSA

The Witch of Edmonton
Thomas Dekker, John Ford, and William Rowley

Drama
Available Now
Methuen Drama
New Mermaids
5⅛ x 7¾ | 156 pp
TP US $14.95 | CAN $18.00
978-0-7136-4253-7 CUSA

Women Beware Women
Thomas Middleton

Drama
Available Now
Methuen Drama
New Mermaids
5⅛ x 7¾ | 160 pp
TP US $14.95 | CAN $18.00
978-0-7136-6663-2 CUSA

The Way of the World
William Congreve

Drama
Available Now
Methuen Drama
New Mermaids
5⅛ x 7¾ | 120 pp
TP US $14.95 | CAN $18.00
978-0-7136-6662-5 CUSA

An Actor's Guide to Getting Work
Simon Dunmore

Business &
Economics
Available Now
A&C Black
5⅜ x 8½ | 224 pp
TP $14.95
978-0-7136-6822-3
USA

Competition for acting work is fierce, and although talent is important, actors need all the help they can get. Now in its fourth edition, this practical, comprehensive guide contains invaluable information and advice to enable actors to make the most of drama schools.

Anagram Solver
Over 200,000 Anagrams at Your Fingertips
Edited by John Daintith

Games
Available Now
A&C Black
5⅛ x 7¾ | 720 pp
TP $22.95
978-0-7136-7510-8
USA

Anagram Solver is the essential guide to cracking all types of quizzes and crosswords featuring anagrams. Containing over 200,000 words and phrases, *Anagram Solver* includes plural noun forms, palindromes, idioms, first names, and all parts of speech.

Check Your English Vocabulary for Law
A&C Black

Language Arts
Available Now
A&C Black
8⅜ x 11¾ | 80 pp
TP $14.95
978-0-7136-7592-4
USA

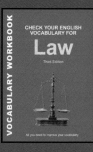

Check Your English Vocabulary for Law is a workbook designed to help non-native English speakers improve their knowledge and understanding of core legal terminology. The workbook includes crosswords, puzzles, and word games to test English vocabulary and a combination of self-study exercises.

Check Your English Vocabulary for Medicine
A&C Black

Language Arts
Available Now
A&C Black
8⅜ x 11¾ | 80 pp
TP $14.95
978-0-7136-7590-0
USA

Check Your English Vocabulary for Medicine is a workbook designed to help learners of English improve their knowledge and understanding of core medical terminology.

A&C Black

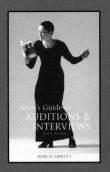

Business &
Economics
Available Now
A&C Black
5½ x 8½ | 128 pp
TP $12.95
978-0-7136-6821-6
USA

Actor's Guide to Auditions & Interviews
Third Edition
Margo Annett

Now in its third edition, this guide outlines the techniques needed to achieve success in getting acting work. It covers all aspects of casting, including gaining a place on a drama course; landing a part in a film, TV commercials, or theater; and becoming a radio or TV presenter.

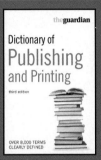

Business &
Economics
Available Now
A&C Black
5⅛ x 7¾ | 320 pp
TP $19.95
978-0-7136-7589-4
USA

Dictionary of Publishing and Printing
Third Edition
A&C Black

This fully revised edition includes over 8,000 words, expressions, and terminology relating to the publishing and printing industries and allied trades. Topics covered include: papermaking, ink, printing and binding machinery, bookselling, typesetting, desktop publishing and design, copyrights, editing, commissioning, contracts, rights, and electronic publishing.

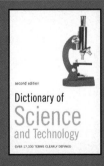

Reference
Available Now
A&C Black
5⅛ x 7¾ | 672 pp
TP $14.95
978-0-7475-6620-5
USA

Dictionary of Science and Technology
Second Edition
A&C Black

The popular *Dictionary of Science and Technology* offers over 17,000 terms from all aspects of science and technology, including chemistry, physics and biology, earth sciences, engineering, astronomy, electronics, medicine, and telecommunications.

Sports & Recreation
Available Now
A&C Black
5⅜ x 8½ | 160 pp
TP $14.95
978-0-7136-9133-7
USA

Jiu Jitsu
Blue Belt to Brown Belt
Robert Clark

This training guide is dedicated to students of Jiu-Jitsu worldwide. It is the only up-to-date and official training manual of the World Jiu-Jitsu Federation, and it covers blue belt to brown. With over three hundred photographs, this manual is an invaluable source of reference for more advanced students and coaches.

Songs of a Sourdough
Robert Service

Poetry
Available Now
A&C Black
4⅞ x 7⅜ | 128 pp
TP $9.95
978-0-7136-5081-5
USA

Songs of a Sourdough is Robert Service at his best! This is nature poetry at its finest. Here, the "Bard of the Yukon" uses picture words that place the reader right in the Yukon of old. As you read you can see the stranger stagger in to the Malamute saloon and feel the fifty-below gush of air until he closes the door behind him.

Writing a Thriller
André Jute

Writing
Available Now
A&C Black
5⅜ x 8½ | 188 pp
TP $12.95
978-0-7136-5093-8
USA

This book guides the reader through a number of identifiable stages of writing a thriller, including the following: choosing the initial theme of a story, the creation of characters, detailed plotting, research, cutting and rewriting, and common writer's block.

Writing Poetry
John Whitworth

Writing
Available Now
A&C Black
5⅜ x 8½ | 208 pp
TP $12.95
978-0-7136-5822-4
USA

A wonderful, positive, and practical handbook packed with advice, exercises, and information. Beginning with what makes poetry, the author describes the different forms, how and what to start writing, finding an audience, and getting published.

Writing Romantic Fiction
Daphne Clair and Robyn Donald

Writing
Available Now
A&C Black
5⅜ x 8½ | 122 pp
TP $15.95
978-0-7136-4887-4
USA

A handbook for writers that includes chapters on fiction techniques, heroes and heroines, plot and subplots, emotional impact, tension, focus, pace, setting, and language. Combining two writers' styles, this book follows the premise that there is no one way to write.

Actor's Yearbook 2007
Simon Dunmore
978-0-7136-7385-2 USA TP $42.95

Career Handbook for Broadcast Media
Shiona Llewellyn
978-0-7136-6320-4 USA TP $14.95

Check Your English Vocabulary for TOEIC
Rawdon Wyatt
978-0-7136-7508-5 USA TP $14.95

**Check Your English Vocabulary/
Phrasal Verbs and Idioms**
Rawdon Wyatt
978-0-7136-7805-5 USA TP $14.95

Children's Writer's And Artist's Yearbook 2007
Foreword by Meg Cabot
978-0-7136-7711-9 USA TP $36.25

Complete Guide to Cross Training
Fiona Hayes
978-0-7136-4883-6 USA TP $16.95

Complete Guide to Exercise to Music
Debbie Lawrence
978-0-7136-4995-6 USA TP $14.95

Creative Web Writing
Jane Dorner; Foreword by Terry Pratchett
978-0-7136-5854-5 USA TP $12.95

Developing Characters for Script Writing
Rib Davis
978-0-7136-6950-3 USA TP $12.95

**Dictionary of Information and Library Management
2nd Edition**
A&C Black
978-0-7136-7591-7 USA TP $19.95

**Dictionary of Leisure, Travel and Tourism
3rd Edition**
A&C Black
978-0-7475-7222-0 USA TP $19.95

Dictionary of Media Studies
A&C Black
978-0-7136-7593-1 USA TP $19.95

Filmmaker's Yearbook 2007
A&C Black
978-0-7136-7552-8 USA TP $48.50

First Steps Towards Acting
Nigel Rideout
978-0-7136-4130-1 USA TP $13.95

Freelance Copywriting
Diana Wimbs
978-0-7136-4822-5 USA TP $12.95

Ghostwriting
Andrew Crofts
978-0-7136-6786-8 USA TP $12.95

Jiu Jitsu: Black Belt Syllabus
Robert Clark
978-0-7136-9134-4 USA TP $14.95

Musician's and Songwriter's Yearbook 2007
Jonathan Little
978-0-7136-7531-3 USA TP $42.50

Pocket Crossword Dictionary
B.J. Holmes
978-0-7136-7503-0 USA TP $9.95

Poetry Writer's Yearbook 2007
Gordon Kerr
978-0-7136-7576-4 USA TP $36.25

Shotokan Karate 1st to 6th KYU
Sensei K. Enoeda
978-0-7136-9135-1 USA TP $14.95

Shotokan Karate 5th KYU to Black
Sensei K. Enoeda
978-0-7136-9136-8 USA TP $14.95

Tae Kwon Do Black Belt Syllabus
Senior Instructors of the Tagb
978-0-7136-9139-9 USA TP $14.95

Tae Kwon Do Green to Red
Tae Kwon-do Association of Great Britain
978-0-7136-9138-2 USA TP $14.95

Traditional Kobujutsu
Robert Clark
978-0-7136-4381-7 USA TP $19.95

Word Origins
John Ayto
978-0-7136-7498-9 USA TP $16.96

Writer's and Artist's Yearbook 2007
Ian Rankin
978-0-7136-7712-6 USA TP $19.95

Writing for Soaps
Chris Curry
978-0-7136-6121-7 USA TP $12.95

My Mother Wears Combat Boots
A Parenting Guide for the Rest of Us
Jessica Mills

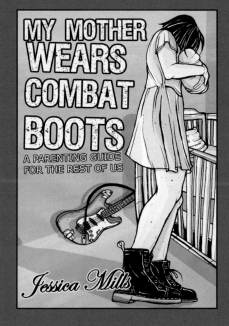

A parenting guide like no other! Jessica Mills, a touring punk musician, artist, and political activist, gives readers a delightful, information-packed guide to having and raising kids without giving up your politics, art, or life.

Based on the popular column of the same name in *MaximumRocknRoll* magazine, *My Mother Wears Combat Boots* is filled with a clever and engaging mix of anecdotes, political analysis, and factual sidebars. Despite its "alternative" presentation, it remains fundamentally a practical guide for parents of all stripes. Amid stories about bringing kids (and their grandparents) to women's rights demonstrations, the evil economics of the infant formula industry, taking baby on tour with your band, how to score free infant gear, and ideas for starting cooperative daycare centers, Mills delivers sound, nuts-and-bolts advice for new and expecting parents. Covering issues like weaning, sex during pregnancy, cloth versus disposable diapers, and psychological debates about whether children should sleep in their parents' bed—among countless others—*My Mother Wears Combat Boots* offers a unique, funny, helpful, and hip approach to parenting for a new generation of moms and dads.

Jessica Mills writes a punk-parenting column for *MaximumRocknRoll,* plays saxophone for Citizen Fish, directed a birth center in Hollywood, Florida, makes jewelry in her metalworking studio, is mom to seven-year-old Emma-Joy and one-year-old Maya-Rae, and organizes childcare cooperatives. She lives with her partner and daughters in Seattle, Washington.

Punk, politics, and parenting: a guide for moms (and dads) who want it all.

Parenting
October
A Paperback Original
5½ x 8½ | 260 pp
TP US $16.95 | CAN $20.50
978-1-904859-72-7 CUSA

Marketing Plans

Co-op available
National advertising:
Bitch

Author Events

San Francisco, CA • Portland, OR •
Seattle, WA

Author Hometown: Seattle, WA

Making A Killing
The Political Economy of Animal Rights
Bob Torres

"He's my kinda man."—Sarah Kramer, co-author of *How it all Vegan*

Suggest to the average leftist that animals should be part of broader liberation struggles, and—once they stop laughing—you'll find yourself casually dismissed. Starting from this skepticism regarding animal liberation, Bob Torres draws broadly upon Left theory to show how human oppression and animal oppression are intertwined through the exploitative dynamics of capitalism. With a focus on labor, property, and the life of commodities, *Making a Killing* contains key insights on the nature of domination, power, and hierarchy, and argues for a critical social theory that understands the human domination of nature in terms of the domination of human by human. An eye-opener for readers concerned with progressive politics, animal welfare—or both.

Concluding with an analysis of the political praxis of veganism, the book puts forth an abolitionist theory of animal rights that challenges thinking both within the broader Left and the animal rights movement.

Bob Torres is assistant professor of sociology at St. Lawrence University, received his PhD from Cornell University, and is co-author of *Vegan Freak: Being Vegan in a Non-Vegan World*. His writings have appeared in *Critical Sociology*, *Journal of Latinos and Education*, *International Journal of Occupational and Environmental Health*, and *Satya* magazine.

Why animal liberation needs the Left and the Left needs animal liberation.

Current Affairs /
Political Science & Government
November
A Paperback Original
5½ x 8½ | 185 pp
TP US $17.95 | CAN $20.50
978-1-904859-67-3 CUSA

Marketing Plans

AK Press

Possibilities
Essays on Hierarchy, Rebellion, and Desire
David Graeber

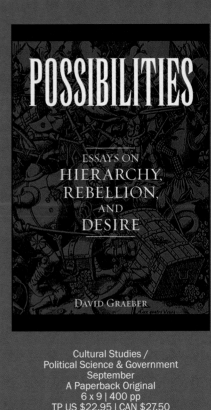

"Graeber's ideas are rich and wide-ranging; he pushes us to expand the boundaries of what we admit to be possible, or even thinkable."—Steven Shaviro, Wayne State University

In this new collection, David Graeber revisits questions raised in his popular book, *Fragments of an Anarchist Anthropology.* Written in an unpretentious style that uses accessible and entertaining language to convey complex theoretical ideas, these twelve essays cover a lot of ground, including the origins of capitalism, the history of European table manners, love potions in rural Madagascar, and the phenomenology of giant puppets at street protests. But they're linked by a clear purpose: to explore the nature of social power and the forms that resistance to it have taken, or might take in the future.

Anarchism is currently undergoing a worldwide revival, in many ways replacing Marxism as the theoretical and moral center of new revolutionary social movements. It has, however, left little mark on the academy. While anarchists and other visionaries have turned to anthropology for ideas and inspiration, anthropologists are reluctant to enter into serious dialogue. David Graeber is not. These essays, spanning almost twenty years, show how scholarly concerns can be of use to radical social movements, and how the perspectives of such movements shed new light on debates within the academy.

David Graeber has written for *Harper's, New Left Review,* and numerous scholarly journals. He is the author or editor of four books and currently lives in New York City.

An anthropologist investigates the revolution of everyday life.

Cultural Studies /
Political Science & Government
September
A Paperback Original
6 x 9 | 400 pp
TP US $22.95 | CAN $27.50
978-1-904859-66-6 CUSA

AK Press

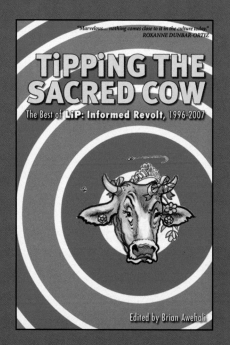

Tipping the Sacred Cow
The Best of LiP: Informed Revolt, 1996–2007
Edited by Brian Awehali

Tipping the Sacred Cow is a flabbergastingly refreshing smarty-pants collection of iconoclastic politics, culture, sex, and humor culled from the uncompromising, eclectic, and frequently laugh-out-loud pages of *LiP* magazine. Author Roxanne Dunbar-Ortiz describes *LiP* as "Marvelous! . . . Witty, but substantial . . . there's simply nothing that comes close to it in the culture today."

Gleefully skewering shibboleths across the political continuum, the radical brain trust gathered here by editor Brian Awehali takes critical aim at everything from women-first feminism, green capitalism, and queer assimilation and gay marriage, to the uses and abuses of shoplifting, the currently fashionable cult of catastrophism, and the prefabrication of political speech. Between broadsides, stops are made for a lively community flag burning, intentionally comedic genderqueer erotica, and other items of pointed mirth.

Contributors include Lisa Jervis, Winona LaDuke, Tim Wise, Heather Rogers, Iain Boal, Mattilda a.k.a. Matt Bernstein Sycamore, Neal Pollack, Guillermo Gómez-Peña, Michael Eric Dyson, damali ayo, Tim Kreider, Christopher Hitchens, and Mary Roach, among others.

Brian Awehali is an award-winning journalist whose work has appeared in or on Britannica.com, *Z* magazine, AlterNet, *Tikkun,* The Black World Today, and *High Times.* He is a tribal member of the Cherokee Nation of Oklahoma but makes his home in Oakland, California. Under his editorial guidance, *LiP* garnered a host of awards and nominations, including Best Online Cultural Coverage and Best New Title from *Utne,* People's Choice from South by Southwest, Best Magazine from *Clamor* magazine, Best Political Magazine from *East Bay Express,* and two Project Censored selections.

A collection of essays and ephemera that proves politics minus fun equals banal zealotry.

Political Science & Government /
Cultural Studies
October
A Paperback Original
6 x 9 | 240 pp
6 B&W illustrations
TP US $18.00 | CAN $21.95
978-1-904859-73-4 CUSA

Marketing Plans

National advertising:
Arthur • Bitch • The Progressive •
Punk Planet • Rain Taxi • Z Magazine

Author Hometown: San Francisco, CA

AK Press

Partisanas
Women in the Armed Resistance to Fascism and German Occupation (1936–1945)
Ingrid Strobl
Foreword by Martha Ackelsberg

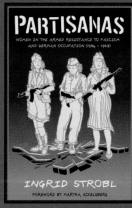

Common perception of women in wartime relegates them to the sidelines of history—working in munitions factories or waiting for their men to return. The truth is that much of the resistance to fascism should be chalked up to the people about whom official accounts have nothing to say. *Partisanas* excavates the history of women who planted bombs, shouldered guns, and were among the most active participants in the European resistance.

Ingrid Strobl is a well-known filmmaker, artist, lecturer, and writer. She makes her home in Cologne, Germany.

Martha Ackelsberg is the author of *Free Women of Spain*.

Marketing Plans
National advertising: BUST • The Indypendent • Library Journal • The Progressive • Tikkun

Women's Studies / History
March
A Paperback Original
6 x 9 | 320 pp
25 B&W photographs
TP US $19.95 | CAN $24.00
978-1-904859-69-7 CUSA

A compelling picture of the women who risked everything in the fight against fascism.

Global Fire
150 Fighting Years of International Anarchism and Syndicalism (Counter-Power vol 2)
Michael Schmidt and Lucien van der Walt

History /
Political Science &
Government
March
A Paperback Original
6 x 9 | 500 pp
TP US $24.95
CAN $30.00
978-1-904859-68-0
CUSA

This is the second of two volumes reexamining the history of anarchism in both theory and practice. Focusing on anarchism's global impact—on five continents over 150 years—this is the most complete and detailed scholarly book on the topic.

Michael Schmidt is a Johannesburg-based senior investigative journalist.

Lucien van der Walt teaches at the University of the Witwatersrand, Johannesburg.

Live from the Armed Madhouse
Greg Palast

Current Affairs /
Popular Culture
Available Now
AK Press Audio
5½ x 5 | 70 minutes
CD 50% US $13.98
CAN $21.50
978-1-904859-64-2
CUSA

Armed with over fifty classified documents, confidential memos, and secret plans, Greg Palast cuts through the TV news baby-talk. It was he who first uncovered how Jeb Bush and Katherine Harris stole the 2000 election. Harris calls him "twisted," but here's the new twist revealed in this CD: John Kerry won in 2004, and 2008 is already fixed.

AK Press

GRANNY MADE ME AN ANARCHIST

GENERAL FRANCO, THE ANGRY BRIGADE AND ME

STUART CHRISTIE

Biography & Autobiography / History
September
A Paperback Original
5½ x 8½ | 400 pp
50 B&W photographs
TP US $19.95 | CAN $24.00
978-1-904859-65-9 CUSA

Marketing Plans

National advertising:
Alternative Press Magazine • BOMB •
International Socialist Review •
The Northeastern Anarchist •
The Progressive • Z Magazine

Granny Made Me An Anarchist
General Franco, The Angry Brigade and Me
Stuart Christie

"Stuart Christie's anarchist activities and brushes with the law make the Sex Pistols look like choir boys."—*Sunday Express*

"A fascinating personal account . . . a remarkable picture of the late-twentieth century, seen through sensitive eyes and interpreted by a compassionate, searching soul."—Noam Chomsky

In 1964, a fresh-faced, eighteen-year-old Glaswegian named Stuart Christie became the most famous anarchist in Britain. He was arrested delivering explosives to Madrid to be used in the assassination of Spanish dictator General Franco. After serving three years of his twenty-year sentence, he was released due to international pressure from supporters like Bertrand Russell and Jean Paul Sartre. Eight years later, he was arrested again in England on suspicion of membership in the Angry Brigade—an armed group hell-bent on overthrowing the government—but was this time acquitted. Christie's warm and witty memoir, from the tough streets of post-World War II Glasgow to the heady ideals of the Generation of '68, reads like a cloak-and-dagger political thriller.

Granny Made Me an Anarchist chronicles clandestine political maneuverings, life behind bars, and flirtations with radical youth who were convinced the government could be toppled and their country made anew. Avoiding the self-centered trappings of many 1960s memoirs, Christie's lamentations shine light into the darkness and illuminate the human soul.

Stuart Christie was a founder of the Anarchist Black Cross, *Black Flag* magazine, and Cienfuegos Press. He has written numerous books on Left and anarchist history.

An extraordinary story with the pace and excitement of a good political thriller.

AK Press

Born Under a Bad Sky
Notes from the Dark Side of the Earth
Jeffrey St. Clair

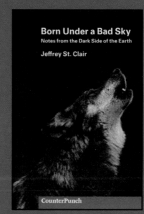

In this chilling survey of the American landscape, investigative journalist Jeffrey St. Clair guides readers through the environmental wreckage of North America, from the plutonium-contaminated fields of the Hanford Nuclear Reservation to Indian Point Energy Center, the world's most dangerous nuclear plant. St. Clair, co-editor of the popular *CounterPunch* newsletter and website, exposes the corrupt political machinery driving the exploitation of the American outback. From the clear-cutting of ancient forests to the damming of some of the world's wildest rivers, he outs the politicians, Democratic and Republican alike, who are profiting from the poisoning of the planet.

Marketing Plans
Co-op available
National advertising: Earth First! Journal • The Ecologist

Author Events
Oakland, CA • San Francisco, CA • Portland, OR • Seattle, WA

Author Hometown: Oregon City, OR

Environmental Studies /
Political Science & Government
December
A Paperback Original
CounterPunch
5 x 7½ | 300 pp
TP US $15.00 | CAN $18.00
978-1-904859-70-3 CUSA

Environmental muckraking by one of America's most acclaimed radical journalists.

I, Claud
Memoirs of a Subversive
Claud Cockburn
Foreword by Alexander Cockburn

The memoirs of British radical journalist Claud Cockburn are sardonic, hilarious, and filled with rich historical detail. They tell the story of an Oxford-educated Communist who rubbed elbows with everyone from Al Capone to Charles de Gaulle. From *Times* correspondent to foreign editor of the *Daily Worker,* Cockburn witnessed many of the twentieth century's most important events. He shares his insights with unparalleled, and decidedly irreverent, authorial skill. Includes a new foreword by Alexander Cockburn.

Claud Cockburn (1904–1981) was a renowned journalist and novelist. His novel *Beat the Devil* was made into a film directed by John Huston.

Marketing Plans
Co-op available
National advertising: CounterPunch • Monthly Review • Mother Jones • The Nation • The Progressive • Z Magazine

Biography & Autobiography /
Political Science & Government
January
CounterPunch
6 x 9 | 410 pp
TP US $18.95 | CAN $21.95
978-1-904859-71-0 CUSA

A classic of radical autobiography.

AK Press

My First Time
A Collection of First
Punk Show Stories
Edited by Chris Duncan

Music / Popular Culture
6 x 9 | 225 pp
50 B&W illustrations and photographs
TP US $17.95 | CAN $21.50
978-1-904859-17-8 CUSA

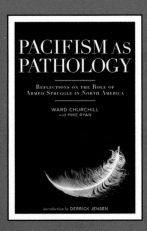

Pacifism as Pathology
Reflections on the Role of Armed
Struggle in North America
Ward Churchill with Mike Ryan
Introduction by Derrick Jensen

Political Science & Government /
Cultural Studies
5 x 8 | 228 pp
TP US $12.95 | CAN $15.50
978-1-904859-18-5 CUSA

Realizing the Impossible
Art Against Authority
**Edited by Josh MacPhee and
Erik Reuland**

Cultural Studies / Art
8 x 8 | 320 pp
125 Color and B&W illustrations
TP US $23.95 | CAN $29.00
978-1-904859-32-1 CUSA

The Price of Fire
Resource Wars and
Social Movements in Bolivia
Benjamin Dangl

Latin American Studies /
Political Science & Government
5½ x 8½ | 240 pp
TP US $15.95 | CAN $19.50
978-1-904859-33-8 CUSA

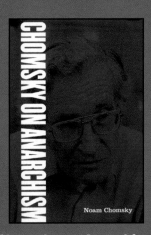

Chomsky on Anarchism
Noam Chomsky
Edited by Barry Pateman

Political Science & Government
6 x 9 | 256 pp
TP US $16.95 | CAN $20.50
978-1-904859-20-8 CUSA

Vision on Fire
Emma Goldman on the
Spanish Revolution
Edited by David Porter

History / Political Science & Government
6 x 9 | 347 pp
19 B&W photographs and maps
TP US $18.95 | CAN $23.00
978-1-904859-57-4 CUSA

The Swing Voter of Staten Island
Arthur Nersesian

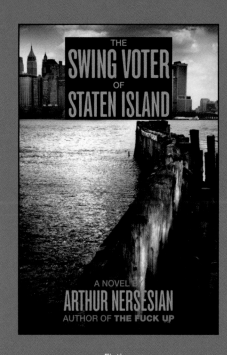

Until now, Arthur Nersesian's previous six novels (including *The Fuck-up*, MTV/ Pocket Books, which has sold over 100,000 copies) have focused on the tragicomedy of fin de siècle New York City. Now, in his boldest novel yet, he has broken into a new landscape that at once fuses the real with the surreal, the psychological with the psychedelic. Actual characters from the 1960s and 1970s—Allen Ginsberg, Timothy Leary, Daniel Ellsberg, and the Berrigan Brothers—are but a few of the folks who populate this alternate version of American history.

The Swing Voter of Staten Island takes place over the course of a week in November 1981. Uli, suffering from amnesia, finds himself on a mission but isn't quite sure what it is, who sent him, or even who he is. He ventures across the perilous wilds of New York City, through abandoned neighborhoods and burned-out battlefields. But Uli soon awakens to the awful fact that this isn't New York City at all. He is a key player in a strange, alternate history of both his city and his country.

Uli has found himself trapped in New York, Nevada, isolated in the center of an impenetrable desert—where the US military was able to transform one of its "military situation cities" into a temporary refuge center, designed to resemble New York City. While battling to make sense of his surroundings, Uli slowly remembers who he is and his own culpability in creating the current situation.

Arthur Nersesian is the author of six novels, including the smash hit *The Fuck-Up* (MTV/Pocket Books), *Unlubricated* (HarperCollins), *Chinese Takeout* (HarperCollins), *Manhattan Loverboy* (Akashic Books), *Suicide Casanova* (Akashic Books), and *dogrun* (MTV/ Pocket Books). He lives in New York City.

The much-anticipated new novel from New York City's most celebrated downtown hit novelist.

Also Available

Suicide Casanova
Arthur Nersesian
Fiction
5¼ x 8¼ | 368 pp
TP US $15.95 | CAN $19.50
978-1-888451-66-5 CUSA

Manhattan Loverboy
Arthur Nersesian
Fiction
5¼ x 8¼ | 202 pp
TP US $13.95 | CAN $17.00
978-1-888451-09-2 CUSA

Fiction
October
Akashic Urban Surreal Series
6 x 9 | 280 pp
TC US $22.95 | CAN $27.50
978-1-933354-34-7 CUSA

Marketing Plans

Co-op available
Advance reader copies
10,000-copy print run

Author Events

Los Angeles, CA • San Francisco, CA •
Washington, DC • Boston, MA •
New York, NY • Portland, OR • Seattle, WA

Author Hometown: New York, NY

Akashic Books

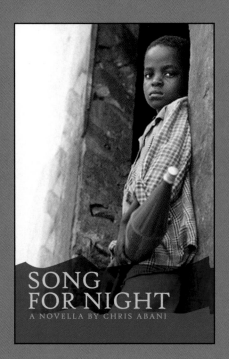

Song for Night
Chris Abani

"Chris Abani might be the most courageous writer working right now. There is no subject matter he finds daunting, no challenge he fears. Aside from that, he's stunningly prolific and writes like an angel. If you want to get at the molten heart of contemporary fiction, Abani is the starting point."—Dave Eggers, author of *What is the What*

"Not since Jerzy Kosinski's *The Painted Bird* or Agota Kristof's *Notebook* trilogy has there been such a harrowing novel about what it's like to be a young person in a war. That Chris Abani is able to find humanity, mercy, and even, yes, forgiveness, amid such devastation is something of a miracle."—Rebecca Brown, author of *The End of Youth*

In *Song for Night,* My Luck, a West African boy soldier who has lost his voice, leads us on a terrifying yet beautiful journey through the nightmare landscape of a brutal war in search of his lost platoon. Masterful, haunting, and written in a ghostly yet lyrical voice, this is a remarkable and empathetic story of courage, grace, morality, and triumph.

Chris Abani is a Nigerian poet and novelist and the author of *The Virgin of Flames*, *Becoming Abigail* (a *New York Times* Editors' Choice), and *GraceLand* (a selection of the *Today Show* Book Club, winner of the 2005 PEN/Hemingway Prize, and the Hurston/Wright Legacy Award). His other prizes include a PEN Freedom to Write Award, a Prince Claus Award, and a Lannan Literary Fellowship. He lives and teaches in California.

Chris Abani's new novella furthers his tremendous success in becoming today's most acclaimed young African writer.

Fiction / African Studies
September
A Paperback Original
5¼ x 8¼ | 164 pp
TP US $12.95 | CAN $15.50
978-1-933354-31-6 CUSA

Marketing Plans

Co-op available
Advance reader copies
10,000-copy print run

Author Events

Los Angeles, CA • San Francisco, CA • Washington, DC • Chicago, IL • Boston, MA • New York, NY • Portland, OR • Seattle, WA

Also Available

Becoming Abigail
Chris Abani
Fiction / African Studies
5¼ x 8¼ | 120 pp
TP US $11.95 | CAN $14.50
978-1-888451-94-8 CUSA

Akashic Books

Ending the War in Iraq

Tom Hayden

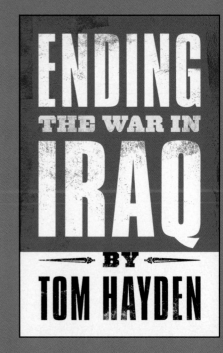

"Hayden stands for the voice of the people being heard, as it must in these difficult times."—Congresswoman Barbara Lee

"My generation owes a great debt to the intellectual courage and moral leadership provided by Hayden's example. Now an entirely new generation has the opportunity to learn from his wisdom."—Marc Cooper, author of *Pinochet and Me*

A leading antiwar figure in the 1960s, Tom Hayden wrote extensively on Vietnam and was one of the small number of Americans engaged in dialogue with both sides during the Paris Peace Talks. As an Irish American, he spent ten years supporting and writing about the peace process leading up to the Good Friday Agreement; and during his eighteen years as a California legislator, he devoted himself to writing about and trying to prevent inner-city violence. Hayden remains a stalwart antiwar activist, is credited with initiating the 2005 congressional exit strategy hearings, and has interviewed Iraqi exiles in the Middle East and London. His urgent new book comes from a patient understanding of how conflicts end.

Hayden argues that the Iraq War will end through the application of public pressure against the pillars of the policy. A new kind of antiwar movement, delineated in this groundbreaking original work, can overturn those pillars. For the first time in American history, he writes, an American majority voted against a war in progress in November 2006. This is a book for millions of peace activists, for the undecided public, and for the 2008 presidential candidates.

Tom Hayden was a founding member of the Students for a Democratic Society and author of its visionary call, the Port Huron Statement, described by Howard Zinn as "one of those historic documents which represents an era." Hayden was also one of the famous "Chicago Seven" protesters during the 1968 Democratic Convention. He was elected to the California State Assembly in 1982, and to the state senate ten years later, serving eighteen years in all.

Tom Hayden brings a lifetime of experience to the challenges of ending the Iraq War—and preventing future wars.

Current Affairs /
Political Science & Government
Available Now
A Paperback Original
5¼ x 8¼ | 250 pp
TP US $14.95 | CAN $18.00
978-1-933354-45-3 CUSA

Marketing Plans

Co-op available
Advance reader copies
15,000-copy print run

Author Events

Los Angeles, CA • San Francisco, CA •
Chicago, IL • Boston, MA • Minneapolis/
St. Paul, MN • New York, NY

Author Hometown: Los Angeles, CA

Detroit Noir
Edited by E.J. Olsen and John C. Hocking

From crime stories in the classic, hard-boiled style to the vividly experimental, from the determination of those risking everything to the desperation of those with nothing left to lose, *Detroit Noir* delivers unforgettable tales that capture the city's dark vitality.

Includes stories by Joyce Carol Oates, Loren D. Estleman, Craig Holden, P.J. Parrish, Desiree Cooper, Nisi Shawl, Craig Bernier, Joe Boland, Megan Abbott, Dorene O'Brien, Lolita Hernandez, Peter Markus, Roger K. Johnson, Michael Zadoorian, Melissa Preddy, and E.J. Olsen.

Mystery / Fiction Anthology
November
A Paperback Original
Akashic Noir Series
5¼ x 8¼ | 300 pp
TP US $14.95 | CAN $18.00
978-1-933354-39-2 CUSA

Motor City's finest literary talents—including Oates, Estleman, Holden, and Parrish—offer a shadowed spectrum of gripping, haunting visions.

Marketing Plans
Co-op available • Advance reader copies

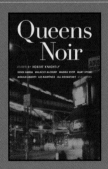

Mystery / Fiction
Anthology
October
A Paperback Original
Akashic Noir Series
5¼ x 8¼ | 300 pp
TP US $14.95
CAN $18.00
978-1-933354-38-5
CUSA

Havana Noir
Edited by Achy Obejas

Brand-new stories by Leonardo Padura, Pablo Medina, Alex Abella, Arturo Arango, Lea Aschkenas, Moisés Asís, Arnaldo Correa, Mabel Cuesta, Paquito D'Rivera, Yohamna de los Ángeles Depestre Corcho, Michel Encinosa Fu, Mylene Fernández Pintado, Carolina Garcia-Aguilera, Miguel Mejides, Achy Obejas, Oscar Ortiz, Ena Lucia Portela, Mariela Varona Roque, and Yoss.

Achy Obejas is the award-winning author of *Days of Awe, Memory Mambo,* and *We Came all the Way from Cuba So You Could Dress Like This?* She was born in Havana.

Mystery / Fiction
Anthology
January
A Paperback Original
Akashic Noir Series
5¼ x 8¼ | 350 pp
TP US $15.95
CAN $19.50
978-1-933354-40-8
CUSA

Queens Noir
Edited by Robert Knightly

Brand-new stories by Denis Hamill, Maggie Estep, Megan Abbott, Robert Knightly, Liz Martínez, Jill Eisenstadt, Mary Byrne, Tori Carrington, Shailly P. Agnihotri, k.j.a. Wishnia, Victoria Eng, Alan Gordon, Beverly Farley, Joe Guglielmelli, and Glenville Lovell.

Robert Knightly is a trial lawyer in the Criminal Defense Division of the Queens Legal Aid Society. In another life, he was a lieutenant in the New York City Police Department. The former president of the New York chapter of Mystery Writers of America, he was born and raised in New York City and lives in Queens.

Akashic Books Noir Series

Paradoxia
A Predator's Diary
Lydia Lunch

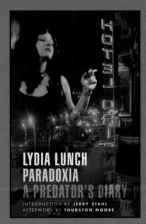

"Paradoxia reveals that Lunch is at her best when she's at her worst . . . [and] gives voice to her sometimes scary, frequently funny, always canny, never sentimental siren song."—Barbara Kruger, *Artforum*

Lydia Lunch relays in graphic detail the true psychic repercussions of sexual misadventure. From New York to London to New Orleans, *Paradoxia* is an uncensored, novelized account of one woman's assault on the males of the species.

Lydia Lunch was the primary instigator of the No Wave Movement and the focal point of the Cinema of Transgression. A musician, writer, and photographer, she exposes the dark underbelly of passion confronting the lusty demons whose struggle for power and control forever stalk the periphery of our collective obsessions.

Marketing Plans
Co-op available • Advance reader copies

Author Events
Los Angeles, CA • San Francisco, CA • Washington, DC • Chicago, IL • Boston, MA • New York, NY • Portland, OR • Seattle, WA

Popular Culture / Biography & Autobiography
September
5¼ x 8¼ | 160 pp
TP US $13.95 | CAN $17.00
978-1-933354-35-4 CUSA

The unspeakable sexual confessions of underground legend Lydia Lunch. With an introduction by Jerry Stahl and an afterword by Thurston Moore.

Silent Pictures
Photographs by Pat Graham

Modest Mouse, Fugazi, Bikini Kill, Blonde Redhead, and Shellac are just a few of the subjects in Pat Graham's visually stunning first book. Many of these photographs have shaped the iconography of underground rock over the past two decades.

Pat Graham has been a photographer for eighteen years. His work has centered on musicians and has been used on dozens of records, as well as in every major music publication in Europe and the United States. His work is part of the permanent collection in the Experience Music Project in Seattle. He currently lives in London.

Marketing Plans
Co-op available • Advance reader copies

Author Events
Los Angeles, CA • San Francisco, CA • Washington, DC • Chicago, IL • Boston, MA • New York, NY • Portland, OR • Philadelphia, PA • Seattle, WA

Photography / Popular Culture
September
A Paperback Original
10 x 11¼ | 132 pp
140 Color and B&W photographs
TP US $22.95 | CAN $27.50
978-1-933354-42-2 CUSA

The first collection of work from the acclaimed underground music photographer Pat Graham.

Akashic Books

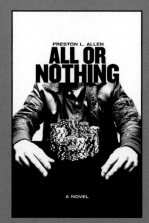

Fiction / African American Studies
November
A Paperback Original
6 x 8 | 280 pp
TP US $14.95 | CAN $18.00
978-1-933354-41-5 CUSA

What William S. Burroughs'
***Junky* was to heroin addiction,**
***All or Nothing* is to gambling, only**
darker and more prophetic.

All or Nothing
Preston L. Allen

While other gambling novels seek either to sermonize on the addiction or glorify it by highlighting its few prosperous celebrities, *All or Nothing* explores the hope and magical thinking that sustains gamblers even at their lowest.

A recipient of a State of Florida Individual Artist Fellowship, Preston L. Allen is the author of the thriller *Hoochie Mama* and the collection *Churchboys and Other Sinners.* His stories have appeared in numerous magazines and journals and have been anthologized in *Brown Sugar* (Penguin) and *Miami Noir* (Akashic Books). He lives in south Florida.

Marketing Plans
Co-op available • Advance reader copies

Author Events
Miami, FL • New York, NY

Author Hometown: Miami, FL

Fiction
February
A Paperback Original
Punk Planet Books
5¼ x 7½ | 250 pp
TP US $14.95 | CAN $18.00
978-1-933354-43-9 CUSA

Denial, God, dystopia,
academia, and reality TV collide
in acclaimed author Elizabeth
Crane's third story collection.

You Must Be This Happy to Enter
Elizabeth Crane

"Crane has a distinctive and eccentric voice that is consistent and riveting."
—*The New York Times Book Review*

Whether breathlessly enthusiastic, serenely calm, or really concentrating on their personal zombie issues, Elizabeth Crane's happy cast explores the complexities behind personal satisfaction.

Elizabeth Crane is the author of two previous story collections, *When the Messenger Is Hot* and *All This Heavenly Glory.* Her work has also been featured in numerous publications, including *Chicago Reader* and *The Believer,* as well as several anthologies, including *McSweeney's Future Dictionary of America* and *The Best Underground Fiction.* A winner of the Chicago Public Library's 21st Century Award, Crane lives in Chicago.

Marketing Plans
Co-op available • Advance reader copies

Author Events
Los Angeles, CA • San Francisco, CA • Washington, DC • Chicago, IL • Boston, MA • New York, NY • Portland, OR • Seattle, WA

Author Hometown: Chicago, IL

PUNK PLANET BOOKS

Akashic Books

The Duppy
Anthony C. Winkler

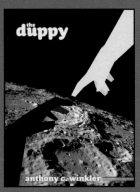

"Every country (if she's lucky) gets the Mark Twain she deserves, and Winkler is ours, bristling with savage Jamaican wit, heart-stopping compassion, and jaw-dropping humor all at once."—Marlon James, author of *John Crow's Devil*

With his characteristic outrageousness, Anthony C. Winkler subverts conventional thinking in this entertaining, thought-provoking, and ultimately uplifting novel about one Jamaican man's surprising trip to heaven.

Anthony C. Winkler was born in Kingston, Jamaica, in 1942, and is widely recognized as one of the island's finest and most hilarious exports. His Caribbean classic *The Lunatic* (Akashic Books) was turned into a feature film, and his last novel, *Dog War,* was published in June 2007 by Akashic Books. He lives with his wife in Atlanta, Georgia.

Fiction / African American Studies
March
A Paperback Original
5 x 7¾ | 175 pp
TP US $13.95 | CAN $17.00
978-1-933354-33-0 CUSA

Oddball sexuality, acts of perversion, and out-of-order behavior from the acclaimed Jamaican author of *The Lunatic* and *Dog War.*

Marketing Plans
Co-op available • Advance reader copies

Author Events
Washington, DC • Atlanta, GA • New York, NY

Author Hometown: Atlanta, GA

The Musical Illusionist
and Other Tales
Alex Rose

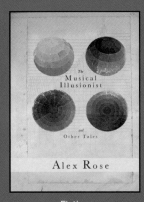

In the tradition of Borges and Calvino, *The Musical Illusionist* is an interwoven collection of postmodern folk tales—disappearing manuscripts, neurological anomalies, teleporting bacteria, and an unforgettable composer who manipulates sound to bend perception—that masterfully blend scientific curiosity with magical-realist caprice.

Alex Rose has published stories and essays for *McSweeney's,* the *North American Review,* the *Providence Journal,* the *Forward,* the *Science Creative Quarterly,* and *DIAGRAM.* He has also directed a number of short films that have appeared on HBO, MTV, Comedy Central, Showtime, and the BBC.

Fiction
September
A Paperback Original
Hotel St. George
5 x 7¼ | 160 pp
30 Color and B&W illustrations
and photographs
TP US $14.95 | CAN $18.00
978-0-9789103-1-0 CUSA

The second installment from the daring Hotel St. George imprint.

Marketing Plans
Co-op available • Advance reader copies

Author Events
Los Angeles, CA • San Francisco, CA • Washington, DC • Amherst, MA • Boston, MA • Portland, ME • New York, NY • Portland, OR • Philadelphia, PA • Providence, RI

Author Hometown: New York, NY

Akashic Books

Gomer's Song
Kwame Dawes

Poetry / African Studies
September
A Paperback Original
Black Goat
6 x 9 | 72 pp
TP US $14.95 | CAN $18.00
978-1-933354-44-6 CUSA

Award-winning Kwame Dawes explores the insidious nature of power and the limits of protest.

Gomer's Song is a re-rendering of the Bible story. In Gomer, a harlot who was the wife of the Old Testament prophet Hosea, Kwame Dawes finds the subject for a beautiful, contemporary exploration on freedom and sacrifice.

Kwame Dawes is an award-winning, Ghanaian-born Jamaican author of several books of poetry, nonfiction, and fiction (including his debut novel, *She's Gone,* published by Akashic Books in 2007). He teaches at the University of South Carolina, where he is distinguished poet in residence and director of the USC Arts Institute and the South Carolina Poetry Initiative. Dawes is the programmer for the annual Jamaican Calabash International Literary Festival.

Marketing Plans
Co-op available • Advance reader copies

Author Events
Los Angeles, CA • San Francisco, CA • Washington, DC • New York, NY • Columbia, SC

Author Hometown: Columbia, SC

Auto Mechanic's Daughter
Karen Harryman

Poetry
September
A Paperback Original
Black Goat
6 x 9 | 84 pp
TP US $14.95
CAN $18.00
978-1-933354-36-1
CUSA

"In Karen Harryman's hands everything becomes a blessing."—Ellen Bass, author of *Mules of Love*

Charting the vicissitudes of her own life, and the travails and triumphs of the lives of those whom she knows and loves, Karen Harryman's poems travel great distances, both internally and geographically.

Karen Harryman lives in Burbank, California, with her husband Kirker Butler. *Auto Mechanic's Daughter* is her first book.

eel on reef
Uche Nduka

**Poetry /
African Studies**
September
A Paperback Original
Black Goat
6 x 9 | 152 pp
TP US $15.95
CAN $19.50
978-1-933354-37-8
CUSA

In *eel on reef,* Uche Nduka challenges every expectation of an African poet. His unique voice is a heady amalgam of Christopher Okigbo, A.R. Ammons, John Ashbery, Kamau Brathwaite, and that which only Nduka can bring.

Uche Nduka was born and raised in Nigeria. His published books include *Flower Child, Second Act,* and *Chiraoscuro* (winner of the Association of Nigerian Authors Poetry Prize in 1997). He lives in Bremen, Germany.

Akashic Books

The World in Place of Itself

Bill Rasmovicz

"Incredibly moving and smart, this book is indeed a world in place of itself, and more, in place of the world we thought we knew. With stunning metaphors, fast-paced leaps and tone shifts within a seamless art, we discover new ways of seeing at almost every line, a palimpsest of visions in every poem of this fabulous book."—Richard Jackson

With fervent physical and metaphysical detail, and narrating from an unexpected angle of perception, Bill Rasmovicz plumbs the world ghosting this one, exposing the true nature of the unconscious—a superconscious whose language is startlingly apt imagery and ecstatic description.

From "On Becoming Light":

And there it was, the moth;
a child's hand wrestling itself in the grass.
Delirious, it fumbled its way out from the dark umbrella
of a tree, then landed on the stoop.

A frayed rope of light swung from the porch.
The moon was gorged on the dewy foment of summer.

I set my hand near, and it fluttered into my palm:
its weight no more than breath, its wings,
laments hammered into sheets of dust.

Bill Rasmovicz is a graduate of the MFA writing program at Vermont College and Temple University School of Pharmacy. His poetry has appeared in *Mid-American Review, Nimrod, Hunger Mountain, Third Coast,* and other magazines. He lives in New York City.

This neo-baroque, hypnotic debut reads like transcribed fever dreams, employing elements of film noir and surrealism.

Poetry
September
A Paperback Original
5½ x 8½ | 80 pp
TP US $14.95 | CAN $18.00
978-1-882295-64-7 CUSA

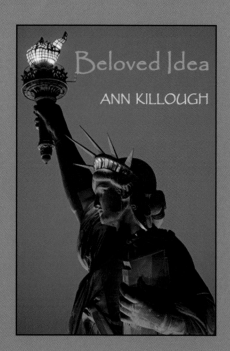

Poetry
November
A Paperback Original
5½ x 8½ | 80 pp
TP US $14.95 | CAN $18.00
978-1-882295-65-4 CUSA

Marketing Plans

National advertising:
The American Poetry Review •
Poetry • Poets & Writers • Rain Taxi •
The Writer's Chronicle

Author Events

Boston, MA • Brookline, MA •
Cambridge, MA • Raleigh, NC

Author Hometown: Brookline, MA

Beloved Idea
Ann Killough

"Ann Killough's voice is self-aware, skeptical, and inconsolable. With bracketed lower-case titles and long strophic lines, with fragmented echoes of the white whale and the open road, and with proliferating metaphors that question the worth and nature of metaphor itself, Killough probes the soul of twenty-first century America and gives our own quiet desperation a name and vivid shape."—Fred Marchant

This brave and remarkable debut functions as one long poem and achieves extension through Stein-like repetition, and meaning through accretion and excess. In seeking a metaphorical ideal, Ann Killough's struggle to write is a struggle to understand her feelings for her nation—a process akin to a mother learning that her child is a murderer, a truth from which there can be no refuge or respite.

From "[stuffed animal]":

*She imagined the beloved nation with its sheep's face and the other wolves
around it like dependent clauses. Or the other dependent clauses around it
like sheep.*

*She could never keep straight who was who in the sentences. At times she
felt like a simple noun in apposition, Red Riding Hood's grandmother hiding
in the closet or the first witch with only her red shoes sticking out.*

Ann Killough's work has appeared in *Fence, FIELD, Poetry Ireland Review, Sentence,* and elsewhere. Her chapbook *Sinners in the Hands: Selections from the Catalog* received the 2003 Robert Phillips Poetry Chapbook Prize. Killough lives in Brookline, Massachusetts, and coordinates the Brookline Poetry Series and the Mouthful Reading Series in Cambridge.

Ann Killough's insistent debut is a quest to lovingly deconstruct,
and construct anew, a nation ideal.

Alice James Books

Door to a Noisy Room
Peter Waldor

Poetry
January
A Paperback Original
5½ x 8½ | 80 pp
TP US $14.95 | CAN $18.00
978-1-882295-66-1 CUSA

"It's such a delight when something catches you by surprise and makes you read on and on. So it is with Waldor, a superb lyric, gnomic and Gnostic poet."
—Gerald Stern

Peter Waldor's spare irony—sometimes tender, sometimes bawdy—deals in dichotomies: love and hate, frailty and strength, fear and faith. These elliptical and colloquial lyrics draw equally from parable, prayer, and elegy. Hesitating on the threshold between isolation and community, the poet focuses a distortingly accurate microscope on what matters in our lives.

"Lips"

My love, our lips
are four knives
asleep in the drawer.

Last four left.
The rest out for
the usual butchery.

The craftsmen—
the woodworker,
silversmith,

gone for good,
even the glassblower
who puffed the knob

that has gone
unheld all evening
is gone.

Peter Waldor's poems have been published or are forthcoming in many magazines, including *The American Poetry Review, Ploughshares,* and *The Iowa Review.* Waldor lives with his wife and three children in northern New Jersey, where he works in the insurance business.

This pithy debut collection negotiates, through playful meditations, our uneasy coexistence in the marketplace and home.

Marketing Plans

National advertising:
The American Poetry Review •
Boston Review • Poetry • Poets & Writers •
Rain Taxi • The Writer's Chronicle

Author Events

Washington, DC • Iowa City, IA •
Boston, MA • Medford, MA • Detroit, MI •
Whippany, NJ • New York, NY

Author Hometown: Short Hills, NJ

Alice James Books

A Thief of Strings
Donald Revell

Poetry
5½ x 8½ | 80 pp
TP US $14.95 | CAN $18.00
978-1-882295-61-6 CUSA

Take What You Want
Henrietta Goodman

Poetry
5½ x 8½ | 80 pp
TP US $14.95 | CAN $18.00
978-1-882295-62-3 CUSA

Equivocal
Julie Carr

Poetry
5½ x 8½ | 80 pp
TP US $14.95 | CAN $18.00
978-1-882295-63-0 CUSA

The Glass Age
Cole Swensen

Poetry
5½ x 8½ | 80 pp
TP US $14.95 | CAN $18.00
978-1-882295-60-9 CUSA

The Case Against Happiness
Jean-Paul Pecqueur

Poetry
5½ x 8½ | 64 pp
TP US $14.95 | CAN $18.00
978-1-882295-59-3 CUSA

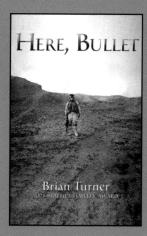

Here, Bullet
Brian Turner

Poetry
5½ x 8½ | 80 pp
TP US $14.95 | CAN $18.00
978-1-882295-55-5 CUSA

Nightlight: A Memoir
Janine Avril

A spare and beautiful memoir of family secrets and their consequences.

While in her twenties, Janine Avril learned a shocking family secret, one that set her on a deeply personal journey into her past. When Janine was twelve, growing up in the wealthy and predominantly Jewish suburb of Roslyn, New York, her mother was diagnosed with a deadly cancer and died three years later. While a junior at Cornell University, Janine learned that her father, a popular French chef and entrepreneur, was ill with full-blown AIDS. It was nearly five years later when Janine received an unexpected phone call from her uncle, forcing her to reevaluate her childhood. Inspired to understand as much as she can about her parents, she finally discovers a powerful link between her father and herself, and her past becomes illuminated like the nightlight that once protected her from the darkness of her youth.

Janine Avril teaches high school English and has taught college writing at Brooklyn College and New York City College of Technology. Janine is the founder and host of Girlsalon, a forum for lesbian/queer writers to showcase their talents. She has been published in the *Los Angeles Times Magazine, Velvetpark Magazine,* and, for her piece "Eavesdropping," *Topic Magazine.* She has also been featured in *Time Out New York, Gay City News* and www.lesbiannation.com. Janine's websites are www.janinesays.com and www.girlsalon.org.

**Secrets are revealed and truths are unearthed
in this beautifully written memoir of one woman's family.**

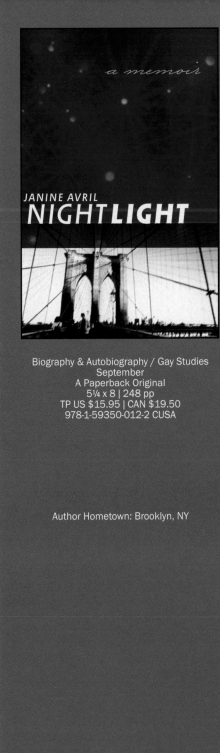

Biography & Autobiography / Gay Studies
September
A Paperback Original
5¼ x 8 | 248 pp
TP US $15.95 | CAN $19.50
978-1-59350-012-2 CUSA

Author Hometown: Brooklyn, NY

Alyson Books

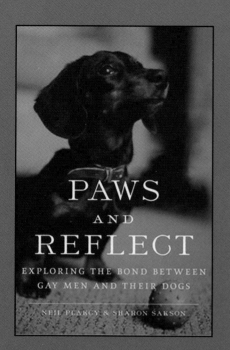

Pets & Pet Care
November
6 x 9 | 273 pp
TP US $15.95 | CAN $19.50
978-1-59350-034-4 CUSA

Paws and Reflect
Exploring the Bond Between Gay Men and Their Dogs
Neil Plakcy and Sharon Sakson

"*Paws and Reflect* is an eloquent, moving testament that this unconditional love has helped form a great emotional and spiritual connection between dogs and their humans that just simply makes our lives healthier and more complete."—David Frei, co-host of *The Westminster Kennel Club Dog Show,* USA Network

"Anyone—gay, straight, bi, transsexual, asexual—who has a dog will appreciate these stories of love, trust, caring and commitment."—*The Bark* magazine

Paws and Reflect explores and celebrates the special and powerful bond between gay man and dog through twenty-five stories of personal experiences in this well-crafted collection. Touching, powerful, and often humorous, this is a must-read for all dog lovers.

The book includes interviews with Edward Albee, Jonathan Caouette, Ron Nyswaner, Charles Busch, and contributions from Jay Quinn, Hal Campbell, and others.

A new, eight-page black-and-white photo insert is included with this paperback edition.

Neil Plakcy is the author of the gay detective novels *Mahu* and *Mahu Surfer,* and his fiction has appeared in many publications. Neil is owned by a golden retriever named Sam with whom he lives, along with his partner, Marc, in Hollywood, Florida.

Sharon Sakson is a writer and producer for NBC News, and the author of *Brussels Griffons: A Complete Pet Owner's Manual.* Sharon lives in Princeton, New Jersey.

**True stories of unconditional love and devotion:
a celebration of man and man's best friend.**

Alyson Books

Paws & Effect
The Healing Power of Dogs
Sharon Sakson

For the dog lovers everywhere who believe that the unconditional love of a dog has changed their world.

In *Paws & Effect,* interviewees explain how the bond they share with their dogs has transported them through terrible illnesses, both physical and psychological. Not only are their dogs faithful, intuitive companions, but they are also often spiritual guides to good health. The introduction relates the unique relationship between dogs and humans dating back to the Stone Age and is followed by individual accounts of dogs that have played a special, healing role in the lives of their human families. *Paws & Effect* also covers new scientific findings on how dogs can save lives, sniff out cancerous tumors, and warn epileptics of impending seizures. Included are interviewees from the United States and Canada.

Sharon Sakson is an NBC News producer and writer, and the author of *Paws and Reflect: Exploring the Bond Between Gay Men and Their Dogs* and *Brussels Griffons: A Complete Pet Owner's Manual.* An American Kennel Club dog show judge and breeder of champions, Sharon lives in Princeton, New Jersey.

Stories that explore how the bond between dog and human works healing miracles in human lives.

Pets & Pet Care
December
6 x 9 | 288 pp
TC US $24.95 | CAN $30.00
978-1-59350-038-2 CUSA

The Portable Queer Series
By Erin McHugh

Attending a dinner party and need that perfect gift? A friend on the mend needs that ideal pick-me-up? Need a party game for that long car ride? Or simply want to treat yourself? Alyson Books introduces The Portable Queer, a charming, informative, and ultimately entertaining new series of gift books that is chock full of clever quotes, revealing biographies, and surprising history. The perfect blend of style and substance, The Portable Queer will likely become your best gay friend.

Erin McHugh is a longtime gay activist and fundraiser, former publishing executive, and author of several books. Erin lives in New York, New York.

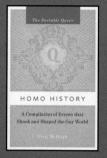

Gay Studies /
Reference
October
4 x 6 | 160 pp
TC US $9.95
CAN $12.00
978-1-59350-031-3
CUSA

The Portable Queer: Homo History
A Compilation of Events that Shook and Shaped the Gay World

From the Old Testament to the New World Order, the centuries have not always championed homosexuality. But the past has also been checkered with surprising liberal periods. From ancient Rome to gay pride, here is a time capsule of gay history, presented in quick, short takes. Strange, fascinating, and historically revealing!

Gay Studies /
Reference
October
4 x 6 | 160 pp
TC US $9.95
CAN $12.00
978-1-59350-032-0
CUSA

The Portable Queer: Out of the Mouth of Queers
A Compilation of Bon Mots, Words of Wisdom and Sassy Sayings

Thoughts from the gays of yesteryear to today's "friends of queers." Observations on love and sex, politics, fashion, and much more, these are the words that have endured through the centuries. But it's not all wisecracks and witticisms—included are some of the most scandalous remarks ever made! Riotous, moving, and definitively quotable.

Gay Studies /
Reference
October
4 x 6 | 160 pp
TC US $9.95
CAN $12.00
978-1-59350-033-7
CUSA

The Portable Queer: A Gay in the Life
A Compilation of Saints and Sinners in Gay History

Those who have changed the face of homosexuality over the centuries are not always heroic. Learn about the first great gay activist Karl Heinrich Ulrichs, read of brave men and women of the Matachine Society and of the Stonewall riot, and relive the stories of the writers and artists who pushed a movement forward. Intriguing, shocking, and ultimately hopeful!

Alyson Books

The Advocate Guide to Gay Men's Health and Wellness

Frank Spinelli, MD

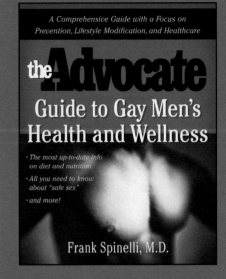

Gay Studies / Health & Fitness
January
A Paperback Original
7 x 9 | 304 pp
TP US $21.95 | CAN $26.50
978-1-59350-040-5 CUSA

Focusing on prevention, lifestyle modification, and healthcare, Dr. Frank Spinelli has channeled his years of experience and research in order to create a comprehensive medical guide for gay men. Covering such diverse topics as immunization, physical exams, sex, the male pap smear, and andropause, New York City's "hottest gay doctor" has compiled his knowledge into an invaluable guide, created specifically for gay men over forty years of age.

The volume also gives gay men of *all* ages the blueprint to become active participants in their own healthcare. *The Advocate Guide* provides a quick reference, along with Dr. Spinelli's tips on the essentials:

- coming out to your doctor
- the gay male physical exam
- safe sex
- depression/anxiety
- substance abuse and the party circuit
- nutrition
- everything you'd want to know about the male body
- and more

Frank Spinelli, MD, is a board certified internist in private practice in New York City, in addition to serving as clinical director of the HIV program at Cabrini Medical Center. Dr. Spinelli has made frequent television appearances, is the gay health expert on *Radio with a Twist,* a national talk show, and is a contributing health writer for *Instinct* magazine. Dr. Spinelli currently lives in the Chelsea district of Manhattan.

An invaluable resource for gay men to live happier, healthier lives by becoming active participants in their healthcare.

Author Hometown: New York, NY

A Push and a Shove
A Novel
Christopher Kelly

A mesmerizing debut novel of vengeance.

Tortured by memories of being bullied at school, Ben Reilly sets out to put his demons to rest. Terrence O'Connor, the beautiful boy who tormented him, is now a successful writer in Manhattan, but he is also a man searching out his own identity. As Ben and Terrence form an unlikely friendship, hidden motives and long-kept secrets bubble to the surface. And can Terrence admit to his own confused feelings? Darkly disturbing and brilliantly written, here is a chilling depiction of the once-victim who unwittingly becomes the bully.

Author Hometown: Fort Worth, TX

Gay Literature / Fiction
September
A Paperback Original
5½ x 8½ | 288 pp
TP US $14.95 | CAN $18.00
978-1-59350-048-1 CUSA

What if you got a chance to exact revenge on the bully from your childhood?

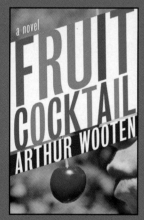

Fruit Cocktail
A Novel
Arthur Wooten

Men are like a box of chocolates—you like what's on the outside.

Hop on board for this delicious, freshly squeezed sequel to the acclaimed *On Picking Fruit,* where Curtis Jenkins once again braves the fickle dating scene in his continuing search for the perfect man. After writing the successful *101 Ways to Collide Into Your Gay Soul Mate,* Jenkins finds on his book tour that men—whether in Provincetown, Los Angeles, or somewhere in between—rarely wear their hearts on their biceps . . . unless it's a tattoo. Funny, unpredictable, and strangely moving, *Fruit Cocktail* is, like its feckless hero, ripe for the picking.

Arthur Wooten has also written for theater, film, and television.

Author Hometown: New York, NY

Gay Literature
December
A Paperback Original
5½ x 8½ | 224 pp
TP US $14.95 | CAN $18.00
978-1-59350-047-4 CUSA

Determined, hopeless romantic Curtis Jenkins finds more bad apples in this hilarious sequel to *On Picking Fruit.*

Alyson Books

Loving Ourselves
The Gay and Lesbian Guide to Self-Esteem
Dr. Kimeron Hardin

Love the inside, embrace the outside.

First published in 1999, this thoroughly revised and updated edition now presents the issues and concerns relating to self-esteem in the LGBT world to a new generation of men and women. This compassionate guide delves into the unique problems of self-esteem in the gay community, and shows how understanding your own self-worth can allow you to function better in this complex world. With advice for every demographic, this is the most comprehensive book for building a better you.

Dr. Kimeron Hardin is a licensed clinical psychologist and director of the Bay Area Pain & Wellness Center.

Author Hometown: San Francisco, CA

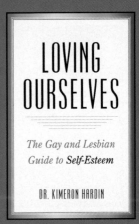

Gay Studies / Self-Actualization & Self Help
March
A Paperback Original
5½ x 8½ | 248 pp
TP US $16.95 | CAN $20.50
978-1-59350-045-0 CUSA

**A revised and updated version
of the definitive book on self-esteem
for the LGBT community.**

The 7-Day Dating and Relationship Plan for Gay Men
Practical Advice from the Gay Matchmaker
Grant Wheaton with Dennis Courtney

Matchmaker, matchmaker, find me a match!

How does a single gay guy find his way to a right, lasting relationship? Our dating expert shares authentic sagas straight (so to speak) from his clients' experiences to illuminate his seven principles, developed to help navigate today's dating challenges. From numerous tips and amazing but true anecdotes to fun-filled facts about where the boys are, readers will find escape from the dating minefields and find relationship success.

Grant Wheaton is the founder and owner of ManMate, Inc., New York's largest dating and relationship service for gay men.

Dennis Courtney is a writer whose critically acclaimed revues have been produced across the United States.

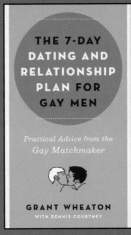

Gay Studies / Relationships
February
A Paperback Original
5 x 8 | 224 pp
TP US $16.95 | CAN $20.50
978-1-59350-049-8 CUSA

**A handy book for men who are looking
for a fresh angle on the dating scene.**

Alyson Books

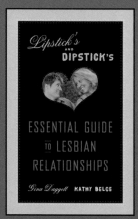

Relationships / Lesbian Studies
November
A Paperback Original
5½ x 8½ | 248 pp
TP US $16.95 | CAN $20.50
978-1-59350-022-1 CUSA

Straight women have Dr. Phil. Now lesbians have their own sassy, straight-talking experts—Lipstick and Dipstick.

Lipstick's and Dipstick's Essential Guide to Lesbian Relationships
Gina Daggett and Kathy Belge

It's point/counterpoint for the lesbian set!

Lipstick is the femmey-femme of the pair, while Dipstick is the eternal tomboy. Together, they are here to help whip into shape the most precious lesbian commodity—relationships. From finding a date to staying together, they help readers navigate the wild world of discovery that pulls up shortly after the U-haul drives away—how to deal with exes, emotional baggage, and sexual dilemmas. Along with pointers about what not to wear, the authors provide a list of the ten signs it's not going to work out.

Gina Daggett and **Kathy Belge** write the "Lipstick & Dipstick" column for *Curve* magazine.

Author Hometown: Portland, OR

Lesbian Studies / Sexuality
February
A Paperback Original
7 x 9 | 304 pp
TP US $21.95 | CAN $26.50
978-1-59350-021-4 CUSA

The most thorough, comprehensive guide to lesbian sex updated in its latest incarnation.

The New Lesbian Sex Book, 3rd Edition
Wendy Caster

The New Lesbian Sex Book, 3rd Edition includes interviews and tips from over thirty women who discuss their lives and experiences in extreme and honest detail. With no assumptions or limits on experience or definition of "sex" or the label of "lesbian," this is an open, friendly, informative, and accessible guide to sex and sexual techniques.

Wendy Caster has authored erotica, a novel, three plays, and much more.

Author Hometown: New York, NY

Alyson Books

The Platypus Ploy
A Kylie Kendall Mystery
Claire McNab

Stone the crows—Aussie Kylie Kendall returns!

Kylie's relationship with paramour Ariana Creeling has reached a new level—until she disappears. There's no sign of violence, no ransom demand—she simply vanishes. Kylie is distraught, not knowing whether she's alive or dead. Convinced there's a link to the prestigious Clarice Turner Evenstar Home, where aged show business stars fade not-so-gently away, Kylie disguises herself as a volunteer and finds herself on the trail of the culprit—but will she be too late to save the woman she loves?

Claire McNab is a transplanted Aussie who has written many mysteries for both children and adults.

Author Hometown: Los Angeles, CA

Mystery / Lesbian Literature
December
A Paperback Original
An Alyson Mystery
5 x 8 | 272 pp
TP US $13.95 | CAN $17.00
978-1-59350-026-9 CUSA

A friend's disappearance has Kylie going undercover at a private nursing clinic.

Murder in the Rue Chartres
A Chanse MacLeod Mystery
Greg Herren

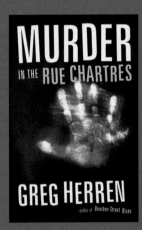

Murder hits the Big Easy.

In the wake of Hurricane Katrina, Chanse MacLeod returns to a different, shattered New Orleans in an attempt to rebuild his own life and face his own future. When he discovers that his last client before the storm was murdered the very night she hired him to find her long-missing father, Chanse is drawn into a web of intrigue and evil.

Greg Herren is the author of six mysteries set in the city of New Orleans, including *Murder in the Rue Dauphine* and *Murder in the Rue St. Ann,* and he co-edited *Love, Bourbon Street.*

Author Hometown: New Orleans, LA

Mystery / Gay Literature
November
A Paperback Original
An Alyson Mystery
5½ x 8½ | 248 pp
TP US $14.95 | CAN $18.00
978-1-55583-966-6 CUSA

Chanse MacLeod returns to a Katrina-ravaged New Orleans— and a puzzling murder case.

Broadway Nights
A Romp of Life, Love, and Musical Theatre
Seth Rudetsky

Welcome to life *beneath* the wicked stage!

Stephen Sheerin was born to play on Broadway—or, at least, under it. He's a musician and conductor, and his dream is to music direct a big Broadway musical. After years of toiling in the pit of some of the most loved (and loathed) hits on the Great White Way, he's just been given his big break. Can life really be going that well? Of course not—his family is driving him crazy and his boyfriend can't seem to get rid of his other boyfriend. Then there's Stephen himself—neurotic and bitchy—who realizes that maybe total happiness is overrated.

Author Hometown: New York, NY

Gay Literature
October
A Paperback Original
5½ x 8½ | 248 pp
TP US $14.95 | CAN $18.00
978-1-59350-010-8 CUSA

In this dishy *roman à clef*, get the inside scoop on making a Broadway show.

OutPlays
Landmark Gay and Lesbian Plays of the Twentieth Century
Edited by Ben Hodges

Twentieth-century theater has been a powerful force in bringing gay and lesbian characters and themes out of the closet and into the spotlight. These dramatic selections share themes of oppression and suppression, countered by love, fear, anger, and humor—universally human, not just gay or lesbian.

Included are Terrence McNally's *The Ritz*, Harvey Fierstein's *Torch Song Trilogy*, Paula Vogel's *The Baltimore Waltz*, John Herbert's *Fortune and Men's Eyes*, and more.

Ben Hodges is an actor, director, author, producer, former managing director for Fat Chance Productions and the Ground Floor Theatre, and a board member of the Theatre World Awards.

Author Hometown: New York, NY

Drama / Gay Literature
March
A Paperback Original
6 x 9 | 560 pp
TP US $21.95 | CAN $26.50
978-1-59350-044-3 CUSA

A collection of landmark plays by gay and lesbian playwrights of the twentieth century.

Alyson Books

Die, Mommie, Die! and Pyscho Beach Party
The Screenplays of Charles Busch
Charles Busch

Part of Alyson Books' new screenplay series, this volume of the final scripts of two cult classics will provide endless enjoyment to fans and students of film. Renowned playwright and filmmaker Charles Busch, whose work has graced the stage from Off-Off Broadway to Broadway, provides commentary on the making of these two films and discusses what it's like to be both behind the camera and to star as a leading lady.

Charles Busch is the author of *Our Leading Lady* and the award-winning Broadway play *The Tale of the Allergist's Wife.* He starred in such plays as *The Lady in Question, Red Scare on Sunset,* and *Vampire Lesbians of Sodom,* which ran for five years Off-Broadway. In 2003, Busch received a special Drama Desk award for career achievement as both a performer and a playwright.

Author Hometown: New York, NY

Film & TV
February
A Paperback Original
5½ x 8½ | 224 pp
TP US $14.95 | CAN $18.00
978-1-59350-025-2 CUSA

The complete screenplays of the cult favorite films from the legendary Charles Busch.

The Dying Gaul and Other Screenplays by Craig Lucas
Craig Lucas
Edited by Steven Drukman

Craig Lucas is a premier American dramatist and now a major film director. These are his scripts for *The Dying Gaul, The Secret Lives of Dentists,* and *Longtime Companion*—which *The New York Times* called "the truest fictional screen chronicle of the advent of AIDS."

Commentary by Lucas and luminaries such as Mary-Louise Parker and Alan Rudolph provide further insight into Lucas' work.

Craig Lucas wrote both the plays and screenplays for *Reckless* and *Prelude to a Kiss.* He has won the award for excellence in literature from the American Academy of Arts and Letters, the PEN/Laura Pels mid-career achievement award, and the Sundance Audience Award.

Film & TV
September
A Paperback Original
5½ x 8½ | 224 pp
TP US $14.95 | CAN $18.00
978-1-59350-050-4 CUSA

Three screenplays by a premier gay American dramatist and major film director.

Alyson Books

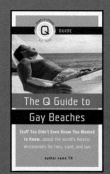

Gay Studies /
Travel & Travel Guides
January
A Paperback Original
5 x 8½ | 172 pp
TP US $12.95
CAN $15.50
978-1-59350-041-2
CUSA

The Q Guide to Gay Beaches
David Allyn

Get out your Speedo—or take it all off—as the Q Guide seeks out fun in the sun all around the globe. From the Mediterranean to the Caribbean to heat-soaked lands the world over, find out which beaches offer the ultimate gay experience.

David Allyn frequently writes travel pieces for *The New York Blade* and www.advocate.com. He lives in New York, New York.

Popular Culture
November
A Paperback Original
5 x 8½ | 172 pp
TP US $12.95
CAN $15.50
978-1-59350-036-8
CUSA

The Q Guide to Designing Women
Allen Crowe

The classic 1980s sitcom goes Q Guide! Learn the truth about the backstage drama that nearly overshadowed the runaway success story of southern-bred ladies, Julia, Mary Jo, Charlene, and Suzanne. Features interviews with the cast and crew.

Allen Crowe has written for numerous television series, including *Hearts Afire* and *Evening Shade,* and he penned the *Designing Women Reunion Show* for Lifetime Television. He lives in Studio City, California.

Gay Studies /
Film & TV
September
A Paperback Original
5 x 8½ | 186 pp
TP US $12.95
CAN $15.50
978-1-59350-006-1
CUSA

The Q Guide to Classic Monster Movies
Douglas McEwan

Dracula, The Invisible Man, Frankenstein, The Mummy—they are the legendary creatures that society has shunned and feared. Now read all about their early movies and what inspired a generation of gay cinema buffs to so embrace them. Features biographies of the films' stars.

Douglas McEwan is the author of the classic movie-themed novel *My Lush Life.* He lives in Reseda, California.

Popular Culture
March
A Paperback Original
5 x 8½ | 172 pp
TP US $12.95
CAN $15.50
978-1-59350-052-8
CUSA

The Q Guide to Buffy the Vampire Slayer
Gregory L. Norris

Go behind the scenes of the smash hit television show that just won't die! From its origins as a reviled movie to its seven-year reign on the WB and UPN networks, Buffy spawned a new generation of vampire lovers.

Gregory L. Norris has written episodes of *Star Trek: Voyager,* and writes a blog about science fiction/fantasy television at www.meetee.com. He lives in Amherst, Massachusetts.

Alyson Books Q Guides Series

The Fame Game
Charles Casillo

"Catchy and mesmerizing. You can't put the book down."—*EDGE New York City*

A hip, modern-day cautionary tale of the trappings of celebrity and its deadly consequences. When Hollywood calls, Mikki stops at nothing to achieve her quest for ultimate fame. In her way is Carla Christaldi, a Hollywood daughter who will do anything to escape her father's shadow. When Mario DeMarco enters their lives, fame takes on a deadly edge.

Charles Casillo is also the author of *Outlaw: The Lives and Careers of John Rechy*. He lives in Brooklyn, New York.

Fiction
September
A Paperback Original
5½ x 8½ | 320 pp
TP US $14.95
CAN $18.00
978-1-59350-043-6
CUSA

ME2
A Novel of Horror
M. Christian

He looks just like you. He acts exactly like you. Every day he becomes more and more like you, taking away that what was yours . . . until there's nothing left. You may think you've met your match—or your double—but that's not even close.

M. Christian has written numerous short stories as well as the novel *Running Dry*. He lives in San Francisco, California.

Gay Literature /
Horror
March
A Paperback Original
5 x 8 | 224 pp
TP US $13.95
CAN $17.00
978-1-55583-963-5
CUSA

My First Time: Volume 5
Edited by Jack Hart

Four volumes and one hundred thousand copies later, Jack Hart's revolutionary series returns for a fifth round of true, gay erotic tales of early encounters. Here are over twenty stories of sexual awakenings, all of which serve as steamy reminders that everyone, no matter how experienced, has had a first time.

Jack Hart most recently edited *Treasure Trail: Erotic Tales of Pirates on the High Seas*. He lives in New York, New York.

Gay Literature /
Erotica
September
A Paperback Original
5½ x 8½ | 224 pp
TP US $15.95
CAN $19.50
978-1-59350-030-6
CUSA

Fast Balls
Erotic Tales of America's Favorite Pastime
Edited by Jesse Grant

They are the boys of summer: pitchers and catchers, home run hitters, and free swingers. From the baseball diamond to the showers, the hotel rooms to the luxury boxes, here are eighteen hot stories of men in uniform—who, after a diving catch, a game-winning run, or an impressive strikeout, like to take it all off. Hotter than August and steamier than the locker room, *Fast Balls* will make you want to play on their team.

Erotica
Available Now
A Paperback Original
5½ x 8½ | 288 pp
TP US $15.95
CAN $19.50
978-1-59350-029-0
CUSA

Alyson Books

Gay Literature
November
A Paperback Original
5½ x 8½ | 272 pp
TP US $15.95
CAN $19.50
978-1-59350-037-5
CUSA

Best Gay Love Stories: Summer Flings
Edited by Brad Nichols

Everyone loves to fall in love, and there's no better time than summer. From beachfront bunking to cruising the ocean's waves, this year's edition of gay love stories explores the electric connection between men and men and the sultry sun that melts their hearts.

Brad Nichols also edited *Best Gay Love Stories: New York City* and the Travelrotica series. He lives in New York, New York.

Gay Literature /
Erotica
December
A Paperback Original
5½ x 8½ | 272 pp
TP US $15.95
CAN $19.50
978-1-59350-039-9
CUSA

Ultimate Gay Erotica 2008
Edited by Jesse Grant

Hot, sexy, and always ready for action, the men who populate this year's edition of the ever-popular series truly represent the ultimate in gay desire. In these twenty-five tales of love and lust, we unleash all types of man and reveal their most secret sexual fantasies.

Jesse Grant, the master of gay erotica, has edited many anthologies, including *Fast Balls*. He lives in New York, New York.

Lesbian Literature
October
A Paperback Original
5½ x 8½ | 272 pp
TP US $15.95
CAN $19.50
978-1-59350-035-1
CUSA

Best Lesbian Love Stories: Summer Flings
Edited by Simone Thorne

Everyone loves to fall in love, and there's no better time than summer. From languid, lazy days to hot, humid nights, this year's edition of lesbian love stories explores the passionate connection between women and women, and the sultry sun that sizzles their skin.

Simone Thorne also edited *Best Lesbian Love Stories: New York City* and the Travelrotica series. She lives in New York, New York.

Lesbian Literature /
Erotica
January
A Paperback Original
5½ x 8½ | 272 pp
TP US $15.95
CAN $19.50
978-1-59350-042-9
CUSA

Ultimate Lesbian Erotica 2008
Edited by Nicole Foster

Lovely, lively, and alluring, the ladies who populate this year's edition of the ever-popular series truly represent the ultimate in lesbian desire. In these twenty-five tales of love and lust, we unleash all types of women and reveal their most secret sexual fantasies.

Nicole Foster, the queen of lesbian erotica, has edited many anthologies, including *Wet* and *Show & Tell*. She lives in New York, New York.

Alyson Books

Charms
And Other Pieces
Paul Valéry
Translated by Peter Dale

The poems of Paul Valéry (1871–1945) have been surprisingly little translated, except for famous anthology pieces like "Le Cimetière marin" (The Graveyard by the Sea). His fascinatingly complex attitudes to poetry were deeply influenced by the impression made on him as a young man by the poems of Stéphane Mallarmé. Peter Dale's skillful and inventive translations face the French text in this fresh version of Valéry's most significant collection, originally published in France in 1922. Dale also provides a lucid introduction and notes.

Peter Dale is the acclaimed translator of Dante's *Divine Comedy* and French poets François Villon, Jules Laforgue, and Tristan Corbière, all from Anvil Press.

Poetry
September
A Paperback Original
5½ x 8½ | 192 pp
TP US $18.95 | CAN $23.00
978-0-85646-398-3 CUSA

A bilingual text of a famous work by a trusted translator.

Fortune's Prisoner
The Poems of *The Consolation of Philosophy*
Boethius
Translated by James Harpur

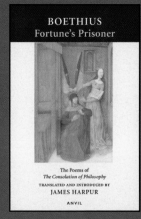

James Harpur argues for the reappraisal of Boethius as poet with his imaginative treatment of the poems from *The Consolation of Philosophy.* His free versions and persuasive introduction encourage their reading as a coherent sequence outside their original context in a work of prose and verse.

An aristocratic scholar and influential member of the court of Theodoric, **Boethius** (born ca. 480 AD) was arrested for alleged treason and executed in ca. 526. He wrote his masterpiece during this imprisonment.

James Harpur is an Anglo-Irish poet living in Ireland. His fourth collection of poems, *The Dark Age,* is published simultaneously.

Poetry
October
A Paperback Original
5½ x 8½ | 112 pp
TP US $15.95 | CAN $19.50
978-0-85646-403-4 CUSA

Boethius' reputation as a poet is reestablished in these fresh and thoughtful versions.

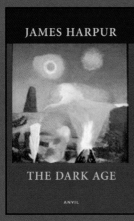

The Dark Age
James Harpur

James Harpur's poetry explores faith and vision in searching and unsentimental terms. His powerful collection, inspired by a vivid historical imagination, focuses on the Dark Ages of Europe and the struggles of early Christianity, especially in the title sequence, which concentrates on early Irish saints.

James Harpur was born in 1956 of Anglo-Irish parentage. He studied at Trinity College, Cambridge, and has worked as an English teacher, lexicographer, and editor. He now lives in Ireland. He is author of *Love Burning in the Soul: The Story of the Christian Mystics, from Saint Paul to Thomas Merton* (Shambhala Publications, 2005).

Poetry / Spirituality
October
A Paperback Original
5½ x 8½ | 72 pp
TP US $13.95 | CAN $17.00
978-0-85646-404-1 CUSA

A new perspective on early Irish history with the travels and travails of saints.

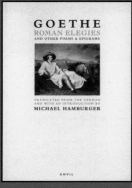

Roman Elegies
And Other Poems & Epigrams
Johann Wolfgang von Goethe
Translated by Michael Hamburger

"Michael Hamburger is exactly the poet one would choose to perform the valuable service of bringing Goethe into focus for us."—Gavin Ewart

This collection of Michael Hamburger's beautifully crafted versions from all periods of Goethe's creative life, including the erotic masterpiece *Roman Elegies,* forms an ideal introduction to a writer "so many-sided as to constitute a whole literature."

Born in Frankfurt in 1749, **Johann Wolfgang von Goethe** trained as a lawyer. His long, creative career encompassed plays, fiction, poetry, and theoretical and critical writings. His lifelong preoccupation was the drama *Faust,* completed shortly before his death in 1832.

Poetry
September
6¼ x 9¼ | 128 pp
TP US $15.95 | CAN $19.50
978-0-85646-274-0 CUSA

A perfect introduction to the great German poet, with a useful introduction by his superb translator.

Anvil Press

Yalo

Elias Khoury

Translated by Peter Theroux

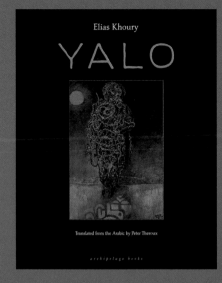

"A heartbreaking book and sometimes hypnotic in beauty. . . . With both gentle and cruel images, Khoury wrote a lamentation for the generation that was corrupted and lost its children, and for the children themselves."—*Haaretz*

Praise for *Gate of the Sun*:

"Few have held to the light the myths, tales and rumors of both Israel and the Arabs with such discerning compassion. *Gate of the Sun* is an imposingly rich and realistic novel, a genuine masterwork."—*The New York Times Book Review*

Elias Khoury's most recent novel propels us into a fantastic universe of skewed reality. We follow the path of a young man, Yalo, who is growing up like a stray dog on the streets of Beirut during the long years of the Lebanese civil war. Living with his mother, who "lost her face in the mirror," he falls in with a dangerous gang whose violent escapades he treats as a game. The game becomes a frightening reality, however, when Yalo is accused of rape and imprisoned. He is forced to confess to crimes of which he has no recollection. As he writes, and rewrites, his testimony, he begins to grasp his family's past and recall all that his psyche has buried, and the true Yalo begins to emerge.

Elias Khoury is the author of twelve novels, four volumes of literary criticism, and three plays. Editor of the cultural pages of Beirut's *An-Nahar*, Khoury is also a global distinguished professor at New York University. *Gate of the Sun* was a *New York Times* Notable Book of the Year in 2006.

Peter Theroux translated Abdelrahman Munif's *Cities of Salt*, Naguib Mahfouz's *Children of the Alley*, and Alia Mamdouh's *Naphtalene: A Novel of Baghdad*. He has lived and traveled throughout the Middle East and is currently based in Washington, DC.

An adolescent on the streets awakens to his own history when he is forced to confess.

Fiction / Literature & Essay
January
6½ x 7½ | 260 pp
TC US $25.00 | CAN $30.00
978-0-9793330-4-0 CUSA

Marketing Plans

Co-op available
Advance reader copies
NPR's *Book Worm*
National advertising:
Bookforum • Los Angeles Times
Book Review • Mother Jones • The Nation •
The New York Review of Books • Tikkun

Plants Don't Drink Coffee

Unai Elorriaga

Translated by Amaia Gabantxo

Unai Elorriaga
Plants Don't
Drink Coffee

Translated from the Basque by Amaia Gabantxo

archipelago books

Fiction
October
6½ x 7½ | 200 pp
TC US $24.00 | CAN $29.00
978-0-9778576-8-5 CUSA

Marketing Plans

Co-op available
Advance reader copies
National advertising:
American Book Review • The Bloomsbury Review • Bookforum • The Boston Book Review • Boston Review • New England Review • The New York Review of Books • The Paris Review • Tikkun • World Literature Today • The Yale Review

Author Events

Los Angeles, CA • San Francisco, CA • Boise, ID • Chicago, IL • Boston, MA • Minneapolis/St. Paul, MN • Reno, NV • New York, NY • Seattle, WA

"I read Unai Elorriaga's latest novel almost without stopping to breathe. Breathlessly, yes, but not quickly, because Elorriaga's books are not the kind you read in two or three hours and put back on the shelf. It is a very good novel. Incredibly good."
—Gorka Bereziartua

Plants Don't Drink Coffee achieves a graceful balance between playfulness (in both language and character) and depth of emotion and thought. Unai Elorriaga gives voice to unassuming characters, to "small" people with "small" lives, magnifying things that often go unnoticed. Four stories narrated from different perspectives crisscross throughout the novel. In the first person, the young Tomas—who wants above all else to be intelligent—tells us why it is so important for him to catch a blue dragonfly and introduces his extended (and eccentric) family to us one by one. We observe the surrealist creation of a rugby field on a golf course, unravel the mystery of why a couple of forty years never married, and delve into the intrigue surrounding a European carpentry competition that Tomas' grandfather had taken part in. *Plants Don't Drink Coffee* is teaming with dreamers, free spirits, and nonconformists who follow their inner voices. Beneath the novel's lighthearted and balletic ways lies a gentle wisdom, a lucid vision of human emotion.

Unai Elorriaga's first novel, *A Streetcar to SP,* won Spain's prestigious National Narrative Prize in 2002. The jury was taken by the freshness of his voice and the book's utter uniqueness. Elorriaga is the most celebrated young Basque author in the Spanish literary landscape. Although influenced by Julio Cortázar and Juan Rulfo, Elorriaga stands alone in both the inventiveness of his narrative and in the particular way his characters reveal their humanity. Elorriaga is truly breaking new ground.

Amaia Gabantxo is a literary translator, writer, and reviewer. Her work has appeared in many journals and newspapers, including *The Times Literary Supplement* and *The Independent,* as well as in *An Anthology of Basque Short Stories* and *Spain: A Traveler's Literary Companion* (Whereabouts Press). Her translation of Anjel Lertxundi's *Perfect Happiness* is forthcoming.

Weaving the invisible with the unspeakable, a young Basque boy lets us into his private world.

Archipelago Books

The Waitress was New

Dominique Fabre

Translated by Jordan Stump

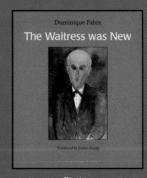

Pierre, a lifelong Parisian waiter, watches people come and go, sizing them up with great accuracy and empathy. Pierre doesn't look outside too much; he prefers to let the world come to him. When the café goes under, Pierre finds himself at a loss. As we follow his stream of thought over three days, Pierre's humanity and profound solitude are revealed.

Dominique Fabre is the author of six novels. He won the Marcel Pagnol Prize for *Fantômes* in 2001. *The Waitress was New* is his first book to appear in English.

Jordan Stump is a noted translator of modern French novelists, including Marie Redonnet and Eric Chevillard.

Marketing Plans
Co-op available • Advance reader copies
National advertising: The Bloomsbury Review • Bookforum • Bookslut.com • Boston Review • The Paris Review

Author Events
San Francisco, CA • Washington, DC • New York, NY • Seattle, WA

Translator Hometown: Lincoln, NE

Fiction
October
A Paperback Original
6 x 7¼ | 160 pp
TP US $16.00 | CAN $19.50
978-0-9778576-9-2 CUSA

**A veteran waiter is set adrift
when his café closes its doors.**

Autonauts of the Cosmoroute

Julio Cortázar and Carol Dunlop

Translated by Anne McLean

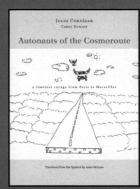

"Anyone who doesn't read Cortázar is doomed."—Pablo Neruda

Autonauts of the Cosmoroute is a love story, an irreverent travelogue of elaborate tales and snapshots detailing Julio Cortázar and Carol Dunlop's thirty-three-day voyage on the Paris-Marseilles freeway in 1982. Uncovering the freeway's hidden underbelly, they push life and literature to surreal extremes. This shot of sun is a satire on modern travel and the great explorers, and an intimate look into one of the greatest literary spirits of our time.

Julio Cortázar (1914–1984) was a true giant of twentieth-century Latin American literature. He met and married Carol Dunlop in France in 1982.

Anne McLean has translated the work of Carmen Martín Gaite, Javier Cercas, Ignacio Padilla, Orlando Gonzáles Esteva, and Luis Sepúlveda, as well as Julio Cortázar's *Diary of Andrés Fava* (Archipelago Books).

Marketing Plans
Co-op available • Advance reader copies
National advertising: Bookforum • Boston Review • The New York Review of Books

Literature & Essay / Travel & Travel Guides
February
A Paperback Original
7 x 9 | 350 pp
130 Color and B&W illustrations
and photographs
TP US $22.00 | CAN $26.50
978-0-9793330-0-2 CUSA

**A life-altering road trip with
one of the greatest writers of the
twentieth century.**

Archipelago Books

Marked
Magdalena Tulli
Translated by Bill Johnston

A single streetcar line runs around the sleepy square of an unnamed city. One day— out of nowhere—refugees pour from the streetcar and set up camp in the square. The residents grow hostile and eventually take extreme action. *Marked* is Magdelana Tulli's most personal novel yet.

Magdalena Tulli's novels include *Moving Parts, Dreams and Stones,* and *In Red. Dreams and Stones* won Poland's Koscielski Foundation Prize in 1995, and *Moving Parts* was shortlisted for the 2002 NIKE Prize. Tulli lives in Warsaw.

Bill Johnston is director of the Polish Studies Center at Indiana University. In 2005, he won an ASTEEL translation prize for Tulli's *Dreams and Stones.* His translation of Tulli's *Moving Parts* is a finalist for the IMPAC Dublin Award.

Marketing Plans
Co-op available • Advance reader copies
National advertising: AGNI • Boston Review • Fence • The New York Review of Books

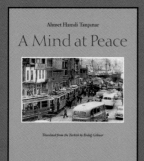

Fiction
January
A Paperback Original
5½ x 6½ | 140 pp
TP US $14.00 | CAN $17.00
978-0-9793330-1-9 CUSA

Refugees cause a surreal disruption in a quiet suburb. A prescient allegory of extermination.

A Mind at Peace
Ahmet Hamdi Tanpinar
Translated by Erdag Göknar

Set on the eve of World War II, *A Mind at Peace* captures the anxieties of a Turkish family facing the difficult reality entrenched in the early republic, founded on the ashes of the Ottoman Empire in 1923. Poetically drawing on the effects of cultural upheaval on the individual, Ahmet Hamdi Tanpinar illuminates the precarious balance between tradition and modernity, East and West.

Ahmet Hamdi Tanpinar (1901–1962) is considered one of the most important Turkish novelists of the twentieth century. He created a cultural universe in his work, bringing together a Western literary voice and the sensibilities of the Ottoman culture.

Erdag Göknar was the recipient of the Oceans Connect Grant and a Fulbright Fellowship. He teaches at Duke University.

Marketing Plans
Co-op avaiable • Advance reader copies
National advertising: Bookforum • The Nation • The New York Review of Books

Translator Hometown: Durham, NC

Fiction
October
A Paperback Original
6½ x 7½ | 450 pp
TC US $25.00 | CAN $30.00
978-0-9793330-5-7 CUSA

A lyrical tribute to Istanbul, set on the eve of World War II.

Archipelago Books

Eat, Drink & Be Vegan
Great Vegan Food for Special and Everyday Celebrations
Dreena Burton

In Dreena Burton's first two best-selling vegan cookbooks, *The Everyday Vegan* and *Vive le Vegan!*, she offered a dazzling array of healthy, animal-free recipes, many of which were based on her experience as a mother of two young girls she and her husband are raising as vegans. Dreena also maintains an active website (www.everydayvegan.com) and blog (www.vivelevegan.blogspot.com) and has cultivated an enthusiastic audience for her family-oriented, nutritious recipes. In this, her third cookbook, Dreena turns her attention to celebratory food—imaginative, colorful, and delectable vegan fare perfect for all kinds of events, from romantic meals for two to dinner parties to full-on galas. Many of the recipes are kid-friendly, and all are appropriate for everyday meals as well.

The book includes 125 recipes and sixteen full-color photographs, as well as meal plans and cooking notes. Recipes include Lentil & Veggie Chimichangas, Thai Chick-Un Pizza, White Bean Soup with Basil & Croutons, Tomato Dill Lentil Soup, Olive & Sundried Tomato Hummus, "Creamy" Cashew Dip with Fruit, Crêpes with Maple Butter Cream, 5-Star Ice "Cream" Sandwiches, and Hemp-anola (Dreena's take on granola).

Come celebrate with Dreena and impress your guests with these sensational animal-free recipes.

Tempting animal-free recipes for parties and celebrations, by the author of *The Everyday Vegan*.

Cookbooks & Cookery
October
A Paperback Original
7½ x 10 | 176 pp
16 Color photographs
TP $22.95
978-1-55152-224-1 USA

Marketing Plans

Co-op available
Advance reader copies
National advertising:
E / The Environmental Magazine •
Geist • Publishers Weekly • Utne •
Vegetarian Times • VegNews

Author Hometown: White Rock, BC

Also Available

The Everyday Vegan
Recipes & Lessons for
Living the Vegan Life
Dreena Burton
Cookbooks & Cookery
7½ x 10 | 205 pp
TP $21.95
978-1-55152-106-0 USA

Vive le Vegan!
Simple, Delectable Recipes for the
Everyday Vegan Family
Dreena Burton
Cookbooks & Cookery
7½ x 10 | 208 pp
TP $19.95
978-1-55152-169-5 USA

Arsenal Pulp Press

New World Provence
Modern French Cooking for Friends and Family
Alessandra Quaglia and Jean-Francis Quaglia

Cookbooks & Cookery
September
A Paperback Original
8½ x 11 | 192 pp
32 Color photographs
TP $24.95
978-1-55152-223-4 USA

Marketing Plans

Co-op available
Advance reader copies
National advertising:
Geist • Publishers Weekly

Author Events

San Francisco, CA •
Portland, OR • Seattle, WA

Author Hometown: Vancouver, BC

French cuisine is considered among the world's best, but its traditional ingredients like butter and cream aren't always appropriate for today's heart-healthy diets. *New World Provence* is a new-style French cookbook designed with contemporary North American audiences in mind, featuring healthy, easy-to-find ingredients prepared using traditional French techniques tweaked with the home cook in mind.

The book includes beautiful yet simple recipes that take advantage of meats, seafood, and vegetables abundant in North American markets; in keeping with their contemporary flair, pan-cultural influences abound, yet all the while the recipes remain faithful to French traditions.

Authors Alessandra Quaglia and Jean-Francis Quaglia are the husband-and-wife chefs and owners of Provence and Provence Marinaside, two fine dining establishments in Vancouver. Their recipes reflect not only North American sensibilities, but familial ones as well; they are the parents of two young sons, and Jean-Francis' mother owned the famed Le Patalain restaurant in Marseilles, France. These relationships pervade the book, which reveals how a common love and respect for food can be passed on from generation to generation, from the old world to the new.

The book features thirty-two stunning, full-color photographs and over 120 recipes, including prawns with chickpea gallette, whole rabbit barbecue, bean and wild mushroom ragout, fresh crab with tomatoes and fresh herbs, roasted vegetable tart, poached sea urchin on bread, and new-style bouillabaisse.

**Fabulous, family-friendly French cuisine for cooks
on this side of the Atlantic.**

Arsenal Pulp Press

Fame Us
The Culture of Celebrity
Photographs by Brian Howell
Introduction by Norbert Ruebsaat with Stephen Osborne

"Hollywood is a place where they'll pay you $50,000 for a kiss and 50 cents for your soul."—Marilyn Monroe

"Washington is Hollywood for ugly people."—Chuck Todd, Hotline.com

"Fame: It's only a punch, a drug bust, or a public defecation away."—Adrianne Curry, winner of the first *America's Next Top Model*

Why do we care so desperately about famous people? In this stunning book, photographs of celebrity impersonators are juxtaposed with narratives and quotations dealing with our cultural obsession with fame, in an era in which tabloids and gossip blogs reign supreme, and personalities like Paris, Lindsay, and Jessica are superstars because of—not in spite of—their personal lives.

Brian Howell's amazing photographs, taken at impersonator conventions held throughout North America, feature an array of would-be stars—from fat Elvises and Michael Jackson à la mug shot to the real wedding of Arnold Schwarzenegger's impersonator to Shania Twain's. The photos' startling intimacy hints at the artifice of celebrity culture, in which the *idea* of celebrity supersedes all else, and the accompanying essays and quotations reveal the true power (and cost) of stardom.

Photos, narratives, and quotations on the nature of fame and celebrity.

Popular Culture / Photography
November
A Paperback Original
8 x 8 | 196 pp
120 B&W photographs
TP $18.95
978-1-55152-228-9 USA

Marketing Plans

Co-op available
Advance reader copies
National advertising:
Bookforum • Geist • The Journal
of Popular Culture • The Progressive •
Publishers Weekly • Utne

Author Hometown: Delta, BC

Also Available

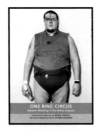

One Ring Circus
Extreme Wrestling in the Minor Leagues
Photographs by Brian Howell
Sports & Recreation / Photography
6 x 8 | 160 pp
100 Black and White photographs
TP $16.95
978-1-55152-132-9 USA

Arsenal Pulp Press

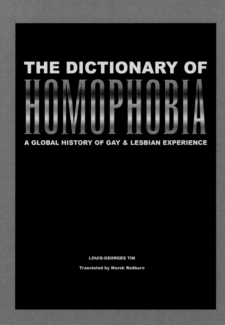

The Dictionary of Homophobia
A Global History of Gay & Lesbian Experience
Edited by Louis-Georges Tin
Translated by Marek Redburn

Based on the work of seventy researchers in fifteen countries, *The Dictionary of Homophobia* is a mammoth, encyclopedic book that documents the history of homosexuality and various cultural responses to it from all regions of the world. It is a masterful, engaged, and wholly relevant study that traces the political and social emancipation of a culture.

The book is the first English translation of *Dictionnaire de L'Homophobie,* published in France in 2003 to worldwide acclaim; its editor, Louis-Georges Tin, launched the first International Day Against Homophobia in 2005, now celebrated in more than fifty countries around the world. *The Dictionary of Homophobia* includes over 175 essays on various aspects of gay rights and homophobia as experienced in all regions of Africa, the Americas, Asia, Europe, and the South Pacific, from the earliest epochs to present day.

Subjects include religious and ideological forces such as the Bible, Communism, Judaism, Hinduism, and Islam; historical subjects, events, and personalities such as AIDS, Stonewall, J. Edgar Hoover, Matthew Shepard, Oscar Wilde, Pat Buchanan, Joseph McCarthy, Pope John Paul II, and Anita Bryant; and other topics such as coming out, adoption, deportation, ex-gays, lesbiphobia, and bi-phobia. In a world where gay marriage remains a hot-button political issue, and where adults and even teens are still being executed by authorities for the "crime" of homosexuality, *The Dictionary of Homophobia* is a both a revealing and a necessary history lesson for us all.

A comprehensive, global history of homophobia, available in English for the first time.

Gay Studies / Lesbian Studies
November
A Paperback Original
7 x 9¾ | 448 pp
100 B&W photographs
TP $39.95
978-1-55152-229-6 USA

Marketing Plans

Co-op available
Advance reader copies
National advertising:
The Bloomsbury Review •
Bookforum • Booklist • The Gay & Lesbian Review Worldwide • Geist • GLQ • Kirkus Reviews • Lambda Book Report • Library Journal • The Progressive • Rain Taxi

Author Hometown: Montreal, QC

Arsenal Pulp Press

Comin' at Ya!
The Homoerotic 3-D Photographs of Denny Denfield
David L. Chapman and Thomas Waugh

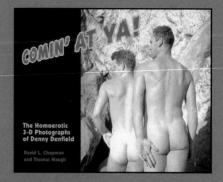

An amazing collection of full-color, sexually explicit 3-D photographs of men taken in the early 1950s by Denny Denfield. Denfield was an amateur physique photographer in California who worked as an accountant for the US Army. His photographs, never distributed publicly given their illegality at the time, display a skill, wit, and daring rarely seen, and with their rich Kodachrome colors and mid-century decors, can now be appreciated for their roguish, almost naïve charm.

The essay by David L. Chapman, from whose own private collection these photographs appear, sheds fascinating light on Denfield's secret life and work (stereography had been invented in 1850, but the advent of a compact, easy-to-use 3-D camera in 1947 allowed amateurs like Denfield to produce their own). A narrative by acclaimed writer Thomas Waugh (*Lust Unearthed, Out/Lines, Gay Art: A Historic Collection*) places Denfield's work in the historical context of homoerotic photography over the last century.

The 3-D photographs comprise dual images that "come alive" when viewed through the 3-D glasses that come with the book. Equal parts kitschy, informed, and sexy, *Comin' at Ya!* is a collection that is both fun and historically fascinating.

The thrill, the spectacle—full-color gay erotic photographs in 3-D.

Gay Studies / Erotica
October
10 x 8 | 176 pp
130 Color and B&W photographs
Includes 3-D glasses
COIL BOUND $27.95
978-1-55152-225-8 USA

Marketing Plans

Co-op available
Advance reader copies
National advertising:
The Gay & Lesbian Review Worldwide •
Geist • GLQ • Lambda Book Report

Author Events

San Francisco, CA •
New York, NY • Seattle, WA

Author Hometown: Seattle, WA

Also Available

Gay Art
A Historic Collection
Felix Lance Falkon and Thomas Waugh
Gay Studies / Art
8½ x 10½ | 255 pp
170 B&W illustrations and photographs
TP $24.95
978-1-55152-205-0 USA

Lust Unearthed
Vintage Gay Graphics From
the DuBek Collection
Thomas Waugh
Gay Studies / Art
8 x 9⅝ | 320 pp
220 B&W Illustrations
TP $23.95
978-1-55152-165-7 USA

Arsenal Pulp Press

73

Gay Studies / Biography & Autobiography
October
6 x 9 | 224 pp
50 Color photographs
TC $24.95
978-1-55152-231-9 USA

A vivid, ecstatic memoir of the author's association with the Angels of Light.

Flights of Angels
My Life with the Angels of Light
Adrian Brooks
Photographs by Dan Nicoletta

The Angels of Light were more than a queer performance troupe in the 1970s; growing out of the equally legendary Cockettes in San Francisco, the Angels were a way of life, putting on trashy, fantastical drag fairy tales in a city and an era that was in the blissful throes of early gay liberation. Adrian Brooks was a charter member of the Angels and the author of most of their shows. In this vivid memoir, San Francisco in the 1970s comes to life as Brooks recounts amazing stories from behind closed doors. He also describes his early years as a Pennsylvania youth whose life is transformed working with Martin Luther King, then subsequently cavorting in Andy Warhol's world in Manhattan, before heading west, where the Angels made perfect, beautiful sense of the world. Featuring fifty full-color photographs, *Flights of Angels* is a remarkable, elegiac ode to the ecstasy and defiance of queer life and culture before the AIDS crisis.

Marketing Plans
Co-op available • Advance reader copies
National advertising: Bookforum • Booklist • The Gay & Lesbian Review Worldwide • Geist • GLQ • Hungry Mind Review • Lambda Book Report • Library Journal • Rain Taxi

Author Events
Los Angeles, CA • Boston, MA • New York, NY

Author Hometown: San Francisco, CA

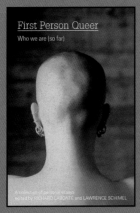

Gay Studies / Biography & Autobiography
November
A Paperback Original
6 x 9 | 224 pp
TP $17.95
978-1-55152-227-2 USA

An anthology of first-person essays depicting the diversity, complexity, and experience of contemporary GLBTQ life.

First Person Queer
Who We Are (So Far)
Edited by Richard Labonté and Lawrence Schimel

In this amazing, wide-ranging anthology of nonfiction essays, contributors write intimate and honest first-person accounts of queer experience, from coming out to "passing" as straight to growing old to living proud. These are the stories of contemporary gay and lesbian life—and are by definition funny, sad, hopeful, and truthful. Representing a diversity of genders, ages, races, and orientations, and edited by two acclaimed writers and anthologists (who between them have written or edited almost one hundred books), *First Person Queer* puts the "personal" back into "queer."

Contributors include Kate Bornstein, Sharon Bridgforth, Katherine V. Forrest, Tim Miller, Achy Obejas, and Simon Sheppard.

Marketing Plans
Co-op available • Advance reader copies
National advertising: The Bloomsbury Review • BOMB • Bookforum • Booklist • The Gay & Lesbian Review Worldwide • Geist • GLQ • Lambda Book Report

Author Events
New York, NY

Arsenal Pulp Press

The Carnivorous Lamb

Agustin Gomez-Arcos

Introduction by Jamie O'Neill

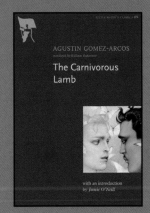

The latest in the Little Sister's Classics series resurrecting gay and lesbian literary gems: a viciously funny, shocking yet ultimately moving 1975 novel. An allegory of Franco's Spain, the novel is about a young gay man (the self-described "carnivorous lamb") coming of age with a mother who despises him, a father who ignores him, and a brother who loves him.

Author Agustin Gomez-Arcos left his native Spain for France in the 1960s to escape its censorship policies. *The Carnivorous Lamb,* originally written in French, won the Prix Hermes. Jamie O'Neill is the acclaimed author of *At Swim, Two Boys.*

Marketing Plans
Co-op available • Advance reader copies
National advertising: The Bloomsbury Review • Bookforum • The Gay & Lesbian Review Worldwide • Geist • GLQ • Lambda Book Report • Library Journal

Gay Literature / Fiction
September
Little Sister's Classics
5½ x 8 | 272 pp
TP $16.95
978-1-55152-230-2 USA

**A Little Sister's Classic:
a stunning, award-winning 1975
novel from Spain.**

Soucouyant

David Chariandy

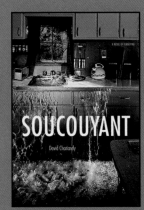

A "soucouyant" is an evil spirit in Caribbean lore, a reminder of past transgressions that refuses to diminish with age. In this beautifully told novel that crosses borders, cultures, and generations, a young man returns home to care for his aging mother, who suffers from dementia. In his efforts to help her and by turn make amends for their past estrangement from one another, he is compelled to re-imagine his mother's stories for her before they slip completely into darkness. In delicate, heartbreaking tones, a beautiful, haunted life is revealed.

Marketing Plans
Co-op available • Advance reader copies
National advertising: The Bloomsbury Review • BOMB • Bookforum •
Hungry Mind Review • Library Journal • Rain Taxi

Author Events
San Francisco, CA • New York, NY • Seattle, WA

Author Hometown: Vancouver, BC

Fiction
September
A Paperback Original
5½ x 8½ | 220 pp
TP $16.95
978-1-55152-226-5 USA

**A beautiful cross-cultural
novel about loss, remembrance,
and the unbreakable ties between
mother and son.**

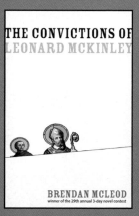

Fiction
September
A Paperback Original
5 x 7 | 144 pp
TP $14.95
978-1-55152-222-7 USA

A 3-Day Novel Contest winner: a comic novel about a young man trying to make sense of God, family, and his own heart of darkness.

The Convictions of Leonard McKinley
Brendan McLeod

Winner of the 29th Annual International 3-Day Novel Contest: By the age of thirteen, Leonard McKinley's failure to follow his own moral compass has caused his father's heart attack and triggered an epileptic fit in his dog. How can he learn to suppress his dark, subversive tendencies and balance virtue with fitting in? Leonard's story is both poignant and hilarious as he compels himself through a series of increasingly complex ethical trials in order to become a better human being. More on the 3-Day Novel Contest can be found at www.3daynovel.com.

Marketing Plans
Co-op available • Advance reader copies
Author Events
Portland, OR • Seattle, WA

Author Hometown: Vancouver, BC

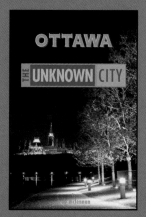

Travel & Travel Guides
October
A Paperback Original
6 x 9 | 224 pp
75 B&W photographs
TP $17.95
978-1-55152-232-6 USA

A subcultural guide to Canada's capital city.

Ottawa: The Unknown City
rob mclennan

Ottawa is Canada's capital city, home to numerous historic sites, museums, and galleries, and the birthplace of such diverse lights as Alanis Morissette, Rich Little, and Paul Anka; it also has a small-town charm lurking beneath its frozen tundra. This witty and urbane Unknown City book—one of only a handful guides available on Ottawa—charts a course through the city's hidden landmarks, shopping and dining hotspots, and secret histories.

Marketing Plans
Co-op available • Advance reader copies
National advertising: Geist

Arsenal Pulp Press

The Aunt Lute Anthology of U.S. Women Writers, Volume Two
20th Century
Edited by Lisa Maria Hogeland and Shay Brawn

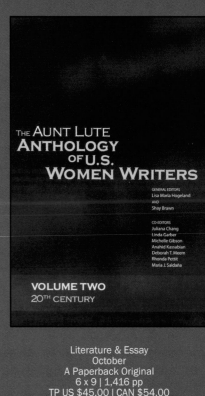

A comprehensive collection of twentieth-century US women's writing, this volume contains works by over two hundred women writing in a variety of genres. Works include not only fiction, drama, and poetry, but various nonfiction forms (autobiography, movement writing, journalism, essay) as well as other creative forms (opera libretto, spoken word, song lyrics).

A sample of the writers, **A** through **C**: Elmaz Abinader, Jane Addams, Etel Adnan, Marjorie Agosin, Ai, Elizabeth Alexander, Paula Gunn Allen, Dorothy Allison, Maya Angelou, Gloria Anzaldúa, Harriette Arnow, Mary Austin, Toni Cade Bambara, Djuna Barnes, Gwendolyn Bennett, Mei-mei Berssenbrugge, Bikini Kill, Elizabeth Bishop, Louise Bogan, Lucille Bogan, Marita Bonner, Kay Boyle, Gwendolyn Brooks, Rita Mae Brown, Minnie Bruce Pratt, Octavia Butler, Patrick Califia-Rice, Janet Campbell Hale, Dorothy Canfield Fisher, Luisa Capetillo, Ana Castillo, Willa Sibert Cather, Lorna Dee Cervantes, Theresa Hak Kyung Cha, Alice Childress, Marilyn Chin, Meg Christian, Chrystos, Frances Chung, Sandra Cisneros, Amy Clampitt, Michelle Cliff, Lucille Clifton, Judith Ortiz Cofer, Wanda Coleman, Lucha Corpi, Ida Cox, Ina Cumpiano, Agnes Cunningham, and Silvia Curbelo. The writers **D** through **Z** are just as diverse, just as comprehensive. The volume includes a preface, headnotes, annotations, and author/title index.

Co-editors: Juliana Chang, assistant professor of English, Santa Clara University; Linda S. Garber, associate professor of English, Santa Clara University; Michelle Gibson, associate professor of women's studies, University of Cincinnati; Anahid Kassabian, James and Constance Alsop chair of music at the University of Liverpool; Deborah Meem, professor of English, University of Cincinnati; Rhonda Pettit, associate professor of English and women's studies, University of Cincinnati; and Maria J. Saldaña, associate professor of English, Rutgers University.

Literature & Essay
October
A Paperback Original
6 x 9 | 1,416 pp
TP US $45.00 | CAN $54.00
978-1-879960-77-0 CUSA

Author Hometown: Cincinnati, OH

The most comprehensive collection of twentieth-century US women's writing ever produced.

Also Available

The Aunt Lute Anthology of U.S. Women Writers
Volume One: 17th through 19th Centuries
Edited by Lisa Maria Hogeland and Mary Klages
Women's Literature
6 x 9 | 1,416 pp
TP x US $45.00 | CAN $54.00
978-1-879960-68-8 CUSA

Aunt Lute Books

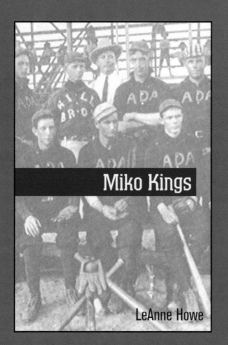

Fiction / Native American Studies
September
A Paperback Original
5½ x 8½ | 206 pp
TP US $11.95 | CAN $14.50
978-1-879960-78-7 CUSA

Author Events

San Francisco, CA • Washington, DC •
Oxford, MI • New York, NY • Cincinnati, OH •
Oklahoma City, OK

Author Hometown: Urbana-Champaign, IL

Miko Kings
An Indian Baseball Story
LeAnne Howe

"This is where the twentieth-century Indian really began . . . not in the abstractions of congressional acts, but on the prairie diamond."—Henri Day

Miko Kings is set in Indian Territory's queen city, Ada, Oklahoma, during the baseball fever of 1903 and simultaneously in 1969, the Vietnam era. The story centers on the lives of Hope Little Leader, a Choctaw pitcher for the Miko Kings baseball team; Lucius Mummy, a switch hitter; and Ezol Daggs, the postal clerk in Indian Territory. It is Daggs who, in attempting to patent her Choctaw theory of relativity, inadvertently changes the course of history for the Indians and their baseball team.

   Though a lively and humorous contemporary work of fiction, the narration draws heavily on LeAnne Howe's careful historical research: boarding schools for Native American children, Native American participation in the Vietnam War, and—most centrally—the story of the little-known Indian Baseball League of the late 1800s and early 1900s.

LeAnne Howe, an enrolled member of the Choctaw Nation of Oklahoma, is an author, playwright, and scholar. Born and educated in Oklahoma, she has read and lectured throughout the United States, Japan, and the Middle East. Her first novel, *Shell Shaker,* earned her a 2002 American Book Award and a Wordcraft Circle Writer of the Year in Creative Prose award. In 2004, *Shell Shaker* was published in French.

   Howe is a recipient of a National Endowment for the Humanities award for research and a Smithsonian Native American internship for research. She has written and directed for theater, radio, and film. Her most recent film project as the narrator/host of *Spiral of Fire* aired on PBS in the fall of 2006. She is currently an associate professor at the University of Illinois at Urbana-Champaign.

The game isn't over till it's over.

Also Available

Shell Shaker
LeAnne Howe
Fiction / Native American Studies
5½ x 8½ | 216 pp
TP US $11.95 | CAN $14.50
978-1-879960-61-9 CUSA

Aunt Lute Books

Lilies Without
Laura Kasischke

Laura Kasischke in her own words: "I realized while ordering and selecting the poems for this collection that much of my more recent work concerns body parts, dresses, and beauty queens. These weren't conscious decisions, just the things that found their way into my poems at this particular point in my life, and which seem to have attached to them a kind of prophetic potential. The beauty queens especially seemed to crowd in on me, in all their feminine loveliness and distress, wearing their physical and psychological finery, bearing what body parts had been allotted to them. For some time, I had been thinking about beauty queens like Miss Michigan, but also the Rhubarb Queen, and the Beauty Queens of abstraction—congeniality. And then—Brevity, Consolation for Emotional Damages, Estrogen—all these feminine possibilities to which I thought a voice needed to be given."

Laura Kasischke is the author of six books of poetry, including *Gardening in the Dark* (Ausable Press, 2004) and *Dance and Disappear* (winner of the 2002 Juniper Prize), and four novels. Her work has received many honors, including the Alice Fay Di Castagnola Award from the Poetry Society of America, the Beatrice Hawley Award, the Pushcart Prize, and the Elmer Holmes Bobst Award for Emerging Writers. She teaches at the University of Michigan in Ann Arbor.

Laura Kasischke's dark myths return to us here more frightening and more exciting than ever.

Poetry
September
A Paperback Original
8½ x 5½ | 80 pp
TP US $14.00 | CAN $17.00
978-1-931337-36-6 CUSA

Marketing Plans

Co-op available
Advance reader copies
National advertising:
Poetry • Poets & Writers

Author Hometown: Chelsea, MI

Some Nights No Cars At All
Josh Rathkamp

This is the first book by a poet whose imagination is intimately related to the physical world around him, which he describes as "a wholly new and startling landscape that is the acolyte deserts of Arizona. Living here on the moon, as it were, and for half of the year in nearly unbearable temperatures, something altogether interior visited me. The experience of this landscape is confused by its actual history—on the one hand, geological, on the other hand, recent and territorial, and in the great middle ranges, the profound consciousness of Anasazi and Hohokam. They say, here, just to walk on the ground is to dream."

Josh Rathkamp's language is plainspoken but emotionally charged. He writes about love (both its pleasures and its difficulties) and of the strangeness of consciousness itself with a confidence that can only come from experience that's been scrutinized and distilled. At first glance quiet and modest, these poems gather considerable force as the book takes us deeper and deeper into questions essential to us all: Can love survive our limitations? What is art, and why do we need it? How can we speak of human consciousness?

Josh Rathkamp was born in Saginaw, Michigan. He received his BA from Western Michigan University and his MFA from Arizona State University. His work has appeared in numerous literary journals, including *Indiana Review, Fugue, Meridian, Passages North, Puerto del Sol, Rhino,* and *Drunken Boat.* He currently teaches at Arizona State University and Phoenix College.

The first book by a poet with a curiosity that's both fierce and modest.

Poetry
September
A Paperback Original
8½ x 5½ | 80 pp
TP US $14.00 | CAN $17.00
978-1-931337-35-9 CUSA

Marketing Plans

Co-op available
Advance reader copies
National advertising:
American Poet • The American
Poetry Review • Poetry • Poets & Writers •
The Writer's Chronicle

Author Hometown: Tempe, AZ

Ausable Press

Natural Selections
Selfish Altruists, Honest Liars, and Other Realities of Evolution
David P. Barash

"Combining humane sensibility with common sense, wisdom, knowledge, wit, and sheer intelligence, David Barash's writing is a tonic for the mind."—Richard Dawkins, author of *The God Delusion*

"Entertaining and thought-provoking."—Steven Pinker, author of *The Blank Slate*

If we are, in part, a product of our genes, can free will exist? Incisive and engaging, this indispensable tour of evolutionary biology runs the gamut of contemporary debates, from science and religion to our place in the universe.

David P. Barash is the author of *The Myth of Monogamy* and *Madame Bovary's Ovaries.* He lives in Redmond, Washington.

Marketing Plans
Co-op available • Advance reader copies
National advertising: Bellevue Literary Review • Booklist • Choice • Kirkus Reviews • Library Journal • Publishers Weekly

Author Hometown: Redmond, WA

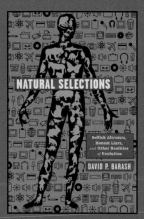

Science
September
6 x 9 | 192 pp
TC US $25.00 | CAN $30.00
978-1-934137-05-5 CUSA

What happens when evolutionary and cultural imperatives clash and what we can do about it.

The Leper Compound
Paula Nangle

"*The Leper Compound* will . . . remain with the reader long after the book has been closed."—Stuart Dybek, author of *I Sailed with Magellan*

For Colleen, motherless at seven, isolated from her schizophrenic younger sister, illness unleashes the uncanny and essential of human identity. Growing into womanhood in Rhodesia's final conflict-ridden years, she transgresses social, racial, and political boundaries in her search for connection. This masterly novel is a searing evocation of late-twentieth-century African life.

Paula Nangle was raised by missionaries in the United States and southern Africa and now lives in Benton Harbor, Michigan. This is her first novel.

Marketing Plans
Co-op available • Advance reader copies
National advertising: Bellevue Literary Review • Booklist • Choice • Kirkus Reviews • Library Journal • Publishers Weekly • Rain Taxi

Author Hometown: Benton Harbor, MI

Fiction / African Studies
January
A Paperback Original
5 x 8 | 192 pp
TP US $14.95 | CAN $18.00
978-1-934137-06-2 CUSA

The psychic geography of conflict in southern Africa is revealed in this arrestingly imaginative first novel.

Bellevue Literary Press

Psychology & Psychiatry /
Biography & Autobiography
January
6 x 9 | 256 pp
110 Color and B&W photographs
TC US $25.00 | CAN $30.00
978-1-934137-07-9 CUSA

**A treasure trove of abandoned
possessions conjures forgotten lives
of twentieth-century mentally ill and
institutionalized patients.**

The Lives They Left Behind
Suitcases from a State Hospital Attic
Darby Penney and Peter Stastny
Photographs by Lisa Rinzler

"A stunning achievement [that] . . . illuminates the tragedy of our treatment of those with mental and emotional problems."—Robert Whitaker, author of *Mad in America*

More than four hundred abandoned suitcases filled with patients' belongings were found when Willard Psychiatric Center closed in 1995 after 125 years of operation. In this fully-illustrated social history, they are skillfully examined and compared to the written record to create a moving—and devastating—group portrait of twentieth-century American psychiatric care.

Darby Penney is a leader in the human rights movement for people with psychiatric disabilities. **Peter Stastny** is a psychiatrist and documentary filmmaker. **Lisa Rinzler** is a prizewinning cinematographer.

Marketing Plans
Co-op available • Advance reader copies
National advertising: Bellevue Literary Review • Booklist • Choice • Kirkus Reviews • Library Journal • Publishers Weekly • Rain Taxi

Author Hometown: Albany, NY/New York, NY

Literature & Essay / Fiction Anthology
February
A Paperback Original
6 x 9 | 320 pp
TP US $16.95 | CAN $20.50
978-1-934137-04-8 CUSA

**Selections from the
well-regarded magazine featuring
fiction, nonfiction, and poetry.**

The Best of the Bellevue Literary Review
Edited by Danielle Ofri
Foreword by Sherwin B. Nuland

"A kaleidoscope of creativity . . . unsentimental and sometimes unpredictable."
—*Journal of the American Medical Association*

Founded just six years ago, *Bellevue Literary Review* is already widely recognized as a rare forum for emerging and celebrated writers—among them Julia Alvarez, Rafael Campo, Rick Moody, and Abraham Verghese—on issues of health and healing. Gathered here are poignant and prizewinning stories, essays, and poems, the voices of patients and those who care for them, which form the journal's remarkable dialogue on "humanity and the human experience."

Danielle Ofri, MD, PhD, author of *Incidental Findings* and *Singular Intimacies,* is the editor in chief of *Bellevue Literary Review.* She lives in New York City.

Marketing Plans
Co-op available • Advance reader copies
National advertising: Bellevue Literary Review • Booklist • Choice • Kirkus Reviews • Library Journal • Publishers Weekly

Author Hometown: New York, NY

Bellevue Literary Press

Reasonable Doubts

Gianrico Carofiglio

Translated by Howard Curtis

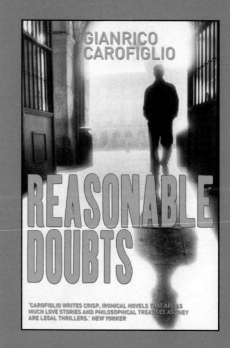

"Carofiglio writes crisp, ironical novels that are as much love stories and philosophical treatises as they are legal thrillers."—*The New Yorker*

"Guerrieri could have just gotten off an Alitalia flight from the land of Grisham or the Los Angeles of Michael Connelly's *The Lincoln Lawyer*. Sharp writing will keep readers turning the pages."—*Publishers Weekly*

Praise for the Guerrieri series:

"*Involuntary Witness* is a stunner."—*The Times*

"Every character in Carofiglio's fiction has a story to tell and they are always worth hearing. As the author himself is an anti-mafia prosecutor, this powerfully affecting series benefits from veracity as well as tight writing."—*Daily Mail*

Lawyer Guerrieri is asked to handle the appeal of Fabio Paolicelli, sentenced to sixteen years for smuggling drugs into Italy. Everything seems stacked against the accused, not least because he initially confessed to the crime. His past as a neo-fascist thug also adds credence to the case against him. Only the intervention of Paolicelli's beautiful half-Japanese wife finally overcomes Guerrieri's reluctance. Matters get more complicated when Guerrieri ends up in bed with her.

Gianrico Carofiglio, born in 1961, is a judge and anti-Mafia prosecutor in the southern Italian city of Bari. Bitter Lemon Press introduced him to English-speaking readers with his best-selling debut novel, *Involuntary Witness*.

The third in the Guerrieri series: a legal thriller by an Italian prosecutor. Turow with wry humor.

Mystery / Fiction
October
A Paperback Original
5¼ x 7¾ | 275 pp
TP US $14.95 | CAN $18.00
978-1-904738-24-4 CUSA

Marketing Plans

Co-op available
Advance reader copies

Author Events

New York, NY

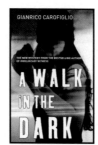

Also Available

Involuntary Witness
Gianrico Carofiglio
Translated by Patrick Creagh
Mystery / Fiction
5⅜ x 7⅜ | 340 pp
TP US $13.95 | CAN $17.00
978-1-904738-07-7 CUSA

A Walk in the Dark
Gianrico Carofiglio
Translated by Howard Curtis
Mystery / Fiction
5¼ x 7¾ | 215 pp
TP US $14.95 | CAN $18.00
978-1-904738-17-6 CUSA

Bitter Lemon Press

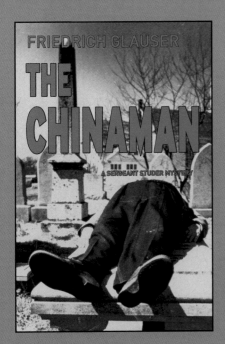

Mystery / Fiction
January
A Paperback Original
5¼ x 7¾ | 186 pp
TP US $14.95 | CAN $18.00
978-1-904738-21-3 CUSA

Marketing Plans

Co-op available
Advance reader copies

The Chinaman
A Sergeant Studer Mystery
Friedrich Glauser
Translated by Mike Mitchell

"After reading Friedrich Glauser's dark tour de force *In Matto's Realm*, it's easy to see why the German equivalent of the Edgar Allan Poe Award is dubbed 'The Glauser.'"
—*The Washington Post*

Praise for the Sergeant Studer series:

"*Thumbprint* is a fine example of the craft of detective writing in a period which fans will regard as the golden age of crime fiction."—*The Sunday Telegraph*

"*In Matto's Realm* is a gem that contains echoes of Dürrenmatt, Fritz Lang's film *M* and Thomas Mann's *The Magic Mountain*. Both a compelling mystery and an illuminating, finely wrought mainstream novel."—*Publishers Weekly*

When, in later years, Sergeant Studer told the story of the Chinaman, he called it the story of three places, as the case unfolded in a Swiss country inn, in a poorhouse, and in a horticultural college. Three places and two murders. Anna Hungerlott, supposedly dead from gastric influenza, left behind handkerchiefs with traces of arsenic. One foggy November morning the enigmatic James Farny, nicknamed the Chinaman by Studer, was found lying on Anna's grave. Murdered, a single pistol shot to the heart that did not pierce his clothing. This is the fourth in the Sergeant Studer series.

Friedrich Glauser is a legendary figure in European crime writing. He was a morphine and opium addict much of his life and began writing crime novels while an inmate of the Swiss asylum for the insane at Waldau.

Three murders in a small village. The fourth Sergeant Studer mystery by the Swiss Simenon.

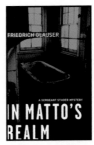

In Matto's Realm
A Sergeant Studer Mystery
Friedrich Glauser
Translated by Mike Mitchell
Mystery / Fiction
5⅜ x 7⅜ | 334 pp
TP US $13.95 | CAN $17.00
978-1-904738-06-0 CUSA

**Also
Available**

Thumbprint
Friedrich Glauser
Translated by Mike Mitchell
Fiction / Mystery
5⅜ x 7⅜ | 200 pp
TP US $13.95 | CAN $17.00
978-1-904738-00-8 CUSA

Bitter Lemon Press

The Sinner

Petra Hammesfahr

Translated by John Brownjohn

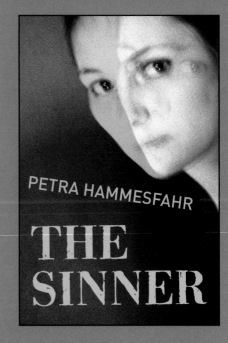

PETRA HAMMESFAHR

THE SINNER

"In this intelligent novel Hammesfahr has etched with precision the thoughts of a woman on the edge of madness."—*Der Spiegel*

Cora Bender killed a man. But why? What could have caused this quiet, lovable young mother to stab a stranger in the throat, again and again, until she was pulled off his body? For the local police it was an open-and-shut case. Cora confessed; there was no shortage of proof or witnesses. But Police Commissioner Rudolf Grovian refused to close the file and began his own maverick investigation. So begins the slow unraveling of Cora's past, a harrowing descent into a woman's private hell.

Hailed as Germany's Patricia Highsmith, Petra Hammesfahr has written a dark, spellbinding novel. At the top of the bestseller list, *The Sinner* has been reprinted sixteen times and sold over 760,000 copies at home. Translated into eleven languages, this is the first Hammesfahr title published in English.

Petra Hammesfahr, born in 1951, left school at thirteen, became pregnant by an alcoholic at seventeen, and began writing novels at the age of forty. Her first thriller was turned down 159 times, but eventually success arrived. Hammesfahr has written over twenty crime and suspense novels. She also writes scripts for television and film. She is married with three children and lives near Cologne.

**She cut the throat of stranger in broad daylight.
In front of her family. But why?**

Mystery / Fiction
February
A Paperback Original
5¼ x 7¾ | 442 pp
TP US $14.95 | CAN $18.00
978-1-904738-25-1 CUSA

Marketing Plans

Co-op available
Advance reader copies

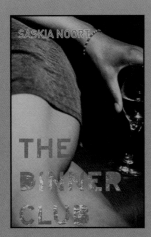

The Dinner Club
Saskia Noort
Translated by Paul Vincent

Mystery / Fiction
5 x 8 | 276 pp
TP US $14.95 | CAN $18.00
978-1-904738-20-6 CUSA

Havana Blue
Leonardo Padura
Translated by Peter Bush

Mystery / Fiction
5 x 8 | 286 pp
TP US $14.95 | CAN $18.00
978-1-904738-22-0 CUSA

Framed
Tonino Benacquista
Translated by Adriana Hunter

Mystery / Fiction
5⅜ x 7⅜ | 240 pp
TP US $14.95 | CAN $18.00
978-1-904738-16-9 CUSA

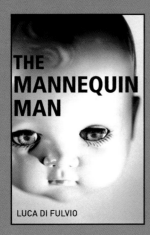

The Mannequin Man
Luca Di Fulvio
Translated by Patrick McKeown

Mystery / Fiction
5¼ x 7¾ | 368 pp
TP US $14.95 | CAN $18.00
978-1-904738-13-8 CUSA

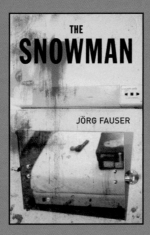

The Snowman
Jörg Fauser
Translated by Anthea Bell

Fiction / Mystery
5⅜ x 7⅜ | 190 pp
TP US $13.95 | CAN $17.00
978-1-904738-05-3 CUSA

Black Ice
Hans Werner Kettenbach
Translated by Anthea Bell

Mystery / Fiction
5⅜ x 7⅜ | 334 pp
TP US $14.95 | CAN $18.00
978-1-904738-08-4 CUSA

The Commonwealth of Life
New Environmental Economics—
A Treatise on Stewardship
Peter G. Brown

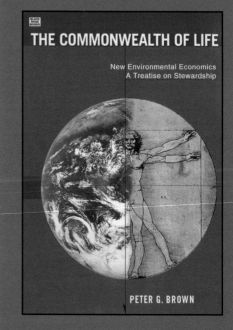

"Convincing analysis; empowering vision."—David Suzuki, scientist and host of CBC's *The Nature of Things*

"A pioneering work in ethics and economics for the new global era raising all the hard questions that we need to think about in the coming decades, and proposing a radically new way of thinking about how the global community should function." —Peter Singer, Ira W. DeCamp professor of bioethics, Princeton University

"Peter Brown has given us a structure that unites an economics of stewardship with a politics of trusteeship, based on an ethics of rights and corresponding duties. Highly recommended!"—Herman E. Daly, University of Maryland

In this important book Peter G. Brown seeks to chart a new future for all who share this planet. Through a series of careful arguments, he identifies three challenges ahead of us: first, to come up with an adequate account of our minimal obligations to each other and to the rest of the natural order; second, to redefine and reshape the institutions of economics, government, and civil society to reflect these obligations; and third, to reconceptualize and redirect the relations between nations to foster these institutions and discharge these obligations. Brown also argues that we have direct moral obligations to non-humans—this he calls "respect for the commonwealth of life."

Peter G. Brown is a professor at McGill University and director of the McGill School of Environment in Montreal, Quebec. He is the author of *Restoring the Public Trust: A Fresh Vision for Progressive Government in America*.

The book that seeks to chart a new future for all who share this planet.

Environmental Studies
September
6 x 9 | 204 pp
TP $19.99
978-1-55164-304-5 USA
TC x $48.99
978-1-55164-305-2 USA

Marketing Plans

National advertising:
E / The Environmental Magazine •
Earth First! Journal • The Ecologist

Author Hometown: Montreal, QC

Black Rose Books

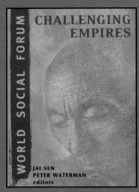

Political Science & Government
September
7 x 10 | 475 pp
TP $28.99
978-1-55164-308-3 USA
TC x $57.99
978-1-55164-309-0 USA

Experimenting with politics that can cope with uncertainty.

World Social Forum
Challenging Empires
Edited by Jai Sen and Peter Waterman

"A stellar collection of essays. Indispensable reading."—Immanuel Wallerstein, Fernand Braudel Center

This comprehensive volume provides a glimpse into the wide-ranging discussions, debates, and arguments that have gone into making the World Social Forum (WSF) one of the more prominent platforms of alternative ideas and practices in the present world.

Jai Sen, an independent researcher living in New Delhi, has contributed to a number of works documenting the World Social Forum.

Peter Waterman worked for the Institute of Social Studies, The Hague, for nearly thirty years. He is the author of *Globalisation, Social Movements, and the New Internationalisms.*

Marketing Plans
National advertising: The Nation • The Progressive • Utne

Author Hometown: Montreal, QC

Asian Studies / History
October
6 x 9 | 204 pp
30 B&W photographs
TP $19.99
978-1-55164-306-9 USA
TC x $48.99
978-1-55164-307-6 USA

Subtle insights into Japan that are different from the usual catalog of descriptions and analyses.

21st Century Japan
A New Sun Rising
Trevor W. Harrison

During 2006, Trevor W. Harrison lived, worked, and traveled in Japan. Written on the cusp of several notable events that shook Japan while he was there, this work begins with an overview of Japan's history and politics, from post-World War II up until the present day, then examines the reality of Japan's geographic location within Asia, as well as its political and economic ties with the West.

Trevor W. Harrison is a professor and chair in the Department of Sociology at the University of Lethbridge in Alberta, and the editor of *Return of the Trojan Horse: Alberta and the New World (Dis)Order.*

Marketing Plans
Co-op available
National advertising: The Nation • The New York Review of Books • Publishers Weekly

Author Hometown: Lethbridge, AB

Black Rose Books

Anarchism

A Documentary History of Libertarian Ideas, Volume Two: The Anarchist Current (1939–2007)

Edited by Robert Graham

Continuing where volume one left off, this anthology documents anarchist writings from World War II up until the present day. Many of the translations (from Africa, India, China, Latin America, and Europe) have never before been published in English.

Contributors include Noam Chomsky, Murray Bookchin, Emma Goldman, George Woodcock, Marie Louise Berneri, Herbert Read, Alex Comfort, Martin Buber, Paul Goodman, Carole Pateman, Colin Ward, Paul Feyerabend, Pierre Clastres, Chaia Heller, Ivan Illich, Daniel Guerin, Luce Fabbri, and many more.

Robert Graham is the editor of *Anarchism: A Documentary History of Libertarian Ideas, Volume One: From Anarchy to Anarchism (300CE to 1939)*.

Marketing Plans
National advertising: Anarchy • Perspectives on Anarchist Theory • Social Anarchism

Author Hometown: Vancouver, BC

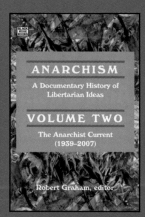

Philosophy / History
October
6 x 9 | 500 pp
TP $28.99
978-1-55164-310-6 USA
TC x $57.99
978-1-55164-311-3 USA

Explores an elaborate genealogy of anti-authoritarian thought.

Faith in Faithlessness

An Anthology of Atheism

Edited by Andrea Levy and Dimitrios Roussopoulos

With the rise of religious fundamentalism worldwide, express disbelief in God(s) has become taboo. In the last few years, however, atheism has witnessed a resurgence. This book contributes to the reassertion of "godlessness" as a philosophical and moral stance. Part One includes historic defenses of atheism (from Baron d'Holbach, Feuerbach, Nietzsche, Marx, Emma Goldman, Bakunin, Paine, Russell, and Freud), while contributions from contemporary nonbelievers from the political and arts communities make up Part Two.

Andrea Levy has published widely on the ecology and peace movements.

Dimitrios Roussopoulos is an author and editor whose most recent work documents the New Left.

Marketing Plans
National advertising: The Progressive • Radical Philosophy • Z Magazine

Author Hometown: Montreal, QC

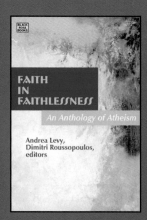

Philosophy / Religion
November
6 x 9 | 224 pp
TP $19.99
978-1-55164-312-0 USA
TC x $48.99
978-1-55164-313-7 USA

Asks freethinkers to declare their atheism in defiance of the stigmatization of disbelief.

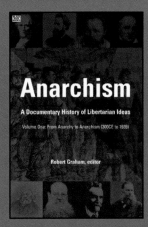

Anarchism
A Documentary History of
Libertarian Ideas, Volume One
Edited by Robert Graham

Philosophy / Political Science & Government
6 x 9 | 536 pp
TP $28.99
978-1-55164-250-5 USA

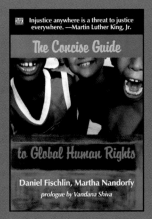

The Concise Guide to
Global Human Rights
**Daniel Fischlin and
Martha Nandorfy**

Current Affairs
6 x 9 | 268 pp
16 B&W photographs
TP $24.99
978-1-55164-294-9 USA

Ghost Strasse
Germany's East Trapped
Between Past and Present
Simon Burnett

Cultural Studies / History
6 x 9 | 256 pp
50 B&W photographs
TP $24.99
978-1-55164-290-1 USA

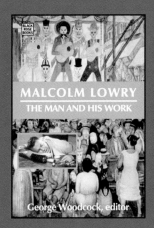

Malcolm Lowry
The Man and His Work
Edited by George Woodcock

Biography & Autobiography
6 x 9 | 224 pp
TP $19.99
978-1-55164-302-1 USA

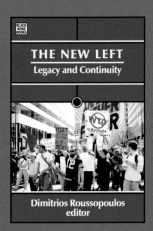

The New Left
Legacy and Continuity
Edited by Dimitrios Roussopoulos

History / Cultural Studies
6 x 9 | 224 pp
20 B&W photographs
TP $19.99
978-1-55164-298-7 USA

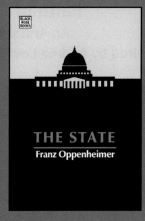

The State
Franz Oppenheimer

Political Science & Government /
Cultural Studies
6 x 9 | 224 pp
TP $19.99
978-1-55164-300-7 USA

Peeping Tom's Cabin
Comic Verse 1928–2008
X.J. Kennedy

Comic Verse 1928–2008
by
X. J. Kennedy

"X.J. Kennedy's well-known travels between the realms of the comic and the serious qualify him for dual citizenship in the world of poetry. Here, the playful is on full display in verse not just 'light' but bright and delightful."—Billy Collins

Peeping Tom's Cabin is the first full-length collection of light verse for adults composed by one of America's most celebrated poets. An uncompromising formalist, X.J. Kennedy uses a broad range of longstanding poetic forms, including limerick, nursery rhyme, ballad, rhymed epitaph, and clerihew. This collection includes many poems previously published in poetry and popular journals, including *The Sewanee Review, The Atlantic Monthly, The New Yorker,* and *Poetry*. These poems honor and skewer all classes of citizen, regardless of their revered place in society. Parents, lovers, poetry critics, students, and especially notable literary figures receive Kennedy's astute comic attention.

"To Someone Who Insisted I Look Up Someone"

I rang them up while touring Timbuktu,
Those bosom chums to whom you're known as "Who?"

X.J. Kennedy has published six collections of verse, including *Nude Descending a Staircase,* which received the Lamont Award from the Academy of American Poets. His newest collection, *The Lords of Misrule,* received the 2004 Poets' Prize. Kennedy has also authored eighteen children's books and several textbooks on fiction and poetry. Other recognitions include the Los Angeles Book Award for Poetry, the Aiken-Taylor Award, and Guggenheim and National Arts Council fellowships. Kennedy was also given the first Michael Braude Award for light verse by the American Academy and Institute of Arts and Letters.

The first light verse collection by the internationally recognized (and hilarious) master of the form.

Poetry
September
American Poets Continuum 105
6 x 9 | 120 pp
TP US $17.00 | CAN $20.50
978-1-929918-96-6 CUSA
TC y US $22.00 | CAN $26.50
978-1-929918-95-9 CUSA

Also Available

You and Yours
Naomi Shihab Nye
Poetry
American Poets Continuum 93
6 x 9 | 104 pp
TP US $15.50 | CAN $18.95
978-1-929918-69-0 CUSA

Blessing the Boats
New and Selected Poems
1988–2000
Lucille Clifton
Poetry
American Poets Continuum 60
6 x 9 | 145 pp
TP US $17.00 | CAN $20.50
978-1-880238-88-2 CUSA

BOA Editions, Ltd.

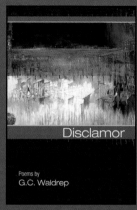

Poetry
September
A Paperback Original
American Poets Continuum 106
6 x 9 | 104 pp
TP US $16.00 | CAN $18.95
978-1-929918-97-3 CUSA

Meditations on war and beauty by a celebrated, fiercely intelligent, and startlingly original young poet.

Disclamor
G.C. Waldrep

"Here is a gorgeous book of the most subtle and vivid mysteries, weighted with earth and time."—Li-Young Lee

While hiking the Marin Headlands north of San Francisco, G.C. Waldrep became fascinated with how the military installations there impact the landscape's spectacular natural beauty. Thus, Waldrep produced "The Batteries," a sequence of nine poems that probe the interrelationship between beauty and violence.

Poems from *Disclamor* have garnered G.C. Waldrep the 2006 Alice Fay Di Castagnola Award from the Poetry Society of America and a 2007 NEA Fellowship. He holds a PhD in American History from Duke University and an MFA from the Iowa Writers' Workshop.

Marketing Plans
Advance reader copies

Author Events
Iowa City, IA • Lewisburg, PA

Author Hometown: Lewisburg, PA

Poetry
October
American Poets Continuum 107
6 x 9 | 72 pp
TP US $16.00 | CAN $18.95
978-1-929918-98-0 CUSA
TC y US $23.00 | CAN $27.95
978-1-934414-02-6 CUSA

Winner of the Isabella Gardner Poetry Award for 2007.

Encouragement for a Man Falling to His Death
Christopher Kennedy

Christopher Kennedy's poetry is funny, deadpan, self-effacing, and revelatory in the way of a man with nothing to lose. Mixing sonnets and prose poems, Kennedy lampoons the absurdities of contemporary American life using ironic fables and surreal parables. Kennedy's poems also reflect his obsession with the idea of transformation—from the ordinary to the extraordinary, from life to death.

Christopher Kennedy is director of the Syracuse University MFA Program in Creative Writing. He has received writing awards from the New York Foundation for the Arts and the Saltonstall Foundation. This is his third full-length poetry collection.

Marketing Plans
Advance reader copies
National advertising: Poets & Writers

Author Events
Louisville, KY • Syracuse, NY

Author Hometown: Syracuse, NY

BOA Editions, Ltd.

Sleeping with Houdini
Nin Andrews

Nin Andrews is arguably the leading female voice in American prose poetry. In a 2005 feature on Andrews in *Moby Lives,* Denise Duhamel wrote, "Nin Andrews is a complete original. Gender-bending and genre-blurring, Andrews is a fabulous fabulist. . . . Her work is always surprising, sharp and wild." In *Sleeping with Houdini,* Andrews speaks as a little girl who wishes she could vanish at will, just as Houdini did. As she grows, Houdini becomes a personal icon, a magical being, a muse, an ultimate lover, and a metaphor for longing.

Nin Andrews is the author of the highly acclaimed *The Book of Orgasms* and other collections.

Marketing Plans
Advance reader copies
National advertising: Poets & Writers

Author Events
Miami, FL • Cleveland, OH • Eugene, OR • Erie, PA • Providence, RI • Seattle, WA

Author Hometown: Poland, OH

Poetry
October
American Poets Continuum 108
6 x 9 | 92 pp
TP US $16.00 | CAN $18.95
978-1-929918-99-7 CUSA

The leading female voice of American prose poetry reinvents Houdini as a metaphor for girlhood and longing.

I Don't Believe in Ghosts
Moikom Zeqo
Translated by Wayne Miller

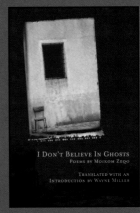

Between 1970 and 1974, Moikom Zeqo wrote a collection of poems called *Meduza* that challenged the core tenets of Albanian socialist realism. When samples were published, Zeqo's work was denounced as "hermetic, with modern influences, dangerous, [and] foreign." *Meduza* was suppressed until 1995, after the collapse of the Albanian communist system. *I Don't Believe in Ghosts* gathers the best and most translatable poems from *Meduza.*

Moikom Zeqo is Albania's former minister of culture and directed Albania's National History Museum. He now works as a freelance writer and journalist in Tirana.

Wayne Miller teaches at the University of Central Missouri, where he co-edits *Pleiades.*

Marketing Plans
Advance reader copies
National advertising: Poets & Writers

Author Events
Los Angeles, CA • San Francisco, CA • Chicago, IL • Columbia, MO • Kansas City, MO • St. Louis, MO • New York, NY • Oberlin, OH • Houston, TX

Translator Hometown: Kansas City, MO

Poetry
November
Lannan Translations Selection Series 12
6 x 9 | 160 pp
TP US $21.95 | CAN $26.50
978-1-934414-01-9 CUSA
TC y US $26.95 | CAN $32.50
978-1-934414-00-2 CUSA

Banned in Albania from 1974 to 1995, this collection introduces a seminal world poet to US readers.

BOA Editions, Ltd.

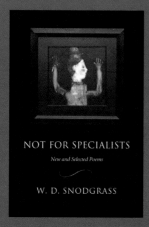

Not for Specialists
New and Selected Poems
W.D. Snodgrass

Poetry
6 x 9 | 251 pp
TP US $21.95 | CAN $26.50
978-1-929918-77-5 CUSA

Darling Vulgarity
Michael Waters

Poetry
6 x 9 | 96 pp
TP US $15.50 | CAN $18.95
978-1-929918-85-0 CUSA

The Rooster's Wife
Russell Edson

Poetry
6 x 9 | 88 pp
TP US $14.95 | CAN $18.00
978-1-929918-63-8 CUSA

Flowers of a Moment
Ko Un
**Translated by Brother Anthony,
Young-moo Kim, and Gary Gach**

Poetry / Asian Studies
9¾ x 8⅜ | 140 pp
12 B&W illustrations
TP US $17.95 | CAN $21.50
978-1-929918-88-1 CUSA

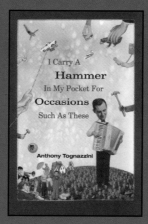

I Carry A Hammer In
My Pocket For Occasions
Such As These
Anthony Tognazzini

Fiction
7 x 10 | 144 pp
TP US $14.95 | CAN $18.00
978-1-929918-90-4 CUSA

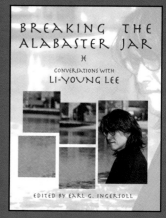

Breaking the Alabaster Jar
Conversations with Li-Young Lee
Li-Young Lee
Edited by Earl Ingersoll

Poetry / Literature & Essay
6 x 9 | 191 pp
TP US $19.95 | CAN $24.00
978-1-929918-82-9 CUSA

Adventure Dad
Rescuing Families from the Couch
One Expedition at a Time
Edited by Joe Kurmaskie

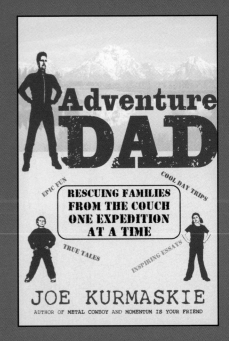

These are first-person stories of dads who haven't let real life (mortgage, marriage, career, kids) destroy their sense of adventure. If you're anything like Joe Kurmaskie and his legion of Adventure Dads, you're not going down without a fight. It's time to adapt and evolve, to turn your yearning for the wild into something for the good of the whole family. Bringing kids on outdoor expeditions leads to closer relationships, trust, respect, and physically and emotionally confident kids. Getting everyone up off the couch and out the door is an investment in your children that will pay dividends throughout their lives.

Each inspiring story from two dozen different Adventure Dads is bookended by lively practical guides for anyone who needs guidance in a new activity, with tips, resources, how-to advice, pitfalls, age and ability considerations, safety tips, and more. You'll be prepared for daytrips, weekend outings, weeklong trips, or epic season-length expeditions.

Subjects covered include sailing, sledding, surfing, rock climbing, bicycle touring, canoeing, hiking, snowshoeing, kayaking, dog sledding, dune riding, snorkeling, rafting, backpacking, mountain biking, snowboarding, geocaching, fly fishing, and skiing.

Joe Kurmaskie is the author of *Metal Cowboy* (Breakaway Books, 1999), *Riding Outside the Lines* (Crown, 2001), and *Momentum Is Your Friend* (Breakaway Books, 2006).

Stories of parents who bring kids along for great outdoor adventures.

Sports & Recreation / Family & Parenting
October
6 x 9 | 320 pp
40 B&W illustrations and photographs
TC US $23.95 | CAN $29.00
978-1-891369-71-1 CUSA

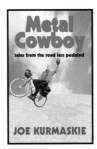

Also Available

Momentum Is Your Friend
The Metal Cowboy and His Pint-Sized
Posse Take on America
Joe Kurmaskie
Sports & Recreation /
Travel & Travel Guides
6 x 9 | 272 pp
50 B&W photographs
TC US $23.95 | CAN $29.00
978-1-891369-65-0 CUSA

Metal Cowboy
Tales from the Road Less Pedaled
Joe Kurmaskie
Literature & Essay / Sports & Recreation
6 x 9 | 304 pp
TC US $23.00 | CAN $27.95
978-1-891369-10-0 CUSA

Breakaway Books

Ultimate
The Greatest Sport Ever Invented by Man
Pasquale Leonardo

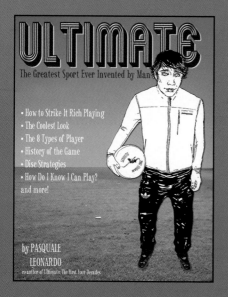

Sports & Recreation / Popular Culture
September
A Paperback Original
5½ x 8½ | 224 pp
100 B&W illustrations and photographs
TP US $14.00 | CAN $17.00
978-1-891369-75-9 CUSA

Marketing Plans

Co-op available

Author Hometown: New York, NY

A tongue-in-cheek guide to playing Ultimate and to Ultimate culture (they don't say *Frisbee*). Full of swanky illustrations, photographs, and some high camp, the book covers the origins of the game, techniques, taxonomy of players, and a style guide. Chapters include: "What Is Ultimate and Why Is It So Cool?," "A Guide to the Five Types of Ultimate Player," "Where to Find Ultimate in Your Hood," "How to Score at an Ultimate Tournament," "How You, Too, Can Train Like a Pro Ultimate Player," "Style Matters: Look Good When You Score," "Parlez-Vous Disc?—The International Scene," "Tricks of the Game," "Best Ultimate Colleges," "Ultimate Was Invented by Aliens (Ultimate Trivia)," and "Ultimate in Popular Culture." This is the first and only book to capture why exactly Ultimate is the greatest sport ever invented by man.

Pasquale Leonardo is the author of *Ultimate: The First Four Decades,* a comprehensive history of the sport. He has been writing about Ultimate since 1996 for the national governing body (Ultimate Players Association) and the international governing body (World Flying Disc Federation), as well as for magazines and tournaments. He is widely known as the premier writer on the sport.

A humorous illustrated guide to Ultimate.

Breakaway Books

God on the Starting Line

The Triumph of a Catholic School Running Team and Its Jewish Coach

Marc Bloom

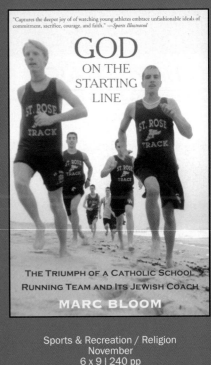

"It captures the deeper joy of watching young athletes embrace unfashionable ideals of commitment, sacrifice, courage, and faith."—*Sports Illustrated*

"Marc Bloom coaches as every coach in the sport should. I recommend this book without reservation. Read it, commit it to memory, and you will be better for it." —*American Track & Field*

"At its core a spiritual book. It will inspire the reader who values small works of goodness and the courage to face big challenges."—*Jewish Book World*

"More than a story of different religions, Jewish and Catholic, meeting on the cross-country course. There is an even more eternal struggle: old versus new. Bloom preaches the value of pain, hard work, suffering, and delayed gratification. His cross-country kids are, well, kids. They want to have fun, chase girls, and enjoy the loosey-goosey life. In Bloom's inspiring tale, both coach and kids learn surprising lessons from each other."—Amby Burfoot, executive editor of *Runner's World*

Marc Bloom, an observant Jew, winds up the coach of a local Catholic high school cross-country team. The common ground he finds between the two faiths helps to propel his team to a state championship.

Marc Bloom, an award-winning journalist, is a features writer for *The New York Times* and a contributing editor of *Runner's World*.

Reflections on the role of faith in a rag-tag team turned state champion.

Sports & Recreation / Religion
November
6 x 9 | 240 pp
TP US $14.00 | CAN $17.00
978-1-891369-74-2 CUSA

Marketing Plans

Co-op available
National advertising:
Runner's World

Author Hometown: Marlboro, NJ

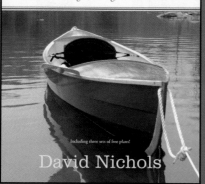

Lapstrake Canoes
Everything You Need to Know to Build a Light, Strong, Beautiful Boat
David Nichols

Lapstrake boats are built by partially overlapping, successive thin planks the length of the boat to make a gorgeous rounded shape that is lightweight, very strong, and stable. This building technique can be done with materials found at any lumberyard or home center. David Nichols makes "advanced" boatbuilding accessible to all ages and skill levels. He has written it so that "any junior high schooler with a bit of focus can build herself a stunning canoe."

Lapstrake Canoes is illustrated with color photographs and line drawings throughout, taking the reader step-by-step through every part of the process. It also includes free foldout plans for three different canoes, from thirteen feet to seventeen feet, plus plans for making your own paddle and making a downwind sail—an astonishing bargain in a world where a set of canoe plans alone can cost fifty to one hundred dollars.

David Nichols has been designing and building boats for the last fifteen years. A graduate of the University of Texas at Austin, he has written for boating magazines, including *WoodenBoat* and *Boatbuilder,* and has written and produced boatbuilding videos. He is the author of *The Working Guide to Traditional Small-Boat Sails.*

A lavishly illustrated guide to building a lapstrake canoe— with free foldout plans included.

Crafts & Hobbies
September
A Paperback Original
8½ x 11 | 112 pp
150 Color photographs and illustrations
TP US $21.95 | CAN $26.50
978-1-891369-72-8 CUSA

Marketing Plans

Co-op available
National advertising:
Messing About in Boats • Paddler •
WoodenBoat

Author Hometown: Austin, TX

Also Available

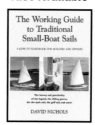

The Working Guide to Traditional Small-Boat Sails
A How-to Handbook for Builders and Owners
David Nichols
Crafts & Hobbies / Sports & Recreation
8½ x 11 | 96 pp
80 Color photographs
TP US $21.95 | CAN $26.50
978-1-891369-67-4 CUSA

Breakaway Books

The Journals of Constant Waterman
Paddling, Poling, and Sailing for the Love of It
Matthew Goldman

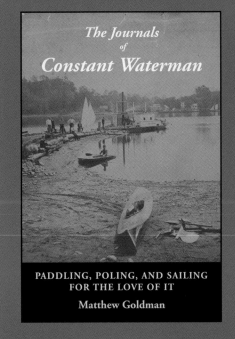

This is a collection of short memoirs about all the boating Matthew Goldman has done in his life—in sailboats, canoes, rowboats, and assorted other floating craft. Most of it is nearly true; the rest has been embellished to make it worthwhile reading. It is descriptive, lyrical, wistful, and, at times, introspective.

Although it is about boating, it includes other aspects of waterfront life: fishing, swimming, building an octagonal cottage on an island, repairing boats, and pursuing mermaids—all have parts to play. In the end, the book is about the decision to either grow old and die or continue boating.

Matthew Goldman has worked as a toolmaker, a woodworker, and a land surveyor. He has written serious drama, black comedy, and farce. Three of his one-act plays have been staged, and his full-length comedy, *Shades of Darkness, Shades of Light,* was included in Tennessee Stage's 2002 Playwrights' Festival. He was one-time editor of the poetry quarterly *A Letter Among Friends,* which flourished for several years, and he has published a number of poems. He currently writes a semi-monthly column in *Messing About in Boats,* and his work has appeared in *Good Old Boat* and *WindCheck.* He resides in Stonington, Connecticut, and works repairing boats in nearby Noank.

**Jubilant, funny essays on paddling and sailing—
making small boats a vital part of life.**

Sports & Recreation /
Biography & Autobiography
October
A Paperback Original
6 x 9 | 304 pp
50 B&W illustrations
TP US $14.00 | CAN $17.00
978-1-891369-73-5 CUSA

Author Hometown: Stonington, CT

Momentum Is Your Friend
The Metal Cowboy and His
Pint-Sized Posse Take on America
Joe Kurmaskie

Sports & Recreation / Travel & Travel Guides
6 x 9 | 272 pp
50 B&W photographs
TC US $23.95 | CAN $29.00
978-1-891369-65-0 CUSA

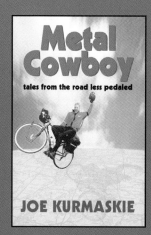

Metal Cowboy
Tales from the Road Less Pedaled
Joe Kurmaskie

Literature & Essay / Sports & Recreation
6 x 9 | 304 pp
TC US $23.00 | CAN $27.95
978-1-891369-10-0 CUSA

Hell's Half Mile
River Runners' Tales of Hilarity
and Misadventure
Edited by Michael Engelhard

Sports & Recreation / Travel & Travel Guides
6 x 9 | 272 pp
TP US $15.00 | CAN $18.00
978-1-891369-47-6 CUSA

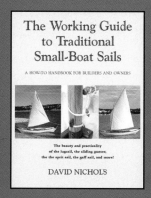

The Working Guide to
Traditional Small-Boat Sails
A How-to Handbook for
Builders and Owners
David Nichols

Crafts & Hobbies / Sports & Recreation
8½ x 11 | 96 pp
80 Color photographs
TP US $21.95 | CAN $26.50
978-1-891369-67-4 CUSA

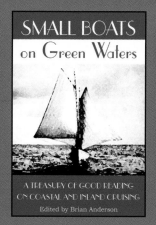

Small Boats on Green Waters
A Treasury of Good Reading on
Coastal and Inland Cruising
Edited by Brian Anderson

Sports & Recreation / Travel & Travel Guides
6 x 9 | 344 pp
40 B&W illustrations
TP US $15.00 | CAN $18.00
978-1-891369-70-4 CUSA

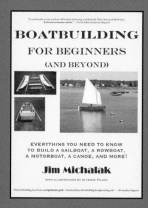

Boatbuilding for Beginners
(and Beyond)
Everything You Need to Know
to Build a Sailboat, a Rowboat, a
Motorboat, a Canoe, and More!
Jim Michalak

Crafts & Hobbies / Technology & Industrial Arts
9 x 12 | 176 pp
200 B&W illustrations & halftones
TP US $24.95 | CAN $30.00
978-1-891369-29-2 CUSA

Lonely Hearts
The 1st Charles Resnick Mystery
John Harvey

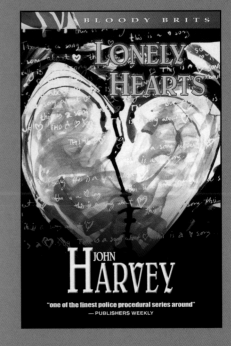

"Harvey's series about Charlie Resnick, the jazz-loving, melancholy cop in provincial Nottingham, England, has long been one of the finest police procedural series around."—*Publishers Weekly*

"The characters in John Harvey's urban crime novels are so defiantly alive and unruly that they put these British police procedurals on a shelf by themselves." —Marilyn Stasio, *The New York Times Book Review*

"Harvey reminds me of Graham Greene, a stylist who tells you everything you need to know while keeping the prose clean and simple. It's a very realistic style that draws you into the story without the writer getting in the way."—Elmore Leonard

"Charlie Resnick is one of the most fully realized characters in modern crime fiction."—Sue Grafton

The first major case for Charles Resnick and his team concerns a number of increasingly serious attacks on women who have been using the "Lonely Hearts" column of the local newspaper. Simultaneously, Resnick becomes involved with Rachel Chaplin, the social worker assigned to a family caught up in allegations of child abuse.

John Harvey's Charles Resnick is British crime fiction's best-kept secret. In the ten novels Harvey wrote about Resnick before ending the series, he established his character as a believable, ordinary policeman who investigated ordinary, everyday crime, rooted in the socioeconomic plight and drab lives of many people in the city of Nottingham.

Bloody Brits Press will reissue the entire Inspector Charles Resnick series in the next three seasons.

The first Charles Resnick mystery back in print by popular demand.

Mystery
September
Bloody Brits Press
A Charles Resnick Mystery 1
5½ x 8½ | 288 pp
TP $13.95
978-1-932859-44-7 USA

Marketing Plans

National advertising:
Mystery News

Rough Treatment
The 2nd Charles Resnick Mystery
John Harvey

"Harvey's police procedurals are in a class by themselves—near Dickensian in their portrayal of human frailty, cinematic in their quick changes of scene and character, totally convincing in their plotting and motivation."—*Kirkus Reviews*

Grice and Grabianski are an ill-matched pair of burglars working Charlie Resnick's patch. When they break into the house of television director Harold Roy, they get more than they bargained for. Grabianski falls in love—or is it lust—with the director's wife, and the pair become enmeshed in a dangerous plot to sell the cocaine that was in the safe back to its supplier.

Marketing Plans
National advertising: Mystery News

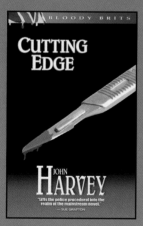

Mystery
October
Bloody Brits Press
A Charles Resnick Mystery 2
5½ x 8½ | 288 pp
TP $13.95
978-1-932859-45-4 USA

Charles Resnick follows a trail of murder and illegal drugs.

Cutting Edge
The 3rd Charles Resnick Mystery
John Harvey

"If John Harvey's novels were songs, Charlie Parker would play them. *Cutting Edge* sings the blues for people too bruised to carry the tune for themselves. Writing in a minor key to tell this moody revenge tragedy, Mr. Harvey creates characters of astonishing psychological diversity. Their voices are abrasive and often husky with pain; but in the end, they all sing their song."—*The New York Times Book Review*

Several members of staff at the local hospital have been seriously attacked at night with a scalpel. Charlie Resnick strives to find a connection between them before assault becomes murder.

Marketing Plans
National advertising: Mystery News

Mystery
November
Bloody Brits Press
A Charles Resnick Mystery 3
5½ x 8½ | 288 pp
TP $13.95
978-1-932859-46-1 USA

Charles Resnick must outwit a deranged attacker.

Bywater Books

Off Minor
The 4th Charles Resnick Mystery
John Harvey

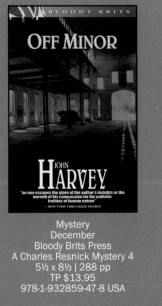

"*Off Minor* by John Harvey is a police procedural story plotted on acts of gross inhumanity yet infused with uncommon humanity. These characters are breathing entities, so convincing and so compelling, that crime detection and absorbing personal dramas become one and the same in this book."—*New York Daily News*

Little Gloria Summers' body has been found in a disused warehouse, and a week later, there are still no clues. Years of patient police work have taught Inspector Charlie Resnick that those who jump to easy conclusions are often the last ones to solve a crime.

Marketing Plans
National advertising: Mystery News

Mystery
December
Bloody Brits Press
A Charles Resnick Mystery 4
5½ x 8½ | 288 pp
TP $13.95
978-1-932859-47-8 USA

Charles Resnick must stop a child-killer before he strikes again.

Foreign Body
The 2nd Fizz and Buchanan Mystery
Joyce Holms

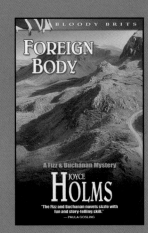

"For Joyce's stories you don't need a strong stomach, though you may find your sides aching with laughter. Her humor is sharp without being nasty; her characters are well drawn."—Ian Rankin

When "Fizz" Fitzgerald suggests a connection between two cases, the police can barely conceal their amusement. Fizz takes matters into her own hands, enlisting the reluctant help of lawyer Tam Buchanan. Soon Tam is mingling with the locals, whose friendly banter conceals all manner of secrets. And it begins to look as though Bessie Anderson knew more than was good for her about one of her neighbors.

Marketing Plans
National advertising: Mystery News

Mystery
January
A Paperback Original
Bloody Brits Press
A Fizz and Buchanan Mystery 2
5½ x 8½ | 288 pp
TP $13.95
978-1-932859-48-5 USA

The brilliant and hilarious follow-up to *Payment Deferred*.

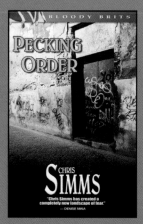

Mystery
February
A Paperback Original
Bloody Brits Press
5½ x 8½ | 288 pp
TP $13.95
978-1-932859-50-8 USA

How far would you go to survive?

Pecking Order
Chris Simms

"Chris Simms has created a completely new landscape of fear."—Denise Mina

Rubble lives in a trailer and works on a chicken farm. Totally oblivious to the outside world, he spends his days disposing of the sick and injured birds. One day, a mysterious visitor arrives and sees Rubble's childlike naiveté combined with an ability to kill without compunction. Soon Rubble is employed on a sinister secret project.

In this chilling thriller, Chris Simms plunges once again into the darkest reaches of human psychology: what it is that drives one person to kill another.

Marketing Plans
National advertising: Mystery News

Mystery
March
A Paperback Original
Bloody Brits Press
A Cairnburgh Mystery 2
5½ x 8½ | 288 pp
TP $13.95
978-1-932859-51-5 USA

A tough and gritty mystery set in the granite streets of Cairnburgh and Aberdeen, Scotland.

Rough Justice
The 2nd Cairnburgh Mystery
Bill Kirton

Floyd Donnelly's dead body is discovered outside the only nightclub in Cairnburgh, Scotland. Detective Chief Inspector Carston thinks he knows who's behind the killing: David Burchill, self-made man and Carston's personal *bête noire*. Burchill is also a possible suspect in another of Carston's cases: a protection racket. An antiques dealer named Hilden has endured a vicious beating from a thug who also destroyed his merchandise.

Carston desperately wants to nail Burchill, but his prey always seems one stop ahead. And with Hilden reluctant to identify his attackers, Carston fears that both cases are destined to remain unsolved for a very long time.

Marketing Plans
National advertising: Mystery News

Bywater Books

Liddy-Jean, Marketing Queen
Mari SanGiovanni

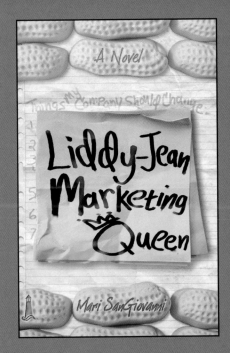

"Liddy-Jean, Marketing Queen is a warm and witty reminder that romance and reading can be fun."—Marianne K. Martin, author of *Under the Witness Tree* and *Dance in the Key of Love*

Liddy-Jean Carpenter has a plan. She is going to write a book. Liddy-Jean Carpenter also has Down syndrome. Working in the marketing department of a large corporation completing basic tasks, no one takes any notice when she starts making a detailed list of what is wrong with the way the company operates.

Enlisting the aid of her coworker Rose and friend Jenny, Liddy-Jean writes an advice book for corporate America called *Wand-Wavers & Worker Bees.* Rose worries what will happen if Liddy-Jean's clever book is published and fears that it will be *The Devil Wears Nada* if the book actually becomes a hit and people find out that the guru of all things wrong with corporate America is really a young woman with Down syndrome. Meanwhile, Liddy-Jean is cooking up another plan—a plan to get Rose away from her dangerous boyfriend.

The way Liddy-Jean sees it, love is love, and she becomes convinced that Rose belongs with Jenny and that she must hatch the perfect scheme to fix both their lives (and maybe a few others along the way).

Liddy-Jean, Marketing Queen is the winner of the second-annual Bywater Prize for Fiction.

Mari SanGiovanni's first book, *Greetings From Jamaica, Wish You Were Queer,* was published by Bywater Books in March 2007. She lives in Rhode Island.

A comical lesbian tale of misbegotten fame à la Chance, the gardener, in the film *Being There*.

Also Available

Greetings From Jamaica, Wish You Were Queer
Mari SanGiovanni
Lesbian Literature
5½ x 8½ | 240 pp
TP US $13.95 | CAN $17.00
978-1-932859-30-0 CUSA

Fiction
January
A Paperback Original
5½ x 8½ | 240 pp
TP US $13.95 | CAN $17.00
978-1-932859-49-2 CUSA

Marketing Plans

National advertising:
The Lesbian Connection

Author Hometown: Providence, RI

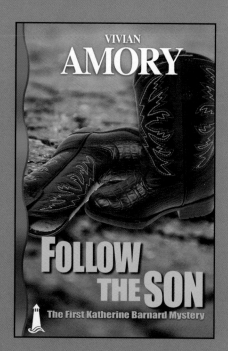

Lesbian Literature / Mystery
March
A Paperback Original
A Katherine Barnard Mystery 1
5½ x 8½ | 288 pp
TP US $13.95 | CAN $17.00
978-1-932859-52-2 CUSA

Marketing Plans

National advertising:
The Lesbian Connection

Follow the Son
The First Katherine Barnard Mystery
Vivian Amory

So was it the sneezing that rang the alarm bells or was it those legs or the incongruity of the cowboy boots with the rest of her outfit or was it seeing a stranger in the middle of the day in Kleinstad? Maybe it just my natural curiosity that made me decide to follow her.

Well, the "following" thing is a long story—a family saga—that is very boring, but the gist of it is that we are a following kind of people. Like some people drum it into their kids' heads that they are winners? We are followers. I sort of understood from my father that his family was indoctrinated with the "Never leaders, always followers" credo. I grew up with this dismal fact of life, knowing I was destined for followingness, until that cold winter day about four years ago when I realized that I could create my own destiny and turn the following thing into a career—so I became a PI.

Kleinstad, the town of my birth, (roughly translated as Little City) is not really a place one drives through—one drives to it, well some people do. And I wondered as I walked on the familiar cracked pavement with the weeds growing through the cracks, what the hell brought her here.

Vivian Amory lives in Durban, South Africa, and writes political speeches for a living. This is her first novel.

Meet Katherine Barnard, a white lesbian PI in today's dynamic and dangerous South Africa.

Bywater Books

Far Beyond Triage
Sarah Lantz

"Large-hearted, linguistically inventive, historically engaged—these poems have a disarming and daft magic, an unlikely mix of sophistication and folk tale—at times, Chagallian; at others, darkened by historical sorrow. In ruined olive groves, in long-deserted villages whose church bells keep tolling, on distant plains where the drumming of wild herds is the percussion of freedom—in all these, a world, fabled and for real, shapes itself, one that looks in time's two directions at once. By the volume's close, it is clear that what has taken root 'far beyond triage' is joy."—Eleanor Wilner

This collection of deeply spiritual poetry explores the longings of the soul and tests the penetrable boundary between the living world and the ethereal. Sarah Lantz articulates complex emotions in a manner that makes her poetry accessible while remaining elusive, heartbreaking and yet hopeful, romantic and yet startlingly real. She creates a world in which small, ordinary moments possess elements of divinity and a greater purpose. Her poetry meanders through time as she writes of "all I knew before I was born" and explores her past and the pasts of her ancestors to help make sense of the present.

Sarah Lantz has been published in the *Denver Quarterly, The Marlboro Review, CALYX Journal, Paris Atlantic,* and *Sister Stew,* among others. She is a secondary school teacher and has taught poetry as a Poet in the Schools in Oregon and Hawaii. She received her MFA from Warren Wilson College and is a member of the Pearl Poets in Portland, Oregon.

A new voice offering sensual, lyrical poetry and dazzling imagery with Rumi's sense of the divine.

Poetry / Jewish Studies
October
A Paperback Original
6 x 9 | 100 pp
TP US $14.95 | CAN $18.00
978-0-934971-91-1 CUSA

Marketing Plans

Advance reader copies

Author Events

Eugene, OR • Newport, OR • Portland, OR • Salem, OR • Bainbridge Island, WA • Bellingham, WA • Olympia, WA • Seattle, WA

Author Hometown: Portland, OR

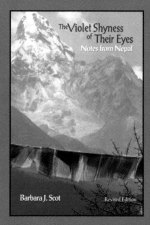

The Violet Shyness of Their Eyes
Notes from Nepal
Barbara J. Scot

Travel & Travel Guides /
Biography & Autobiography
6 x 9 | 290 pp
55 B&W photographs
TP US $16.95 | CAN $20.50
978-0-934971-88-1 CUSA

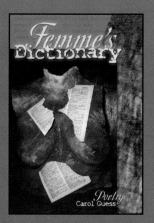

Femme's Dictionary
Carol Guess

Poetry / Lesbian Literature
6 x 9 | 80 pp
TP US $13.95 | CAN $17.00
978-0-934971-86-7 CUSA

Going Home to A Landscape
Writings by Filipinas
Edited by Marianne Villanueva and Virginia Cerenio

Asian Studies / Women's Literature
6 x 9 | 300 pp
TP US $17.95 | CAN $21.50
978-0-934971-84-3 CUSA

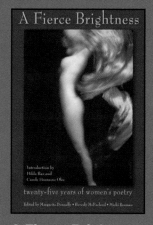

A Fierce Brightness
Twenty-five Years of Women's Poetry
Edited by Margarita Donnelly, et al.

Poetry Anthology / Women's Literature
6 x 9 | 200 pp
TP US $14.95 | CAN $18.00
978-0-934971-82-9 CUSA

A Line of Cutting Women
Edited by Beverly McFarland, et al.

Fiction Anthology / Women's Studies
6 x 9 | 256 pp
TP x US $16.95 | CAN $20.50
978-0-934971-62-1 CUSA

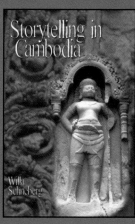

Storytelling in Cambodia
Willa Schneberg

Poetry / Asian Studies
6 x 9 | 132 pp
TP US $13.95 | CAN $17.00
978-0-934971-89-8 CUSA

Full House 4
Revelation
Soo Yon Won

"A fun title and a good read."—AnimeOnDVD.com

The unstable relationship between Alley Ji and Ryder Bay takes an unexpected twist as long-kept secrets are finally revealed! Will Ryder renovate Full House just to spite Alley? Is Alley as helpless as she seems? Will the mysteries surrounding her father be resolved? All this, plus a shocking cliffhanger!

Manga
Available Now
CPM Manhwa
5 x 7⅜ | 192 pp
192 B&W illustrations
TP US $9.99 | CAN $12.00
978-1-57800-707-3 CUSA

Two hardheaded opposites can't seem to realize that they're in love with each other.

Full House 5
Unrequited
Soo Yon Won

Manga
Available Now
CPM Manhwa
5 x 7⅜ | 192 pp
192 B&W illustrations
TP US $9.99
CAN $12.00
978-1-57800-738-7
CUSA

"Quite likable."—*Publishers Weekly*

With a sudden change of heart, narcissistic movie star Ryder Bay gives Full House back to Alley, thereby dissolving their fictitious engagement. But Alley suddenly realizes she has feelings for Ryder! Will she reveal her feelings before he leaves forever?

Full House 6
Soo Yon Won

Manga
September
A Paperback Original
CPM Manhwa
5 x 7⅜ | 200 pp
200 B&W illustrations
TP US $9.99
CAN $12.00
978-1-57800-740-0
CUSA

"As frothy as any paperback romance."—*School Library Journal*

Chased by Henry, Alley and Ryder end up at an empty country house. With nowhere else to hide, they decide to stay there. Now alone with each other, Ryder tells Alley the story of the love of his life—Jasmine. Once again, it seems like the two are finally getting along, when yet another misunderstanding leads Alley to think that Ryder has been toying with her. But this time, with Full House out of the picture once and for all, Alley decides to leave Ryder for good.

Central Park Media

Otogi Matsuri 1
Dark Offering
Junya Inoue

A teenaged outsider with strange new powers is Earth's only hope against a horde of demonic invaders! When high school student Yousuke Suruga accidentally breaks an ancient shinto shrine, his physical body merges with the Bow of Suzaku, an enigmatic weapon from ancient times. Yousuke's only hope lies with Ezo, the eccentric history teacher who wields the Spear of Seiryuu, another mystic weapon that, when combined with the Bow of Suzaku, may be the world's only hope against the ever-growing threat of the monster realm.

Manga
September
A Paperback Original
CPM Manga
5 x 7⅜ | 184 pp
184 B&W illustrations
TP US $9.99 | CAN $12.00
978-1-57800-727-1 CUSA

A teenager with strange new powers is Earth's only hope against a horde of demons.

Otogi Matsuri 2
Blood Rites
Junya Inoue

This second blood-soaked volume includes more monsters, miscreants, and murder! Yousuke's life has gone from bad to worse as demons continue to spill forth from the Monster Realm, causing mayhem and horror. Even worse, his fledgling skills at monster fighting are still amateurish at best, and he can't be sure if his eccentric mentor, Ezo, will be a help or a hindrance.

Manga
January
A Paperback Original
CPM Manga
5 x 7⅜ | 184 pp
184 B&W illustrations
TP US $9.99 | CAN $12.00
978-1-57800-730-1 CUSA

The second blood-soaked volume includes more monsters, more miscreants, and more murder!

Central Park Media

The Sword of Shibito 2

Hideyuki Kikuchi

Art by Missile Kakurai

Manga
September
A Paperback Original
CPM Manga
5 x 7⅜ | 216 pp
216 B&W illustrations
TP US $9.99
CAN $12.00
978-1-57800-720-2
CUSA

"Its weirdness will win you over."—DVDVisionJapan.com

The undead warrior Shibito's mission of revenge is interrupted by a band of pilgrims who've become the targets of bloodthirsty bandits. Will the man-monster put aside his bloody agenda long enough to help them? And are the pilgrims better off with the bandits or this newfound ally stitched together from a dozen corpses?

The Sword of Shibito 3

Hideyuki Kikuchi

Art by Missile Kakurai

Manga
February
A Paperback Original
CPM Manga
5 x 7⅜ | 224 pp
224 B&W illustrations
TP US $9.99
CAN $12.00
978-1-57800-721-9
CUSA

The mystery of Shibito's death is finally revealed! How and why did Shibito die all those years ago? Why did he wake up from his eternal sleep? What is the real reason behind Shibito's resurrection? The mysteries of Shibito's past life—and death—are finally revealed in the climactic chapter of this supernatural epic.

Kung Fu Jungle Boy 1

Jae Kyung Uhm

Art by Choong Ho Lee

Manga
October
A Paperback Original
CPM Manhwa
5 x 7⅜ | 192 pp
192 B&W illustrations
TP US $9.99
CAN $12.00
978-1-57800-708-0
CUSA

The pre-pubescent (yet super-strong) Kakoong is the official protector of the peaceful Cloud Island. He's called into action when the diabolical (and very flatulent) Lord Kojak attacks, hoping to free his imprisoned evil leader. What follows next is all-out martial arts action with funny animals, handsome warriors, potty humor, and Kakoong's sexy girlfriend! This one's got it all!

Kung Fu Jungle Boy 2

Jae Kyung Uhm

Art by Choong Ho Lee

Manga
February
A Paperback Original
CPM Manhwa
5 x 7⅜ | 184 pp
184 B&W illustrations
TP US $9.99
CAN $12.00
978-1-57800-709-7
CUSA

The insanity continues as the Kung Fu Jungle Boy Kakoong falls into a hidden underground dungeon, where he finds a mysterious sleeping maiden. He better hope his girlfriend doesn't find out—she's the jealous type! Then he meets up with a murderous assassin, a monster made of sugar, and his ultimate arch-enemy: the resurrected Evil King Ma!

Manga
October
A Paperback Original
CPM Manga
5 x 7⅜ | 184 pp
184 B&W illustrations
TP US $9.99
CAN $12.00
978-1-57800-731-8
CUSA

Script Downers 1
Ryu Tmr

Hina works for a high-tech agency that battles the evil Artificial Intelligences threatening network servers across the globe. The only way for Hina to combat these beasties is to enter the virtual world, but the dangers there are no less real! This explosive action-comedy will have you keeping one eye on your hard drive every time you check your E-mail!

Manga
February
A Paperback Original
CPM Manga
5 x 7⅜ | 184 pp
184 B&W illustrations
TP US $9.99
CAN $12.00
978-1-57800-732-5
CUSA

Script Downers 2
Ryu Tmr

The cataclysmic conclusion to the adventures of the web-surfing, reality-bending secret agent Hina. The adventures continue Hina travels to even more bizarre worlds in the Artificial Intelligence universe. No assignment is too deadly, no foe is too scary, and no outfit is too tight or tiny for our heroine!

Manga
November
A Paperback Original
CPM Manhwa
5 x 7⅜ | 264 pp
264 B&W illustrations
TP US $9.99
CAN $12.00
978-1-57800-711-0
CUSA

Nambul War Stories 4
Desperation
Hyun Se Lee

"A must-read!"—SequentialTart.com

The best-selling manhwa series of all time continues as Korean citizens are herded into concentration camps. Things are especially difficult for Hae-Sung, as he is tortured for the guards' amusement while his family endures unspeakable brutality. Can he unite the imprisoned families and overthrow the guards, or will they all die anonymously behind the barbed wire fences?

Manga
March
A Paperback Original
CPM Manhwa
5 x 7⅜ | 240 pp
240 B&W illustrations
TP US $9.99
CAN $12.00
978-1-57800-744-8
CUSA

Nambul War Stories 5
Desperation
Hyun Se Lee

News of the atrocities in the Japanese war camp spreads as the fugitive Hae-Sung treks across the country. Caught between government soldiers and hired mercenaries, Hae-Sung retreats to the mountains, where he hopes to stay alive long enough to plan his next move. Will he be able to organize a grassroots campaign to overthrow the invaders?

Central Park Media

Angel Shop 1
Sook Ji Hwang

Manga
October
A Paperback Original
CPM Manhwa
5 x 7⅜ | 200 pp
200 B&W illustrations
TP US $9.99
CAN $12.00
978-1-57800-702-8
CUSA

"The story is interesting."—SequentialTart.com

In a futuristic world, teenaged Boris is annoyed that his cute (yet strange) classmate Yuri Angel has created a robot that looks just like him! His plan is simple: revenge! He steals the automaton and takes its place as a servant at Yuri's house. But now Boris has no idea what to do next!

Wedding Eve
Keiko Honda

Manga
October
A Paperback Original
CPM Manga
5 x 7⅜ | 216 pp
216 B&W illustrations
TP US $9.99
CAN $12.00
978-1-57800-724-0
CUSA

Yui is a wedding gown designer with a problem: Her reputation's at stake because the last four brides to wear her designs have gone through painful divorces. Have her designs become bad luck for the brides-to-be? This leads the passionately single Yui to wonder why a woman who makes her living from love has no love to call her own.

Dystopia
Suzushi Katsuragi

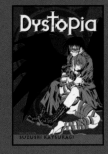

Manga
November
A Paperback Original
CPM Manga
5 x 7⅜ | 256 pp
256 B&W illustrations
TP US $9.99
CAN $12.00
978-1-57800-728-8
CUSA

Something is killing humans who have received mysterious powers through a seemingly divine source, and only the vampire Angela stands between them and utter annihilation. Her only friend is the vampire known only as Alliance, who secretly desires to create a vampire world called Dystopia. Will he use his unique abilities to assist Angela . . . or to destroy her?

Pretty Road 1
Junko Sasaki

Manga
November
A Paperback Original
CPM Manga
5 x 7⅜ | 216 pp
216 B&W illustrations
TP US $9.99
CAN $12.00
978-1-57800-736-3
CUSA

Yuki is a successful executive with a secret: She works as a golf caddie on weekends hoping to meet Mr. Right. Her dream almost comes true when a handsome executive chooses her to caddy for him, until Yuki discovers that he's a vice president at her company! Will this be the love she's been hoping for or a career disaster?

Prince Standard 1
Betten Court

Manga
December
A Paperback Original
CPM Manga
5 x 7⅜ | 200 pp
200 B&W illustrations
TP US $9.99
CAN $12.00
978-1-57800-733-2
CUSA

Bright-eyed Prince Star left the comfortable lifestyle of his father's castle behind in order to search the lands of his kingdom for thrills and adventure. Of course, he should've been more careful for what he wished for, because the young prince soon finds himself surrounded by a slew of unsavory characters and even a cute girl or two.

Couple 4
Jae Sung Park
Art by Sung Jae Park

Manga
December
A Paperback Original
CPM Manhwa
5 x 7⅜ | 176 pp
176 B&W illustrations
TP US $9.99
CAN $12.00
978-1-57800-705-9
CUSA

"A cute and fun manhwa."—SequentialTart.com

First kisses are supposed be special, but when a Peeping Tom photographs Young Ho and Yu Mi's intimate moment and posts the photo on a bulletin board, their lives are cast into turmoil. Who did this . . . and why? Will Young Ho and Yu Mi's love be dashed to pieces before it can even begin?

Oath To Love And Passion 2
Sook Ji Hwang

Manga
January
A Paperback Original
CPM Manhwa
5 x 7⅜ | 216 pp
216 B&W illustrations
TP US $9.99
CAN $12.00
978-1-57800-737-0
CUSA

The nastiest romantic comedy ever returns with more spite, jealousy, backstabbing, and polar bears than you can shake a stick at! The twins have their hands full when their new boyfriends take them out for a night on the town. Things are just fine, as long as everyone's lying, but when truth rears its ugly head, things get bad fast!

Kururi From the Sea
Jukki Hanada
Art by Hiyohiyo

Manga
January
A Paperback Original
CPM Manga
5 x 7⅜ | 192 pp
192 B&W illustrations
TP US $9.99
CAN $12.00
978-1-57800-729-5
CUSA

A sexy fantasy jam-packed with beautiful maidens as undersea girl Kururi comes to the surface world seeking love and adventure. But this isn't a *Little Mermaid* fantasy. Kururi is a butt-kicking supervixen who doesn't take crap from anybody, especially her undersea rival, who follows her to the surface world to make her life miserable.

Central Park Media

Hard Boiled Angel: Angel Detective 1
Hyun Se Lee

Manga
February
A Paperback Original
CPM Manhwa
5 x 7⅜ | 352 pp
352 B&W illustrations
TP US $9.99
CAN $12.00
978-1-57800-741-7
CUSA

"A powerhouse."—PopCultureShock.com

Someone has been using hardened criminals in a deadly experiment, injecting them with cancerous cells that yield catastrophic results. Is this the first stage of some fearsome biological weapon, or something far more sinister? It's up to Detective Jiran Ha of the Hard Crimes Unit to unravel the mystery before innocent people become the target of a mysterious killer.

Yongbi the Invincible 4
Ki Woon Ryu
Art by Jung Who Moon

Manga
March
A Paperback Original
CPM Manhwa
5 x 7⅜ | 192 pp
192 B&W illustrations
TP US $9.99
CAN $12.00
978-1-57800-742-4
CUSA

The stupid samurai Yongbi continues his quest for the mysterious Golden Castle, but there are obstacles aplenty: Armies of assassins prepare an all-out assault on our dimwitted hero in order to wrest a priceless amulet from his grasp. Meanwhile, Yongbi's faithful horse Bi-Yong engages in an interspecies carnal romp that defies description. Plus, there's the heart-stopping return of the Assassin Weasel!

Masca 2
Young Hee Kim

Manga
March
A Paperback Original
CPM Manhwa
5 x 7⅜ | 208 pp
208 B&W illustrations
TP US $9.99
CAN $12.00
978-1-57800-710-3
CUSA

The shocking backstory of the master mage Eliwho is revealed! In a mystical land in another universe many years ago, the novice sorcerer Eliwho is forced into a shady contract with the sinister Devil of Sibilla. Now, five hundred years later, minor details of that encounter will have a lasting impact on not only Eliwho's life, but his entire kingdom!

Tag—You're It! 2
Sook Kim

Manga
March
A Paperback Original
CPM Manhwa
5 x 7⅜ | 192 pp
192 B&W illustrations
TP US $9.99
CAN $12.00
978-1-57800-743-1
CUSA

Four outrageous stories designed to snap your funny bone in half! See an ill-conceived matchmaking attempt, laugh at a pompous rock band that can't get anything right, guffaw at a nerdy teen in love with another man's wife, and snicker when the babies of a devil and an angel get mismatched at Heaven Hospital. We told you this was nuts!

Full House 1
Incompatible
Soo Yon Won

Manga
Available Now
CPM Manhwa
5 x 7⅜ | 192 pp
192 B&W illustrations
TP US $9.99
CAN $12.00
978-1-58664-970-8
CUSA

Alley is an aspiring screenwriter determined to make it big. Ryder is a famous actor at the center of media scrutiny. When Ryder buys Alley's house (without her knowledge!), they're forced to live together, despite their undeniable contempt for each other. Alley and Ryder might turn out to be a very happy couple—if they don't kill each other first!

Couple 1
Jae Sung Park
Art by Sung Jae Park

Manga
Available Now
CPM Manhwa
5 x 7⅜ | 192 pp
192 B&W illustrations
TP US $9.99
CAN $12.00
978-1-58664-951-7
CUSA

After being evicted, college freshman Yu Mi must find a place to stay or she'll be forced to return to her home in the country. Can she convince shallow senior Young Ho to allow her to stay at his grimy place until she finishes college? Get a glimpse into the outrageous lives of the most unlikely couple ever!

Couple 2
Jae Sung Park
Art by Sung Jae Park

Manga
Available Now
CPM Manhwa
5 x 7⅜ | 176 pp
176 B&W illustrations
TP US $9.99
CAN $12.00
978-1-58664-952-4
CUSA

Young Ho didn't think having the cute freshman girl Yu Mi move in with him would be any big deal, but he'd better think again! Ever since she moved in his life has been a mass of conflicting emotions. Are they just friends? Could their relationship turn into something else? The answers to these (and other) questions will probably remain unanswered in this hilarious saga of the most mismatched couple ever.

Couple 3
Jae Sung Park
Art by Sung Jae Park

Manga
Available Now
CPM Manhwa
5 x 7⅜ | 176 pp
176 B&W illustrations
TP US $9.99
CAN $12.00
978-1-58664-953-1
CUSA

"*Couple* is a cute and fun manhwa."—SequentialTart.com

No matter what Young Ho does he ends up in hot water with his roommate, the petite farm girl Yu Mi. Sure, they're *supposed* to "just be friends," but things don't always go as planned. For example, there's Young Ho's infatuation with the blonde girl down the hall that's making Yu Mi jealous, not to mention Yu Mi's unbelievably hunky date who makes Young Ho squid-chomping mad. These developments (and others!) lead to a sexual tension that you could cut with a chainsaw!

Central Park Media

Goodbye Madame Butterfly
Sex, Marriage & the Modern Japanese Woman
Sumie Kawakami
Translated by Yuko Enomoto

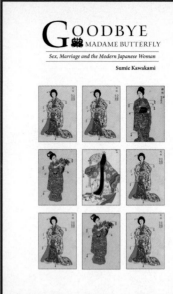

"[Kawakami's essays are] brilliantly written, and a perfect example of how similar bad marriages are, regardless of their setting."—Bookslut.com

Who's to blame for Japan's shrinking birthrate? Too often, politicians and the media pin the blame on young women, whom they call "parasite singles" for living with their parents. Japanese females need to return to their roles as "good wives and wise mothers," the argument goes.

Sumie Kawakami destroys this line of thinking through intimate portraits of women, all in their own way struggling under the country's contorted views of female sexuality.

Women deal with meddling mothers-in-law, coddled momma's-boy husbands, and a society that did not officially outlaw sexual discrimination until 1999. The result is often sexual dysfunction and physical and emotional abuse behind closed doors.

Kawakami shines a light on these troubled relationships and finds a surprising amount of inspiration as women talk of their struggles to find equilibrium and their hopes for a brighter future.

Sumie Kawakami is a Japanese journalist and single mother who has written extensively on marriage and sex, including a 2004 book titled *Tsuma no Koi (Wives in Love)* with Astra, Inc., and three essays in *Kuhaku & Other Accounts from Japan* (Chin Music Press, 2005).

Japan's sexual hang-ups exposed as women liberate themselves from joyless, sexless marriages.

Also Available

Kuhaku & Other Accounts from Japan
Edited by Bruce Rutledge
Illustrated by Craig Mod and kozyndan
Asian Studies / Cultural Studies
4¾ x 7⅜ | 224 pp
43 Color and B&W illustrations
TC US $28.50 | CAN $34.50
978-0-9741995-0-4 CUSA

Asian Studies / Women's Studies
September
5¼ x 7½ | 260 pp
10 B&W illustrations
TC US $20.00 | CAN $24.00
978-0-9741995-3-5 CUSA

Marketing Plans

Co-op available
Advance reader copies

Author Events

San Francisco, CA • Denver, CO •
New York, NY • Portland, OR • Seattle, WA

Chin Music Press

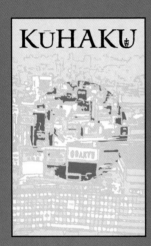

Kuhaku & Other Accounts from Japan
Edited by Bruce Rutledge
Illustrated by Craig Mod and kozyndan

Asian Studies / Cultural Studies
4¾ x 7⅜ | 224 pp
43 Color and B&W illustrations
TC US $28.50 | CAN $34.50
978-0-9741995-0-4 CUSA

Do You Know What It Means to Miss New Orleans?
Toni McGee Causey, Colleen Mondor, and Jason Berry

Literature & Essay / Cultural Studies
5 x 7 | 160 pp
TC US $18.50 | CAN $22.50
978-0-9741995-1-1 CUSA

Last of the Red Hot Poppas
Jason Berry

Mystery / Fiction
4½ x 7 | 302 pp
TC US $24.50 | CAN $29.50
978-0-9741995-2-8 CUSA

The Memory of Pablo Escobar
James Mollison

The extraordinary story of the richest and most violent gangster in history—his youth, his bid for political power, his domination of the world's cocaine trade, his campaign against the Colombian state during which thousands died, his imprisonment in a luxurious private jail, his escape, and his eventual capture and shooting—is told in hundreds of photographs gathered by photographer James Mollison in Colombia. Exhaustively researched, this visual biography includes photographs from Escobar family albums, pictures by Escobar's bodyguards, pictures from police files (both shot by the police and taken in raids of Escobar's premises), and snapshots by the Federal Drug Administration officer who helped hunt Escobar down.

The book contains illuminating interviews with family members, other gangsters, Colombian police and judges, and survivors of Escobar's killing sprees. The text is supplemented by contemporary photographs by Mollison of Escobar's fleet of planes, his private zoo, arms caches captured by the police, and even Escobar's prison jukebox. It is both a compelling picture story and a landmark in visual journalism.

This is the original follow-up to James Mollison's *James and Other Apes* (Chris Boot, 2004). Born of British origin in Kenya, Mollison now lives in Venice. He works as an advertising and editorial photographer, and his work has been widely published throughout the world, including in *Colors*, *The New York Times*, the *Guardian*, and *Le Monde*.

Photography / True Crime
October
7 x 9¼ | 368 pp
800 Color and B&W illustrations
and photographs
TC US $60.00 | CAN $72.00
978-1-905712-06-9 CUSA

**The life and crimes of the gangster Pablo Escobar,
in hundreds of previously unpublished photographs.**

The death of Pablo Escobar, from the private album of Hugo Martinez,
the Colombian policeman who led the team that shot him.

Chris Boot

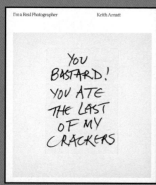

I'm a Real Photographer
Keith Arnatt Photographs 1976–2002
Photographs by Keith Arnatt
Introduction by David Hurn
Afterword by Clare Grafik

Photography / Art
September
8 x 9½ | 176 pp
180 Color and B&W illustrations
and photographs
TC US $45.00 | CAN $54.00
978-1-905712-05-2 CUSA

**The first comprehensive
survey of the photographic works
of Keith Arnatt.**

This is the first comprehensive survey of the photography of Keith Arnatt. Born in Oxford, England, in 1930 and now retired, Arnatt established an international reputation in the late 1960s as a conceptual performance artist. In the mid-1970s, however, he surprised the art establishment by abandoning conceptual art. Feeling he had exhausted its possibilities, Arnatt announced his conversion to the then-unfashionable medium of photography. He subsequently worked prolifically over twenty-five years within a short radius of his home in South Wales, making photographic series—mainly of cats, dogs, and the debris of everyday life—that are conceptually sharp, often very funny, and offer a rich commentary on the history of photography. With a personal essay by Magnum photographer David Hurn and an illustrated, contextual essay by curator Clare Grafik, *I'm a Real Photographer* is published alongside the first major survey of Arnatt's photographs at the Photographers' Gallery in London.

The Power Book
Jacqueline Hassink

Photography / Art
October
13½ x 10¾ | 192 pp
160 Color photographs and illustrations
TC US $60.00 | CAN $72.00
978-1-905712-07-6 CUSA

**A travelogue featuring ten years
of work by a leading conceptual
photographer.**

Jacqueline Hassink is a Dutch-born, New York-based conceptual artist whose widely exhibited photographs deal methodically and precisely with the themes of globalization and economic power. In Table of Power (1996), for instance, Hassink photographed the boardroom tables of Europe's forty largest multinationals, while Female Power Stations: Queen Bees (2000) is about the business and domestic environments of leading women executives. *The Power Book,* the first survey of Hassink's photography, takes the form of a travelogue—the best of her photographs from America, Europe, the Middle East, and Japan are presented chronologically alongside illuminating diary notes and sketches. *The Power Book* is published to accompany Hassink's major exhibition The Power Show (opening in Amsterdam, Rotterdam, and New York before touring internationally).

Author Hometown: New York, NY

Chris Boot

Pitch Black
Youme Landowne and Anthony Horton

On the subway, do you ever notice that people are always looking, but they only see what they want to? Things can be sitting right in front of them and still they can't see it.

That's your guide Anthony speaking. He'll show you how he lives in the tunnels underneath the New York City subway system—that is, if you'll let him. Which is exactly what Youme decided she would do one afternoon when she and Anthony began a conversation in the subway about art. It turns out that both Youme and Anthony Horton are artists. While part of Youme's art is listening long and hard to the stories of the people she meets, part of Anthony's is making art out of what most people won't even look at. Thus began a unique collaboration and conversation between these two artists over the next year, which culminated in Anthony's biography, the graphic novel *Pitch Black*. With art and words from both of them, they map out Anthony's world—a tough one from many perspectives, startling and undoing from others, but from Anthony's point of view, a life lived as art.

Youme Landowne (known as **Youme**) is a painter and book artist who thrives in the context of public art. She studied cross-cultural communication through art at the New School for Social Research and Friends World College. She has interned in public schools and has been a student at the Friends World College at the Nairobi and Kyoto campuses.

Born in 1968, **Anthony Horton** is a homeless artist who lives underneath New York City. His work can be seen along the tunnel walls in the darkest parts of the transit system.

A graphic novel, a true story—a life lived underneath the New York City subway system.

Graphic Novels
September
11 x 6½ | 40 pp
50 B&W illustrations
TC US $17.95 | CAN $21.50
978-1-933693-06-4 CUSA

Marketing Plans

Co-op available
Advance reader copies

Author Events

San Francisco, CA • Washington, DC •
Miami, FL • New York, NY • Baltimore, MD •
Philadelphia, PA

Author Hometown: New York, NY

The Resurrection of Bert Ringold

Harvey Goldner

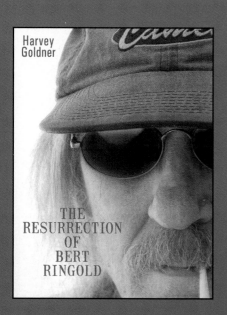

Poetry
January
A Paperback Original
6 x 9 | 112 pp
TP US $13.95 | CAN $17.00
978-1-933693-16-3 CUSA

Marketing Plans

Co-op available
Advance reader copies

Author Events

San Francisco, CA • Portland, OR •
Seattle, WA

Author Hometown: Seattle, WA

Harvey Goldner is a poet neglectorino in the classic sense, with his poems rising up out of the fecund Seattle underground, wisely irritated with the stupid Republicanized world but lucky enough to remember the 1950s Memphis dreams that Little Richard, Gandhi, and Elvis promised us all.

*"The 70s, 80s and 90s were
such a bummer; and the new
millennium's creeping forth
even dumber, so I'm warping
back to the 60s. Will you
come too?" Jack said, sitting
backwards on his chair.*

*"But let's do it right this time:
no drugs of any kind, no pro
miscuous sex, no jungle jabber jazz,
Stones nor Grateful Dead, no pigeon
politics, no Zen, no Hin-
doo gooroo razzmatazz."*

*"What's left?" I said, scratching
my old bald head.*

*"Well, there's travel, hos-
pitality, patchouli, gen
erosity, DayGlo poetry,
long hair laughter and
Ravi Shankar records."*

*"Alright, Jack, I'll go,
but on one condition—no
Ravi Shankar records!"*

*"OK, man, fuck a bunch of
Ravi Shankar records—let's go!"*

Harvey Goldner is that old guy who drives cab on Sundays in Seattle to keep body and soul together. To do this, he says, he must transform himself into a R.A.T. The rest of the week he is himself—underground poet and curmudgeon who is mapping out the narrow, perilous road to immortality on the Internet. No luck so far.

**Harvey Goldner is not Bukowski because Bukowski is dead
and Harvey lives in Seattle.**

Cinco Puntos Press

A Perfect Season for Dreaming /
Una temporada perfecta para soñar

Benjamin Alire Sáenz
Art by Esau Andrade

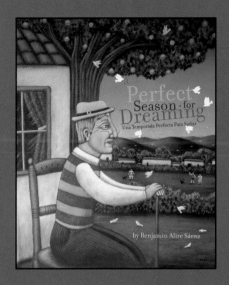

Ninety-two-year-old Octavio Rivera is a beautiful dreamer. And lately he has been visited by some very interesting dreams—dreams about piñatas that spill their treasures before him, revealing kissing turtles, winged pigs, hitchhiking armadillos, and many more fantastic things! Octavio doesn't tell anyone about his dreams except his young granddaughter Regina because she alone understands beautiful and fantastic dreams. On the ninth afternoon, Octavio prepares for his daily siesta, hoping to be blessed with one last lovely dream. That afternoon he dreams of a sky full of sweet and perfect hummingbirds calling his name over and over again . . .

Like Margaret Wild's marvelous book *Old Pig, A Perfect Season for Dreaming* unfolds the sweet possibilities in the relationships between the very old and the very young.

Benjamin Alire Sáenz—novelist, poet, essayist, and writer of children's books—is at the forefront of emerging Latino literature. He has received both the Wallace Stegner Fellowship and the Lannan Fellowship, and an American Book Award. He teaches at the University of Texas at El Paso, and considers himself a "fronterizo," a person of the border.

Born in Mexico, **Esau Andrade** comes from a family of folk artists. Although still young, he is increasingly recognized as a master artist in the tradition of the great painters Diego Rivera and Rufino Tamayo, in whose footsteps he follows. Andrade's paintings are included in the collection of the Museum of Latin American Art in Long Beach, California, as well as in the Downey Museum of Art in Downey, California.

An old man tells his granddaughter about the nine most beautiful dreams of his lifetime.

Children's Fiction / Hispanic Studies
March
8½ x 11 | 40 pp
18 Color illustrations
TC US $17.95 | CAN $21.50
978-1-933693-01-9 CUSA

Marketing Plans

Co-op available
Advance reader copies

Author Events

Los Angeles, CA •
Las Cruces, NM • El Paso, TX

Author Hometown: El Paso, TX

Also Available

A Gift from Papá Diego
Un regalo de Papá Diego
Benjamin Alire Sáenz
Illustrated by Geronimo Garcia
Children's Fiction / Hispanic Studies
10 x 8 | 40 pp
20 Color Illustrations
TP US $10.95 | CAN $13.50
978-0-938317-33-3 CUSA

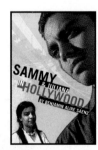

Sammy & Juliana in Hollywood
Benjamin Alire Sáenz
Fiction / Hispanic Studies
5½ x 8¼ | 240 pp
TC US $19.95 | CAN $24.00
978-0-938317-81-4 CUSA

Cinco Puntos Press

ABeCedarios
Mexican Folk Art ABCs in Spanish and English
Cynthia Weill
Photographs by K.B. Basseches
Art by Moisés and Armando Jiménez

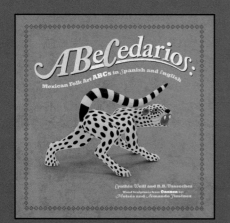

Children's Nonfiction
November
7½ x 7½ | 32 pp
30 Color photographs
TC US $14.95 | CAN $18.00
978-1-933693-13-2 CUSA

Marketing Plans

Co-op available
Advance reader copies

Author Hometown: New York, NY

Every ABC book worth its cover price is bound to have bright colors and big letters. But not every ABC book has magical hand-carved animals to illustrate every letter. And very few alphabet books present those letters in more varieties than English! Very few alphabet books except the *ABeCedarios,* that is! In this brightly colored book, the alphabet is presented in both Spanish and English, and includes the four additional letters—and whimsical animals—that make the Spanish alphabet so much fun.

The famous folk artists, brothers Moisés and Armando Jiménez, carved the wonderful animal figures that illustrate each letter in *ABeCedarios.* Working with their wives and children in the beautiful village of Arrazola in Oaxaca, Mexico, they carved and painted each enchanting animal by hand. For many centuries, people in Oaxaca have carved wood to make toys and household objects. However, it was Moisés and Armando's grandfather Manuel who started making animal figures. Now more than sixty families in Arrazola make their living from wood carving.

Cynthia Weill works at Teachers College, Columbia University in New York City. She is the co-author with Pegi Deitz Shea of *Ten Mice for Tet* (Chronicle Books, 2003), a book inspired by the Vietnamese embroidery she saw while working in international relief in Hanoi, Vietnam. She is trained as an art historian and studies the process of folk artisans around the world.

K.B. Basseches is an artist, photographer, and art educator. She was an assistant professor at Virginia Commonwealth University in the Department of Art Education, and served as a staff photographer at the Smithsonian Institution in the Portrait Gallery in Washington, DC. Basseches has exhibited throughout the mid-Atlantic region and in the Los Angeles area. She lives in Richmond, Virginia, with her young son and husband.

Delicate hand-painted animals from Oaxaca lead little ones through a bilingual alphabet.

Cinco Puntos Press

Little Zizi

Thierry Lenain

Illustrated by Stéphane Poulin
Translated by Daniel Zolinsky

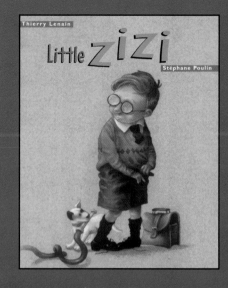

Like all boys, Martin had a zizi, and this zizi didn't cause him any problems. Of course, from time to time, Martin worried a little. He wondered if one day his zizi would look like his dad's zizi. But that's normal, all boys wonder about that. So, everything was going quite well.

That is, everything was going well until one day in the locker room the big bully Adrian started making fun of Martin's zizi in front of everybody! Poor Martin. And to make matters worse, Martin and the bully both wanted to be the boyfriend of Anäis, the prettiest girl in school. Push came to shove, and the boys decided to have a pissing contest. So how does our story end? Is it true that in the littlest of packages come the greatest gifts? Thierry Lenain's jolly text is joined happily with Stéphane Poulin's exquisite but hilarious illustrations to make this a wonderful book for parents and children to share and enjoy together.

Thierry Lenain taught handicapped children before becoming a writer. He has published more than fifty children's books in Europe. In 1992, he became editor of *Citrouille,* a magazine about children's literature. He has three children, and, after eighteen years at the foot of the mountains, he has moved to the edge of the sea.

Stéphane Poulin is a Canadian author and illustrator. He's been drawing passionately since he was a kid. He has published over one hundred books in North America and Canada and has won many international prizes.

Daniel Zolinsky is a photographer who is currently working on a collection of photographs that traces Odysseus' journey home from the Trojan War.

A story about acceptance and appreciation of . . . well . . . the little things in life. Remember: "small is beautiful."

Children's Fiction
February
8¼ x 10¼ | 32 pp
TC US $16.95 | CAN $20.50
978-1-933693-05-7 CUSA

Author Hometown: Las Cruces, NM

Young Adult Fiction / Jewish Studies
October
5½ x 8½ | 262 pp
TP US $8.95 | CAN $11.00
978-1-933693-15-6 CUSA

Marketing Plans

Co-op available
Advance reader copies

Double Crossing
Eve Tal

"Outstanding in both its structure and its questioning of faith, this offering is not to be missed."—*Kirkus Reviews* (starred review)

"Best of all is the shocking surprise that changes everything, even Papa—a haunting aspect of the immigrant story left too long untold."—*Booklist* (starred review)

The future for Jews in rural villages in Russia in 1905 held little promise. So Benjamin Balaban, a poor but very devout Jew, determines to flee to America with Raizel, his daughter. Once they are settled he will send for the rest of his family. Raizel doesn't understand the reasons for leaving—her village is full of magic and the stories and poems that her grandmother tells her. Her odyssey with her father across Russia and Europe and on to America is full of adventure, adversity, and hardship. When they finally board a ship for America, a terrible storm makes Raizel and her father sick. All their food is stolen, and Benjamin won't eat non-kosher food. At Ellis Island, his haggard appearance, deep cough, and emaciated frame get them turned away from America. Raizel, though, is now determined to get back to America and the hope of a new life for her whole family.

Double Crossing is the winner of the Paterson Prize for Books for Young People, a Notable Book for a Global Society, and was included in Booklist's Top Ten First Novels for Youth.

Eve Tal was born in 1947 in New York City. After receiving her BA from Oberlin College, she moved to Israel in the early 1970s. She lives on Kibbutz Hatzor with her husband and three sons.

In 1905 a young Jewish girl and her father flee Czarist Russia for America.

Also Available

Double Crossing
Eve Tal
Young Adult Fiction / Jewish Studies
5½ x 8¼ | 262 pp
TC US $16.95 | CAN $20.50
978-0-938317-94-4 CUSA

Cinco Puntos Press

Writings for a Democratic Society
The Tom Hayden Reader
Tom Hayden

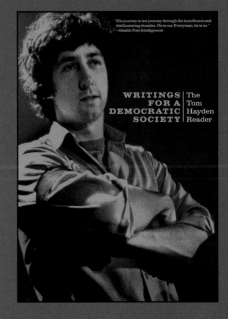

"His journey is our journey through the tumultuous and disillusioning decades. He is our Everyman, he is us."—*Seattle Post-Intelligencer*

Praise for Tom Hayden:

"One comes away enthralled by Hayden's odyssey."—*The Boston Sunday Globe*

From his earliest days as a Freedom Rider and leader of Students for a Democratic Society, through decades as a state senator, to contemporary notes on the Iraq war, the global South, immigration, and spirituality, Tom Hayden's writings constitute nothing less than an alternative history of our times.

Writings for a Democratic Society is the only book that encapsulates Tom Hayden's writings over fifty years, a time in which he has been a reflective eyewitness to American history in the making. The book is composed of sections about the New Left of the 1960s, the Chicago 8, Vietnam, electoral politics, gang violence, Ireland, the environment, global justice, and US foreign policy today.

"Tom Hayden changed America," the national correspondent of *The Atlantic*, Nicholas Lemann, has written. He created the "blueprint for the Great Society programs," according to presidential assistant Richard Goodwin. He was the "single greatest figure of the 1960s student movement," according to *The New York Times Book Review*. Forty years later he was described as "the conscience of the Senate."

Tom Hayden is the author of more than a dozen critically acclaimed books, including *Reunion* and *Street Wars*.

The best of Tom Hayden's writings from the turbulent 1960s to the Iraq war.

Political Science & Government / History
November
A Paperback Original
6 x 8½ | 450 pp
TP US $18.95 | CAN $23.00
978-0-87286-461-0 CUSA

City Lights Publishers

You'll Be Okay
My Life with Jack Kerouac
Edie Kerouac-Parker

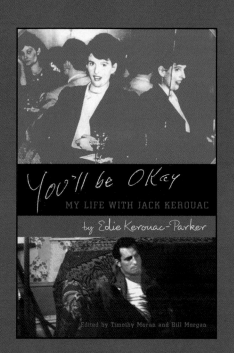

Biography & Autobiography /
Literature & Essay
September
A Paperback Original
5¼ x 8 | 200 pp
30 B&W photographs
TP US $14.95 | CAN $18.00
978-0-87286-464-1 CUSA

Marketing Plans

Co-op available
Advance reader copies

"You have a unique viewpoint from which to write about Jack as no one else has or could write. I feel very deeply that this book must be written. And no one else, I repeat, can write it."—William S. Burroughs

Edie Parker was eighteen years old when she met Jack Kerouac at Columbia University in 1940. A young socialite from Grosse Pointe, Michigan, she had come to New York to study art and quickly found herself swept up in the excitement and new freedoms that the big city offered a sheltered young woman of that time.

Jack Kerouac was also eighteen, attending Columbia on a football scholarship, impressing his friends with his intelligence and knowledge of literature. Introduced by a mutual friend, Jack and Edie fell in love and quickly moved in together, sharing an apartment with Joan Adams (who would later marry William S. Burroughs). This is the story of their life together in New York, where they began lifetime friendships with Allen Ginsberg, William S. Burroughs, and others. Edie's memoir provides the only female voice from that nascent period, when the leading members of the Beat Generation were first meeting and becoming friends.

In the end, Jack and Edie went their separate ways, keeping in touch only on rare occasions through letters and late-night phone calls. In his last letter to Edie, written a month before his death, Kerouac ended it with the encouraging phrase: "You'll be okay." It was from that note that the title of this book was taken.

**Jack Kerouac's first wife gives an insider's view
of the nascent Beat Generation.**

The year 2007 marks the fiftieth anniversary of Kerouac's *On the Road*.

City Lights Publishers

State of Exile

Cristina Peri Rossi

Translated by Marilyn Buck

Cristina Peri Rossi was born in Uruguay and is considered a leading light of the "Latin American Boom" generation. In 1972, after her work was banned by a repressive military regime, she left her country and moved to Spain.

This collection of poems, written during her journey and the first period of her self-exile, was so personal that it remained unpublished for almost thirty years. It is accompanied here by two brilliant essays on exile, one by Peri Rossi and the other by translator Marilyn Buck, who is an American political prisoner, exiled in her own land.

Cristina Peri Rossi is the author of thirty-seven works, including *The Ship of Fools*.

Marketing Plans
Co-op available • Advance reader copies

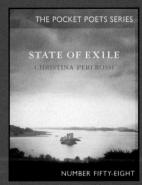

Poetry / Latin American Literature
March
A Paperback Original
City Lights Pocket Poets Series 58
4⅞ x 6¼ | 200 pp
TP US $14.95 | CAN $18.00
978-0-87286-463-4 CUSA

A tender, moving, and multi-layered portrait of the pain, loneliness, and permanent nostalgia of exile.

---

187 Reasons Mexicanos Can't Cross the Border

Undocuments 1971–2007

Juan Felipe Herrera

A hybrid collection of texts written and performed on the road, from Mexico City to San Francisco, from Central America to central California, illustrated throughout with photos and artwork. Rants, manifestos, newspaper cutups, street theater, anti-lectures, love poems, and riffs tell the story of what it's like to live outlaw and brown in the United States.

Juan Felipe Herrera is a professor of creative writing at the University of California, Riverside. The author of twenty-one books, he is also a community arts leader and a dynamic performer and actor. He is the son of Mexican immigrants and grew up in the migrant fields of California.

Marketing Plans
Co-op available • Advance reader copies

Author Events
Fresno, CA • Los Angeles, CA • San Francisco, CA • Austin, TX

Author Hometown: Redlands, CA

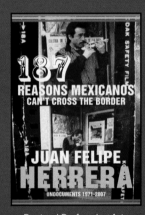

Poetry / Performing Arts
November
A Paperback Original
5¾ x 8¼ | 278 pp
15 B&W photographs
TP US $16.95 | CAN $20.50
978-0-87286-462-7 CUSA

The collected performance poetry from a progenitor of Chicano spoken word, spanning thirty-seven years.

The Haunted House
Rebecca Brown

Long out of print, Rebecca Brown's brilliant debut novel explores the psychic repercussions of growing up in an alcoholic family and the ways in which one woman's past continues to inform and inhabit her life. Robin Daley's childhood is dominated by a sense of impermanence: Her hard-drinking father disappears as suddenly and unexpectedly as he arrives; her adulthood offers an escape, but strange things happen when the dark corners and locked rooms of family life are revealed.

Rebecca Brown is the author of *The Gifts of the Body, The Last Time I Saw You,* and *The End of Youth.* She lives in Seattle.

Marketing Plans
Co-op available • Advance reader copies

Author Events
Los Angeles, CA • San Francisco, CA • Boulder, CO • New York, NY • Portland, OR • Seattle, WA

Author Hometown: Seattle, WA

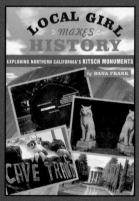

Fiction / Lesbian Literature
September
5 x 7¼ | 196 pp
TP US $13.95 | CAN $17.00
978-0-87286-460-3 CUSA

Rebecca Brown's novel explores how a woman's life is affected by growing up in an alcoholic family.

Local Girl Makes History
Exploring Northern California's Kitsch Monuments
Dana Frank

A historian's nostalgic trip to a series of local daytrip sites takes an unexpected turn as she explores the mysterious draw of these places. Childhood memories and urban myths lead to research into hidden stories, and what's revealed tells much about the politics of history-making.

Writing in a personal, humorous, and engaging style, Dana Frank brings the reader along on her process of discovery. Full of surprises and plot twists along the way, her adventures are quirky, fun, and informative. Each essay is accompanied by a map and illustrated with photos, news clippings, and memorabilia.

Dana Frank is a professor of history at the University of California, Santa Cruz.

Marketing Plans
Co-op available • Advance reader copies

Author Events
San Francisco, CA • Santa Cruz, CA

Author Hometown: Santa Cruz, CA

Travel & Travel Guides / History
November
A Paperback Original
City Lights Foundation Books
5¾ x 8 | 278 pp
TP US $16.95 | CAN $20.50
978-1-931404-09-9 CUSA

A professor's nostalgic journey to childhood tourist attractions reveals their hidden histories and universal relevance.

City Lights Publishers

The Meat and Spirit Plan
Selah Saterstrom

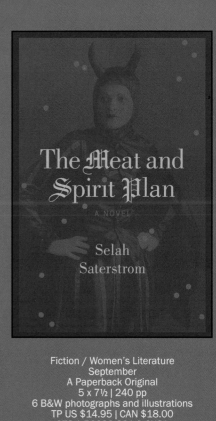

"*The Meat and Spirit Plan* is ferocious and dazzling, the work of a savage poet. Every scene is a hard polished gem of raunch and revelation. Strung together they build a force of piercing tenderness. It's an impressive achievement, and a real pleasure to read."—Katherine Dunn, author of *Geek Love*

"Like an experimentally inclined Annie Proulx, Saterstrom tersely renders the effects of social violence on individual lives . . . the effect is shattering and transcendent."—Modern Times Bookstore newsletter

In lyric, diamond-cut prose, Selah Saterstrom revisits the mythic, dead-end Southern town of Beau Repose. This time, the story follows a strung-out American teenager influenced by heavy metal, inspired by Ginger Rogers, hell-bent on self-destruction, and more intelligent than anyone around her realizes. Forced into rehab and private school, her life, at least on the surface, changes course, eventually leading to theology studies in Scotland. But as the feverish St. Vitus's dance of her adolescence morphs into slow-motion inertia abroad, an illness brings her home again—to face the legacy of pain she left behind and to find a way to become the lead in a dance of her own creation.

An heir to William Faulkner and Toni Morrison, Saterstrom soars above the traditional boundaries of the American novel with "exquisite, cut-to-the-quick language" (*Raleigh News & Observer*) that makes her novels "impossible to put down."

Selah Saterstrom is the author of *The Pink Institution,* a debut novel praised across the country for "letting gusts of fresh, tart air blow into the old halls of Southern Gothic" (*The Believer*). A Mississippi native, she is currently on the faculty of the University of Denver's Creative Writing Program. Visit her website at www.selahsaterstrom.com.

A searing coming-of-age novel set to the music of chance.

Also Available

The Pink Institution
Selah Saterstrom
Fiction / Women's Literature
5 x 7½ | 140 pp
15 Duotone photographs
TP US $15.00 | CAN $18.00
978-1-56689-155-4 CUSA

Fiction / Women's Literature
September
A Paperback Original
5 x 7½ | 240 pp
6 B&W photographs and illustrations
TP US $14.95 | CAN $18.00
978-1-56689-201-8 CUSA

Coffee House Press

Night Train
Lise Erdrich

Fiction / Native American Studies
February
A Paperback Original
5½ x 8½ | 152 pp
TP US $14.95 | CAN $18.00
978-1-56689-202-5 CUSA

Marketing Plans

Co-op available
Advance reader copies
National advertising:
BOMB • Bookmarks • MultiCultural Review

Author Events

Iowa City, IA • Minneapolis/St. Paul, MN •
Bismarck, ND • Fargo, ND • Sioux Falls, SD

Author Hometown: Wahpeton, ND

What does it mean to be a "fully processed" Indian in America today? In *Night Train*, Lise Erdrich offers a sharp-humored and powerful primer. Largely set in the small towns and reservations of northwestern Minnesota and western North Dakota, her literary snapshots capture the characters' lives playing out against a backdrop of emergency rooms, supermarket aisles, backwoods parties, family breakfast tables, booze-soaked taverns, and sterile but emotionally fraught offices.

Taken at the very moment when the pressures of daily life collide with the insidiousness of history, these stories reveal the personal struggle and small triumphs of people facing the absurdities of bureaucracy, cycles of poverty and addiction, and out-sized notions of Indian legends and culture.

It takes love, fortitude, and no small amount of humor to survive the sun-starved winters of the Great Plains, where finding reasons to keep going (and keep growing) can be the most profound accomplishment. Erdrich's flashbulb-quick stories provide it all in cathartic doses, and within the many voices of her tales, all the crazy starts to make sense.

Lise Erdrich has worked in the fields of Indian health and education since the 1980s and is currently a school health officer at the Circle of Nations School in Wahpeton, North Dakota. Her stories have received a number of awards, including the *Minnesota Monthly* Tamarack Award, the *Many Mountains Moving* Flash Fiction Contest, and Best of Show at the North Dakota State Fair. *Night Train* is her highly anticipated first collection.

The most exciting addition to American Indian fiction since Sherman Alexie hit the scene.

Coffee House Press

How to Be Perfect
Ron Padgett

"Ron Padgett makes the most quiet and sensible of feelings a provocatively persistent wonder."—Robert Creeley

Ron Padgett has reenergized modern poetry with exuberant and tender love poems, exceptionally lucid and touching elegies, and imaginative and action-packed homages to American culture and visual art. He has paid tribute to Woody Woodpecker and the West, to friends and collaborators, to language and cowslips, to beautiful women and chocolate milk, to paintings and small-time criminals. His poems have always imparted a contagious sense of joy.

In these new poems, Padgett hasn't forsaken his beloved Woody Woodpecker, but he has decided to heed the canary and sound the alarm. Here, he asks, "What makes us so mean?" And he really wants to know. Even as these poems cajole and question, as they call attention to what has been lost and what we still stand to lose, they continue to champion what makes sense and what has always been worth saving. "Humanity," Padgett generously (and gently) reminds us, still "has to take it one step at a time."

Ron Padgett is a celebrated translator, memoirist, teacher, and, as Peter Gizzi says, "a thoroughly American poet, coming sideways out of Whitman, Williams, and New York Pop with a Tulsa twist." His poetry has been translated into more than a dozen languages and has appeared in *The Best American Poetry, Poetry 180, The Norton Anthology of Postmodern American Poetry, The Oxford Book of American Poetry,* and on Garrison Keillor's *The Writer's Almanac.* Visit his website at www.ronpadgett.com.

Required reading for humans.

Poetry
September
A Paperback Original
6 x 9 | 128 pp
TP US $15.00 | CAN $18.00
978-1-56689-203-2 CUSA

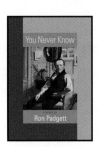

Also Available

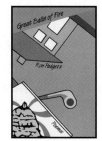

You Never Know
Ron Padgett
Poetry
7 x 10 | 96 pp
TP US $14.95 | CAN $18.00
978-1-56689-128-8 CUSA

Great Balls of Fire
Ron Padgett
Poetry
6 x 9 | 96 pp
TP US $14.00 | CAN $17.00
978-0-918273-80-2 CUSA

Poetry
October
A Paperback Original
6 x 9 | 140 pp
TP US $15.00 | CAN $18.00
978-1-56689-204-9 CUSA

Investigative poet Brenda Coultas unearths the eccentricities and tragedies that congregate along humanity's borders.

The Marvelous Bones of Time
Excavations and Explanations
Brenda Coultas

Incorporating memoir, folktales, fact, and hearsay into two distinctly moving poems, this collection attests to history's manifestation in the present moment. Beginning in the author's Indiana hometown, not far from the birthplace of Abraham Lincoln, and along the Kentucky border where "looking from the free state / there is a river then a slave state," Brenda Coultas uncovers a land still troubled by the specter of slavery. In the second section, Coultas investigates tales of UFO sightings, legendary monsters, and poltergeists, exploring the very nature of narrative truth through the lens of the ghost story.

Brenda Coultas is the author of *A Handmade Museum,* winner of the Poetry Society of America's Norma Farber First Book Award.

Marketing Plans
Co-op available • Advance reader copies
National advertising: Bookslut.com • Poets & Writers • The Village Voice
Literary Supplement
Author Events
San Francisco, CA • Boulder, CO • Minneapolis/St. Paul, MN • New York, NY

Author Hometown: New York, NY

Poetry
September
A Paperback Original
6 x 9 | 86 pp
TP US $15.00
CAN $18.00
978-1-56689-205-6
CUSA

Vertigo
Martha Ronk

A National Poetry Series winner, chosen by C.D. Wright.

This visionary seventh collection by the PEN USA Award-winning poet pivots around uncertainties, mysteries, and the unexpected to find the language of the mind's theater. Melancholy and playful, analytic and lyrical, *Vertigo* immerses the reader in a dense realm of memory and multiple perspectives, repositioning our relations to daily life, the past, and the future.

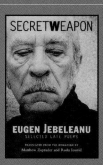

Poetry
February
A Paperback Original
6 x 9 | 116 pp
TP US $15.00
CAN $18.00
978-1-56689-206-3
CUSA

Secret Weapon
Selected Late Poems of Eugen Jebeleanu
Translated by Matthew Zapruder and Radu Ioanid
Introduction by Andrei Codrescu

These spare and allegorical later poems of Romania's great poet, Eugen Jebeleanu (1911–1991), are deeply moving expressions of collective and personal guilt from an artist whose early participation in and later disillusionment with the regime lend his work a particular, searing authenticity. Appearing in English for the first time, these profoundly unsentimental poems are politically and artistically significant lyric testimonies.

Coffee House Press

Minnesota State Fair
An Illustrated History
Kathryn Strand Koutsky and Linda Koutsky
Foreword by Garrison Keillor

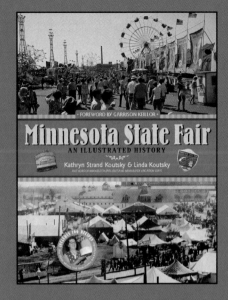

"A joyful book for us fair lovers—it brings to mind the joys of the fair itself and those Twelve Thrilling Days and Fun-Filled Nights."—Garrison Keillor

State fairs are cornerstones of the American tradition, and few are as beloved as the Minnesota State Fair. Since 1854, Minnesota has reveled in promoting the rich bounty of its land and the magnificent talents of its citizens. From the legendary horse Dan Patch, whose record-breaking races kept the country on the edge of its seat, to Teddy Roosevelt's famous grandstand speech suggesting that America should "speak softly and carry a big stick," and from the invention of mini-donuts to the discovery of batter-fried cheese curds, the Minnesota State Fair has captured the imagination—and the taste buds—of the entire nation.

As you travel through time imagining stolen kisses along the dark and romantic canals of Ye Old Mill and the thrills and chills of the Midway, as you explore the innovations found atop Machinery Hill and dig into a hearty breakfast at the Epiphany Diner, you will also uncover the history of this wonderful state. Filled with more than one hundred concessionaire and Blue Ribbon recipes, fascinating facts, and over 1,200 photographs from the Great Minnesota Get-Together, this treasury of Minnesota's happiest memories will keep you looking forward to the fair all year long.

Mother and daughter team Kathryn Strand Koutsky and Linda Koutsky are the authors of the best-selling illustrated histories *Minnesota Eats Out* and *Minnesota Vacation Days*. Lifelong fairgoers, they worked in collaboration with the Minnesota State Fair to bring us this irresistible, first-of-its-kind compendium.

A lavishly illustrated, fun-filled history of the Minnesota State Fair complete with Blue Ribbon recipes!

History
September
9 x 12 | 224 pp
1,200 Color and B&W illustrations and photographs
TC US $35.00 | CAN $42.00
978-1-56689-207-0 CUSA

Marketing Plans

Co-op available
20,000-copy print run

Author Events

Duluth, MN • Mankato, MN • Minneapolis/St. Paul, MN • Red Wing, MN • Rochester, MN • St. Cloud, MN • Winona, MN

Author Hometown: Minneapolis, MN

Coffee House Press

Visit Teepee Town
Native Writings After the Detours
**Edited by Diane Glancy and
Mark Nowak**

Poetry Anthology / Native American Studies
6 x 9 | 392 pp
TP US $17.95 | CAN $21.50
978-1-56689-084-7 CUSA

The Moon in Its Flight
Gilbert Sorrentino

Fiction
6 x 8 | 300 pp
TP US $16.00 | CAN $19.50
978-1-56689-152-3 CUSA

From Baghdad to Brooklyn
Growing Up in a Jewish-Arabic
Family in Midcentury America
Jack Marshall

Biography & Autobiography / Jewish Studies
6 x 9 | 260 pp
8 B&W photographs
TP US $16.00 | CAN $19.50
978-1-56689-174-5 CUSA

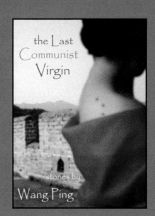

The Last Communist Virgin
Wang Ping

Fiction / Asian Studies
5 x 7½ | 218 pp
TP US $14.95 | CAN $18.00
978-1-56689-195-0 CUSA

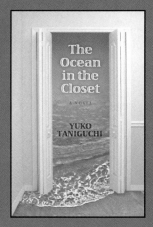

The Ocean in the Closet
Yuko Taniguchi

Fiction / Asian Studies
5 x 7½ | 268 pp
TP US $14.95 | CAN $18.00
978-1-56689-194-3 CUSA

A Visit from St. Alphabet
Dave Morice

Children's Fiction / Sidelines & Gift Books
6½ x 5 | 24 pp
9 Color illustrations
TC US $9.95 | CAN $12.00
978-1-56689-179-0 CUSA

People Make Movements

Lessons from Freedom Summer

Kathy Emery, Linda Reid Gold, and Sylvia Braselmann

Introduction by Howard Zinn

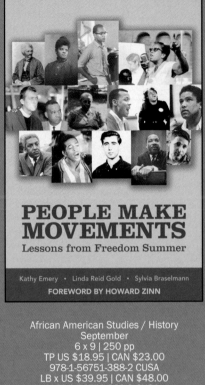

"Can we bring teachers and students together, not through the artificial sieve of certification and examination, but on the basis of their common commitment to an exciting social goal? Can we solve the old educational problem of how to teach children crucial values, while avoiding a blanket imposition of the teacher's ideas? *People Make Movements* asks the questions that get at the heart of what education should be about."—Howard Zinn, from the introduction

"Part history text, part curriculum, part invitation to activism, when our students consider who 'we' are, *People Make Movements* will provide important insights. Every social studies or language arts teacher can benefit from this new resource." —Bill Bigelow, editor of *Rethinking Schools* magazine and author of *The Line Between Us: Teaching About the Border and Mexican Immigration*

"By looking at past achievements, all the human connections made in the struggle against racism, and the possibilities ahead, the message comes across: You Are History."—Elizabeth Martínez, editor of *Letters from Mississippi*

People Make Movements provides the historical context to the Freedom Schools of Mississippi in 1964. It tells the story of how the four major civil rights organizations ended up joining together in Mississippi to break the back of segregation in the South. It is a case study illustrating important elements that are crucial to the success of a social movement. It behooves social justice advocates today to know these lessons if we are to contribute to the creation of the next social movement.

People Make Movements provides the historical context to the Freedom Schools of Mississippi in 1964.

African American Studies / History
September
6 x 9 | 250 pp
TP US $18.95 | CAN $23.00
978-1-56751-388-2 CUSA
LB x US $39.95 | CAN $48.00
978-1-56751-389-9 CUSA

Author Hometown: San Francisco, CA

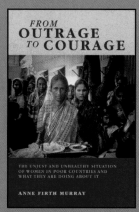

Political Science & Government /
Women's Studies
September
6 x 9 | 400 pp
TP US $24.95 | CAN $30.00
978-1-56751-390-5 CUSA
LB x US $39.00 | CAN $47.00
978-1-56751-391-2 CUSA

Women in poorer countries face daunting health injustices—and they are fighting back.

From Outrage to Courage
The Unjust and Unhealthy Situation of Women in Poor Countries and What They are Doing About It
Anne Firth Murray

From sex-selective abortions to millions of girls who are "disappeared," from ninety million girls who do not go to school to HIV/AIDS spreading fastest among adolescent girls, women face unique health challenges, writes Anne Firth Murray. In this searing cradle-to-grave review, Murray tackles health issues from prenatal care to challenges faced by aging women. Looking at how gender inequality affects basic nutrition, Murray makes clear the issues are political more than they are medical.

In an inspiring look, *From Outrage to Courage* shows how women are organizing the world over. Women's courage to transform their situations and communities provides inspiration and models for change. From China to India, from Indonesia to Kenya, Anne Firth Murray takes readers on a whirlwind tour of devastation—and resistance.

Author Hometown: Palo Alto, CA

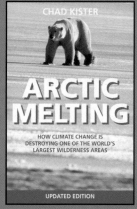

Environmental Studies
September
5 x 7⅝ | 212 pp
TP US $16.95 | CAN $20.50
978-1-56751-386-8 CUSA
LB x US $39.95 | CAN $48.00
978-1-56751-387-5 CUSA

Notes on the ground from an activist-traveler.

Arctic Melting
How Climate Change is Destroying One of the World's Largest Wilderness Areas, Updated Edition
Chad Kister

"This little book shares amazing on-site details only the Alaskans and intent visitors know firsthand. [Author Chad Kister] tells of seeing the shocking differences of melting from warmer and shorter winters. Chad documents how the Arctic is suffering more varied ecospasms than any large bioregion on earth. Chad reports on vast global and local trends, like 160 species of birds that migrate to the Arctic from all US states and six continents. The native traditional lives and values are stressed because their homes and food supplies are disappearing. Chad is a true adventurer, reporter, and advocate for respecting the integrity of Arctic ecosystems. This is the best little 'screaming tales' book from the Arctic wilderness we need to learn NOW."—Michael Sunanda

Author Hometown: Athens, OH

Common Courage Press

William Klein Contacts
Photographs by William Klein

Contacts is the first collection of William Klein's famous contact sheets, revamped and over-painted. The most important and famous works of this great artist have been chosen and printed from these contact sheets—those very same works that have made him one of the most acclaimed all-around photographers and artists in the last thirty years. The large prints in the book, some of which have never been published, are reproductions of painted contact sheets, and can be either detached and framed or kept in their original form in the book.

Photography
March
16⅝ x 13⅜ | 36 pp
38 Color and B&W photographs
TC US $55.00 | CAN $66.00
978-88-6965-064-2 CUSA

A collection of William Klein's hand-painted contacts shows where his genius comes from.

Rajasthan
Photographs by Tito Dalmau

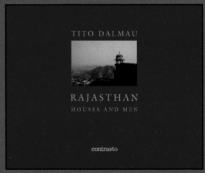

Rajasthan is a book on the love of a man for this beautiful land and the breathtaking impression the images he shot have produced on a woman.

With the images in this book, architect and photographer Tito Dalmau leads us gently through the fascinating scenario of the different forms of the inhabited landscape in Rajasthan. The pictures are accompanied by historical circumstances and geographical notes by Maka Abraham, whose words provide us with all the data about the reality that will bring us back into this timeless world, where the house is conceived as home for the extended family.

Photography / Travel & Travel Guides
September
11⅞ x 9½ | 176 pp
95 Color photographs
TC US $49.00 | CAN $59.00
978-88-6965-062-8 CUSA

The magnificient pictures of Tito Dalmau take us on a trip around Rajasthan.

My brother's keeper

Edited by Alessandra Mauro

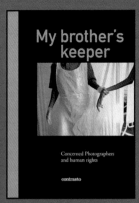

Photography / Cultural Studies
September
6¾ x 9½ | 320 pp
177 Color and B&W photographs
TC US $50.00 | CAN $60.00
978-88-6965-061-1 CUSA

A visual compendium of human rights and concerned photography.

Their names are Lewis Hine, Sebastião Salgado, Eugene Smith, Tom Stoddart, and Igor Kostin. They tackled hunger, drought, ecological catastrophes, and HIV. They are documentary photographers, authors, and journalists who decided to aim their cameras at a series of unknown stories that had to be revealed, told, understood, and denounced.

My brother's keeper gathers twenty exemplary stories of documentary photography. Each one is presented with an introductory text, and a selection of photographs conveys the sense and value of these extremely important reports. It is a peculiar way to track the history of our days, as well as the one of photography, of those *concerned* authors who "wanted to show things that had to be corrected, who wanted to show things that had to be appreciated."

The introduction to the book is written by Susie Linfield, director of the Cultural Reporting & Criticism Program at New York University. Also includes photographs by Bob Adelman, Gianni Berengo Gardin, Carla Cerati, Luciano D'Alessandro, Lucinda Devlin, Donna Ferrato, Marc Garanger, Philip Jones Griffith, Ulrik Jantzen, Josef Koudelka, Peter Magubane, Juan Medina, Gilles Peress, Raghu Rai, Jacob Riis, David Seymour, and Li Zhensheng.

The Ninth Floor

Photographs by Jessica Dimmock

Photography
November
8¼ x 10¼ | 128 pp
60 Color photographs
TC US $38.00 | CAN $45.95
978-88-6965-059-8 CUSA

Jessica Dimmock's documentation of drug users in a New York shooting gallery.

Over the past two years, Jessica Dimmock has photographed a group of die-hard heroin users living on "The Ninth Floor" of a Manhattan building in a surprising, powerful, and intimate way. The tale of the terrible consequences of heroin abuse has been documented many times before, but Dimmock epitomizes the attitude of the concerned photographer by her deep compassion for the people she portrays. The photographs brilliantly capture the chaotic atmosphere of human lives spinning out of control. Dimmock's contemporary visual language, coupled with a strong narrative approach, compels the viewer to understanding and care.

Migration
New & Selected Poems
W.S. Merwin

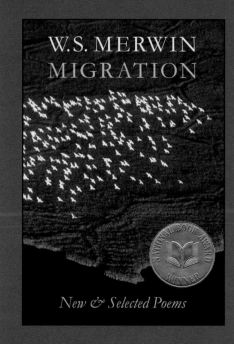

Named one of the 100 Notable Books of the Year by *The New York Times.*

"The poems in *Migration* speak a life-long belief in the power of words to awaken our drowsy souls and see the world with compassionate interconnection."—National Book Award judges' statement

"The publication of W.S. Merwin's selected and new poems is one of those landmark events in the literary world."—*Los Angeles Times*

W.S. Merwin is the most influential American poet of the last half-century—an artist who has transfigured and reinvigorated the vision of poetry for our time. *Migration: New and Selected Poems* is that case. This 570-page distillation—selected by Merwin from fifteen diverse volumes—is a gathering of the best poems from a profound body of work, accented by a selection of distinctive new poems.

As an undergraduate at Princeton University, Merwin was advised by John Berryman to "get down on your knees and pray to the muse every day." *Migration* represents the bounty of those prayers. Over the last fifty years, Merwin's muse has led him beyond the formal verse of his early years to revolutionary open forms that engage a vast array of influences and possibilities. As Adrienne Rich wrote of Merwin's work: "I would be shamelessly jealous of this poetry if I didn't take so much from it into my own life."

W.S. Merwin is the author of over fifty books of poetry, prose, and translation. He lives in Hawaii, where he raises endangered palm trees.

Poetry
September
6 x 9 | 570 pp
TP US $24.00 | CAN $29.00
978-1-55659-261-4 CUSA

Winner of the National Book Award, *Migration* is the definitive Merwin volume. Now in paperback.

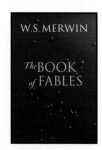

**Also
Available**

Present Company
W.S. Merwin
Poetry
6 x 9 | 152 pp
TP US $16.00 | CAN $19.50
978-1-55659-233-1 CUSA

The Book of Fables
W.S. Merwin
Poetry / Literature & Essay
6 x 9 | 400 pp
TP US $20.00 | CAN $24.00
978-1-55659-256-0 CUSA

Copper Canyon Press

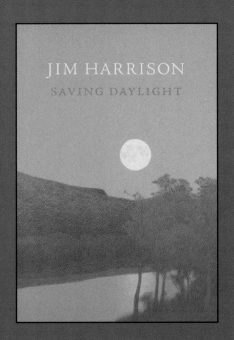

Poetry
September
6 x 9 | 124 pp
TP US $16.00 | CAN $19.50
978-1-55659-267-6 CUSA

Marketing Plans

Co-op available
National advertising:
American Poet • The American Poetry
Review • Poetry • Poetry Flash

Author Hometown: Livingston, MT

Saving Daylight
Jim Harrison

Now in paperback, *Saving Daylight* was named to the Notable Books of the Year lists from *The Kansas City Star* and the Michigan Library Association.

"This is [Harrison's] most robust, sure-footed, and blood-raising poetry collection to date."—*Booklist*

Jim Harrison—one of America's most beloved writers—calls his poetry "the true bones of my life." Although he is best known as a fiction writer, it is as a poet that *Publishers Weekly* famously called him an "untrammeled renegade genius."

   Saving Daylight, Harrison's tenth collection of poetry, is his first book of new poems in a decade. All of Harrison's abundant passions for life are poured into suites, prose poems, letter-poems, and even lyrics for a mariachi band.

   The subjects and concerns are wide-ranging—from the heart-rending "Livingston Suite," where a boy drowns in the local river and the body is discovered by the poet's wife—to some of the most harrowing political poems of Harrison's career. There is also a cast of creature characters—bears, dogs, birds, fish—as well as the woodlands, thickets, and occasional cities of Arizona, Montana, Michigan, France, and Mexico.

   "Imagination is my only possession," Harrison once said. And *Saving Daylight* is an imagination in full, exuberant bloom.

Jim Harrison is the author of over thirty books of poetry, fiction, and nonfiction. His work has been translated into dozens of languages. Born and raised in Michigan, he now lives in Montana and Arizona.

"Jim Harrison is a writer with immortality in him."—*The Times* (London)

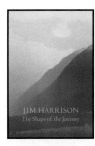

Also Available

The Shape of the Journey
New & Collected Poems
Jim Harrison
Poetry
6 x 9 | 484 pp
TP US $20.00 | CAN $24.00
978-1-55659-149-5 CUSA

Braided Creek
Jim Harrison and Ted Kooser
Poetry
5½ x 7 | 90 pp
TP US $15.00 | CAN $18.00
978-1-55659-187-7 CUSA

Copper Canyon Press

Letters to Yesenin
Jim Harrison

"The way Harrison has embedded his entire vision of our predicament implicitly in the particulars of two poetic lives, his own and Yesenin's, is what makes the poem not only his best but one of the best in the past twenty-five years of American writing."—Hayden Carruth, *Sulfur*

"Harrison inhabits the problems of our age as if they were beasts into which he had crawled, and *Letters to Yesenin* is a kind of imaginative taxidermy that refuses to stay in place up on the trophy room wall, but insists on walking into the dining room."
—*The American Poetry Review*

Jim Harrison's gorgeous, desperate, and harrowing "correspondence" with Sergei Yesenin—a Russian poet who hanged himself after writing his final poem in his own blood—is considered an American masterwork.

In the early 1970s, Harrison was living in poverty on a hardscrabble farm, suffering from depression and suicidal tendencies. In response he began to write daily prose-poem letters to Yesenin. Through this one-sided correspondence, Harrison unloads to this unlikely hero, ranting and raving about politics, drinking problems, family concerns, farm life, and a full range of daily occurrences. The rope remains ever present.

Yet sometime through these letters there is a significant shift. Rather than feeling inextricably tied to Yesenin's fate, Harrison becomes furious, arguing about their imagined relationship: "I'm beginning to doubt whether we ever would have been friends."

In the end, Harrison listened to his own poems: "My year-old daughter's red robe hangs from the doorknob shouting *Stop.*"

Harrison was suicidal while writing *Letters to Yesenin*; these poems saved his life.

Poetry
November
Copper Canyon Classics
5 x 7 | 60 pp
TP US $12.00 | CAN $14.50
978-1-55659-265-2 CUSA

Marketing Plans

Co-op available
Advance reader copies
National advertising:
American Poet • The American
Poetry Review • Poetry • Poetry Flash •
The Writer's Chronicle

Author Hometown: Livingston, MT

Insomniac Liar of Topo
Norman Dubie

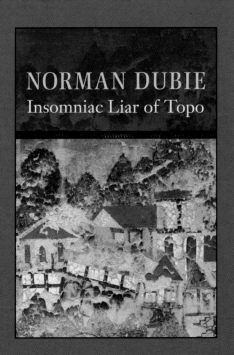

Poetry
October
A Paperback Original
6 x 9 | 110 pp
TP US $16.00 | CAN $19.50
978-1-55659-263-8 CUSA

Marketing Plans

Co-op available
Advance reader copies
National advertising:
American Poet • The American Poetry
Review • Poetry • The Writer's Chronicle

Author Hometown: Tempe, AZ

"Dubie has already been recognized as one of the most powerful and influential American poets . . . his poems have always been generous and inclusive, capable of containing multiple and conflicting worlds—of memory and the present, of the artistic and the daily."—*The Washington Post Book World*

The poems in Norman Dubie's *Insomniac Liar of Topo* behave much like that of a linear accelerator: exploding worlds into each other, from opposite poles, with tremendous speed, to discover the worlds within. Populated by an eccentric menagerie of mystics, holy men, and brilliant artists, Dubie brings together the grotesque and beautiful, to call forth the sincere within the context of war and human dissonance.

Dubie, a master purveyor of trickster protest and psychological release, uses an array of voices to highlight the splinter and shatter of wartime, of destroyed art and sacred texts, and the specific and various destructions that have made humans themselves aliens of their own planet.

So, the sun's down, the ship's lights
are like obvious fat jewels. And
if we want to have commerce
with the lizard men in their blue suits,
then we must eat more of these slouching animals
and faster too.

Norman Dubie is the author of nineteen books of poetry and served as poetry editor for *The Iowa Review* and director of the graduate poetry workshop at the University of Iowa. He helped found the MFA program at Arizona State University in Tempe, where he teaches as a regents professor for creative writing.

Norman Dubie is a trickster purveyor of illusions
whose devout readership expects the unexpected.

Also
Available

The Mercy Seat
Collected and New Poems 1967–2001
Norman Dubie
Poetry
6 x 9 | 424 pp
TP US $18.00 | CAN $21.95
978-1-55659-212-6 CUSA

Ordinary Mornings of a Coliseum
Norman Dubie
Poetry
6 x 9 | 144 pp
TP US $15.00 | CAN $18.00
978-1-55659-213-3 CUSA

Copper Canyon Press

Ambition and Survival
Becoming a Poet
Christian Wiman

"Blazing high style" is how *The New York Times* describes the prose of Christian Wiman, the young editor transforming *Poetry*, the country's oldest literary magazine.

Ambition and Survival is a collection of stirring personal essays and critical prose on a wide range of subjects: reading Milton in Guatemala, recalling violent episodes of his youth, and traveling in Africa with his eccentric father, as well as a series of penetrating essays on writers as diverse as Thomas Hardy and Janet Lewis. The book concludes with a portrait of Wiman's diagnosis of a rare form of incurable and lethal cancer, and how mortality reignited his religious passions.

When I was twenty years old I set out to be a poet. That sounds like I was a sort of frigate raising anchor, and in a way I guess I was, though susceptible to the lightest of winds. . . . When I read Samuel Johnson's comment that any young man could compensate for his poor education by reading five hours a day for five years, that's exactly what I tried to do, practically setting a timer every afternoon to let me know when the little egg of my brain was boiled. It's a small miracle that I didn't take to wearing a cape.

Christian Wiman is the editor of *Poetry* magazine. His poems and essays appear regularly in *The New Yorker, The Atlantic Monthly, Harper's,* and *The New York Times Book Review.*

An intimate first book of personal essays and incisive commentary from the editor of *Poetry*.

Literature & Essay / Poetry
September
A Paperback Original
6 x 9 | 280 pp
TP US $18.00 | CAN $21.95
978-1-55659-260-7 CUSA

Marketing Plans

Co-op available
Advance reader copies
National advertising:
American Poet • The American
Poetry Review • Poetry • Poetry Flash •
The Writer's Chronicle

Author Hometown: Chicago, IL

Also Available

Now Available from Copper Canyon Press

The Long Home
Christian Wiman
Poetry
6 x 9 | 88 pp
TP US $16.00 | CAN $19.50
978-1-55659-269-0 CUSA

Hard Night
Christian Wiman
Poetry
6 x 9 | 96 pp
TP US $14.00 | CAN $17.00
978-1-55659-220-1 CUSA

Copper Canyon Press

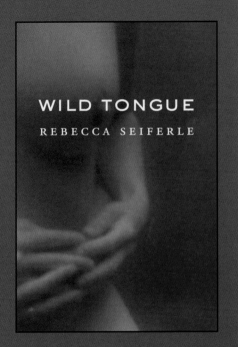

WILD TONGUE
REBECCA SEIFERLE

Poetry
September
A Paperback Original
6 x 9 | 196 pp
TP US $17.00 | CAN $20.50
978-1-55659-262-1 CUSA

Marketing Plans

Co-op available
Advance reader copies
National advertising:
American Poet • The American
Poetry Review • Poetry

Author Hometown: Tucson, AZ

Wild Tongue
Rebecca Seiferle

"With a bitter and withering irony and an eye for shocking beauty . . . Seiferle cuts straight to the emotionally honest kernel within family, spirit and myth."
—*Publishers Weekly*

Poet Rebecca Seiferle once said that "one should always read a poem as if it was a matter of life and death." Seiferle's fourth book of poems, *Wild Tongue*, suggests a similar belief about *writing* poems.

The tongue is both voice and body, and *Wild Tongue* rages against these global bits, bridles, and palliatives that attempt to calm and control. Combining shocking beauty and compelling directness, Seiferle counterbalances divorce and domestic violence with newfound love and cathartic wit. Her poems, like cave drawings, are inspired by urgency and concern, working into the cracks and contours of truth and wound.

So, it came to this, she could barely bear
to be touched, though she was glad for that
moment in the kitchen, tense with containers,
scrapings of delicacies adhering, floating
in the sink, and the other woman who turned and walked toward
her, holding out her arms, extended
from her shoulders, those most human wings,
to gather her up . . .

Rebecca Seiferle is the editor of the online journal *Drunken Boat* and has published six volumes of poetry and translation. She lives in Tucson, Arizona.

Rebecca Seiferle's fourth book displays wild rage, maternal instincts, and poetic talent at rolling boil.

Also Available

Bitters
Rebecca Seiferle
Poetry
6 x 9 | 120 pp
TP US $14.00 | CAN $17.00
978-1-55659-168-6 CUSA

The Black Heralds
César Vallejo
Translated by Rebecca Seiferle
Poetry / Latin American Studies
6 x 9 | 250 pp
TP US $16.00 | CAN $19.50
978-1-55659-199-0 CUSA

Copper Canyon Press

A Red Cherry on a White-tiled Floor

Selected Poems

Maram al-Massri

Translated by Khaled Mattawa

"Maram al-Massri comes as a shock. She writes about all the taboo subjects—physical passion, faithlessness, adultery, loneliness, despair—with candor and intensity that would mark her out even to Westerners."—*The Times* (London)

"Her direct, unadorned writing, with its emphasis on the quotidian, and utilization of simple, almost child-like metaphors, contrast sharply with the conventions of traditional Arabic love poetry."—*Banipal: Magazine of Modern Arab Literature*

Syrian poet Maram al-Massri writes of love and the place of women in the modern age with striking candor and intensity. "I am this mix between the submissive and rebellious woman," she writes, "my freedom is so difficult and so desired." Her poems invoke a world where women are trapped and men flow freely, of the intoxicating power of seduction and the intensity of lust, of the security of relationships and muffled explosions of emotion.

Like grains of salt
they shone
then melted.
This is how they disappeared,
those men
who did not love me.

Al-Massri herself straddles racial, religious, and cultural worlds. Born in Latakia, Syria, she moved to Paris in 1984 and has since refused to return: "I divorced from my past, my religion, my land, and even from my language." Despite being fluent in French and English, she writes in Arabic, following traditional forms.

A Red Cherry on a White-tiled Floor is al-Massri's first book published in the United States, and appears as a bilingual Arabic-English edition.

The first American publication of Syrian poet Maram al-Massri, presented in a bilingual Arabic-English edition.

Poetry
November
A Paperback Original
5½ x 8½ | 114 pp
TP US $15.00 | CAN $18.00
978-1-55659-264-5 CUSA

Copper Canyon Press

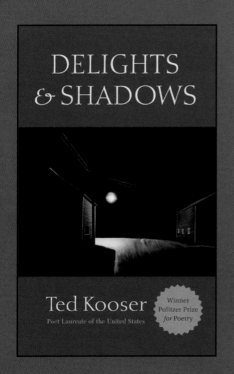

Poetry
September
5½ x 9 | 96 pp
TC y NR US $75.00 | CAN $90.00
978-1-55659-243-0 CUSA

Author Hometown: Garland, NE

Delights & Shadows
Ted Kooser

"Kooser is straightforward, possesses an American essence, is humble, gritty, ironic and has a gift for detail and a deceptive simplicity."—*Seattle Post-Intelligencer*

This signed, limited edition celebrates the Pulitzer Prize-winning collection by former Poet Laureate Ted Kooser.

Delights & Shadows is one of the best-selling poetry books in America, and Ted Kooser—editor of the weekly column "American Life in Poetry"—is a beloved poet. While serving as poet laureate, he stated, "I hope to interest more people in poetry. I hope to perform a service as a poet, giving people something they can use." Kooser certainly succeeded.

While *Delights & Shadows* has been lavishly reviewed in major media throughout the country, reader responses to the book have poured into Copper Canyon Press. A reader from rural New York wrote, "Kooser's tenth book of poems is a work of profound insight into the core of human existence and feeling." Another from Virginia wrote, "An instantly attractive collection by a poet unknown to me, who sees remarkable things in everyday objects. Today I ordered five more of his previous books at a local store."

Ted Kooser, author of thirteen books of poetry and nonfiction, is the former Poet Laureate of the United States. He lives in Nebraska.

A signed, limited edition of Ted Kooser's Pulitzer Prize-winning collection. Limited to 250 numbered copies.

Also Available

Braided Creek
Jim Harrison and Ted Kooser
Poetry
5½ x 7 | 90 pp
TP US $15.00 | CAN $18.00
978-1-55659-187-7 CUSA

Copper Canyon Press

Cuckoo's Blood
Versions of Zen Poetry
Stephen Berg

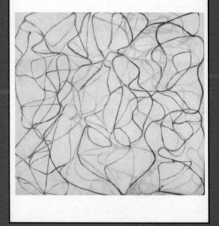

"We need poets like this. Mr. Berg relentlessly describes what we would often prefer to forget but can't allow ourselves to forget."—*The New York Times Book Review*

Certain poems of Zen masters, including work by Ikkyū, Bashō, and Dōgen, have haunted and nourished readers from around the world for centuries—and Stephen Berg for fifty years. Driven to know "what these people thought, believed, felt," Berg rewrote existing translations to create provocative, energized, and multilayered versions.

These are not new poems, nor are they old poems. These are explorations into the deeper resonances of Zen masters, expounding on the simple themes of the minute and overpowering them. This is Zen poetry to the core, nodding to the poets who came before while breathing new life into the forms and meanings.

"Deathsong," by Hakuin

Punch your fist mind of a fist through this black wall al-
ways in front of you always the next step you can't
take as you walk into it through it but can't
because it's who you are but can't be do not want
to be nothing but the place where you were are won't
be slam this fist of a fist into the wall that
isn't even here built of the billion nows yous
which when it finally is you finally face it you
pass through like a raw black breath

Stephen Berg is the founder and co-editor of *The American Poetry Review* and author of numerous collections of poetry and translations. He lives in Philadelphia.

Idiosyncratic and energized versions of Zen poems by the editor of *The American Poetry Review*.

Also Available

The Steel Cricket
Versions: 1958–1997
Stephen Berg
Poetry
6 x 9 | 240 pp
TP US $16.00 | CAN $19.50
978-1-55659-075-7 CUSA

Ikkyū: Crow With No Mouth
15th Century Zen Master
Stephen Berg
Poetry / Asian Studies
5½ x 8½ | 80 pp
TP US $14.00 | CAN $17.00
978-1-55659-152-5 CUSA

Copper Canyon Press

Poetry / Buddhism
December
A Paperback Original
5½ x 7½ | 136 pp
TP US $16.00 | CAN $19.50
978-1-55659-268-3 CUSA

Marketing Plans

Poetry / African American Studies
September
A Paperback Original
American Poetry Review
APR/Honickman First Book Prize
6 x 9 | 96 pp
TP US $14.00 | CAN $17.00
978-0-9776395-3-3 CUSA

Marketing Plans

Co-op available
Advance reader copies
National advertising:
American Book Review

Author Hometown: Brooklyn, NY

Totem
Gregory Pardlo

"Gregory Pardlo . . . wants to explore the druidic function of art, the works of jazz musicians, painters, poets, and others who live imaginatively, expand reality, and make imagination free."—Brenda Hillman, from the introduction

Totem, winner of the APR/Honickman First Book Prize, is the debut of a poet who has been *listening* for decades. In his youth, Gregory Pardlo heard stories of factory hours and picket lines from his father; in the bars, clubs, and on the radio he listens to jazz and blues, the rhythms, beats, and aspirations of which seep into his poems.

 A former Cave Canem fellow, Pardlo creates work that is deeply autobiographical, drifting between childhood and adult life. He speaks a language simultaneously urban and highbrow, seamlessly switching from art analysis to sneakers hung over the telephone lines.

From "Vincent's Shoes":

. . . I hung
the hightops from a power line.
It was in me to do. I felt it in my gut
the way Vincent might have felt
the wheat fields and the smoking socket
of the sun rattling, tweezed days
late into the ear of an aluminum bowl

Gregory Pardlo teaches at Medgar Evers College, The City University of New York, and lives in Brooklyn.

**Winner of the APR/Honickman First Book Prize,
with an introduction by Brenda Hillman.**

**Also
Available
APR/Honickman
First Book Prize
Winners**

Blue Colonial
David Roderick
Introduction by Robert Pinsky
Poetry
6 x 9 | 96 pp
TP US $14.00 | CAN $17.00
978-0-9776395-1-9 CUSA

In the Surgical Theatre
Dana Levin
Poetry
6 x 9 | 96 pp
TC y US $23.00 | CAN $27.95
978-0-9663395-2-9 CUSA

Copper Canyon Press

American Music
Chris Martin

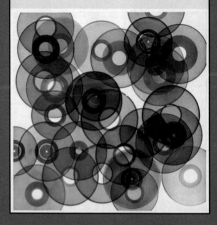

"Chris Martin . . . takes the O'Hara city poet eye in his own direction, showing a sweet vision for the distance between public and private spaces."—*Jacket*

American Music, selected by C.D. Wright from over one thousand manuscripts as winner of the Hayden Carruth Award for New and Emerging Poets, is uniquely attuned to the feedback symphony of a modern city, the lyrical product of "an earnest rage born of the absurd."

Chris Martin's poems reflect all things found in the urban environment: asphalt, subways, technology, strangers, the drudgery of work, the garbage trucks and open parks, fist fights and snapshots, fears and paranoia, loves and joys. Here is the constant sense of life hurtling forward without the time to reflect, within a city rife with opportunities: "I can practically / Hear all those words out / There amassing to make the journey / Inward."

American Music is a jostling of the senses; a decadent descent into the throbbing of a metropolitan world filled with familiar yet unresolved queries:

. . . it strikes me
That every person in every passenger
Seat in every car in
Every town in every country
Is having some goddamn
Thought—this is mine.

Chris Martin is a rapper, teacher, and editor of *Puppy Flowers,* an online magazine of the arts. He holds an MA in poetry, performance, and education from the Gallatin School of Individualized Study at New York University. He lives in Brooklyn.

A winner of the Hayden Carruth Award and selected for publication from over one thousand manuscripts.

Poetry
November
A Paperback Original
6 x 9 | 96 pp
TP US $15.00 | CAN $18.00
978-1-55659-266-9 CUSA

Also Available

Hayden Carruth Award Winners

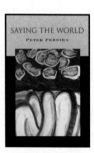

The Lichtenberg Figures
Ben Lerner
Poetry
6 x 9 | 96 pp
TP US $14.00 | CAN $17.00
978-1-55659-211-9 CUSA

Saying the World
Peter Pereira
Poetry / Gay Literature
6 x 9 | 96 pp
TP US $14.00 | CAN $17.00
978-1-55659-197-6 CUSA

Copper Canyon Press

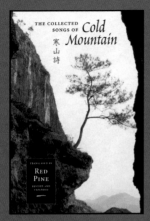

The Collected Songs of Cold Mountain
Cold Mountain (Han Shan)
Translated by Red Pine

Poetry / Asian Studies
6 x 9 | 320 pp
4 B&W photographs
TP US $17.00 | CAN $20.50
978-1-55659-140-2 CUSA

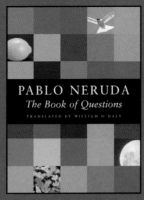

The Book of Questions
Pablo Neruda
Translated by William O'Daly

Poetry / Latin American Literature
5 x 8 | 96 pp
TP US $14.00 | CAN $17.00
978-1-55659-160-0 CUSA

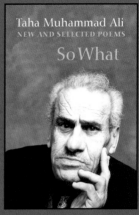

So What
New and Selected Poems
1973–2005
Taha Muhammad Ali
Translated by Peter Cole

Poetry
6 x 9 | 280 pp
TP US $18.00 | CAN $21.95
978-1-55659-245-4 CUSA

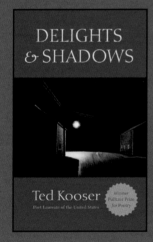

Delights & Shadows
Ted Kooser

Poetry
6 x 9 | 96 pp
TP US $15.00 | CAN $18.00
978-1-55659-201-0 CUSA

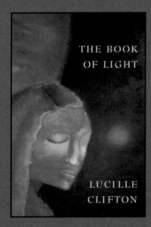

The Book of Light
Lucille Clifton

Poetry / African American Studies
6 x 9 | 80 pp
TP US $13.00 | CAN $15.95
978-1-55659-052-8 CUSA

Spring Essence
The Poetry of Hô Xuân Huong
Hô Xuân Huong
Translated by John Balaban

Poetry / Asian Studies
6 x 9 | 140 pp
TP US $15.00 | CAN $18.00
978-1-55659-148-8 CUSA

Margarita, How Beautiful the Sea

Sergio Ramírez

Translated by Michael Miller

León, Nicaragua, 1907. During a tribute he delivers during his triumphal return to his native city, Rubén Darío writes on the fan of a little girl one of his most famous poems, "Margarita, How Beautiful the Sea."

In 1956 in a cafe in León, a group of literati gather, dedicated, among other things, to the rigorous reconstruction of the legend surrounding Darío—but also to conspire. There will be an attempt against dictator Somoza's life, and that little girl with the fan a half-century before will not be a disinterested party.

In *Margarita, How Beautiful the Sea,* Sergio Ramírez encompasses, in a complete metaphor of reality and legend, the entire history of his country. The narrative moves along paths fifty years apart, which inevitably converge. The story becomes a fascinating exercise on the power of memory, on the influence of the past, fictitious or not, in the finality of reality.

Sergio Ramírez is a leading Nicaraguan writer and intellectual who served in the Junta of National Reconstruction and as vice president of the country from 1984 until 1990. He is the author of over thirty books, among them nine works of fiction, and he is the recipient of numerous honors, including the L'Ordre du Chevalier des Arts et des Lettres in France.

Michael B. Miller, former professor of Spanish and Latin American literatures, holds a PhD from George Washington University. He has translated numerous works from Spanish, including *A Place Called Milagro de la Paz* by Manlio Argueta.

**Winner of the coveted Alfaguara Prize, a rich, poetic novel
from a major Latin American author.**

Fiction / Latin American Literature
September
5½ x 8½ | 320 pp
TP US $15.95 | CAN $19.50
978-1-931896-41-2 CUSA
TC US $24.95 | CAN $30.00
978-1-931896-42-9 CUSA

Marketing Plans

Co-op available
Advance reader copies

**Also
Available**

Hatful of Tigers
Reflections on Art, Culture and Politics
Sergio Ramírez
Literature & Essay / Current Affairs
5 x 7½ | 148 pp
TC US $15.00 | CAN $18.00
978-0-915306-98-5 CUSA

A Place Called Milagro de la Paz
Manlio Argueta
Translated by Michael Miller
Fiction / Latin American Literature
5½ x 8½ | 160 pp
TP US $14.95 | CAN $18.00
978-1-880684-68-9 CUSA

Curbstone Press

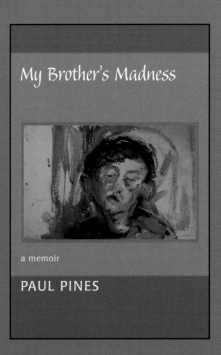

My Brother's Madness

a memoir

PAUL PINES

Biography & Autobiography /
Psychology & Psychiatry
October
A Paperback Original
5½ x 8½ | 318 pp
TP US $15.95 | CAN $19.50
978-1-931896-34-4 CUSA

Marketing Plans

Co-op available
Advance reader copies

Author Events

Phoenix, AZ • Tucson, AZ • Los Angeles, CA •
San Francisco, CA • Denver, CO • Hartford, CT
• New London, CT • Miami, FL • Coral
Gables, FL • Chicago, IL • Notre Dame, IN
• New Orleans, LA • Alberquerque, NM •
Albany, NY • Glens Falls, NY • New York, NY
• Queensbury, NY • Saratoga Springs, NY •
Manchester, VT

Author Hometown: Glens Falls, NY

My Brother's Madness
A Memoir
Paul Pines

"Few books nourish the psyche and stir the heart as much as *My Brother's Madness*."
—David Unger, author of *Life in the Damn Tropics*

My Brother's Madness is based on the author's relationship with his brother—who had a psychotic breakdown in his late forties—and explores the unfolding of two intertwined lives and the nature of delusion. Circumstances lead one brother from juvenile crime on the streets of Brooklyn to war-torn Vietnam, to a fast-track life as a Hollywood publicist to owning and operating The Tin Palace, one of New York's most legendary jazz clubs, while his brother falls into, and fights his way back from, a delusional psychosis.

My Brother's Madness is part thriller, part exploration that not only describes the causes, character, and journey of mental illness, but also makes sense of it. It is ultimately a story of our own humanity, and answers the question, *Am I my brother's keeper?*

Paul Pines grew up in New York City and is the author of five books of poetry, including his most recent, *Adrift on Blinding Light.* His novel, *The Tin Angel,* was critically very well received. He currently lives with his wife Carol and daughter Charlotte in Glens Falls, New York, where he teaches American literature and creative writing at Adirondack Community College, practices psychotherapy at Glens Falls Hospital, and hosts the annual Lake George Jazz Weekend.

**A story of the struggle to survive a family life that
includes extortion, murder, and madness.**

Curbstone Press

America's Child
A Woman's Journey through the Radical Sixties
Susan Sherman

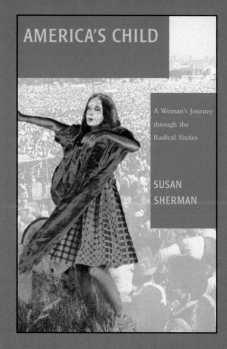

"*America's Child* is not only a chronicle of the sixties, it's a book of interior and exterior voyages, a book of transformations, a courageous, honest and illuminating book."
—Claribel Alegría

America's Child is the story of the journey of a child of first-generation immigrant parents from a working-class neighborhood in Philadelphia to the mythic avenues of 1940s Hollywood, through the transformative years of Berkeley, to the avant-garde art world of New York, and to a Cuban movie theater filled with Vietnamese students and the turbulence of the sixties.

Susan Sherman's journey, during a period in which the world was in ferment and large sections of the population were engaged in active self-examination and agitating for social change, is one of discovery and introspection.

From the cultural renaissance of the late 1950s, through the sexual revolution, to political activism that starts with world issues and ends with struggles around sexism and homophobia, *America's Child* is simultaneously cultural history, social discourse, and a deeply personal narrative.

Poet, playwright, and founding editor of *Ikon* magazine, Susan Sherman has published three collections of poetry, a translation, and *The Color of the Heart* (Curbstone Press). *America's Child* was completed thanks to the help of a New York Foundation for the Arts Fellowship in Creative Nonfiction Literature, a Puffin Foundation grant, and a residency at Blue Mountain Center.

A young woman's chronicle of the radical sixties.

Also Available

The Color of the Heart
Writing from Struggle & Change 1959–1990
Susan Sherman
Literature & Essay / History
5½ x 8½ | 224 pp
TP US $10.95 | CAN $13.50
978-0-915306-90-9 CUSA

Biography & Autobiography / Cultural Studies
October
A Paperback Original
5½ x 8½ | 280 pp
TP US $15.95 | CAN $19.50
978-1-931896-35-1 CUSA

Marketing Plans

Co-op available
Advance reader copies

Author Events

Hartford, CT • New London, CT • New York, NY

Author Hometown: New York, NY

Curbstone Press

Measured by Stone
Sam Hamill

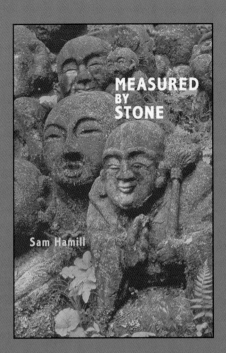

Poetry / Buddhism
September
A Paperback Original
5½ x 8½ | 90 pp
TP US $13.95 | CAN $17.00
978-1-931896-40-5 CUSA

These poems exhibit the range of Sam Hamill's celebrated practice and vision, from philosophical and discursive elements to the intensely lyrical, from his continuing poems of praise (and elegies) for fellow poets to the clear influence of the Zen classics he has so notably translated.

"To Gray on Our Anniversary"

I've relished years of bliss with you
despite the nefarious Hells
this suffering world has put us through.
I know you're not fond of growing old,
and what pain's to come, only time will tell.
Still, you are my comfort in the cold
of Odyssean storm–tossed seas,
my bride, my muse, my Penelope.

Sam Hamill is the author of fourteen volumes of original poetry. He has published three collections of essays and two dozen volumes translated from ancient Greek, Latin, Estonian, Japanese, and Chinese. He is the founding editor of Copper Canyon Press and director of Poets Against War. His work has been translated into more than a dozen languages.

New poems by the director of Poets Against War.

Marketing Plans

Co-op available
Advance reader copies

Author Events

Hartford, CT • Washington, DC •
Baltimore, MD • Portland, OR •
Pittsburgh, PA • Seattle, WA

Author Hometown: Port Townsend, WA

Also Available

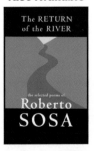

Return of the River
The Selected Poems of Roberto Sosa
Roberto Sosa
Introduction by Sam Hamill
Translated by JoAnne Engelbert
Poetry / Latin American Literature
5½ x 8½ | 100 pp
TP US $16.95 | CAN $20.50
978-1-880684-80-1 CUSA

Curbstone Press

NEVER SLEEP
Graduating to Graphic Design
Andre Andreev and Dan Covert
Introduction by Michael Vanderbyl

There is a major disconnect between the life of a design student and the transition to being a design professional. To demystify the transition, we share the failures, successes, and surprises during our years in college and progression into the field: the creative process, monetary problems, internships, interviews, mistakes, and personal relationships. We include the work from our first design class to our most current client work, along with side stories and interviews from our mentors, teachers, and peers. This book will serve as the ultimate companion for design students, educators, and anyone breaking into a creative field.

At the combined age of forty-six, Andre Andreev and Dan Covert have been recognized by *I.D., BDA, Communication Arts, PRINT, Graphis,* Taschen, *Metropolis,* the Type Directors Club, The Art Directors Club, *CMYK, HOW,* Adobe, *STEP Field Guide to Emerging Design Talent,* and *Young Guns.* They met while studying graphic design at California College of the Arts and currently work for MTV's on-air design department in New York, while operating their firm dress code at night. They also co-teach typography and design courses at Pratt Institute in Brooklyn. Andre eats no meat, and Dan dislikes puppies.

**The ultimate companion for design students,
educators, and anyone breaking into a creative field.**

Art
September
7 x 9 | 250 pp
150 Color and B&W photographs
TC US $29.99 | CAN $36.00
978-0-9791800-1-9 CUSA

Author Events

Los Angeles, CA • San Francisco, CA • Boston, MA • New York, NY

Author Hometown: New York, NY

Tsunami
A Document of Devastation
Photographs by VII

Photography / Current Affairs
26 x 19 | 72 pp
53 Color and B&W photographs
LOOSE SHEETS US $54.00 | CAN $65.00
978-0-9742836-0-9 CUSA

Flip o Rama
Italia
Elliott Erwitt

Photography / Art
4½ x 6 | 504 pp
BOX SET US $96.00 | CAN $115.50
978-0-9705768-4-2 CUSA

Vanishing
**Antonin Kratochvil with
Michael Persson**

Environmental Studies / Photography
14 x 18¾ | 240 pp
119 B&W photographs
TC US $54.00 | CAN $65.00
978-0-9705768-3-5 CUSA

Wonderland
A Fairytale of the Soviet Monolith
Jason Eskenazi

Photography / History
5 x 7 | 224 pp
80 B&W photographs
TC US $32.00 | CAN $38.50
978-0-9742836-7-8 CUSA

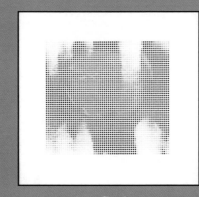

Nonfiction
Christopher Anderson

Photography
8 x 7 | 104 pp
BOXED TP US $45.00 | CAN $54.00
978-0-9705768-1-1 CUSA

9/11 Box
**Photographs by VII Photo Agency
with Susan Sontag, Dalai Lama,
and others**

Photography / Current Affairs
11 x 9½ | 760 pp
185 Color and B&W photographs
BOXED TC 50% NR US $120.00 | CAN $144.00
978-0-9742836-6-1 CUSA

Small World
Photographs by Martin Parr

Small World is a biting and very funny satire in which Martin Parr observes global tourism and the tourist's search for authentic cultures that are themselves destroyed in that search.

Martin Parr has worked on numerous photographic projects and developed an international reputation for his innovative imagery, his oblique approach to social documentary, and his input to photographic culture within the United Kingdom and abroad. In 2002 a major retrospective exhibition was initiated by The Barbican in London and is touring internationally to 2008.

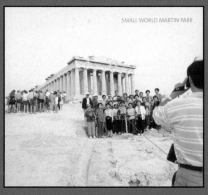

Photography
November
11¾ x 10¾ | 96 pp
70 Color photographs
TC US $45.00 | CAN $54.00
978-1-904587-40-8 CUSA

The new edition of a classic book from Britain's most successful and influential contemporary photographer.

Beijing: Theatre of the People
Photographs by Ambroise Tézenas
Foreword by Patrick Zackmann

Winner of the Leica European Publishers Award.

In the streets of Beijing, Ambroise Tézenas discovered a landscape that offered an unexpected vision: its spaces almost stage sets in which contemporary Beijing plays out a complex struggle. It is a city caught between two worlds—an ancient past and a frenzied present. Included are images of the construction of major projects such as the Opera House, Grand National Theatre, and the Olympic Stadium—all part of the city's furious redevelopment.

Ambroise Tézenas, based in Paris, has worked extensively for the French and international press.

Photography
September
11 x 12 | 120 pp
70 Color photographs
TC US $45.00 | CAN $54.00
978-1-904587-36-1 CUSA

Beijing—a city caught between two worlds, an ancient past and a frenzied present.

Dewi Lewis Publishing

Mouthpiece
Photographs by Justin Quinnell

As one of the world's leading pinhole photographers, Justin Quinnell takes the technique to new extremes. The results are surreal, revealing, and hilarious. He captures on film his visit to the dentist, portraits of friends and family, and the everyday acts of having a bath, cleaning his teeth, and eating his dinner. More surreal are the landscapes, the icons of world travel; included are the Lincoln Memorial and the Twin Towers.

Justin Quinnell is a recognized expert on pinhole photography and has tirelessly promoted it for over twenty years. He regularly lectures on the subject internationally.

Photography
September
6 x 4¾ | 96 pp
60 Color photographs
TC US $15.00 | CAN $18.00
978-1-904587-33-0 CUSA

Open wide! Astonishing pictures taken by a pinhole camera that sits on the tongue.

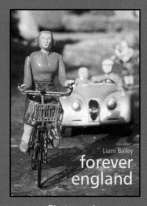

Forever England
Photographs by Liam Bailey
Foreword by Ally Ireson

This is a world of elderly ladies and shopping bags, firemen battling blazing thatched roofs, days out at the seaside, and cricket on the village green. The people, only inches tall, are all residents of Bekonscot, a model village set firmly in a 1930s time warp. Everyday life, from the mundane to the extraordinary, carries on unchanged. Originally built by a London accountant to entertain his house guests, it opened to the public in 1929. This is a fascinating photographic tour through this world-famous folly that stands as a tribute to English eccentricity, humor, determination, and craftsmanship.

Photography
September
5½ x 7¾ | 160 pp
145 Color photographs
TC US $18.00 | CAN $21.95
978-1-904587-30-9 CUSA

The oldest model village in the world—a tribute to English eccentricity.

Dewi Lewis Publishing

Between Dogs and Wolves
Growing up with South Africa
Photographs by Jodi Bieber

Photography
October
6 x 8 | 144 pp
80 B&W photographs
TC US $30.00
CAN $36.00
978-1-904587-32-3
CUSA

Between Dogs and Wolves is a moving portrait of the harsh realities of Johannesburg's toughest neighborhoods. Jodi Bieber focuses on a generation of young people growing up on the fringes of South African society.

Jodi Bieber's work has appeared in *The New York Times Magazine, U.S. News & World Report, GEO, Mare,* and *L'Express.* She works for Amnesty International, Médecins Sans Frontières, and Positive Lives.

A Record of England
Sir Benjamin Stone & The National Photographic Record Association, 1897–1910
Photographs by Sir Benjamin Stone
Text by Elizabeth Edwards and Peter James

Photography / Art
October
10 x 9 | 156 pp
122 B&W
photographs
TC US $39.95
CAN $48.00
978-1-904587-37-8
CUSA

This is England in the late nineteenth century through the eyes of the photographic survey movement. In 1897 Sir Benjamin Stone announced the formation of the National Photographic Record Association. Its objective was to make a record of England for future generations. This book examines Stone's central role in the project and presents over 120 of his photographs.

Knock Three Times
Working Men, Social Clubs and Other Stories
Photographs by Chris Coekin
Foreword by David Campany

Photography
October
10 x 10 | 96 pp
60 Color photographs
and illustrations
TC 50% NR
US $39.95
CAN $48.00
978-1-904587-28-6
CUSA

"Warm and engaging—filled with images that are both poignant and often very, very funny. This really is a sensational book."—*The Times* (London)

Through photographs and archive material, Chris Coekin explores the cultural roots and identity of the Working Men's Club and examines the complexity of working-class culture, as well as ideas of masculinity, relationships, and work ethic.

The Mother Of All Journeys
Photographs by Dinu Li

Photography
November
8½ x 11¾ | 96 pp
60 Color photographs
and illustrations
TC US $45.00
CAN $54.00
978-1-904587-41-5
CUSA

This is a journey from China to England; it is a reflection on identity and the passage of time. Dinu Li traces his family's journey from rural China, via Hong Kong, to the industrial north of England. Inspired by the memories of Li's mother, the story is told through photographs, personal recollections, and family snapshots.

Dewi Lewis Publishing

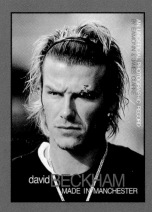

David Beckham
Made in Manchester.
An Unofficial Photographic Record
**Photographs by Eamonn Clarke
and James Clarke**

Sports & Recreation / Photography
7½ x 10½ | 144 pp
160 Color photographs
TC US $35.00 | CAN $42.00
978-0-9546843-0-3 CUSA

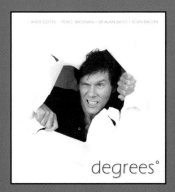

Degrees
Photographs by Andy Gotts
Foreword by Sir Alan Bates
with Pierce Brosnan
Afterword by Kevin Bacon

Photography / Popular Culture
12 x 13 | 180 pp
162 B&W photographs
TC US $49.95 | CAN $60.00
978-0-9546843-6-5 CUSA

Common Sense
Martin Parr

Photography / Cultural Studies
12 x 8 | 160 pp
158 Color photographs
TC US $50.00 | CAN $60.00
978-1-899235-07-0 CUSA

Rough Beauty
Photographs by Dave Anderson
Introduction by Anne Tucker

Photography / Current Affairs
9¾ x 9¾ | 120 pp
80 B&W photographs
TC US $40.00 | CAN $48.00
978-1-904587-29-3 CUSA

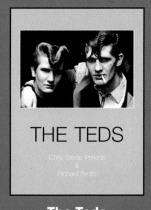

The Teds
Photographs by Chris Steele-Perkins
with Richard Smith

Photography / Popular Culture
7 x 9¼ | 128 pp
72 duotone photographs
TC US $26.95 | CAN $32.50
978-1-899235-44-5 CUSA

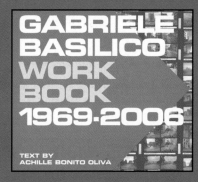

**Gabriele Basilico.
Workbook 1969–2006**
Photographs by Gabriele Basilico
**Introduction by Achille
Bonito Oliva**

Photography / Architecture
11 x 10 | 240 pp
300 Color and B&W photographs
TC US $55.00 | CAN $66.00
978-1-904587-35-4 CUSA

Beyond The Secret

The Definitive Unauthorized Guide to *The Secret*

Alexandra Bruce

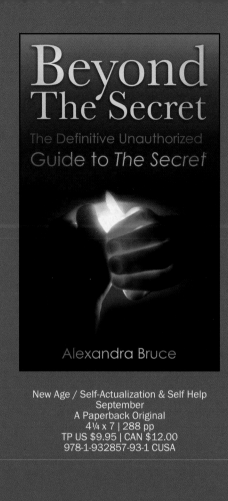

The Secret is the biggest book since *The Purpose Driven Life.* Based on a best-selling documentary film of the same name, it presents the "Law of Attraction," which, according to the tagline, "has traveled through centuries to reach you." By synthesizing "how to get rich" ideas from classic self-help books by Wallace D. Wattles *(The Science of Getting Rich),* Napoleon Hill *(Think and Grow Rich!),* and Charles Haanel *(The Master Key System)* with twenty-five modern-day self-improvement gurus like Jack Canfield, Bob Proctor, Michael Bernard Beckwith, James Ray, Lisa Nichols, and Joe Vitale, author Rhonda Byrne and her team have created an almost alchemically rich and compelling promise.

They claim that "The Secret" was discovered by such historical luminaries as Plato, da Vinci, Galileo, Napoleon, Hugo, Beethoven, Newton, Edison, and Einstein; that "The Secret" has existed in fragments in religions, philosophies, and oral traditions for centuries . . . but only now has it all been put together. "The Secret is everything you have dreamed of . . . and is beyond your wildest dreams," trumpet the marketing materials. Could it really be true, or is it just a new spin on the very old (and decidedly *not* secret) "power of positive thinking" wedded to "ask and you shall receive"?

Alexandra Bruce goes behind the scenes to investigate the phenomenon, from its roots in Australia to the sales bonanza that has seen creator Rhonda Byrne become the most successful debut author in memory. Bruce takes a hard but fair look at the "teachers" featured in *The Secret* and the "Law of Attraction" that is the central theme. To truly understand the significance of *The Secret,* perspective is needed. *Beyond The Secret* delivers that and much more.

The Secret is the biggest self-help phenomenon since Dale Carnegie—this book explains why.

Also Available

Beyond the Bleep
The Definitive Unauthorized Guide to What the Bleep Do We Know!?
Alexandra Bruce
New Age / Spirituality
4¼ x 7 | 228 pp
TP US $9.95 | CAN $12.00
978-1-932857-22-1 CUSA

The Disinformation Company

New Age / Self-Actualization & Self Help
September
A Paperback Original
4¼ x 7 | 288 pp
TP US $9.95 | CAN $12.00
978-1-932857-93-1 CUSA

Marketing Plans

Co-op available
15,000-copy print run
National advertising:
Leading Edge Review • Magical Blend •
New Age Retailer • Publishers Weekly

Author Events

New York, NY

Author Hometown: Southampton, NY

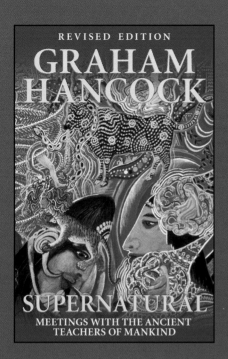

Spirituality / New Age
October
6 x 9 | 540 pp
120 Color and B&W illustrations
and photographs
TP $18.95
978-1-932857-84-9 USA

Marketing Plans

Co-op available
15,000-copy print run

Author Events

Esalen, CA • Los Angeles, CA •
San Francisco, CA • New York, NY •
Rhinebeck, NY

Supernatural
Meetings with the Ancient Teachers of Mankind
Graham Hancock

Less than fifty thousand years ago mankind had no art, no religion, no sophisticated symbolism, no innovative thinking. Then, in a dramatic and electrifying change, described by scientists as "the greatest riddle in human history," all the skills and qualities that we value most highly in ourselves appeared already fully formed, as though bestowed on us by hidden powers. In *Supernatural* Graham Hancock sets out to investigate this mysterious "before-and-after moment" and to discover the truth about the influences that gave birth to the modern human mind.

His quest takes him on a detective journey from the stunningly beautiful painted caves of prehistoric France, Spain, and Italy to rock shelters in the mountains of South Africa, where he finds extraordinary Stone Age art. He uncovers clues that lead him to the depths of the Amazon rainforest to drink the powerful hallucinogen Ayahuasca with shamans, whose paintings contain images of "supernatural beings" identical to the animal-human hybrids depicted in prehistoric caves. Hallucinogens such as mescaline also produce visionary encounters with exactly the same beings. Scientists at the cutting edge of consciousness research have begun to consider the possibility that such hallucinations may be real perceptions of other "dimensions." Could the "supernaturals" first depicted in the painted caves be the ancient teachers of mankind? Could it be that human evolution is not just the "meaningless" process that Darwin identified, but something more purposive and intelligent that we have barely begun to understand? This newly revised edition of *Supernatural* is now available for the first time as a paperback.

Graham Hancock is the author of the international bestsellers *The Sign and The Seal, Fingerprints of the Gods,* and *Heaven's Mirror.* His books have sold more than five million copies.

The latest book from international best-selling author Graham Hancock.

Also Available

Supernatural
Meetings with the Ancient Teachers of Mankind
Graham Hancock
History / Spirituality
6½ x 9½ | 720 pp
120 Color and B&W illustrations and photographs
TC $29.95
978-1-932857-40-5 USA

The Disinformation Company

50 Facts That Should Change The World 2.0
Jessica Williams

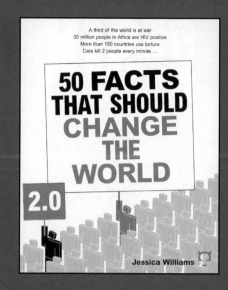

Jessica Williams revisits her classic series of snapshots of life in the twenty-first century. Revised and updated with lots of new material, this book is every bit as vital as the first edition. From the inequalities and absurdities of the so-called developed world to the vast scale of suffering wreaked by war, famine, and AIDS in developing countries, it paints a picture of incredible contrasts.

This 2.0 edition again contains an eclectic selection of facts addressing a broad range of global issues, now with added emphasis on climate change, the decline in human rights and democratic freedoms around the world, the unexpected global impact of corporate growth, sports and media madness and inequality, and lots of updated facts and figures. Each is followed by a short essay explaining the story behind the fact, fleshing out the bigger problem lurking behind the numbers. Real-life stories, anecdotes, and case studies help to humanize the figures and make clear the human impact of the bald statistics.

All of the facts remind us that whether we like to think of it or not, the world is interconnected and civilization is a fragile concept. Williams makes us think about some of the hard facts about our civilization and what we can do about them.

Jessica Williams is a journalist and producer of the BBC's flagship international interview program, *HARDTalk with Tim Sebastian,* where she has researched and produced interviews with such disparate figures as the political philosopher Noam Chomsky, President Paul Kagame of Rwanda, Sir David Attenborough, and the academic Edward Said.

Revised, updated, and every bit as vital as the first edition!

Current Affairs / Cultural Studies
November
A Paperback Original
6¼ x 7½ | 288 pp
TP $14.95
978-1-932857-90-0 USA

Also Available

50 Facts That Should Change the World
Jessica Williams
Current Affairs / Cultural Studies
6 x 8 | 352 pp
TP $14.95
978-0-9729529-6-5 USA

The Disinformation Company

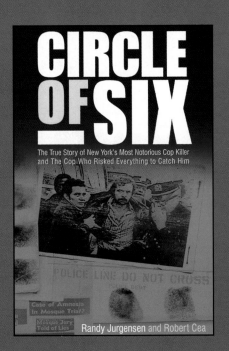

True Crime
September
6 x 9 | 296 pp
15 B&W photographs
TP US $15.95 | CAN $19.50
978-1-932857-85-6 CUSA

Circle of Six

The True Story of New York's Most Notorious Cop Killer and The Cop Who Risked Everything to Catch Him

Randy Jurgensen and Robert Cea

Circle of Six is the true story of what is perhaps the most notorious case in the history of the New York Police Department. It details Randy Jurgensen's determined effort to bring to justice the murderer of Patrolman Phillip Cardillo.

Cardillo was shot and killed inside Harlem's Mosque #7 in 1972, in the midst of an all-out assault on the NYPD from the Black Liberation Army. The New York of this era was a place not unlike the Wild West, in which cops and criminals shot it out on a daily basis.

Despite the mayhem on the streets and the Machiavellian corridors of Mayor Lindsay's City Hall, Detective Jurgensen single-handedly took on the Black Liberation Army, the Nation of Islam, NYPD brass, and City Hall, capturing Cardillo's killer, Lewis 17X Dupree. He broke the case with an unlikely accomplice, Foster 2X Thomas, a member of the Nation of Islam who became Jurgensen's witness. The relationship they formed during the time before trial gave each of the two men a greater perspective of the two sides in the street war and changed them forever. In the end, Jurgensen had to settle for a conviction on other charges, and Dupree served a number of years. The murder case is still officially unsolved. In 2006 the NYPD reopened the case, and it is once again an active investigation with full media attention.

The book has received acclaim from current New York City Police Commissioner Ray Kelly, as well as from former Commissioner William Bratton.

Randy Jurgensen's co-author is **Robert Cea** (*No Lights, No Sirens*), also a former NYPD detective.

A New York City detective's relentless search for a cop killer no one wanted caught.

Marketing Plans

Co-op available
National radio tour

Author Events

Atlantic City, NJ • New York, NY • Westchester, NY

Author Hometown: New York, NY

The Disinformation Company

Far Out
101 Strange Tales From Science's Outer Edge
Mark Pilkington

Mark Pilkington charts some of the more curious byways, scenic detours, and inspired failures of scientists, inventors, and, yes, crackpots, over the past few hundred years.

From the Aquatic Ape Hypothesis to zero-point energy, via the Hieronymous Machine and Phlogiston, *Far Out* tells the stories that are all too often ignored, lost, or simply forgotten by conventional science books. Some of them are perhaps best left languishing in the margins of history, but others may yet change our future. Entries cover physics, chemistry, biology, archaeology, parapsychology, and other areas yet to be inducted into mainstream science, including radionics, keranography, erotoxin, and remote viewing.

Written in a succinct and engaging style, each piece provides a useful, self-contained introduction to its topic, and provides enough information to allow readers to discover more if they so desire.

Far Out is the latest in the unique CD-sized book format from Disinformation, following the best-selling *50 Things You're Not Supposed To Know* series by Russ Kick. Once again, the book is printed in two colors, with the entries arranged into sections, many with appropriate illustrations, diagrams, or photographs.

Mark Pilkington is a freelance journalist, writer, and editor. As well as writing the "Far Out" column for the *Guardian* on which this book is based, he has also written for *The Times* (London), *Fortean Times, Arthur,* and *The Wire,* among others. He also edits the highly praised anthology of cultural marginalia, *Strange Attractor,* and runs Strange Attractor Press.

The most curious byways, scenic detours, and inspired failures of scientists, inventors, and crackpots.

Science / Occultism & Parapsychology
October
A Paperback Original
5½ x 5 | 208 pp
100 B&W illustrations and photographs
TP US $11.95 | CAN $14.50
978-1-932857-87-0 CUSA

Marketing Plans

Co-op available
Advance reader copies

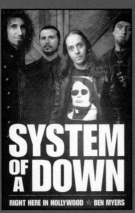

Music / Popular Culture
September
A Paperback Original
6 x 9 | 208 pp
17 B&W photographs
TP US $19.95 | CAN $24.00
978-1-932857-88-7 CUSA

**The first and only book on one of
the world's biggest bands.**

System Of A Down
Right Here In Hollywood
Ben Myers

System of a Down has evolved from a cult band whose demo tapes swapped hands voraciously on the metal underground to one of the world's biggest bands, having sold in excess of forty million albums. It's not just well-informed music fans that love them—the CIA certainly knows about them . . . and trails them closely.

Featuring exclusive new interviews with the band and major players involved in their story, Ben Myers' book is the first definitive account of this remarkable band.

Ben Myers is a highly respected music journalist and is currently a features editor at *Kerrang!* He is the author of several books, including *Green Day*. His work has appeared in numerous publications, including *Kerrang!*, *Melody Maker*, and *Q*.

Marketing Plans
Co-op available
National advertising: AMP • CMJ • Kerrang!

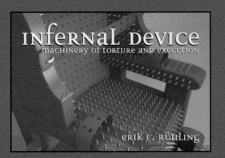

Cultural Studies / History
November
9 x 6 | 96 pp
40 Color photographs and illustrations
Paper over Board US $14.95 | CAN $18.00
978-1-932857-89-4 CUSA

**A fully illustrated collection of torture
devices used throughout the ages in
the pursuit of "truth."**

Infernal Device
Machinery of Torture and Execution
Erik Ruhling

Erik Ruhling assembles an unmatched array of torture tools invented exclusively for the infliction of pain and the ending of life, each carefully researched with an accompanying full-color, highly detailed rendering. This beautifully presented book features classics like the Iron Maiden and the Guillotine, as well as more rarified connoisseur's fare such as the Scavenger's Daughter and the Ear Chopper. And if the Tongue Tearer is not to your taste, there's always the Breast Ripper or the Drunkard's Cloak.

Erik Ruhling is a graphic designer and the curator of www.occasionalhell.com. He holds degrees in anthropology and English and lives in Atlanta, Georgia, in a house without a dungeon (unfortunately).

Marketing Plans
Co-op available • National radio tour

Author Hometown: Atlanta, GA

The Disinformation Company

SM Hunter v02
(Action)
You Na

Welcome to the future, where spam mails are living organisms, and the fight against the viruses they harbor is an incalculable threat in lives and money. The only defense citizens, corporations, and governments have against these spam and viruses are the Hunters.

SM Hunter is the newest series by author You Na, and it is currently continuing in her native South Korea. It is a fast-paced, action- and character-driven graphic novel that appeals to all manhwa and manga enthusiasts. You Na's artwork is crisp, her characters' costumes are bold, and the overall impression is that of a full-bodied graphic novel.

Manga
November
A Paperback Original
5¼ x 7½ | 184 pp
TP US $11.99 | CAN $14.50
978-1-933809-14-4 CUSA

The hunt continues in the never-ending war against spam mail!

SM Hunter v03
(Action)
You Na

The spam-mail boom of the near future: The great advances of technology, a new generation of improved systems, and ideal computer programs have caused a backlash. In the near future, hundreds of thousands of spammers have caused incalculable destruction to the mainframe of the lives of everyday citizens. Spam mail hunters have become their only defense.

But now the Hunters have become restless. All it took was one error in judgment, the momentary loss of momentum. A spam has survived and is now a captive. Was it conscience that stopped his blade? Or perhaps a bout of pity?

Manga
January
A Paperback Original
5¼ x 7½ | 184 pp
TP US $11.99
CAN $14.50
978-1-933809-15-1 CUSA

Erotic Manga
September
A Paperback Original
5¼ x 7½ | 200 pp
TP US $12.99
CAN $15.95
978-1-933809-66-3
CUSA

Cage of Thorns
(Yaoi)
Sonoko Sakuragawa

Kujou Tsurugi is a young executive at a construction company. One day, while attending a party, he is assaulted by an acquaintance. However, he is saved by Katsuragi Takaya, the son of a lower-house parliamentarian. But the politician's son expects a payment for saving him. Tsurugi is shocked at Katsuragi's demand, but he's even more unnerved by his response.

Erotic Manga
September
A Paperback Original
5¼ x 7½ | 200 pp
TP US $12.99
CAN $15.95
978-1-933809-57-1
CUSA

Maiden Rose v01
(Yaoi)
Fusanosuke Inariya

Two soldiers caught on opposing sides of a war between nations must choose between their country and an oath of fealty made long before. But the world that they live in is hard, distrustful, and cold. What will happen to their innocent love as they are tangled ever deeper inside the terrible ravages of war?

Erotic Manga
October
A Paperback Original
5¼ x 7½ | 200 pp
TP US $12.99
CAN $15.95
978-1-933809-74-8
CUSA

White & Black
(Yaoi)
Kumiko Misasagi

White Angel Kouki and Black Angel Eiji must deliver departed souls into the afterlife. The angels age as they consume the souls in order to ferry the souls either to heaven or to hell. The unexpected happens as Eiji begins to age rapidly, leaving Kouki to wonder about the short time they have left together.

Erotic Manga
November
A Paperback Original
5¼ x 7½ | 200 pp
TP US $12.99
CAN $15.95
978-1-933809-34-2
CUSA

Illicit Contract
(Yaoi)
Kei Momoyama

A gentlemanly business affair that involves old rivals in a most unlikely deal. Tomoyuki and Tsuzuki have been rivals since their school days. But when their companies merge, it looks like they'll have to learn to work together for a change. Then, Tsuzuki discovers Tomoyuki's secret. How long can Tomoyuki bear the blackmail?

Chronicle of the Divine Sword v01

(Yaoi)

Uki Ogasawara

Erotic Manga
November
A Paperback Original
5¼ x 7½ | 184 pp
TP US $12.99
CAN $15.95
978-1-933809-03-8
CUSA

The ninja, Shinkai Sumida, gained immortality from Shiva, god of a magical sword. Four hundred years later, he meets Tsunaie Hirasaka, a man whom he's already killed once, and has vowed to continue killing through the endless cycle of reincarnations. What was the oath that compels Shinkai to continue living such an existence?

Chronicle of the Divine Sword v02

(Yaoi)

Uki Ogasawara

Erotic Manga
February
A Paperback Original
5¼ x 7½ | 184 pp
TP US $12.99
CAN $15.95
978-1-933809-51-9
CUSA

As Shinkai attempts to fulfill his vow against his enemy, Tsunaie Hirasaka, he is thwarted each time by his own conflicting emotions. Why was the vow made, and can Shinkai continue on this path of destruction? In the last installment of the series, the oath is revealed through Shinkai's efforts to change his destiny.

La Vita Rosa

(Yaoi)

Akira Honma

Erotic Manga
November
A Paperback Original
5¼ x 7½ | 200 pp
TP US $12.99
CAN $15.95
978-1-933809-86-1
CUSA

Miyamoto works for the sales division of a major insurance company. He's attracted to his cool and beautiful boss, Himuro. However, his courtship is thwarted by the return of the company president, Takarada. It's now become a three-way parley in a fierce battle for Himuro's affections!

Office love and hijinx from *Publishers Weekly* 2006 Top Ten Manga author Akira Honma!

Spirit of the Roses

(Yaoi)

Norikazu Akira

Erotic Manga
November
A Paperback Original
5¼ x 7½ | 200 pp
TP US $12.99
CAN $15.95
978-1-933809-64-9
CUSA

Prodigal son Reiji Naruse returns home to inherit the family business of Naruse Corporation (aka The Naruse Yakuza Group). Along with the assets, he also inherits the company's skillful, seductive, and fiercely loyal negotiator, Kikuchi. Kikuchi has pledged his life to the Naruse family, but where will that loyalty lead when it concerns Reiji's personal life?

Erotic Manga
December
A Paperback Original
5¼ x 7½ | 184 pp
TP US $12.99
CAN $15.95
978-1-933809-16-8
CUSA

10K ¥ Lover

(Yaoi)

Dr. Ten

A homeless boy is taken in one night by a stranger, but this stranger doesn't give charity. So, what does he want? *Sex!*

Can our homeless hero handle his master's libido? What will he do when his master wants to sell him? What about his master's horny younger brother? And most importantly—what the heck are their names?!

Erotic Manga
December
A Paperback Original
5¼ x 7½ | 200 pp
TP US $12.99
CAN $15.50
978-1-933809-52-6
CUSA

Temptation

(Yaoi)

Momiji Maeda

Alvere is a jaded aristocrat, Nicolae a naïve young priest. Their paths cross when fate throws Nicolae in front of Alvere's carriage, and the nobleman finds himself entranced with Nicolae's beauty and purity. Nicolae believes he can offer Alvere solace in God, but this wolf in sheep's clothing wants nothing to do with God, and everything to do with Nicolae.

Erotic Manga
December
A Paperback Original
5¼ x 7½ | 200 pp
TP US $12.99
CAN $15.95
978-1-933809-62-5
CUSA

Awakening Desires

(Yaoi)

Bohra Naono

What do you do when the person you're in love with is too old for you? Or your best friend? Or you're the one who's too old? This is a collection of romantic stories about the sweetness that is first love.

Bohra Naono is a very popular author and has a large fan base in both the United States and Europe.

Erotic Manga
December
A Paperback Original
5¼ x 7½ | 184 pp
TP US $12.99
CAN $15.95
978-1-933809-63-2
CUSA

Devil x Devil

(Yaoi)

Sachiyo Sawauchi

Hotei is a low-level devil living on Earth. Being a devil in disguise is harder than it seems, especially when Hotei has to compete with a fallen angel, Suzaku. For Suzaku, life on Earth is quite heavenly, and it's made sweeter by his conquest of one very unlucky devil.

DramaQueen

KinZetsu x Eden

(Yaoi)

Inami Hajime

Erotic Manga
January
A Paperback Original
5¼ x 7½ | 200 pp
TP US $12.99
CAN $15.95
978-1-933809-90-8
CUSA

Here are six stories about high school boys, their romantic antics, and their sexual libidos. The secret life of high school boys (in uniforms!) is exposed: What are their fears? Their aspirations? And find out the answer to the most pressing question on their minds: What comes first, lust or sex? Does it matter?

Possessive Love

(Yaoi)

Ruri Fujikawa

Erotic Manga
January
A Paperback Original
5¼ x 7½ | 200 pp
TP US $12.99
CAN $15.95
978-1-933809-67-0
CUSA

Takano is an art teacher who was almost raped by one of his students, but is rescued by his colleague, Ogata. Takano expresses his gratitude, only to have Ogata blackmail him. Takano thinks he has no choice but to consent to Ogata's request. However, as time passes, Takano discovers Ogata's true motives for their "relationship."

Instinctively a Man

(Yaoi)

Takashi Kanzaki

Erotic Manga
January
A Paperback Original
5¼ x 7½ | 200 pp
TP US $12.99
CAN $15.95
978-1-933809-59-5
CUSA

Yasukuni is the heir of a distinguished family, one that prizes masculinity and stoicism. He also happens to be crazy about one of his private instructors, Kiyoi. Among the many lessons Kiyoi gives him is the art of sexual pleasures. However, Yasukuni wants Kiyoi to make love with him earnestly, not just as a form of instruction.

Can't Help Gettin' Hurt

(Yaoi)

Mika Sadahiro

Erotic Manga
February
A Paperback Original
5¼ x 7½ | 200 pp
TP US $12.99
CAN $15.50
978-1-933809-69-4
CUSA

Shouji thinks his boyfriend's first love, Terumi, might still have feelings for Honami, so he goes to investigate. He discovers that Terumi is happily married. Now, it's Shouji who can't get Terumi out of his head. Things become more complicated when Honami's lingering feelings for Terumi surface.

Cult author **Mika Sadahiro** is known for her style of angst-infused and sex-driven plots.

Erotic Manga
February
A Paperback Original
5¼ x 7½ | 200 pp
TP US $12.99
CAN $15.95
978-1-933809-65-6
CUSA

Wicked Love Song

(Yaoi)

Kaoru Kyogoku

Choco and Aasan met on a heavenly tropical island. Aasan seduced Choco with his sweet words, but in reality he's completely vicious! Choco's fiancé had left him on the rocks; what surprising path will he take in the midst of this sadness?

Included in this volume are three short stories that highlight the things we do for love.

Erotic Manga
February
A Paperback Original
5¼ x 7½ | 200 pp
TP US $12.99
CAN $15.95
978-1-933809-56-4
CUSA

A Love That Conquers Gods

(Yaoi)

Akira Honma

On his trip to New York City, college student Takeru gets lost in the wrong part of town. He gets attacked, but is rescued by a man named Rei. Touched by Rei's kindness, Takeru can't help being attracted to him. But then Takeru discovers that Rei is the second-highest-ranking mafia man in New York City. Can love overcome such odds?

Erotic Manga
March
A Paperback Original
5¼ x 7½ | 200 pp
TP US $12.99
CAN $15.95
978-1-933809-79-3
CUSA

NOT FOR SALE!

(Yaoi)

Sanae Rokuya

Nozomi is a boring and late-blooming college student. His classmate, Ryuji, is an extremely dangerous delivery host. When Nozomi witnesses a steamy kiss between Ryuji and a male teacher, he's thunderstruck! His eyes can't seem to stop following Ryuji's movements. If Ryuji has any say (and he does!), Nozomi is just about to get a taste of paradise.

Manga
December
A Paperback Original
5¼ x 7½ | 184 pp
TP US $11.99
CAN $14.50
978-1-933809-12-0
CUSA

8 MM v03

(Romance)

You Na

When Suk-hyun's young cousins come to visit him, Suk-hyun can't believe his bad luck. Will he be able to take care of them well? How will Suk-hyun pretend to be a good role model? What happens when he realizes the truth about his young cousin, Eunjee? As if that wasn't enough, Auntie is in love!

8 MM v04
(Romance)
You Na

Manga
February
A Paperback Original
5¼ x 7½ | 184 pp
TP US $11.99
CAN $14.50
978-1-933809-13-7
CUSA

A mysterious fortuneteller tells Jae-young that the three men she is destined to meet will die because of her! Jae-young is worried that Suk-hyun is one of them, and Suk-hyun certainly does seem to get into more accidents than he can handle. Is Suk-hyun one of the men in Jae-young's destiny? If so, does it mean his death?

Audition v07
(Romance)
Kye Young Chon

Manga
January
A Paperback Original
5¼ x 7½ | 184 pp
TP US $11.99
CAN $14.50
978-1-933809-49-6
CUSA

The fourth level of the audition: The Recycle Band has hung on amidst the shaky support they have received. The team has become eager. They must be careful not to let their guard down. But will they survive the next level? Or will personal issues and difficulties get in the way of reaching their goal?

Vision v08
(Romance)
Lin Yu-Chin

Manga
February
A Paperback Original
5¼ x 7½ | 184 pp
TP US $10.99
CAN $13.50
978-1-933809-11-3
CUSA

A mysterious prince from a faraway land enters the lives of our fragile lovers. What troubles will he bring? Will the Tang Kingdom be saved? Or will this plummet Nurhan onto the brink of destruction?

DVD v07
(Romance)
Kye Young Chon

Manga
February
A Paperback Original
5¼ x 7½ | 184 pp
TP US $11.99
CAN $14.50
978-1-933809-41-0
CUSA

Sajang has voluntarily resigned from school. He has decided to study with Ddam for the college-entrance exam. But where is she? Can she trust him? Can Sajang get back with Ddam? In the meantime, although Ddam was warned about the relationship with Venu, she can't help falling for him.

Vision of the Other Side v02
(Manga)
Lin Yu-Chin

Erotic Manga
5 x 8 | 176 pp
TP US $10.99 | CAN $13.50
978-1-933809-05-2 CUSA

Audition v02
(Romance)
Kye Young Chon

Manga
5 x 8 | 176 pp
TP US $11.99 | CAN $14.50
978-1-933809-44-1 CUSA

Your Honest Deceit v02
(Yaoi)
Sakufu Ajimine

Erotic Manga
5 x 8 | 200 pp
TP US $12.99 | CAN $15.95
978-1-933809-21-2 CUSA

Lovely Sick v02
(Yaoi)
Shoko Ohmine

Erotic Manga
5 x 8 | 176 pp
TP US $12.99 | CAN $15.95
978-1-933809-01-4 CUSA

The Tyrant Falls in Love v01
(Yaoi)
Hinako Takanaga

Erotic Manga
5 x 8 | 200 pp
TP US $12.99 | CAN $15.95
978-1-933809-31-1 CUSA

The Summit v01
(Boys' Love)
Young Hee Lee

Manga
5 x 8 | 192 pp
TP US $12.99 | CAN $15.95
978-1-933809-53-3 CUSA

India Notes
Photographs by Raghu Rai
with Tiziano Terzani

India Notes is a dialogue between two wonderful visions of India, between two almost magically matching points of view: one from a Westerner in love with the country, and one from a local, perhaps the greatest Indian photographer, who spent his life reporting on this huge territory and its recent changes. It's about India in all its complexity, its contrasts, its immemorial culture, and its people.

Photography
September
10 x 9 | 144 pp
70 Color and B&W photographs
TC US $54.00 | CAN $65.00
978-2-916355-11-5 CUSA

**Legendary photographer Raghu Rai
tells us about India, his country.**

Cinema
Photographs by Xavier Lambours

For more than twenty-five years, Xavier Lambours has portrayed those who made cinema a myth: actors (Robert De Niro, Clint Eastwood, Harvey Keitel, Sean Connery, Harrison Ford, Nicole Kidman, Liz Taylor), directors (Martin Scorsese, David Lynch, Orson Welles, François Truffaut, Wong Kar-Wai), screenwriters, cinematographers, and set decorators; they all played the portrait game under the direction of this hugely talented eye.

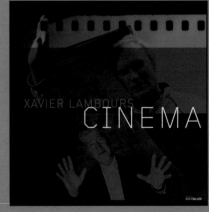

Photography / Film & TV
November
11 x 11 | 224 pp
200 B&W photographs
TC US $60.00 | CAN $72.00
978-2-916355-13-9 CUSA

**Two hundred portraits of the
biggest movie stars from the
last three decades.**

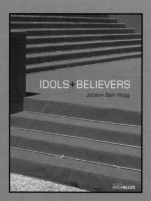

Idols+Believers
Photographs by Jocelyn Bain Hogg

Photography / Film & TV
9½ x 11½ | 224 pp
200 Color and B&W photographs
TC US $45.00 | CAN $54.00
978-2-916355-00-9 CUSA

Children of Abraham
Photographs by Abbas

Photography
7 x 9 | 240 pp
140 B&W photographs
TP US $34.00 | CAN $41.00
978-2-916355-01-6 CUSA

Tokyo Love Hello
Photographs by Chris Steele-Perkins
Foreword by Donald Richie

Photography
9 x 7 | 240 pp
100 Color photographs
TC US $40.00 | CAN $48.00
978-2-916355-05-4 CUSA

Chalk Lines: The Caucasus
Photographs by Stanley Greene

Photography
10 x 9 | 128 pp
100 B&W photographs
TC US $40.00 | CAN $48.00
978-2-916355-10-8 CUSA

The Kravchenko Case
One Man's War On Stalin
Gary Kern

Based on the private, unpublished papers of Victor Kravchenko, never before available to researchers and historians; hundreds of FBI documents won after a six-year lawsuit under the Freedom of Information Act; and extensive interviews with the defector's sons and associates, *The Kravchenko Case* tells the story of a man who broke away from the closed Soviet society, defected to America, and then waged a one-man war against Stalin's dictatorial regime.

Marketing Plans
Co-op available

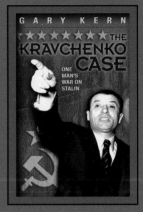

History
October
A Paperback Original
6 x 9 | 760 pp
TP US $28.00 | CAN $33.95
978-1-929631-73-5 CUSA

Victor Kravchenko—the most discussed case of a Soviet defector at the height of the Cold War.

The Mafia and the Allies
Sicily 1943 and the Return of the Mafia
Ezio Costanzo
Translated by George Lawrence

Within weeks of the Pearl Harbor attack and the declaration of war on the United States by Germany and Italy, US war plans included the defense of the East Coast and the invasion of Sicily. Here, Ezio Costanzo examines the many elements of this secret scenario, which includes long-suppressed information about cooperation between the Mafia and the US Army. The results came in the aftermath of the invasion, during the new military government that gave many Mafia leaders important administrative positions. Seen from an Italian standpoint, the success of US forces is examined in detail and many questions are finally answered.

Marketing Plans
Co-op available

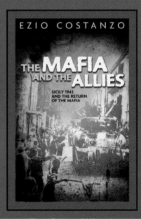

True Crime / History
September
A Paperback Original
6 x 9 | 250 pp
40 B&W photographs
TP US $17.00 | CAN $20.50
978-1-929631-68-1 CUSA

The Mafia returns to Sicily with the Allies in 1943. The whole story told by a Sicilian historian.

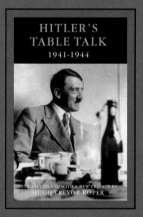

Hitler's Gift to France
The Return of the Ashes of Napoleon II
Georges Poisson
Translated by Robert L. Miller

In the dead of the winter of 1940, Hitler decided to return from its burial place in Vienna the ashes of Napoleon II, known as the "Aiglon," the only son of the emperor Napoleon. The gesture was intended to win the support of the French people, but only managed to precipitate a political crisis at Vichy, where Marshal Pétain ordered the pro-German Deputy Prime Minister Pierre Laval arrested. Based on new research and previously unknown documents, the author, historian Georges Poisson, at last sheds light on an incident most historians—including Robert O. Paxton—have been at a loss to explain.

Marketing Plans
Co-op available

History
November
A Paperback Original
6 x 9 | 250 pp
30 B&W photographs
TP US $19.00 | CAN $23.00
978-1-929631-67-4 CUSA

A mystery of the Nazi occupation of France is at last explained by new research.

Hitler's Table Talk 1941–1944
Secret Conversations
Edited by H.R. Trevor-Roper
Introduction by Gerhard L. Weinberg

This is a new edition of a major document from World War II with additional, previously unavailable texts assembled from the stenographic record of Hitler's informal conversations ordered by Martin Bormann. These texts remain the classic collection of Hitler's nighttime monologues with his entourage, covering mostly nonmilitary subjects and long-range plans. Hitler lets his thoughts wander, never failing to provide an opinion on every subject. Additional documents from various archives make this the most complete English-language edition in print.

History
December
6 x 9 | 750 pp
TP US $24.00 | CAN $30.00
978-1-929631-66-7 CUSA

New material adds value to this classic edition, with a new introduction by historian Gerhard L. Weinberg.

Enigma Books

Paris Weekend
A Spy Novel
Sergei Kostin
Translated by Todd Bludeau

KGB operative Paco Araya is a mole who runs a travel agency in Manhattan, where he's been living for many years. Suddenly, on a secret mission in Paris, he discovers by accident that the man he's wanted to kill for many years happens to be within reach. Why does Paco want to kill this man, a known international terrorist very much reminiscent of the infamous Carlos the Jackal? Espionage and personal vengeance provide a deadly mix in this masterful Russian version of John Le Carré.

Marketing Plans
Co-op available

Fiction
January
A Paperback Original
Enigma Thrillers
5½ x 8¼ | 250 pp
TP US $15.00 | CAN $18.00
978-1-929631-70-4 CUSA

A KGB mole in New York City finds a long-lost enemy during a Paris trip.

The Shattered Sky
Bernard Uzan
Translated by Robert L. Miller

Fiction
February
A Paperback Original
Enigma Thrillers
5½ x 8¼ | 250 pp
TP US $15.00
CAN $18.00
978-1-929631-71-1
CUSA

To be down and out in Paris as a young man: The twenty-one-year-old hero struggles to survive, taking multiple jobs, including that of secret agent for the French government. After the untimely deaths of his father and his brother, he takes on the struggle for daily existence, overcoming enormous handicaps as a polio survivor, living as a Jew in anti-Semitic France, and the desperate search for work and for love, while the call of adventure opens up the long road toward finding himself. A first novel translated from the French.

Operation Neptune
The Secret Attack on New York
Arno Baker

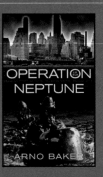

Fiction
March
A Paperback Original
Enigma Thrillers
5½ x 8¼ | 300 pp
TP US $15.00
CAN $18.00
978-1-929631-72-8
CUSA

Weeks before the attack on Pearl Harbor, a secret offensive is underway. Vital convoys bound for England and Russia are subjected to the stealth weapons of Mussolini's frogmen operating inside a peaceful New York harbor with the Mafia's assistance. A young FBI agent takes the case all the way to J. Edgar Hoover and President Franklin Delano Roosevelt.

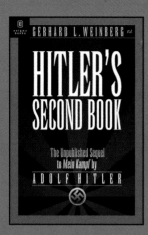

Hitler's Second Book
The Unpublished Sequel to
Mein Kampf
Edited by Gerhard L. Weinberg

History
6 x 9 | 330 pp
TP US $15.00 | CAN $18.00
978-1-929631-61-2 CUSA

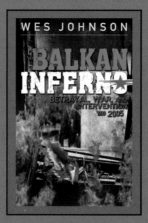

Balkan Inferno
Betrayal, War, and Intervention
1990–2005
Wes Johnson

Current Affairs
6 x 9 | 525 pp
40 B&W photographs, charts and maps
TP US $26.00 | CAN $31.50
978-1-929631-63-6 CUSA

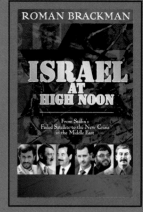

Israel at High Noon
From Stalin's Failed Satellite to the
New Crisis in the Middle East
Roman Brackman

History
6 x 9 | 320 pp
TP US $23.00 | CAN $27.95
978-1-929631-64-3 CUSA

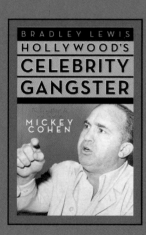

Hollywood's Celebrity
Gangster
The Incredible Life and Times
of Mickey Cohen
Bradley Lewis

True Crime
6 x 9 | 425 pp
50 B&W photographs
TP US $22.00 | CAN $26.50
978-1-929631-65-0 CUSA

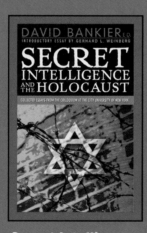

Secret Intelligence
and the Holocaust
Essays from the Colloquium at the City
University of New York, May 2003
Edited by David Bankier
Introduction by Gerhard L. Weinberg

History
6 x 9 | 320 pp
16 B&W photographs
TP US $23.00 | CAN $27.95
978-1-929631-60-5 CUSA

The Origins of the
War of 1914
Luigi Albertini

History
6 x 9 | 2,100 pp
TP US $95.00 | CAN $114.00
978-1-929631-26-1 CUSA
A three-volume set

Lions at Lamb House
Edwin M. Yoder Jr.

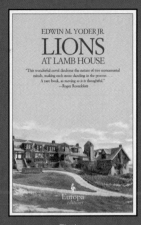

"This wonderful novel discloses the nature of two monumental minds, making each more dazzling in the process. . . . A rare book, as moving as it is thoughtful."
—Roger Rosenblatt

In 1908, an Austrian psychiatrist visits southern England at the urgent request of a Boston colleague, who fears his brother's intention to rewrite his early novels may be the sign of debilitating neuroses. The Austrian doctor is Sigmund Freud. The Boston psychologist is William James, and the novelist is his brother Henry. Over ten days, the worlds of psychology and literature collide—giving rise to this charming novel of ideas.

Marketing Plans
Co-op available • Advance reader copies • 10,000-copy print run

Author Hometown: Washington, DC

Fiction
September
A Paperback Original
5¼ x 8¼ | 280 pp
TP US $14.95 | CAN $18.00
978-1-933372-34-1 CUSA

A thoughtful and vibrant historical novel written by a Pulitzer Prize-winning author.

The Lost Sailors
Jean-Claude Izzo
Translated by Howard Curtis

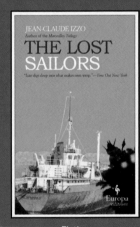

"Izzo digs deep into what makes men weep."—*Time Out New York*

In this moving investigation into the human comedy, the men aboard an impounded freighter in the port of Marseilles are divided: Wait for the money owed them, or accept their fate and abandon ship? Captain Abdul Aziz is determined to save his charge and do the right thing by his men. In these close quarters charged with physical and emotional tension, each life begins to resemble a chapter in the complex, colorful, and tragic story of the Mediterranean Sea itself—rich with romance, legend, passion, and drama.

Marketing Plans
Co-op available • Advance reader copies • 10,000-copy print run

Fiction
September
A Paperback Original
5¼ x 8¼ | 280 pp
TP US $14.95 | CAN $18.00
978-1-933372-35-8 CUSA

A richly textured, bittersweet investigation into the human comedy.

The Queen of the Tambourine
Jane Gardam

Fiction
September
5¼ x 8¼ | 226 pp
TP $14.95
978-1-933372-36-5 USA

A Whitbread Award-winning, darkly comic novel of a woman losing and regaining control of her life.

"Funny and moving."—*The New York Times*

In prose vibrant and witty, *The Queen of the Tambourine* traces the emotional breakdown—and eventual restoration—of Eliza Peabody, a smart and wildly imaginative woman who has become unbearably isolated in her prosperous London neighborhood. Eliza must reach the depths of her downward spiral before she can once again find health and serenity. This story of a woman's confrontation with the realities of sanity will delight readers who enjoy the works of Anita Brookner, Sybille Bedford, Muriel Spark, and Sylvia Plath. Winner of the Whitbread Award for Best Novel of the Year.

Marketing Plans
Co-op available • Advance reader copies • 12,000-copy print run

Broken Colors
Michele Zackheim

Fiction / Women's Literature
October
A Paperback Original
5¼ x 8¼ | 300 pp
TP US $14.95 | CAN $18.00
978-1-933372-37-2 CUSA

An accomplished woman's journey toward the making of great art and the nature of love.

"A profoundly original, beautifully written work, so emotionally accurate that it tears at the heart. I read it without stopping."—Gerald Stern

Sophie Marks' path to artistic and personal fulfillment takes her from World War II England to postwar Paris and the Italian countryside. She leaves Europe in 1967 and spends the next two decades in the American Southwest. Acclaimed at last as an artist, she returns to England to confront the hidden memories of her childhood and test the possibilities of a renewed love, a passion ripened by maturity.

Marketing Plans
Co-op available • Advance reader copies • 10,000-copy print run
Author Hometown: New York, NY

Europa Editions

Fairy Tale Timpa

Altan

Translated by Michael Reynolds

"Altan is one of the geniuses of Italian illustration . . . for years he has made Italians of all ages think and dream."—*RAI Books*

"A veritable classic that every home must have on its bookshelves. . . . Timpa is a friend to wile away the hours with. . . . She speaks with animals, adults, objects, plants, even with shoes, she observes the world with interest, deep feeling, respect and wonder. [Timpa] continues to attract and fascinate children that belong to widely divergent generations."—*La Stampa*

In this new series of nine short Timpa adventures, our little pink-spotted heroine doesn't just read fairy tales, she inhabits them—stepping right into the world of Sleeping Beauty, Pinocchio, and even the Frog Prince.

Timpa has been the best-loved children's character in Italy for decades, spawning television programs, animated films, all manner of merchandising, and dozens of imitators. *Fairy Tale Timpa* includes nine new Timpa adventures accompanied by Altan's captivating full-color illustrations. For readers aged two to six.

Nine new Timpa adventures for our youngest readers featuring Altan's full-color illustrations.

Children's Fiction
November
A Paperback Original
8¼ x 11½ | 48 pp
42 Color illustrations
TP US $14.95 | CAN $18.00
978-1-933372-38-9 CUSA

Marketing Plans

Co-op available
Publishers Weekly BEA galley program

Also Available

Here Comes Timpa
Altan
Translated by Michael Reynolds
Children's Fiction
8¼ x 11½ | 48 pp
42 Color illustrations
TP US $14.95 | CAN $18.00
978-1-933372-28-0 CUSA

Timpa Goes to the Sea
Altan
Translated by Michael Reynolds
Children's Fiction
8¼ x 11½ | 48 pp
42 Color illustrations
TP US $14.95 | CAN $18.00
978-1-933372-32-7 CUSA

Europa Editions

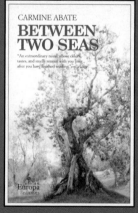

Zeroville
Steve Erickson

"Erickson is as unique and vital and pure a voice as American fiction has produced."—Jonathan Lethem

A film-obsessed ex-seminarian with images of Elizabeth Taylor and Montgomery Clift tattooed on his head arrives on Hollywood Boulevard in 1969. Vikar Jerome enters the vortex of a cultural transformation: rock and roll, sex, drugs, and—most important to him—the decline of the movie studios and the rise of independent directors. Jerome becomes a film editor of astonishing vision. Through encounters with former starlets, burglars, political guerrillas, punk musicians, and veteran filmmakers, he discovers the secret that lies in every movie ever made.

Marketing Plans

Co-op available • Advance reader copies • 10,000-copy print run

Author Hometown: Los Angeles, CA

Fiction
November
A Paperback Original
5¼ x 8¼ | 380 pp
TP US $15.95 | CAN $19.50
978-1-933372-39-6 CUSA

Nathanael West meets Tarantino when a movie-obsessed ex-seminarian turns into a film editor of astonishing skill.

Between Two Seas
Carmine Abate
Translated by Antony Shugaar

The US debut of one of Italy's great contemporary storytellers: The photographer Hans Heumann travels to southern Italy in search of the light that has long attracted artists. There he meets Giorgio Bellusci, who dreams of rebuilding the south's most famous inn. The dark secret behind Giorgio's obsession will change the course of both men's lives.

The first of Carmine Abate's novels to appear in English and the winner of the Fenice-Europa Prize for fiction, this is a touching journey that takes readers to the storied heart of Italy and accompanies them on an exploration into the meaning of memory.

Marketing Plans

Co-op available • Advance reader copies • 10,000-copy print run

Fiction / Mystery
January
A Paperback Original
5¼ x 8¼ | 196 pp
TP US $14.95 | CAN $18.00
978-1-933372-40-2 CUSA

A journey to the heart of Italy and an exploration into the meaning of memory.

Europa Editions

The Have-Nots
Katharina Hacker
Translated by Helen Atkins

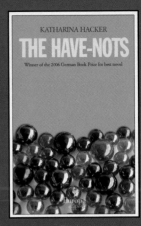

The Have-Nots is the winner of the 2006 German Book Prize for best novel and was praised by the jury for having confronted our age's most pressing issues: "[Katharina Hacker's] protagonists are in their thirties, they know it all but know nothing of themselves. . . . Their questions are our questions."

In one of three interweaving storylines, Jakob and Isabelle move to London, where Jakob will fill the post of a colleague killed in the World Trade Center attack. But their relationship, like the world they once knew and the happiness they once shared, becomes more fragile with each passing day.

Marketing Plans
Co-op available • Advance reader copies • 10,000-copy print run

Fiction
February
A Paperback Original
5¼ x 8¼ | 300 pp
TP US $14.95 | CAN $18.00
978-1-933372-41-9 CUSA

A *Bright Lights, Big City* for the post-9/11 generation.

The Lost Daughter
Elena Ferrante
Translated by Ann Goldstein

"Elena Ferrante will blow you away."—Alice Sebold, author of *The Lovely Bones*

From the author of *The Days of Abandonment*, *The Lost Daughter* is Elena Ferrante's most compelling and perceptive meditation on womanhood and motherhood yet. Leda, a middle-aged divorcée, is alone for the first time in years when her daughters leave home to live with their father. Her initial, unexpected sense of liberty turns to ferocious introspection following a seemingly trivial occurrence. Ferrante's language is as finely tuned and intense as ever, and she treats her theme with a fierce, candid tenacity.

Marketing Plans
Co-op available • Advance reader copies • 12,000-copy print run

Fiction / Women's Literature
March
A Paperback Original
5¼ x 8¼ | 204 pp
TP US $14.95 | CAN $18.00
978-1-933372-42-6 CUSA

A complex, controlled, piercing meditation on womanhood and motherhood.

Europa Editions

Margherita Dolce Vita
Stefano Benni
Translated by Antony Shugaar

Fiction
5¼ x 8¼ | 208 pp
TP US $14.95 | CAN $18.00
978-1-933372-20-4 CUSA

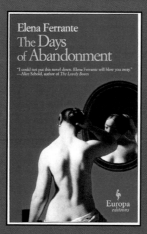

The Days of Abandonment
Elena Ferrante
Translated by Ann Goldstein

Fiction
5¼ x 8¼ | 192 pp
TP US $14.95 | CAN $18.00
978-1-933372-00-6 CUSA

Old Filth
Jane Gardam

Fiction
5¼ x 8¼ | 256 pp
TP $14.95
978-1-933372-13-6 USA

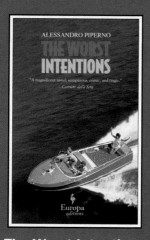

The Worst Intentions
Alessandro Piperno
Translated by Ann Goldstein

Fiction
5¼ x 8½ | 320 pp
TP US $14.95 | CAN $18.00
978-1-933372-33-4 CUSA

Cooking with Fernet Branca
James Hamilton-Paterson

Fiction
5¼ x 8¼ | 288 pp
TP US $14.95 | CAN $18.00
978-1-933372-01-3 CUSA

The Goodbye Kiss
Massimo Carlotto
Translated by Lawrence Venuti

Fiction
5¼ x 8¼ | 194 pp
TP US $14.95 | CAN $18.00
978-1-933372-05-1 CUSA

The Amputated Memory
A Novel
Werewere Liking
Translated by Marjolijn de Jager
Afterword by Michelle Mielly

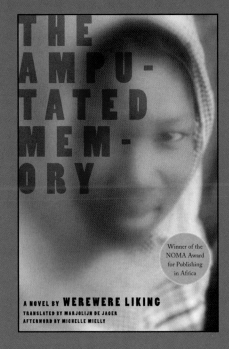

A modern-day *Things Fall Apart, The Amputated Memory* explores the ways in which an African woman's memory preserves, and strategically forgets, moments in her tumultuous past as well as the cultural past of her country.

Pinned between the political ambitions of her philandering father, the colonial and global influences of encroaching and exploitive governments, and the traditions of her Cameroon village, Halla Njokè recalls childhood traumas and reconstructs forgotten experiences to reclaim her sense of self. Winner of the Noma Award—previous honorees include Mamphela Ramphele, Ngugi wa Thiong'o, and Ken Saro-Wiwa—*The Amputated Memory* was called by the Noma jury "a truly remarkable achievement . . . a deeply felt presentation of the female condition in Africa; and a celebration of women as the country's memory."

Since 1978, Cameroon-born *artiste extraordinaire* **Werewere Liking** has been living in the Ivory Coast, where she established the Village Ki-Yi, a self-supporting center for the performing and fine arts. A singer, dancer, actor, playwright, songwriter, and author of two titles previously published in the United States, Liking has been honored across the globe for her writing and theater work; she has performed at such venues as the Kennedy Center.

Marjolijn de Jager teaches French, Dutch, and literary translation at New York University and works as an independent literary translator, most recently on Assia Djebar's *Children of the New World.*

Michelle Mielly received her PhD from Harvard University and now teaches in the Department of Comparative Literature at Pennsylvania State University.

A Noma Award-winning novel called "a deeply felt presentation of the female condition in Africa."

Fiction / African Studies
November
Women Writing Africa
5½ x 8½ | 400 pp
TC US $24.95 | CAN $30.00
978-1-55861-555-7 CUSA

Marketing Plans

Co-op available

Also Available

You Can't Get Lost in Cape Town
Zoë Wicomb
Afterword by Carol Sicherman
Fiction
5½ x 8½ | 240 pp
TP US $15.95 | CAN $19.50
978-1-55861-225-9 CUSA

David's Story
Zoë Wicomb
Afterword by Dorothy Driver
Fiction
5½ x 8½ | 288 pp
TP US $14.95 | CAN $18.00
978-1-55861-398-0 CUSA

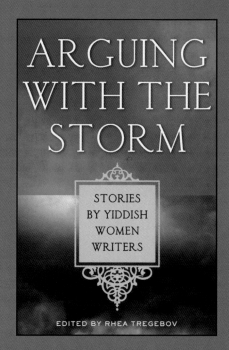

Fiction / Jewish Studies
November
Jewish Women Writers
5½ x 8½ | 128 pp
9 B&W photographs
TP $14.95
978-1-55861-558-8 USA
LB x $55.00
978-1-55861-559-5 USA

Marketing Plans

Co-op available

Author Hometown: Vancouver, BC

Arguing with the Storm
Stories by Yiddish Women Writers
Edited by Rhea Tregebov

From the *shtetl* to the New World, from failed revolutions in tsarist Russia to the Holocaust, these Yiddish tales illuminate a lost world from a woman's distinctive perspective. For decades, stories by Yiddish women writers were available only to those who spoke the "mother tongue" of Eastern European Jews. This translation brings some of the women writers of the golden age of Yiddish to English-speaking readers.

Their stories range from the wryly humorous—a girl seeking a wet nurse for her cousin brings him to a *shiksa,* with dire consequences—to the bittersweet, as a once-idealistic revolutionary now sees her hopes for humanity as "fantasy." The title is from a poem that describes a widow arguing with a storm that threatens her harvest. It is a metaphor for the Holocaust, whose dark cloud was rising. *Arguing with the Storm* is a joy to read and a tribute to all those women, who, in arguing with the storm, fought to protect their families and way of life.

The anthology includes works by Sarah Hamer-Jacklyn, Bryna Bercovitch, Anne Viderman, Malka Lee, Frume Halpern, Rochel Bruches, Paula Frankel-Zaltzman, Chava Rosenfarb, and Rikuda Potash.

Rhea Tregebov teaches creative writing at the University of British Columbia and is the author of six critically acclaimed books of poetry, most recently *(alive): Poems New and Selected.* She collected these tales with the help of the Winnipeg Women's Yiddish Reading Circle.

From the *shtetl* to the Holocaust, lost voices from a rich and lively tradition.

Also Available

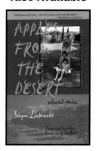

Apples from the Desert
Selected Stories
Savyon Liebrecht
Foreword by Grace Paley
Introduction by Lily Rattok
Fiction / Jewish Studies
5¼ x 8½ | 240 pp
TP US $13.95 | CAN $17.00
978-1-55861-235-8 CUSA

The Feminist Press at CUNY

The Loved Ones
A Modern Arabic Novel
Alia Mamdouh
Translated by Marilyn L. Booth
Foreword by Hélène Cixous

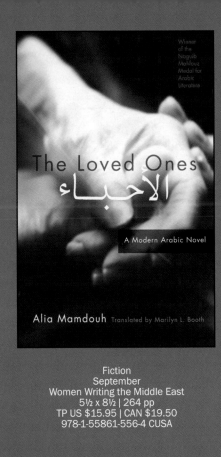

"Leaves an indelible impression. [*The Loved Ones*] is rich with family and neighbors and [Alia Mamdouh] notes all of their subtle interactions and secrets."—*Library Journal*

"Often intense and lyrical."—*Kirkus Reviews*

This winner of the Naguib Mahfouz Medal for Literature mingles memories of the past with the shifting voices of the present when the estranged son of an Iraqi exile flies from his home in Toronto to visit her in Paris. As his ailing mother, the once-vibrant Suhaila, lies in a hospital bed, he acquaints himself with her constellation of close friends. Immediately, he becomes immersed in the complex relationships he has fought so hard to avoid with both his mother and his war-torn homeland. Alia Mamdouh weaves a magical tale of the human condition in this stunning and beautifully written novel of faith, family, and hope.

Alia Mamdouh is the author of essays, short stories, and four novels, including the most widely translated, *Naphtalene.* Born in Iraq, she now lives in exile in Paris.

Marilyn Booth is a translator of Middle Eastern fiction and autobiographies. She received her BA from Harvard-Radcliffe and her DPhil from Oxford University, and has taught at Brown University and the American University in Cairo. Currently, she is visiting associate professor of comparative literature at the University of Illinois at Urbana-Champaign.

Hélène Cixous is a world-renowned French feminist theorist, critic, essayist, novelist, and playwright.

A Mahfouz Medal-winner that weaves together a tender tale of bittersweet love between a mother and son.

Fiction
September
Women Writing the Middle East
5½ x 8½ | 264 pp
TP US $15.95 | CAN $19.50
978-1-55861-556-4 CUSA

Marketing Plans

Co-op available

Also Available

Naphtalene
Alia Mamdouh
Translated by Peter Theroux
Foreword by Hélène Cixous
Fiction
5½ x 8½ | 214 pp
TP US $15.95 | CAN $19.50
978-1-55861-493-2 CUSA

Children of the New World
A Novel of the Algerian War
Assia Djebar
Translated by Marjolijn de Jager
Afterword by Clarisse Zimra
Fiction / African Studies
5½ x 8½ | 224 pp
TP US $15.95 | CAN $19.50
978-1-55861-510-6 CUSA

The Feminist Press at CUNY

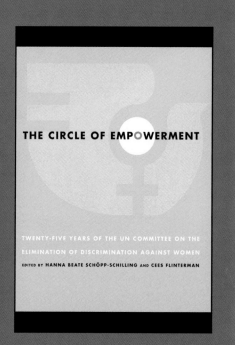

Current Affairs /
Political Science & Government
December
6 x 9 | 392 pp
TP US $24.95 | CAN $30.00
978-1-55861-563-2 CUSA
LB x US $55.00 | CAN $66.00
978-1-55861-564-9 CUSA

The Circle of Empowerment
Twenty-five Years of the UN Committee on the Elimination of Discrimination against Women
Edited by Hanna Beate Schöpp-Schilling and Cees Flinterman

The Convention on the Elimination of All Forms of Discrimination against Women (CEDAW) is one of the most important human rights tools ever created. Adopted in 1979 by the United Nations General Assembly, it is often described as an international bill of rights for women. These essays and personal reflections, from individuals who have served on the committee that monitors CEDAW, introduce readers to the issues and the activism.

Only a handful of countries have refused to ratify CEDAW; the United States is the only industrialized country among them. *The Circle of Empowerment* reveals the profound impact the convention has had on women's lives around the world and its potential to affect US women. With examples and moving reminiscences from Japan to Tunisia to the Caribbean and beyond, this readable collection addresses CEDAW's impact on women in Islam, labor markets, migration, violence against women, human trafficking, women in politics, and more.

Hanna Beate Schöpp-Schilling has, since 1989, been a member of the CEDAW committee, where she has held the positions of rapporteur and vice chair. She is a lecturer and consultant on women, gender, youth, and human rights in Europe and Asia.

Cees Flinterman, a member of the CEDAW committee since 2002, is a professor of international law at Utrecht University in the Netherlands. He is director of the Netherlands Institute of Human Rights (SIM) and the School of Human Rights Research. He has served as a representative of the Netherlands to several UN human rights commissions.

Essays and personal reflections from former and current CEDAW committee members on discrimination against women.

Also Available

Developing Power
How Women Transformed International Development
Edited by Irene Tinker and Arvonne Fraser
Women's Studies
6 x 9 | 320 pp
TP US $26.95 | CAN $32.50
978-1-55861-484-0 CUSA

The Feminist Press at CUNY

Rites of Compassion

"Old Mrs. Harris" and "A Simple Heart"

Willa Cather and Gustave Flaubert

Edited by Mary Gordon

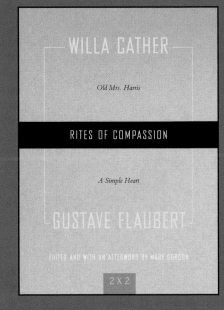

Personally selected by award-winning writer Mary Gordon, these two stories by Willa Cather and Gustave Flaubert render subtle portraits of characters whose sacrifices achieve nobility as they willingly serve people who take them for granted.

Set in a house Cather modeled on her own childhood home, "Old Mrs. Harris" depicts the staunch matriarch of a busy household; her tale and her life revolve around her ineffectual son-in-law, her displaced southern debutante daughter, and a bevy of grandchildren whose dreams seem out of reach. In "A Simple Heart," written by Flaubert at the request of George Sand, Félicité is a faithful servant first to a family fallen on hard times and then, shockingly, to a stuffed parrot she confuses with the Holy Spirit.

Cruel and honest, these two stories explore the ways in which families treat their aging members, the harsh impatience of the young, and the patient compassion of women who make their family's everyday lives possible.

Willa Cather (1873–1947), the Pulitzer Prize-winning author of more than fifteen books including *My Antonia, O Pioneers!,* and *One of Ours,* was one of the most distinguished American writers of the early twentieth century.

Gustave Flaubert (1821–1880) had limited writing success while he lived, but his works, *Madame Bovary* and *A Sentimental Education* in particular, are now recognized as masterpieces.

Mary Gordon is the author of six novels and the recipient of many awards, most recently the Story Prize for *The Stories of Mary Gordon.* She teaches at Barnard College in New York City.

Willa Cather and Gustave Flaubert's ultimate "servants" provide piercing commentary on aging and individuals taken for granted.

Fiction Anthology
October
A Paperback Original
Two By Two
5 x 7 | 152 pp
TP US $9.95 | CAN $12.00
978-1-55861-562-5 CUSA

Marketing Plans

Co-op available

Also Available

Here and Somewhere Else
Stories by Grace Paley and Robert Nichols
Introduction by Marianne Hirsch
Fiction Anthology
5 x 7 | 128 pp
TP US $12.95 | CAN $15.50
978-1-55861-537-3 CUSA

The Riddle of Life and Death
"Tell Me a Riddle" and
"The Death of Ivan Illych"
Tillie Olsen and Leo Tolstoy
Introduction by Jules Chametzky
Fiction Anthology
5 x 7 | 240 pp
TP US $12.95 | CAN $15.50
978-1-55861-536-6 CUSA

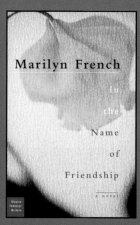

Fiction
February
Classic Feminist Writers
5½ x 8½ | 408 pp
TP US $15.95 | CAN $19.50
978-1-55861-520-5 CUSA

Updates Marilyn French's classic bestseller *The Women's Room* to explore the realities of contemporary women.

In the Name of Friendship
A Novel
Marilyn French
Afterword by Stéphanie Genty

"Shows [women's friendships] to be the saving grace of civilization."—Gloria Steinem

"Set in Steventon, an affluent town in the Berkshires, this finely detailed group portrait [of four disparate women] . . . celebrates women's cherishing friendships and creativity . . . the intelligent and openhearted women and men [French] warmly portrays are compelling."—*Booklist*

Now available in paperback, this updated edition by the author of the classic novel *The Women's Room* (21 million copies sold worldwide) explores the realities behind women's lives during the landmark year 2000.

Marilyn French is the best-selling author of six novels.

Stéphanie Genty is an associate professor at the Université d'Evry-Val d'Essonne, France.

Author Hometown: New York, NY

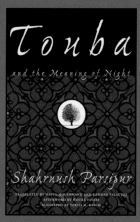

Fiction
January
Women Writing the Middle East
5½ x 8½ | 368 pp
TP US $16.95 | CAN $20.50
978-1-55861-557-1 CUSA

Now available in paperback: the epic masterpiece by Iran's most celebrated living author, Shahrnush Parsipur.

Touba and the Meaning of Night
Shahrnush Parsipur
Translated by Havva Houshmand and Kamram Talattof
Afterword by Houra Yavari

"[With this] bold, insightful novel . . . [Shahrnush] Parsipur makes a stylishly original contribution to modern feminist literature."—*Publishers Weekly* (starred review)

"Parsipur should be admired both as a courageous woman who endured jail and torture . . . and as a writer and innovator."—Azar Nafisi, author of *Reading Lolita in Tehran*

Now available in paperback, this complex epic captures the changing fortunes of Iranian women in the twentieth century from the era of colonialism through the rule of two shahs to the 1980 Islamic Revolution.

The Iranian best-selling author of eleven books, including *Women Without Men*, **Shahrnush Parsipur** now lives in exile in the United States.

Author Hometown: Berkeley, CA

The Feminist Press at CUNY

Mistress of Herself
Speeches and Letters of Ernestine Rose, Early Women's Rights Leader
Ernestine Rose
Edited by Paula Doress-Worters

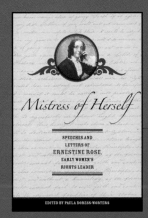

Susan B. Anthony hung a picture of her on the wall. Elizabeth Cady Stanton publicly eulogized her invaluable contributions to the women's rights movement. Unique among her peers as an immigrant of Jewish background, celebrated orator Ernestine Rose won the title "Queen of the Platform" for her brilliant speeches advocating, and linking together, women's rights, the abolition of slavery, and religious freedom. This first collection of her extant papers reclaims her place with Anthony and Stanton.

Paula Doress-Worters, a veteran activist, co-wrote the groundbreaking *Our Bodies, Ourselves* in 1970 and each subsequent edition.

Marketing Plans
Co-op available

History
October
6 x 9 | 328 pp
6 B&W photographs
TP US $18.95 | CAN $23.00
978-1-55861-543-4 CUSA
LB x US $55.00 | CAN $66.00
978-1-55861-544-1 CUSA

The first collection of impassioned speeches and writings from the nineteenth century's US women's rights leader.

Activisms
WSQ: Fall / Winter 2007
Edited by Dorothy L. Hodgson and Ethel C. Brooks

Contributors from Africa, Asia, Latin America, Australia, Canada, and more explore social justice and gender equality, particularly in the global south. This issue includes photo-essays about US and South African performance art, an interview with renowned feminist activist Charlotte Bunch, and a discussion forum on Mary Wollstonecraft. Articles and fiction examine how art, humor, protests, detective novels, and transnational networks promote progressive agendas.

Dorothy L. Hodgson, author of *Once Intrepid Warriors,* is a professor of anthropology at Rutgers University.

Ethel C. Brooks, author of *Unraveling the Garment Industry,* is an assistant professor of women's and gender studies and sociology at Rutgers University.

Cultural Studies / Women's Studies
December
A Paperback Original
Women's Studies Quarterly
6 x 9 | 352 pp
10 B&W illustrations and photographs
TP US $22.00 | CAN $26.50
978-1-55861-566-3 CUSA

Focusing on the global south, international contributors explore women's activism around social and political issues.

Taking On the Big Boys
Or Why Feminism Is Good for
Families, Business, and the Nation
Ellen Bravo

Current Affairs
6 x 9 | 176 pp
TP US $15.95 | CAN $19.50
978-1-55861-545-8 CUSA

Behind Closed Doors
Her Father's House and
Other Stories of Sicily
Maria Messina
Translated by Elise Magistro
Introduction by Fred Gardaphe

Fiction
5 x 7 | 144 pp
2 B&W photographs
TC US $19.95 | CAN $24.00
978-1-55861-553-3 CUSA

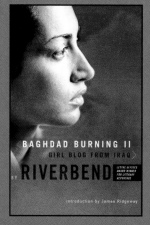

Baghdad Burning II
More Girl Blog from Iraq
Riverbend
Introduction by James Ridgeway
and Jean Casella

Current Affairs
5½ x 8½ | 240 pp
TP US $14.95 | CAN $18.00
978-1-55861-529-8 CUSA

Born in the Big Rains
A Memoir of Somalia and Survival
Fadumo Korn
Translated by Tobe Levin

Biography & Autobiography
6 x 9 | 192 pp
TP US $23.95 | CAN $29.00
978-1-55861-531-1 CUSA

To Stir the Heart
Four African Stories
Bessie Head and Ngugi wa Thiong'o
Introduction by Tuzyline Jita Allan

Fiction Anthology
5 x 7 | 96 pp
TP US $9.95 | CAN $12.00
978-1-55861-547-2 CUSA

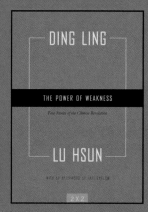

The Power of Weakness
Four Stories of the
Chinese Revolution
Ding Ling and Lu Hsun
Introduction by Tani Barlow

Fiction Anthology
5 x 7 | 96 pp
TP US $9.95 | CAN $12.00
978-1-55861-548-9 CUSA

Dark Mission
The Secret History of NASA
Richard C. Hoagland and Mike Bara

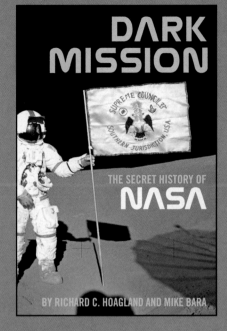

For most Americans, the word *NASA* suggests a squeaky-clean image of technological infallibility.

Yet the truth is that NASA was born in a lie and has concealed the truths about its occult origins. *Dark Mission* documents this seemingly wild assertion.

Why is the Bush administration intent on returning to the moon as quickly as possible? What are the reasons for the current "space race" with China, Russia, even India? Remarkable images reproduced within this book provided to author Richard C. Hoagland by disaffected NASA employees provide clues why, including information about suppressed lunar discoveries.

Mystical organizations quietly dominate NASA, carrying out their own secret agendas behind the scenes. This is the story of men at the very fringes of rational thought and conventional wisdom, operating at the highest levels of our country. Their policies are far more aligned with ancient religions and secret mystery schools than the façade of rational science NASA has successfully promoted to the world for almost fifty years.

Dark Mission is proof of the secret history of the National Aeronautics and Space Administration and the astonishing, seminal discoveries it has repeatedly suppressed for decades.

Richard C. Hoagland is the former science advisor to *CBS News,* author of *The Monuments of Mars,* and a frequent guest on the popular radio programs *Coast To Coast* and *The Art Bell Show.*

Mike Bara is a consulting engineer for Boeing aircraft. This is his first book.

The secret agenda of NASA suppressing true spectacular lunar and Mars-based discoveries.

Science / Current Affairs
October
A Paperback Original
6 x 9 | 550 pp
84 Color and B&W illustrations
and photographs
TP US $24.95 | CAN $30.00
978-1-932595-26-0 CUSA

Marketing Plans

Co-op available
15,000-copy print run

Author Events

Los Angeles, CA • Las Vegas, NV • Laughlin, NV • Albuquerque, NM

Author Hometown: Albuquerque, NM

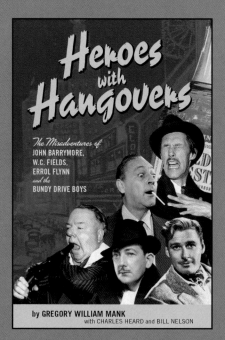

by GREGORY WILLIAM MANK
with CHARLES HEARD and BILL NELSON

Film & TV / Biography & Autobiography
October
A Paperback Original
7 x 10 | 280 pp
92 Color and B&W illustrations
and photographs
TP US $22.95 | CAN $27.50
978-1-932595-24-6 CUSA

Marketing Plans

10,000-copy print run

Author Events

Hollywood, CA • Pasadena, CA •
Riverside, CA • New York, NY •
Philadelphia, PA • Dallas, TX •
Fort Worth, TX

Author Hometown: Philadelphia, PA

Heroes With Hangovers
The Misadventures of John Barrymore, W.C. Fields, Errol Flynn and the Bundy Drive Boys
Gregory William Mank, Charles Heard, and Bill Nelson

They carried on like pirates, pranked like the Marx Brothers, and had dark sides worthy of Dracula.

They were the Bundy Drive Boys—hard-drinking, brilliantly talented, world-famous men of golden-age Hollywood. John Barrymore, W.C. Fields, and Errol Flynn all roistered at the Bundy Drive studio of the profane artist John Decker. All were hell-bent on scaring away film industry boogeymen even while creating sordid monsters of their own.

Heroes with Hangovers tells the uncensored and ultimately moving story of these lost-soul geniuses. Their group meetings inspired and emboldened them to greater heights of folly, fun, lunacy, and even criminal behavior. The partying and antics of the Rat Pack seem tame in comparison.

Illustrated with many rare, never-before-seen photos and material from the private archives of Barrymore, Decker, Gene Fowler, and Fields, *Heroes with Hangovers* provides the full-blooded saga of these blessed and cursed men, their legacy and their ghosts. At night they were heroes of the theater, but in the morning they were *Heroes with Hangovers*.

Gregory William Mank is the author of *It's Alive!* and *Karloff and Lugosi: The Story of a Haunting Collaboration,* as well as magazine features and DVD commentaries. He lives in Delta, Pennsylvania.

Charles Heard is a Dallas stockbroker. He is a Hollywood historian and archivist who collects John Decker artwork.

Bill Nelson is co-owner of the rare and out-of-print Internet bookstore Oddball Books, and is an avid collector and researcher of Hollywood history.

The gorgeously illustrated, uncensored stories of Hollywood's most tormented and talented circle of friends.

Feral House

The Ministry of Truth
Kim Jong-Il's North Korea
Christian Kracht, Eva Munz, and Lukas Nikol

The few dozen tourists—and a few journalists—who come annually to the North Korean capital of Pyongyang are accompanied by guides and are only allowed to see what the regime blinders for their viewing. For the visitors, actors often represent pedestrians, and the consumer goods seen in stores are unavailable to the public at large. The statistics heaped upon the visitors are dubious at best.

Kim Jong-Il's People's Republic of North Korea is a gigantic installation, a simulation, a play. Eva Munz, Christian Kracht, and Lukas Nikol traveled to this land to take pictures of a country from which there are no pictures. What they show in *The Ministry of Truth* is a window view of the gigantic 3-D production of Kim Jong-Il, who writes the nation's statistics and authors its film script. Because no accurate view is available of this total installation, the authors make the only one possible: They comment on their photos with quotations from a didactic book on the art of film written by the dictator, who not only collects wine and Mazda RX-7 sports cars, but also has an enormous film library.

Christian Kracht is a celebrated journalist and author and the editor of the German cultural magazine *Der Freund*. The photographs of Eva Munz and Lukas Nikol have had numerous international exhibitions.

This book of photographs brings you North Korea as chillingly envisioned by dictator Kim Jong-Il.

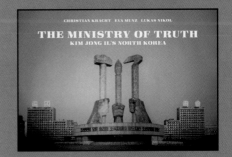

Photography / Current Affairs
October
A Paperback Original
10½ x 8 | 132 pp
88 Color photographs
TP US $22.95 | CAN $27.50
978-1-932595-27-7 CUSA

Marketing Plans

Co-op available

Author Events

Los Angeles, CA • San Francisco, CA • New York, NY

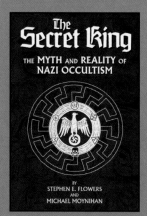

History / Occultism & Parapsychology
September
5½ x 8¼ | 320 pp
24 B&W illustrations and photographs
TP US $16.95 | CAN $20.50
978-1-932595-25-3 CUSA

**Here are the links between
the Nazi high command and a bizarre
netherworld of esoteric beliefs.**

The Secret King
The Myth and Reality of Nazi Occultism
Stephen E. Flowers and Michael Moynihan

The Secret King is the first book to explode many myths surrounding the popular idea of Nazi occultism, while presenting the actual esoteric rituals used by Heinrich Himmler's SS under the influence of rune magician Karl-Maria Wiligut, the "Secret King of Germany."

Stephen E. Flowers, PhD, is a prolific writer and translator in the fields of runology and the history of occultism. He is also the author of books on magical runic traditions under the pen name Edred Thorsson.

Michael Moynihan co-authored the best-selling, award-winning book *Lords of Chaos*. He also co-edits the esoteric journal *Tyr*.

Author Hometown: Burlington, VT

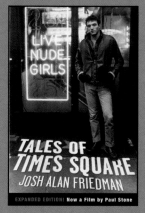

Cultural Studies / Sexuality
September
5¼ x 8½ | 320 pp
14 B&W photographs
TP US $16.95 | CAN $20.50
978-1-932595-28-4 CUSA

**The classic account of New York City's
sleaziest district returns with seven
new chapters.**

Tales of Times Square
Expanded Edition
Josh Alan Friedman

"Friedman has drawn a vivid picture of the Times Square area and its denizens. He writes about the porn palaces with live sex shows, and the men and women who perform in them, prostitutes and their pimps, the runaways who will likely be the next decade's prostitutes, the clergymen who fight the smut merchants and the cops who feel impotent in the face of the judiciary."—*Publishers Weekly*

This classic account of the ultra-sleazy, pre-Disneyfied era of Times Square is now the subject of a documentary film of the same name to be theatrically released this year. With this edition, *Tales of Times Square* returns to print with seven new chapters.

Author Hometown: Dallas, TX

Feral House

Design: Isamu Noguchi and Isamu Kenmochi

Foreword by Katarina Posch

Essays by Bonnie Rychlak, Tetsu Matsumoto, Hiroshi Mori, and Nina Murayama

"Let the East learn from Western civilization. Let the West learn from the Eastern culture. In the world of freedom, we naturally create a relationship to each other." —Isamu Noguchi, in an address to the staff at the Industrial Arts Research Institute in Tokyo

Isamu Kenmochi (1912–1971) was one of the pioneers of industrial design in Japan. Postwar Japanese artists struggled to create their own original industrial products. Kenmochi sought to establish Japanese modern design while reinventing traditional techniques and materials. Like many Japanese artists of his generation, Kenmochi was inspired by Isamu Noguchi (1904–1988), a pivotal figure in twentieth-century sculpture and design. Through Noguchi's influence and subsequent introductions to creative masters such as Alexander Girard, Walter Gropius, George Nelson, and Ludwig Mies van der Rohe, Kenmochi traveled abroad and collected furniture, household products, and thousands of color slides documenting American and European design, which he brought back to Japan to share with contemporaries in the field.

Noguchi and Kenmochi first met at the architect Kenzo Tange's office at Tokyo University on June 24, 1950. In August of that year, Noguchi spent two weeks teaching with Kenmochi at the Industrial Arts Research Institute in Tokyo. Basing his approach on Japanese design traditions, Noguchi persuaded the artists at the institute to look beyond the mere exotic. The ideology they developed came to be known as Japanese Modern, or Japonica Design.

Bonnie Rychlak is a curator and director of collections at the Noguchi Museum in New York. An artist herself, Rychlak worked as Isamu Noguchi's assistant until his death in 1988, and is a leading authority on Noguchi's life and art.

Beautiful furniture and household objects designed by Isamu Noguchi and Isamu Kenmochi.

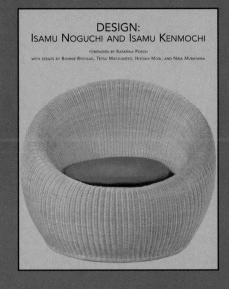

Design
September
9 x 11½ | 240 pp
140 Color and B&W illustrations
and photographs
TC US $50.00 | CAN $60.00
978-0-9794727-0-1 CUSA

Marketing Plans

Co-op available

Author Events

A national museum exhibition tour, beginning at the Noguchi Museum in New York in October 2007

The Full Body Project
Photographs by Leonard Nimoy

Photography / Women's Studies
November
8 x 10 | 96 pp
40 B&W photographs
TC US $45.00 | CAN $54.00
978-0-9794727-2-5 CUSA

**Interpretive nude photographic studies
of full-bodied women.**

In his provocative new book, photographer and actor Leonard Nimoy captures images of full-bodied women, some of whom are involved in what is known as the "fat acceptance" movement. "The average American woman," Nimoy writes, "weighs 25 percent more than the models selling the clothes. There is a huge industry built up around selling women ways to get their bodies closer to the fantasy ideal. Pills, diets, surgery, workout programs. . . . The message is 'You don't look right. If you buy our product, you can get there.'"

Leonard Nimoy, best known to the public from his role as Spock on *Star Trek*, has been a lifelong photographer. His work has been widely exhibited and is in numerous private and public collections. A previous book of his photographs, *Shekhina*, was published in 2002.

Marketing Plans
Co-op available

Author Events
Los Angeles, CA • New York, NY

Author Hometown: Los Angeles, CA

Wheels on Waves
California Skate Parks
Photographs by Arthur Tress

Photography / Popular Culture
November
10 x 10 | 112 pp
50 Color and B&W photographs
TC US $45.00 | CAN $54.00
978-0-9794727-1-8 CUSA

**Abstract forms captured by
Arthur Tress from the world of
California skateboard parks.**

For more than three years, Arthur Tress photographed dynamic forms in California skateboard parks and captured skaters in motion on swelling pools of concrete. Best known for his staged photographs, Tress breaks new ground in this series by capturing rapid motion in the moment with his square-format Hasselblad camera. "Visually, skateboarding is extraordinary," Tress says. "I love the graceful movements of the skaters against the strong curves and shadows of the concrete bowls. I was happy to have discovered this as a subject matter."

Born in Brooklyn, New York, **Arthur Tress** has exerted a profound influence on American photography since the 1960s. His work is in numerous major museum collections, and has been published and exhibited around the world.

Marketing Plans
Co-op available

Author Events
Los Angeles, CA • New York, NY

Author Hometown: Cambria, CA

Five Ties Publishing

Duke, the Dog Priest
Domício Coutinho
Translated by Clifford E. Landers

Fiction /
Latin American
Literature
November
A Paperback Original
Green Integer 175
4¼ x 6 | 416 pp
TP US $14.95
CAN $18.00
978-1-933382-89-0
CUSA

Born in Brazil, novelist Domício Coutinho immigrated to the United States in 1959. His first novel, *Duke, the Dog Priest,* comically explores Nova Eboracense, Brazilian New York, with its dazzling mix of priests, brothers, nuns, students, church workers, parishioners, city luminaries, and a dog named Duke who wants to become a priest—making for a wonderfully fantastic novel.

The New York Trilogy
Paul Auster

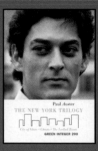

Fiction / Mystery
September
Green Integer 200
4¼ x 6 | 586 pp
TC US $29.95
CAN $36.00
978-1-933382-88-3
CUSA

Paul Auster's great trilogy of 1985–1986 broke ground in its mix of serious fictional techniques and detective and mystery genres. Since that time it has become one of the most successful series of novels of the last two decades, and is now republished in a beautiful cloth edition.

The Untameables
F.T. Marinetti
Translated by Jeremy Parzen

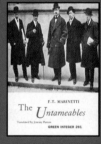

Fiction
September
Green Integer 231
4 x 6 | 200 pp
TP US $12.95
CAN $15.50
978-1-933382-23-4
CUSA

"How could one define *The Untameables*? Adventure novel? Symbolic poetry? Science fiction? Fable? Philosophical-social vision? . . . It's a free-word book. Nude crude synthesizing. Simultaneous polychromatic polyhumourous. Vast violent dynamic." —F.T. Marinetti

Merciless Beauty
Sam Eisenstein

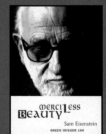

Fiction / True Crime
September
A Paperback Original
Green Integer 166
4¼ x 6 | 272 pp
TP US $13.95
CAN $17.00
978-1-933382-87-6
CUSA

The author of *Cosmic Cow* and *Rectification of Eros* once more explores unknown realms of the heart in this novel about a young, beautiful woman imprisoned for having murdered her husband and lover—again and again! A lyrical story of love and revenge.

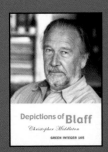

Literature & Essay /
Fiction
November
A Paperback Original
Green Integer 165
4¼ x 6 | 216 pp
TP US $12.95
CAN $15.50
978-1-933382-90-6
CUSA

Depictions of Blaff
Christopher Middleton

In the tradition of Henri Michaux's Plume and Julio Cortázar's Lucas, British author Christopher Middleton presents hilarious anecdotes of the great economist Blaff—a bold, bluffing, blunderbuss character.

Poetry
September
A Paperback Original
Green Integer 244
4¼ x 6 | 224 pp
TP US $13.95
CAN $17.00
978-1-933382-91-3
CUSA

Blood of the Quill
Azem Shkreli
Translated by Robert Elsie

With an introduction by Janice Mathie-Heck, this brilliant collection of bilingual poetry represents the major work of one of Kosovo's most noted poets, a work that celebrates life in a world where war has brutally torn apart the lives of its citizens.

Poetry /
Women's Literature
January
A Paperback Original
Green Integer 174
4¼ x 6 | 224 pp
TP US $13.95
CAN $17.00
978-1-933382-94-4
CUSA

The Complete Early Poems
Rae Armantrout

Rae Armantrout (author of *The Pretext*) is one of contemporary America's most beloved poets of wit. Her early collections, from 1978's *Extremities* to 1995's *Made to Seem,* are presented together in this important volume.

Poetry
October
A Paperback Original
Green Integer 197
4¼ x 6 | 184 pp
TP US $13.95
CAN $17.00
978-1-933382-86-9
CUSA

Tussi Research
Dieter M. Gräf
Translated by Andrew Shields

As part of its ongoing Villa Aurora series, Green Integer presents the second collection of poetry (after the first, *Tousled Beauty*) by the major young German poet, Dieter M. Gräf. This volume explores history and Western, especially German, myths.

Green Integer

My Year 2006: Serving
Douglas Messerli

Biography &
Autobiography /
Popular Culture
October
A Paperback Original
Green Integer 261
4¼ x 6 | 375 pp
30 B&W photographs
TP US $15.95
CAN $19.50
978-1-933382-93-7
CUSA

In this, the third volume of his ongoing cultural memoir, Douglas Messerli explores figures and issues of 2006—the films of Robert Altman and Jean Renoir; *The Queen*; the writing of Guest, Hauser, Sorrentino, and others; and Southern myths—all centered on the topic of "serving."

1001 Great Stories, No. 3
10 Norwegian Tales
Edited by Douglas Messerli

Fiction Anthology
December
A Paperback Original
Green Integer 302
4¼ x 6 | 256 pp
8 B&W photographs
TP US $12.95
CAN $15.50
978-1-933382-92-0
CUSA

Collected here are ten tales by significant Norwegian writers: Tarjei Vesaas, Sigurd Hoel, Aksel Sandemose, Thorvald Steen, Finn Carling, Johan Borgen, Kjell Askildsen, Øystein Lønn, and Roy Jacobsen.

North of Hell
Miguel Correa Mujica
Translated by Alexis Romay

Fiction /
Hispanic Studies
February
A Paperback Original
Green Integer 191
4¼ x 6 | 86 pp
TP US $11.95
CAN $14.50
978-1-933382-95-1
CUSA

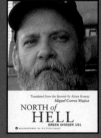

In his introduction to this novel, noted Cuban novelist Reinaldo Arenas suggests that there are two kinds of good literature—the second of which, exemplified by *North of Hell,* is an "unstoppable fury of the condemned." This is satiric literature at its best.

Tristia
Osip Mandelshtam
Translated by Kevin J. Kinsella

Poetry
October
A Paperback Original
Green Integer 169
4¼ x 6 | 96 pp
TP US $11.95
CAN $14.50
978-1-933382-96-8
CUSA

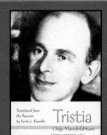

The great twentieth-century Russian poet's second volume of poetry, *Tristia,* explores myths of Orpheus and Eurydice in a brilliantly symbolic manner. This is one of the most important books of Russian poetry.

The Vicar's Passion
Honoré de Balzac
Translated by Ed Ford

Fiction / Mystery
4¼ x 6 | 400 pp
TP US $14.95 | CAN $18.00
978-1-931243-47-6 CUSA

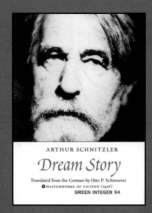

Dream Story
Arthur Schnitzler
Translated by Otto Schnnerer

Fiction
4¼ x 6 | 167 pp
TP US $11.95 | CAN $14.50
978-1-931243-48-3 CUSA

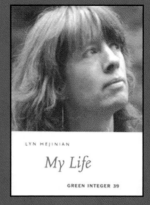

My Life
Lyn Hejinian

Poetry / Biography & Autobiography
4¼ x 6 | 120 pp
TP US $10.95 | CAN $13.50
978-1-931243-33-9 CUSA

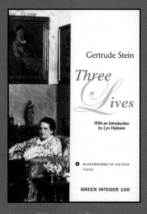

Three Lives
Gertrude Stein
Introduction by Lyn Hejinian

Fiction
4½ x 6 | 280 pp
TP US $12.95 | CAN $15.50
978-1-892295-33-0 CUSA

A Tragic Man Despite Himself
The Complete Short Plays
Anton Chekhov

Drama
4½ x 6 | 600 pp
TP US $25.00 | CAN $30.00
978-1-931243-17-9 CUSA

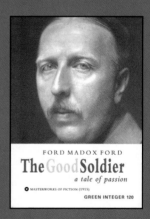

The Good Soldier
Ford Madox Ford

Fiction
4¼ x 6 | 315 pp
TP US $10.95 | CAN $13.50
978-1-931243-62-9 CUSA

Math in Minutes
Easy Activities for Children Ages 4–8
Sharon MacDonald

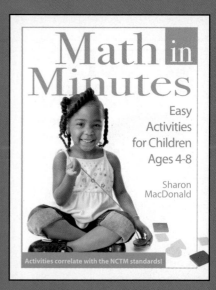

This engaging, exciting introduction to early math concepts will be a sure-fire hit with young children. They can go on a Geometric Shape Hunt, measure with Pompoms, or find the Missing Numbers—just a few of the fun, simple activities you'll find in *Math in Minutes.*

The activities progress in difficulty within each chapter. Some activities offer a way to "Take It Up a Level" for children who want a challenge. Organized by math concept, each of the activities relates to the National Council of Teachers of Mathematics standards and uses easy-to-find materials available in any classroom. Because assessment has become so important in education, each activity begins with "Math Objectives that Meet Standards" to help teachers meet the specific standards set by their state. The book's unique tips and insights from an experienced teacher will help new and veteran teachers alike.

Sharon MacDonald has been training teachers for over fifteen years. She is a frequent keynote speaker and workshop presenter at early childhood conferences. This is her fifth book with Gryphon House. Her other titles include *Sanity Savers for Early Childhood Teachers; Squish, Sort, Paint, and Build; Block Play;* and *Everyday Discoveries.* Sharon lives in San Antonio, Texas.

The perfect introduction to early math concepts for young children!

Education & Teaching / Childcare
September
A Paperback Original
8½ x 11 | 224 pp
150 B&W illustrations
TP $19.95
978-0-87659-057-7 USA

**Also
Available**

Everyday Discoveries
Amazingly Easy Science and Math Using Stuff You Already Have
Sharon MacDonald
Education & Teaching / Family & Parenting
8½ x 11 | 256 pp
111 B&W Illustrations
TP $19.95
978-0-87659-196-3 USA

Sanity Savers for Early Childhood Teachers
200 Quick Fixes for Everything from Big Messes to Small Budgets
Sharon MacDonald
Education & Teaching / Family & Parenting
8½ x 11 | 160 pp
50 B&W Illustrations
TP $14.95
978-0-87659-236-6 USA

Gryphon House

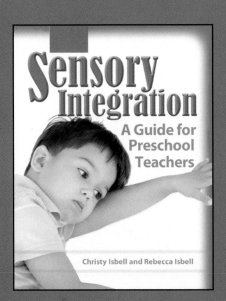

Childcare / Education & Teaching
September
A Paperback Original
8½ x 11 | 160 pp
63 B&W illustrations and photographs
TP $19.95
978-0-87659-060-7 USA

Marketing Plans

Co-op available
National advertising:
Publishers Weekly

Author Hometown: Johnson City, TN/
Jonesborough, TN

Sensory Integration
A Guide for Preschool Teachers
Christy Isbell and Rebecca Isbell

Do you have a child in your early childhood classroom who:

- Climbs on top of furniture and jumps off?
- Covers his ears when children are singing?
- Refuses to touch clay, paint, or sand?
- Often falls down and skins her knees?
- Refuses to play on outdoor playground equipment?

If so, it is possible the child is having trouble with sensory integration. How can you help children with these problems so they can enjoy learning and grow in positive ways? *Sensory Integration* helps you identify children who have difficulties with sensory processing, and it offers easy-to-use solutions to support the sensory needs of young children in the preschool classroom. Solutions include adaptations and activities for children with different types of sensory processing disorder. This book has a bonus chapter with instructions for creating low-cost items to help children with sensory issues.

Christy Isbell is a pediatric occupational therapist with specialized training in both sensory integration and neuro-developmental treatment. She lives in Johnson City, Tennessee.

Rebecca Isbell is director of the Center of Excellence in Early Childhood Learning and Development. She is a professor of early childhood education at East Tennessee State University, where she was recognized as a distinguished professor for teaching. She lives in Jonesborough, Tennessee.

**Help children with sensory processing problems learn and grow
with the adaptations and activities in this book.**

**Also
Available**

The Inclusive Learning Center Book
for Preschool Children With Special Needs
Christy Isbell and Rebecca Isbell
Education & Teaching / Family & Parenting
8½ x 11 | 320 pp
169 B&W illustrations and photographs
TP $29.95
978-0-87659-294-6 USA

The Complete Learning Spaces
Book for Infants and Toddlers
54 Integrated Areas with Play Experiences
Christy Isbell and Rebecca Isbell
Education & Teaching / Childcare
8½ x 11 | 352 pp
223 B&W illustrations and photographs
TP $29.95
978-0-87659-293-9 USA

Gryphon House

Read! Move! Learn!

Active Stories for Active Learning

Carol Totsky Hammett and Nicki Collins Geigert

Enhance literacy skills, bring the magic of a good book to the classroom, and encourage healthy, active lifestyles in young children with *Read! Move! Learn!* This new book has over 150 active learning experiences based on more than seventy popular children's books. The authors provide complete plans that include theme connections, related books and music, lesson objectives, a vocabulary list, a concept list, and activities for each children's book, providing hours of fun in the classroom!

A few of the children's books included are:

- *Barn Dance*
- *Harold and the Purple Crayon*
- *Head, Shoulders, Knees, and Toes*
- *I'm a Little Teapot*
- *In the Tall, Tall Grass*
- *Monkey See, Monkey Do*
- *Quick as a Cricket*
- *Snowball Fight!*
- *Ten Terrible Dinosaurs*
- *We're Going on a Bear Hunt*

Carol Totsky Hammett began her teaching career over twenty-five years ago and has worked as a physical education specialist, pre-kindergarten teacher, and an early childhood special education teacher. She is currently an elementary school principal in Bend, Oregon.

Nicki Collins Geigert has worked as an educator for the past thirty-six years. She has led workshops for the National Association for the Education of Young Children (NAEYC), various state early childhood organizations, and the American Alliance of Health, Physical Education, Recreation, and Dance (AAHPERD). She lives in Carlsbad, California.

Energize your classroom with lively literacy lessons based on more than seventy popular children's books!

Childcare / Education & Teaching
September
A Paperback Original
8½ x 11 | 232 pp
150 B&W illustrations
TP $19.95
978-0-87659-058-4 USA

Marketing Plans

Co-op available
National advertising:
Publishers Weekly

Author Hometown: Bend, OR/Carlsbad, CA

Gryphon House

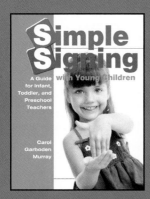

Simple Signing with Young Children
A Guide for Infant, Toddler, and Preschool Teachers
Carol Garboden Murray

Education & Teaching / Childcare
9 x 11 | 192 pp
TP $24.95
978-0-87659-033-1 USA

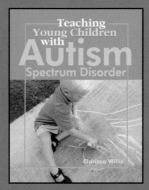

Teaching Young Children With Autism Spectrum Disorder
A Practical Guide for the Preschool Teacher
Clarissa Willis

Education & Teaching / Childcare
8½ x 11 | 192 pp
70 B&W illustrations and photographs
TP $24.95
978-0-87659-008-9 USA

Inclusive Lesson Plans Throughout the Year
Laverne Warner, Sharon Lynch, Cynthia Simpson, and Diana Kay Nabors

Education & Teaching / Childcare
9 x 11 | 352 pp
150 B&W illustrations
TP $29.95
978-0-87659-014-0 USA

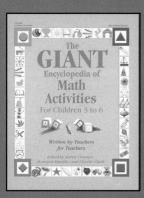

The GIANT Encyclopedia of Math Activities
Over 600 Activities Created by Teachers for Teachers
Edited by Kathy Charner, Maureen Murphy, and Charlie Clark

Education & Teaching / Childcare
9 x 11 | 528 pp
120 B&W illustrations
TP $34.95
978-0-87659-044-7 USA

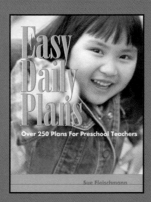

Easy Daily Plans
Over 250 Plans for Preschool Teachers
Sue Fleischmann

Education & Teaching / Childcare
9 x 11 | 408 pp
20 B&W illustrations
TP $29.95
978-0-87659-005-8 USA

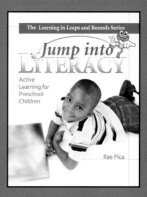

Jump into Literacy
Active Learning for Preschool Children
Rae Pica

Education & Teaching / Childcare
9 x 11 | 136 pp
39 B&W illustrations
TP $14.95
978-0-87659-009-6 USA

Are You Ready for Me?

Claire Buchwald

Illustrated by Amelia Hansen

Getting a dog can be a wonderful moment in a family's life—or the beginning of a bad situation for everyone. In *Are You Ready for Me?*, engaging text and colorful, detail-filled pictures describe the responsibilities and joys of dog ownership in the lives of two children. A dog and a pup waiting to be chosen at an animal adoption center pose questions that show what it will mean to bring a dog into one's family.

The book's final page offers a We Are Ready to Have a Dog Contract with questions to check off; children and parents together will be able to decide whether they really are ready. A link to The Gryphon Press website offers bonuses, including a Ready for Dog Ownership Certificate, and even an award certificate for children who are mature enough to realize that they and a dog are not a good match at this point in the child's life.

Are You Ready for Me? is a book that every dog-loving family will want to own. Parents and grandparents will enjoy giving the book as a delightful way to lead up to both the exhilarating moment of adoption and a lifetime of mutual happiness.

Claire Buchwald, author of four children's picture books, including *Max Talks to Me* (The Gryphon Press, 2007), has a PhD in communications and significant background as an educator.

Artist Amelia Hansen has illustrated twenty previous titles, including *At the Dog Park with Sam and Lucy* (The Gryphon Press, 2006).

Children and parents together will be able to decide whether they are ready for a dog.

Children's Fiction / Pets & Pet Care
October
Sit! Stay! Read!
9 x 9¾ | 24 pp
24 Color illustrations
Ages 5 and up
TC US $15.95 | CAN $19.50
978-0-940719-04-0 CUSA

Marketing Plans

Advance reader copies
National advertising:
School Library Journal • The Bark

Author Events

San Diego, CA • Minneapolis, MN •
Philadelphia, PA

Author Hometown: Bloomington, MN

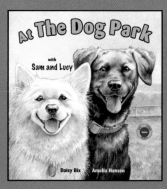

At the Dog Park
with Sam and Lucy
Daisy Bix
Illustrated by Amelia Hansen

Children's Fiction / Pets & Pet Care
9 x 9¾ | 24 pp
24 Color illustrations
TC US $15.95 | CAN $19.50
978-0-940719-00-2 CUSA

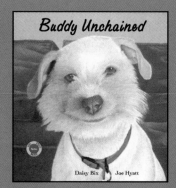

Buddy Unchained
Daisy Bix
Illustrated by Joe Hyatt

Children's Fiction / Pets & Pet Care
9 x 9¾ | 24 pp
24 Color illustrations
TC US $15.95 | CAN $19.50
978-0-940719-01-9 CUSA

Max Talks to Me
Claire Buchwald
Illustrated by Karen Ritz

Children's Fiction / Pets & Pet Care
9 x 9¾ | 24 pp
24 Color illustrations
TC US $15.95 | CAN $19.50
978-0-940719-03-3 CUSA

Beyond the Green Zone

Dispatches from an Unembedded Journalist in Occupied Iraq

Dahr Jamail

Foreword by Amy Goodman

"Dahr Jamail does us a great service, by taking us past the lies of our political leaders, past the cowardice of the mainstream press, into the streets, the homes, the lives of Iraqis living under US occupation. If what he has seen could be conveyed to all Americans, this ugly war in Iraq would quickly come to an end. A superb journalist." —Howard Zinn

We walk slowly under the scorching sun along dusty rows of humble headstones. She continues reading them aloud to me, "Old man wearing jacket with dishdasha, near industrial center. He has a key in his hand." Many of the bodies were buried before they could be identified. Tears welling up in my eyes she quietly reads, "Man wearing red track suit." She points to another row, "Three women killed in car leaving city by American missile."

As the occupation of Iraq unravels, the demand for independent reporting is growing. Since 2003, unembedded journalist Dahr Jamail has filed indispensable reports from Iraq that have made him this generation's chronicler of the unfolding disaster there. In these collected dispatches, Jamail presents never-before-published details of the siege of Fallujah and examines the origins of the Iraqi insurgency.

Dahr Jamail makes frequent visits to Iraq and has published his accounts in newspapers and magazines worldwide. He has regularly appeared on *Democracy Now!,* as well as the BBC, Pacifica Radio, and numerous other networks.

The most important unembedded US reporter in Iraq takes us inside the Iraq we never see.

Also Available

Friendly Fire
The Remarkable Story of a Journalist Kidnapped in Iraq, Rescued by an Italian Secret Service Agent, and Shot by U.S. Forces
Giuliana Sgrena
Introduction by Amy Goodman
Political Science & Government / Current Affairs
5½ x 8½ | 280 pp
12 B&W photographs and maps
TC US $20.00 | CAN $24.00
978-1-931859-39-4 CUSA

Current Affairs
October
5½ x 7½ | 240 pp
15 B&W photographs
TC US $22.00 | CAN $26.50
978-1-931859-47-9 CUSA

Haymarket Books

Diary of Bergen-Belsen

Hanna Lévy-Hass

Introduction by Amira Hass

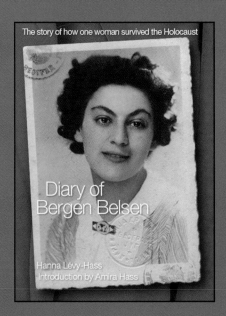

The story of how one woman survived the Holocaust

Diary of Bergen Belsen

Hanna Lévy-Hass
Introduction by Amira Hass

History / Jewish Studies
September
5½ x 7½ | 140 pp
TC US $20.00 | CAN $24.00
978-1-931859-48-6 CUSA

Marketing Plans

National advertising:
ForeWord Magazine • Heeb •
The New York Times Review of Books • Tikkun

Hanna Levy-Hass, a Yugoslavian Jew, emerged a defiant survivor of the Holocaust. Her observations, recorded in her own incomparable voice, shed new light on the lived experience of Nazi internment. Levy-Hass stands alone as the only resistance fighter to report on her own experience inside the camps, and she does so with unflinching clarity in dealing with the political and social divisions inside Bergen-Belsen.

Amira Hass, an indispensable voice in her own right as the only Israeli journalist living and writing from the Occupied Territories, offers a substantial introduction to her mother's work that addresses the meaning of the Holocaust for Israelis and Palestinians today.

Born in Sarajevo in 1913, Hanna Lévy-Hass became involved in the clandestine Communist movement while studying in Belgrade in the 1930s. There, she was instilled with a passion for freedom and equality, which would guide her work and her perspective throughout the rest of her life. Even the misuse of the memory of the Holocaust as legitimization of the Israeli occupation of Palestine did not dissuade her from a determination to fight for a better world based on justice and liberty.

A unique, deeply political survivor's diary from the final year inside the notorious concentration camp.

Haymarket Books

Vietnam
The (Last) War the United States Lost
Joe Allen

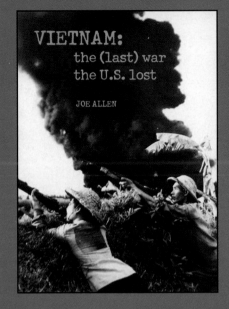

As the United States now faces a major defeat in its occupation of Iraq, the history of the Vietnam War, as a historic blunder for US military forces abroad, and the true story of how it was stopped, takes on a fresh importance. Unlike most books on the topic, constructed as specialized academic studies, *Vietnam: The (Last) War the United States Lost* examines the lessons of the Vietnam era for a popular audience. Joe Allen writes as both a dedicated historian and an engaged participant in today's antiwar movement.

Many damaging myths about the Vietnam era persist, including the accusations that antiwar activists routinely jeered and spat at returning soldiers or that the war finally ended because Congress cut off its funding. Writing in a clear and accessible style, Allen reclaims the stories of courageous GI revolt; its dynamic relationship with the civil rights and peace movements; the development of coffeehouses where these groups came to speak out, debate, and organize; and the struggles waged throughout barracks, bases, and military prisons to challenge the rule of military command.

Allen's analysis of the US failure in Vietnam is also the story of the hubris of US imperial overreach, a new chapter of which is unfolding in the Middle East today.

Joe Allen is a regular contributor to the *International Socialist Review* and a longstanding social justice fighter, involved in the ongoing struggles in the labor movement for the abolition of the death penalty, and to free the political prisoner Gary Tyler.

As the connection between Vietnam and Iraq grows more urgent, Joe Allen presents lessons for today's antiwar movement.

History / Asian Studies
December
A Paperback Original
5½ x 8½ | 150 pp
15 B&W photographs
TP US $14.00 | CAN $17.00
978-1-931859-49-3 CUSA

Marketing Plans

Co-op available
National advertising:
In These Times • The Nation •
The Progressive

Author Events

Chicago, IL • Boston, MA • New York, NY

Author Hometown: Chicago, IL

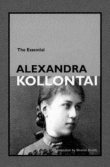

Women's Studies
January
5 x 8 | 250 pp
TP US $15.00
CAN $19.50
978-1-931859-31-8
CUSA

The Essential Alexandra Kollontai
Alexandra Kollontai
Introduction by Sharon Smith

This is a collection of the work of Alexandra Kollontai, a leading member of Russia's Bolshevik Party and an integral part of the international women's movement. It encompasses her groundbreaking writings on sexual morality under capitalism, women's oppression, the family, and women's role in the Russian Revolution. This book is now available to today's activists and scholars with a new introduction by Sharon Smith.

History
September
6 x 9 | 240 pp
TP US $20.00
CAN $24.00
978-1-931859-50-9
CUSA

Revolution and Counterrevolution
Class Struggle in a Moscow Metal Factory
Kevin Murphy

Nearly all recognition of the unparalleled democracy the Russian Revolution established has been destroyed by the legacy of the Stalinist regime that followed. Kevin Murphy's writing, based on exhaustive research, is the most thorough investigation to date on working-class life during the revolutionary era, reviving the memory of the incredible gains for liberty and equality that the 1917 revolution brought about.

History /
Political Science &
Government
January
6 x 9 | 700 pp
TP y US $50.00
CAN $60.00
978-1-931859-51-6
CUSA

The Revolution and the Civil War in Spain
Pierre Broué and Émile Témine

The tragic defeat of the Spanish Civil War has long fascinated those who continue to struggle for social justice. Pierre Broué and Émile Témine's long out-of-print history details the internal political dynamics that led the popular front to hold back radical measures that would have galvanized the working class and the peasant base of the revolution and decisively weakened Franco's fascist forces.

History
February
A Paperback Original
5½ x 8 | 220 pp
TP US $15.00
CAN $18.00
978-1-931859-52-3
CUSA

The Comintern
Duncan Hallas

This history of the Communist (Third) International, from its beginnings in 1919 as the center of world revolution through its degeneration at the hands of the Stalinist bureaucracy, draws out lessons valid today to unite and rebuild a Left capable of fighting for radical social change.

Haymarket Books

Definite Space

Poems

Ann Iverson

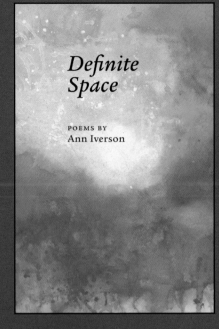

Poetry / Women's Studies
September
A Paperback Original
6 x 9 | 96 pp
TP US $15.95 | CAN $19.50
978-0-9779458-4-9 CUSA

"While Ann Iverson makes direct references to contemporary political events, she mutes their potential polarizing effect by considering them within a non-politicized context: her life. Consequently, no matter one's position on our nation's response to September II, to the war on terror, or the president, one can appreciate these compassionate poems."—Rachel Lintula

Ann Iverson's second collection of poetry conveys the emotional journey of a son's first and second deployment to Baghdad, as well as the spiritual and physical adjustment to a move from the inner city to a country-like suburb. In spare, distinctive imagery, Iverson ponders the personal, familial, and social transitions brought about by life's changes. She thoughtfully considers the tension within relationships that change often engenders and by doing so, personalizes a national tragedy and the subsequent war in Iraq.

In "Even Though" she juxtaposes the surreal war and its reality with her common life experience: "I cleared my throat and raised my voice, / though the city did not respond. / And the soldiers stay away too long, / for years and years and years / Even though we call to them. / Even though they hear."

Ann Iverson received her MALS and MFA from Hamline University in Minnesota. Her writing has been featured on *The Writer's Almanac* with Garrison Keillor and has appeared in *The Oklahoma Review* and *MARGIE: The American Journal of Poetry.* Her first collection, *Come Now to the Window,* was published by the Laurel Poetry Collective. She currently is the director of arts and sciences at Dunwoody College of Technology in Minneapolis. She and her husband live in East Bethel, Minnesota.

A mother's conflicted poetry about her son's deployment to Baghdad during the Iraq War.

Marketing Plans

Co-op available

Author Events

Duluth, MN • Minneapolis, MN • St. Paul, MN

Author Hometown: East Bethel, MN

Holy Cow! Press

Poetry / Asian Studies
October
A Paperback Original
6 x 9 | 120 pp
1 Woodcut
TP US $15.95 | CAN $19.50
978-0-9779458-5-6 CUSA

Marketing Plans

Co-op available

Author Events

Berkeley, CA • Los Angeles, CA • Ojai, CA •
Oxnard, CA • San Francisco, CA •
Boston, MA • Mackinac Island, MI • Petosky,
MI • Traverse City, MI • Minneapolis, MN •
St. Paul, MN • Sante Fe, NM • Portland, OR •
Seattle, WA

Author Hometown: Minneapolis, MN

A Cartload of Scrolls
100 Poems in the Manner of T'ang Dynasty Poet Han-shan
James P. Lenfestey

"These aren't translations of Han-shan's poems; they're *transmissions* of his spirit!"
—Eric Utne, founder of *Utne Reader*

"I love this book!"—Jim Moore

In 1974, author James P. Lenfestey came upon the book *Cold Mountain: 100 Poems of the T'ang Dynasty Poet Han-shan,* translated by Burton Watson, and it cured his warts. It also turned out to be the voice he had "missed" all his life. For the first and only time in his writing life, Lenfestey began to "write back" to another author. The result thirty-three years later is this collection of one hundred poems, inspired by the form and sensibility of that 1,200-year-old Chinese hermit, yet brimming with Lenfestey's own humor, wisdom, insight, and delight in language. Titles such as "Han-shan is the Cure for Warts," "Thinking of Sex Like the Chinese," and "Oracle Bones" provide a glimpse into Lenfestey's poetic landscape. This book is dedicated to poetic translator Burton Watson, eighty-one, whom Lenfestey visited in Tokyo on a pilgrimage to China to pay homage to Han-shan at his hermit cave.

James P. Lenfestey has worked as a college literature instructor, alternative school administrator, salesman, marketing communications professional, and editorial writer for the Minneapolis *Star Tribune,* where he won several Page One Awards. He has published three previous collections of poetry and a collection of personal essays, including *The Urban Coyote: Howlings on Family, Community and the Search for Peace and Quiet* (Nodin Press). He coordinates poetry festivals and a reading series in California, Michigan, and Minneapolis, where he and his wife currently reside.

One hundred poems in the form and sensibility of the eighth-century Chinese hermit poet Han-shan.

Holy Cow! Press

Youth to Power

How Today's Young Voters Are Building Tomorrow's Progressive Majority

Michael Connery

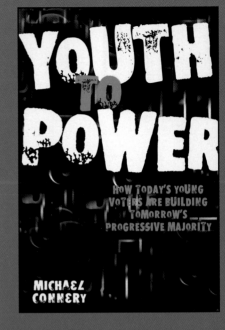

Nearly half of today's young voters under thirty—known as the Millennial Generation—identify themselves as Democrats, and they voted overwhelmingly Democratic in the 2006 election. Since youthful voting habits are a strong indicator of future party loyalty, we may be seeing the beginning of a progressive resurgence in American politics.

In combination with their progressive ideals, the millennials are both civic-minded and entrepreneurial, having come of age in the safety of a post-Cold War world marked by an unprecedented revolution in technology. Using their unsurpassed social and technological skills, they have fostered a community spirit that is beginning to reverse the decades-long decline in social capital that was famously recorded by Robert Putnam in *Bowling Alone*.

Youth to Power: How Today's Young Voters Are Building Tomorrow's Progressive Majority examines how today's young people are combining technology with a vigorous social spirit to revive progressive politics. In addition to recounting the history of youth politics since its emergence in the 1972 election, as well as showing where the movement still lags behind its more organized conservative counterpart, the book features interviews with many of the major figures in the youth political movement, and identifies strategies that the Democratic Party can use to capitalize on its new advantages with young voters. *Youth to Power* is a must-read for anyone who wants to understand the political and cultural future of America.

An expert in youth politics, Michael Connery is co-founder of Music for America, a get-out-the-vote organization. He blogs about progressive youth politics at www.futuremajority.com.

How the Millennial Generation is reigniting progressive politics in America.

Current Affairs /
Political Science & Government
February
A Paperback Original
5½ x 8¼ | 200 pp
TP US $14.95 | CAN $18.00
978-0-9788431-3-7 CUSA

Marketing Plans

Advance reader copies

Author Events

San Francisco, CA • Boulder, CO •
Denver, CO • New York, NY •
Portland, OR • Seattle, WA

Sandrine's Letter to Tomorrow
Dedra Johnson

Fiction
November
A Paperback Original
5½ x 8 | 220 pp
TP US $14.95 | CAN $18.00
978-0-9788431-2-0 CUSA

In the tradition of Toni Morrison and Alice Walker, the next great female African American novelist.

Set in 1970s-era New Orleans, *Sandrine's Letter to Tomorrow* is the disturbingly powerful and uplifting story of a young African American girl named Sandrine, whose only refuge against a world of poverty, racial discrimination, and parental abuse are the letters she writes to her dead grandmother. In the tradition of Toni Morrison's *The Bluest Eye* and Alice Walker's *The Color Purple*, *Sandrine's Letter to Tomorrow* is a brilliant debut from an important new voice in African American fiction.

A professor of English at Dillard University, Dedra Johnson received her MFA from the University of Florida, where she was a finalist for the Hurst-Wright Award. *Sandrine's Letter to Tomorrow* was a finalist for the 2006 William Faulkner-William Wisdom Creative Writing Award.

Marketing Plans
Advance reader copies

Author Events
Miami, FL • Tampa, FL • Decatur, GA • New Orleans, LA • Oxford, MS • New York, NY

Mortarville
Grant Bailie

Fiction / Science Fiction & Fantasy
January
A Paperback Original
5½ x 8 | 225 pp
TP US $14.95 | CAN $18.00
978-0-9788431-1-3 CUSA

A *Brave New World* for the twenty-first century.

A dark commentary on conformity in American society, *Mortarville* is the story of "Jack Smith," a man created from a test tube. Raised in a secret underground government facility with other test-tube boys who are punished harshly for any minor infraction, Jack is taught to understand the outside world by reading comic books and watching old television shows. After repeated escape attempts, he is programmed to believe that he once had a family, and is released to live in Mortarville, a decaying industrial city. However, no matter how hard he tries to belong to the real world, he cannot shake the memories of his past, which leads to a spectacular and moving conclusion.

Grant Bailie's first novel, *Cloud 8,* was published by Ig Publishing in 2003 to substantial critical acclaim.

Marketing Plans
Advance reader copies

Author Events
Berkeley, CA • Chicago, IL • New York, NY • Cleveland, OH • Portland, OR

Ig Publishing

Julie Black Belt
The Kung Fu Chronicles
Oliver Chin
Illustrated by Charlene Chua

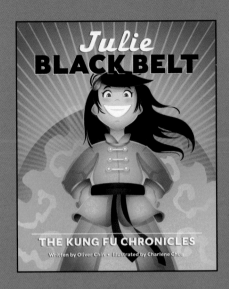

"*Julie Black Belt* is a great introduction for young readers into the world of martial arts."—Phillip Wong, Wushu Grand Champion, and Zhang Hong Mei, International Games gold medalist

"When a child learns about his body and also learns discipline, it can't help but benefit all of his everyday habits"—*Los Angeles Times*

"It's a kick! Kids look to martial arts for skills and attitudes missing from team sports."—*The Christian Science Monitor*

When Julie takes a kung fu class, she thinks getting a black belt will be easy. But her bold teacher says guess again! As reality doesn't match her expectations, Julie wonders, what would her matinee idol Brandy Wu do?

Can Julie take her lessons to heart? Only then can this "white belt" pass her next test to show her brother, parents, and heroine this sport's true spirit.

Colorful and energetic illustrations capture both high-flying action and purposeful reflection. Julie is a refreshing female character whom children everywhere will identify with. This engaging adventure of "kung fu enlightenment" displays what real kid power is!

Oliver Chin has written *Timmy and Tammy's Train of Thought,* the acclaimed Tales of the Chinese Zodiac series, *The Adventures of WonderBaby,* and other books. Residing in San Francisco, California, he is married with two sons.

Charlene Chua is an award-winning illustrator who has designed advertising for Dentsu and Saatchi & Saatchi, and editorial art for *FHM, Maxim,* and IGN.com. She resides in Toronto with her husband.

Kim Possible meets the Karate Kid.

Children's Fiction / Sports & Recreation
September
8½ x 10½ | 36 pp
36 Color illustrations
TC US $15.95 | CAN $19.50
978-1-59702-009-1 CUSA

Author Events

Los Angeles, CA • San Francisco, CA • Toronto, ON

Author Hometown: San Francisco, CA
Illustrator Hometown: Toronto, ON

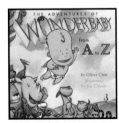

Also Available

The Adventures of WonderBaby
From A to Z
Oliver Chin
Illustrated by Joe Chiodo
Children's Fiction
7 x 7 | 32 pp
32 Color illustrations
BD US $8.95 | CAN $11.00
978-1-59702-001-5 CUSA

Timmy and Tammy's Train of Thought
Oliver Chin
Illustrated by Heath McPherson
Children's Fiction / Crafts & Hobbies
11 x 8 | 36 pp
36 Color illustrations
TC US $15.95 | CAN $19.50
978-1-59702-008-4 CUSA

Immedium

The Octonauts
& the Sea of Shade
Meomi

"There are also more Octonaut adventures to come, and I for one cannot wait to read them."—SuperCoolBaby.com

In this sequel, the Octonauts notice the ocean's shadows are missing! So these eight brave teammates travel to the mysterious Sea of Shade to learn why. Can they convince the proud Shade King to return everyone's shadows? Find out!

These entertaining explorers appeal to children, and their sophisticated design and subversive humor delight appreciative adults.

Meomi's artwork has appeared in clothing, toys, and merchandise worldwide. Its clients include Fisher-Price/Mattel, Electronic Arts, Google, *Time Out* magazine, Cingular, and the Canadian Broadcasting Corporation.

Marketing Plans
Co-op available

Author Events
Vancouver, BC • Los Angeles, CA • San Francisco, CA

Author Hometown: Los Angeles, CA/Vancouver, BC

Children's Fiction / Sidelines & Gift Books
October
11 x 8 | 36 pp
36 Color illustrations
TC US $15.95 | CAN $19.50
978-1-59702-010-7 CUSA

The second episode of "Hello Kitty meets *Star Trek* under the sea."

The Year of the Rat
Tales from the Chinese Zodiac
Oliver Chin
Illustrated by Miah Alcorn

"Absolutely adorable . . . what a fabulous cast of characters your books contain!"
—Kate Ferguson, Book Passage

The year 2008 is the Year of the Rat! Ralph the rat explores the world with the boy Bing. But when Bing's birthday party goes awry, can Ralph rescue him using qualities that others frowned upon? The third in the popular series introduces the twelve charismatic animals from the Chinese calendar.

Oliver Chin has written this series and other children's picture books. His family lives in San Francisco.

Miah Alcorn illustrated *The Year of the Dog* and *The Year of the Pig*. He and his family reside in Birmingham, Alabama.

Marketing Plans
Co-op available

Author Events
Birmingham, AL • Los Angeles, CA• San Francisco, CA

Author Hometown: San Francisco, CA | Illustrator Hometown: Birmingham, AL

Children's Fiction / Asian Studies
January
Tales from the Chinese Zodiac
9⅝ x 10 | 36 pp
36 Color illustrations
TC US $15.95 | CAN $19.50
978-1-59702-011-4 CUSA

Stuart Little meets *The Red Balloon*.

Immedium

Gifts from the Heart
Simple Ways to Make Your Family's Christmas More Meaningful
Virginia Brucker

Are you overwhelmed by the frantic commercialism of our modern Christmas? Do you long for a more meaningful celebration? *Gifts from the Heart* contains hundreds of simple ideas that will help you create a warmer, more loving celebration focused on sharing and giving. Parents, grandparents, early childhood educators, teachers, and youth group leaders will love the imaginative ideas in this book. *Gifts from the Heart* is filled with:

- Time-saving tips for busy families
- Delightful kid-tested craft projects
- Heartwarming ideas for family traditions and capturing memories
- Fun-filled activities that help grandparents connect with their grandchildren
- Terrific suggestions for gifts that develop imagination, creativity, and literacy
- Practical ideas for helping our planet and our animal friends
- Delicious tried-and-true recipes for cooks of all ages
- Presentation tips and fabulous recipes for gifts from the kitchen
- Party and potluck tips and recipes
- Easy-to-do volunteer activities that make a difference to others during the holidays
- Tips for divorced parents and blended families
- Meaningful ways to help friends and families struggling with illness or loss at Christmas

A primary teacher for more than twenty-five years, **Virginia Brucker** is the recipient of the National Council of the Cancer Society's Community Champion Award for her support of cancer research. She lives and works in beautiful Nanoose Bay on Vancouver Island.

Simple ways to make your family's Christmas more meaningful.

Sidelines & Gift Books
October
A Paperback Original
5 x 8 | 336 pp
125 B&W illustrations
TP $14.95
978-1-897178-30-0 USA

Marketing Plans

Co-op available

Author Events

Portland, OR • Seattle, WA

Author Hometown: Nanoose Bay, BC

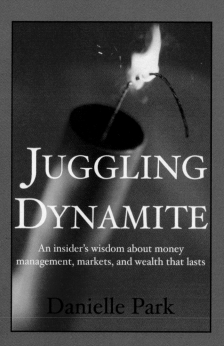

Business & Economics
September
A Paperback Original
6 x 9 | 203 pp
37 B&W illustrations
TP $16.95
978-1-897178-34-8 USA

Marketing Plans

Co-op available

Author Events

Chicago, IL • Seattle, WA

Author Hometown: Barrie, ON

Juggling Dynamite

An insider's wisdom about money management, markets, and wealth that lasts

Danielle Park

This book shows you how to bulletproof your investments so that neither you nor your money are trampled by the herd mentality of the marketplace. Investing can be challenging, and compounding the problem are the pressures that stem from the profit-oriented investment sales industry and the attention-seeking business media. In *Juggling Dynamite,* portfolio manager Danielle Park reveals not only how to protect your money but also how to actively make it grow.

Park explains how investors can benefit from understanding market cycles, the cost of mutual funds, and the evaluation of stock prices. This book will equip you with the tools to make your portfolio grow using active investing and an understanding of market timing. *Juggling Dynamite* will enable you to reach that elusive brass ring: lasting financial success.

Danielle Park is a chartered financial analyst with over sixteen years of professional consulting experience. She helps manage millions of dollars as a portfolio manager and partner at the independent investment counsel firm she co-founded. She is also an avid health and fitness buff. She lives in Barrie, Ontario.

How to put investors in control of their money.

Insomniac Press

The Prosperity Factor for Kids
A comprehensive parent's guide to developing positive saving, spending, and credit habits
Kelley Keehn

This book will help parents teach their children about money and financial responsibility. It is divided by age group, from five-year-olds using a piggy bank to teenagers preparing to leave home for the first time.

Inside you will find many exercises, examples, and tips to help parents and children become financially fit. *The Prosperity Factor for Kids* details incremental lessons and skills needed to turn your kids into mini money managers.

Learning about money and finance can be both easy and fun. In this book, you will find all of the tools necessary to lay the foundation for the financial health and well-being of your child.

Kelley Keehn has been a successful investment professional and speaker for over a decade. Her work has been published in a multitude of media formats around the world. She has spent many years in the financial industry studying the psychology of the ultra-wealthy and now breaks their secrets down into simple steps that anyone can follow.

The definitive guide to teaching children financial responsibility.

Also Available

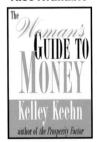

The Woman's Guide to Money
Kelley Keehn
Finance / Business & Economics
6 x 9 | 256 pp
TP $16.95
978-1-897178-08-9 USA

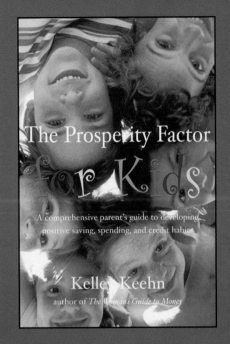

Business & Economics / Parenting
September
A Paperback Original
6 x 9 | 224 pp
24 B&W illustrations
TP $14.95
978-1-897178-42-3 USA

Marketing Plans

Co-op available

Author Events

Washington, DC • Atlanta, GA

Author Hometown: Edmonton, AB

Insomniac Press

Fiction
January
A Paperback Original
6 x 9 | 311 pp
TP $16.95
978-1-897178-36-2 USA

The words don't tell the whole story . . .

Delible
Anne Stone

Sixteen-year-old Melissa Sprague has a lot on her mind: The A-bomb. Acid rain. Where her dad's been hiding out for the last fifteen years. Mel's younger sister, Lora, knows that despite her sister's talent for misery, Mel's preoccupations aren't unusual. But when Mel vanishes, what were the diversions of a teenage girl are taken up as evidence, casting questions over Mel's disappearance. Lora *knows* that someone has taken her sister and it was *not* a stranger who took her. In a narrative both gutsy and intimate, Anne Stone draws us deep into Lora's world, reminding us what it is to be that young and lucid, that vulnerable to a world so much bigger than ourselves.

Anne Stone is a contributing editor at *Matrix* magazine. She has written two other novels: *jacks: a gothic gospel* and *Hush*. She lives in Vancouver.

Marketing Plans
Co-op available

Author Events
Portland, OR • Seattle, WA

Author Hometown: Vancouver, BC

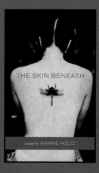

Mystery / Lesbian
Literature
February
A Paperback Original
6 x 9 | 265 pp
TP $16.95
978-1-897178-39-3
USA

The Skin Beneath
Nairne Holtz

Five years ago, Sam O'Connor's sister Chloe died in New York, just another accidental overdose at the Chelsea Hotel. But now, someone has sent Sam a mysterious postcard claiming that Chloe actually died of gunshot wounds and that she was investigating a political conspiracy. Sam has to find out what really happened. As she navigates the twisted trail between fact and fantasy, she is forced to confront some difficult truths about her sister and, more frightening, about herself.

Nairne Holtz, a writer, librarian, and bibliographer, lives in Montreal. This is her first novel.

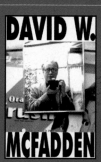

Poetry
October
A Paperback Original
6 x 9 | 328 pp
TP $16.95
978-1-897178-41-6
USA

Selected Poems
David W. McFadden

David W. McFadden's life in Canadian poetry has spanned five decades, and he's still going strong. This selection from his career to date brings back into print many of the greatest poems from nearly two dozen books. McFadden is that rare and precious breed of artist: he is both a poet's poet and a people's poet.

David W. McFadden is the author of many poetry, fiction, and travel books. He lives in Toronto.

Insomniac Press

Raymond Pettibon: V-Boom

Art by Raymond Pettibon

Text by Aaron Rose, F. J. San Martin,
and Frank-Thorsten Moll

Raymond Pettibon is one of the most distinctive and highly regarded American artists of his generation. In the thousands of drawings he has produced over the last two decades, Pettibon stakes out a thematic territory that combines the bright, shiny world of American mass culture with its darkly complex undertows. Pettibon's imagery largely derives from the world of cartoons and popular culture: surfers, trains, baseball players, and cartoon characters. His prolific skill lies in his ability to make powerful and poetic associations between word and image. An avid reader, he isolates a phrase or word and inserts it into his drawing, not as a commentary but as an active graphic element, often written in capitals like a caption to the image. His works range in tone from the polemical to the confessional and introspective and explore the extremes of the human condition from the abject to the sublime.

Pettibon's work was originally produced for the attention of his friends—fellow artists and musicians in the punk scene in Los Angeles in the 1970s and early 1980s. At that time he combined painting, songwriting, performing, and video-making for bands like Sonic Youth, Minutemen, and Black Flag.

Today his works are included in the permanent collections of public galleries throughout the world and have been shown in many solo exhibitions, including the Philadelphia Museum of Art, the Whitney Museum of American Art, and the Museum of Contemporary Art in Los Angeles.

Current work by one of the world's most significant innovators of figurative art.

Art
September
9 x 11 | 272 pp
244 Color illustrations
TC US $65.00 | CAN $78.00
978-3-939583-26-4 CUSA
German bilingual

Artist Hometown: Hermosa Beach, CA

Kehrer Verlag

Frank Rothe: China Naked
Photographs by Frank Rothe
Text by Christoph Tannert and Celina Lunsford

Photography / Art
October
11⅞ x 9½ | 120 pp
60 Color photographs
TC US $40.00
CAN $48.00
978-3-939583-11-0
CUSA
German bilingual

German photographer Frank Rothe has created an unusual and unique portrait of modern China. He breaks through the cliché that we think of "the Chinese" only collectively and shows nude portraits of young and old individuals of Beijing and Shanghai. Rothe then juxtaposes each portrait with a long-exposed cityscape photograph reflecting China's mass society.

Alexander Hahn: Works 1976–2006
Art by Alexander Hahn
Edited by Christoph Vögele

Art
September
9⅝ x 8 | 216 pp
252 Color and B&W
illustrations and
photographs
TC with DVD
US $40.00
CAN $48.00
978-3-939583-20-2
CUSA
German bilingual

This catalog provides the first extensive overview of the works of Swiss video artist Alexander Hahn. The "new media pioneer" has compiled here a representative sampling from his *oeuvre*: works on paper, films and videos, objects, video sculptures, and installations. The accompanying DVD contains videos incorporating a fusion of images and sound, along with poetic texts.

John M Armleder: Too Much is Not Enough
Art by John M Armleder
Edited by Stephan Berg and Raphaela Platow

Art
September
10⅞ x 9⅝ | 128 pp
80 Color photographs
TC US $36.00
CAN $43.50
978-3-939583-02-8
CUSA
German bilingual

John M Armleder is one of the most important Swiss artists today. He deals with art itself by means of his wide-ranging stylistic and formulaic vocabulary, thereby creating an inimitable universe of impressive works that vary between the fields of art, design, concept, Neo Geo, Pop, and Trash. This publication documents the first comprehensive presentation of Armleder's *oeuvre* in the United States.

Fabrizio Plessi: Lava
Art by Fabrizio Plessi
Introduction by Thomas Elsen

Art
September
11⅞ x 9½ | 240 pp
210 Color and B&W
illustrations and
photographs
TC US $40.00
CAN $48.00
978-3-939583-19-6
CUSA
German bilingual

Lava is the title of renowned Italian media artist Fabrizio Plessi's new monumental installation. Lava is a powerful and tremendously fresh work, perhaps one of Plessi's most poetic works. This volume presents the installation and shows drawings for Lava. Plessi achieved international acclaim with the documenta 8 and participation in several Venice Biennials.

Kehrer Verlag

Losing Kei

Suzanne Kamata

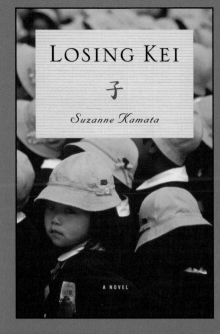

A young mother fights impossible odds to be reunited with her child in this acutely insightful first novel about an intercultural marriage gone terribly wrong.

Jill Parker is an American painter living in Japan. Far from the trendy *gaijin* neighborhoods of downtown Tokyo, she's settled in a remote seaside village where she makes ends meet as a bar hostess. Her world appears to open when she meets Yusuke, a savvy and sensitive art gallery owner who believes in her talent. But their love affair, and subsequent marriage, is doomed to a life of domestic hell, for Yusuke is the *chonan,* the eldest son, who assumes the role of rigid patriarch in his traditional family while Jill's duty is that of a servile Japanese wife. A daily battle of wills ensues as Jill resists instruction in the proper womanly arts. Even the long-anticipated birth of a son, Kei, fails to unite them. Divorce is the only way out, but in Japan a foreigner has no rights to custody, and Jill must choose between freedom and abandoning her child.

Told with tenderness, humor, and an insider's knowledge of contemporary Japan, *Losing Kei* is the debut novel of an exceptional expatriate voice.

Suzanne Kamata's work has appeared in over one hundred publications. She is the editor of *The Broken Bridge: Fiction from Expatriates in Literary Japan* and a forthcoming anthology from Beacon Press on parenting children with disabilities. A five-time nominee for the Pushcart Prize, she has twice won the Nippon Airways/Wingspan Fiction Contest.

An American ex-patriot in Japan goes to desperate lengths to be reunited with her son.

Fiction / Asian Studies
January
A Paperback Original
6 x 9 | 216 pp
TP US $14.95 | CAN $18.00
978-0-9728984-9-2 CUSA

Marketing Plans

Co-op available
Advance reader copies
National advertising:
Asian Week • LA Weekly •
Mothering Magazine • Ms. • Oxygen.com •
Utne Reader

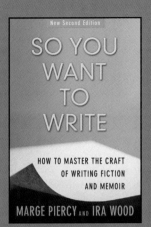

**Confessions of a
Memory Eater**
Pagan Kennedy

Fiction / Women's Literature
6 x 9 | 248 pp
TP US $14.95 | CAN $18.00
978-0-9728984-8-5 CUSA

**So You Want to Write
(2nd Edition)**
How to Master the Craft of
Writing Fiction and Memoir
Marge Piercy and Ira Wood

Writing / Self-Actualization & Self Help
6 x 9 | 288 pp
TP US $16.95 | CAN $20.50
978-0-9728984-5-4 CUSA

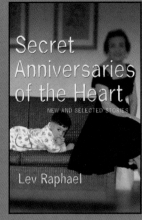

**Secret Anniversaries
of the Heart**
New and Selected Stories
Lev Raphael

Fiction / Jewish Studies
6 x 9 | 300 pp
TP US $15.95 | CAN $19.50
978-0-9728984-7-8 CUSA

**The Devil and
Daniel Silverman**
Theodore Roszak

Fiction / Current Affairs
6 x 9 | 320 pp
TP US $15.95 | CAN $19.50
978-0-9679520-7-9 CUSA

**Louder:
We Can't Hear You (Yet!)**
The Political Poems of Marge Piercy
Marge Piercy

Poetry
5½ x 5
CD 50% US $15.95 | CAN $19.50
978-0-9728984-2-3 CUSA

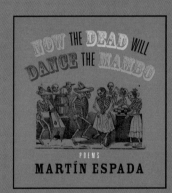

**Now the Dead Will Dance
the Mambo**
The Poems of Martín Espada
Martín Espada

Poetry / Hispanic Studies
5½ x 6⅛
CD 50% US $15.95 | CAN $19.50
978-0-9728984-3-0 CUSA

Sisters of Heaven
China's Barnstorming Aviatrixes: Modernity, Feminism, and Popular Imagination in Asia and the West
Patti Gully

In the late 1930s, as the world moved closer to war, three vivacious Chinese women defied gender perceptions by becoming pilots. Driven by a fierce independent spirit, they realized their dream of flying, completed barnstorming goodwill missions across the Western Hemisphere, and captured the imagination of all those whose lives they touched.

They were Hilda Yan, once China's representative at the League of Nations; Li Xiaqing, known as film actress Li Dandan before becoming China's "First Woman of the Air"; and Jessie Zheng, the only commissioned female officer in the Chinese Air Force.

In a story almost forgotten to history, Patti Gully's exhaustive research delves into the personal lives of these women, uncovering their fascinating personalities, loves, passions, and above all their overwhelming sense of patriotism and duty. In a time when no Chinese woman could even drive a car, these aviatrixes used flight as a metaphor for their own freedom as well as a symbol of empowerment.

Gully shows how, despite their success, their relationships with men were checkered and stormy, leaving behind the wreckage of broken marriages and the children they abandoned—the price they ultimately paid to realize their dream of flying.

With an uncanny eye for detail and technical accuracy, *Sisters of Heaven* offers a rare look at a lost era in aviation history, gender studies, and the history of China and the West.

Patti Gully is a graduate of the University of Winnipeg. She holds a BA in arts with an emphasis on English, religious studies, and classics. She also holds an MLIS from the University of British Columbia. She is an amateur pilot and aviation history scholar and lives in Vancouver.

A League of Their Own meets *The Joy Luck Club* meets *Memphis Belle.*

Asian Studies / Biography & Autobiography
September
6 x 9 | 448 pp
60 B&W photographs
TP US $24.95 | CAN $30.00
978-1-59265-075-0 CUSA

Marketing Plans

Co-op available
Advance reader copies
National advertising:
The New York Times Book Review •
The Women's Review of Books

Author Hometown: Vancouver, BC

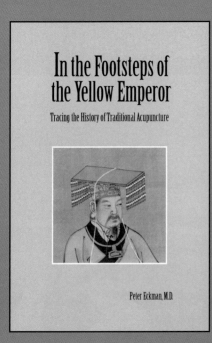

In the Footsteps of the Yellow Emperor
Tracing the History of Traditional Acupuncture
Peter Eckman, MD

Asian Studies / Biography & Autobiography
September
6 x 9 | 248 pp
250 B&W illustrations and photographs
TP US $18.95 | CAN $23.00
978-1-59265-074-3 CUSA

Marketing Plans

Co-op available
Advance reader copies

Author Hometown: San Francisco, CA

Praise for the hardcover edition:

"[Eckman] traces acupuncture through Chinese antiquity with a very readable clarity absent in other scholarly accounts of the same material. This story blossoms in the twentieth-century convergence of acupuncture traditions in Europe, and stands as the only articulate comprehensive account of this migration."—J. Helms, *American Academy of Medical Acupuncture Review*

"A product of monumental research into the tale of how acupuncture has been transmitted from East to West."—Alan Hext, *European Journal of Oriental Medicine*

Acupuncture now enjoys immense popularity as a major form of alternative healing in the West. Once considered mysterious and exotic, acupuncture dates from before the first century BC and the *Huang Di Nei Jing* (*The Yellow Emperor's Internal Classic*), one of ancient China's earliest philosophical and medicinal texts. What makes it so popular today? How did the traditions of acupuncture evolve, migrate, and adapt to different societies worldwide?

Originally published in 1996 to great acclaim, this updated paperback edition of *In the Footsteps of the Yellow Emperor* offers a fascinating and highly readable account of one doctor's personal and professional quest to explore the healing traditions of Asia, its rich historical lineage, and its subsequent transmission to contemporary Europe and North America. It is a must-have book in the healing arts for all practitioners and general-interest readers.

Peter Eckman, MD, PhD (New York University), MAc (College of Traditional Acupuncture, Leamington Spa, England) is editor of *The Essential Book of Traditional Chinese Medicine* and co-author of *Closing the Circle: Lectures on the Unity of Traditional Oriental Medicine.* He has a medical practice in San Francisco.

One doctor's journey of discovering the transmission of medical knowledge from East to West.

Long River Press

Flash Forward 2007
Emerging photographers from Canada, the United Kingdom and the United States
Susan Bright

Flash Forward is The Magenta Foundation's annual emerging photographers competition. Now in its third year, this compelling look at the next generation of artists from three countries brings to light the talent and promise of an exceptional group.

Photographers from Canada, the United States, and the United Kingdom are invited to submit. The jury comprises top industry professionals; this year's jurors are Daniel Faria from the Monte Clark Gallery in Toronto, Simon Bainbridge from the *British Journal of Photography* in the United Kingdom, Darren Ching from *Photo District News* in New York, and new this year, Rebecca McClelland from *The Sunday Times* in the United Kingdom.

Flash Forward showcases the future of photography, focusing on emerging talent that jurors have identified as having great potential. This small volume is essential for curators, collectors, advertising professionals, and artists who wish to stay fully informed about up-and-coming photographers.

Susan Bright is an independent writer, lecturer, and curator. She is a former curator of photographs at the National Portrait Gallery and director of The Association of Photographers Gallery.

Highlighting the young stars of tomorrow. Jurors include *The Sunday Times* (United Kingdom) and *Photo District News* (New York).

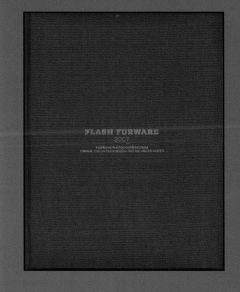

Photography
October
7 x 9 | 192 pp
160 Color photographs
TC US $25.00 | CAN $30.00
978-0-9739739-2-1 CUSA

The Magenta Foundation

Carte Blanche
Photography Vol. 1
**Foreword by Douglas Coupland
with MaryAnn Camilleri**

Photography
9½ x 13 | 260 pp
230 Color and B&W photographs
TC US $65.00 | CAN $78.00
978-0-9739739-0-7 CUSA

Phantom Shanghai
**Photographs by Greg Girard
Foreword by William Gibson
with Leo Rubinfien**

Photography
10 x 13 | 240 pp
120 Color photographs
TC US $50.00 | CAN $60.00
978-0-9739739-1-4 CUSA

Selected Backlist from The Magenta Foundation

Imaginationally
Michael's Lovable Fun of Dictionaries
Michael Bernard Loggins

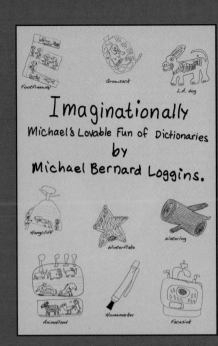

Praise for *Fears of Your Life*:

"Written in a lively, lucid, meticulous hand . . . reminiscent of early Matt Groening, not only in spirit and subject matter, but in style."—*The San Francisco Bay Guardian*

Have you ever felt *terrifical*? Are you in the habit of *uncluding* things you don't like? Maybe you live in *troublemakerhood*. Author Michael Bernard Loggins, an adult with developmental disabilities, gives new meaning to familiar feelings in *Imaginationally*, an illustrated dictionary of words he created to describe his daily experiences and thoughts.

From *afholicatic* (somebody obsessed with things they've never seen before) to *zincky* (when food is spoiled and nasty to eat), customized words are handwritten in alphabetical order with Loggins' own definitions, examples of how you would use them in a sentence, and hand-drawn illustrations. It's a totally original lexicon of *funable* and *laughterful* terms that you just might find yourself using soon. With the special, do-it-yourself pages included in the book, you can add your own personal patois.

Michael Bernard Loggins is the author of *Fears of Your Life*, a handwritten, illustrated book that chronicles more than 180 of his fears both great and small. *Fears of Your Life* was read on National Public Radio's *This American Life*, excerpted in *Harper's Magazine*, and adapted for the stage and performed at Yerba Buena Center for the Arts. Loggins has worked with Creativity Explored, an art studio for adults with developmental disabilities, since 1984. He lives in San Francisco.

The most entertaining imaginary dictionary ever!

Humor / Art
November
6 x 9 | 156 pp
50 B&W illustrations
Paper over Board $14.95
978-1-933149-18-9 USA

Also Available

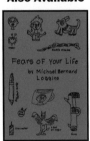

Fears of Your Life
Michael Bernard Loggins
Humor / Art
6 x 9 | 138 pp
TC $12.95
978-0-916397-90-6 USA

Manic D Press

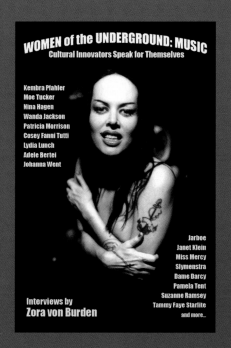

Music / Women's Studies
September
A Paperback Original
5½ x 8½ | 192 pp
22 B&W photographs
TP $15.95
978-1-933149-19-6 USA

Marketing Plans

Co-op available
Advance reader copies
National advertising:
Bitch • Bookslut.com • Bust •
Morbid Curiosity • Nerve • Spin

Author Events

Berkeley, CA • Los Angeles, CA •
San Francisco, CA • Portland, OR •
Bellingham, WA • Olympia, WA • Seattle, WA

Author Hometown: San Francisco, CA

Women of the Underground: Music
Cultural Innovators Speak for Themselves
Interviews by Zora von Burden

"To be truly strong, a performer/artist must enter into extreme vulnerability. If you embrace vulnerability, you emerge fearless from staring your fear in the face. The more open you are in your work as a performer/artist, the more strength you gather."—Jarboe (Swans)

In a series of thirty candid interviews with radical women musicians, author Zora von Burden gives the forerunners of this generation a voice and probes the depths of how and why they broke through society's limitations to create works of outstanding measure. Among the musical genres covered are rock, punk, goth, industrial, electronica, performance art, lounge, and more. An inspiration to young women and fascinating to music fans of all ages and genders, these musical innovators are unconventional, exceptional groundbreakers who have strong followings and have influenced generations for the past fifty years and beyond. An essential reference work for libraries, universities, contemporary art museums, and cultural institutions.

Includes interviews with: Wanda Jackson, Moe Tucker (Velvet Underground), Teresa Nervosa (Butthole Surfers), Nina Hagen, Lydia Lunch, Adele Bertei (The Contortions), Cosey Fanni Tutti (Throbbing Gristle), Jarboe (Swans), Slymenstra (Gwar), Patricia Morrison (Sisters of Mercy, The Damned), Johanna Went, Kembra Pfahler (The Voluptuous Horror of Karen Black), Pamela Tent (The Cockettes), and many others.

Zora von Burden was born and raised in San Francisco, California. A frequent contributor to the *San Francisco Herald,* von Burden also wrote the screenplay for Geoff Cordner's underground cult classic film, *Hotel Hopscotch.*

In their own words: influential women musicians talk about shattering stereotypes and changing the world.

From left to right: Wanda Jackson, Moe Tucker, and Jarboe

Manic D Press

Juicy Mother 2
How They Met
Edited by Jennifer Camper

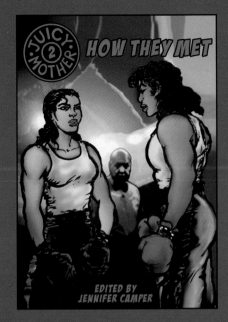

"*Juicy Mother* is what underground comics used to be. Lesbians and homosexuals populate these electric pages, and the scenes can be disturbing. Enlightening, too."
—*The Boston Globe*

The only current publication that showcases comix by queer artists, the groundbreaking graphic novel *Juicy Mother 2* contains richly drawn tales that examine LGBT life from new perspectives: killer dykes chasing romance, a superhero tranny, how Hothead met Chicken, homeboys in love, lesbian internet hook-ups, West Hollywood parties, kids with queer parents, and many other unexpectedly funny depictions of how like-minded individuals have found each other for love, lust, and heartbreak. Thoroughly entertaining adult comix for gender pirates and sexual outlaws, *Juicy Mother 2* contains depictions of sweet sex, rough sex, and confusing sex.

Featuring new work by: Alison Bechdel (*Fun Home*), Tristan Cowen, Howard Cruse (*Stuck Rubber Baby*), Diane DiMassa (*Hothead Paisan*), Jamaica Dyer, Michael Fahy, Lawrence Ferber, Fly, Leanne Franson, Katie Fricas, Chitra Ganesh, Justin Hall, Joan Hilty, Victor Hodge, David Hooper, G.B. Jones, David Kelly, Robert Kirby, Carrie McNinch, Erika Moen, Sara Rojo Parez, Karen Platt, Carlo Diego Quispe, Lawrence Schimel, Serpilla, Ariel Schrag (*Potential*), and Scott Treleaven.

Jennifer Camper is a New York cartoonist and graphic artist. Her books include *Rude Girls and Dangerous Women,* and *subGURLZ.* Her cartoons and illustrations have appeared in many publications, including *The Village Voice, Ms., Out,* and *The Advocate,* and her work has been exhibited across the United States and Europe. She lives in Brooklyn, New York.

The highly anticipated second volume of *Juicy Mother* examines queer life from new perspectives.

Graphic Novels / Lesbian Literature
October
A Paperback Original
7 x 10 | 160 pp
160 B&W illustrations
TP $14.95
978-1-933149-20-2 USA

Manic D Press

The Beatles in Rome 1965
Photographs by Marcello Geppetti

Music / Photography
6¼ x 8¼ | 44 pp
40 B&W photographs
Paper over Board $12.95
978-1-933149-12-7 USA

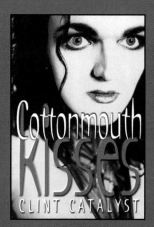

Cottonmouth Kisses
Clint Catalyst

Fiction / Gay Studies
6 x 9 | 160 pp
TP $12.95
978-0-916397-65-4 USA

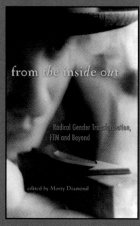

From the Inside Out
Radical Gender Transformation,
FTM and Beyond
Edited by Morty Diamond

Gay Studies / Gender Studies
5½ x 8½ | 168 pp
TP $13.95
978-0-916397-96-8 USA

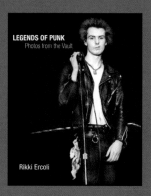

Legends of Punk
Photos from the Vault
Rikki Ercoli

Music / Photography
7 x 10 | 128 pp
TC $19.95
978-0-916397-86-9 USA

Devil Babe's Big Book of Fun!
Isabel Samaras

Popular Culture / Art
8 x 10 | 64 pp
TP $11.95
978-0-916397-52-4 USA

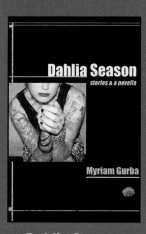

Dahlia Season
stories & a novella
Myriam Gurba

Fiction / Lesbian Literature
6 x 9 | 224 pp
TP $14.95
978-1-933149-16-5 USA

The Concubine of Shanghai
Hong Ying

Praise for *K: The Art of Love*:

"Like all Hong Ying's work, *K* is written with a wonderfully intense simplicity—it's tough, uncompromising, direct and tense with strong emotion, but also full of poetry and grace."—Andrew Motion

Sold by her uncle in 1907 to the First Salon of Gifted Girls, a reputable brothel, sixteen-year-old Cassia is plucked from the ranks of servant girl by a powerful client. Power Chang is the boss of the fearsome Shanghai Triad. In spite of her large feet and pendulous breasts, both unbound, Cassia swiftly becomes his favorite mistress and enjoys her first passionate encounters as well as her first taste of luxurious living.

The story follows Cassia after the violent death of Power Chang and her subsequent rise to "godmother" of Shanghai. She not only seduces the next Triad boss, Huang, after he hears her opera troupe, but also his lacky, Yu, who replaces the murdered Huang as the next Triad leader.

This novel will appeal to anyone interested in China, triad politics and history, and the position of women as sexual slaves to men in Shanghai's houses of ill repute.

Hong Ying grew up in the 1960s in the slums of Chongquing on the Yangtze River in China. An author and poet, she is best known in the English-speaking world for her novels *K: The Art of Love, Peacock Cries, Summer of Betrayal,* and her autobiography, *Daughter of the River*.

From the best-selling author of *K: The Art of Love*—sex, love, and survival in the Shanghai underworld.

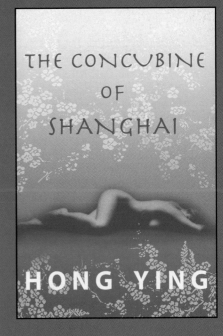

Fiction / Women's Literature
February
A Paperback Original
5½ x 8½ | 288 pp
TP US $14.95 | CAN $18.00
978-0-7145-3150-2 CUSA

Marketing Plans

Co-op available
Advance reader copies
10,000-copy print run
National advertising:
The New York Times Book Review

Peacock Cries
Hong Ying
Translated by Mark Smith
Fiction
5 x 8 | 250 pp
TP US $14.95 | CAN $18.00
978-0-7145-3100-7 CUSA

Also Available

K: The Art of Love
Hong Ying
Translated by Henry Zhao and Nicky Harman
Fiction / Erotica
7¾ x 5 | 262 pp
TP US $14.95 | CAN $18.00
978-0-7145-3072-7 CUSA

Marion Boyars Publishers, Ltd.

Current Affairs / African Studies
October
A Paperback Original
5½ x 8½ | 256 pp
16 Color photographs
TP US $17.95 | CAN $21.50
978-0-7145-3142-7 CUSA

Marketing Plans

15,000-copy print run

More Than Eyes Can See
A nine month journey through the AIDS pandemic
Rhidian Brook

Sent in 2006 by the Salvation Army to bear witness to the work they were doing in response to the AIDS pandemic, Rhidian Brook, his wife, and two children follow a trail of devastation through communities still shattered and being broken by the disease—truck stop sex workers in Kenya, victims of rape in Rwanda, child-headed families in Soweto, children of prostitutes in India. It is a remarkable journey among the infected and the affected through a world that, despite seeming on the brink of collapse, is being held together not by power, politics, guns, or money, but by small acts of kindness performed by unsung people who choose to live in hope.

The problem of AIDS and HIV is a cause supported by many well-known people and events. The recent RED campaign has received publicity due in part to its spokesman, Bono of U2. This book is aimed at a young, politically aware audience who wants to make a difference.

Rhidian Brook is an award-winning novelist, the previous winner of the Somerset Maughan Award and a Betty Trask Award, and a scriptwriter for *Silent Witness* on an ongoing basis. He has written articles on faith, travel, social issues, and education for newspapers including *The Observer,* the *Guardian,* and *Daily Telegraph*. He is also a regular contributor to Radio 4's *Thought for the Day* program.

Rhidian Brook and his family travel through lands devastated by AIDS, including India, Africa, and the Far East.

Marion Boyars Publishers, Ltd.

This May Help You Understand the World
The People and Facts Behind the Headlines
Lawrence Potter

Everyone has insecurities about what they think they should know—the popularity of Lawrence Potter's previous book, *Mathematics Minus Fear*, proves that. With its humorous style, his book makes knowledge accessible to anyone.

Each day, newspapers deliver fresh information on conflicts all around the world. *This May Help You Understand the World* assures you that it is okay to need more information than what is carried in today's papers. People do want to understand the facts behind the headlines, and Potter makes it his business to enable this by discussing the following topics:

- Who has won more battles: the autocrat, plutocrat, theocrat, meritocrat, bureaucrat, democrat, or pornocrat?
- What did you say this country was called? Identity crises in Eastern Europe.
- Charisma or coercion: leaders we fell out of love with.
- Who's kicking now? Political footballs.
- Buckle up: ideology through the window of a private jet.

Lawrence Potter studied classics at Magdalen College in Oxford and has since travelled to Central America, taught English in Romania, and taught math in Rwanda. He is the author of the best-selling title *Mathematics Minus Fear,* also published by Marion Boyars.

From Bush's blunderings to global glitches— the problems of a troubled world made easy.

Current Affairs
October
A Paperback Original
5½ x 8½ | 256 pp
TP US $17.95 | CAN $21.50
978-0-7145-3137-3 CUSA

Also Available

Mathematics Minus Fear
Lawrence Potter
Education & Teaching / Mathematics
5½ x 8½ | 180 pp
20 Graphs
TP US $17.95 | CAN $21.50
978-0-7145-3115-1 CUSA

Marion Boyars Publishers, Ltd.

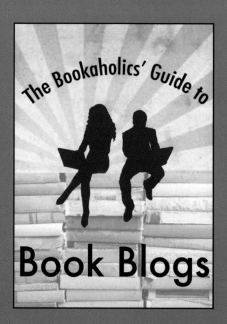

Literature & Essay
September
A Paperback Original
5½ x 8½ | 288 pp
TP US $17.95 | CAN $21.50
978-0-7145-3151-9 CUSA

Marketing Plans

Co-op available
Advance reader copies
10,000-copy print run

The Bookaholics' Guide to Book Blogs
the new literary force
Catheryn Kilgarriff, Rebecca Gillieron, and Meryl Zegarek

As more and more bloggers write about books and with some of their websites receiving thousands of hits a day, this is an easy-to-follow guide to the top, book-related blogs.

With the current craze for blogs, the phenomenon of book blogging is of interest from an objective standpoint as well as to those keen to read book reviews. How much influence do these bloggers have? Is there any kind of censorship or quality control? Are booksellers aware of them? Does Oprah Winfrey take note?

Many people develop a real fondness for book bloggers who write reviews for love and not money. Taking in small, quirky websites like Book Slut, dovegreyreader, Bluestalking Reader, and MoorishGirl as well as large, well-known sites like salon.com, this book will show readers how to investigate literature from distant lands, to find the sites of authors who are yet to be discovered by the mainstream, and to find the pages of book industry pundits who have opened their daily lives to a wider world. Welcome to the honest world of book blogs.

Catheryn Kilgarriff and Rebecca Gillieron are editors at Marion Boyars Publishers, and Meryl Zegarek is a book publicist of many years standing. All three have seen the book industry from the inside and are happy that blogs are now opening this world up to ordinary readers.

The first-ever guide to the top book blogs—includes interviews and sample reviews.

Marion Boyars Publishers, Ltd.

I Could Tell You But Then You Would Have to be Destroyed by Me

Emblems from the Pentagon's Black World

Trevor Paglen

Shown here for the first time, these seventy-five patches reveal a secret world of military imagery and jargon, where classified projects are known by peculiar names ("Goat Suckers," "None of Your Fucking Business," "Tastes Like Chicken") and illustrated with occult symbols and ridiculous cartoons. Although the actual projects represented here (such as the notorious Area 51) are classified, these patches— which are worn by military units working on classified missions—are precisely photographed, strangely hinting at a world about which little is known.

By submitting hundreds of Freedom of Information requests, the author has also assembled an extensive and readable guide to the patches included here, making this volume the best available survey of the military's black world—a $40 billion industry that has quietly grown by almost 50 percent since 9/11.

Trevor Paglen is a geographer by training, and an expert on clandestine military installations. He leads expeditions to the secret bases of the American West and is the author, with A.C. Thompson, of *Torture Taxi: On the Trail of the CIA's Rendition Flights*, which *The New York Times* praised as "the real thing . . . and not on the evening news."

A catalog of military patches representing secret US projects— a sure cult hit.

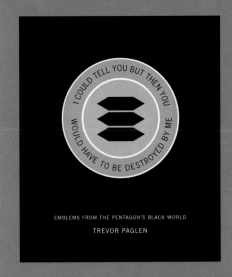

Current Affairs /
Political Science & Government
November
6 x 8 | 136 pp
75 Color illustrations
TC US $20.00 | CAN $24.00
978-1-933633-32-9 CUSA

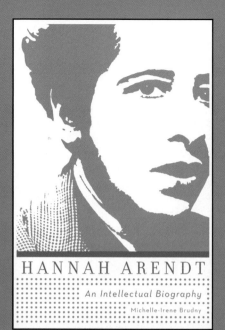

Biography & Autobiography / Philosophy
March
5½ x 7½ | 250 pp
TC US $24.95 | CAN $30.00
978-1-933633-35-0 CUSA

Marketing Plans

Co-op available
Advance reader copies
10,000-copy print run

Author Events

New Haven, CT • New York, NY

Hannah Arendt
An Intellectual Biography
Michelle-Irene Brudny

With her discovery that Hannah Arendt wrote her masterpiece, *The Origins of Totalitarianism,* years earlier than previously thought—well before World War II and anticipating the horrors of Nazism—Michelle-Irene Brudny overturns traditional Arendt scholarship. Based on that groundbreaking discovery, Brudny rejects the claim that Arendt is primarily a polemical writer and shows instead that she was a true visionary.

In this first intellectual biography of Arendt, Brudny traces the development of Arendt's philosophy, showing her wide-ranging interests and her intellectual growth. She clearly delineates the influence of Arendt's philosophy teacher and lover, Martin Heidegger, and illuminates Arendt's complex relationship with Judaism—which Arendt never saw as her "repellant doppelganger," as has been sometimes said. Brudny also examines the importance of Arendt's American years—an area that, until now, has been little explored.

The writings and philosophies of Hannah Arendt have never been more relevant, especially in the context of today's violence and barbarism. With fascinating details about her life and her influence on contemporary philosophy, this brief biography— one of only two Arendt biographies available in English—is an excellent guide to the life and work of one of the twentieth century's most important thinkers.

Michelle-Irene Brudny is a philosopher and American studies professor at the University of Rouen. She is one of a team of scholars charged with editing and publishing Hannah Arendt's posthumous work.

New scholarship reveals Hannah Arendt to be a true visionary.

Melville House

Biting the Wax Tadpole
Adventures in Word Travel
Elizabeth Little

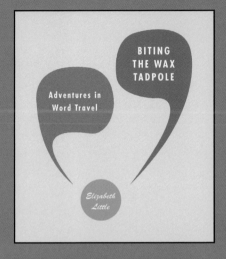

Biting the Wax Tadpole is a decidedly unstuffy look at the staid world of learning languages. Using examples from languages dead, difficult, and just plain made-up, grammar fanatic Elizabeth Little shares all of the irresistible "dirty bits"—irregular verbs, unusual spellings, and evolutionary quirks—that give languages their character and comprise what she calls "word travel."

Using unexpected comparisons, Little reveals the finer points of the spoken and written word—such as how American rap lyrics illustrate the way middle voice works in Hungarian. Or how literal translation of movie titles explains the use of verbal adjectives in Mandarin. Burning topics in modern linguistics are also addressed, including: Is Klingon or Vulcan the more legitimate language? Does Britney Spears' poetry mean anything to anyone in any language anywhere?

The fully illustrated book also includes funny, informative sidebars about classic cases of mistranslation, such as when Coca-Cola tried to find its phonetic equivalent in Chinese: pronounced "ke-kou-ke-le." Though it sounded right, the characters literally translated to "bite the wax tadpole." Not what Coke had in mind, but in Elizabeth Little's off-kilter travel guide, it's just another example of language taking you someplace interesting.

Elizabeth Little is a writer and editor living in New York City. She has worked as a literary agent and as a writer and editor for the travel guide *Let's Go: China,* and her writing has appeared in *The New York Times.* This is her first book.

A grammar fanatic explores her peculiar love for learning the quirks and curiosities of foreign languages.

Reference
November
7½ x 8½ | 275 pp
TC US $21.95 | CAN $26.50
978-1-933633-33-6 CUSA

Marketing Plans

Co-op available
Advance reader copies
15,000-copy print run

Author Events

St. Louis, MO • New York, NY

Author Hometown: New York, NY

Melville House

The Confessions of Noa Weber

Gail Hareven

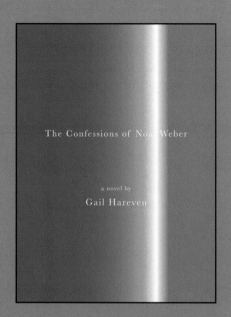

The Confessions of Noa Weber

a novel by

Gail Hareven

Fiction / Women's Studies
January
A Paperback Original
5½ x 7½ | 300 pp
TP US $16.95 | CAN $20.50
978-1-933633-37-4 CUSA

Marketing Plans

Co-op available
Advance reader copies

Author Events

San Francisco, CA • Washington, DC •
Chicago, IL • New York, NY

This award-winning novel by major Israeli novelist Gail Hareven is, by turns, a funny, self-mocking, brutally honest, and always absorbing account of one woman's quest to understand her longtime obsessive love for one mysterious man.

Middle-aged writer Noa Weber—acclaimed both as a writer and as one of Israel's leading feminists—has all the trappings of a successful "feminist" life: She has a strong career, a wonderful daughter she raised alone, and she's a respected cultural figure. Yet her interior life is inextricably bound by her love for a man—Alek, a Russian émigré and the father of her child, who, over the years, has drifted in and out of her life.

Trying to understand—as well as free herself from—this lifelong obsession, Noa turns her pen upon herself, and with relentless honesty dissects her life. Against the evocative setting of turbulent, modern-day Israel, the examination becomes a quest to transform the nature of her love from irrational desire to a greater, transcendent comprehension of the sublime.

The Confessions of Noa Weber introduces to the English-speaking world a startlingly talented writer in a rich tale that illuminates the desires, yearnings, and complexities of life in Israel, and of people trying to balance the needs of the secular world with the ultimate need and desire for transcendence.

Gail Hareven is one of Israel's leading writers; the author of five novels, three short story collections, plays, a nonfiction book, and two children's books; and the winner of the prestigious Sapir Prize for The Confessions of Noa Weber. She teaches writing and feminist theory in Jerusalem. This is her first book to be translated into English.

One woman's unflinching look at emotional, spiritual, and physical obsession.

Melville House

Close to Jedenew
Kevin Vennemann

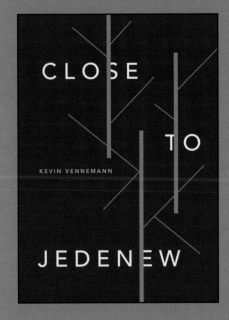

"A stunning debut."—*Die Zeit*

"Vennemann intertwines the tenderest memories of childhood and friendship with the denial that the murderers have already entered the house. Who would have thought the novel capable of this profoundly original way to examine anti-Semitism and the formation of atrocity?"—Lore Segal, author of *Her First American*

It begins like a classic German fable: Children from the rural village of Jedenew, Poland, get together late at night to play together in the dark woods. But their game is to pretend they live in the imaginary world of the Jedenew that came before them—when it wasn't occupied by the Nazis, and when their Jewish friends weren't mysteriously disappearing one by one.

Kevin Vennemann's writing—already a sensation with the major publishing houses of Europe—is evocative of W.G. Sebald for its lyrical style and bold intelligence. The innovative simultaneous plot—consisting of the real *and* imaginary worlds of the children—has been compared to the piercing analogies of Kafka. But the accessible and absorbing narrative of *Close to Jedenew*, as well as its beautifully lush prose, signals the emergence of one of the most original and masterful young writers to appear in decades.

Kevin Vennemann was born in 1977 in Germany and today lives in Vienna and Paris. Melville House will publish his second novel, *Mara Kogoj,* in 2008.

The writer heralded as the next W.G. Sebald in a searing debut novel.

Fiction
February
5½ x 7 | 200 pp
TC US $22.95 | CAN $27.50
978-1-933633-39-8 CUSA

Marketing Plans

Co-op available
Advance reader copies

In Hoboken
Christian Bauman

"Bauman writes with precision, in prose that reverberates . . . strong, compelling work."—Robert Stone

As the son of a folk singer whose suicide gained him cult status, Thatcher has a leg up on New York's music scene. Instead, he decides to keep his parentage secret and take his guitar across the river to seedy Hoboken, New Jersey, to form a band.

There, amidst the tenements and dive bars and all-night diners, Thatcher and his friends struggle to make meaningful music in a culture turning away from it.

A wicked sense of humor turns out to be key for the motley crew: manager Marsh, the beloved, polio-stricken local rock-and-roll kingpin; lesbian singer/songwriter Lou, to whom Thatcher is deeply attracted; James, guitar virtuoso and daytime World Trade Center employee, not to mention owner of the floor Thatcher is sleeping on; and locals such as Orris, the overweight, half-blind prophet of Hoboken's west side and patient at the mental clinic where Thatcher is a clerk.

As in Roddy Doyle's *The Commitments* and Nick Hornby's *High Fidelity,* the music is at the heart of it all. But in *In Hoboken* the place and the people turn out to be just as inspiring.

Christian Bauman's acclaimed debut *The Ice Beneath You,* and his second novel, *Voodoo Lounge,* were both based on his experiences as an American soldier in the mid-1990s fighting in Somalia. He now lives outside Philadelphia, Pennsylvania.

Apparently, it takes all kinds to make a rock band in working-class America . . .

Fiction
March
A Paperback Original
5½ x 7½ | 250 pp
TP US $15.95 | CAN $19.50
978-1-933633-47-3 CUSA

Marketing Plans

Co-op available
Advance reader copies

Melville House

Reporting Iraq

An Oral History of the War by the Journalists who Covered It

Edited by Mike Hoyt, John Palatella, and the editors of the *Columbia Journalism Review*

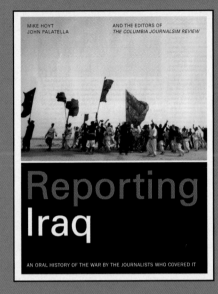

"Never in the fifty years that I have been in or around the news business have I read a better record of a historic event than this."—Reese Schonfeld, founding president of CNN

"This should be required reading in every journalism class from high school to graduate school."—James W. Crawley, president of Military Reporters and Editors

Following in the footsteps of best-selling books about the war, *Reporting Iraq* is a fully illustrated narrative history of the war by the world's best-known reporters and photojournalists. Included are contributions from fifty journalists, including Dexter Filkins (the *New York Times* correspondent who won widespread praise for his coverage of Fallujah), Rajiv Chandrasekaran (author of *Imperial Life in the Emerald City*), Anthony Shadid (the *Washington Post* reporter awarded a Pulitzer Prize for his Iraq reporting), and Patrick Cockburn (from London's *Independent*).

In this, the first book to tell the history of the war through the end of 2006, the deadliest period of the conflict, we learn that most journalists saw a disaster in Iraq before they were allowed to report it. This revelation, along with hundreds of untold first-person stories and numerous censored photographs, makes *Reporting Iraq* a fascinating look at the war and an important critique of international press coverage.

Reporting Iraq is published in conjunction with the *Columbia Journalism Review*, America's premier media monitor and a watchdog of the press in all its forms, from newspapers and magazines to radio, television, wire services, and the Internet.

A major event: first-person stories of the war by the world's best-known correspondents.

Current Affairs / History
October
7 x 9 | 300 pp
25 Color photographs
TP US $18.95 | CAN $23.00
978-1-933633-34-3 CUSA
LB y US $60.00 | CAN $72.00
978-1-933633-38-1 CUSA

Marketing Plans

Co-op available
Advance reader copies

Author Events

New York, NY

Author Hometown: New York, NY

Melville House

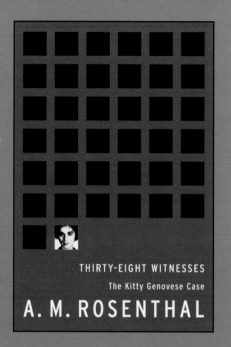

THIRTY-EIGHT WITNESSES
The Kitty Genovese Case

A. M. ROSENTHAL

True Crime / History
January
Melville House Classic Journalism
5 x 7 | 100 pp
10 B&W photographs
TP US $14.95 | CAN $18.00
978-1-933633-29-9 CUSA

Marketing Plans

Co-op available
Advance reader copies

Author Hometown: New York, NY

Thirty-Eight Witnesses
The Kitty Genovese Case
A.M. Rosenthal
Introduction by Samuel Freedman
Foreword by Arthur Ochs Sulzberger

"The most important book by perhaps the most important newspaper editor of the last half century."—Gay Talese

"Abe Rosenthal told a stunning, tragic story and called each one of us to account for averting our eyes—and hearts—and voices."—Mike Wallace

"A memorable book that needs to be available to anyone who struggles to live an honorable life."—Robert Coles

It's one of the most oft-cited murders in US history: Thirty-eight people in Queens, New York, watched from their windows as twenty-eight-year-old Kitty Genovese was chased by a madman with a knife up and down their respectable, middle-class street, screaming for help while she was attacked, again and again, until she was dead. The murder took over half an hour. Not one of the thirty-eight witnesses did a thing to help her.

Legendary newsman Abe Rosenthal was metro editor of *The New York Times* then, and the murder occurred on his beat.

Thirty years after its first publication, his *Thirty-Eight Witnesses* remains the only book on the subject, as well as the only book ever written by the great journalist. It is part memoir, part investigative journalism, and part public service.

A.M. Rosenthal was, for many years, the executive editor of *The New York Times* who decided to run the Pentagon Papers, among other notable stories. Before that, he won the Pulitzer Prize for his journalism. He died in 2005.

The only book by the fabled journalist is the only book on the famous murder.

Melville House

The Secret History of the English Language

M.J. Harper

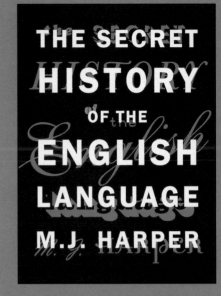

"The most outrageous book I have ever read, and one of the funniest."—*The Oldie*

"Unusual, funny, and provocative. . . . This fascinating book is a useful investigation into the ways in which history is constructed and the dangers of 'unassailable' academic truths."—*New Statesman*

"The best rewriting of history since *1066 And All That*."—*Fortean Times*

"Mind-blowing, incredibly entertaining stuff. . . . A well-written and funny book."—*Daily Mail*

In a hugely enjoyable read with gloriously corrosive prose, M.J. Harper slashes and burns through the whole of accepted academic thought about the history of the English language. According to Harper:

- The English language does not derive from an Anglo-Saxon language.
- French, Italian, and Spanish did not descend from Latin.
- Middle English is a wholly imaginary language created by well-meaning but deluded academics.
- Most of the entries in the *Oxford English Dictionary* are wrong.

And that's just the beginning. Part revisionist history, part treatise on the real origins of the English language, and part impassioned argument against academia, *The Secret History of the English Language* is essential reading for language lovers, history buffs, Anglophiles, and anyone who has ever thought twice about what they've learned in school.

M.J. Harper is an applied epistemologist. He lives in London.

A snarkily original, blistering attack that shows how everything you know about the origins of the English language is wrong.

Reference / History
February
5½ x 7½ | 225 pp
TC $21.95
978-1-933633-31-2 USA

Melville House

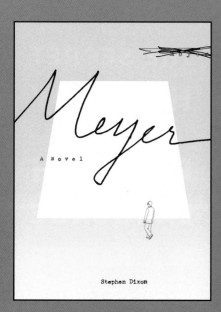

Fiction
September
A Paperback Original
5½ x 7½ | 300 pp
TP US $16.95 | CAN $20.50
978-1-933633-30-5 CUSA

Marketing Plans

Co-op available
Advance reader copies

Author Events

Washington, DC • Baltimore, MD •
New York, NY • Philadelphia, PA

Author Hometown: Baltimore, MD

Meyer
Stephen Dixon

"One of the great secret masters."—Jonathan Lethem

"A hip Saul Bellow."—*Publishers Weekly*

The twenty-seventh book of fiction by the award-winning Baltimore writer sets up a situation that the protagonist—Meyer, a prolific fiction writer from Baltimore—finds preposterous: writer's block. After numerous books, Meyer has never experienced writer's block before, and panic sets in.

In a story rife with Stephen Dixon's trademark zest and style, Meyer proceeds to rifle through all the possible aspects of his life that could make for good fiction, and to try whatever it takes to get writing again. Sometimes sex with his wife helps, so he tries that without luck—several times, just to be sure. He wonders if he should try sex with one of the neighbors. He wonders if he should try writing about his parents' death . . . again. He wonders about concocting awful things for himself and his family. He wonders about concocting wonderful things for himself and his family. He wonders what he's doing, and tries sex with his wife again.

It is, in short, Stephen Dixon at his best: stylish, funny, moving, and relentless as ever in his pursuit of the small, meaningful, and ultimately powerful revelations of everyday life.

Stephen Dixon is the author of *Old Friends*, *Phone Rings*, and numerous other books. He has twice been a finalist for the National Book Award and has won honors from the Guggenheim Foundation, the National Endowment for the Arts, and The American Academy of Arts and Letters.

A master novelist confronts writer's block with sex, coffee, and an eraser.

Phone Rings
Stephen Dixon
Fiction
5½ x 8 | 280 pp
TP US $15.00 | CAN $18.00
978-0-9761407-8-8 CUSA

**Also
Available**

Old Friends
Stephen Dixon
Fiction
4¾ x 7½ | 220 pp
TC US $22.95 | CAN $27.50
978-0-97496-092-0 CUSA

Melville House

The Lemoine Affair
Marcel Proust

It is surprising but true: a polished, mature work by Marcel Proust that was unavailable in English translation—until now. In this overlooked comedic gem based on a true story, the author considered one of the most important writers of the twentieth century tells the tale of a con artist who claimed he could manufacture diamonds, with each chapter of the tale written in the style of a different French writer.

This delicious spoof of Balzac, Flaubert, Chateaubriand, and others is presented in a sparkling, nuanced translation by the award-winning Charlotte Mandell, exclusively for The Art of the Novella series.

Marketing Plans
Co-op available

Fiction
February
The Art of the Novella
5 x 7 | 100 pp
TP US $9.00 | CAN $11.00
978-1-933633-41-1 CUSA

The only available translation of Marcel Proust's masterful spoof of French masters Balzac, Flaubert, and others.

The Coxon Fund
Henry James

The first stand-alone edition of this lesser-known novella from the master of the form is a wry comedy about the fine line between making art and freeloading. Henry James examines one of his favorite topics—the artist's place in society—by profiling a "genius" who just can't seem to support himself. A dazzling intellectual and brilliant speaker, Mr. Saltram has become the most sought-after houseguest in England. As the society ladies compete to see who can host him more lavishly, Saltram warms to the many comforts of English country house living. And, as his intellectual labors slacken, it becomes harder and harder to get him to leave.

Marketing Plans
Co-op available

Fiction
February
The Art of the Novella
5 x 7 | 100 pp
TP US $9.00 | CAN $11.00
978-1-933633-42-8 CUSA

A wry, edgy comedy on the fine line between making art and freeloading.

May Day
F. Scott Fitzgerald

Fiction
February
The Art of the Novella
5 x 7 | 100 pp
TP US $9.00 | CAN $11.00
978-1-933633-43-5 CUSA

The only stand-alone volume of a rare political study by the American master F. Scott Fitzgerald.

Although F. Scott Fitzgerald is known for the kind of subtle, polished social commentary found in his masterpiece *The Great Gatsby*, his little-known novella *May Day* is unique in that it is the most raw, direct socio-political commentary he ever wrote, and one of the most desperate works in his *oeuvre*. It is a dark, biting story in which rich, drunken Yale students in town for a reunion, hordes of soldiers returning from the First World War, and the workers of a small socialist newspaper all converge in New York City on May Day. This is the first and only stand-alone version of this rarity.

Marketing Plans
Co-op available

Rasselas, Prince of Abyssinia
Samuel Johnson

Fiction
February
The Art of the Novella
5 x 7 | 100 pp
TP US $9.00
CAN $11.00
978-1-933633-44-2
CUSA

The other great book by the man who wrote the dictionary: This is Dr. Samuel Johnson's beautiful, engaging, and ultimately inspiring story of a royal brother and sister who escape the castle and, traveling in disguise, search for knowledge and a way to feel more useful to society. It is a masterpiece of English literature.

The Deceitful Marriage
Miguel de Cervantes

Fiction
March
The Art of the Novella
5 x 7 | 100 pp
TP US $9.00
CAN $11.00
978-1-933633-04-6
CUSA

The first stand-alone edition of this wicked satire by the great author is a strikingly experimental, humorous, and racy story about a cheating husband sent to the hospital after his wife gives him syphilis. Shocked, he is further stunned to overhear the hospital's guard dogs having a rather interesting conversation.

Melville House The Art of the Novella Series

The Centaur's Son
Stories
Philip Daughtry

Philip Daughtry writes, both autobiographically and fictionally, of love, intellectuality, danger, and farce.

Daughtry trespasses federal land in Oregon to greet a wild stallion; follows a young cheating husband through pagan Ireland as he attempts to heal a wounded bird to win back the trust of his wife; visits a doomed drunken poet in Helsinki; finds first love, for a night, in 1960s Paris; works with an insane cowhand in lawless Belize backcountry; traffics special cargo into Ireland; describes the lives of children living and playing in an abandoned prison camp in northern England; travels with gypsies along Spain's Gold Coast; and speculates on a flooded world where haunted men sail between mountaintops of islands:

In my experience few men embraced this quietude and so confused human will with human being. Whole nations charged arrogantly onward at the directives of pragmatic reason over earthly evidence denying dominion to all species under meaningless flags of suicidal faith. These still, final hours tell me I am among the last of a race that awakened too late to the forces of air, earth, fire and water. Men have no name among galaxies gathering dust where dust began and I will not sign one as this paper runs out.

Philip Daughtry was born in England in 1942 and is a descendant of American outlaws Frank and Jesse James. He was involved in the Baby Beat Generation during the 1970s San Francisco Renaissance. He teaches at Santa Monica College in southern California.

Stories describing the observations and world travels of poet and Beat writer Philip Daughtry.

Literature & Essay / Travel & Travel Guides
October
A Paperback Original
5½ x 8½ | 140 pp
TP US $15.00 | CAN $18.00
978-1-56279-131-5 CUSA

Marketing Plans

Co-op available
Advance reader copies

Walking with Nobby
Conversations with Norman O. Brown
Dale Pendell

"Dr. Brown was a master of philosophical speculation, mixing Marx, Freud, Jesus and much else to raise and answer immense questions."—Douglas Martin, *The New York Times*

Dale Pendell and retired professor Norman O. Brown, during walks taken along the coast of California, discuss many concepts and characters, including paganism and world religions, Dionysus, Marx, and Freud, presented here as footnoted conversations.

Norman O. Brown (1913–2002) was an American scholar born in El Oro, Mexico. He studied at Oxford University and the University of Wisconsin, Madison, and taught at Wesleyan University and the University of California, Santa Cruz.

Writer Dale Pendell was a student and friend of Brown.

Marketing Plans
Co-op available • Advance reader copies

Author Hometown: Penn Valley, CA

Literature & Essay / Philosophy
October
A Paperback Original
5½ x 8½ | 170 pp
TP US $18.00 | CAN $21.95
978-1-56279-132-2 CUSA

Discussions, transcribed after five walks, between author Dale Pendell and retired professor Norman O. Brown.

The Harp and the Shadow
Alejo Carpentier
Translated by Thomas Christensen and Carol Christensen

"An extraordinary display of historical inquisitiveness and stylistic maturity."
—*The New York Times Book Review*

Exploring the consequences of the European discovery of the Americas and challenging the myth of Columbus, Alejo Carpentier—"the father of magical realism"—studies the first meetings of the Western and American cultures and the tragic consequences of tarnished and abandoned idealism.

Alejo Carpentier (1904–1980) is considered one of the fathers of modern Latin American literature. He lived in Cuba, France, and Venezuela.

Thomas Christensen and Carol Christensen have translated the works of Julio Cortázar, Laura Esquivel, and Carlos Fuentes.

Marketing Plans
Advance reader copies

Fiction / History
October
5½ x 8½ | 170 pp
TP US $17.00 | CAN $20.50
978-1-56279-133-9 CUSA

A fictional exploration of the characters involved in the European discovery of the Americas.

Mercury House

The Brand New Monty Python Papperbok
Monty Python

One of the most original and groundbreaking humor classics of all time, the *Papperbok* was compiled for Methuen in the early 1970s by the young Monty Python team at the height of their surreal powers and was published on the heels of the improbable success of *Monty Python's Flying Circus*.

A surreal delight, the *Papperbok* was a testing ground for ideas equally as fresh and funny as the *Flying Circus* material. It is full of colorful and rude illustrations by Terry Gilliam, oddball instruction sheets, cod schoolboy stories about adventure and mischief, misleading horoscopes, informative and thrilling features—such as "Hamster: A Warning," "The Python Book of Etiquette," and "The London Casebook of Detective René Descartes"—zany competitions, fake editorials, spurious film reviews, and some of the oddest miscellany ever pressed between the pages of a book.

The extraordinary comic genius of Monty Python is on full display in this humor classic, too-long unavailable and now back by popular demand.

**One of the most original humor books ever written,
from the creators of Monty Python.**

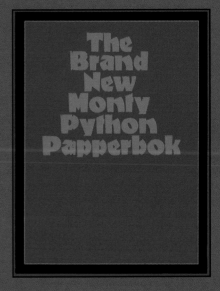

Humor / Film & TV
September
Methuen Humour
8½ x 11 | 96 pp
90 Color and B&W illustrations
and photographs
TP US $24.95 | CAN $30.00
978-0-413-77642-6 CUSA

Marketing Plans

Co-op available
Advance reader copies
10,000-copy print run

**Also
Available**

Monty Python and the
Holy Grail Screenplay
Drama
5 x 8 | 92 pp
TP US $14.95 | CAN $18.00
978-0-413-74120-2 CUSA

The Very Best of Monty Python
Monty Python
Film & TV / Humor
5 x 6 | 320 pp
320 Color and B&W illustrations and
photographs
TP US $16.95 | CAN $20.50
978-0-413-77615-0 CUSA

Methuen Publishing, Ltd.

Treasure Hunt
Peter Earle

History
September
6¼ x 9½ | 256 pp
TC US $30.00 | CAN $36.00
978-0-413-77638-9 CUSA

An astonishing history of the British obssession with hunting sunken treasure, by a world-renowned naval historian.

In 1687 Captain William Phips arrived in English waters with forty tons of treasure rescued from the wreck of the Concepción, sunk forty years before in the middle of the ocean. The great British treasure-hunting boom had begun. Over the next two centuries, many such adventures, most based on extremely dubious information, were begun. World-renowned historian Peter Earle returns with an extraordinary history of outstanding bravery, exceptional recklessness, and above all, dreams of treasure.

Peter Earle is emeritus reader in economic history at the University of London and the author of *The Pirate Wars*.

Marketing Plans
Co-op available • Advance reader copies

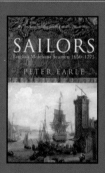

History
October
5 x 7½ | 256 pp
TP US $13.95
CAN $17.00
978-0-413-77634-1
CUSA

Sailors
English Merchant Seamen 1650–1775
Peter Earle

Sailors is the history of the English seaman in the seventeenth and eighteenth centuries, a period during which England rose to dominance in world commerce and became the greatest naval power in the world. Drawing on primary documents and memoirs, this is an exemplary history of those who lived and toiled on the sea.

Humor
February
A Paperback Original
Methuen Humour
5 x 7½ | 500 pp
TP US $15.95
CAN $19.50
978-0-413-77648-8
CUSA

Michael Frayn Collected Columns
Michael Frayn

Playwright and novelist Michael Frayn originally came to prominence as the writer of short, surreal, razor-sharp explorations of human foibles, sex, politics, manners, and the events of the day. Here are 110 of his finest and funniest pieces, selected and introduced by himself.

Michael Frayn is the author of plays including *Copenhagen*, novels including *Headlong*, and the recent philosophy work *The Human Touch*.

Methuen Publishing, Ltd.

Nothing Happens in Carmincross
Benedict Kiely

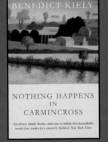

Fiction
January
A Paperback Original
5 x 7½ | 240 pp
TP US $13.95
CAN $17.00
978-0-413-77641-9
CUSA

At the height of the Troubles, Mervyn returns from America to his native Ulster, only to find the specter of bombs and political murder hanging over his idyllic Carmincross. This is the timely reissue of Benedict Kiely's novel about a land riven by terrorism.

Benedict Kiely was one of the most celebrated Irish writers of the twentieth century. He died in February 2007.

Building Radar
Forging Britain's Early-Warning Chain, 1935–1945
Colin Dobinson

Military History
January
6¼ x 9½ | 356 pp
36 B&W photographs
and illustrations
TC US $45.00
CAN $54.00
978-0-413-77229-9
CUSA

This is the first detailed study of the patterning and design of Britain's early-warning radar stations of the Second World War, without which the Battle of Britain could not have been won. The book draws upon extensive new research in wartime papers.

Colin Dobinson is a renowned British historian and archeologist.

AA Command
Britain's Anti-Aircraft Defences of the Second World War
Colin Dobinson

Military History
February
6¼ x 9½ | 320 pp
TP US $30.00
CAN $36.00
978-0-413-77633-4
CUSA

This first full-length history of Britain's anti-aircraft defenses during the Second World War draws upon original documents and firsthand accounts from men and women who defended the home front during the Battle of Britain, the Blitz, and the Luftwaffe's cruel campaigns against cathedral cities and coastal resorts.

Fields of Deception
Britain's Bombing Decoys of World War II
Colin Dobinson

Military History
February
6½ x 9½ | 320 pp
TP US $30.00
CAN $36.00
978-0-413-77632-7
CUSA

During the Second World War, Britain's Air Ministry secretly coordinated a strategy to defeat German bombers with the aid of film industry technicians, by means of ingeniously designed decoy airfields, towns, and military bases built throughout the island. This is the only available study of this unique secret history.

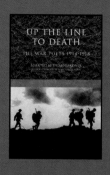

Up The Line To Death
The War Poets 1914–1918
Edited by Brian Gardner

Poetry Anthology
October
5 x 7½ | 230 pp
TP US $13.95
CAN $17.00
978-0-413-59570-6
CUSA

The most complete and compelling anthology of First World War poetry, this book includes poems by Wilfred Owen, Siegfried Sassoon, Rupert Brooke, Edward Thomas, and many others who beautifully convey the horror, fear, and pity of war.

Brian Gardner was a noted writer and historian of the First and Second World Wars.

The Terrible Rain
The War Poets 1939–1945
Edited by Brian Gardner

Poetry Anthology
November
A Paperback Original
5 x 7½ | 230 pp
TP US $13.95
CAN $17.00
978-0-413-15010-3
CUSA

The poetry of the Second World War has often been dismissed as inferior to that of the First World War. This book shows how wrong that assessment is. Poets of the home front—Louis MacNeice, W.H. Auden, Dylan Thomas, Laurie Lee—responded to create a remarkable record of the spirit of their time.

The Dictionary of Liberal Thought
Edited by Duncan Brack and Ed Randall

Political Science &
Government /
Reference
September
Politicos
6¼ x 9½ | 416 pp
TC US $50.00
CAN $60.00
978-1-84275-167-1
CUSA

This is a comprehensive guide to the key figures and ideas of the liberal-democratic tradition from the seventeenth century to the present. With a broad compass, taking in liberal, social democrat, and libertarian thinkers, movements, and concepts, this is the first dictionary of its kind. Each article includes a biography, key ideas, key works, and further reading.

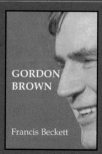

Gordon Brown
Francis Beckett

Biography &
Autobiography /
Current Affairs
September
Politicos
6¼ x 9½ | 240 pp
TC US $30.00
CAN $36.00
978-1-84275-213-5
CUSA

What sort of man is Gordon Brown? What do his life and career tell us about the sort of prime minister he will be? Will a Brown government be fundamentally different from a Blair government? Here, the most revealing portrait yet of Britain's next prime minister.

Francis Beckett is a highly experienced journalist, writer, and contemporary historian.

Methuen Publishing, Ltd.

Videodrome
Studies in the Horror Film
Tim Lucas

Released in 1983, David Cronenberg's *Videodrome* is one of his most original and provocative works, fusing social commentary with shocking elements of sex and violence. Crossing the boundary between science fiction, horror, and social criticism, *Videodrome* remains a unique and brilliant work in the *oeuvre* of cinema's greatest maverick.

Tim Lucas had behind-the-scenes access to every facet of production when *Videodrome* was filmed in 1981. His unique perspective provides interviews with cast and crew, including exclusive, never-before-published interviews with Cronenberg, commentary and analysis of the film, and over sixty black-and-white and color photographs, many never before seen.

Videodrome is the first in the Studies in the Horror Film series, which aims to present critical and popular discussion of the great horror films in affordable, attractive packages.

Tim Lucas is the editor of *Video Watchdog* magazine, which specializes in critical discussions of popular and obscure horror, fantasy, and science fiction films. He is also a renowned and astute film critic and award-winning writer.

The first in a new series on horror films keyed to this expanding market.

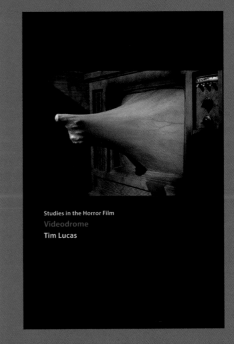

Studies in the Horror Film
Videodrome
Tim Lucas

Film & TV
November
Studies in the Horror Film
5½ x 8½ | 144 pp
50 B&W illustrations & Color and B&W film stills
TP US $19.95 | CAN $24.00
978-1-933618-28-9 CUSA
TC 50% NR US $50.00 | CAN $60.00
978-1-933618-29-6 CUSA

Marketing Plans

Co-op available
Advance reader copies

Author Hometown: Cincinnati, OH

Falling Angel
William Hjortsberg
Introduction by James Crumley
Foreword by Ridley Scott

Horror
5½ x 8½ | 302 pp
TP US $14.00 | CAN $17.00
978-1-933618-08-1 CUSA

Some of Your Blood
Theodore Sturgeon
Introduction by Steve Rasnic Tem

Horror / Fiction
5½ x 8½ | 192 pp
TP US $12.00 | CAN $14.50
978-1-933618-00-5 CUSA

Frankenstein
or The Modern Prometheus
Mary Shelley
Introduction by Patrick McGrath

Fiction / Horror
6 x 9 | 420 pp
TP US $16.00 | CAN $19.50
978-1-933618-12-8 CUSA

Street of No Return
David Goodis
Introduction by Robert Polito

Fiction
6 x 9 | 240 pp
TP US $14.00 | CAN $17.00
978-1-933618-22-7 CUSA

Nightfall
David Goodis
Introduction by Bill Pronzini

Fiction
6 x 9 | 220 pp
TP US $14.00 | CAN $17.00
978-1-933618-17-3 CUSA

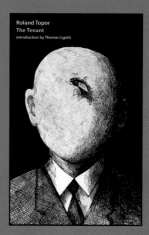

The Tenant
Roland Topor
Introduction by Thomas Ligotti

Horror / Fiction
5½ x 8½ | 224 pp
8 B&W illustrations
TP US $13.00 | CAN $15.95
978-1-933618-06-7 CUSA

Bridging the Divide
The Continuing Conversation between a Mormon and an Evangelical
Dr. Robert L. Millet and Rev. Gregory C.V. Johnson
Foreword by Craig L. Blomberg and Stephen E. Robinson

Inspired by the groundbreaking publication of *How Wide the Divide? A Mormon and an Evangelical in Conversation,* this is an engaging dialogue between two scholars of "opposing" religious communities. Dr. Robert L. Millet, a Mormon and former dean of religious education at Brigham Young University, and Rev. Gregory C.V. Johnson, a Baptist pastor, meet and begin their own conversation. Eventually they take their dialogues public, appearing in both Mormon and Baptist venues. The first part of the book is a Q&A between the two authors; the second part is a Q&A with Mormon and Baptist audiences. Lastly, they provide guiding principles of constructive conversation.

Author Events
New York, NY • Salt Lake City, UT

Religion
November
A Paperback Original
6 x 9 | 160 pp
TP US $14.95 | CAN $18.00
978-0-9766843-6-7 CUSA

The meetings between Mormons and Evangelicals break new ground in this interfaith dialogue.

America Needs a Woman President
Brett Bevell
Illustrated by Eben Dodd

"*America Needs a Woman President* will appeal to any woman or man of any political persuasion (or none at all) who hungers for wise and bold leadership. It is a love poem, a visionary rant, a call to action, a cry for sanity. America needs this funny, brilliant, and beautiful book."—Elizabeth Lesser, author of *The New American Spirituality*

Imagine a president who leads with a mother's love, the forgiving humor of a grandmother, and the wisdom of a medicine woman. These words, beautifully illustrated by artist Eben Dodd, give hope for a new paradigm of leadership at a time when we need it most.

Marketing Plans
Co-op available • Advance reader copies

Author Events
Washington, DC • New York, NY • Philadelphia, PA

Political Science & Government /
Women's Studies
September
A Paperback Original
6 x 6 | 48 pp
18 B&W illustrations
TP US $8.95 | CAN $11.00
978-0-9766843-5-0 CUSA

America needs a woman president, giving birth to a new America, embracing the world.

Parmenides and the Way of Truth
Richard G. Geldard

Parmenides was a philosopher, healer, and spiritual guide in fifth-century BC Elea, a Greek outpost on the western coast of Italy. Around 450 BC he and a young Socrates engaged in a debate on the nature of reality, later immortalized by Plato in *The Parmenides,* the dialogue that recreated that meeting. Richard Geldard's inspiring account brings new life and contemporary understanding to Parmenides, allowing us to understand his thought and benefit from his wisdom.

Richard G. Geldard earned his PhD in dramatic literature and classics at Stanford University. He is the author of *Remembering Heraclitus* and *The Traveler's Key to Ancient Greece.*

Philosophy / Spirituality
September
A Paperback Original
6 x 9 | 240 pp
TP US $16.95 | CAN $20.50
978-0-9766843-4-3 CUSA

An inspiring account gives new life to the Greek philosopher immortalized in his dialogues with Socrates.

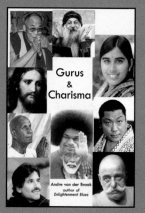

Gurus & Charisma
André van der Braak

Is the charismatic guru a liberator or pied piper? Psychologist and guru expert André van der Braak analyzes the dangerous aspects of the relationship between the guru and his students and explains their appeal. He then uses examples to differentiate between healthy and unhealthy charisma. The last part of the book guides the reader to more healthy forms of discipleship and concludes with a quick guide for knowing whether *your* guru is leading you down the wrong track.

André van der Braak, PhD, lived in the spiritual community of American guru Andrew Cohen, as documented in his compelling memoir *Enlightenment Blues.*

Spirituality
January
A Paperback Original
6 x 9 | 220 pp
TP US $15.95 | CAN $19.50
978-0-9766843-7-4 CUSA

The author of *Enlightenment Blues* digs deeper into the appeal of contemporary charismatic spiritual leaders.

Monkfish Book Publishing

Planet Ocean

Photo stories from the 'Defending our Oceans' voyage

Sara Holden

Photographs by Daniel Beltrá, Todd Warshaw, and Lester V. Ledesma

"How inappropriate to call this planet Earth, when clearly it is Ocean."
—Arthur C. Clarke

Three-quarters of the planet is ocean, 80 percent of all life lives here, and every second breath of air each of us takes is provided by the ocean. It gives us so much, yet we know relatively little about it.

Planet Ocean is a window onto this secret world. Through stunning photographs, taken on a sixteen-month Defending Our Oceans expedition, Greenpeace reveals wonderful sights that few people have seen, and also some that certain people would like us not to see.

Despite the vastness of the oceans, we now know that they are in crisis, struggling to absorb the impact of our destructive ways. This is the story of our oceans—their extraordinary beauty and diversity of life—and the equally astounding ways in which they are exploited.

Millions have watched this story unfold, following the most ambitious ocean expedition ever undertaken by Greenpeace. It's a photographic journey that reveals the mysteries of the deep, explores seamounts and their ecosystems, identifies the biggest predators, circles the corals, and breaks through the surface to meet the people whose lives depend on the oceans.

The photographs in this book are the work of a team of world-class photographers assigned to the Defending our Oceans voyage.

Sara Holden has worked for Greenpeace International since 2000. She previously worked for Reuters Television as a political journalist.

Daniel Beltrá has documented a number of Greenpeace expeditions. His work has appeared in *TIME, Business Week, Der Spiegel, Geo, Paris Match, Stern,* and many others. He recently won a 2007 World Press Photo Award.

Greenpeace photography brings the drama of the ocean to shore and calls for protected marine reserves.

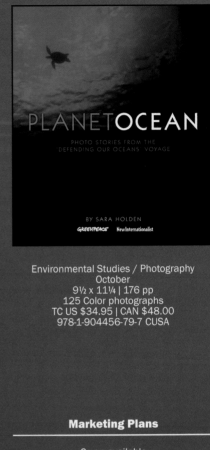

Environmental Studies / Photography
October
9½ x 11¼ | 176 pp
125 Color photographs
TC US $34.95 | CAN $48.00
978-1-904456-79-7 CUSA

Marketing Plans

Co-op available

Author Hometown: San Diego, CA
Photographer Hometown: Seattle, WA

The No-Nonsense Guide to World Health
Shereen Usdin

A clear yet wide-ranging introduction to the state of health worldwide explores the ways in which health provision is often determined by ethnicity, class, and gender. Starting with a brief history of medical progress, this guide delves into current politics of health in the contexts of big business and private health provision, media, gender, and the environment.

Shereen Usdin is a medical doctor and a public health specialist. She is co-founder of the internationally acclaimed Soul City for Health and Development Communication in South Africa and works in the areas of development communication, HIV/AIDS, violence against women, and human rights.

Marketing Plans
Co-op available

Current Affairs / Health & Fitness
September
A Paperback Original
No-Nonsense Guides
4¼ x 7 | 144 pp
15 B&W illustrations, charts, and graphs
TP $11.95
978-1-904456-65-0 USA

A history of modern healthcare shows that public health is largely determined by socio-economic factors.

The No-Nonsense Guide to World Poverty
Jeremy Seabrook

This guide questions conventional thinking about wealth and poverty—is the opposite of poverty really wealth, or is it safety and sufficiency?

Drawing on experience of poor people all over the world, the author gives voice to those whose views are rarely sought and shows how we all need to live more modestly to make poverty history.

Jeremy Seabrook has written more than thirty books (including *Travels in the Skin Trade* and *Children of Other Worlds*), and has worked as a teacher, social worker, journalist, lecturer, and playwright. He has contributed to many magazines, including the *New Statesman* and *The Ecologist.*

Marketing Plans
Co-op available

Current Affairs /
Political Science & Government
September
No-Nonsense Guides
4¼ x 7 | 144 pp
10 B&W illustrations, charts, and graphs
TP $11.95
978-1-904456-66-7 USA

Economic growth and wealth creation will never meet the poor's need for sufficiency and safety.

New Internationalist No-Nonsense Guides

The No-Nonsense Guide to International Development
Maggie Black

"Overseas aid" and "international development" are catch-all terms that cover a multitude of activities—and abuses. This guide explains what "development" actually is and explores its political and economic roots. It shows what can happen in the name of development and argues for a more organic, social approach with those it seeks to serve as equal partners in the process.

Maggie Black has written books for the Oxford University Press, UNICEF, and Oxfam. She has worked as a consultant for UNICEF, Anti-Slavery International, and WaterAid, among others, and has written for the *Guardian, The Economist,* and BBC World Service.

Marketing Plans
Co-op available

Current Affairs /
Political Science & Government
October
No-Nonsense Guides
4¼ x 7 | 144 pp
20 B&W illustrations, charts, and graphs
TP $11.95
978-1-904456-63-6 USA

An exploration of all aspects of "development" that shows it should be more social than political.

The No-Nonsense Guide to Sexual Diversity
Vanessa Baird

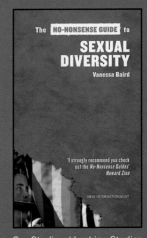

The treatment of sexual minorities—whether lesbian, gay, bisexual, or transgender—varies significantly in different parts of the world. In some countries, equal rights have been achieved and progress is being made against discrimination; in others, being gay still incurs the death penalty.

This guide examines all the colors of the sexual rainbow, unearths hidden histories, and looks at contributions from medicine and science. It also includes a unique global survey of laws that affect sexual minorities.

Vanessa Baird has been co-editor at *New Internationalist* magazine since 1986. Her previous books include, as compiler and editor, *Eye to Eye Women.*

Marketing Plans
Co-op available

Gay Studies / Lesbian Studies
October
No-Nonsense Guides
4¼ x 7 | 144 pp
10 B&W illustrations, charts, and graphs
TP $11.95
978-1-904456-64-3 USA

This book demystifies all the colors of the sexual rainbow, tracking the campaigns for rights and equality worldwide.

The World of Street Food
Easy Quick Meals to Cook at Home
Troth Wells

Cookbooks & Cookery
September
8½ x 8½ | 176 pp
150 Color photographs
TP $19.95
978-1-904456-50-6 USA

Marketing Plans

Co-op available

This is the book to take the taste buds traveling. Arepas from Venezuela, tom yam soup from Thailand, delicious mezze from the Middle East—*The World of Street Food* offers the best in fast food from Africa, Latin America, the Middle East, and Asia. Over a hundred recipes have been chosen for their popularity at street stalls and markets around the world.

A collective effort by the author and fans of street food worldwide, this book combines thorough research with personal stories from the people and places the recipes come from: for instance, how the South African bunny chow was invented through a combination of Asian curry, European bread, and apartheid; or the stories from Penang, Malaysia, said by many to be the street food capital of the world.

Each recipe is accompanied by award-winning food photography and evocative travel pictures. The majority of recipes are vegetarian, and many are vegan or vegan-adaptable. As with all New Internationalist food books, *The World of Street Food* includes information on nutrition and organic and fair-trade ingredients.

Troth Wells has been with the *New Internationalist* since 1972. She has written a number of world food books, and is an editor of *The World Guide,* a global reference source that focuses on majority-world issues.

World street food favorites, selected because they are popular, fresh, and easy to cook.

Also Available

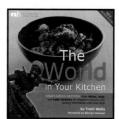

The Bittersweet World of Chocolate
Troth Wells and Nikki van der Gaag
Cookbooks & Cookery / Current Affairs
9 x 9 | 176 pp
150 Color photographs
TC US $24.95 | CAN $30.00
978-1-904456-25-4 CUSA

The World in your Kitchen
Vegetarian recipes from Africa, Asia and
Latin America for Western kitchens
Troth Wells
Cookbooks & Cookery
8 x 8 | 176 pp
175 Color and B&W photographs
TP US $19.95 | CAN $24.00
978-1-904456-20-9 CUSA

New Internationalist

Cars Go Fast
John Chattin

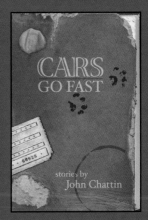

Fiction
October
A Paperback Original
Many Voices Project 111
6 x 9 | 220 pp
TP US $14.95 | CAN $18.00
978-0-89823-234-9 CUSA

**Hopeful stories despite lives
destroyed by various forms of escape;
the toll of work on the soul.**

"Written with descriptive simplicity and easy grace."—Joseph Caldwell

Characters leave: They hunker into cars and head out of town, book flights and hit the skies, or leave by drink or drugs or acts of violence. But they're all going—loners by default, part Jack Kerouac, part James Dean, part Charles Bukowski.

John Chattin earned an MFA in creative writing from The New School. His work has appeared in *Bayou Magazine, The Powhatan Review,* and *Bellevue Literary Review.* He is a human resources associate with The Vera Institute of Justice in New York. This is his first book.

Marketing Plans
Co-op available • Advance reader copies
National advertising: Bellevue Literary Review • The Minnesota Review • Poets & Writers

Author Events
Washington, DC • Bowling Green, KY • Louisville, KY • Moorhead, MN • Fargo, ND • Brooklyn, NY • Manhattan, NY • New York, NY • Cincinnati, OH • Seattle, WA

Signaling for Rescue
Marianne Herrmann

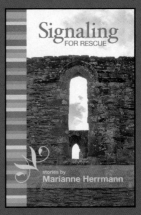

Fiction
October
A Paperback Original
Many Voices Project 112
6 x 9 | 180 pp
TP US $14.95 | CAN $18.00
978-0-89823-235-6 CUSA

**Men and women in Europe
and the United States struggle to
find love and meaning.**

These stories dramatize the harrowing path from fear or abuse to hope and redemption. Whether mourning miscarried children while caring for a pregnant sister, surviving childhood sexual abuse in the Wisconsin woods, traveling in Italy after the death of a sister, or dealing with a mother's death by torturing a father's new girlfriend, characters confront the strangeness lurking beneath familiar domestic situations.

Marianne Herrmann holds a BA from Georgetown University and an MA in English/creative writing from the University of Minnesota. She studied art history at the Florence, Italy, campus of the University of Michigan. This is her first book.

Author Events
Minneapolis, MN • Fargo, ND

New Rivers Press

The Tender, Wild Things
Diane Jarvenpa

"Organic lyricism . . . subtle narratives. . . . A wonderful book and a gorgeous journey not to be missed."—Lee Ann Roripaugh

This rapturous journey through poetry takes the reader through reclaiming a Finnish heritage, seasons of a childless marriage, the decision to adopt a child from China, nurturing the poet's mother through a final illness, and finding consolation in "the wild, tender things."

Diane Jarvenpa is a Minnesota native whose grandparents all emigrated from Finland. She has received grants from the Minnesota State Arts Board and, as Diane Jarvi, performs folk and world music in Europe, Australia, and the United States.

Poetry / Women's Studies
October
A Paperback Original
Many Voices Project 113
6 x 9 | 60 pp
TP US $13.95 | CAN $17.00
978-0-89823-236-3 CUSA

Diane Jarvenpa, the acclaimed singer known as Diane Jarvi, publishes a second book of lush, lyrical poems.

Towards the Forest
Holaday Mason

"[Mason] bravely explores the interior life of the mind and imagination . . . the poems ravel, unravel as hauntingly as Kodaly or Bartok."—Sarah Maclay

Edgy and lyrical expressions of the human heart set in a landscape of palms and avocados, of ocean and forest, of Hollywood billboards and noir passion, Holaday Mason's poetry is haunted and nocturnal, with broken dreaming and falling blossoms, an erotic and dangerous and beautiful place, a world dark and graceful. She writes with extravagant passion and unflinching nerve.

Holaday Mason is a clinical psychologist living in Venice, California, and is active in the literary scene there.

Marketing Plans
Co-op available • Advance reader copies

Poetry
October
A Paperback Original
New American Poetry
6 x 9 | 60 pp
TP US $13.95 | CAN $17.00
978-0-89823-237-0 CUSA

A brave, risk-taking poet who explores the interior life of the mind and imagination.

New Rivers Press

Peak Everything
Waking Up to the Century of Declines
Richard Heinberg

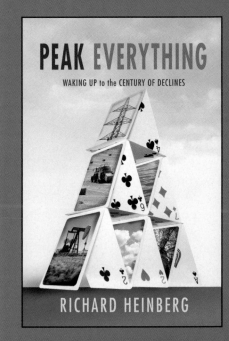

The twentieth century saw unprecedented growth in population, energy consumption, and food production. As the population shifted from rural to urban, the impact of humans on the environment increased dramatically.

The twenty-first century ushered in an era of declines, in a number of crucial areas, including global oil, natural gas, and coal extraction; yearly grain harvests; climate stability; population; economic growth; fresh water; and minerals and ores, such as copper and platinum.

To adapt to this profoundly different world, we must begin now to make radical changes to our attitudes, behaviors, and expectations.

Peak Everything addresses many of the cultural, psychological, and practical changes we will have to make as nature rapidly dictates our new limits. This latest book from Richard Heinberg, author of three of the most important books on Peak Oil, touches on the most important aspects of the human condition at this unique moment in time.

A combination of wry commentary and sober forecasting on subjects as diverse as farming and industrial design, this book tells how we might make the transition from the Age of Excess to the Era of Modesty with grace and satisfaction, while preserving the best of our collective achievements. A must-read for individuals, business leaders, and policymakers who are serious about effecting real change.

Richard Heinberg is a journalist, lecturer, and the author of seven books, including *The Party's Over, Powerdown,* and *The Oil Depletion Protocol.* He is one of the world's foremost Peak Oil educators.

How to transition gracefully from the Age of Excess to the Era of Modesty.

Environmental Studies / Current Affairs
September
6 x 9 | 224 pp
TC $24.95
978-0-86571-598-1 USA

Marketing Plans

Co-op available
10,000-copy print run

Author Hometown: Santa Rosa, CA

Also Available

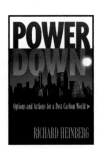

The Oil Depletion Protocol
A Plan to Avert Oil Wars, Terrorism and Economic Collapse
Richard Heinberg
Current Affairs / Environmental Studies
6 x 9 | 208 pp
10 B&W illustrations, charts and graphs
TP $16.95
978-0-86571-563-9 USA

Powerdown
Options and Actions for a Post-Carbon World
Richard Heinberg
Current Affairs / Environmental Studies
6 x 9 | 224 pp
TP $16.95
978-0-86571-510-3 USA

New Society Publishers

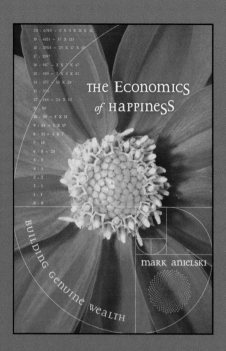

Business & Economics / Current Affairs
September
A Paperback Original
6 x 9 | 288 pp
30 B&W illustrations, photographs,
and charts
TP $17.95
978-0-86571-596-7 USA

Marketing Plans

Co-op available

The Economics of Happiness
Building Genuine Wealth
Mark Anielski

We all know that money can't buy you love or happiness, but we have been living our lives as though the accumulation of wealth is the key to our dreams. Why, in spite of increasing economic prosperity over the past fifty years, are many conditions of well-being in decline and rates of happiness largely unchanged since the 1950s?

Why do our measures of economic progress not reflect the values that make us happy: supportive relationships, meaningful work, a healthy environment, and our spiritual well-being?

Economist Mark Anielski has developed a new and practical economic model called Genuine Wealth to measure the real determinants of well-being and help redefine progress.

The Economics of Happiness shows:

- How economics, capitalism, accounting, and banking, which dominate our consciousness, can be reoriented toward the pursuit of genuine happiness
- How to rediscover the original meaning of the language of economics
- How to measure the five capitals of Genuine Wealth: human, social, natural, built, and financial
- How nations, governments, communities, and businesses are using the Genuine Wealth model to build a new economy of well-being
- How you and your family can apply the Genuine Wealth model in your lives

Anielski's road map toward this vision of flourishing economies of well-being will resonate with individuals, communities, and governments interested in issues of sustainability and quality of life.

Mark Anielski is an ecological economist and president of his family-owned corporation, which specializes in the economics of well-being.

Practical solutions for building economies of well-being based on Genuine Wealth.

New Society Publishers

Not Just a Pretty Face
The Ugly Side of the Beauty Industry
Stacy Malkan

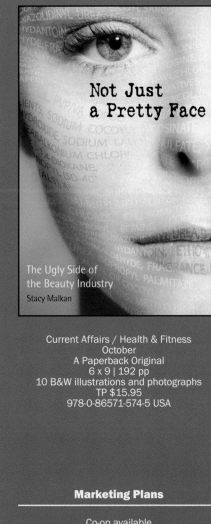

Coal tar in dandruff shampoo, lead in lipstick, and 1,4-dioxane in baby soap? How is this possible? Simple: The $35 billion cosmetics industry is so powerful that they've kept themselves unregulated for decades.

Not one cosmetic product has to be approved by the US Food and Drug Administration before hitting the market. Incredible? Consider this:

- The European Union has banned more than 1,100 chemicals from cosmetics. The United States has banned just nine.
- Only 11 percent of chemicals used in cosmetics in the United States have been assessed for health and safety—leaving a staggering 89 percent with unknown or undisclosed effects.
- More than 70 percent of all cosmetics contain phthalates, which are linked to birth defects and infertility.
- Many baby soaps are contaminated with the cancer-causing chemical 1,4-dioxane.

It's not just women who are affected by this chemists' brew. Shampoo, deodorant, face lotion, and other products used daily by men, women, and children contain hazardous chemicals that the industry claims are "within acceptable limits." But there's nothing acceptable about daily multiple exposures to carcinogenic chemicals—from products that are supposed to make us feel healthy and beautiful.

Not Just a Pretty Face delves deeply into the dark side of the beauty industry and looks to hopeful solutions for a healthier future. This scathing investigation peels away less-than-lovely layers to expose an industry in dire need of an extreme makeover.

Stacy Malkan is the communications director for Health Care Without Harm and founding member of Campaign for Safe Cosmetics.

The girls' guide to giving the cosmetics industry a makeover.

Current Affairs / Health & Fitness
October
A Paperback Original
6 x 9 | 192 pp
10 B&W illustrations and photographs
TP $15.95
978-0-86571-574-5 USA

Marketing Plans

Co-op available

New Society Publishers

How Green is Your City?
The SustainLane US City Rankings
SustainLane

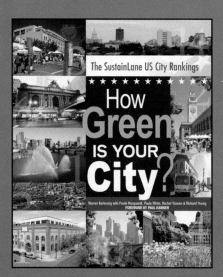

Urban Planning / Current Affairs
Available Now
A Paperback Original
7½ x 9 | 224 pp
75 Color photographs and charts
TP $22.95
978-0-86571-595-0 USA

Marketing Plans

Co-op available
10,000-copy print run

Author Hometown: San Francisco, CA

In our Peak Oil, post-Katrina world, how do America's largest cities stack up in terms of sustainability? Which cities are self-sufficient and well-prepared for our uncertain future, and which cities are operating business-as-usual?

How Green is Your City? examines the outcome of a sustainability study of the fifty largest US cities, compiled by SustainLane. The 2006 SustainLane Sustainable Cities Ranking employed fifteen standards to measure each city's performance and ranked them according to the cumulative results. Among those standards:

- Public transit use
- Air and tap water quality
- Planning/land use
- City innovation
- Affordability
- Energy/climate change policy
- Local food/agriculture
- Green economy
- Sustainability management

Leading the pack is Portland, Oregon, with its high quality of life and commitment to green building, local food, alternative fuels, and renewable energy, while Columbus, Ohio, with its dependence on the automobile and poor public transit, ranks at the bottom.

How Green is Your City? offers an in-depth analysis of each city's policies, strengths, and challenges, as well as the emerging job and tax base expansion with the growth of clean technologies. *How Green is Your City?* will appeal to city planners, councilors, and anyone interested in making their city a more sustainable place.

SustainLane.us was designed as an online community-driven site devoted to green businesses, government, products, and services. Writers Warren Karlenzig, Frank Marquardt, Paula White, Rachel Yaseen, and Richard Young of SustainLane.com contributed to this project.

A sustainability ranking for the fifty largest US cities—
a national competition for city sustainability.

New Society Publishers

The New Village Green
Living Light, Living Local, Living Large
Edited by Stephen Morris

The village green is the focal point of any community, a gathering place where the best ideas take root and the brightest voices are heard. *The New Village Green* gathers some of the best ideas and brightest voices of the green community, some famous and familiar, others fresh and unknown. Each tells an absorbing story, and collectively they comprise a powerful chorus that profiles the current state of the environment.

This remarkable book gathers wisdom and insight from a compelling and thought-provoking virtual community. Each contributor brings a unique perspective that mingles reverence for the environment with provocative thoughts for the future. Topics range from spirituality to solar panels and, just like a real village green, are juxtaposed with opinions from "the new village people," including:

- Writers Bill McKibben and Michael Pollan
- Scientists James Lovelock and Donella Meadows
- Spiritual leaders Gandhi and Buddha

And practical, homespun topics are given equal time:

- Good reasons to embrace alternative currencies
- Tips for growing great garlic

Meant to be devoured in one sitting or sipped a little at a time, this book springboards the green movement into the future by acknowledging its roots in the past. Rachel Carson, Paul Ehrlich, and Helen and Scott Nearing are as relevant today as the Slow Food Movement and Peak Oil. This book will touch the heart of anyone who lives with conscience and hope.

Stephen Morris is editor and publisher of *Green Living Magazine* and co-founder of The Public Press.

The revolutionary ideas, values, and attitudes of the green chorus.

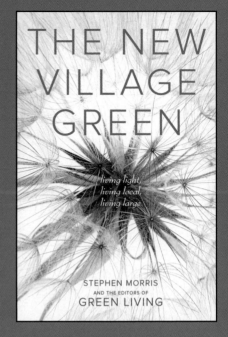

Environmental Studies / Current Affairs
September
A Paperback Original
6 x 9 | 288 pp
TP $17.95
978-0-86571-599-8 USA

Marketing Plans

Co-op available
10,000-copy print run

Author Hometown: Randolph, VT

New Society Publishers

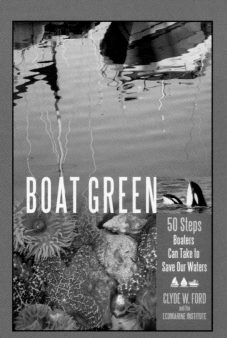

Sports & Recreation
February
A Paperback Original
6 x 9 | 224 pp
15 B&W illustrations and photographs
TP $16.95
978-0-86571-590-5 USA

Marketing Plans

Co-op available
10,000-copy print run

Boat Green
50 Steps Boaters Can Take to Save Our Waters
Clyde W. Ford

Recreational boating is a pastime enjoyed by millions. Yet the waters and marine environment that boaters so love are in serious jeopardy from pollution, resource mismanagement, and misunderstanding. Boaters can help change that. Although a relatively small part of the problem of marine environmental degradation, recreational boaters can be a huge part of the solution, writes Clyde W. Ford, an avid boater of over twenty years, whose encounters with polluted waters galvanized him to explore workable solutions.

Boat Green provides a host of environmentally sound boating practices, based on scientific research and practical boating experience. In this book, boaters will learn ways to:

- Reduce vessel operation and maintenance costs
- Improve vessel performance
- Increase safety and health of vessel operators and crew
- Increase awareness of marine issues
- Enhance enjoyment of the marine environment

All of these steps will help lessen the impact of recreational boating on the marine environment. These are practical solutions that have been field-tested and refined on actual vessels cruising the Pacific Northwest waters.

Boat Green is an essential guide for recreational boaters and for all those concerned about protecting the marine environment.

Clyde W. Ford is the executive director of EcoMarine Institute and author of nine books, including the award-winning *The Long Mile* and the Charlie Noble series of contemporary nautical suspense novels. Ford enjoys cruising the waters of the Inside Passage aboard his single-engine biodiesel trawler.

Why "green boating" saves money, increases fun, and helps the planet.

New Society Publishers

Building an Ark
101 Solutions to Animal Suffering
Ethan Smith with Guy Dauncey

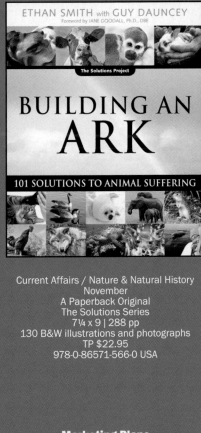

Building an Ark: 101 Solutions to Animal Suffering is a first-of-its-kind, inspiring look at practical solutions to the impact humans have on animals and the natural world.

Factory farms, habitat destruction, animal product testing, the abuse and neglect of companion animals, the illegal trade in endangered species, unsustainable fishing, and climate change all create unnecessary suffering for animals.

For several decades there has been a global movement building, an ever-increasing consciousness that will soon affect animal welfare and the future of life on Earth—if it's given time to do so. *Building an Ark* is the story of this movement. Extensively researched and drawing on practical examples from around the world, it provides a voice for both the animals and the humans who have dedicated their lives to building a sustainable future for all species.

The ark is ready for all to board. Individuals, action groups, schools, businesses, governments, farmers, fishers, developing nations—there's a role for everyone on this journey. *Building an Ark* offers a host of solutions that, if adopted, will ensure that animals will suffer less today, and that humans and animals will share a more sustainable planet tomorrow.

Ethan Smith is a writer, animal welfare advocate, and author/editor of the anthology *Softly On This Earth: Joining Those Who Are Healing Our Planet.*

Guy Dauncey founded the Solutions Project and is author of several books, including *Stormy Weather: 101 Solutions to Global Climate Change.*

The voice for all animals and people dedicated to a sustainable future for all species.

Current Affairs / Nature & Natural History
November
A Paperback Original
The Solutions Series
7¼ x 9 | 288 pp
130 B&W illustrations and photographs
TP $22.95
978-0-86571-566-0 USA

Marketing Plans

Co-op available

Author Hometown: Pender Island, BC

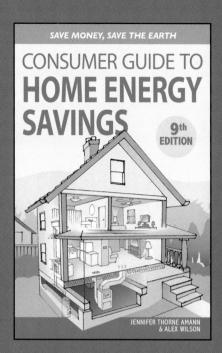

Home Improvement & Construction /
Environmental Studies
October
5½ x 8½ | 256 pp
100 B&W illustrations and photographs
TP $16.95
978-0-86571-602-5 USA

Marketing Plans

Co-op available
10,000-copy print run

Author Hometown: Washington, DC

Consumer Guide to Home Energy Savings, 9th Edition
Save Money, Save the Earth
Jennifer Thorne Amann and Alex Wilson

How efficient are front-loading washing machines? When is it time to replace your old refrigerator? These questions and many more are answered in *The Consumer Guide to Home Energy Savings,* a one-stop resource for consumers who want to improve their home's energy performance and reduce costs. Zeroing in on the most useful response can be a challenge; this ninth edition cuts through the confusion.

Well-organized and highly readable, *The Consumer Guide to Home Energy Savings* begins with an overview of the interrelationships between energy use, economics, and the environment. Chapters focus on specific areas in the home, such as electronics, lighting, heating, cooling, ventilation, kitchen, and laundry, and provide helpful explanations for each, including:

- Describing energy use characteristics
- Drawing comparisons between available technologies
- Outlining the most cost-effective repair and replacement options
- Providing step-by-step guidance for finding the right equipment
- Describing how the equipment operates
- Summarizing how much energy is used or lost

Included are tips on improving existing equipment and guidance for when and why consumers should purchase new energy-efficient equipment, as well as a reminder to check local government and utility incentives for purchase or retrofit grants.

This guide will be an invaluable resource to all consumers concerned about reducing both their energy bills and their environmental impact.

Jennifer Thorne Amann is a senior associate in the ACEEE (American Council for an Energy-Efficient Economy) Buildings and Equipment Program.

Alex Wilson is president of BuildingGreen, Inc., author of *Your Green Home,* and executive editor of *Environmental Building News.*

A new edition of this two hundred thousand copy bestseller.

New Society Publishers

How to Re-imagine the World
A Pocket Guide for Practical Visionaries
Anthony Weston

Who says that all possible social and political systems have already been invented? Or that work—or marriage, or environmentalism, or anything else—must be just what they are now?

This book is a conceptual toolbox for imagining and initiating radical social change. Chapters offer specific, focused, and shareable techniques:

- Seeking a Whole Vision: creating a pull and not just a push toward change
- Generative Thinking: looking for "seeds" and "sparks," stretching and twisting ideas, and going two steps too far
- Looking for Unexpected Openings: "weeds" and "wild cards," inside tracks, leverage points, and hidden possibilities
- Working at the Roots: reconstructing the built world, cultural practices, and even worldviews
- Building Momentum: playing to our strengths, reclaiming the language, "allying everywhere," doing it now, and going for broke

Leap-frogging new kinds of cars and better mass transit in turn, why not a world in which "transportation" itself is unneeded? What about remaking New Orleans as a floating city, or putting only extreme surfers in the path of hurricanes? And why not dream of the stars? The question is not whether radical change is coming. It is already well underway. The only question is who will make it. Why not us?

Anthony Weston is a professor of philosophy at Elon University in North Carolina, where he teaches ethics, environmental studies, and "Millennial Imagination." He is the author of ten other books, including *Back to Earth, Jobs for Philosophers,* and *Creativity for Critical Thinkers.*

**A guide to big ideas—
to reawakening the radical imagination for social transformation.**

Current Affairs
October
A Paperback Original
4½ x 7 | 160 pp
TP $11.95
978-0-86571-594-3 USA

Marketing Plans

Co-op available

Author Hometown: Elon, NC

New Society Publishers

Extreme Weather Hits Home
Protecting Your Buildings from Climate Change
John Banta

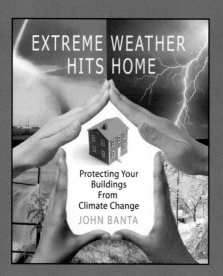

Home Improvement & Construction
November
A Paperback Original
7½ x 9 | 256 pp
90 B&W illustrations and photographs
TP $22.95
978-0-86571-593-6 USA

Marketing Plans

Co-op available

Author Hometown: Vacaville, CA

We know how to prepare our homes for each seasonal change, but do we know how to prepare for climate change? Violent weather events like floods, tornadoes, ice storms, and hurricanes only tell part of the story. Climate change is frequently more subtle, but its effects on our homes and properties can still be devastating.

Nearly 50 percent of North America has a potential for structural damage from shifting moisture in expansive clay soils, a condition that is already costing billions of dollars each year. Humidity is projected to increase, trapping moisture in wall cavities and resulting in deterioration. As the climate changes and moisture levels adjust, there are a number of proactive steps that can be taken to prevent or lessen expensive repairs.

Extreme Weather is the only book of its kind, showing how to protect your home or business from climate change by focusing on the following areas:

- Risk and causal assessment, due to region and soil
- Extreme weather's rapid and slow effects
- Site, foundation, wall, and roof considerations and modifications
- Insurance options
- Anticipated changes for the United States, Canada, and Mexico

Our homes are one of the most expensive investments we will ever make. They are also our refuge from the elements, and we must protect them so they can protect us. This book is a valuable resource for all property owners.

John Banta is an indoor environmental consultant with twenty years of experience in building biology, building science, and indoor environmental quality.

How to spot early warning signs of costly climate change damage to your home.

New Society Publishers

Green Building, A to Z
Understanding the Language of Green Building
Jerry Yudelson

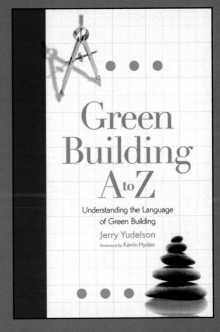

Green building is the fastest-growing trend to hit since the Internet, bringing with it an enormous range of new products, systems, and technologies. *Green Building A to Z* is an informative, technically accurate, and highly visual guide to green building, for both decision-makers and interested citizens. It begins with an introduction to the importance of green buildings and a brief history of the green building movement, outlines the benefits and costs of green buildings, and shows how you can influence the spread of green buildings. The book touches on key issues, such as enhancing water conservation, reducing energy use, and creating a conservation economy.

The book examines all aspects of green buildings, including:

- Architecture 2030
- Locally sourced materials
- Natural ventilation
- Solar energy
- Zero-net-energy buildings

More than just a reference, this book emphasizes the importance of green buildings and green developments for a sustainable future. It will be an invaluable resource for businesspeople, homeowners, product manufacturers, developers, building industry professionals, and government officials.

Jerry Yudelson is a professional engineer with an MBA. He has trained three thousand people in the LEED (Leadership in Energy and Environmental Design) Green Building Rating System, and has chaired Greenbuild, the world's largest green building conference, for the past four years. The founder of a green building consulting firm, he is the author of three books on green building marketing, and is an advisor to manufacturers, venture capital firms, design firms, and developers.

The first book for anyone interested in understanding green buildings and technology.

Home Improvement & Construction
October
A Paperback Original
6 x 9 | 160 pp
30 B&W illustrations and photographs
TP $14.95
978-0-86571-572-1 USA

Marketing Plans

Co-op available
10,000-copy print run

Author Hometown: Tucson, AZ

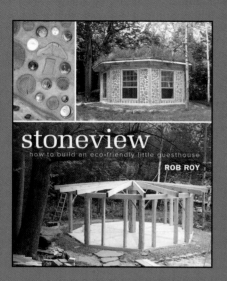

Home Improvement & Construction
February
A Paperback Original
7½ x 9 | 240 pp
130 Color and B&W illustrations
and photographs
TP $24.95
978-0-86571-597-4 USA

Marketing Plans

Co-op available

Author Hometown: West Chazy, NY

Stoneview
How to Build an Eco-Friendly Little Guesthouse
Rob Roy

Stoneview is an octagonal, cordwood masonry timber-framed guesthouse with a living roof located in upstate New York, fully constructed and finished for just $6,000. In response to the enormous interest in this unique little home, author and builder Rob Roy has written *Stoneview*.

Over 130 clear line drawings and step-by-step images provide the reader with all the information needed to build this three hundred-square-foot cabin from start to finish, and a full-color section shows off the beautiful design features of this charming "green" cabin. All design considerations are covered, as well as an interesting and thorough discussion of the geometry of the octagon.

Separate chapters are devoted to:

- Site preparation
- Forming and pouring the slab
- Timber framing
- The lightweight living roof
- The cordwood masonry walls

Full instructions for the interior floor and wall finishing are included, as well as a basic plumbing system featuring the "humanure" composting toilet system. *Stoneview* concludes with a performance evaluation of the building and a complete costing analysis. Best of all, the house is appropriate for any climate.

Rob Roy and his wife Jaki started the Earthwood Building School in 1981. Earthwood specializes in alternative building methods such as cordwood masonry and earth-sheltered housing. Roy is the author of twelve books, including *Earth–Sheltered Houses, Timber Framing for the Rest of Us,* and *Cordwood Building* (New Society Publishers).

Step-by-step instructions for building an octagonal, cordwood masonry guesthouse.

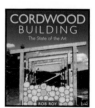

Also Available

Timber Framing for the Rest of Us
A Guide to Contemporary Post and
Beam Construction
Rob Roy
Home Improvement & Construction
7½ x 9 | 192 pp
120 B&W photographs and illustrations
TP $22.95
978-0-86571-508-0 USA

Cordwood Building
The State of the Art
Edited by Rob Roy
Home Improvement & Construction /
Design
8 x 9 | 240 pp
90 Color and B&W photographs
TP $26.95
978-0-86571-475-5 USA

New Society Publishers

Green Building Products, 3rd Edition
The GreenSpec® Guide to Residential Building Materials
Edited by Alex Wilson and Mark Piepkorn

Interest in sustainable, green building practices is greater than ever. Whether concerned about allergies, energy costs, old-growth forests, or durability and long-term value, homeowners and builders are looking for ways to ensure that their homes are healthy, safe, beautiful, and efficient.

In these pages are descriptions and manufacturer contact information for more than 1,400 environmentally preferable products and materials. All phases of residential construction are covered. Products are grouped by function, and each chapter begins with a discussion of key environmental considerations and what to look for in a green product. Over 40 percent revised, this updated edition includes over 120 new products. Categories of products include:

- Sitework and landscaping
- Decking
- Foundations, footers, and slabs
- Structural systems and components
- Sheathing
- Doors and windows
- Insulation
- Flooring and floor coverings
- Interior/exterior finish and trim
- Paints and coatings
- Mechanical systems/HVAC
- Plumbing, electrical, and lighting
- Furniture and furnishings
- Distributors and retailers

Editor **Alex Wilson** is president of BuildingGreen, Inc., an authoritative source for information on environmentally responsible design and construction, which also publishes *Environmental Building News.* Co-editor **Mark Piepkorn** has extensive experience with natural and traditional building methods.

The most comprehensive directory of green building products available—now in its third edition.

Also Available

Your Green Home
A Guide to Planning a Healthy, Environmentally Friendly New Home
Alex Wilson
Home Improvement & Construction
6 x 9 | 256 pp
150 B&W illustrations
TP $17.95
978-0-86571-555-4 USA

Home Improvement & Construction
March
8½ x 11 | 352 pp
250 B&W illustrations and photographs
TP $34.95
978-0-86571-600-1 USA

Marketing Plans

Co-op available
10,000-copy print run

Author Hometown: Brattleboro, VT

New Society Publishers

Making a Living While Making a Difference, Revised Edition

Conscious Careers in an Era of Independence

Melissa Everett

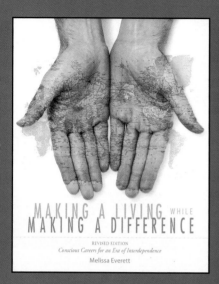

Making a Living While Making a Difference is a timely and highly informative guide to a working life built on principled choices and an entrepreneurial attitude. It's about greener enterprises and technologies, socially responsible business, innovative nonprofit work, and reinventing government. It's *really* about putting the pieces together with creativity and hope.

Working people everywhere are realizing that personal success is interconnected with healthy communities and the environment. We are all looking for our unique "creative edge" with work that allows us to make an impact close to home and in the world.

The substantially revised third edition of *Making a Living While Making a Difference* acknowledges that while the path to finding a life's work that is satisfying, sustainable, and financially feasible is not easy, there are simple steps to follow. An empowering ten-step program includes:

- Paying attention to what you care most about
- Stabilizing your life with regard to time, money, and relationships
- Assessing your core aptitudes and attitudes
- Cultivating the entrepreneurial skills to create the workplace you want, whether or not you are in business for yourself

With dozens of rich personal stories and a thorough look at the options, this is the comprehensive life and work guide for people who care about their communities and the planet.

Melissa Everett is a career counselor, group facilitator, and educator in the field of sustainable development, and is the executive director of Sustainable Hudson Valley.

The career-life guide for people who care about their communities and the planet.

Careers
November
7¼ x 9 | 240 pp
15 B&W illustrations, charts, and graphs
TP $22.95
978-0-86571-591-2 USA

Marketing Plans

Co-op available

Author Hometown: Kingston, NY

New Society Publishers

Real Goods Solar Living Source Book—Special 30th Anniversary Edition
Your Complete Guide to Renewable Energy Technologies and Sustainable Living
John Schaeffer

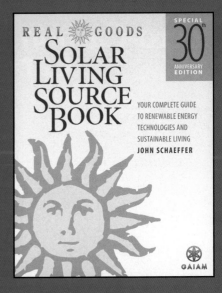

Concerns over dwindling resources and environmental degradation are driving many to seek alternatives to our wasteful, polluting lifestyle. Clean technologies such as solar power, wind power, and biofuels are soaring in popularity.

Real Goods Solar Living Source Book—Special 30th Anniversary Edition is the ultimate guide to renewable energy, sustainable living, green building, homesteading, off-grid living, and alternative transportation, written by experts with decades of experience and a passion for sharing their knowledge. This fully updated edition includes brand-new sections on Peak Oil, climate change, relocalization, natural burial, biodynamics, and permaculture. It also boasts the latest product listings and completely rewritten and expanded chapters on:

- Land and shelter
- Natural building
- Passive solar
- Biofuels
- Sustainable transportation
- Grid-tied photovoltaics
- Solar hot water systems
- Plus, over 150 pages of maps, wiring diagrams, formulae, charts, solar sizing worksheets, and much more

Whether you're a layperson or a professional, novice or longtime aficionado, the new sourcebook puts the latest research and products at your fingertips—all the information you need to make sustainable living a reality.

John Schaeffer is the president and founder of Real Goods, the oldest and largest catalog company devoted to the sale and service of renewable energy products. Now merged with Gaiam, Real Goods has converted over sixty thousand homes to solar energy since 1978, when it sold the very first photovoltaic module in the United States. Real Goods hosts the annual SolFest at its Solar Living Center headquarters in Hopland, California.

The essential renewable energy resource, completely revised and updated for 2008.

Home Improvement & Construction
September
Gaiam Real Goods
8½ x 11 | 608 pp
1200 B&W illustrations, photographs, and charts
TP $35.00
978-0-916571-06-1 USA

Marketing Plans

20,000-copy print run

Author Hometown: Hopland, CA

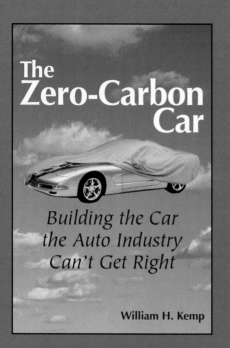

The Zero-Carbon Car
Building the Car the Auto Industry Can't Get Right
William H. Kemp

The transportation sector, dominated by the personal automobile, is responsible for over a quarter of North America's total energy consumption. Motor vehicles account for the overwhelming majority of harmful atmospheric emissions. In addition, rising fuel, road, and infrastructure costs are beginning to converge, driving us to the end of Autopia.

The Zero-Carbon Car reviews the issues of climate change and carbon rationing, Peak Oil, urban sprawl, and geopolitical and socioeconomic disruption related to fossil fuel use. The book argues that, while there is no way to avoid the eventual demise of the automobile, there is an opportunity for the automotive industry to develop—and governments to support—an ultra-efficient, zero-carbon-emission automobile.

The second half of the book documents the successful design and construction of a zero-carbon vehicle, proving that the technology is not only possible, it is viable today. For those who wish to fabricate their own vehicles, plans and software are provided in the book and at the accompanying website.

The Zero-Carbon Car is a must-read for automotive enthusiasts, environmentalists, and anyone who cares about how their transportation choices affect the planet. The book may not solve the world's fuel, transportation, and energy supply problems, but it could help pave the way to a cleaner, more sustainable future.

William H. Kemp is the vice president of engineering for an energy sector corporation, a sustainable living and clean energy advocate, a leading expert in renewable energy technologies, and the author of *The Renewable Energy Handbook*, *Smart Power*, and *Biodiesel Basics and Beyond*.

**A complete guide to the zero-carbon car,
costing less than a tankful of gas.**

Transportation
October
A Paperback Original
Aztext Press
6 x 9 | 500 pp
600 B&W illustrations, photographs,
and charts
TP $34.95
978-0-9733233-4-4 USA

Author Hometown: Tamworth, ON

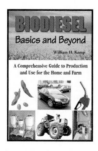

Also Available

Biodiesel Basics and Beyond
A Comprehensive Guide to Production
and Use for the Home and Farm
William H. Kemp
Technology & Industrial Arts
6 x 9 | 300 pp
200 B&W illustrations and photographs
TP $29.95
978-0-97332-333-7 USA

The Renewable Energy Handbook
A Guide to Rural Energy Independence,
Off-Grid and Sustainable Living
William H. Kemp
Home Improvement & Construction
6 x 9 | 592 pp
250 B&W illustrations, photographs,
and charts
TP $29.95
978-0-97332-332-0 USA

New Society Publishers

Sustainability by Design
A Vision for a Region of 4 Million
Design Centre for Sustainability

The Greater Vancouver region's population is expected to double in the next fifty years, with a 250 percent increase in citizens over sixty-five.

Sustainability by Design addresses the challenge of transforming livability into sustainability while accommodating this demographic change. Focusing on jobs, housing, transportation, infrastructure, parks, and open space, this beautifully illustrated and designed book is an invaluable resource for city planners, design professionals, elected officials, and citizens interested in a sustainable future.

The **Design Centre for Sustainability** at the University of British Columbia is an internationally recognized organization that pursues sustainable approaches to building communities through the lens of collaborative design.

Author Hometown: Vancouver, BC

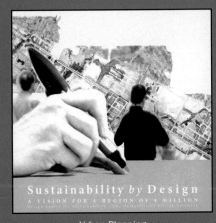

Urban Planning
September
A Paperback Original
Design Centre for Sustainability
8 x 8 | 80 pp
120 Color photographs and illustrations
TP $19.95
978-0-97809-662-5 USA

A case study that projects a livable future for Greater Vancouver using smart growth principles.

As If the Earth Matters
Recommitting to Environmental Education
Thom Henley and Kenny Peavy

Is environmental education succeeding in producing an eco-aware and conscientious population, or has it "flat-lined"?

Lavishly illustrated and packed with fun-filled outdoor educational activities, *As If the Earth Matters* shows how, through immersing our children in the beauty of nature, we can motivate them to take an active role in conservation.

Perfect for parents, teachers, camp leaders, and nature clubs, this book reawakens a childlike joy and sense of wonder in the natural world.

Thom Henley and **Kenny Peavy** have introduced thousands of students to the wonders of nature. Henley is the author of nine previous books.

Author Hometown: Victoria, BC

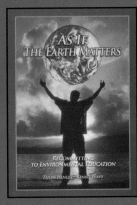

Education & Teaching
September
A Paperback Original
Thom Henley and Kenny Peavy
5¾ x 8¼ | 256 pp
300 Color photographs
TP $19.95
978-974-90749-7-8 USA

A global approach to environmental education and action.

New Society Publishers

287

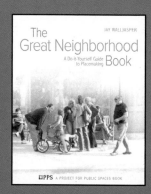

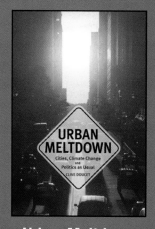

The Great Neighborhood Book
A Do-it-Yourself Guide to Placemaking
Jay Walljasper with Project for Public Spaces

Urban Planning / Cultural Studies
7½ x 9 | 192 pp
125 B&W photographs, charts and maps
TP $19.95
978-0-86571-581-3 USA

Urban Meltdown
Cities, Climate Change and Politics as Usual
Clive Doucet

Current Affairs / Urban Planning
6 x 9 | 240 pp
TP $17.95
978-0-86571-584-4 USA

Guerrilla Gardening
A Manualfesto
David Tracey

Gardening & Horticulture / Urban Planning
7½ x 9 | 240 pp
50 B&W photographs, charts, and maps
TP $19.95
978-0-86571-583-7 USA

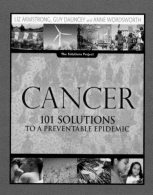

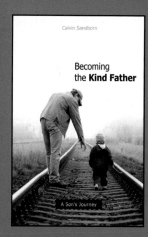

Branded!
How the 'Certification Revolution' is Transforming Global Corporations
Michael E. Conroy

Business & Economics / Environmental Studies
6 x 9 | 320 pp
50 B&W illustrations, photographs, and charts
TP $19.95
978-0-86571-579-0 USA

Cancer
101 Solutions to a Preventable Epidemic
Liz Armstrong, Guy Dauncey, and Anne Wordsworth

Health & Fitness / Environmental Studies
7½ x 9 | 336 pp
125 B&W photographs, charts, and maps
TP $22.95
978-0-86571-542-4 USA

Becoming the Kind Father
A Son's Journey
Calvin Sandborn

Family & Parenting / Psychology & Psychiatry
5½ x 9½ | 176 pp
TP $15.95
978-0-86571-582-0 USA

Undoing the Silence
Six Tools for Writing to Make a Difference
Louise Dunlap

This comprehensive and engaging training book helps both amateurs and professionals influence the democratic process through letters, articles, proposals, and more. It's a "you-can-do-it" approach combined with strategies to articulate personal vision and frame messages that are truly heard.

Healing as much as teaching, the author uncovers the culture of silence—how gender, race, education, class, and family values work to quiet dissent.

Since the Free Speech Movement of the 1960s, Louise Dunlap, PhD, has been training citizen groups as well as university scholars internationally in writing for social change. She is currently a lecturer at Tufts University.

Author Hometown: Cambridge, MA

Writing / Political Science & Government
September
A Paperback Original
7 x 9¼ | 288 pp
24 B&W illustrations, charts and graphs
TP US $20.01 | CAN $24.00
978-0-9766054-9-2 CUSA

Practical methods for citizen activists to put their most powerful ideas into words and effect change.

Art and Upheaval
Artists on the World's Frontlines
William Cleveland
Foreword by Clarissa Pinkola Estés

Artists in communities in crises the world over are working to resolve conflict, promote peace, and rebuild civil society. Here are six remarkable stories of artists in Northern Ireland, Cambodia, South Africa, the United States (Watts, Los Angeles), aboriginal Australia, and Serbia, who heal unspeakable trauma, give voice to the forgotten and disappeared, and re-stitch the cultural fabric of their communities.

Author William Cleveland is an activist, teacher, facilitator, lecturer, and director of the Center for the Study of Art & Community. He is the author of *Art in Other Places,* which explores the emerging community arts movement in the United States.

Author Hometown: Bainbridge Island, WA

Cultural Studies / Art
March
A Paperback Original
7 x 9¼ | 288 pp
60 Color and B&W illustrations
and photographs
TP US $20.01 | CAN $24.00
978-0-9766054-6-1 CUSA

Citizen artists successfully rebuild the social infrastructure in six cities devastated by war, repression, and dislocation.

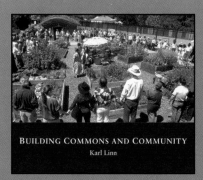

Building Commons and Community
Karl Linn

Cultural Studies / Urban Planning
10 x 8½ | 224 pp
200 Color photographs
TC US $29.95 | CAN $36.00
978-0-9766054-7-8 CUSA

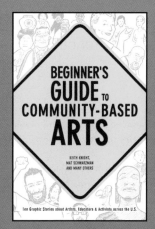

Beginner's Guide to Community-Based Arts
Mat Schwarzman
Illustrated by Keith Knight

Cultural Studies / Art
6⅝ x 10⅛ | 200 pp
200 B&W illustrations
TP US $19.95 | CAN $24.00
978-0-9766054-3-0 CUSA

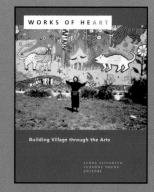

Works of Heart
Building Village through the Arts
Lynne Elizabeth and Suzanne Young

Cultural Studies / Art
7 x 9 | 144 pp
96 Color photographs
TC US $24.95 | CAN $30.00
978-0-9766054-0-9 CUSA

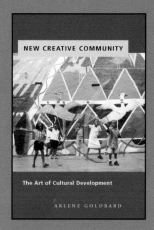

New Creative Community
The Art of Cultural Development
Arlene Goldbard

Cultural Studies / Art
6 x 9¼ | 268 pp
24 B&W photographs
TP US $19.95 | CAN $24.00
978-0-9766054-5-4 CUSA

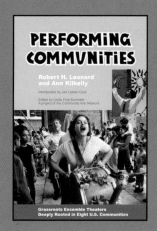

Performing Communities
Grassroots Ensemble
Theaters Deeply Rooted in
Eight U.S. Communities
Robert H. Leonard and Ann Kilkelly

Performing Arts / Cultural Studies
6 x 9 | 240 pp
15 B&W photographs
TP US $19.95 | CAN $24.00
978-0-9766054-4-7 CUSA

Doing Time in the Garden
Life Lessons through
Prison Horticulture
James Jiler

Gardening & Horticulture /
Education & Teaching
7 x 9 | 176 pp
60 Color photographs and
16 B&W illustrations
TC US $24.95 | CAN $30.00
978-0-9766054-2-3 CUSA

Political Portraits
Fidel Castro reflects on famous figures in history
Fidel Castro

A prominent figure himself on the world stage for fifty years, Fidel Castro offers some fascinating and perceptive comments on historical figures and some of his contemporaries, including Nelson Mandela, Che Guevara, José Martí, Simón Bolívar, John F. Kennedy, Abraham Lincoln, Pablo Neruda, Gabriel García Márquez, Oswaldo Guayasamín, Ernest Hemingway, Karl Marx, Friedrich Engels, Joseph Stalin, and Jesus Christ.

With remarkable objectivity, and surprisingly little rancor or bitterness toward his foes, this selection offers as much insight into Fidel Castro as it does into those he discusses.

This is the perfect complement to other Ocean Press books by Fidel Castro, such as *Fidel Castro Reader* (Spring 2007), *Fidel and Religion,* and *My Early Years.* The book includes twelve pages of photographs of Fidel with some of the personalities he discusses here.

This title is also published in Spanish.

**Prominent himself on the world stage for fifty years,
Fidel Castro offers insights on some other famous figures.**

Biography & Autobiography /
Political Science & Government
March
A Paperback Original
5½ x 8½ | 200 pp
12 B&W photographs
TP US $16.95 | CAN $20.50
978-1-920888-94-7 CUSA

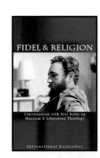

**Also
Available**

Fidel Castro Reader
Edited by David Deutschmann
Political Science & Government / History
6 x 9 | 650 pp
TP US $19.95 | CAN $24.00
978-1-920888-88-6 CUSA

Fidel and Religion
Fidel Castro in Conversation with Frei Betto
Political Science & Government /
Biography & Autobiography
6 x 9 | 300 pp
TP US $19.95 | CAN $24.00
978-1-920888-45-9 CUSA

Ocean Press

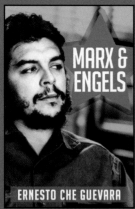

Marx & Engels
An Introduction
Ernesto Che Guevara

This new Che Guevara book makes an insightful contribution to the revival of interest in Marxism.

Commenting on Marx's humanism, Che writes: "Such a humane man, whose capacity for affection extended to all those suffering throughout the world, offering a message of committed struggle and indomitable optimism, has been distorted by history and turned into a stone idol."

A thoughtful and provocative introduction to the lives and work of Marx and Engels by a famous revolutionary practitioner of Marxism, this book includes Che's recommended reading list of essential Marxist classics, making it a popular choice for students and political activists alike.

Political Science & Government /
Biography & Autobiography
October
A Paperback Original
Che Guevara Publishing Project
5 x 7¾ | 100 pp
TP US $9.95 | CAN $12.00
978-1-920888-92-3 CUSA

The unpublished book by Che Guevara that makes an insightful contribution to the revival of interest in Marxism.

Marketing Plans
Co-op available • Advance reader copies • 10,000-copy print run
National advertising: NACLA Report on the Americas • The Nation • Rethinking Marxism

Contemporary Guerrilla Movements in Latin America
Alberto Prieto

The guerrilla fighter has become a defining image of Latin America. This book reviews recent guerrilla movements across the continent, providing a perceptive analysis of their methods and motivations. Alberto Prieto compares and contrasts the experiences of Sandino in Nicaragua, Fidel and Che in Cuba, the decades-long civil war in Colombia, and the current situation in Central America, Peru, Mexico, and elsewhere.

In particular, the author considers whether the guerrilla era is now over in Latin America, and if social change is possible through more peaceful means.

Alberto Prieto is a professor of history at the University of Havana.

Political Science & Government / History
February
A Paperback Original
5½ x 8½ | 290 pp
TP US $18.95 | CAN $23.00
978-1-920888-96-1 CUSA

A comprehensive review of guerrilla movements that have characterized recent Latin American history.

Marketing Plans
Co-op available • Advance reader copies
National advertising: Latin American Perspectives • Latin American Politics and Society • Latin American Research Review • NACLA Report on the Americas • The Nation

Ocean Press

Retratos Políticos
Fidel Castro habla de los grandes personajes de la historia mundial
Fidel Castro

Spanish Language /
Biography &
Autobiography
March
A Paperback Original
Ocean Sur
5½ x 8½ | 210 pp
12 B&W photographs
TP US $16.95
CAN $20.50
978-1-921235-51-1
CUSA

Fidel Castro offers some fascinating and perceptive comments on historical figures and some of his contemporaries, including Nelson Mandela, Che Guevara, José Martí, Simón Bolívar, John F. Kennedy, Abraham Lincoln, Pablo Neruda, Gabriel García Márquez, Oswaldo Guayasamín, Ernest Hemingway, Karl Marx, and Jesus Christ.

This selection offers as much insight into Fidel Castro as it does into those he discusses.

Marx-Engels
Esbozo biográfico
Ernesto Che Guevara

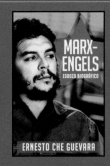

Spanish Language /
Biography &
Autobiography
October
A Paperback Original
Ocean Sur
Che Guevara
Publishing Project
5 x 7¾ | 100 pp
TP US $9.95
CAN $12.00
978-1-921235-25-2
CUSA

This new Che Guevara book makes an insightful contribution to the revival of interest in Marxism.

A thoughtful and provocative introduction to the lives and work of Marx and Engels by a famous revolutionary practitioner of Marxism, this book includes Che's recommended reading list of essential Marxist classics, making it a popular choice for students and political activists alike.

¿Guerra o paz en Colombia?
Cincuenta años de un conflicto sin solución
Carlos A. Lozano Guillén

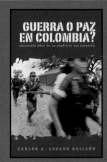

Spanish Language /
Political Science &
Government
September
A Paperback Original
Ocean Sur
5½ x 8½ | 184 pp
TP US $15.95
CAN $19.50
978-1-921235-14-6
CUSA

This is a critical interpretation of the fifty years of unresolved conflict and civil war in Colombia, analyzing the role of the United States and the war on drugs, the right-wing paramilitaries and the left-wing guerrilla movements, and finally discussing the real possibilities for achieving peace.

Carlos A. Lozano Guillén is a journalist and the editor of Colombia's only left-wing daily newspaper, *Voz.*

El Socialismo y el Hombre en Cuba
Ernesto Che Guevara

Spanish Language /
Political Science &
Government
September
A Paperback Original
Ocean Sur
Che Guevara
Publishing Project
5 x 7½ | 50 pp
16 B&W photographs
TP US $9.95
CAN $12.00
978-1-921235-17-7
CUSA

Che Guevara's classic work on social change and human nature, reviewing the early years of Cuba's revolution and analyzing the role of the individual in transforming the social, economic, and political structures of capitalist society. One of the most important political and philosophical documents to emerge from the Cuban Revolution and the 1960s, featuring photographs taken by Che in Cuba.

Spanish Language /
Political Science &
Government
September
A Paperback Original
Ocean Sur
5½ x 8½ | 236 pp
TP US $16.95
CAN $20.50
978-1-921235-43-6
CUSA

La Historia me Absolverá
Fidel Castro

This is Fidel Castro's brilliant courtroom defense speech, offering a foretaste of the oratory for which he would become famous. During his trial for initiating an uprising against Batista's dictatorship in 1953, Castro was sentenced to fifteen years of imprisonment. He was released twenty months later due to public pressure, and within six years he marched triumphantly into Havana at the head of the Cuban Revolution.

Spanish Language /
Political Science &
Government
October
A Paperback Original
Ocean Sur
5½ x 8½ | 215 pp
TP US $16.95
CAN $20.50
978-1-921235-56-6
CUSA

El Pensamiento Político de Ernesto Che Guevara
María del Carmen Ariet-García

An analysis of the political thought of Che Guevara, this book shows Che, best known as a guerrilla fighter, as a profound thinker, incisive political and economic strategist, and a creative, distinctly Latin American Marxist. The book explains Che's internationalism and motivation to participate, and ultimately offer his life, in the struggle to create a better world.

Spanish Language /
Biography &
Autobiography
September
A Paperback Original
Ocean Sur
6 x 9 | 500 pp
TP US $24.95
CAN $30.00
978-1-921235-57-3
CUSA

Miguel Mármol
Los sucesos de 1932 en El Salvador
Roque Dalton

"*Miguel Mármol* is an extraordinary literary document and political resource."—*The Nation*

This is the classic Latin American testimony of a shoemaker and revolutionary. Miguel Mármol devoted his life to organizing El Salvador's poor, narrowly escaping capture and death several times for his political activities. In Prague in 1966, poet Roque Dalton interviewed Mármol, producing a remarkable first-person account of Mármol's life.

Spanish Language /
Political Science &
Government
October
A Paperback Original
Ocean Sur
5½ x 8½ | 310 pp
TP US $19.95
CAN $24.00
978-1-921235-54-2
CUSA

Las Guerrillas Contemporáneas en América Latina
Alberto Prieto

The guerrilla fighter is a defining image of Latin America. This book reviews recent guerrilla movements across the continent, providing a perceptive analysis of their methods and motivations. Alberto Prieto compares and contrasts the experiences of Sandino in Nicaragua, Fidel and Che in Cuba, the civil war in Colombia, and the current situation in Central America, Peru, Mexico, and elsewhere.

Ocean Press

Una Guerra para Construir la Paz
Schafik Handal

Spanish Language /
Political Science &
Government
September
A Paperback Original
Ocean Sur
5½ x 8½ | 151 pp
TP US $14.95
CAN $18.00
978-1-921235-13-9
CUSA

Schafik Handal reflects on the peace process in El Salvador, analyzing the causes of the long, brutal war and the negotiations that finally resulted in the signing of peace accords in 1992. Schafik also reviews subsequent contraventions of the accords.

Schafik Handal was a guerrilla commander in El Salvador in the 1980s and a leading participant in the peace negotiations.

¿Por qué soy Chavista?
Razones de una revolución
Farruco Sesto

Spanish Language /
Political Science &
Government
September
A Paperback Original
Ocean Sur
5½ x 8½ | 89 pp
TP US $11.95
CAN $14.50
978-1-921235-16-0
CUSA

This memoir by Venezuela's minister for culture relates a personal vision of Hugo Chávez and the reforms sweeping Venezuela today, describing the reasons for the transformation of Venezuelan society and the importance of culture in Venezuela's development. Above all, the author asserts the importance of revolutionary values and ethics as the basis for the political, social, and cultural changes in Venezuela.

Chile y Allende
Fidel Castro

Spanish Language /
Political Science &
Government
January
A Paperback Original
Ocean Sur
6 x 9 | 300 pp
TP US $19.95
CAN $24.00
978-1-921235-42-9
CUSA

Chile y Allende is Fidel Castro's analysis of the Chilean road to socialism in the 1970s. In 1971, Castro spent a month in Chile, addressing public meetings and discussing with President Salvador Allende Cuba's experience in combating US-inspired counterrevolutionary forces. On departure, he handed Allende a rifle. The book includes Castro's speech following the US-sponsored coup by Augusto Pinochet in 1973, in which Allende lost his life.

Diez Días que Estremecieron al Mundo
John Reed

Spanish Language /
Political Science &
Government
January
A Paperback Original
Ocean Sur
5½ x 8½ | 280 pp
TP US $18.95
CAN $23.00
978-1-921235-07-8
CUSA

This is the first and best eyewitness account of the 1917 Russian Revolution. With the immediacy of a cinema script, US radical journalist John Reed captures the turmoil and optimism that swept away the Czarist regime. Reed's account remains an unsurpassed classic of inspired reporting.

This title, **John Reed**'s most famous work, formed the basis of Warren Beatty's Oscar-winning film *Reds*.

Contexto Latinoamericano no.1
septiembre-diciembre 2006
Edited by Roberto Regalado

Contexto Latinoamericano is a new quarterly Spanish-language magazine from Latin America and by Latin Americans, which aims to facilitate and promote the exchange of ideas among activists and political and social movements throughout the continent. It offers a timely forum for debate on current political and cultural issues in Latin America.

This launch issue of *Contexto Latinoamericano* reviews the success of progressive or left-wing candidates in recent presidential elections in Colombia, Bolivia, Chile, Mexico, and Peru. Other articles cover Puerto Rico's struggle for independence, Monroeism versus Bolivarianism, and artists and the commercialization of art.

Spanish Language /
Political Science & Government
September
A Paperback Original
Ocean Sur
Contexto Latinoamericano
6½ x 9½ | 254 pp
TP US $14.95 | CAN $18.00
978-1-921235-15-3 CUSA

Contexto Latinoamericano no.2
enero-marzo 2007
Edited by Roberto Regalado

Contexto Latinoamericano is edited by Roberto Regalado, a leading Cuban political analyst and author of *Latin America at the Crossroads/América Latina entre siglos.* The editorial advisory board of *Contexto* includes representatives of a broad range of political currents and individuals of the Latin American Left.

This second issue focuses on the Panama Canal and elections in Nicaragua, Ecuador, Brazil, Mexico, and Venezuela. Contributors include Schafik Handal (El Salvador), Roberto Fernández Retamar (Cuba), and Armando Bartra (Mexico).

Contexto Latinoamericano is a crucial, up-to-date resource for US academics, students, and activists interested in contemporary Latin America.

Spanish Language /
Political Science & Government
September
A Paperback Original
Ocean Sur
Contexto Latinoamericano
6½ x 9½ | 210 pp
TP US $14.95 | CAN $18.00
978-1-921235-44-3 CUSA

Contexto Latinoamericano no.3
abril-junio 2007
Edited by Roberto Regalado

Spanish Language /
Political Science & Government
September
A Paperback Original
Ocean Sur
Contexto Latinoamericano
6½ x 9½ | 210 pp
TP US $14.95 | CAN $18.00
978-1-921235-45-0 CUSA

Contexto Latinoamericano no.4
julio-septiembre 2007
Edited by Roberto Regalado

Spanish Language /
Political Science & Government
October
A Paperback Original
Ocean Sur
Contexto Latinoamericano
6½ x 9½ | 210 pp
TP US $14.95 | CAN $18.00
978-1-921235-46-7 CUSA

Ocean Press

Sacco y Vanzetti

Vidas Rebeldes

Nicola Sacco and Bartolomeo Vanzetti

Edited by John Davis

Italian immigrants and anarchists Nicola Sacco and Bartolomeo Vanzetti were framed by the state and executed for murder amid anti-immigrant hysteria in 1920s Boston. This book illustrates how anarchists and immigrants were the "terrorists" of yesteryear, and explores the consequences of using fear as a political weapon.

Features contributions from John Dos Passos, Emma Goldman, Joan Baez and Ennio Morricone, H.G. Wells, and Howard Zinn.

Spanish Language / Political Science & Government
September
A Paperback Original
Ocean Sur
Vidas Rebeldes
5 x 7¾ | 140 pp
TP US $11.95
CAN $14.50
978-1-921235-06-1
CUSA

En el Borde de Todo

El hoy y el mañana de la revolución en Cuba

Julio César Guanche

What will become of the Cuban Revolution? With Fidel Castro's decline, many outside of Cuba have predicted the end of the revolution. Here, ordinary Cubans of various ages and backgrounds are interviewed on life in Cuba, the current political situation, and their hopes for the future. A unique opportunity to hear ordinary Cubans' views during a time of change and uncertainty.

Spanish Language / Current Affairs
October
A Paperback Original
Ocean Sur
6 x 9 | 375 pp
TP US $21.95
CAN $26.50
978-1-921235-50-4
CUSA

Introducción al Pensamiento Socialista

Néstor Kohan

This is a clear, accessible, and highly informative history of socialist thought, seen from a uniquely Latin American perspective.

Includes excerpts from the great rebel thinkers, including Karl Marx, Che Guevara, Fidel Castro, Rosa Luxemburg, José Carlos Mariátegui, Camilo Torres, Roque Dalton, Jean-Paul Sartre, Julio Antonio Mella, Antonio Gramsci, Albert Einstein, and more.

Spanish Language / Political Science & Government
September
A Paperback Original
Ocean Sur
5½ x 8½ | 255 pp
TP US $17.95
CAN $21.50
978-1-921235-52-8
CUSA

Colombia: laboratorio de embrujos

Democracia y terrorismo de estado

Hernando Calvo

This book, by Colombian journalist and former political prisoner Hernando Calvo, combines a history of the fifty-year guerrilla war in Colombia with personal accounts of the victims of dictatorship and terror.

Hernando Calvo, author of *The Cuban Exile Movement* (Ocean Press, 1996) and several other books on Latin America, lives in exile in France.

Spanish Language / Political Science & Government
January
A Paperback Original
Ocean Sur
6 x 9 | 311 pp
TP US $19.95
CAN $24.00
978-1-921235-55-9
CUSA

Ocean Press

Self Portrait
A photographic and literary memoir
Ernesto Che Guevara

Biography & Autobiography /
Latin American Studies
8½ x 9½ | 305 pp
200 Duotone photographs
TP US $29.95 | CAN $36.00
978-1-876175-82-5 CUSA

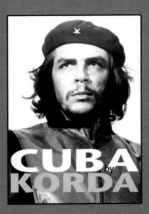

Cuba
by Korda
Alberto Korda

Photography / Latin American Studies
9 x 12¼ | 160 pp
82 Duotone photographs
TP US $24.95 | CAN $30.00
978-1-920888-64-0 CUSA

Che
A Memoir
Fidel Castro

Biography & Autobiography /
Latin American Studies
5½ x 8½ | 237 pp
16 B&W photographs
TP US $16.95 | CAN $20.50
978-1-920888-25-1 CUSA

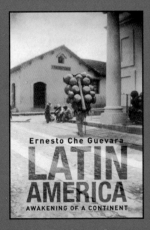

Latin America
Awakening of a Continent
Ernesto Che Guevara

Political Science & Government /
Latin American Studies
6 x 9 | 450 pp
TP US $24.95 | CAN $30.00
978-1-920888-38-1 CUSA

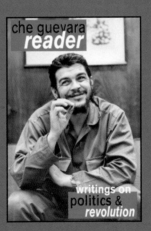

Che Guevara Reader
Writings on Politics and Revolution
Ernesto Che Guevara

Political Science & Government /
Latin American Studies
6 x 9 | 437 pp
TP US $23.95 | CAN $29.00
978-1-876175-69-6 CUSA

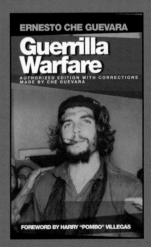

Guerrilla Warfare
Authorized Edition
Ernesto Che Guevara

Political Science & Government /
Latin American Studies
5½ x 8½ | 157 pp
TP US $11.95 | CAN $14.50
978-1-920888-28-2 CUSA

Literary Genius
25 Classic Writers Who Define English & American Literature
Edited by Joseph Epstein
Illustrated by Barry Moser

What constitutes literary genius? This collection of essays focuses on twenty-five English-language writers whose original and enduring works enrich our lives. Renowned portraitist Barry Moser provides a handsome engraving of each writer, together with illustrations based upon their texts.

Contents:

1. Tom Shippey on Geoffrey Chaucer
2. Lois Potter on William Shakespeare
3. Reynolds Price on John Milton
4. Anthony Hecht on Alexander Pope
5. David Bromwich on Samuel Johnson
6. David Womersley on Edward Gibbon
7. Dan Jacobson on William Wordsworth
8. Hilary Mantel on Jane Austen
9. Frederic Raphael on William Hazlitt
10. Eavan Boland on John Keats
11. Daniel Mark Epstein on Nathaniel Hawthorne
12. A.N. Wilson on Charles Dickens
13. Justin Kaplan on Walt Whitman
14. William Pritchard on Herman Melville
15. Paula Marantz Cohen on George Eliot
16. Bruce Floyd on Emily Dickinson
17. David Carkeet on Mark Twain
18. Joseph Epstein on Henry James
19. Elizabeth Lowry on Joseph Conrad
20. Stephen Cox on Willa Cather
21. Robert Pack on Robert Frost
22. Joseph Blotner on William Faulkner
23. John Gross on James Joyce
24. John Simon on T.S. Eliot
25. James L. W. West III on Ernest Hemingway

Joseph Epstein, former editor of the *American Scholar,* teaches writing and literature at Northwestern University. He is the author of seventeen books.

Barry Moser is world-renowned for his children's illustrations, engravings, water-colors, and reinterpretations of the classics.

Profiles of twenty-five great writers whose works help us see the world in new ways.

Literature & Essay / Literary Criticism
October
A Paperback Original
7⅜ x 9¼ | 256 pp
59 Wood Engravings
TP US $18.95 | CAN $23.00
978-1-58988-035-1 CUSA

Marketing Plans

Co-op available
Advance reader copies

Paul Dry Books

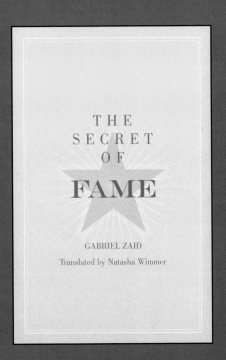

Literature & Essay / Cultural Studies
March
4½ x 7 | 195 pp
TC US $14.95 | CAN $18.00
978-1-58988-038-2 CUSA

Marketing Plans

Co-op available
Advance reader copies

The Secret of Fame
Gabriel Zaid
Translated by Natasha Wimmer

Fame. Why do authors seek it? How does one acquire it? What are the consequences of attaining it? Gabriel Zaid examines the methods and motivations, from ancient times to the present day. He shines a critical, yet humorous, light on today's literary world, whose denizens find it "more interesting to talk about writers than to read them," and he takes a serious look at the desire for fame and the disillusionment and objectification that can accompany it. Along the way, Zaid pokes fun at literary and scholarly traditions, including the unwritten rules of quoting other authors, the ascendancy of the footnote, and the practice of publishing "foolishly complete works."

The author can manage his literary name like a brand, with a whole line of products: books published under his name (but not necessarily entirely written by him), with all their subsidiary rights; as well as a line of services. . . . There's no reason that toys, clothes, and many other things should be the sole province of characters like Harry Potter and Mickey Mouse. At the Günter Grass Museum, established with the participation of the writer, Günter Grass t–shirts or Günter Grass tin drums could surely be sold.

Gabriel Zaid's poetry, essays, and cultural criticism have been widely published throughout the Spanish-speaking world. In 2003, Paul Dry Books published Zaid's *So Many Books,* which Leon Wieseltier called "genuinely exhilarating."

Natasha Wimmer is an editor and a translator in New York City. She recently translated *The Savage Detectives* by Roberto Bolano (Farrar, Straus and Giroux Publishers).

An entertaining and provocative look at the way writers write and why some achieve celebrity status.

Also Available

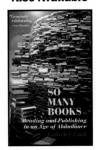

So Many Books
Reading and Publishing in an Age of Abundance
Gabriel Zaid
Translated by Natasha Wimmer
Literature & Essay
4½ x 7 | 144 pp
TP US $9.95 | CAN $12.00
978-1-58988-003-0 CUSA

Paul Dry Books

Infinity
Beyond the Beyond the Beyond
Lillian R. Lieber
Illustrated by Hugh Gray Lieber
Foreword by Barry Mazur

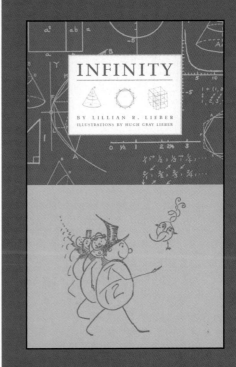

"Another excellent book for the lay reader of mathematics. . . . In explaining [infinity], the author introduces the reader to a good many other mathematical terms and concepts that seem unintelligible in a formal text but are much less formidable when presented in the author's individual and very readable style."—*Library Journal*

"The interpolations tying mathematics into human life and thought are brilliantly clear."—*Booklist*

"Mrs. Lieber, in this text illustrated by her husband, Hugh Gray Lieber, has tackled the formidable task of explaining infinity in simple terms, in short line, short sentence technique popularized by her in *The Education of T.C. MITS.*"—*Chicago Sunday Tribune*

Infinity, another delightful mathematics book from the creators of *The Education of T.C. MITS,* offers an entertaining, yet thorough, explanation of the concept of, yes, infinity. Accessible to non-mathematicians, this book also cleverly connects mathematical reasoning to larger issues in society. The new foreword by Harvard mathematics professor Barry Mazur is a tribute to the Liebers' influence on generations of mathematicians.

Lillian R. Lieber was a professor and head of the Department of Mathematics at Long Island University. She wrote a series of light-hearted (and well-respected) math books, many of them illustrated by her husband.

Barry Mazur is the Gerhard Gade University Professor of Mathematics at Harvard University and is the author of *Imagining Numbers.*

This elegant, accessible, and playful book artfully illuminates the concept of infinity with its striking drawings.

Mathematics / Science
November
5 x 8 | 359 pp
26 B&W illustrations
TP US $14.95 | CAN $18.00
978-1-58988-036-8 CUSA

Also Available

The Education of T.C. Mits
What modern mathematics means to you
Lillian R. Lieber
Illustrated by Hugh Gray Lieber
Mathematics / Science
5 x 8 | 230 pp
53 B&W illustrations
TP US $11.95 | CAN $14.50
978-1-58988-033-7 CUSA

Paul Dry Books

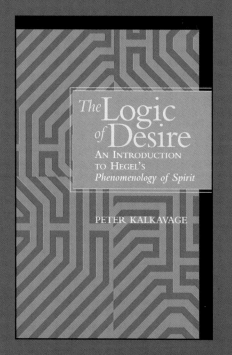

Philosophy
December
A Paperback Original
5½ x 8½ | 500 pp
TP US $35.00 | CAN $42.00
978-1-58988-037-5 CUSA

Marketing Plans

Co-op available

The Logic of Desire
An Introduction to Hegel's *Phenomenology of Spirit*
Peter Kalkavage

Peter Kalkavage's *The Logic of Desire: An Introduction to Hegel's Phenomenology of Spirit* guides the reader through Georg Wilhelm Friedrich Hegel's great work. Given the book's legendary difficulty, one may well ask, "Why even try to read the *Phenomenology*?" In his preface, Kalkavage explains why he thinks a reader should try.

There is much to commend the study of Hegel: his attentiveness to the deepest, most fundamental questions of philosophy, his uncompromising pursuit of truth, his amazing gift for characterization and critique, his appreciation for the grand sweep of things and the large view, his profound admiration for all that is heroic, especially for the ancient Greeks, those heroes of thought in whom the philosophic spirit first dawned, his penetrating gaze into modernity in all its forms, the enormous breadth of his interests, and the sheer audacity of his claim to have captured absolute knowing in the form of a thoroughly rational account.

No genuine philosophic education can omit a serious encounter with this giant of the modern age, the giant who absorbed all the worlds of spiritual vitality that came before him and tried to organize them into a coherent whole.

Anyone who is interested in Hegel will want to own this book.

Peter Kalkavage is a member of the senior faculty at St. John's College in Annapolis, Maryland, where he has taught for thirty years. He is the author of numerous articles on philosophy. He translated Plato's *Timaeus* and co-translated Plato's *Phaedo* and *Sophist*.

The best introduction for the general reader to Georg Wilhelm Friedrich Hegel's great book, *Phenomenology of Spirit*.

Paul Dry Books

The Malice Box

Martin Langfield

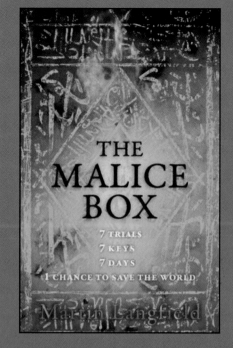

"One of the best novels I have read in a very long time. A thrilling journey of self discovery. . . . Splendidly rewarding."—*Shots Magazine* (London)

When Robert is sent what seems to be a simple copper puzzle box, he has no idea his life is about to undergo a violent transformation. That night, an acquaintance kills himself under curious circumstances; the following day, an old friend reveals the existence of an arcane weapon that could endanger the fate of the Western world.

The responsibility for hunting down and destroying this weapon, this Malice Box, lies with Robert. The weapon is primed to explode in seven days, and Robert must undergo a spiritual and physical quest—a series of trials around Manhattan—in order to track down the keys that will prevent detonation. In a desperate race against the clock, Robert scours the streets of Manhattan under the constant gaze of a sinister figure known as the Watchman. He has only Teri, a beautiful and mysterious psychic, to guide him.

The Malice Box is a thriller unlike any other. Crack the clues with Robert and join in the quest to close the Malice Box once and for all at www.maliceboxquest.com.

Martin Langfield is the global head of journalistic training at Reuters. He headed the New York bureau for seven years, most recently as East Coast bureau chief, and also worked as foreign correspondent and bureau chief for Reuters in Miami, Mexico, and El Salvador. He lives in New York.

**An ancient conspiracy links the secret alchemy of
Isaac Newton to modern-day New York.**

Fiction / Mystery
September
6 x 9 | 432 pp
TC $25.00
978-1-933648-48-4 USA

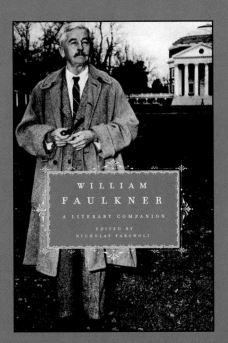

William Faulkner
A Literary Companion
Edited by Nicholas Fargnoli

The novels of William Faulkner continue to fascinate and inspire. This compendium of critical thought—including Robert Penn Warren, Graham Greene, Lionel Trilling, Malcolm Cowley, and George Orwell, among others—will aid fans and students alike in understanding the great author and giant of American literature.

More than simply a renowned Mississippi writer, the Nobel Prize-winning novelist is acclaimed throughout the world as one of the twentieth century's greatest artists, one who transformed his home state into an apocryphal setting in which he explored and challenged "the old verities and truths of the heart."

It is one of the more remarkable feats of American literature: how a young man who never graduated from high school, never received a college degree, living in a small town in the poorest state in the nation, could, during the Great Depression, write a series of novels all set in the same small Southern county—books that include *As I Lay Dying, Light in August,* and above all, *Absalom, Absalom!*—that would one day be recognized as among the greatest literature ever produced by an American.

Nicholas Fargnoli is the author of many books, including *James Joyce: A Literary Reference, Ulysses in Critical Perspective,* and *William Faulkner A to Z: The Essential Reference to His Life and Work.* Fargnoli is a professor of theology and English at Molloy College in New York.

**A monumental critical resource on William Faulkner—
the perfect companion to the Nobel Prize-winning author's life and work.**

Literary Criticism
September
A Paperback Original
6 x 9 | 512 pp
TP US $16.95 | CAN $20.50
978-1-933648-58-3 CUSA

Marketing Plans

Co-op available
Advance reader copies
National advertising:
American Scholar • The New Yorker

Pegasus Books

The Road to Blue Heaven

An Insider's Diary of North Carolina's 2007 Basketball Season

Wes Miller

Introduction by Adam Lucas

Wes Miller grew up in the shadow of the Atlantic Coast Conference, college basketball's most powerful league. But as a high school senior, none of those elite programs offered him a scholarship—they thought he was too small and too slow.

After a year at a mid-major program, he chose to attend North Carolina without a basketball scholarship. Over the next four years, Miller's hard work resulted in a major role on the Carolina team. He earned a starting spot as a junior, displacing more highly touted players.

He began his senior year with a mission—to chronicle all aspects of his final season in Chapel Hill. Off the court, it is a glimpse of a life few will ever enjoy. At a basketball-crazy school like the University of North Carolina, basketball players are the Beatles. On the court, Miller had to find his place in one of the most talented Carolina teams in history. This is the story of his senior year in his own words, as he takes you inside the locker room, on the court, and behind the scenes in the most unique book ever written about one of the most famous college sports dynasties of all time—Carolina basketball.

Wes Miller is a senior on the men's basketball team at North Carolina, one of the nation's most elite programs.

Adam Lucas is the author of three books on North Carolina basketball: *Going Home Again, Led By Their Dreams,* and *The Best Game Ever.* He lives in Chapel Hill.

An intimate account—and a powerful individual story of triumph over diversity—of the North Carolina Tar Heels' dramatic 2007 basketball season.

Sports & Recreation
September
5½ x 8¼ | 256 pp
16 Color photographs
TC US $24.00 | CAN $29.00
978-1-933648-57-6 CUSA

Marketing Plans

Co-op available
Advance reader copies
10,000-copy print run
National advertising:
Raleigh News & Observer •
Sports Illustrated • Tar Heel Monthly

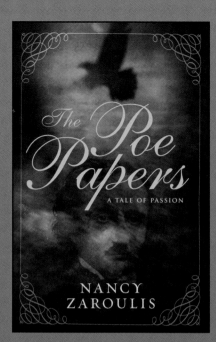

Mystery
September
5½ x 8¼ | 240 pp
TP US $13.95 | CAN $17.00
978-1-933648-64-4 CUSA

Marketing Plans

Co-op available
National advertising:
Mystery Scene • The Strand Magazine

The Poe Papers
a tale of passion
Nancy Zaroulis

"A macabre, terrifying thriller."—*Library Journal*

"A nightmare of sex, murder, and madness."—*Kirkus Reviews*

"Told with great power. . . . A stunning achievement."—*The Boston Globe*

"Nancy Zaroulis has a fierce sense of history. . . . A magnificent storyteller."
—*The Plain Dealer*

"Fascinating. . . . It would be interesting to see what Alfred Hitchcock would do with this material."—*Publishers Weekly*

A woman with a secret of adulterous love in her past and a still-ravenous desire burning within her; a daughter who has grown to be her mother's rival in voluptuous beauty and rapacious lust; and the young man who comes to their old New England mansion on a scholar's visit—and is willing to do anything in exchange for the forbidden secret they possess—stays to be seduced body and soul.

Nancy Zaroulis is the author of five novels, as well as three Beacon Hill Mysteries, published under the pseudonym Cynthia Peale. Her sole nonfiction work, *Who Spoke Up?*, a history of the anti-Vietnam War movement, was a *New York Times* Notable Book of the Year. She lives with her family in Massachusetts. Visit Nancy at www.thepoepapers.com.

A diabolical love story between a mother, a daughter, and an obsessed treasure hunter—with Edgar Allan Poe's legacy hanging in the balance.

Pegasus Books

The Dark Water
The Strange Beginnings of Sherlock Holmes
David Pirie

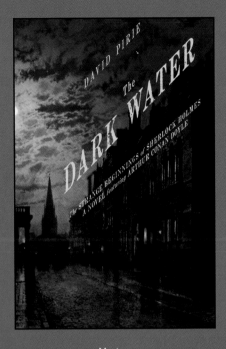

"The third novel in an imaginative Victorian series narrated by the young Arthur Conan Doyle. As the inspirational model for Sherlock Holmes, the brilliant and eccentric Dr. Bell properly takes charge of the cryptic codes that figure in this ingenious mystery."—Marilyn Stasio, *The New York Times Book Review*

"Pirie's knowledge of Doyle's biography, as well as of the Holmes canon, makes him an intellectual treat and a downright guilty pleasure."—*The Washington Post*

"I was utterly hooked. It's not just Thomas Harris; it's also Raymond Chandler and Arthur Conan Doyle himself. All of these great writers are echoed in a way that is not merely wonderful and absolutely gripping, but completely original. The series has huge commercial potential."—Sarah Dunant, #1 *New York Times* best-selling author of *In the Company of the Courtesan*

In a literary tour de force worthy of Sir Arthur Conan Doyle himself, author David Pirie brings his rich familiarity with both the Doyle biography and the Sherlock Holmes canon to a mystifying Victorian tale of vengeance and villainy. The howling man on the heath, a gothic asylum, the walking dead, the legendary witch of Dunwich—perils lurk in every turn of the page throughout this ingenious novel, as increasingly bizarre encounters challenge the deductive powers of young Doyle and his mentor, the pioneering criminal investigator Dr. Joseph Bell.

David Pirie is the author of two other critically praised novels featuring Arthur Conan Doyle, *The Patient's Eyes* and *The Night Calls*. He lives in Bath.

The creator of Sherlock Holmes pursues his own fiendish nemesis in this ingenious novel of detection.

Mystery
October
6 x 9 | 320 pp
TP US $14.95 | CAN $18.00
978-1-933648-59-0 CUSA

Marketing Plans

Co-op available
10,000-copy print run
National advertising:
The Strand Magazine

Also Available

The Patient's Eyes
The Dark Beginnings of Sherlock Holmes
David Pirie
Mystery / Fiction
6 x 8 | 256 pp
TP $14.95
978-1-933648-43-9 USA

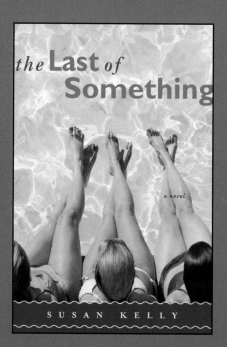

Fiction
October
5½ x 8¼ | 208 pp
TP US $12.95 | CAN $15.50
978-1-933648-60-6 CUSA

Marketing Plans

Co-op available
10,000-copy print run

Author Events

Chapel Hill, NC • Charlotte, NC •
Greensboro, NC • Raleigh, NC •
Wilmington, NC • Greenville, SC

The Last of Something
a novel
Susan Kelly

"A reflective, smoothly written novel. . . . The denouement is strong and affecting."—*Publishers Weekly*

"Kelly writes like there's an angel hiding in her pen. . . . A winner all the way."
—*The News & Observer*

"An affecting novel . . . a smoothly written tale. Kelly hones in on both the big and small things that draw women together."—*Orlando Sentinel*

They've been friends since their college days—Shotsie, Bess, and Claire—and the twenty years since have gotten themselves husbands, children, mortgages, assorted body patches, one handgun, a hysterectomy, and lots of neurosis. Still, at least once a year they again have each other. And Ian.

This year, in this affecting, sly, bittersweet novel, they are gathering along with their husbands at Dune Ridge on the coast of North Carolina near the close of summer. Only this year their circle is incomplete. Because Ian—wildly irresponsible Ian, "the enigma" Ian—does not show. His young, new wife does, however, and no matter what romance Ian may in the past have shared with Shotsie, Bess, and Claire, it's the dewily beautiful Nina who is bearing his child.

For sure, a hurricane is heading menacingly their way, and neither friendship nor memory, any more than a creaky seaside cottage, can grant them safe harbor. In old stories new truths unfold.

Susan Kelly is the author of the novels *Even Now* and *How Close We Come*, winner of the Carolina Novel Award and an alternate selection of the Book of the Month Club. She lives in Greensboro, North Carolina.

Three women, two decades of friendship, one summer weekend, and a hurricane: Some things last, others end.

Pegasus Books

Now You Know
a novel
Susan Kelly

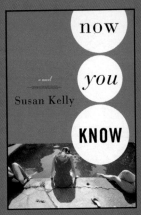

Fiction
October
5½ x 8¼ | 224 pp
TC US $22.00 | CAN $26.50
978-1-933648-61-3 CUSA

"Susan Kelly has a quiet dignity and honesty."—*Atlanta Journal-Constitution*

College roommates in 1947, Frances and Libba forge an unlikely friendship that only ends with Frances' lingering death. As secrets and betrayals begin to emerge, Frances' three children strive to resolve their resentment toward their mother's best friend.

A poignant, stylish novel about the darker side of Southern mores, by the incomparable Susan Kelly.

Susan Kelly is the author of the novels *The Last of Something, Even Now,* and *How Close We Come,* winner of the Carolina Novel Award and an alternate selection of the Book of the Month Club. She lives in Greensboro, North Carolina.

Marketing Plans
Co-op available • Advance reader copies

Author Events
Chapel Hill, NC • Charlotte, NC • Debordieux, NC • Greensboro, NC • Lichfield, NC • Raleigh, NC • Wilmington, NC • Winston Salem, NC • Greenville, SC • Richmond, VA

An emotionally vibrant story of family secrets and the sacrifices that love compels us to make.

The Tibetan Art of Serenity
How to Conquer Fear and Gain Contentment
Christopher Hansard

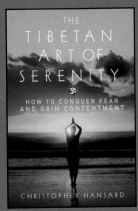

Self-Actualization & Self Help
October
A Paperback Original
5½ x 8¼ | 240 pp
TP $14.95
978-1-933648-62-0 USA

"As life becomes more hectic, it's important to stop and think about the way we are living. Christopher's book is the best possible starting point."—*Vogue* (United Kingdom)

In this inspiring book, leading Tibetan Bon practitioner Christopher Hansard explains the twelve types of fear that affect our lives. He shares age-old techniques for overcoming these fears to find increased peace and confidence.

Christopher Hansard was trained in the spiritual traditions of Tibetan Bon from the age of four and is now a leading practitioner in the field. He is director of clinical affairs at the Eden Medical Centre in London.

Marketing Plans
Co-op available • Advance reader copies • 10,000-copy print run

Tibetan spiritual traditions show us how to start living life with increased peace, humor, and confidence.

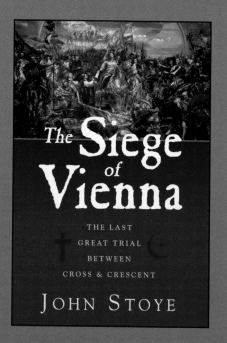

History
November
5½ x 8¼ | 240 pp
TP US $14.95 | CAN $18.00
978-1-933648-63-7 CUSA

Marketing Plans

Co-op available
10,000-copy print run
National advertising:
The Economist •
The Washington Post Book World

The Siege of Vienna
The Last Great Trial Between Cross & Crescent
John Stoye

"In his splendid study *The Siege of Vienna,* the Oxford historian John Stoye provides a detailed account of the intricate machinations between the Habsburgs and the Ottomans. Mr. Stoye's description of the siege itself is masterly. He seems to know every inch of ground, every earthwork and fortification around the Imperial City, and he follows the action meticulously."—*The Wall Street Journal*

"Worthy of the pen of Herodotus. . . . It is a measure of the fascination of Mr. Stoye's subject that one should think of comparing his treatment of it with the work of the greatest historians."—*The Times Literary Supplement*

"John Stoye is the master of every aspect of his subject."—*Daily Telegraph*

The siege of Vienna in 1683 was one of the turning points in European history. So great was its impact that countries normally jealous and hostile sank their differences to throw back the armies of Islam and their savage Tartar allies.

The consequences of defeat were momentous: The Ottomans lost half of their European territories, which led to the final collapse of their empire, and the Habsburgs turned their attention from France and the Rhine frontier to the rich pickings of the Balkans. That hot September day in 1683 witnessed the last great trial of strength between the East and the West—and opened an epoch in European history that lasted until the First World War.

John Stoye, the author of several books on European history, is a fellow at Magdalen College, Oxford, where he lives.

The definitive account of the last serious threat to western Europe by the armies of Islam.

Pegasus Books

Bone Machine
A Joe Donovan Thriller
Martyn Waites

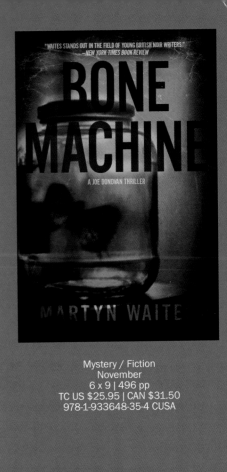

"Waites stands out in the field of young British noir writers . . . with his bruised characters, raw-edged dialogue, and extraordinary night vision."—Marilyn Stasio, *The New York Times Book Review*

The body is discovered in an abandoned burial ground: a young woman, blond, ritualistically mutilated, apparently. Her eyes and mouth have been crudely sewn shut.

The police come up with a suspect quick enough: the victim's boyfriend, Michael Nell, who has a notoriously uncontrollable temper as well as an incriminating record of violence against women. His lawyer, however, is not convinced that Nell is a killer.

All Joe Donovan has to do is prove the truth of Michael Nell's alibi. The job proves not to be routine, as Donovan's inquiries lead him and his crack team of operatives deep into Newcastle's murky underworld of child-trafficking and prostitution. When the second body shows up, the former investigative journalist knows he's up against more than local gangsters.

Still bearing the scars of his own crushing history since the disappearance of his six-year-old son three years before, Donovan now finds himself enmeshed in the dark biography of an elusive, deranged serial killer whom he can profile but cannot identify. The killer meanwhile obliges the authorities with maddeningly cryptic clues to his twisted, deadly intents, but all the while time for the next young, unsuspecting victim is fast running out.

Martyn Waites is emerging as one of the leading writers of British noir fiction. He lives in London.

Joe Donovan is back, in a riveting new urban thriller from a frontrunner in the field of contemporary noir.

Also Available

The Mercy Seat
A Joe Donovan Thriller
Martyn Waites
Mystery / Fiction
5½ x 8¼ | 432 pp
TC US $25.00 | CAN $30.00
978-1-933648-00-2 CUSA

Mystery / Fiction
November
6 x 9 | 496 pp
TC US $25.95 | CAN $31.50
978-1-933648-35-4 CUSA

Marketing Plans

Co-op available
Advance reader copies
National advertising:
Los Angeles Times • Publishers Weekly

Author Events

Author appearance at Bouchercon

Pegasus Books

"RARE AND FANTASTIC." —*THE PHILADELPHIA INQUIRER*

Fiction / Mystery
November
5½ x 8¼ | 432 pp
TP US $14.95 | CAN $18.00
978-1-933648-33-0 CUSA

Marketing Plans

10,000-copy print run

Author Events

Author appearance at Bouchercon

The Mercy Seat
A Joe Donovan Thriller
Martyn Waites

"Rare and fantastic."—*The Philadelphia Inquirer*

"London's dark heart has seldom been exposed with such surgical precision. Brutal, mesmerizing stuff."—Ian Rankin

"Highly recommended for adult mystery collections."—*Library Journal* (starred review)

"A beautifully written and constructed thriller. . . . Raw violence explodes on almost every page, and there are some artfully awful villains."—*Publishers Weekly* (starred review)

"A powerful writer who creates memorable characters who live in the memory as well as on the page. *The Mercy Seat* flies, with no stop in the action and tension. The skillful dialogue reminds me of Ken Bruen."—Otto Penzler

"An ambitious, tautly plotted thriller that offers a stark antidote to P.D. James' cozy world of middle-class murder. A huge talent."—*Time Out London*

"A sometimes brutal, sometimes poetic journey through the dark heart of modern London, and confirms Waites as of the brightest stars in British crime writing."—John Connolly

A research scientist has gone missing. An ace newspaper reporter has disappeared and so has a minidisk, along with its incriminating evidence. And a teenage hustler is on the run. In his pursuer, the Hammer, a skin-headed professional killer, the principle of evil has indeed been made flesh.

Unsettling and unpredictable, this compelling page-turner delivers point-blank its every unexpected narrative hit, twist, and turn as it leads protagonist Joe Donovan to the terror of the mercy seat.

Martyn Waites is emerging as one of the leading writers of British noir fiction. He lives in London.

Now in paperback: the taut, unpredictable urban crime thriller by the British neo-noir star.

Pegasus Books

A Beginner's Guide to Philosophy
Dominique Janicaud

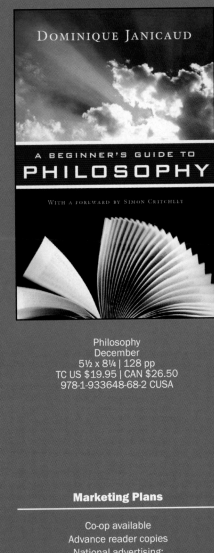

"Janicaud opens up his subject in the most immediate way I have ever seen."
—*Daily Telegraph*

"Janicaud sees philosophy first as a habit of mind close to Plato's original conception of the discipline as the best way of unmasking received ideas."—*The Observer* (London)

"Enticing and charming. . . . By seeking, daring to know the essence of beauty, truth, and goodness we can achieve illumination and satisfaction. This book points us in the right direction."—*The Good Book Guide*

"Its elegance of expression and exposition will appeal also to more mature seekers after enlightenment who are gently, subtly led from Socrates to Nietzsche. Janicaud equips us to face down the conformist pressures of modern life."—*The Times* (London)

A small marvel, *A Beginner's Guide to Philosophy* provides an instructive and delightful introduction to philosophy. Despite its brevity, this beginner's guide covers a vast range of authors and topics. The reader will find discussions of ancient and modern philosophy, beginning with the pre-Socratic thinkers, before moving on to Plato and Aristotle. The narrative then proceeds to an elegant survey of modern philosophers: Descartes, Nietzsche, Kant, and Hegel. Dominique Janicaud finally comes to the problems that have occupied thinkers through the ages: the existence of God, the meaning of life, human nature, and the question of freedom.

Dominique Janicaud, a renowned French philosopher, taught at the University of Nice. He died of a heart attack after swimming in the Mediterranean in 2002, after only just completing this book, written to introduce his daughter to philosophy.

A brief yet illuminating history of Western philosophy, from Plato to Descartes to Nietzsche.

Philosophy
December
5½ x 8¼ | 128 pp
TC US $19.95 | CAN $26.50
978-1-933648-68-2 CUSA

Marketing Plans

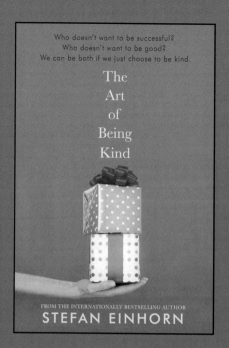

Who doesn't want to be successful?
Who doesn't want to be good?
We can be both if we just choose to be kind.

The
Art
of
Being
Kind

FROM THE INTERNATIONALLY BESTSELLING AUTHOR
STEFAN EINHORN

Self-Actualization & Self Help / Philosophy
October
5½ x 8¼ | 224 pp
TC US $21.95 | CAN $26.50
978-1-933648-70-5 CUSA

Marketing Plans

Co-op available
Advance reader copies
10,000-copy print run
National advertising:
Psychology Today • Publishers Weekly

The Art of Being Kind
Stefan Einhorn

Being kind in a genuine and positive way truly is an art, and it is an art that can be learned. Stefan Einhorn believes it is the single most important factor in achieving success and satisfaction in life—being a good person can make you happier, richer, more successful, and fulfilled.

Although it inevitably plays a part in our everyday actions, being kind is not always easy to put into practice. In all of life's dilemmas we calculate, whether consciously or subconsciously, what the consequences of our behavior—good or bad—is likely to be.

It is this ethical intelligence that Stefan Einhorn believes demonstrates our ability to be a good person. Partially inherited and developed in childhood, ethical intelligence continues to grow throughout our lives. In this groundbreaking book, Einhorn reveals the five life-altering tools we all need to focus on if we are to become better people. He also identifies the common stumbling blocks to be avoided in the process of achieving goodness.

Offering both immediate and long-term solutions to readers who want to be better human beings, this unique book holds a special key to the advantages of being kind.

Stefan Einhorn, MD, PhD, is a chairman of the department of oncology-pathology at the Karolinska Institute in Stockholm. The author of several books in the fields of popular medicine and the philosophy of religion, including *A Concealed God: Religion, Science, and the Search for Truth,* he is also a prominent lecturer in both Sweden and the United States.

A revelatory, groundbreaking key to the rewards and
benefits of being kind.

Pegasus Books

Delusion
a novel
Michèle Roberts

"On the narrative level alone, this is a compelling combination of Victorian pastiche and psychological thriller, fully and vividly imagined and often very funny. Rarely has the creative interaction of past and present been so suggestively and entertainingly conveyed."—*The Independent on Sunday*

"On the surface a gripping mystery story, the novel is a challenging exploration of women's friendships, history, sensuality and passion. Four main characters spanning three moments in history—ancient Egypt, Victorian England, contemporary London—unravel an ambivalent tale of birth, death, exploitation, closeness and betrayal."—*Guardian*

Voices, auras, materializations. Is she a mere trickster, a charlatan who plays on the anguish of the bereaved, or perhaps a hysteric who suffers delusions? No matter, in the shabby brick precincts of East London, the séances have won the pretty, blond medium Flora Milk local acclaim, and soon she will find herself more comfortably situated in the Victorian household of Sir William Preston, a researcher of some renown in psychic phenomena. Indeed, his wife Minny, who is still grieving the loss of her infant daughter, will embrace the gifted sixteen-year-old as her "protégé."

At once a ghost story and a psychological thriller, this elegant novel again demonstrates that Michele Roberts is a literary talent of the highest order.

Michèle Roberts is the author of eleven novels, including *Daughters of the House,* short-listed for the Man Booker Prize and winner of the WHSmith Literary Award, and *Reader, I Married Him,* also published by Pegasus Books. She lives in England.

An affecting novel of hope and betrayal, stretching from ancient Egypt to Victorian England to contemporary London.

Also Available

Reader, I Married Him
Michèle Roberts
Fiction
5½ x 8¼ | 240 pp
TP $13.95
978-1-933648-02-6 USA

Fiction
January
A Paperback Original
5½ x 8¼ | 160 pp
TP US $12.95 | CAN $15.50
978-1-933648-66-8 CUSA

Marketing Plans

Co-op available
Advance reader copies
National advertising:
The New York Times Review of Books

Pegasus Books

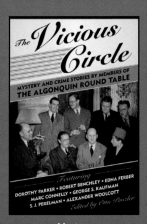

All Shot Up
the classic crime thriller
Chester Himes

"The greatest find in American fiction since Raymond Chandler."—*The Observer* (London)

The shocking and explosive hardboiled classic: From murderers to prostitutes, corrupt politicians and racist white detectives, Coffin Ed Johnson and Gravedigger Jones, Harlem's toughest detective duo, must carry the day against an absurdist world of racism and class warfare.

After arriving on the American literary scene with novels of scathing social protest, Chester Himes created a pioneering pair of dangerously charming African American sleuths, Gravedigger Jones and Coffin Ed Johnson, who attempt to maintain some kind of order on the streets of Harlem. Himes died in Spain in 1984.

Mystery / Fiction
December
5½ x 8¼ | 192 pp
TP US $13.95 | CAN $17.00
978-1-933648-72-9 CUSA

"Pungent, violent, and mordantly funny."—*Newsweek*

Marketing Plans
Co-op available

The Vicious Circle
Mystery and Crime Stories by Members of the Algonquin Round Table
Edited by Otto Penzler

"Otto Penzler knows more about crime fiction than most people know about anything."—Robert B. Parker

An anthology of stylish, clever, often humorous mystery and crime stories by the writers of the Algonquin Round Table, the notorious, vituperative group of American literary figures who gathered at the Algonquin Hotel to drink and match wits with each other.

Otto Penzler is the proprietor of the Mysterious Bookshop in New York City. He is the founder of The Mysterious Press and has won an Edgar Award, an Ellery Queen Award, and a Raven Award for his contributions to the publishing field.

Mystery
January
5½ x 8¼ | 304 pp
TC US $23.95 | CAN $29.00
978-1-933648-67-5 CUSA

A publishing event! The mystery fiction of the Algonquin Round Table.

Marketing Plans
Co-op available • Advance reader copies

Author Events
Launch party at the Algonquin Hotel

Author Hometown: New York, NY

Pegasus Books

Rudyard Kipling's Tales of Horror and Fantasy

With an Introduction by Neil Gaiman

Rudyard Kipling

Afterword by Stephen Jones

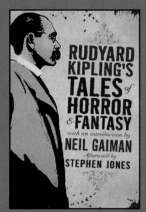

"Rudyard Kipling is one of the finest writers of fantasy in the last one hundred years."—Ray Bradbury

"Kipling has seen a perfect Odyssey of strange experiences."—Andrew Lang

Rudyard Kipling (1865–1936) was born in Bombay, India, but was raised in England until he returned to India in 1881 as a journalist. In 1907, Kipling became the first English writer to win the Nobel Prize in Literature. He is best known for *The Jungle Book* (1894), *Kim* (1902), and *Just So Stories* (1902), which are renowned throughout the world.

Marketing Plans
Co-op available • Advance reader copies

Horror / Literature & Essay
January
A Paperback Original
5½ x 8¼ | 800 pp
TP $17.95
978-1-933648-78-1 USA

From ghost stories to psychological suspense, the complete horror and dark fantasy stories of Rudyard Kipling.

Mafiya

a novel of crime

Charlie Stella

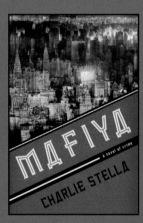

"Stella is a kind of obscene Ring Lardner, finding a lean, rancid poetry in his characters' vernacular, and rendering it with flawless precision and humor."—*The Washington Post Book World*

A hooker gone straight, the street-smart Agnes Lynn declares vengeance on the Mafiya when her best friend turns up dead and mutilated, only to find herself enmeshed in grim plots with Russian mavericks on both sides of the law.

Charlie Stella's first novel drew favorable comparison with such masters of the crime novel as Mario Puzo and Elmore Leonard. *Mafiya* is his sixth novel. Stella lives in New Jersey.

Marketing Plans
Co-op available • Advance reader copies

Author Events
Launch party in Manhattan

Mystery
January
6 x 9 | 336 pp
TC US $25.00 | CAN $30.00
978-1-933648-65-1 CUSA

The masterful crime writer turns his eye to the Russian mob in a New York thriller.

Rules for the Modern Man
Dylan Jones

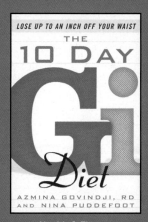

Reference / Popular Culture
January
A Paperback Original
6 x 9 | 432 pp
TP $16.95
978-1-933648-69-9 USA

A clever, practical, and entertaining guidebook of etiquette for the modern, sophisticated man.

It's tough being a man in the twenty-first century. First there are the big dilemmas, like how to get a raise. And there are all those things you ought to know: how to buy lingerie, how to make the perfect martini, how to tie a Windsor knot, how to propose to your girlfriend. The list is endless.

Fear not. The highly respected editor of *GQ* draws on his wealth of experience to give us the final answers.

Dylan Jones is the editor of *GQ*, the most successful up-market men's magazine in Britain. He lives in London.

Marketing Plans
Co-op available • Advance reader copies • 10,000-copy print run

Author Events
Launch party in Manhattan

The 10-Day GI Diet
Lose Up to an Inch Off Your Waist
Nina Puddefoot

Health & Fitness
February
A Paperback Original
6 x 8 | 400 pp
10 B&W illustrations, charts, and graphs
TP $14.95
978-1-933648-45-3 USA

Take an inch off your waistline in just ten days with this new, dynamic diet plan.

With flexible menus and seventy tempting recipes, fitness exercises and inspiring thoughts, this safe, straightforward, nutritionally sound low-GI diet can reduce your body weight in ten days and will change your eating habits forever.

Designed to demonstrate the immediate short-term benefits of eating foods with a low glycemic index (GI)—multigrain breads, bran-based cereals, muesli, fish, chicken, lentils, grains, nuts, fruits, vegetables—this simple, safe, and straightforward diet plan can deliver a healthier, trimmer you in ten days.

Nina Puddefoot is also the author of *The GI Plan,* which was an international best-seller. She lives in London.

Marketing Plans
Co-op available • Advance reader copies • 10,000-copy print run
National advertising: Fitness Magazine • SELF • Shape

Pegasus Books

U2
An Irish Phenomenon
Višnja Cogan

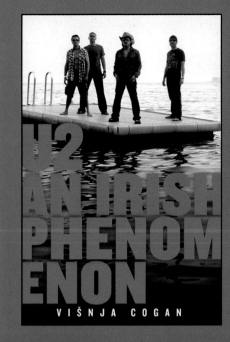

U2 is the biggest band in the world, has sold over 120 million records, played over one thousand concerts in thirty-one countries, and reached number one on the charts with nine studio albums.

The sheer longevity and worldwide success of this Irish rock band, with no change in lineup or manager, continues to confound the critics. Višnja Cogan delves into the personal story of U2, beginning with the members' backgrounds, their days in the 1970s as The Hype and Feedback in Dublin, the arrival of Paul McGuinness, and the charismatic Shalom Group, which nearly caused a split.

Among the features identified and described as central to U2's success: their sense of community, Irish independence, spirituality, creative drive, ambition, and social conscience. The combination of these elements has allowed U2 to conquer the world. Bono has become a powerful human rights campaigner—one of three *TIME* magazine activists of 2005, twenty years after U2 first graced the cover. They broke the mold, avoided the "rock star" scene, and constantly struggled to improve. U2 was part of a generation looking for a voice. This book celebrates and pays homage to a band that has given a voice to the modern era—and reveals the reasons that led to the U2 phenomenon.

Višnja Cogan has spoken about U2 at international music conferences and has been following the group since 1983. She was born in Croatia, raised in France, and currently is a professor of French at Dublin City University.

The inspiring story of how U2's unique qualities have made them the world's most popular band.

Music
March
A Paperback Original
5½ x 8¼ | 304 pp
16 Color photographs
TP US $14.95 | CAN $18.00
978-1-933648-71-2 CUSA

Marketing Plans

Co-op available
Advance reader copies
10,000-copy print run
National advertising:
Rolling Stone

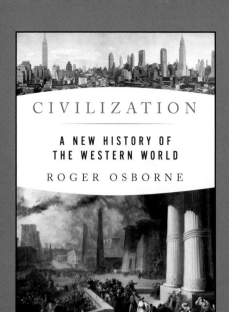

History
March
6 x 9 | 544 pp
TP $16.95
978-1-933648-76-7 USA

Marketing Plans

Co-op available
20,000-copy print run
National advertising:
The Economist • The Wall Street Journal •
The Washington Post Book World

Civilization
A New History of the Western World
Roger Osborne

"An intellectual high-wire act that the author pulls off with deceptive ease. . . . Battles and wars, scientists and inventors, artists and tycoons, all get their turn in a smoothly rolling narrative. Mr. Osborne, with great skill, ties his disparate topics together into a coherent narrative, as absorbing as any novel. . . . It would be hard to imagine a more readable general history of the West that covers so much ground so incisively."—William Grimes, *The New York Times*

Ever since the attacks of September 11, 2001, Western leaders have described a world engaged in "a fight for civilization." But what do we mean by *civilization*? We believe in a Western tradition of freedom that has produced a fulfilling existence for many millions of people and a culture of enormous depth and creative power. But the history of our civilization is also filled with unspeakable brutality—for every Leonardo there is a Mussolini, for every Beethoven symphony a concentration camp, for every Chrysler Building a My Lai massacre.

An ambitious historical assessment of the Western world—tying together the histories of empires, art, philosophy, science, and politics—*Civilization* reexamines and confronts us with all of our glories and catastrophes. At such a dangerous time in the world's history, this brilliant book is required reading.

For many years **Roger Osborne** edited books on medicine, psychology, and history. Since 1992 he has been a full-time writer, using particular subjects to demonstrate new ways of understanding the past. He lives in Yorkshire.

A magnificent, fresh, and thought-provoking history of Western civilization, from its origins to the present.

Pegasus Books

Eye Mind
Roky Erickson and The 13th Floor Elevators
Paul Drummond

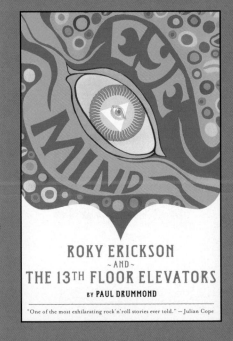

"One of the most exhilarating and important rock 'n' roll stories ever told."
—Julian Cope

The trailblazing 13th Floor Elevators released the first "psychedelic" rock album in America, transforming culture throughout the 1960s and beyond. The Elevators followed their own spiritual cosmic agenda, to change society by finding a new path to enlightenment. Their battles with repressive authorities in Texas and their escape to San Francisco's embryonic counterculture are legendary.

When the Elevators returned to Texas, the band became subject to investigation by Austin police. Lead singer Roky Erickson was forced into a real-life enactment of *One Flew over the Cuckoo's Nest* and was put away in a maximum-security unit for the criminally insane for years. Tommy Hall, their Svengali lyricist, lived in a cave. Guitarist Stacy Sutherland was imprisoned. The drummer was involuntarily subjected to electric shock treatments, and the bassist was drafted into the Vietnam War.

This fascinating biography breaks decades of silence of band members and addresses a huge cult following of Elevators fans in the United States and Europe. The group is revered as a formative influence on Janis Joplin, Led Zeppelin, Patti Smith, Primal Scream, R.E.M, and Z.Z. Top.

Roky Erickson is the subject of a heralded recent documentary feature, *You're Gonna Miss Me*; a box set of remastered Elevators CDs with liner notes by author Paul Drummond will be issued in fall 2007.

Paul Drummond has worked with primary people in the fields of fashion and music as a set designer and art director. He also manages the Roky Erickson Archives.

The wild, untold story of the 13th Floor Elevators, led by the notorious Roky Erickson.

Music
October
A Paperback Original
6 x 9 | 350 pp
140 Color and B&W illustrations
and photographs
TP US $19.95 | CAN $24.00
978-0-9760822-6-2 CUSA

Marketing Plans

Co-op available

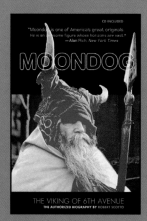

Music
October
6½ x 9 | 280 pp
25 B&W photographs
TC with CD US $24.95 | CAN $30.00
978-0-9760822-8-6 CUSA

The first biography of one of the twentieth century's most fascinating and original artists.

Moondog, The Viking of 6th Avenue
The Authorized Biography
Robert Scotto

"Moondog is one of America's great originals."—Alan Rich, *The New York Times*

Here is one of the most improbable lives of the twentieth century: a blind and homeless man who became the most famous eccentric in New York and who, with enormous diligence, rose to prominence as an internationally respected music presence.

Born Louis Thomas Hardin in 1916, Moondog first made an impression in the late 1940s when his music was played by the New York Philharmonic at Carnegie Hall. His unique, melodic compositions were released on the Prestige jazz label. In the late 1960s the Viking-garbed Moondog was a pop music sensation on Columbia Records. Moondog is the noted inspiration for the contemporary freak folk movement led by Devandra Barnhart.

Moondog's compositional style was, many say, adopted by his former roommate, Philip Glass. Moondog's work transcends labels and redefines the distinction between popular and high culture. A CD compilation with a variety of Moondog's compositions is bound into the book, and a Moondog tribute is planned for the 2007–2008 season of UCLA Live by Hal Willner.

Author Robert Scotto is a professor at New York's Baruch College.

Author Hometown: Brooklyn, NY

New Age / Self-Actualization & Self Help
October
A Paperback Original
5¼ x 8½ | 220 pp
15 B&W illustrations and photographs
TP US $14.95 | CAN $18.00
978-1-934170-07-6 CUSA

Here are the occult teachings that *The Secret* used—and missed.

The Secret Source
The Law of Attraction is One of Seven Hermetic Laws: Here are the Other Six
Edited by Maja D'Aoust, Adam Parfrey, and Jodi Wille

The Secret Source reveals the actual occult doctrines that gave birth to "The Law of Attraction" and inspired the media phenomenon known as *The Secret.*

Why did *The Secret* divulge only one of the seven Hermetic Laws? What are the others, what do they say, and how could they enrich your life?

The Secret Source provides the actual texts and fascinating stories behind the "Emerald Tablet," the Kabbalistic treatise known as "The Kybalion," and Manly P. Hall's essay on the occult movement that produced it.

Maja D'Aoust lectures at the Philosophical Research Society; Adam Parfrey, editor of *Apocalypse Culture,* is writing a history of secret societies in America; and Jodi Wille is editing a book on the mystical commune known as "The Source." Manly P. Hall is the author of *The Secret Teachings of All Ages*.

Marketing Plans
Co-op available

Author Hometown: Los Angeles, CA

Process

Turkey, the US and Iraq
William Hale

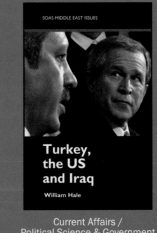

The American-led invasion of Iraq in March 2003 has had an unpredictable impact on the role and policies of Turkey. Although Turkey gave vital support to America in the first Gulf War, in the second, America's only formal ally in the region refused to support US strategy. To explain Turkey's changing foreign policy, William Hale examines the relationship between Turkey, the United States, and Iraq since the 1920s. Published in association with the London Middle East Institute at SOAS (School of Oriental and African Studies).

William Hale is a professor of Turkish politics and former head of the Department of Political and International Studies at the School of Oriental and African Studies, University of London.

Marketing Plans
Co-op available • Advance reader copies

Current Affairs /
Political Science & Government
September
A Paperback Original
Middle East Issues
5¼ x 8¼ | 200 pp
TP US $21.95 | CAN $26.50
978-0-86356-675-2 CUSA

A newsworthy analysis of Turkey's struggle to mediate between its neighbor countries and the United States.

The Gulf Family
Kinship Policies and Modernity
Edited by Alanoud Alsharekh

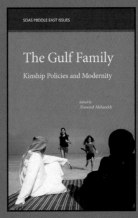

The contributors in *The Gulf Family* examine the paradox of the persisting importance of family and tribe in the face of modernization. They evaluate past and present roles of kinship in the GCC (Gulf Cooperation Council) states, assess the impacts of change, and speculate on likely future patterns of social, economic, and political organization. Published in association with the London Middle East Institute at SOAS (School of Oriental and African Studies).

Alanoud Alsharekh is a member of the Advisory Council of the London Middle East Institute at the School of Oriental and African Studies and a consultant for the United Nations Development Fund for Women.

Marketing Plans
Co-op available • Advance reader copies

Cultural Studies
November
A Paperback Original
5¼ x 8¼ | 180 pp
TP US $21.95 | CAN $26.50
978-0-86356-680-6 CUSA

Examines the paradox of the persisting importance of family and tribe in the face of modernization.

Saqi Books

My Cousin, My Husband
Clans and Kinship in Mediterranean Societies
Germaine Tillion

In this classic work, Germaine Tillion argues that the phenomenon of men killing their daughters, sisters, and wives over matters of sexual honor is not an aberration specific to Islam. Rather, it is part of a pagan Mediterranean legacy of marriage between first cousins that still affects both modern Christian and Muslim societies. Tillion charts the rise of that unique Mediterranean social innovation she calls the "Republic of Cousins."

Germaine Tillion, former director of studies of the École Pratique des Hautes Études in Paris, is an anthropologist with unrivaled knowledge of nomads and settled agriculturalists in North Africa.

Cultural Studies / History
December
A Paperback Original
Saqi Essentials
5¼ x 8¼ | 190 pp
TP US $21.95 | CAN $26.50
978-0-86356-625-7 CUSA

This classic work examines honor killings and their relationship to Islam, Christianity, and Mediterranean culture.

Origins of the Druze People and Religion
Philip K. Hitti

The Druze, who can be traced back to eleventh-century Levant, have long intrigued scholars of the Middle East. Their obscure origins and blending of beliefs from Ismali Shi'ism, animism, Greek philosophy, Jewish and Christian mysticism, Iranian Gnosticism, and Buddhism have set them apart from their neighbors.

The author reveals the remarkable Druze pantheon of semi-deities and investigates their dogmas and rituals. The book also includes rarely seen extracts from the sacred writings of the Druze.

Philip K. Hitti (1886–1978) was born in Lebanon and taught at Princeton University from 1926 to 1954.

Marketing Plans
Advance reader copies

Cultural Studies / History
March
Saqi Essentials
5¼ x 8¼ | 100 pp
TP US $12.95 | CAN $15.50
978-0-86356-690-5 CUSA

Philip K. Hitti reveals the remarkable Druze pantheon of semi-deities and investigates their dogmas and rituals.

Saqi Books Essentials Series

Croatia Through History
Branka Magaš

This comprehensive volume recounts Croatia's development from the early Middle Ages to the present day. Branka Magaš observes that the ties that bound Croatia to other states for centuries have contributed to the state's vitality, with a complex web of Slav, Croat, Dalmatian, Slavonian, Serb, Jewish, Italian, Yugoslav, and other identities emerging as a part of an ongoing social and political dialogue, which at times has included open strife.

Branka Magaš is a historian, journalist, and commentator on the former Yugoslavia. She co-founded the Croatian Peace Forum in 1991 and the Alliance to Defend Bosnia-Herzegovina in 1993.

Marketing Plans
Co-op available • Advance reader copies

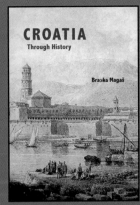

History / Current Affairs
January
6 x 9½ | 680 pp
32 Color illustrations
TC US $60.00 | CAN $72.00
978-0-86356-775-9 CUSA

This comprehensive volume recounts Croatia's development from the early Middle Ages to the present day.

The History of Bosnia
From the Middle Ages to the Present Day
Marko Attila Hoare

Praise for *How Bosnia Armed* (2004):

"Well-searched, thoughtful and provocative . . . required reading for anyone interested in the Bosnian conflict."—*The Journal of Military History*

In this first comprehensive study of national identity in Bosnia-Herzegovina, the author seeks to explain what being Bosnian means to Muslims, Serbs, Croats, and Jews.

Marko Attila Hoare is a senior research fellow in the School of Social Sciences at Kingston University.

Marketing Plans
Co-op available

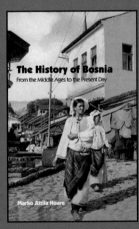

History
September
6 x 9½ | 620 pp
TC US $45.00 | CAN $54.00
978-0-86356-953-1 CUSA

The first comprehensive study of national identity in Bosnia-Herzegovina.

From Baghdad to Bedlam
Maged Kadar

Maged Kadar is working nights as a London taxi driver. By day he's a news junkie, hooked on broadcasts from his native war-torn Iraq and desperate for news of his family. He recalls Saddam Hussein's rise to power and his escape to England, where he meets his future wife, Carole, in the lingerie section of a department store in Liverpool. From the idyll of his Iraqi childhood through the harsh realities of 1980s Britain, Maged's recollections are filled with a deep affection for his Iraqi and British homes.

Maged Kadar, a former London cab driver, now teaches Arabic and Islamic culture to British troops.

Biography & Autobiography / Current Affairs
October
A Paperback Original
5 x 7¾ | 252 pp
TP US $14.95 | CAN $18.00
978-0-86356-635-6 CUSA

A heartbreaking, funny memoir of an Iraqi's exile in the United Kingdom.

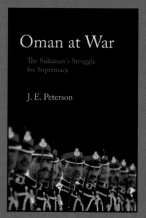

Oman at War
The Sultanate's Struggle for Supremacy
J.E. Peterson

J.E. Peterson takes a detailed look at the crises that have tested the mettle of Oman's army and accelerated its development, surveying its transition from a strictly traditional regime controlling only parts of the country to a modern, inclusive state, particularly in terms of security concerns.

J.E. Peterson is a political analyst specializing in the Arabian Peninsula and the Gulf. He is affiliated with the Center for Middle Eastern Studies at the University of Arizona in Tucson.

Current Affairs / History
February
6 x 9½ | 680 pp
16 B&W photographs
TC US $85.00 | CAN $102.00
978-0-86356-456-7 CUSA

A detailed look at the crises that have tested Oman and accelerated its development.

Marketing Plans
Co-op available • Advance reader copies

Author Hometown: Tuscon, AZ

Saqi Books

The Imagination Unbound
Al-Adab al-'Aja'ibi and the Literature of the Fantastic in the Arabic Tradition
Kamal Abu-Deeb

The fantastic in literature is not a modern European invention; it is present in Arabic narratives dating from the ninth century.

The Imagination Unbound contains an Arabic and English study of *al–Adab al–'Aja'ibi*, with the original Arabic text of *Kitab al–Azama* (The Book of Greatness) and commentary by the author.

Kamel Abu-Deeb holds the chair in Arabic at the University of London. A poet and essayist, he has published many books and papers in both Arabic and English and has been co-editor of the avant-garde journal *Mawaqif*.

Marketing Plans
Co-op available

Literary Criticism
January
7 x 9½ | 240 pp
TC US $60.00 | CAN $72.00
978-0-86356-636-3 CUSA

An essential reference for Arabic literature scholars showing the pre-Islamic tradtions of the fantastic.

Diary of a Country Prosecutor
Tawfik al-Hakim

Who shot Kamar al-Dawar Alwan? Was it a crime of passion? What was the role of the beautiful peasant girl Rim? Is the mysterious Sheikh Asfur as crazy as he seems? Partly autobiographical, *Diary of a Country Prosecutor* is an Egyptian comedy of errors. Imbued with the ideals of a European education, the young public prosecutor encounters a world of poverty and backwardness where an imported legal system is both alien and incomprehensible.

Tawfik al-Hakim was born in Alexandria in 1898 and studied law in Paris. He became the Arab world's leading dramatist, as well as a major short story writer.

Marketing Plans
Co-op available

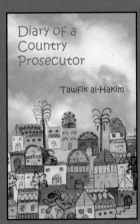

Fiction
October
A Paperback Original
5¼ x 8¼ | 135 pp
TP US $12.95 | CAN $15.50
978-0-86356-549-6 CUSA

A classic comedy of errors set in rural Egypt, with a foreword by P.H. Newby.

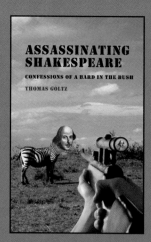

Assassinating Shakespeare
Confessions of a Bard in the Bush
Thomas Goltz

Biography & Autobiography /
Travel & Travel Guides
5¼ x 8¼ | 256 pp
8pp of B&W photographs
TP US $19.95 | CAN $24.00
978-0-86356-718-6 CUSA

Hizbullah (Hezbollah)
The Story from Within
Naim Qassem

Political Science & Government
6 x 9 | 284 pp
TC US $29.95 | CAN $36.00
978-0-86356-517-5 CUSA

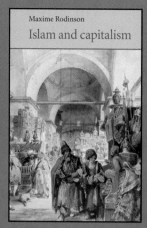

Islam and Capitalism
Maxime Rodinson

Cultural Studies
5 x 8 | 344 pp
TP US $24.95 | CAN $30.00
978-0-86356-471-0 CUSA

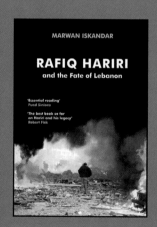

Rafiq Hariri and the
Fate of Lebanon
Marwan Iskandar

Current Affairs
6 x 9 | 239 pp
TC US $24.95 | CAN $30.00
978-0-86356-370-6 CUSA

Sufi Cuisine
Nevin Halici

Cookbooks & Cookery
8¼ x 8¼ | 240 pp
TP US $24.95 | CAN $30.00
978-0-86356-581-6 CUSA

Simple Arabic
A Comprehensive Course
Yousif Haddad and Jack Ingle

Language Arts / Study Aids
6 x 9 | 198 pp
TP US $19.95 | CAN $24.00
978-0-86356-342-3 CUSA

Water
Nine Stories
Alyce Miller

"Alyce Miller has the eye and the skills for getting the short story right. . . . She writes vividly about people in various degrees of emotional extremis, and she avoids the temptation to invent resolutions for the dilemmas they're in. She deftly captures individual psychologies."—From the foreword by Norman Rush

In this startling new collection by prize-winning author Alyce Miller, changing images of water as a force both destructive and healing are woven throughout. Whether giving voice to the nameless wife from a tale by Chekhov or illustrating the fears driving apart black and white communities in small-town Ohio, Miller makes vivid the heart of human interaction. These stories, told from different perspectives of age, race, and gender, acknowledge a common rhythm in each of us—unsettled desire.

Alyce Miller has authored a collection of stories, *The Nature of Longing* (W.W. Norton & Company), winner of the Flannery O'Connor Award for Short Fiction, and a novel, *Stopping for Green Lights* (Anchor Doubleday), as well as more than 120 stories, poems, and essays that have appeared in literary magazines and anthologies. Her other awards include the Lawrence Foundation Prize from *Michigan Quarterly Review, The Kenyon Review* Award for Literary Excellence in Fiction, and distinguished citations in *The Best American Short Stories, The Best American Essays, The O. Henry Prize Stories,* and *The Pushcart Prize*. She leads a double life as an attorney specializing in animal law and a professor in the graduate writing program at Indiana University Bloomington.

The winner of the 2006 Mary McCarthy Prize, selected by Norman Rush.

Fiction
January
A Paperback Original
6 x 9 | 224 pp
TP US $15.95 | CAN $19.50
978-1-932511-56-7 CUSA

Marketing Plans

Co-op available
Advance reader copies
National advertising:
Poets & Writers • Rain Taxi •
The Writer's Chronicle

Author Events

Berkeley, CA • Oakland, CA •
San Francisco, CA • Indianapolis, IN •
Louisville, KY • New York, NY • Cincinnati, OH
• Cleveland, OH • Columbus, OH

Author Hometown: Bloomington, IN

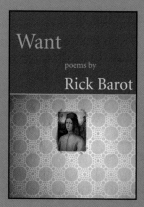

Poetry
February
A Paperback Original
6 x 9 | 88 pp
TP US $13.95 | CAN $17.00
978-1-932511-57-4 CUSA

A stunning new poetry collection from the 2001 Kathryn A. Morton Prize-winner, selected by Stanley Plumly.

Want
Poems
Rick Barot

"Barot's *Want* is dexterous and thrilling, and his capacious and generous vision shows us how the eye survives 'to correct the heart.'"—Michael Collier

"In Rick Barot's hands every poem casts at least two luminous shadows. *Want* is masterfully merciless and merciful at the same time."—Terrance Hayes

"Meticulously wrought, each line in *Want* stands as both brushstroke and musical phrase, as one saunters through the haunting stanzas, room after room, stricken with a retrospective calm."—Timothy Liu

Rick Barot was born in the Philippines and grew up in San Francisco. He currently teaches at Warren Wilson College and Pacific Lutheran University.

Marketing Plans
Co-op available • Advance reader copies
National advertising: Poets & Writers

Author Events
Los Angeles, CA • San Francisco, CA • Miami, FL • Chicago, IL • Iowa City, IA • Boston, MA • New York, NY • Philadelphia, PA • Houston, TX • Seattle, WA

Author Hometown: Tacoma, WA

Poetry
September
A Paperback Original
Quarternote Chapbook Series
6 x 9 | 32 pp
TP US $10.95 | CAN $13.50
978-1-932511-54-3 CUSA

The sixth edition in the Quarternote Chapbook Series by a chancellor of the Academy of American Poets.

The Preacher
A Poem
Gerald Stern

"*The Preacher*'s a poem with polyphonic voices, enormous range, and many of Stern's familiar icons: his animism, his city grit, his philosophical fragments, his irony and justice quest, his reaching for the strain of memory."—Ira Sadoff

Gerald Stern is the author of fourteen poetry books, including *This Time: New and Selected Poems,* which won the 1998 National Book Award. He taught at the Iowa Writers' Workshop for fifteen years, and he is the recipient of many awards, including the Lamont Poetry Prize, the Ruth Lilly Prize, the Wallace Stevens Award, and the National Jewish Book Award for poetry.

Marketing Plans
Advance reader copies
National advertising: The American Poetry Review • Poets & Writers • Rain Taxi • The Writer's Chronicle

Author Hometown: Lambertsville, NJ

Sarabande Books

The Book of Beginnings and Endings
Jenny Boully

"Jenny is the future of nonfiction in America. What an absurdly arrogant statement to make. I make it anyway. Watch."—John D'Agata

"Yes, Aristotle, there can be pleasure without 'complete and unified action with a beginning, middle, and end.' Jenny Boully has done it."—Mary Jo Bang

A book with only beginnings and endings, all invented. Jenny Boully opens and closes more than fifty topics ranging from physics and astronomy to literary theory and love. A brilliant statement on interruption, impermanence, and imperfection.

Jenny Boully is the author of *The Body: An Essay* and *[one love affair]**. Born in Thailand, she currently divides her time between Texas and Brooklyn.

Marketing Plans
Co-op available • Advance reader copies
National advertising: Poets & Writers • Rain Taxi • The Writer's Chronicle

Author Events
Los Angeles, CA • Washington, DC • Boston, MA • New York, NY •
Asheville, NC • San Antonio, TX

Author Hometown: Brooklyn, NY

Literature & Essay
November
A Paperback Original
6 x 9 | 128 pp
TP US $14.95 | CAN $18.00
978-1-932511-55-0 CUSA

The third collection from this thrillingly innovative master of the lyric essay.

Epistles
Poems
Mark Jarman

"To read this book is to be reminded of how many major poems have their root in prayer."—Grace Schulman

"The thirty prose poems that make up *Epistles* are as compellingly modern in their form as they are timeless in their quest for spiritual truths amid radical doubts."
—David Lehman

These are compellingly modern prose poems in the style of Paul's Letters to the Corinthians.

Mark Jarman's book *The Black Riviera* won the 1991 Poets' Prize. *Questions for Ecclesiastes* was a finalist for the 1997 National Book Critics Circle Award. Jarman is a professor at Vanderbilt University in Nashville.

Marketing Plans
Co-op available
National advertising: The American Poetry Review • Poets & Writers •
Rain Taxi • The Writer's Chronicle

Author Events
Chicago, IL • Louisville, KY • Chapel Hill, NC • Nashville, TN

Author Hometown: Nashville, TN

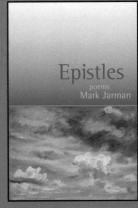

Poetry / Spirituality
October
6 x 9 | 112 pp
TP US $14.95 | CAN $18.00
978-1-932511-53-6 CUSA
TC y US $21.95 | CAN $26.50
978-1-932511-52-9 CUSA

The ninth poetry collection from the 1998 Lenore Marshall Poetry Prize-winner.

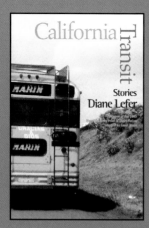

California Transit
Stories and a Novella
Diane Lefer

Fiction
6 x 9 | 256 pp
TP US $15.95 | CAN $19.50
978-1-932511-47-5 CUSA

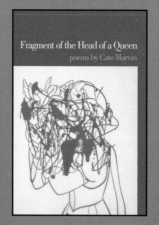

Fragment of the Head of a Queen
Poems
Cate Marvin

Poetry
6 x 9 | 74 pp
TP US $13.95 | CAN $17.00
978-1-932511-51-2 CUSA

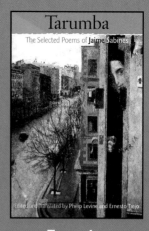

Tarumba
The Selected Poems of
Jaime Sabines
**Translated by Philip Levine
and Ernesto Trejo**

Poetry / Latin American Literature
6 x 9 | 128 pp
TP US $14.95 | CAN $18.00
978-1-932511-48-2 CUSA

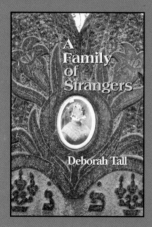

A Family of Strangers
Deborah Tall

Literature & Essay / Jewish Studies
6 x 9 | 260 pp
TP US $16.95 | CAN $20.50
978-1-932511-44-4 CUSA

Legitimate Dangers
American Poets of the New Century
**Edited by Michael Dumanis
and Cate Marvin**

Poetry Anthology
6 x 9 | 500 pp
TP US $24.00 | CAN $29.00
978-1-932511-29-1 CUSA

The Memory Palace of
Isabella Stewart Gardner
Patricia Vigderman

Literature & Essay /
Biography & Autobiography
6 x 9 | 152 pp
25 B&W illustrations
TP US $15.95 | CAN $19.50
978-1-932511-43-7 CUSA

Crossing the Dark
Heidi W. Boehringer

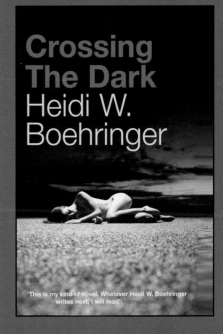

Praise for *Chasing Jordan*:

"With this first novel, Ms. Boehringer gives notice that she is a writer to watch. This is my kind of novel. Whatever Heidi Boehringer writes next, I will read." —Harry Crews

Mona, a high-ranking police officer, has rescued her teenage daughter Perdita from a dangerous criminal who has been using her as a sex slave. As both Mona and Perdita spiral into separate worlds of fear, isolation, and despair, Mona, with the help of her fellow officer and confidant Nick, tries to save Perdita from the depression that threatens to overwhelm her. But what if Mona falls victim to her own fury and despair?

Heidi W. Boehringer lives in Deerfield Beach, Florida. She has appeared on National Public Radio's *The Spoken Word* and has written essays for *The Miami Herald*. She is also a conference speaker and teaches creative writing.

Sea of Love meets *Thelma and Louise.*

Fiction / Mystery
November
A Paperback Original
5 x 8 | 288 pp
TP US $14.95 | CAN $18.00
978-1-85242-498-5 CUSA

Marketing Plans

Co-op available
Advance reader copies
National advertising:
BOMB • Bookforum

Author Events

Miami, Fl • New York, NY • Charlotte, NC

Author Hometown: Deerfield Beach, FL

Also Available

Chasing Jordan
Heidi W. Boehringer
Fiction / Women's Literature
8 x 5 | 240 pp
TP US $15.00 | CAN $18.00
978-1-85242-893-8 CUSA

Serpent's Tail

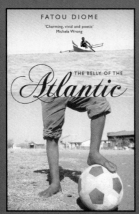

Fiction / African Studies
September
A Paperback Original
5⅝ x 8⅜ | 192 pp
TP US $15.95 | CAN $19.50
978-1-85242-903-4 CUSA

**A powerful debut novel from a
talented young Senegalese author.**

The Belly of the Atlantic
Fatou Diome

"This charming, vivid and poetic book captures the poignancy of immigrant life and all the unresolved pain of Africa's relationship with its former colonial powers."
—Michela Wrong

Salie lives in Paris. Back home on the Senegalese island of Niodior, her football-crazy brother Madické counts on her to get him to France, the promised land where foreign footballers become world famous. The story of Salie and Madické highlights the painful situation of those who emigrate. It is a moving account of one of the great tragedies of our time.

Marketing Plans
Co-op available • Advance reader copies
National advertising: BOMB

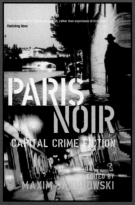

Fiction Anthology
November
A Paperback Original
5 x 8 | 288 pp
TP US $14.95 | CAN $18.00
978-1-85242-966-9 CUSA

The dark side of the City of Light.

Paris Noir
Capital Crime Fiction
Edited by Maxim Jakubowski

Paris Noir is a collection of new stories about the dark side of Paris, with contributions by leading French, British, and American authors who have all lived there. The stories range from quietly menacing to spectacularly violent, and include contributions from some of the most famous crime writers from both sides of the Atlantic.

Contributors include: Cara Black, Jerome Charyn, Stella Duffy, Barry Gifford, Sparkle Hayter, John Harvey, Maxim Jakubowski, Jake Lamar, Dominique Manotti, Michael Moorcock, Jim Nisbet, Jean-Hughes Oppel, Scott Phillips, Romain Slocombe, Jason Starr, Dominique Sylvain, Marc Villard, and John Williams.

Marketing Plans
Co-op available

Serpent's Tail

No More Angels
Ron Butlin

From Ancient Greece, via contemporary Britain, into the future, from childhood to old age and beyond, the stories in *No More Angels* capture the idiosyncrasies of modern life.

Comic, tragic, and sometimes both, Ron Butlin explores individual lives with a lightness of touch that cuts right to the heart. A dramatic follow-up to Butlin's acclaimed *Belonging*, *No More Angels* is a captivating celebration of human frailty.

Includes an introduction by Ian Rankin.

Marketing Plans
Co-op available • Advance reader copies

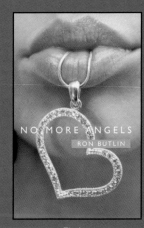

Fiction
January
A Paperback Original
5 x 8 | 224 pp
TP US $15.00 | CAN $18.00
978-1-85242-954-6 CUSA

New short stories from one of contemporary British literature's most distinctive voices.

Perverted by Language
Fiction Inspired by The Fall
Edited by Peter Wild

Mechanical ducks, shark women that taste of licorice, perverted sexual shenanigans in cramped office spaces, double-crossing Nazi apologists, bald-headed cultural subversives, and celebrity deer-culling—this is the wonderful and frightening world of *Perverted by Language*. Twenty-three writers choose a song by The Fall and use it as inspiration for a short story.

Contributors include: Steve Aylett, Matt Beaumont, Nicholas Blincoe, Clare Dudman, Richard Evans, Michel Faber, Niall Griffiths, Andrew Holmes, Mick Jackson, Nick Johnstone, Stewart Lee, Kevin MacNeil, Carlton Mellick III, Rebbecca Ray, Nicholas Royle, Matthew David Scott, Stav Sherez, Mark E. Smith, Nick Stone, Matt Thorne, Jeff VanderMeer, Helen Walsh, and John Williams.

Marketing Plans
Co-op available • Advance reader copies

Fiction Anthology
March
A Paperback Original
5 x 8 | 256 pp
TP US $15.00 | CAN $18.00
978-1-85242-929-4 CUSA

New fiction inspired by the music of the legendary Manchester band The Fall.

A State of Denmark
Derek Raymond

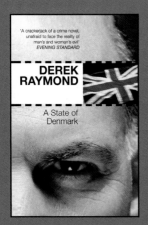

Fiction
September
5 x 8 | 288 pp
TP US $14.95 | CAN $18.00
978-1-85242-947-8 CUSA

A frightening Orwellian vision of a totalitarian England.

"Raymond's novel is rooted firmly in the dystopian vision of Orwell and Huxley, sharing their air of horrifying hopelessness."—*Sunday Times*

It is the 1960s. England has become a dictatorship, governed by a sly, ruthless politician called Jobling. All non-whites have been deported, *The English Times* is the only newspaper, and ordinary people live in dread of nightly curfews and secret police. Derek Raymond's skill is to make all too plausible the transition from complacent democracy to dictatorship in a country preoccupied by consumerism and susceptible to media spin.

Marketing Plans
Co-op available • Advance reader copies

Malvinas Requiem
Rodolfo Fogwill

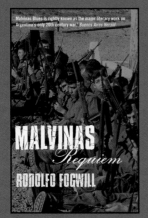

Fiction / Latin American Studies
October
A Paperback Original
5 x 8 | 176 pp
TP US $14.95 | CAN $18.00
978-1-85242-965-2 CUSA

Tells the story of the forgotten Argentine soldiers who fought against the British.

"*Malvinas Requiem* has a well-earned spot as the major literary piece on Argentina's only twentieth-century war."—*Buenos Aires Herald*

It's early June 1982 and winter in the Falkland Islands: twenty-four young soldiers—deserters from the Argentine army—spend the last weeks of the conflict hiding underground in a cave. Inside their refuge, they listen to the radio, stockpile supplies, and exchange stories; outside, under cover of night, they trade with the Argentine quartermaster and with the British. Looking out over the bleak landscape, after weeks of gray skies and horizontal snow, one of them remarks that "you'd have to be English to want this."

Marketing Plans
Co-op available • Advance reader copies
National advertising: Latin American Perspectives

Serpent's Tail

Kath Trevelyan
Jeremy Cooper

Fiction
November
A Paperback Original
5 x 8 | 320 pp
TP US $16.95
CAN $20.50
978-1-85242-938-6
CUSA

Kath Trevelyan intends to remain alive until the moment she dies. At seventy-two, she is still a letterpress printer, visiting arts festivals with her daughters and absorbing the richness of the world. Her beloved husband is long dead, and she believes she has had her share of romantic love. John Garsington feels the same. Though much younger than Kath, he too has a passion for art and work that he loves.

School for Scumbags
Danny King

Fiction
February
A Paperback Original
5 x 8 | 288 pp
TP US $14.95
CAN $18.00
978-1-85242-972-0
CUSA

Habitual teenage delinquent Wayne Banstead is expelled from yet another school and finds himself hauled off to reform school. It plays host to the worst of the worst—thieves, bullies, arsonists, and flashers. But far from rehabilitating the boys, the teachers seem intent on instructing them in how to get away with things. Danny King's latest is definitely not suitable for kids.

The Alpine Fantasy of Victor B
and Other Stories
Edited by Jeremy Akerman and Eileen Daly

Fiction Anthology
October
A Paperback Original
5 x 8 | 256 pp
TP US $15.95
CAN $19.50
978-1-85242-926-3
CUSA

The Alpine Fantasy of Victor B and Other Stories brings together seventeen of Britain's leading contemporary artists in one collection.

Moving, humorous, and sometimes deeply macabre, these stories deal with dementia, mortality, mass murder, and madness. *The Alpine Fantasy of Victor B and Other Stories* is a haunting exploration of the impulses that drive today's artists.

Nineteen Seventy Seven
David Peace

Fiction / Mystery
September
5 x 5 | 352 pp
TP US $12.00
CAN $14.50
978-1-85242-744-3
CUSA

Half-decent copper Bob Fraser and burnt-out hack Jack Whitehead would be considered villains in most people's books. They have one thing in common, though. They're both desperate men dangerously in love with Chapeltown whores. And as the summer moves remorselessly towards the bonfires of Jubilee Night, the killings accelerate, and it seems as if Fraser and Whitehead are the only men who suspect or care that there may be more than one killer at large.

Serpent's Tail

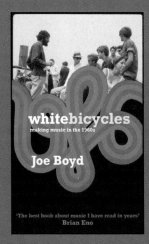

White Bicycles
Making Music in the 1960s
Joe Boyd

Music / Biography & Autobiography
6 x 9 | 304 pp
TP US $18.00 | CAN $21.95
978-1-85242-910-2 CUSA

Cruel Poetry
Vicki Hendricks

Fiction / Mystery
5 x 8 | 320 pp
TP US $14.95 | CAN $18.00
978-1-85242-927-0 CUSA

Double Fault
Lionel Shriver

Fiction
5½ x 8½ | 320 pp
TP US $14.95 | CAN $18.00
978-1-85242-911-9 CUSA

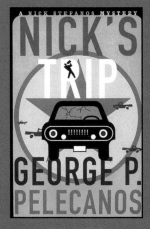

Nick's Trip
George P. Pelecanos

Mystery
5 x 8 | 288 pp
TP US $13.00 | CAN $15.95
978-1-85242-714-6 CUSA

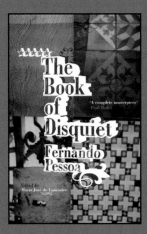

The Book of Disquiet
Fernando Pessoa
Translated by Margaret Jull Costa

Fiction / Literature & Essay
5 x 8 | 288 pp
TP US $14.00 | CAN $17.00
978-1-85242-758-0 CUSA

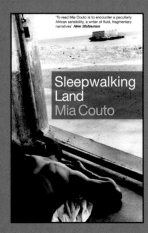

A Sleepwalking Land
Mia Couto
Translated by David Brookshaw

Fiction / African Studies
5 x 8 | 256 pp
TP US $14.95 | CAN $18.00
978-1-85242-897-6 CUSA

The Contenders
Hillary, John, Al, Dennis, Barack, et al.
Laura Flanders, Richard Goldstein, Dean Kuipers, James Ridgeway, and Dan Savage with Eli Sanders

Is there a difference between one Democratic candidate and another? Or has the electoral system leveled the field, so that it always and only comes down to money and powerful friends? For the first time in many years, the Democratic Party contenders—those who want to be president, and those who are impacting the terms of the public discussion—are placing issues and identities at the forefront of their campaigns. A black man, a Latino, and a woman are viable candidates. A populist from the South and a progressive from Cleveland are propelling the party from the center to a more liberal platform. A vice president makes a comeback. But we still have to wonder—and worry—if any of them has what it takes to turn the system around and begin to dig us out of the quagmire that this country has created at home and abroad. Some of the nation's wittiest and best-informed commentators look beyond the campaign promises, the mudslinging, and the personal testimony to present another side of the story: Will any of these politicians be able to transcend politics and make a difference?

Laura Flanders (writing on Hillary Clinton) is the host of *RadioNation* on Air America Radio network. She is the author of *Blue Grit: Democrats Take Back Politics from the Politicians* and *Bushwomen: How They Won the White House for Their Men.*

Richard Goldstein (writing on Barack Obama) writes regularly for *The Nation.* He is the author of *Homocons: The Rise of the Gay Right.*

Dean Kuipers (writing on Al Gore) is the managing editor of *CityBeat,* the alternative weekly of Los Angeles, and is the author of *Burning Rainbow Farm: How a Stoner Utopia Went Up in Smoke.*

James Ridgeway (writing on John Edwards) is *Mother Jones'* Washington, DC, bureau chief and the author of *The Five Unanswered Questions about 9/11.*

Dan Savage (writing on Dennis Kucinich with Eli Sanders) is the author of the internationally syndicated sex column "Savage Love." **Eli Sanders** is the senior staff writer for *The Stranger,* Seattle's weekly newspaper.

The alternative guide to the Democratic presidential candidates of 2008.

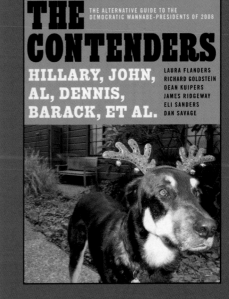

Current Affairs
November
5½ x 8 | 320 pp
TC $22.95
978-1-58322-789-3 USA

Marketing Plans

Co-op available
Advance reader copies
25,000-copy print run

Author Events

Los Angeles, CA • Washington, DC •
New York, NY

Seven Stories Press

Flying Close to the Sun
My Life and Times as a Weatherman
Cathy Wilkerson

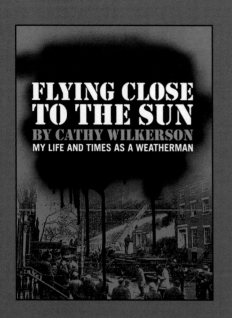

History
September
6 x 8 | 416 pp
16 B&W photographs
TC $24.95
978-1-58322-771-8 USA

Flying Close to the Sun is the memoir of a white middle-class girl from the suburbs who became what today many would call a terrorist—a bomb-making member of the Weather Underground—who then came to learn the lessons of the 1960s that other radicals of all stripes seem not to have learned. Cathy Wilkerson, who famously blew up and escaped from her parents' Greenwich Village townhouse, here wrestles with the contradictions of the movement that still have not been publicly aired before now: the absence of women's voices; the incompetence and the egos; the hundreds of bombs detonated in protest, which caused little loss of life but were also ineffective in fomenting revolution. Years later she realizes that in making decisions from a place of rage and hopelessness, the Weather Underground in effect accepted the same disregard for human life practiced by Richard Nixon, Henry Kissinger, and William Westmoreland. They had abandoned themselves to the sanctimony of hating their enemies. In searching for new paradigms for change, Wilkerson asserts with brave humanity and confessional honesty an assessment of her past—of those heady, iconic times—and finds hope and faith in a world that at times seemed to offer neither.

Cathy Wilkerson was active in the civil rights movement, Students for a Democratic Society, and the Weather Underground. In 1970, she, along with Kathy Boudin, survived an explosion in the basement of her parents' townhouse that killed three Weathermen, forcing the group underground. For the past twenty years she has worked as an educator teaching teachers in New York City schools.

The gentle truth of what went wrong in the sixties.

Marketing Plans

Co-op available
Advance reader copies
10,000-copy print run

Author Events

San Francisco, CA • Boston, MA •
New York, NY • Seattle, WA

Also Available

Sing a Battle Song
The Revolutionary Poetry, Statements, and Communiqués of the Weather Underground
1970–1974
Edited by Bernardine Dohrn, Bill Ayres, and Jeff Jones
History / Political Science & Government
6 x 9 | 390 pp
TP $19.95
978-1-58322-726-8 USA

Seven Stories Press

I Had to Say Something
The Art of Ted Haggard's Fall
Mike Jones with Sam Gallegos

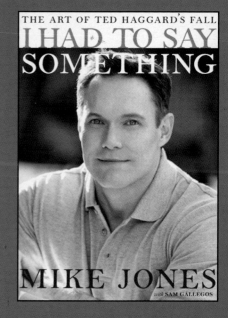

For almost three years, a man named "Art" came to see Mike Jones, an escort, at least once a month. With time, the relationship deepened, including sexual experimentation as well as sincere conversation. Like many of Jones' closeted clients in the clergy or the military, Art revealed his vulnerabilities as he struggled with his true desire for sexual contact and emotional involvement with a man.

One day, Jones recognized Art preaching hate on a religious cable channel. He soon discovered that Art was actually the Reverend Ted Haggard, who, as president of the National Association of Evangelicals, influenced the daily lives of thirty million followers, advocating virulently against gay rights and same-sex unions, with direct access to White House policy makers.

On November 1, 2006, after months of indecision, Jones made public his relationship with Ted Haggard. Within days, Haggard resigned from all his positions of power, admitting to a "sexual immorality" that shook the evangelical world, right before Election Day 2006.

Here is the disarming story of how a sexual relationship became a lightning rod that completely changed two men's lives, as well as, possibly, the history of American governance. Jones' only rules were telling the truth and not being ashamed of who he is.

From 1980 until November 2006, **Mike Jones** worked as an escort and a massage therapist. His story dominated national news, including coverage on *The Today Show, Good Morning America,* MSNBC, CNN, CourtTV, *The Dr. Keith Ablow Show,* in the Associated Press, *People,* and *TIME.* Jones has been credited with turning the midterm election for the Democrats. He was named one of *The Advocate*'s People of the Year for 2006.

Sam Gallegos is a Denver-based freelance writer who worked as a researcher for Randy Shilts, author of *And The Band Played On.*

A male escort calls out for justice from the self-proclaimed gatekeepers of morality.

Current Affairs
Available Now
5½ x 8 | 240 pp
TC $23.95
978-1-58322-768-8 USA

Marketing Plans

Co-op available

Author Events

Los Angeles, CA • San Francisco, CA • Colorado Springs, CO • Denver, CO • New York, NY

Evolution
Jean-Baptiste de Panafieu
Translated by Linda Asher
Photographs by Patrick Gries

Science / Environmental Studies
October
11 x 11 | 288 pp
200 Duotone photographs
TC $65.00
978-1-58322-784-8 USA

Unprecedented in its approach, the number and diversity of the species presented, and the quality of the photographs, *Evolution* is *the* book on how we came to be what we are. Spectacular, mysterious, elegant, or grotesque, the skeletons of the vertebrates that inhabit the earth today carry within them the imprint of an evolutionary process that has lasted several billion years. This book is the result of a dual approach, scientific as well as aesthetic, rigorous yet accessible. Each chapter is made up of a short text that illuminates one theme of the evolutionary process—repetition, adaptation, polymorphism, sexual selection—and a series of exquisitely composed photographs of skeletons against a black background. Approximately three hundred photographs of whole skeletons or their details have been made possible by the French National Museum of Natural History. The reader learns, by experiencing each text and photograph together, how the structure of every creature has been shaped by its environmental and genetic inheritance.

Author **Jean-Baptiste de Panafieu**, a professor of natural sciences and a doctor of biological oceanography, has published a number of popular scientific works for younger readers and has written and directed documentaries.

Linda Asher, a former fiction editor for *The New Yorker,* has translated into English Victor Hugo, Georges Simenon, and Milan Kundera. Her translation of Martin Winckler's *The Case of Dr. Sachs* (*La maladie de Sachs*) won the French-American Foundation Translation Prize in 2000.

Photographer **Patrick Gries** has photographed over two thousand artworks for the new Quai Branly Museum and collaborated with the Cartier Foundation for Contemporary Art, among other recent projects.

Evolution is the book on how we came to be.

Seven Stories Press

Questions
Shere Hite

Gender, sexual violence, and sexual idealism in the world today; the history of sexual stereotypes and gender roles; and the sexualization of globalization and terrorism: These are just some of the topics in this short but wide-ranging portrait of contemporary life.

The preeminent writer of the sexual lives of women and men, **Shere Hite** is a pioneering force as both a feminist and a post-feminist thinker. She is best known for work that has "left an indelible mark on Western civilization" (Reuters), and as a "revolutionary agent of change . . . [whose work] on sexuality, friendship, and love continues to challenge gender stereotypes—and expand the meaning of 'human'" (Barbara Ehrenreich). Her most famous book is *The Hite Report* (reissued by Seven Stories Press in 2004), and her latest is *The Shere Hite Reader* (Seven Stories Press, 2006). Hite is a regular contributor to the *Financial Times* (United Kingdom), *Corriere della Sera* (Italy), and *El País* (Spain). She lives in London.

A road map to our sexual world.

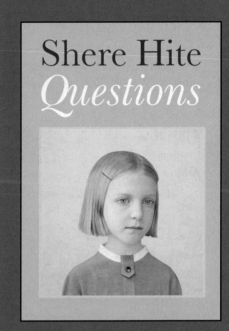

Gender Studies / Women's Studies
March
5 x 8 | 128 pp
TC $18.00
978-1-58322-786-2 USA

Also Available

The Hite Report
Shere Hite
Sexuality / Women's Studies
6 x 9 | 512 pp
TP $17.95
978-1-58322-569-1 USA

The Shere Hite Reader
New and Selected Writings on Sex,
Globalization and Private Life
Shere Hite
Sexuality
6 x 9 | 560 pp
TP $24.95
978-1-58322-568-4 USA

Seven Stories Press

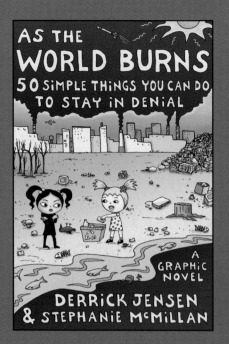

Graphic Novels / Environmental Studies
November
A Paperback Original
6 x 9 | 224 pp
224 B&W illustrations
TP $14.95
978-1-58322-777-0 USA

Marketing Plans

15,000-copy print run

Author Hometown: Crescent City, CA

As the World Burns

50 Simple Things You Can Do to Stay in Denial

Derrick Jensen

Illustrated by Stephanie McMillan

Two of America's most talented activists team up to deliver a bold and hilarious satire of modern environmental policy in this fully illustrated graphic novel. The US government gives robot machines from space permission to eat the earth in exchange for bricks of gold. A one-eyed bunny rescues his friends from a corporate animal testing laboratory. And two little girls figure out the secret to saving the world from both of its enemies (and it isn't by using energy-efficient light bulbs or biodiesel fuel). *As the World Burns* will inspire you to do whatever it takes to stop ecocide before it's too late.

Derrick Jensen, an activist, author, and philosopher, is the author of *Endgame*, volumes one and two; *A Language Older Than Words*; and *The Culture of Make Believe* (a finalist for the 2003 J. Anthony Lukas Book Prize), among other books. Jensen's writing has been described as "breaking and mending the reader's heart" (*Publishers Weekly*).

Activist and artist **Stephanie McMillan** began syndicating her daring political cartoons in 1999. Since then her work has appeared in dozens of publications and has been exhibited in museums across the country. A book based on her comic strip, *Minimum Security*, was published in 2005.

A MORE inconvenient truth.

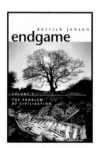

Also Available

Endgame
Volume 1: The Problem of Civilization
Derrick Jensen
Current Affairs / Environmental Studies
6 x 9 | 528 pp
TP $18.95
978-1-58322-730-5 USA

Endgame
Volume 2: Resistance
Derrick Jensen
Current Affairs / Environmental Studies
6 x 9 | 496 pp
TP $18.95
978-1-58322-724-4 USA

Seven Stories Press

The Unraveling of the Bush Presidency
Howard Zinn

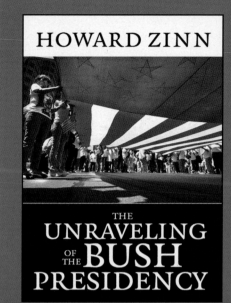

Here, in the magisterial yet plainspoken style of *A People's History of the United States,* is historian Howard Zinn's long-awaited telling of US history during these last six years, a time when catastrophic machinations of war have dictated our foreign and domestic policy, and voices of resistance have appeared in the unlikeliest places.

Perhaps more than any other American, Howard Zinn has helped us understand ourselves by deepening our understanding of our own history. He is the author of numerous books, including his epic masterpiece, *A People's History of the United States,* and a number of recent books published by Seven Stories Press: *Voices of a People's History of the United States* and *Terrorism and War* (both written with Anthony Arnove) and *The Zinn Reader.*

**A pamphlet on the history of our times by
one of our most revered activists.**

History / Current Affairs
Available Now
A Paperback Original
5 x 7 | 48 pp
TP $7.95
978-1-58322-769-5 USA

**Also
Available**

A Young People's History of the
United States, Vol. 1
Columbus to the Spanish-American War
Howard Zinn
Young Adult Nonfiction
6 x 8 | 192 pp
TC $16.95
978-1-58322-759-6 USA

A Young People's History of the
United States, Vol. 2
Class Struggle to the War on Terror
Howard Zinn
Young Adult Nonfiction
6 x 8 | 256 pp
TC $17.95
978-1-58322-760-2 USA

Seven Stories Press

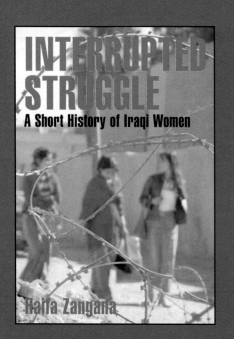

Current Affairs / Women's Studies
November
5½ x 8 | 160 pp
TC $20.00
978-1-58322-779-4 USA

Marketing Plans

Co-op available
Advance reader copies

Interrupted Struggle
A Short History of Iraqi Women
Haifa Zangana

Haifa Zangana, a former political prisoner of the Ba'ath regime, is the first to put the current plight of Iraqi women in context. She traces a long line of daring and vocal activists, resisting foreign aggression and despotism for the past 100 years, from a handful of turn-of-the-century poets, to 1960s activists in armed struggle (of which Zangana was a part), to suicide bombers today.

Zangana contradicts the passive role into which Western media have cast Iraqi women and presents a forceful critique of foreign non-governmental organizations designed to hijack the initiatives of Iraqi women. Addressing the stark realities of Iraq under occupation, Zangana reveals Baghdad as a "city of widows," where more than three hundred thousand women have been left to head households. Just as the sanctions disproportionately affected women and children, the war and occupation have destroyed their ways of life. In the rebuilding of Iraq, as so often before, Zangana suggests, Iraqi women will be left to pick up the pieces of their country after yet another senseless imperial adventure.

Haifa Zangana is an Iraqi political commentator, novelist, and former prisoner of Saddam Hussein's regime. She is a weekly columnist for *al-Quds* newspaper and a commentator for the *Guardian, Red Pepper,* and *al-Ahram Weekly.* She lives in London.

The story of Iraqi women before and after Washington's "liberation."

Seven Stories Press

Censored 2008
The Top 25 Censored Stories
Edited by Peter Phillips and Project Censored

"Carefully orchestrated. . . . This well-researched work is highly recommended for most libraries."—*Library Journal* (starred review)

"Buy it, read it, act on it. Our future depends on the knowledge this collection of suppressed stories allows us."—*The San Diego Review*

"Required reading for broadcasters, journalists, and well-informed citizens."—*Los Angeles Times*

The best-selling Censored series highlights the year's twenty-five most important underreported news stories, alerting readers to the negligence of corporate media and the resurgence of alternative media.

Peter Phillips, director of Project Censored, is an associate professor of sociology at Sonoma State University. He is known for his pieces in the alternative press and in independent newspapers nationwide, such as *Z Magazine* and *Social Policy.*

Project Censored, founded in 1976 by Carl Jensen, has as its principal objective the advocacy for and protection of First Amendment rights and the freedom of information in the United States.

The breaking news stories you won't find anywhere else.

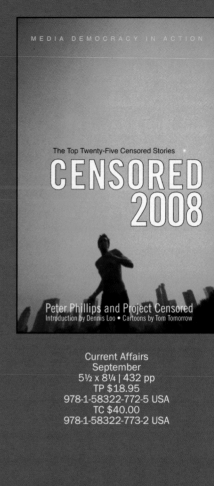

Current Affairs
September
5½ x 8¼ | 432 pp
TP $18.95
978-1-58322-772-5 USA
TC $40.00
978-1-58322-773-2 USA

Marketing Plans

15,000-copy print run

Also Available

Censored 2007
The Top 25 Censored Stories
Edited by Project Censored and Peter Phillips
Current Affairs
5½ x 8¼ | 432 pp
TP $18.95
978-1-58322-738-1 USA

Seven Stories Press

REVISED AND EXPANDED EDITION

GARY NULL

THE

FOOD-
MOOD-
BODY
CONNECTION

NUTRITION-BASED AND ENVIRONMENTAL

APPROACHES TO MENTAL HEALTH AND

PHYSICAL WELL-BEING

Health & Fitness /
Self-Actualization & Self Help
January
6 x 9 | 608 pp
TP $24.95
978-1-58322-788-6 USA

Marketing Plans

Co-op available

The Food-Mood-Body Connection
Nutrition-Based and Environmental Approaches to Mental Health and Physical Well-being (Second Edition)
Gary Null with Amy McDonald

"Null, a longtime champion of alternative health care, makes a good case. . . . His book is sure to find a big audience among those (including families) affected by these conditions."—*Publishers Weekly* (starred review)

"In an increasingly Balkanized medical community, fractured by all manner of alternative therapies, Null, a PhD in human nutrition and public-health science, is leading one of the biggest breakaway republics of all."—Jeffrey Kluger, *TIME*

Now, at a time when the effects of nutrition on mental health are becoming increasingly recognized and accepted by the general public, comes a completely revised and updated tome from an early advocate of the subject. Behold the second edition of *The Food-Mood-Body Connection,* by best-selling health and nutrition expert Gary Null, who was affectionately dubbed "the new Mister Natural" by *TIME* magazine. Drawing from up-to-the-minute research and a wealth of patient testimonials, Null reveals how alternative, nutrition-based approaches can effectively treat many mental disorders, chronic conditions, and a variety of commonly misdiagnosed organic conditions. With participation from more than sixty-five alternative practitioners, this edition includes several new chapters, plus updates on topics ranging from alcoholism and depression to food allergies and PMS.

Best-selling health and nutrition author **Gary Null** is one of America's most popular health and fitness writers. Dr. Null has a PhD in nutrition and is the author of dozens of books and hundreds of medical articles. He is also the host of a popular daily radio show on VoiceAmerica.

No need to brood . . . improve your mood with food!

Also Available

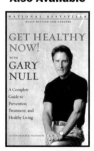

Get Healthy Now! with Gary Null
A Complete Guide to Prevention, Treatment,
and Healthy Living (Second Edition)
Gary Null
Health & Fitness
5½ x 8¼ | 1,146 pp
TP $29.95
978-1-58322-753-4 USA

Seven Stories Press

Fidel
A Graphic Novel Life of Fidel Castro
Néstor Kohan
Illustrated by Nahuel Scherma

The Cuban Revolution of 1959, spearheaded by the young Fidel Castro along with his companion in arms, Ernesto "Che" Guevara, is mythic in both its dream and reality. *Fidel* offers a uniquely readable and illustrated account of the struggle for Castro to define and defend his nation in the face of fear and opposition from the United States, Cuba's neighbor a scant ninety miles away. In addition to discussing the Bay of Pigs and the Cold War, the author examines Cuban influence in Latin American insurgencies, the student protests of 1968 Europe, the African American uprisings of the United States, the liberation of Vietnam, the decolonization of Africa, the end of apartheid, and the rise of Cuban-ally Hugo Chávez, the president of Venezuela. Along with entertaining comics and photographs, this short read traces the ambitions of Castro as he aims to endow the face of socialism with creative, intelligent, and humanitarian features, and shows a man indistinguishable from his revolution and his country.

Néstor Kohan, born in Buenos Aires in 1967, is the author of a number of Spanish-language books on Marxism, Che Guevara, and social movements in Latin America.

Nahuel Scherma is an Argentinian filmmaker and documentarian. *Fidel* is his first book of illustrations.

An illustrated guide through Fidel Castro's Cuba and his revolutionary dream.

Graphic Novels / Current Affairs
September
A Paperback Original
5 x 7½ | 176 pp
TP $14.95
978-1-58322-782-4 USA
Spanish-language edition:
TP $13.95
978-1-58322-783-1 USA

Seven Stories Press

A Field Guide for Female Interrogators
Coco Fusco

A FIELD GUIDE FOR FEMALE INTERROGATORS

BY COCO FUSCO

Current Affairs / Women's Studies
February
A Paperback Original
5½ x 7½ | 128 pp
28 Color illustrations
TP $16.95
978-1-58322-780-0 USA

Marketing Plans

10,000-copy print run

Author Events

Los Angeles, CA • New York, NY

The world was shocked by the images that emerged from Abu Ghraib, the US-controlled prison in Iraq. Lynndie England, the young female army officer shown smiling devilishly as she humiliated male prisoners, became first a scapegoat and then a victim who was "just following orders." Ignored were the more elemental questions of how women are functioning within conservative power structures of government and the military. Why do the military and the CIA use female sexuality as an interrogation tactic, and why is this tactic downplayed and even ignored in internal investigations of prisoner abuse?

Combining an art project with critical commentary, Coco Fusco imaginatively addresses the role of women in the war on terror and explores how female sexuality is being used as a weapon against suspected Islamic terrorists. Using details drawn from actual accounts of detainee treatment in US military prisons, Fusco conceives a field guide of instructional drawings that prompts urgent questions regarding the moral dilemma of torture in general and the use of female sexuality specifically. Fusco assesses what these matters suggest about how the military and the state use sex, sexuality, and originally feminist notions of sexual freedom.

Coco Fusco is a New York-based interdisciplinary artist and writer. She is the author of *English is Broken Here: Notes on Cultural Fusion in the Americas,* and editor of *Corpus Delecti: Performance Art of the Americas* and *Only Skin Deep: Changing Visions of the American Self* (with Brian Wallis). A recipient of a 2003 Herb Alpert Award in the Arts, she is an associate professor at Columbia University.

The strategic uses of female sexuality in the war on terror.

Seven Stories Press

Human Rights Watch World Report 2008
Human Rights Watch

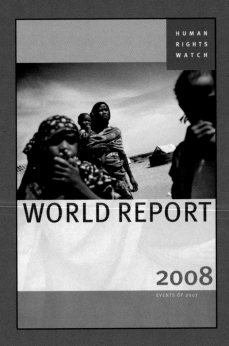

"A wonderful report. An attempt to bring rationality where emotion tends to dominate."—Simon Jenkins, former editor of *The Times* (London)

"The reports of the New York-based Human Rights Watch (HRW) have become extremely important. . . . Cogent and eminently practical, these reports have gone far beyond an account of human rights abuses in the country."—Ahmed Rashid, *The New York Review of Books*

"When Human Rights Watch, a respected organization that has been monitoring the world's behavior since 1978, focuses its annual review on America's use of torture and inhumane treatment, every American should feel a sense of shame. And everyone who has believed in the United States as the staunchest protector of human rights in history should be worried."—*International Herald Tribune*

Human Rights Watch is increasingly recognized as the world's leader in building a stronger awareness for human rights. Their annual *World Report* is the most probing review of human rights developments available anywhere.

Written in straightforward, non-technical language, *Human Rights Watch World Report 2008* prioritizes events in the most affected countries during the year. The backbone of the report consists of a series of concise overviews of the most pressing human rights issues in countries from Afghanistan to Zimbabwe, with particular focus on the role—positive or negative—played in each country by key domestic and international figures.

Highly anticipated and widely publicized by the US and international press every year, the *World Report* is an invaluable resource for journalists, diplomats, and all citizens of the world.

The leading human rights organization's indispensable annual report.

Current Affairs
February
A Paperback Original
6 x 9 | 576 pp
TP $24.00
978-1-58322-774-9 USA

Also Available

Human Rights Watch World Report 2007
Human Rights Watch
Current Affairs
6 x 9 | 560 pp
TP $24.00
978-1-58322-740-4 USA

Seven Stories Press

Goodbye, Mr. Socialism
Antonio Negri and Raf Scelsi

Current Affairs /
Political Science & Government
September
A Paperback Original
5 x 7 | 160 pp
TP $15.95
978-1-58322-775-6 USA

In the current era of war, globalization, and domestic crisis, what is to be made of the global Left? *Goodbye, Mr. Socialism* offers a gripping encounter with one of today's leading leftists, presenting his most up-to-date analysis of global events and insight into the prospects for the Left in an age of neoliberalism.

In his most accessible work yet, Antonio Negri discusses the state of the global Left since the end of the Cold War and suggests a new politics in a series of rousing conversations with Italian journalist Raf Scelsi. Scelsi prompts Negri to critique the episodes in the post-Cold War period that have afforded the Left opportunities to rethink its strategies, in terms of organization and of political programs and objectives. Addressing the twilight of social democracy, Negri offers a compelling defense of the prospects for social transformation.

Antonio Negri was born in Padua in 1933. He is one of the world's leading critics of state power and has been actively involved in political movements to transform society. In 1979 he was arrested for his alleged connection to the Red Brigades and sentenced to a term in prison. In 1983, Negri fled into political exile in France and later returned to Italy in 1997, where he voluntarily served his term and was released in 2003. Among his most important works are *Empire* and *Multitude* (both with Michael Hardt).

Raf Scelsi teaches philosophy and history. He is an editor with the Italian publisher Feltrinelli and his works include *Cyberpunk: Antologia di testi politici* (ShaKe, 1990), and *No copyright: Nuovi diritti nel 2000* (ShaKe, 1994).

**One of the world's leading political thinkers addresses
the worldwide crisis of the Left.**

Seven Stories Press

The Emergence of Memory
Conversations with W.G. Sebald
Edited by Lynne Sharon Schwartz

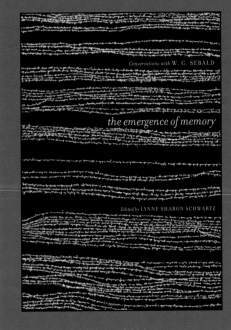

"The novelist and translator Lynne Sharon Schwartz has carefully rendered these subtle currents of belief and sensibility, moving always beneath an airy conversational style, in dexterous prose."—*Virginia Quarterly Review* on *A Place to Live and other selected essays* by Natalia Ginzburg

When German author W.G. Sebald died in a car accident at the age of fifty-seven, the literary world mourned the loss of a writer whose *oeuvre* it was just beginning to appreciate. Through pieces culled from essays, interviews, and reviews, award-winning translator and author Lynne Sharon Schwartz offers a profound portrait of the late Sebald, who has been praised posthumously for his unflinching explorations of historical cruelty, memory, and dislocation in post-Nazi Europe. With contributions from poet, essayist, and translator Charles Simic, *New Republic* editor Ruth Franklin, *Bookworm* radio host Michael Silverblatt, and more, *The Emergence of Memory* offers Sebald's own voice in interviews between 1997 up to a month before his death in 2001. Also included are cogent accounts of almost all of Sebald's books, thematically linked to events in the contributors' own lives.

Contributors include Carole Angier, Joseph Cuomo, Ruth Franklin, Michael Hofmann, Arthur Lubow, Tim Parks, Michael Silverblatt, Charles Simic, and Eleanor Wachtel.

Lynne Sharon Schwartz is the author of nineteen works of fiction, nonfiction, poetry, and memoir. She has been nominated for the National Book Award, the PEN/Hemingway Award for Best First Novel, and the PEN/Faulkner Award for Fiction, and she won the PEN Renato Poggioli Award for Translation in 1991.

The eloquence of W.G. Sebald is revived.

Literary Criticism
October
5 x 8½ | 160 pp
TC $23.95
978-1-58322-785-5 USA

Marketing Plans

Co-op available
Advance reader copies

Also Available

A Place to Live
Natalia Ginzburg
Edited by Lynne Sharon Schwartz
Literature & Essay
6 x 8 | 240 pp
TP $12.95
978-1-58322-570-7 USA

Seven Stories Press

Columbus and Other Cannibals

Jack D. Forbes

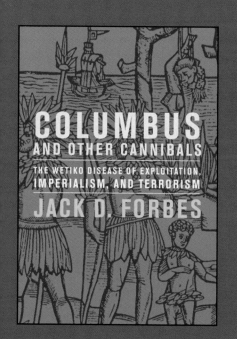

History
March
5 x 7 | 224 pp
TP $14.95
978-1-58322-781-7 USA

Celebrated American Indian thinker Jack Forbes' *Columbus and Other Cannibals* was one of the founding texts of the anti-civilization movement when it was first published in 1978. His history of terrorism, genocide, and ecocide told from a Native American point of view has inspired America's most influential activists for decades. Frighteningly, his radical critique of the modern "civilized" lifestyle is more relevant now than ever before.

Identifying the Western compulsion to consume the earth as a sickness, Forbes writes:

> "Brutality knows no boundaries. Greed knows no limits. Perversion knows no borders. . . . These characteristics all push towards an extreme, always moving forward once the initial infection sets in. . . . This is the disease of the consuming of other creatures' lives and possessions. I call it cannibalism."

This updated edition includes a new preface by the author and an introduction by Derrick Jensen.

Jack D. Forbes is professor emeritus and former chair of Native American Studies at the University of California at Davis. Of Powhatan-Renápe, Delaware-Lenápe, and non-Indian background, he founded the organization Native American Movement in 1961, and started Native American studies programs across the country. He has lectured around the world and is the author of twelve books.

A timely revival of the underground classic that fostered the anti-civilization movement.

Seven Stories Press

Ex Machina
Robert Finn

Robert Finn's writing has achieved "a measure of success rare among new, small publishers" (*The Observer*).

In this sequel to the best-selling *Adept,* Susan Milton and David Braun battle a life-threatening situation. Brought together over the theft of an ancient relic, they begin to unravel its mystical powers.

Robert Finn is emerging as one of the breakthrough British authors of crime and mystery thrillers. *Adept* was his debut novel and prequel to *Ex Machina*. Finn lives and works in London.

Marketing Plans
Co-op available • Advance reader copies • 10,000-copy print run

Mystery / Fiction
March
A Paperback Original
5 x 7¾ | 414 pp
TP US $14.95 | CAN $18.00
978-1-905005-64-2 CUSA

A tense sci-fi thriller and a must-read for all those who loved *Adept*.

Sob Story
Carol Anne Davis

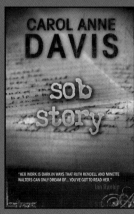

"The queen of noir."—*Booklist*

"Davis writes with dangerous authority about the deadly everyday. Her work is dark in ways that Ruth Rendell and Minette Walters can only dream of. You've got to read her."—Ian Rankin

Amy thinks that Jeff, her prison pen pal, will be behind bars for several years. He lied—his release date is imminent. She believes that he's a gentle, misunderstood young man. She's wrong.

Carol Anne Davis is the author of *Shrouded, Safe As Houses,* and *Noise Abatement* and also writes true-crime nonfiction. Her writing regularly appears in monthly mainstream magazines.

Marketing Plans
Co-op available • Advance reader copies

Mystery / Fiction
January
A Paperback Original
5 x 7¾ | 320 pp
TP US $14.95 | CAN $18.00
978-1-905005-63-5 CUSA

"You've got to read her."—Ian Rankin

The Other Eden
Sarah Bryant

Fiction / Romance
October
A Paperback Original
5 x 7¾ | 462 pp
TP US $14.95 | CAN $18.00
978-1-905005-11-6 CUSA

"Somehow intimate and grand at the same time. Romantic, thrilling, epic and touching."—Booktrust

"Lush, sensual, musical, and dangerously seductive, *The Other Eden* is a rare vision of a corrupt, irresistible paradise. It will haunt you and your dreams."—J.D. Landis, author of *Lying in Bed, Longing,* and *Artist of the Beautiful*

Sarah Bryant is originally from Boston and now lives in the Scottish Borders with her husband and two children. She holds an MLitt in creative writing from the University of St Andrews, and what free time is left between writing and family goes to horses and the Celtic harp.

Marketing Plans
Co-op available • Advance reader copies • 10,000-copy print run

Taking the Plunge
Stacie Lewis

Fiction / Women's Literature
March
A Paperback Original
5 x 7¾ | 192 pp
TP US $14.95 | CAN $18.00
978-1-905005-45-1 CUSA

Sometimes the scariest thing about getting married is your own family!

"A touching and jaw-dropping account that makes a great case for elopement! It had me gripped!"—*Trashionista*

Taking the Plunge is a chronicle of the turbulent events leading up to the author's wedding. Originally written for the website www.weddings.co.uk, thousands followed Stacie Lewis' reports from the frontlines as hits to the site doubled to twenty-five thousand each day. Due to popular request, Stacie used her experiences as the basis for this novel. Funny, heart-breaking, and based on real life, *Taking the Plunge* is a tried-and-tested, sure-fire hit with those both engaged and married.

Stacie Lewis writes regularly for several publications, including weekly articles for the *Detroit News*.

Marketing Plans
Co-op available • Advance reader copies

Snowbooks

The First Wave

James R. Benn

Fiction
September
6 x 9 | 304 pp
TC US $24.00 | CAN $29.00
978-1-56947-471-6 CUSA

Praise for *The First Wave*:

"A triple dose of excitement with a murder mystery within a spy thriller within a World War Two adventure story. . . . A 'rattling good read.'"—Rhys Bowen, author of *In Dublin's Fair City*

"Has all the essential elements: murder, espionage, and romance."—Karen E. Olson, author of the Anne Seymour mysteries

"What a great read, full of action, humor and heart."—Louise Penny, author of *Still Life*

Praise for the Billy Boyle series:

"A meaty, old-fashioned and thoroughly enjoyable tale of WWII-era murder and espionage."—*The Seattle Times*

"The World War II atmosphere and history are expertly handled."—*Denver Post*

"Great fun. Benn knows his war history. . . . A batch of intriguing characters who seem destined to make another appearance."—*The Globe and Mail* (Toronto)

"A memorable debut."—*BookPage*

"If you enjoy World War II mysteries . . . you'll love this book. . . . One of the best books I've read this year."—*Mystery Scene*

Lieutenant Billy Boyle reluctantly accompanies Major Samuel Harding, his boss, in the first boat to land on the shores of Algeria during the Allied invasion. Their task is to arrange the surrender of the Vichy French forces. But there is dissension between the regular army, the local militia, and de Gaulle's Free French. American black marketeers in league with the enemy divert medical supplies to the Casbah, leading to multiple murders that Billy must solve while trying to rescue the girl he loves, a captured British spy.

James R. Benn is the author of *Billy Boyle: A World War II Mystery,* selected by Book Sense as one of the top five mysteries of 2006 and nominated for a Dilys Award. He is a librarian and lives in Hadlyme, Connecticut.

Billy Boyle finds skullduggery ashore in Algeria.

Marketing Plans

Co-op available
Advance reader copies
25,000-copy print run

Billy Boyle

James R. Benn

Fiction
September
6 x 9 | 304 pp
TP US $12.00 | CAN $14.50
978-1-56947-476-1 CUSA

Marketing Plans

Co-op available
12,500-copy print run

"This book has got it all—an instant classic."—Lee Child, author of *The Hard Way*

"A tale as tight as a drum. Doesn't get any better than this."—Mary-Ann Tirone Smith, author of the Poppy Rice mysteries

"It is a pleasure marching off to war with spirited Billy Boyle. He is a charmer, richly imagined and vividly rendered. And he tells a finely suspenseful yarn." —Dan Fesperman, author of *The Prisoner of Guantánamo*

"Rich with atmosphere. . . . A treat from start to finish."—Owen Parry, author of the Abel Jones mysteries

What's a twenty-two-year-old Irish cop from Boston doing at Beardsley Hall having lunch with Haakon, King of Norway, and the rest of the Norwegian government in exile? Billy Boyle himself wonders. Back home, he'd just made detective (with a little help from family and friends) when war was declared. Unwilling to fight—and perhaps die—for England, he was relieved when his mother wrangled a job for him on the staff of a general married to her distant cousin, Mamie. But the general turns out to be Dwight D. Eisenhower; his headquarters are in London, which is undergoing the Blitz; and Uncle Ike has a special assignment for Billy: He wants Billy to be his personal investigator.

Operation Jupiter, the impending invasion of Norway, is being planned. Billy is to catch a spy amongst the Norwegians. He doubts his own abilities, and a theft and two murders test his investigative powers. But to his own surprise, Billy proves to be a better detective than anyone suspected.

James R. Benn's *Billy Boyle: A World War II Mystery* was selected by Book Sense as one of the top five mysteries of 2006 and nominated for a Dilys award. He is a librarian and lives in Hadlyme, Connecticut.

Billy Boyle goes to war.

Soho Press

Little Face
Sophie Hannah

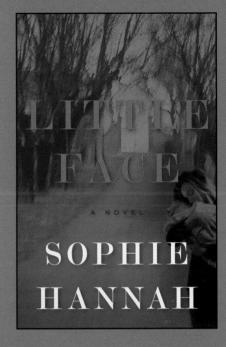

"A taut, seamless thriller with all the dark foreboding of *Rebecca,* an extraordinary chilling tale that grabs the reader from the first page."—Denise Mina, author of *The Dead Hour*

"A stunning tale of murder, madness, and mind-bending duplicity. . . . Resonates long after you've turned the final, masterful page."—Judith Kelman, author of *The Session*

"*Little Face* is a wonderful work, a brilliant use of mirrors and the writer's magic. Chilling, tantalizing, and ultimately fair and deeply satisfying."—Barbara D'Amato, author of *Death of a Thousand Cuts*

"[The] characters are vivid, the novel's challenging double narrative is handled with flair, and its denouement is ingenious."—*The Sunday Times* (London)

"Superb . . . good, old-fashioned spine-tingling stuff, but also a fine modern thriller."—*The Times* (London)

The first time she goes out after their daughter is born, Alice leaves the two-week-old infant at home with her husband, David. When she returns two hours later, she insists that the baby in the crib is not her child. Despite her apparent distress, David is adamant that she is wrong.

The police are called to the scene. Detective Constable Simon Waterhouse is sympathetic, but he doubts Alice's story. His superior, Sergeant Charlie Zailer, thinks Alice must be suffering from some sort of delusion brought on by postpartum depression. With an increasingly hostile and menacing David swearing she must either be mad or lying, how can Alice make the police believe her before it's too late?

Sophie Hannah is an award-winning and best-selling poet in the United Kingdom. She has also previously published fiction. This is her first psychological crime novel. She lives in West Yorkshire with her husband and two children.

It's every mother's nightmare.

Fiction
October
6 x 9 | 320 pp
TC US $25.00 | CAN $30.00
978-1-56947-468-6 CUSA

Marketing Plans

Co-op available
Advance reader copies
25,000-copy print run
National advertising:
Bookslut.com • Mystery Scene

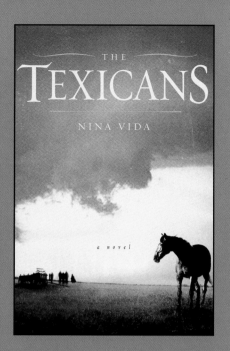

Fiction
October
6 x 9 | 296 pp
TP US $13.00 | CAN $15.95
978-1-56947-477-8 CUSA

Marketing Plans

Co-op available
12,500-copy print run

Author Hometown: Huntington Beach, CA

The Texicans
Nina Vida

"A completely engaging tale following a handful of remarkable settlers."—*Entertainment Weekly*

"Lively. . . . Vivid characters. . . . Enthralling reading."—*The Miami Herald*

"Compelling. . . . That Vida brings so much fresh energy to the timeworn Western genre—complex characters, engaging stories, cutting-edge historical revisionism—is no small feat."—*Austin American-Statesman*

"An imaginative and thoroughly researched tale driven by intriguing characters."—*Denver Post*

"Should be placed on the same shelf with *Lonesome Dove*, *Texas*, and *Pale Horse, Pale Rider.*"—*The Monitor* (Texas)

When cholera strikes San Antonio in 1843, Aurelia Ruiz discovers that she might have the power to heal—and also to curse. Meanwhile, Joseph Kimmel, a school-teacher in Missouri and the son of a Polish Jew, learns of his brother's death in San Antonio and sets off for Texas. On his way, a runaway slave steals his horse. After being rescued by Henry Castro, a man who is importing immigrants to populate his planned city, Castroville, Joseph agrees to marry a young Alsatian girl to save her from a Comanche chief who has demanded her. Then Joseph encounters Aurelia and becomes enamored with her.

Comanches, Tonkaways, Mexican *vaqueros,* immigrant farmers, and runaway slaves all play a part in Joseph's rebirth as a rancher, but when a renegade band of Texas Rangers descends upon the ranch, everything changes.

Nina Vida is the author of six previous novels: *Scam, Return from Darkness, Maximillian's Garden, Goodbye Saigon, Between Sisters,* and *The End of Marriage.* She lives with her husband in Huntington Beach, California.

The birth of Texas through the eyes of underdogs.

Soho Press

God of Luck
Ruthanne Lum McCunn

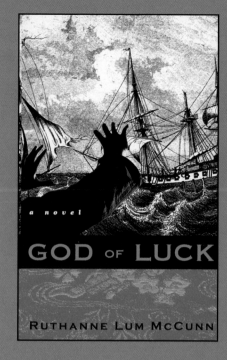

"With *God of Luck*, Ruthanne Lum McCunn has turned her descriptive and sensitive storytelling skills to the little-known coolie trade in Peru. She beautifully combines the hardships and brutality of the kidnapping of a Chinese man, conditions on the slave ships, and the bitterness of back-breaking labor in a foreign land with the sadness and determination of the wife and family back home. Never separating history from its impact on individual people, McCunn has reached into her characters' hearts to bring readers a story of emotional depth and truth."—Lisa See, author of *Snow Flower and the Secret Fan*

"Once again Ruthanne Lum McCunn opens a window onto another little-known chapter in the history of Chinese experience in the Americas. With amazing detail and riveting power, Ah Lung's story will keep readers spellbound and cheering to the final page."—Jeanne Wakatsuki Houston, author of *Farewell to Manzanar*

"Wise and spell-binding."—Gus Lee, author of *China Boy*

Ah Lung and his beloved wife, Bo See, are separated by a cruel fate when, like thousands of other Chinese men in the nineteenth century, he is kidnapped, enslaved, and shipped to the deadly guano mines off the coast of Peru. Using their wits and praying to the God of Luck, they never lose hope of someday being reunited.

Ruthanne Lum McCunn is of Scottish and Chinese ancestry. She is the author of the classic *Thousand Pieces of Gold,* which has sold over two hundred thousand copies, as well as the novels *The Moon Pearl* and *Wooden Fish Songs.* She lives in San Francisco.

**Kidnapped from China and enslaved in Peru, only his own wits—
and luck—can save him.**

Fiction
September
5 x 8 | 256 pp
TC US $23.00 | CAN $27.95
978-1-56947-466-2 CUSA

Marketing Plans

Co-op available
Advance reader copies
15,000-copy print run

Author Events

Washington, DC • Baltimore, MD •
New York, NY • Gettysburg, PA •
Philadelphia, PA

Author Hometown: San Francisco, CA

Soho Press

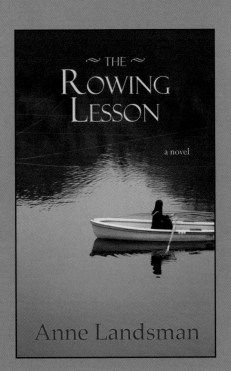

The Rowing Lesson
Anne Landsman

"Anne Landsman's glittering, shimmering new novel is a tour de force. . . . Elation and pain, anxiety and exuberance, and the uneven beat of living are all caught in language as silky and fluid as music."—Roxana Robinson, author of *A Perfect Stranger*

"Like Joyce or William Gass or John Edgar Wideman, Anne Landsman fashions a sensual web of memory and desire, rescuing a world at the brink of extinction through the power of her lyricism."—Stewart O'Nan, author of *The Good Wife*

"An elegy for a lost father and a beloved world on the point of disappearing. Rarely in South African writing will we encounter language of such fire and passion." —J.M. Coetzee, author of *Slow Man*

"A fierce elegy, a daughter's imaginary inhabitation of the memory of her dying father . . . an adventure in language. . . . It makes art of a life."—Louis Menand, author of *American Studies*

Betsy Klein is summoned from her home in the United States to her father's hospital bed in South Africa. Orphaned young, he had to struggle to become a doctor and to win the respect of his Boer patients. We first meet young Harold Klein on an excursion with his friends on the Ebb 'n Flow, a river to which he often returns. That is where he later teaches his little daughter to row and where he finally makes his last metaphoric passage.

Anne Landsman was born and raised in South Africa. Her debut novel, *The Devil's Chimney* (Soho Press, 1997), was published in paperback by Penguin. She lives in Manhattan with her husband and two children.

A passionate and poetic evocation of a man's life.

Fiction
November
5 x 8 | 288 pp
TC US $23.00 | CAN $27.95
978-0-93914-469-3 CUSA

Marketing Plans

Co-op available
Advance reader copies
25,000-copy print run
National advertising:
The New York Times Book Review

Author Hometown: New York, NY

Soho Press

Light Fell
Evan Fallenberg

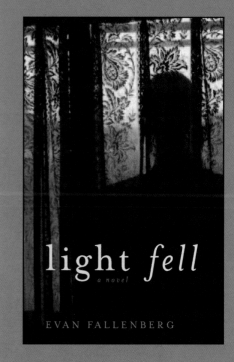

"*Light Fell* illuminates all the complexities, the contradictions, and the collisions of faith, family, and passion. . . . Evan Fallenberg has written an honest and brave book."—Binnie Kirshenbaum, author of *An Almost Perfect Moment*

"*Light Fell* weaves a complex and moving tapestry of a family worn thin and unraveled by a father's choice. . . . Powerful."—Victoria Redel, author of *The Border of Truth* and *Loverboy*

"Exquisite. . . . *Light Fell* helps illuminate, to the great satisfaction of the reader, the ever-complex human condition, the mysteries of desire, and, when we ourselves grant it, the astonishing power of forgiveness."—Aryeh Lev Stollamn, author of *The Illuminated Soul*

Twenty years ago Joseph left behind his entire life—his wife, his five sons, and his religious Israeli community—when he fell in love with a man—a rabbi. Their affair is long over, but its echoes continue to reverberate through the lives of Joseph and his family in ways that none of them could have predicted. Now, for his fiftieth birthday, Joseph is preparing to have his five sons spend the Sabbath with him in his Tel Aviv penthouse. This will be the first time they have all been together in nearly two decades. As they prepare for this reunion, they must confront what was, what is, and what could have been.

Evan Fallenberg is a native of Cleveland, Ohio, and has lived in Israel since 1985, where he is a writer, teacher, and translator. His recent translations include novels by Batya Gur and Meir Shalev. He is the father of two sons.

A story about fathers and sons, faith and sexuality.

Fiction
January
5 x 8 | 240 pp
TC US $22.00 | CAN $26.50
978-1-56947-467-9 CUSA

Marketing Plans

Co-op available
Advance reader copies
12,500-copy print run
National advertising:
The Advocate • Bookslut.com

Soho Crime Display Special Offer

Eligible titles include:

By Jake Arnott
truecrime 978-1-56947-407-5 $12.00
By Cheryl Benard
Moghul Buffet 978-1-56947-179-1 $12.00
By Cara Black
Murder in Belleville 978-1-56947-279-8 $13.00
Murder in Clichy 978-1-56947-411-2 $12.00
Murder in Montmartre 978-1-56947-445-7 $12.00
Murder in the Bastille 978-1-56947-364-1 $13.00
Murder in the Marais 978-1-56947-212-5 $13.00
Murder in the Sentier 978-1-56947-331-3 $13.00
By Colin Cotterill
The Coroner's Lunch 978-1-56947-418-1 $11.00
Disco for the Departed 978-1-56947-464-8 $12.00
Thirty-Three Teeth 978-1-56947-429-7 $12.00
By Garry Disher
The Dragon Man 978-1-56947-395-5 $11.00
Kittyhawk Down 978-1-56947-427-3 $12.00
Snapshot 978-1-56947-460-0 $12.00
By Clare Francis
A Dark Devotion 978-1-56947-357-3 $14.00

By Stan Jones
Shaman Pass 978-1-56947-413-6 $11.00
White Sky, Black Ice 978-1-56947-333-7 $13.00
By Martin Limón
Buddha's Money 978-1-56947-399-3 $14.00
The Door to Bitterness 978-1-56947-435-8 $12.00
Jade Lady Burning 978-1-56947-020-6 $13.00
Slicky Boys 978-1-56947-385-6 $13.00
By Peter Lovesey
Bloodhounds 978-1-56947-377-1 $13.00
The Circle 978-1-56947-432-7 $13.00
Diamond Dust 978-1-56947-322-1 $13.00
Diamond Solitaire 978-1-56947-292-7 $13.00
The False Inspector Dew 978-1-56947-255-2 $12.00
The House Sitter 978-1-56947-361-0 $13.00
The Last Detective 978-1-56947-209-5 $13.00
The Reaper 978-1-56947-308-5 $12.00
The Summons 978-1-56947-360-3 $13.00
Upon a Dark Night 978-1-56947-393-1 $13.00
The Vault 978-1-56947-256-9 $13.00

Soho Press

Soho Crime Display Special Offer

Order 20 or more backlist and frontlist Soho Crime paperbacks at a 50% discount and receive a 24-copy freestanding Soho Crime display.

Soho Crime Marketing Fall/Winter 2007–2008

- National advertising includes:
  Mystery Scene, The New York Times
- Fall/Winter 2007–2008 Soho Crime Sampler
- Features in the Soho Crime Newsletter and in e-mail blasts
- Bookstore co-op is available
- BEA giveaways include: Soho Crime tote bags, bookmarks, shelf talkers, and samplers

By Seicho Matsumoto
Inspector Imanishi Investigates 978-1-56947-019-0 $13.00
By Magdalen Nabb
Death in Autumn 978-1-56947-296-5 $11.00
Death in Springtime 978-1-56947-415-0 $10.00
Death of an Englishman 978-1-56947-254-5 $12.00
The Innocent 978-1-56947-436-5 $12.00
The Marshal and the Madwoman 978-1-56947-340-5 $12.00
The Marshal and the Murderer 978-1-56947-297-2 $12.00
Property of Blood 978-1-56947-310-8 $12.00
Some Bitter Taste 978-1-56947-339-9 $12.00
By Rebecca Pawel
Death of a Nationalist 978-1-56947-344-3 $12.00
Law of Return 978-1-56947-380-1 $12.00
The Summer Snow 978-1-56947-443-3 $12.00
The Watcher in the Pine 978-1-56947-409-9 $12.00
By John Straley
The Curious Eat Themselves 978-1-56947-412-9 $12.00
The Woman Who Married a Bear 978-1-56947-401-3 $12.00

By Akimitsu Takagi
The Tattoo Murder Case 978-1-56947-156-2 $13.00
By Helene Tursten
Detective Inspector Huss 978-1-56947-370-2 $14.00
The Torso 978-1-56947-453-2 $13.00
By Janwillem van de Wetering
Amsterdam Cops 978-1-56947-210-1 $12.00
The Blond Baboon 978-1-56947-063-3 $12.00
The Corpse on the Dike 978-1-56947-049-7 $12.00
Hard Rain 978-1-56947-104-3 $12.00
The Japanese Corpse 978-1-56947-057-2 $12.00
Just a Corpse at Twilight 978-1-56947-075-6 $12.00
The Maine Massacre 978-1-56947-064-0 $12.00
Outsider in Amsterdam 978-1-56947-017-6 $12.00
By Timothy Watts
Cons 978-1-56947-034-3 $10.00
By Qiu Xiaolong
Death of a Red Heroine 978-1-56947-242-2 $14.00
A Loyal Character Dancer 978-1-56947-341-2 $13.00
When Red Is Black 978-1-56947-396-2 $13.00

Soho Press

Chinatown Beat
Henry Chang

Mystery
November
Soho Crime
5 x 7½ | 220 pp
TP US $12.00 | CAN $14.50
978-1-56947-478-5 CUSA

Marketing Plans

Co-op available
10,000-copy print run
National advertising:
Mystery Scene • The New York
Times Book Review

Author Hometown: New York, NY

"This is a nasty, terse slice of noir, and Yu is a fellow whose adventures should be worth following."—*The Washington Post Book World*

"For readers who relish noir suspense, it doesn't get much better than this stunning novel."—*The Boston Globe*

"It is an evocative, often bleak, but fascinating view of being at 'cross-cultural odds' that fuels *Chinatown Beat*, the successful debut by New York author Henry Chang."
—*South Florida Sun-Sentinel*

"*Chinatown Beat* is a classic noir, filled with longing, violence, and that uniquely urban melancholy, but it also brings something new to the table, a loving specificity of a people and place, the multicultures of New York's Chinatown, that has rarely if ever been encountered in fiction before. A real discovery."—Richard Price, author of *Freedomland* and *Clockers*

"An auspicious beginning."—*Richmond Times–Dispatch*

NYPD Detective Jack Yu was raised in Chinatown. Some of his old friends are criminals now; some are dead. Recently transferred to his old neighborhood, where 99 percent of the cops are white, Jack is confronted with a serial rapist who preys on young Chinese girls. Then Uncle Four, an elderly leader of the charitable Hip Ching Society and member of the Hong Kong-based Red Circle Triad, is gunned down. To solve these crimes, Jack turns to both modern police methods and an ancient fortune-teller.

Henry Chang was born and raised in New York City's Chinatown, where he now lives. He is a graduate of the Pratt Institute and the City College of New York and is currently a security director in Manhattan.

**A Chinese American detective takes on the
seedy underworld of New York City's Chinatown.**

Soho Press

The Wandering Ghost
Martin Limón

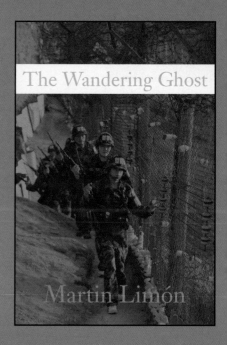

Praise for Martin Limón:

"Easily the best military mysteries in print today."—Lee Child

"It's great to have these two mavericks back. . . . Mr. Limón writes with . . . wonderful, bleak humor, edged in pain, about GI life."—*The New York Times Book Review*

"Limón's crisp, clear storytelling opens a door to another world and leaves one hoping the next installment won't be so long in arriving."—*The Baltimore Sun*

"Limón has the military lingo and ambience down to a T. Plot, pacing, and plausibility are just about perfect."—*The Philadelphia Inquirer* (editor's choice)

"As usual, Limón paints a picture of Korea in the mid-1970s that is so detailed and richly atmospheric that the reader's senses are flooded with the sounds, smells, and tastes of the place. Fans of the Sueño-Bascom series, who have been waiting eagerly for a new novel, can relax. It was well worth the wait."—*Booklist* (starred review)

The only female MP assigned to a base in the DMZ is missing. Has she been abducted, killed, or, possibly, gone AWOL? Eighth Army cops George Sueño and Ernie Bascom, sent to find her, discover a murder that has been concealed, rampant black marketeering and corruption, crooked officers, rioting Korean civilians, and the wandering ghost of a schoolgirl run down by a speeding army truck. It is up to them to right egregious wrongs while being pursued by criminals who want to kill them.

Martin Limón is the author of four earlier books in the Sueño-Bascom series. His debut, *Jade Lady Burning,* was a *New York Times* Notable Book.

Sueño and Bascom, seeking a missing female MP in the Korean DMZ, encounter a wandering ghost.

Mystery
November
Soho Crime
5 x 7½ | 320 pp
TC US $24.00 | CAN $29.00
978-1-56947-481-5 CUSA

Also Available

The Door to Bitterness
Martin Limón
Fiction / Mystery
5 x 7½ | 280 pp
TP US $12.00 | CAN $14.50
978-1-56947-435-8 CUSA

Jade Lady Burning
Martin Limón
Mystery
5 x 7½ | 224 pp
TP US $13.00 | CAN $15.95
978-1-56947-020-6 CUSA

Soho Press

Mystery
December
Soho Crime
5 x 7½ | 220 pp
TP US $12.00 | CAN $14.50
978-1-56947-482-2 CUSA

Marketing Plans

Co-op available
National advertising:
Mystery Scene •
The New York Times Book Review

Death of a Dutchman
Magdalen Nabb

Praise for the Marshal Guarnaccia series:

"This elegant series, which began in 1981 with *Death of an Englishman* . . . is set in Florence, a city that glows in the Tuscan sun. . . . [His] sense of estrangement accounts for Guarnaccia's special perspective on strangers, those 'innocents' among the living and the dead."—*The New York Times Book Review*

"Lean, elegant prose that surpasses the best of Simenon, along with a puckish view of the Florentines from Guarnaccia's Sicilian perspective."—*Kirkus Reviews*

"The richest mystery here, however, is Florence itself, whose intricate politics and class structure Nabb parses with precision and wit."—*The Washington Post*

"Great local atmosphere and rich characterizations."—*Publishers Weekly*

"A superb series. . . . A working-man's Maigret."—*Booklist*

"Crime fiction at its best."—*The Sunday Times* (London)

"Guarnaccia's Florence is a delightful place to visit."—*Mystery Scene*

Summoned by an aged woman to investigate mysterious noises in the vacant flat next to hers, Marshal Guarnaccia discovers a dying Dutch jeweler. The old lady had known him when he was a boy growing up in Florence. Could he have returned to the family home just to commit suicide? Or could the man be the victim of a cunning murderer?

Magdalen Nabb was born in Lancashire. She has lived in Florence since 1975 and has written twelve Marshal Guarnaccia mysteries. This is the second in the series.

Who would come to Florence just to kill himself?

Also Available

The Innocent
Magdalen Nabb
Mystery
5 x 8 | 256 pp
TP US $12.00 | CAN $14.50
978-1-56947-436-5 CUSA

Death in Springtime
Magdalen Nabb
Mystery
5 x 7½ | 156 pp
TP US $10.00 | CAN $12.00
978-1-56947-415-0 CUSA

Soho Press

Blood of the Wicked
Leighton Gage

"Terrifically written, intelligent, and powerfully evocative. . . . A not to be missed debut."—Brian Haig, author of *Man in the Middle*

"*Blood of the Wicked* manages to pack a huge amount into a spare three hundred pages; power politics, petty violence, sexual scandal, saintly courage, staggering poverty and obscene wealth. . . . This is a novel as rich and complex as Brazil itself, with villains who make you want to spit, and heroes whose goodness is heartbreaking." —Rebecca Pawel, Edgar Award-winning author of *Death of a Nationalist*

In the remote Brazilian town of Cascatas do Pontal, where landless peasants are confronting the owners of vast estates, the bishop arrives by helicopter to consecrate a new church and is assassinated. Mario Silva, chief inspector for criminal matters of the federal police of Brazil, is dispatched to the interior to find the killer. The pope himself has called Brazil's president; the pressure is on Silva to perform. Silva must battle the state police and a corrupt judiciary as well as criminals who prey on street kids, the warring factions of the Landless League, the big landowners, and the church itself, in order to solve the initial murder and several brutal killings that follow. Here is a Brazil that tourists never encounter.

Leighton Gage is married to a Brazilian woman and spends part of each year in Santana do Parnaiba, Brazil, and the rest of the year in Florida and Belgium. This is his first novel.

Inspector Mario Silva investigates a series of gory murders in Brazil.

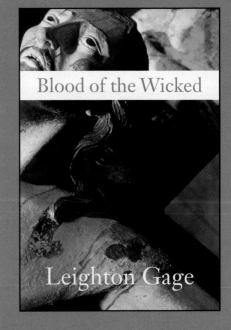

Mystery
January
Soho Crime
5 x 7½ | 304 pp
TC US $24.00 | CAN $29.00
978-1-56947-470-9 CUSA

Marketing Plans

Co-op available
Advance reader copies
15,000-copy print run
National advertising:
Mystery Scene • The New York
Times Book Review

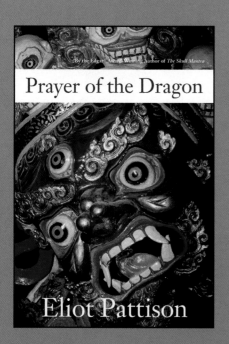

Prayer of the Dragon
Eliot Pattison

Mystery
December
Soho Crime
5 x 7½ | 396 pp
TC US $24.00 | CAN $29.00
978-1-56947-479-2 CUSA

Marketing Plans

Co-op available
Advance reader copies
15,000-copy print run

Author Hometown: Philadelphia, PA

Praise for the Shan series:

"Nothing I've read or seen about how China has systematically crushed the soul of Tibet has been as effective. . . . A thriller of laudable aspirations and achievements."—*Chicago Tribune*

"Shan becomes our Don Quixote. . . . Set against a background that is alternately bleak and blazingly beautiful, this is at once a top-notch thriller and a substantive look at Tibet under siege."—*Publishers Weekly* (starred review)

"A rich and multilayered story that mirrors the complexity of the surrounding land."—*San Francisco Chronicle*

"Pattison thrills both mystery enthusiasts and readers fascinated by, and concerned about, Tibet."—*Booklist*

"Pattison has taken an unknown world and made it come alive."—*Library Journal*

Summoned to a remote village from the hidden lamasery where he lives, Shan, formerly an investigator in Beijing, must save a comatose man from execution for two murders in which the victims' arms have been removed. Upon arrival, he discovers that the suspect is not Tibetan but Navajo. The man has come with his niece to seek ancestral ties between their people and the ancient Bon. The recent murders are only part of a chain of deaths. Together with his friends, the monks Gendun and Lokesh, Shan solves the riddle of Dragon Mountain, the place "where world begins."

Eliot Pattison is an international lawyer based near Philadelphia. His four previous Shan novels, set in Tibet, are *The Skull Mantra* (which won the Edgar Award for Best First Novel), *Water Touching Stone*, *Bone Mountain*, and *Beautiful Ghosts*.

The fifth mystery in this Edgar Award-winning series set in Tibet.

Soho Press

A Grave in Gaza

Matt Beynon Rees

Praise for the Omar Yussef series:

"An astonishing first novel."—*The New York Times Book Review*

"*The Collaborator of Bethlehem* is readable and literate, and offers a vivid portrait of Palestinian life today."—*The Washington Post*

"Matt Beynon Rees has taken a complex world of culture clash and suspicion and placed upon it humanity."—David Baldacci, author of *The Collectors*

"Omar's probe of a West Bank ruled by political intrigue, religious hatred, and militia thugs lets ex-*TIME* Jerusalem Bureau Chief Rees make the Mideast conflict personal."—*Entertainment Weekly*

"*The Collaborator of Bethlehem* is the best—and the rarest—sort of mystery: exciting and compelling, but it is also a deeply moving story that will, for many readers, shed much needed light on the conditions in the Palestinian territories."—David Liss, author of *The Ethical Assassin* and *A Conspiracy of Paper*

"An evocative, compassionate tale."—*San Francisco Chronicle*

"Rees's book vividly captures the fabric of daily Palestinian life."—*The Boston Globe*

As he tries to save the lives of two men, Omar Yussef is confronted with the corruption and violence of Gaza's warring government factions and the criminal gangs with which they are connected.

Matt Beynon Rees was born in South Wales. He was previously the Jerusalem bureau chief for *TIME* magazine, where he is currently a contributor. He is the author of one previous mystery in the Omar Yussef series, *The Collaborator of Bethlehem*, and the nonfiction work *Cain's Field: Faith, Fratricide, and Fear in the Middle East.* He lives in Jerusalem.

In Gaza, death lurks around every corner.

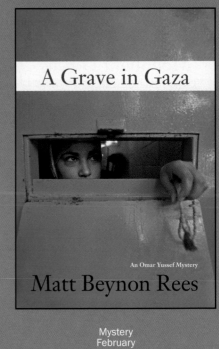

Mystery
February
Soho Crime
5 x 7½ | 368 pp
TC US $24.00 | CAN $29.00
978-1-56947-472-3 CUSA

Marketing Plans

Co-op available
Advance reader copies
20,000-copy print run
National advertising:
Mystery Scene • The New York
Times Book Review

Moonlight Downs

Adrian Hyland

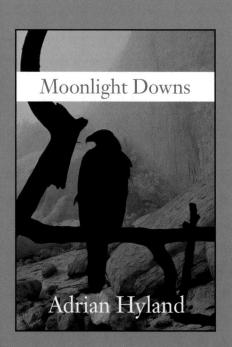

Mystery
February
Soho Crime
5 x 7½ | 304 pp
TC US $24.00 | CAN $29.00
978-0-93914-483-9 CUSA

Marketing Plans

Co-op available
Advance reader copies
12.000-copy print run
National advertising:
Mystery Scene • The New York
Times Book Review

"A hymn to the wit, courage, stark beauty and power of the dreaming of a unique people. One cannot help but be enriched by it."—Anne Perry

"Packs a real wallop. . . . An epic and ambitious mystery set against the vast backdrop of Central Australia, where indigenous and white people live side by side in an uneasy truce."—*Vogue* (Australia)

"Incorporates geophysical data, race politics and aboriginal spirituality into a seamless, often hilarious stream of narrative. [It] has all the hallmarks of a first of a very successful series with the potential to forge a new sub-genre of detective fiction—that of a feisty, female indigenous sleuth whose intelligence and tenacity prove superior to force and ignorance."—*The Sydney Morning Herald*

"Witty, knowing, at times downright hilarious. The plot is absorbing and Hyland's characters are originals. . . . As Emily Tempest untangles the knot of a murder, she also comes to rediscover her past, her belonging and her self."—*Brisbane Courier Mail*

Emily Tempest, a feisty part-aboriginal woman, left home to get an education and has since traveled abroad. She returns to visit the Moonlight Downs "mob," still uncertain if she belongs in the aboriginal world or that of the whitefellers. Within hours of her arrival, an old friend is murdered and mutilated. The police suspect a rogue aborigine, but Emily starts asking questions. Emily Tempest, a modern half-aboriginal sleuth, is a welcome successor to Arthur Upfield's classic detective.

Adrian Hyland worked with aboriginal communities in Central Australia for ten years. He now teaches at LaTrobe University in Melbourne. This is his first novel.

Half Australian aborigine, half white, Emily Tempest sees her worlds collide when an old friend is murdered.

Soho Press

Murder on the Ile Saint-Louis
Cara Black

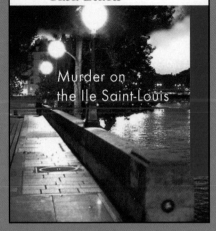

"If its expert plotting and intense characterizations aren't enough, the book is absolutely drenched with the sights, sounds, and smells of Paris and will certainly be treasured by every Francophile lucky enough to read it."—*The Denver Post*

"Gripping. . . . A wonderfully complex plot is lent immediacy by environmental activists agitating against a proposed oil agreement. . . . This Paris has a gritty, edgy feel, and Black's prose evokes the sound of the Seine rising with the spring thaw. Aimée makes an engaging protagonist."—*Publishers Weekly* (starred review)

"Another taut, well-observed, and thoroughly entertaining Aimée Leduc mystery." —*Library Journal*

"Must reading for fans of the jauntier side of European crime fiction."—*Booklist*

Facing a tight deadline on a computer security contract, Aimée responds to a telephone call from a stranger that leads her to an abandoned infant in a courtyard on the Ile Saint-Louis. She brings the baby home with her, calls her Stella, and awaits contact from the mother. But days pass, and no one reclaims the infant.

Meanwhile, a group of environmental protestors is trying to stop the government from entering into a contract with an oil company notorious for pollution. As Aimée attempts to identify the baby's mother, two murders and an abortive bombing involving the protestors lead her—and little Stella—into danger.

On the run in the sewers beneath the Seine, Aimée finally finds the woman she has been looking for, only to discover that the man she has fallen in love with is not who she thought he was.

Aimée Leduc must solve two murders while caring for an abandoned infant.

Mystery
March
Soho Crime
5 x 7½ | 304 pp
TP US $12.00 | CAN $14.50
978-0-93914-475-4 CUSA

Marketing Plans

Co-op available
10,000-copy print run
National advertising:
Mystery Scene • The New York
Times Book Review

Author Hometown: San Francisco, CA

**Also
Available**

Murder in Montmartre
Cara Black
Mystery
5 x 8 | 368 pp
TP US $12.00 | CAN $14.50
978-1-56947-445-7 CUSA

Murder in Clichy
Cara Black
Mystery
5 x 7½ | 320 pp
TP US $12.00 | CAN $14.50
978-1-56947-411-2 CUSA

Soho Press

Murder in the Rue de Paradis
Cara Black

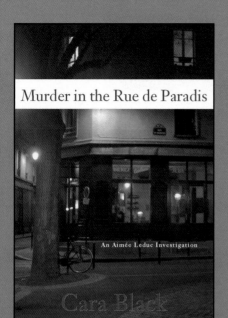

Mystery
March
Soho Crime
5 x 7½ | 288 pp
TC US $24.00 | CAN $29.00
978-1-56947-474-7 CUSA

Marketing Plans

Co-op available
Advance reader copies
12,500-copy print run
National advertising:
Mystery Scene • The New York
Times Book Review

Author Hometown: San Francisco, CA

Praise for the Aimée Leduc series set in Paris:

"Compelling. . . . Aimée makes an engaging protagonist, vulnerable beneath her vintage chic clothing and sharp-witted exterior."—*Publishers Weekly* (starred review)

"Charming. . . . Aimée is one of those blithe spirits who can walk you through the city's historical streets and byways with their eyes closed."—*The New York Times Book Review*

"The buzz is partly about her heroine's hip, next-generation, cutting-edge investigations and partly about Paris, a setting of unrivaled charm."—*Houston Chronicle*

"Cara Black books are good companions. . . . Fine characters, good suspense, but, best of all, they are transcendentally, seductively, irresistibly French. If you can't go, these will do fine. Or, better yet, go and bring them with you."—Alan Furst

"Conveys vividly those layers of history that make the stones of Paris sing for so many of us."—*Chicago Tribune*

"If you've always wanted to visit Paris, skip the air fare and read Cara Black . . . instead."—Val McDermid

Aimée is thrilled when her one-time lover, Yves, an investigative journalist, returns from his assignment in Egypt and proposes marriage. But after a single night of bliss, his body is discovered in a Paris doorway. His throat has been slit. Aimée is determined to avenge him. The trail leads to a sleeper jihadist and embroils her in Turkish and Kurdish politics.

Cara Black is a frequent visitor to Paris; this is her eighth mystery set there. She lives in San Francisco with her husband and son.

Aimée Leduc loses her man to an assassin's blade.

**Also
Available**

Murder in Montmartre
Cara Black
Mystery
5 x 8 | 368 pp
TP US $12.00 | CAN $14.50
978-1-56947-445-7 CUSA

Murder in Clichy
Cara Black
Mystery
5 x 7½ | 320 pp
TP US $12.00 | CAN $14.50
978-1-56947-411-2 CUSA

Soho Press

Heat
How to Stop the Planet From Burning
George Monbiot

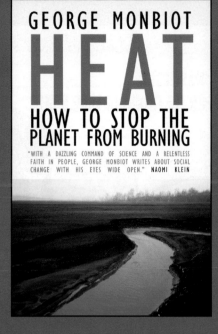

"A dazzling command of science and a relentless faith in people."—Naomi Klein

"The most powerful treatise yet on the gravity of global warming. . . . I defy you to read this book and not feel motivated to change."—*The Times* (London)

"If you care about the future of the planet, you should read *Heat,* and then give a copy to a friend."—Elizabeth Kolbert

Today virtually none of us ask, *Is climate change actually happening?* Only one question is worth asking: *Can it be stopped?*

George Monbiot thinks it can. And with *Heat: How to Stop the Planet From Burning,* he offers us a book that just might save our world.

For the first time, *Heat* demonstrates that we *can* achieve the necessary cut—a 90 percent reduction in carbon emissions by 2030—without bringing civilization to an end. Though he writes with a "spirit of optimism," Monbiot does not pretend it will be easy. Our response will have to be immediate, and it will have to be decisive.

With dazzling intellect and ample wit, Monbiot supports his proposals with a rigorous investigation into what works, what doesn't, how much it costs, and what the problems might be. And he is not afraid to attack anyone—friend or foe—whose claims are false or whose figures have been fudged.

There is no time to waste. Monbiot observes, "We are the last generation that can make this happen, and this is the last possible moment at which we can make it happen."

George Monbiot is one of the world's most influential thinkers. Nelson Mandela presented Monbiot with a United Nations Global 500 Award for outstanding environmental achievement. He is a weekly columnist for the *Guardian.*

A brilliant and terrifying book that forces us to move beyond denial and into action.

Environmental Studies / Current Affairs
Available Now
5⅜ x 8½ | 304 pp
10 B&W illustrations
TC $22.00
978-0-89608-779-8 USA

South End Press

Environmental Studies / Current Affairs
October
A Paperback Original
5 x 7 | 136 pp
TP US $10.00 | CAN $12.00
978-0-89608-777-4 CUSA

Marketing Plans

Advance reader copies
10,000-copy print run
National advertising:
E: The Environmental Magazine •
The Ecologist • Mother Jones • Utne •
Vegetarian Times

Manifestos on the Future of Food and Seed
Edited by Vandana Shiva

"Shiva is a burst of creative energy, an intellectual power."—*The Progressive*

Manifestos on the Future of Food and Seed is a short, pocket-sized collection that goes to the heart of our existence—what we eat and how we grow it.

We live in a world where of the eighty thousand edible plants used for food, only about 150 are being cultivated, and just eight are traded globally. A world where we produce food for 12 billion people when there are only 6.3 billion people living, and still, 800 million suffer from malnutrition and 1.7 billion suffer from obesity. A world where food is modified to travel long distances rather than to be nutritious and flavorful.

Manifestos on the Future of Food and Seed lays out, in practical steps and far-reaching concepts, a program to ensure food and agriculture become more socially and ecologically sustainable. The book harvests the work and ideas produced by thousands of communities around the world. Emerging from the historic gatherings at Terra Madre, farmers, traders, and activists diagnose and offer prescriptions to reverse perhaps the worst food crisis faced in human history.

There is a growing realization that food politics is vital to the health of our bodies, economies, and environment—in other words, a matter of life or death. Carlo Petrini, founder of Slow Food, writes, "Reinstating food as a central, primary element in our lives seems an obvious thing to do, since without food, no living things would exist." Thousands of communities around the world are working to do just this.

A world-renowned environmental leader and thinker, **Vandana Shiva** is the author of many books, including *Earth Democracy, Stolen Harvest,* and *Staying Alive. Manifestos* includes essays by Prince Charles and Carlo Petrini.

An urgent call to strengthen and unify the movements to save seeds, food, and our future.

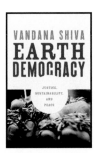

Also Available

Earth Democracy
Justice, Sustainability, and Peace
Vandana Shiva
Environmental Studies / Women's Studies
5⅜ x 8½ | 224 pp
TP US $15.00 | CAN $18.00
978-0-89608-745-3 CUSA

Stolen Harvest
The Hijacking of the Global Food Supply
Vandana Shiva
Science
5⅜ x 8½ | 152 pp
TP US $14.00 | CAN $17.00
978-0-89608-607-4 CUSA

South End Press

Getting Off
Pornography and the End of Masculinity
Robert Jensen

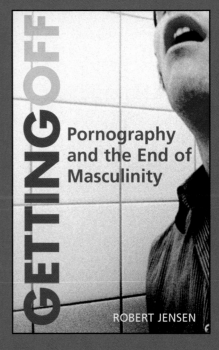

"Jensen's brutally honest assessment of the increasingly pornographic world has never been more difficult to face, or more necessary."—Gail Dines, co-editor of *Gender, Race, and Class in Media*

"Agree or disagree with his analyses or conclusions, but this brave book challenges men—and women—to face this crucial and sometimes painful subject with courage and hope. "—Jackson Katz, author of *The Macho Paradox: Why Some Men Hurt Women and How All Men Can Help*

"Expertly combining 'the personal' with 'the political,' Robert Jensen exposes the shocking misogyny of today's pornography and forces us to face the ugliness of American masculinity. A wake-up call to men and women alike."—Sonali Kolhatkar, host of Pacifica Radio's *Uprising*

Pornography is big business—a multi-billion dollar industry. It also makes for complicated politics. Anti-pornography arguments are frequently dismissed as patently "anti-sex"—and ultimately "anti-feminist"—silencing at the gate a critical discussion of pornography's relationship to violence against women and even what it means to be a "real man."

In his most personal and difficult book to date, Robert Jensen launches a powerful critique of mainstream pornography that promises to reignite one of the fiercest debates in contemporary feminism. At once alarming and thought-provoking, *Getting Off* asks tough but crucial questions about pornography, manhood, and paths toward genuine social justice.

Robert Jensen is the author of *The Heart of Whiteness: Confronting Race, Racism, and White Privilege* and *Citizens of the Empire: The Struggle to Claim Our Humanity*. He is an associate professor in the School of Journalism at the University of Texas, Austin.

Does porn make the man?

Gender Studies / Sexuality
September
A Paperback Original
5⅜ x 8½ | 200 pp
TP US $12.00 | CAN $14.50
978-0-89608-776-7 CUSA

Marketing Plans

Advance reader copies
White Box
BEA Author Signing
National advertising:
Bitch • BUST • ColorLines •
The Indypendent • Ms. Magazine •
The Nation • Utne

Author Hometown: Austin, TX

South End Press

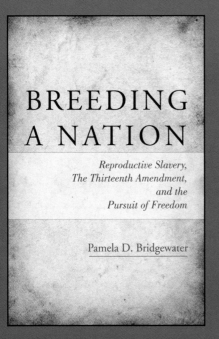

Women's Studies / African American Studies
February
A Paperback Original
5⅜ x 8½ | 220 pp
2 B&W illustrations
TP US $18.00 | CAN $21.95
978-0-89608-778-1 CUSA

Marketing Plans

Advance reader copies
National advertising:
Ms. Magazine • The Nation

Author Hometown: Washington, DC

Breeding a Nation
Reproductive Slavery, the Thirteenth Amendment, and the Pursuit of Freedom
Pamela D. Bridgewater

Law professor and activist Pamela D. Bridgewater argues that the lawmakers who wrote the Thirteenth Amendment with the intent of ending slavery understood that human breeding—forcing women to have babies—was a central element of slavery. Knowing that it was politically dangerous to name reproductive slavery in the amendment, they framed it with enough scope to restrain the government from ever again requiring women to give birth or preventing them from doing so.

In other words, to limit or completely take away reproductive freedom is not only unconstitutional—it reinstitutes slavery.

Breeding a Nation explores a much-denied episode in US history—the deliberate "growing" of humans as a crop for sale. In 2008, two hundred years will have passed since the transatlantic slave trade was outlawed—ironically a victory that caused massive escalation in reproductive coercion. Once the flow of Africans to the United States was cut off, the only way to maintain the economy was to aggressively, even systematically, breed new "slaves" from the men and women already enslaved here. Some plantations even stopped growing crops so they could focus entirely on slave-breeding. In essence, slave-breeding became a vital feeder industry for agribusiness, and the massive wealth it produced undergirds America's position as a global superpower in the world today.

A must-read for activists and academics interested in civil rights, reproductive rights, and reparations. *Breeding a Nation* shows us firsthand how to evoke history to change the laws governing our reproductive lives. Bridgewater's arguments will invigorate legal, women's, and black studies for years to come.

What does the Thirteenth Amendment, intended to abolish slavery, have to do with reproductive rights? Everything!

South End Press

King for a Day
Erin Feinberg

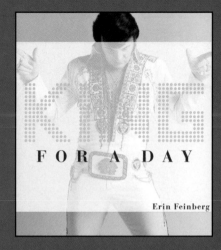

Thirty years after Elvis Presley "left the building," his music and American-icon prominence live on through his legions of past, present, and future fans. Among those devotees who stand out as brightly as Elvis' studded jumpsuits are the impersonators.

Through a deeply personal photographic study, Erin Feinberg focuses on the diverse range of culture, fashion, and persona that Elvis impersonators embrace. By means of one-on-one studio sessions and interviews, *King for a Day* captures the individuals behind the Elvis façade, coaxing from them their personal connection to Elvis, how they came to this form of entertainment, and how this aspect of their life completes them.

Erin Feinberg is a New York City-based freelance photographer whose clients include *Rolling Stone*, PBS, Sipa Press, *Gibson Guitar*, and *The New York Times*, among others. She also works on long-term documentary projects and portrait photography where, both stylistically and emotionally, she continues to show a strong humanistic connection with her subject matter.

August 16 will be the thirtieth anniversary of Elvis' death.

Music / Photography
September
10½ x 11½ | 192 pp
100 Color photographs
TC US $40.00 | CAN $42.00
978-1-933108-14-8 CUSA

Marketing Plans

Co-op available

Author Hometown: New York, NY

Absinthe: Sip of Seduction, A Contemporary Guide
Second Edition
Betina Wittels and Robert Hermesch
Edited by T.A. Breaux

The consumption and enticement of absinthe are not desirous relics of the past. There is a vibrant and devoted contemporary scene focused exclusively on the notorious "green fairy."

Authors Betina Wittels, Robert Hermesch, and T.A. Breaux, all absinthe connoisseurs, have updated their highly acclaimed book with a further-explored historical section, new absinthe reviews to tantalize imbibers, sidebars peeking into various absinthe subcultures, stunning new imagery from both past and present, and more.

For anyone looking to begin their absinthe journey, or those who've been on the path for some time now, this book is a must for all things absinthe.

Betina Wittels is an antiques dealer with a world-renowned specialty in *fin de siècle* French glassware and absinthe spoons. Wittels also has a master's degree in family psychotherapy.

Robert Hermesch is a clinical social worker currently residing in Boston, Massachusetts. In addition to sipping historic libations, Hermesch enjoys studying Eastern philosophy, watching the Red Sox, and listening to the Grateful Dead.

T.A. Breaux is a professional scientist who has perfected the technique of reconstructing the most famous original brands of absinthe. Breaux is also the founder of the Société International d'Absinthe, a worldwide absinthe-connoisseurs organization.

The best-selling absinthe book on the market, entirely updated with fresh content and imagery.

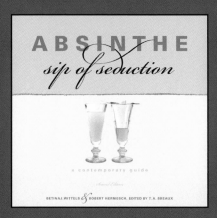

Cookbooks & Cookery / Popular Culture
November
9 x 8½ | 144 pp
200 Color and B&W illustrations and photographs
TP US $22.00 | CAN $26.50
978-1-933108-15-5 CUSA

Marketing Plans

Co-op available

Author Events

Tucson, AZ • New Orleans, LA • Boston, MA

Author Hometown: Tucson, AZ

Speck Press

DeKok and the Somber Nude
A.C. Baantjer

"There are touches of the 87th Precinct, Maigret and Janwillem van de Wetering, but Baantjer is in a category all his own."—*The Globe and Mail*

This latest installment of the internationally popular Inspector DeKok series finds the gray sleuth dealing with a most gruesome murder.

The oldest of the four men turned to DeKok, "You're from homicide?"

DeKok nodded. The seasoned inspector wiped the raindrops from his face, bent down gingerly, and carefully lifted a corner of the canvas. Slowly the head became visible: a severed girl's head. DeKok felt the blood drain from his face, his stomach turning into an icy cold pit. "Is that all you found?" he asked.

"A little farther," the man answered with sad disbelief, "is the rest."

Spread out among the dirt and refuse were the remaining parts of the body: the arms, the long, slender legs, and the petite torso. There was no clothing.

DeKok faces death as an inevitable part of life, but when things turn this macabre, it's a hard reality to stomach.

A.C. Baantjer is the most widely read author in the Netherlands. He is a former detective inspector of the Amsterdam police, and his fictional characters reflect the depth and personality of individuals encountered during his nearly forty-year career in law enforcement.

Reviewers agree that this police procedural series is one of the strongest currently being published.

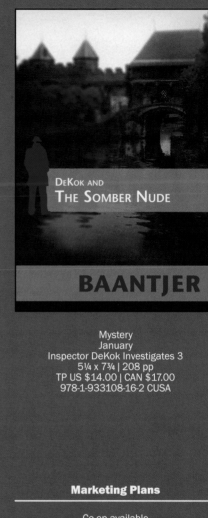

Mystery
January
Inspector DeKok Investigates 3
5¼ x 7¾ | 208 pp
TP US $14.00 | CAN $17.00
978-1-933108-16-2 CUSA

Marketing Plans

Co-op available
Advance reader copies

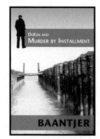

Also Available

DeKok and the Death of a Clown
A.C. Baantjer
Mystery
5¼ x 7¾ | 252 pp
TP US $14.00 | CAN $17.00
978-1-933108-03-2 CUSA

DeKok and Murder by Installment
A.C. Baantjer
Mystery
5¼ x 7¾ | 208 pp
TP US $14.00 | CAN $17.00
978-1-933108-07-0 CUSA

Follies of Science
20th Century Visions of Our
Fantastic Future
Eric Dregni and Jonathan Dregni

Science / Popular Culture
9 x 8½ | 128 pp
112 Color and B&W photographs
and illustrations
TP US $19.00 | CAN $23.00
978-1-933108-09-4 CUSA

Django Reinhardt
and the Illustrated History
of Gypsy Jazz
**Michael Dregni, Alain Antonietto,
and Anne Legrand**

Music / Biography & Autobiography
9 x 8½ | 208 pp
200 Color and B&W illustrations
and photographs
TP US $25.00 | CAN $30.00
978-1-933108-10-0 CUSA

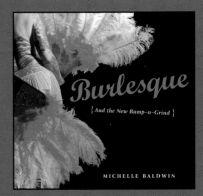

Burlesque and the
New Bump-n-Grind
Michelle Baldwin

Performing Arts
9 x 8½ | 160 pp
160 Color and B&W photographs
TP US $22.95 | CAN $27.50
978-0-9725776-2-5 CUSA

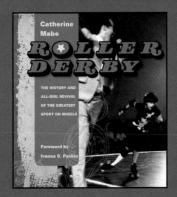

Roller Derby
The History and All-Girl Revival of the
Greatest Sport on Wheels
Catherine Mabe

Sports & Recreation / Cultural Studies
7 x 7¾ | 160 pp
100 Color and B&W illustrations
and photographs
TP US $18.00 | CAN $21.95
978-1-933108-11-7 CUSA

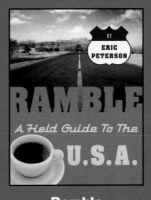

Ramble
A Field Guide to the U.S.A.
Eric Peterson

Travel & Travel Guides
5¼ x 7¾ | 232 pp
100 Color and B&W photographs
TP US $18.00 | CAN $21.95
978-1-933108-08-7 CUSA

Scooters
Red Eyes, Whitewalls &
Blue Smoke
Colin Shattuck with Eric Peterson

Transportation / Cultural Studies
9 x 8½ | 144 pp
120 Color and B&W photographs
TP US $22.00 | CAN $26.50
978-0-9725776-3-2 CUSA

The Astro Boy Essays
Osamu Tezuka, Mighty Atom, and the Manga/Anime Revolution
Frederik L. Schodt

The pioneering genius of Japan's "god of manga," Osamu Tezuka (1928–1989), is examined through his life's masterwork: *Tetsuwan Atomu,* also known as *Mighty Atom* or *Astro Boy,* a comic series featuring a cute little android who yearns to be more human. The history of *Tetsuwan Atomu* and Tezuka's role in it is a road map to understanding the development of new media in Japan and the United States. Topics include Tezuka's life, the art of animation, the connection between fantasy robots and technology, spin-offs, and *Astro Boy*'s cultural impact.

Frederik L. Schodt is a translator and author of numerous books about Japan, including *Manga! Manga!* and *Dreamland Japan.* He often served as Osamu Tezuka's English interpreter.

Marketing Plans
Co-op available

Author Events
San Francisco, CA

Author Hometown: San Francisco, CA

Film & TV / Popular Culture
September
A Paperback Original
5⅜ x 7¾ | 248 pp
40 Color and B&W illustrations
and photographs
TP US $16.95 | CAN $20.50
978-1-933330-54-9 CUSA

A tribute to Japan's "god of manga" by his longtime American friend and translator.

Democracy with a Gun
America and the Policy of Force
Fumio Matsuo

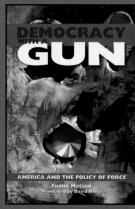

Drawing on the author's experiences growing up in wartime Japan and his forty years covering the United States, *Democracy with a Gun* traces America's current position as the world's sole superpower. Discussions of influential American leaders, the Second Amendment, the Civil War, the dropping of the atomic bomb, the wars in Vietnam and Iraq, and aggressive foreign policies suggest a nation willing to act unilaterally to secure, and impose, its lofty goals of peace and freedom. This timely and important work offers a perspective from abroad rarely provided by the usual media pundits.

Fumio Matsuo, who was Kyodo News Service's bureau chief in Washington, is one of Japan's best-known international journalists.

Author Events
San Francisco, CA

Current Affairs /
Political Science & Government
September
6 x 9 | 306 pp
TC US $26.00 | CAN $36.00
978-1-933330-46-4 CUSA

A foreign journalist's inside look at American culture and history via its use of violence.

Stone Bridge Press

Kyoto
The Forest within the Gate
Photographs by John Einarsen

Photography / Travel & Travel Guides
September
A Paperback Original
7 x 8¾ | 128 pp
70 Duotone photographs
TP US $19.95 | CAN $24.00
978-1-933330-50-1 CUSA

For those who have been touched by the magic of Kyoto.

Over a thousand years old, Kyoto is a city of many layers that are often simultaneously exposed like the geological formations in a long-weathered cliff. This book is a collection of personal encounters, moments, and scenes of Kyoto that have touched the author through the years.

Duotone photographs of temples, landscapes, gardens, and people represent an essential vocabulary of Kyoto that has evolved over centuries through the interplay of culture, climate, and topography. This collection includes contributions by leading Kyoto writers Marc Peter Keane, Edith Shiffert, Diane Durston, and Preston Houser.

John Einarsen is the founding editor and art director of the award-winning *Kyoto Journal*.

The Little Tokyo Subway Guidebook
Everything You Need to Know to Get Around the City and Beyond
Edited by IBC Publishing

Travel & Travel Guides
September
A Paperback Original
IBC Books
4⅛ x 5⅞ | 96 pp
75 Color illustrations
TP US $9.95 | CAN $12.00
978-4-89684-457-3 CUSA

This handy, color-coded guide for tourists makes getting around Tokyo fast and easy.

This handy book was prepared with the official cooperation of Tokyo Metro and the Tokyo Metropolitan Bureau of Transportation to help readers confidently navigate the convenient but complicated Tokyo subway system. Included are color-coded diagrams of all thirteen Tokyo subway lines; information on ticketing, tourist fares, and commuter passes; a landmark finder; an exit finder; and full-color maps that include national railway, Yokohama, and airport connections. Also included are useful words and phrases, a guide to signs, and where to go for help. Concise and thoroughly up to date, this is the one book readers will want for getting around.

Stone Bridge Press

Design Japan
50 Creative Years with the Good Design Awards
Edited by JIDPO

For fifty years, the Good Design Award has been Japan's most coveted achievement for excellence and innovation in industrial design. After introducing the design philosophies, histories, and cutting-edge products of twenty leading Japanese companies—including Sony, Panasonic, Toyota, Yamaha, Muji, and Shiseido—*Design Japan* explores how Japanese businesses and the Good Design Award have evolved together to meet changing tastes.

Included are the works of one hundred past Good Design Award winners and essays by leading designers and architects like Naoto Fukazawa and Kengo Kuma. This full-color volume was produced by the Japan Industrial Design Promotion Organization (JIDPO) to commemorate the fiftieth anniversary of the Good Design Awards.

Design
September
A Paperback Original
10⅛ x 10⅛ | 228 pp
400 Color photographs
TP US $29.95 | CAN $36.00
978-1-933330-48-8 CUSA

How "Made in Japan" became "Designed in Japan," showcasing the best work of today's top designers.

Travels in the East
Donald Richie
Introduction by Stephen Mansfield

Donald Richie's newest collection of travel essays explores all the corners of Asia and slightly beyond as it sweeps through Egypt, India, Bhutan, Mongolia, China, Laos, Cambodia, Vietnam, Borneo, Thailand, Yap, and Japan. Richie is an observer and wanderer, reveling in the freedom to not be himself but always aware of his role as an outsider. Similar to his other works, there remains a sense that these landscapes, cultures, and delights will soon be no more.

Donald Richie is a film critic, the foremost explorer of Japanese culture in English, and the author of the acclaimed travel diary/novel *The Inland Sea*.

Author Events
New York, NY

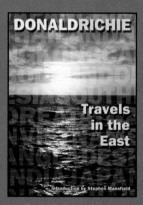

Travel & Travel Guides
September
A Paperback Original
5¼ x 7¼ | 160 pp
1 Map
TP US $14.95 | CAN $18.00
978-1-933330-61-7 CUSA

Adventures and contemplations throughout the world by a master storyteller, critic, and expatriate writer.

Stone Bridge Press

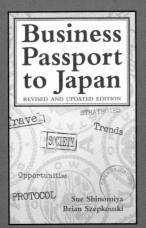

Travel & Travel Guides /
Business & Economics
October
5 x 8 | 248 pp
6 B&W illustrations
TP US $14.95 | CAN $18.00
978-1-933330-47-1 CUSA

A fresh, interactive approach to working in twenty-first century Japan, filled with insight and examples.

Business Passport to Japan
Revised and Updated Edition
Sue Shinomiya and Brian Szepkouski

This updated guide offers a fresh, interactive approach to doing business in Japan by presenting practical tips in an easy-to-read format. It goes beyond the logistical details of meetings, courtesy, and protocol to uncover the thought processes and cultural values behind the behaviors and situations readers may encounter— especially those that are changing as Japan's "blue suit" corporate culture gives way to a younger, laid-back, and more Internet-savvy workforce. Throughout the guide, readers are encouraged to take the long view to develop lasting successes. Indispensable for newcomers and veterans alike.

Sue Shinomiya (Portland, Oregon) and Brian Szepkouski (New York City area) are consultants with extensive experience working in Japan.

Marketing Plans
Co-op available

Author Hometown: Portland, OR/New York, NY

Film & TV / Asian Studies
November
A Paperback Original
6 x 9 | 340 pp
20 B&W photographs
TP US $22.95 | CAN $27.50
978-1-933330-53-2 CUSA

For film lovers and scholars, an essential resource and reference guide.

A Critical Handbook of Japanese Film Directors
From the Silent Era to the Present Day
Alexander Jacoby
Foreword by Donald Richie

This important work fills the need for a reasonably priced yet comprehensive volume on major directors in the history of Japanese film. With clear insight and without academic jargon, Alexander Jacoby examines the works of over 150 filmmakers to uncover what makes their films worth watching.

Included are artistic profiles of everyone from Yutaka Abe to Isao Yukisada, including masters like Kinji Fukasaku, Juzo Itami, Akira Kurosawa, Takashi Miike, Kenji Mizoguchi, Yasujiro Ozu, and Yoji Yamada. Each entry includes a critical summary and filmography, making this book an essential reference and guide.

UK-based Alexander Jacoby is a writer and researcher on Japanese film.

Stone Bridge Press

The Stone Bridge Book of Everyday Kanji
Japanese Character Reference and Writing Guide
Edited by Stone Bridge Press

Anyone studying written Japanese will welcome this comprehensive guide to all 1,945 characters designated for "daily use" (*Joyo Kanji*) in newspapers, magazines, and other common reading materials. Each kanji is presented with clear stroke-by-stroke writing instructions as well as meanings, *onyomi/kunyomi* readings, usage examples, radical classifiers, cross-references, and tips to help readers learn and remember. Also included is an introduction to the written language and multiple indexes to locate every character by stroke count, reading, or radical. An essential first text for beginners, as well as a durable reference for intermediate and advanced students.

Foreign Language Reference
October
A Paperback Original
4¾ x 7 | 800 pp
TP US $18.95 | CAN $20.50
978-1-933330-49-5 CUSA

All 1,945 Japanese characters adopted for daily use, for learning and reference.

Japanese Beyond Words
The Gaijin's Guide to Verbal Skills and Cultural Clues
Andrew Horvat

This new edition of *Japanese Beyond Words* takes the language student into the nonverbal skill zones that must be mastered to communicate effectively in Japanese. Now with an index and expanded chapters, it outlines the ins and outs of polite/rude speech, bowing, disagreeing, intonation, apologies, slang, preconceptions of foreigners, and much more.

Andrew Horvat lives in Tokyo. Formerly a reporter for the Associated Press, Tokyo correspondent for the *Los Angeles Times,* and Tokyo bureau chief for American Public Radio, he is now a visiting professor at Tokyo Keizai University and lecturer at Showa Women's University, where he teaches courses on cross-cultural communication and language policy.

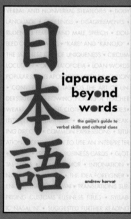

Foreign Language Reference / Asian Studies
November
5½ x 8½ | 200 pp
TP US $16.95 | CAN $20.50
978-1-933330-52-5 CUSA

A knowledge-based approach for students looking to speak—and listen—well.

China Fever
Fascination, Fear, and the World's Next Superpower
Frank Fang

China is poised to be the world's next superpower, but do we really understand what is happening there or what the repercussions of its ascendance could be? In engaging, accessible language, Frank Fang provides a unique insider's look at the fundamental issues faced by China and the West. By exploring key situations and conflicts embroiled in economic, political, and cultural relations, *China Fever* paves the way for understanding China's rapid acceleration onto the world stage.

Frank Fang, an economist, is the director of the International Economics Center, an independent research organization based in Chicago.

Marketing Plans
Co-op available • Advance reader copies

Author Hometown: Chicago, IL

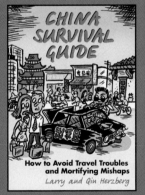

Asian Studies / Business & Economics
October
6 x 9 | 256 pp
TC US $24.95 | CAN $30.00
978-1-933330-55-6 CUSA

Crouching tiger, hidden minefield: The care and feeding of the world's next superpower.

China Survival Guide
How to Avoid Travel Troubles and Mortifying Mishaps
Larry Herzberg and Qin Herzberg

This first-ever humorous travel guide on China both dishes the dirt on the myriad travel mishaps that may befall any unsuspecting tourist and explains how to avoid them! Possible danger zones debunked include airports, hotels, hospitals, taxis, and bathrooms. Readers will learn essential skills like how to haggle, exchange currencies, cross the street, decipher menus, say useful phrases in Chinese, and more. The guide comes complete with survival tips on etiquette, a map, and resource lists. Don't leave home for China without it!

Veteran travelers Larry Herzberg and Qin Herzberg are Chinese language and culture professors at Calvin College in Michigan.

Author Events
Grand Rapids, MI

Travel & Travel Guides / Asian Studies
September
A Paperback Original
4 x 6 | 160 pp
10 B&W photographs and 1 map
TP US $9.95 | CAN $18.00
978-1-933330-51-8 CUSA

The first humorous travel guide to China that spells out tourist problems and solutions with candor.

Stone Bridge Press

Kitsuné
Japan's Fox of Mystery, Romance, & Humor
Kiyoshi Nozaki

Asian Studies /
Folklore
September
Stone Bridge Classics
5¼ x 7½ | 280 pp
60 B&W illustrations
and photographs
TP US $12.95
CAN $15.50
978-1-933330-34-1
CUSA

The classic exposition on Japan's folkloric fox details all appearances of the *kitsuné* found in Japan's rich culture, from religion and superstition to art and literature. Historical illustrations throughout the book reveal an entire nation's enduring fascination for this mysterious animal.

Kiyoshi Nozaki was a writer and Japanese folklorist.

The Flight of the Dragon
An Essay on the Theory and Practice of Art in China and Japan, Based on Original Sources
Laurence Binyon

Asian Studies / Art
September
Stone Bridge Classics
5¼ x 7½ | 112 pp
TP US $9.95
CAN $12.00
978-1-933330-35-8
CUSA

This pioneering essay explains Chinese and Japanese art theory by analyzing original records left by Eastern artists and critics. Not only influential in the Modernism movement and British poetry, it is particularly perceptive on the influence of Zen on art.

Laurence Binyon (1869–1943) was a well-respected poet and the premier Asian art historian of his time.

The Honorable Visitors
Donald Richie

Travel & Travel Guides
September
Stone Bridge Classics
5¼ x 7½ | 192 pp
TP US $11.95
CAN $14.50
978-1-933330-36-5
CUSA

A humorous and revealing work, *The Honorable Visitors* recounts the adventures and observations of famed travelers to Japan, including Aldous Huxley, Rudyard Kipling, Charlie Chaplin, Truman Capote, Jean Cocteau, William Faulkner, and Angela Carter. Donald Richie's artful storytelling offers surprising insights into the East and West.

A converted Tokyoite, Donald Richie is considered today's foremost writer on Japanese culture in English.

The Nightless City
or, The History of the Yoshiwara Yukwaku
J.E. de Becker
Introduction by Donald Richie

History / Asian
Studies
September
Stone Bridge Classics
5¼ x 7½ | 424 pp
55 B&W illustrations,
photographs, and
charts
TP US $14.95
CAN $18.00
978-1-933330-38-9
CUSA

The lives of geisha and courtesans, their employers and clients, and the art of sex and eroticism come to life as this masterpiece of anthropology reveals the history, rituals, etiquette, language, costumes, superstitions, and even medical records of Japan's famous red-light district.

J.E. de Becker (1863–1929) was a British lawyer and longtime resident of Japan.

Kokoro
Hints and Echoes of Japanese Inner Life
Lafcadio Hearn

Asian Studies /
Literature & Essay
October
Stone Bridge Classics
5¼ x 7½ | 248 pp
TP US $12.95
CAN $15.50
978-1-933330-37-2
CUSA

The word *kokoro* translates to heart, capturing a spectrum of meanings such as spirit, courage, resolve, and sentiment. Here Lafcadio Hearn provides fifteen poignant glimpses into the spiritual and emotional makeup of Japan, getting to the "heart" of a proud and often misunderstood nation.

Lafcadio Hearn (1850–1904) was an expatriate and famed writer of Japanese culture.

Kukai the Universal
Scenes from His Life
Ryotaro Shiba
Translated by Akiko Takemoto

Biography &
Autobiography /
Asian Studies
November
Stone Bridge Classics
5¼ x 7½ | 416 pp
17 B&W photographs,
charts, and maps
TP US $14.95
CAN $18.00
978-1-933330-41-9
CUSA

The life's work of famed Japanese writer Ryotaro Shiba, this extensive and inspired biography recounts the life of the visionary monk who founded Shingon Buddhism, invented the *kana* syllabary, and changed the cultural landscape of Japan forever.

Ryotaro Shiba (1923–1996) is Japan's most respected historical novelist of the twentieth century and the winner of the Naoki Prize.

The Inugami Clan
Seishi Yokomizo
Translated by Yumiko Yamazaki

Mystery
September
Stone Bridge Fiction
5¼ x 7½ | 309 pp
TP US $12.95
CAN $15.50
978-1-933330-31-0
CUSA

In 1940s Japan, the wealthy head of the Inugami Clan dies, setting off a chain of bizarre, gruesome murders. Detective Kindaichi must unravel the clan's terrible secrets of forbidden liaisons, monstrous cruelty, and disguised identities to find the murderer.

Seishi Yokomizo is Japan's most popular mystery writer. His novels have been made into numerous movies and television dramas in Japan.

Death March on Mount Hakkoda
A Documentary Novel
Jiro Nitta
Translated by James Westerhoven

Fiction / History
September
Stone Bridge Fiction
5¼ x 7½ | 231 pp
1 Map
TP US $11.95
CAN $14.50
978-1-933330-32-7
CUSA

In a military training mission gone tragically wrong, 210 soldiers ascend Mount Hakkoda in the dead of winter and only eleven return. This fictionalized account of a true incident remains one of Japan's most poignant stories about soldiers' courage and the dangers of reckless leadership.

Jiro Nitta (1912–1980) was one of Japan's most popular authors and a winner of the Naoki Prize.

Stone Bridge Press

Milky Way Railroad
Kenji Miyazawa
Translated by Joseph Sigrist and D.M. Stroud
Illustrated by Ryu Okazaki

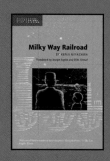

Fiction / Philosophy
October
Stone Bridge Fiction
5¼ x 7½ | 128 pp
16 B&W illustrations
TP US $9.95
CAN $12.00
978-1-933330-40-2
CUSA

One night, alone on a hilltop, a young boy is swept aboard a magical train bound for the Milky Way. A classic in Japan, this tender fable is a book of great wisdom, offering insight into the afterlife.

One of Japan's greatest storytellers, Kenji Miyazawa (1896–1933) was a teacher, author, poet, and scientist.

The Cape
and Other Stories from the Japanese Ghetto
Kenji Nakagami
Translated by Eve Zimmerman

Fiction
October
Stone Bridge Fiction
5¼ x 7½ | 200 pp
1 Chart
TP US $11.95
CAN $14.50
978-1-933330-43-3
CUSA

Born into the *burakumin*—Japan's class of outcasts—Kenji Nakagami depicts the lives of his people in sensual language and stark detail. *The Cape* is a breakthrough novella about a *burakumin* community, their troubled memories, and complex family histories. Includes *House on Fire* and *Red Hair*.

Kenji Nakagami (1946–1992) was a prolific writer admired for his vigorous prose style.

The Name of the Flower
Kuniko Mukoda
Translated by Tomone Matsumoto

Fiction
November
Stone Bridge Fiction
5¼ x 7½ | 160 pp
TP US $10.95
CAN $13.50
978-1-933330-44-0
CUSA

Over a dozen unsettling, eccentric stories about seemingly ordinary Japanese families paint vivid portraits of secret unhappiness and betrayal. Kuniko Mukoda's tales chart the distances between men and women and between people and their memories.

Kuniko Mukoda (1929–1981) gained fame as a television scriptwriter and became a renowned essayist and short story writer.

Wind and Stone
A Novel of Aesthetic Seduction
Masaaki Tachihara
Translated by Stephen W. Kohl

Fiction
November
Stone Bridge Fiction
5¼ x 7½ | 160 pp
7 B&W illustrations
TP US $10.95
CAN $13.50
978-1-933330-42-6
CUSA

Mizue cannot ignore the remarkable sexual energy in the landscapes created by Kase, her husband's garden designer. As an affair with Kase awakens new sensuality in Mizue, the garden silently watches the destruction of her carefully constructed homelife.

Masaaki Tachihara (1926–1980) wrote novels and short stories and was awarded the Naoki Prize for fiction in 1961.

Rokoan Origami
The Art of Connecting Cranes
Masako Sakai and Michie Sahara

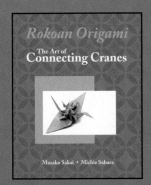

Crafts & Hobbies / Asian Studies
November
A Paperback Original
Heian Origami Favorites
8 x 10 | 72 pp
80 Color photographs and illustrations
TP US $24.95 | CAN $30.00
978-0-89346-954-2 CUSA

Learn to create connected origami cranes in flight with simple cuts and folds.

This new edition combines *Origami: Rokoan Style* and *Origami: Rokoan Style #2* into one book. Learn the centuries-old method of Rokoan origami that allows one to create up to one hundred cranes out of a single sheet of paper. Special patterns of cuts and folds produce stunning, elegant groups of connected cranes captured in mid-flight. Fifty-one intermediate- to advanced-level models are presented in full-color photographs, with step-by-step diagrams that show how to fold each one using textured washi paper.

Masako Sakai and Michie Sahara, a mother and daughter team, taught Rokoan origami and were dedicated to spreading the art of washi and origami for many years.

Money Folding
Florence Temko

Crafts & Hobbies
November
A Paperback Original
Heian Origami Favorites
7¼ x 10¼ | 32 pp
50 Color photographs and illustrations
TP US $12.95 | CAN $15.50
978-0-89346-955-9 CUSA

Save money . . . as art! Learn to fold your next gift out of dollar bills.

Back by popular demand, *Money Folding* and *Money Folding 2* are combined in this volume that contains two additional new figures. Renowned origami expert and best-selling author Florence Temko guides readers through the basics of paper money folding in an easy, step-by-step format. Readers will learn how to turn currency into animals, flowers, classic shapes, and figures they can wear! Figures are intermediate to advanced in difficulty.

San Diego resident Florence Temko is an internationally known author of many how-to books on paper arts and folkcrafts. She loves to share her knowledge of origami through her books, hands-on programs, and television appearances.

Author Events
San Diego, CA

Author Hometown: San Diego, CA

Stone Bridge Press

Shikosha Design Library
Edited by Schio Yoshioka

For many years the Shikosha Publishing Company in Kyoto produced exceptional books featuring the very finest traditional Japanese designs. Now, drawing on its rich storehouse of images of textiles, stencils, prints, and other artworks, it is launching the Shikosha Design Library. Marrying classical designs of timeless beauty with a contemporary sensibility, each volume explores color, pattern, and composition in a stunning visual format for gift-giving, inspiration, and practical use in all the decorative and digital arts.

Cherry Blossoms

Design /
Crafts & Hobbies
September
A Paperback Original
Shikosha Design
Library
8½ x 8½ | 120 pp
110 Color photographs
TP US $16.95
CAN $20.50
978-1-933330-57-0
CUSA

The cherry blossom is a symbol of evanescent beauty in Japan, and its soft pink colorations have been explored countless times by Japanese artists throughout history. Featuring the work of Kyoto kimono design masters, this volume offers splendid examples of the venerable cherry and its variants, with color swatches, line-drawn renderings, image reverses, and other treatments that breathe new life into old conventions.

Stencil Patterns

Design /
Crafts & Hobbies
October
A Paperback Original
Shikosha Design
Library
8½ x 8½ | 120 pp
110 Color photographs
TP US $16.95
CAN $20.50
978-1-933330-58-7
CUSA

Many of the most stunning textile designs in Japan are produced by stenciling, either to apply color or as paste-resist. Stencils are repeatable and thus lend themselves to modern designers looking for visual coherence. This volume features designs from the Edo to Showa periods. Coloration is entirely up to the artist, whether he or she wants to revive the classical approach of Old Japan or aims for a punk, pop, or wild aesthetic.

Sarasa Woodblock Patterns

Design /
Crafts & Hobbies
November
A Paperback Original
Shikosha Design
Library
8½ x 8½ | 120 pp
110 Color photographs
TP US $16.95
CAN $20.50
978-1-933330-59-4
CUSA

Sarasa is decorated cotton cloth, either printed or hand-painted. Developed in India two thousand years ago, sarasa arrived in Japan after the sixteenth century, where it had an enormous artistic influence. This volume features Indian and Persian woodblock print designs and exquisite Persian textiles. In Japan, sarasa is used for everything from common wrapping cloths and futon covers to sophisticated obi for kimono.

The Shikosha Design Library is prepared under the supervision of Sachio Yoshioka, a fifth-generation Kyoto dyer and frequent writer on dyeing techniques and the use of color.

Stone Bridge Press Shikosha Design Library

Crafts & Hobbies
September
A Paperback Original
Heian / OriGrafix
11 x 7⅞ | 128 pp
60 Color illustrations
TP US $16.95 | CAN $20.50
978-0-89346-952-8 CUSA

OriGrafix Japan
Traditional Designs
Studio Cochae

Are you ready for a new kind of origami? Preprinted tear-out paper with colorful pop art designs on the front and folding lines on the back turn into 3-D objects for play and display. Each volume includes twenty designs, sixty all-different sheets of folding paper, and four sheets of backgrounds for staging your creations. With *OriGrafix Japan,* you can make a cicada, turtle, crane, frog, little prince, Daruma, goldfish, and many more.

Crafts & Hobbies
October
A Paperback Original
Heian / OriGrafix
11 x 7⅞ | 128 pp
60 Color illustrations
TP US $16.95 | CAN $20.50
978-0-89346-953-5 CUSA

OriGrafix Fun
Hop, Move, Fly, Play
Studio Cochae

Included in each book are basic techniques, object descriptions, and complete folding instructions for each design. *OriGrafix Fun* showcases designs to play with—airplanes, sumo wrestlers, tops, pinwheels, balls, butterflies, cameras, and many more.

Studio Cochae, based in Tokyo, is a free-thinking and free-moving origami group whose main members are Yosuke Jikuhara and Miki Takeda.

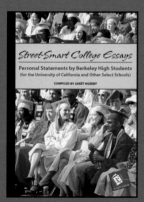

Education & Teaching / Writing
September
A Paperback Original
A Cody's Book
5⅜ x 7½ | 144 pp
TP US $11.95 | CAN $14.50
978-1-933330-60-0 CUSA

**A new imprint from
Cody's Books: great books with a
San Francisco Bay Area angle.**

Street-Smart College Essays
Personal Statements by Berkeley High Students (for the University of California and Other Select Schools)
Compiled by Janet Huseby

Introducing a new series from Cody's Books that captures the energy and activism of the Bay Area. This lively collection of successful college admissions essays from the kids at Berkeley High reflects the diversity and eclectic interests of urban and suburban students at public schools where academic ambition, gender issues, life on the streets, and love for math, music, and art are all a part of the mix. Learn to write . . . and keep it real.

Editor Janet Huseby is a journalist and writer who has been helping students with their college essays for many years.

Author Events
San Francisco, CA

Author Hometown: Berkeley, CA

Stone Bridge Press

Catch That Crocodile!

Anushka Ravishankar

Illustrated by Pulak Biswas

Who will catch that crocodile that's terrifying everyone in town?

Probin policeman with his stick?
Can Doctor Dutta do the trick?
Will Bhayanak Singh drag it away?
Or is the crocodile here to stay?
But then there is another thought:
Who says a crocodile should be caught?

Acclaimed Indian poet Anushka Ravishankar's hilarious nonsense-verse tale of a rampant reptile and his hapless assailants carries a subtle conservationist message. Another classic from the award-winning team behind *Tiger on a Tree*.

Forthcoming: a limited handmade edition, screen-printed and bound by Tara Publishing's team of skilled artisans.

Children's Fiction / Art
December
7¼ x 9½ | 40 pp
40 Color illustrations
TC US $14.95 | CAN $18.00
978-81-86211-63-2 CUSA
Handmade Edition
TC 50% NR US $25.00 | CAN $30.00
978-81-86211-94-6 CUSA

The bold, hilarious, and humane verse-tale of a rampant reptile and his hapless assailants.

The Sacred Banana Leaf

Nathan Kumar Scott

Art by Radhashyam Raut

Kanchil, the beloved trickster mouse-deer of Indonesian folklore, falls into a pit. With only a banana leaf for company, he invents a prophecy to trick some unlikely animals into helping him out—if the world doesn't end first! And if anyone dares sneeze, the consequences will be dire.

This sequel to the popular *Mangoes and Bananas* is illustrated in the Patachitra tradition of Orissa, eastern India, an intricate and colorful painting style that brings a cast of enchanting animals to life.

Born and raised in India, Colorado-based Nathan Kumar Scott is a collector of folktales from around the world.

Author Hometown: Fort Collins, CO

Children's Fiction / Art
November
8¼ x 11 | 32 pp
32 Color illustrations
TC US $16.95 | CAN $20.50
978-81-86211-28-1 CUSA

Beautiful traditional Patachitra artwork animates this unique, mischievous tale, the sequel to the popular *Mangoes and Bananas*.

Matchbook
Indian Matchbox Labels
Shahid Datawala

Sidelines & Gift Books / Design
October
A Paperback Original
4¾ x 6¼ | 196 pp
196 Color photographs
TP US $19.95 | CAN $24.00
978-81-86211-22-9 CUSA

A groundbreaking treasure-trove of striking graphic design curios from the Indian matchbox marketplace.

Designed as a large matchbox, complete with slipcase and striking edge, *Matchbook* is the first-ever collection of Indian matchbox labels.

Curious and visually stunning, matchbox labels come in a staggering variety of designs. A well-established brand quickly spawns imitations and variations as small producers compete with the large in an anarchic marketplace.

The book showcases almost one thousand colorful members of this extended family, including such brands as Cheetah Fight, Judo Deluxe, Tip Top, and New Shit. The introduction provides an insight into India's complex match industry, where an unjust economy throws a shadow over the vibrant graphics it produces.

The Book Book
A Journey into Bookmaking
Sophie Benini Pietromarchi

Children's Nonfiction / Crafts & Hobbies
March
6½ x 9½ | 128 pp
128 Color illustrations
TC US $19.95 | CAN $24.00
978-81-86211-24-3 CUSA

A uniquely poetic and creative craft book, using unlikely materials to bring every story to life.

Artist Sophie Benini Pietromarchi invites children on a fantastic and lyrical journey into the world of bookmaking. Exploring colors, textures, shapes, and feelings, she demonstrates how to turn these intangible elements into pictorial narratives, using such unlikely fodder as pencil shavings, onions, dust, and leaves.

This visual feast of a book evolved from Pietromarchi's bookmaking workshops with children. Playfully narrated, and packed with captivating and inventive illustrations, *The Book Book* is a tribute to the rich imaginative world in all of us.

Tara Publishing

No Word From Gurb
Eduardo Mendoza

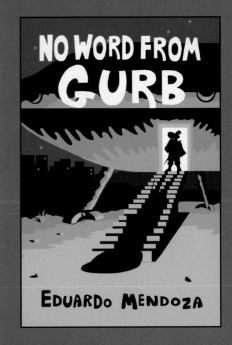

"Literary Prozac."—*Cosmopolitan*

"Eduardo Mendoza is one of contemporary Spain's most important writers."
—*The New York Times Book Review*

"An accomplished literary novelist who knows how to entertain."—*Kirkus Reviews*

A shape-shifting extraterrestrial named Gurb has assumed the form of Madonna and disappeared in Barcelona's back streets. His hapless commander, desperately trying to find him, records the daily pleasures, dangers, and absurdities of our fragile world, while munching his way through enormous quantities of *churros*. No stone is left unturned in the search for his old pal Gurb.

Will Barcelona survive this alien invasion? Will the captain ever find his subordinate? Are there enough *churros* in Barcelona to satisfy his intergalactic appetite?

Eduardo Mendoza was born in 1943 in Barcelona. He spent some years in New York working as an interpreter for the United Nations before returning to his native city. His other novels include *The Truth About the Savolta Case*, *The City of Marvels*, and *The Year of the Flood*.

A hilarious cult classic featuring an extraterrestial Don Quixote bumbling through modern-day Barcelona.

Fiction
October
A Paperback Original
5 x 7¾ | 158 pp
TP US $11.95 | CAN $14.50
978-1-84659-016-0 CUSA

Softcore
Tirdad Zolghadr

Mystery / Fiction
December
A Paperback Original
5 x 7¾ | 215 pp
TP US $14.95 | CAN $18.00
978-1-84659-020-7 CUSA

Fashion collides with politics and conspiracy theories in the frenzied workings of the international art world.

San, a self-proclaimed beatnik and Yale art graduate, is back in his native Tehran. With the financial support of his best friend Stella, he's reopening Aunt Zsa Zsa's infamous cocktail bar, The Promessa.

Arrested while photographing a kitsch flower display in front of the Revolutionary Courthouse, San is forced to sign up as a secret agent. He straddles the worlds of art and espionage with panache in this frenetic tour of modern Tehran, where conspiracy theories flourish and fashion rubs shoulders with the shrinking world of politics.

Tirdad Zolghadr is a self-confessed airline brat and freelance critic/curator.

The Bird
Oh Jung-Hee

Fiction
September
A Paperback Original
5 x 7¾ | 167 pp
TP US $14.95 | CAN $18.00
978-1-84659-021-4 CUSA

A beautifully written, deeply affecting story of a shattered childhood.

"Delicate, understated writing that finds the extraordinary in the ordinary." —Tobias Hill

U-il thinks he can fly like his favourite cartoon character Toto the Astroboy. His older sister, eleven-year-old U-mi, is doing her best to look after him since their mother died and their father deserted them.

Now all they have are their well-meaning but unhelpful neighbors—the Moons, Landlady Grandma, the weightlifting Mr Yi and his squawking widow bird—and despair is leading U-mi to mimic her father's behavior, abusing the one person closest to her.

Oh Jung-Hee is an uncontested master of short fiction in Korea.

Telegram

Katha
Short Stories by Indian Women
Edited by Urvashi Butalia

Part of a successful series that showcases women's writing from around the world.

Indian women's stories have been handed down from generation to generation, enriched and embroidered along the way. This collection reflects the vast and complex cultures of India, through British colonial rule and Partition to the present day.

Urvashi Butalia is co-founder of Kali for Women, India's first feminist publishing house. Her publications include the award-winning *The Other Side of Silence: Voices from the Partition of India*—a "magnificent and necessary book," according to Salman Rushdie.

Women's Literature / Fiction
March
A Paperback Original
5 x 7¾ | 250 pp
TP US $14.95 | CAN $18.00
978-1-84659-030-6 CUSA

An unique collection, featuring some of the best-known names in Indian literature.

Jamilia
Chingiz Aïtmatov

"The most beautiful love story in the world."—Louis Aragon

The Second World War is raging, and Jamilia's husband is off fighting at the front. Accompanied by Daniyar, a sullen newcomer who was wounded on the battlefield, Jamilia spends her days hauling sacks of grain from the threshing floor to the train station in their village in the Caucasus.

Spurning men's advances and wincing at the dispassionate letters she receives from her husband, Jamilia falls helplessly in love with the mysterious Daniyar in this heartbreakingly beautiful tale.

A classic from the award-winning Kyrgyz novelist **Chingiz Aïtmatov**.

Marketing Plans
Advance reader copies

Fiction
January
A Paperback Original
5 x 7¾ | 92 pp
TP US $11.95 | CAN $14.50
978-1-84659-032-0 CUSA

A modern classic of Soviet literature— a love story that ranks alongside Ivan Turgenev's *First Love*.

Telegram

Scéalta
Short Stories by Irish Women
Edited by Rebecca O'Connor

Fiction Anthology / Travel & Travel Guides
5 x 8 | 174 pp
TP US $14.95 | CAN $18.00
978-1-84659-003-0 CUSA

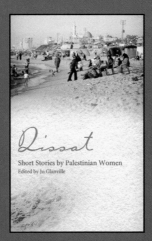

Qissat
Short Stories by Palestinian Women
Edited by Jo Glanville

Fiction
5 x 8 | 188 pp
TP US $18.95 | CAN $23.00
978-1-84659-012-2 CUSA

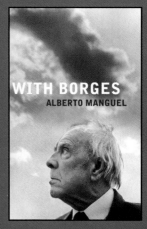

With Borges
Alberto Manguel

Biography & Autobiography
5 x 8 | 77 pp
TP $11.95
978-1-84659-005-4 USA

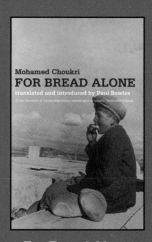

For Bread Alone
Mohamed Choukri
Translated by Paul Bowles

Fiction
5 x 8 | 213 pp
TP US $14.95 | CAN $18.00
978-1-84659-010-8 CUSA

Streetwise
Mohamed Choukri

Fiction
5 x 8 | 222 pp
TP US $14.95 | CAN $18.00
978-1-84659-027-6 CUSA

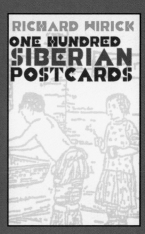

One Hundred Siberian Postcards
Richard Wirick

Fiction
5 x 8 | 239 pp
50 B&W illustrations
TP US $15.95 | CAN $19.50
978-1-84659-015-3 CUSA

Spring Awakening
Text and Lyrics by Steven Sater
Music by Duncan Sheik

"This brave new musical, haunting and electrifying by turns, restores the mystery, the thrill to that shattering transformation that stirs in all our souls."—Charles Isherwood, *The New York Times*

"The staggering purity of this show will touch all open hearts. . . . In its refined, imaginative simplicity, it daringly reverses all the conventional rules by returning the American musical to an original state of innocence."—John Heilpern, *The New York Observer*

"An unexpected jolt of sudden genius, edgy in its brutally honest, unromanticized depiction of human sexuality."—Clive Barnes, *New York Post*

Spring Awakening is an extraordinary new rock musical with book and lyrics by Steven Sater and music by Grammy Award-nominated recording artist Duncan Sheik. Inspired by Frank Wedekind's controversial 1891 play about teenage sexuality and society's efforts to control it, the piece seamlessly merges past and present, underscoring the timelessness of adolescent angst and the universality of human passion.

Steven Sater's plays include the long-running *Carbondale Dreams, Perfect for You, Doll* (Rosenthal Prize/Cincinnati Playhouse), *Umbrage* (Steppenwolf New Play Prize), and a reconceived version of Shakespeare's *Tempest,* which played in London.

Duncan Sheik is a singer/songwriter who also collaborated with Sater on the musical *The Nightingale.* He has composed original music for *The Gold Rooms of Nero* and for The Public Theater's *Twelfth Night* in Central Park.

"The best new musical in a generation."—*The New York Observer*

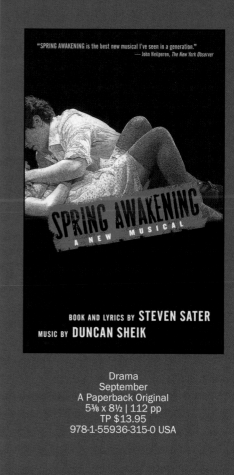

Drama
September
A Paperback Original
5⅜ x 8½ | 112 pp
TP $13.95
978-1-55936-315-0 USA

Marketing Plans

Co-op available
10,000-copy print run
National advertising:
American Theatre magazine

Theatre Communications Group

Drama
February
A Paperback Original
6 x 9 | 440 pp
TP $19.95
978-1-55936-316-7 USA

Marketing Plans

Version 3.0
Contemporary Asian American Plays
Edited by Chay Yew

"The first two generations of Asian American drama articulated experiences and issues of race and identity. Their legacy left an indelible impression. In this anthology, a new generation of Asian American playwrights explores the myriad ways in which Asians live in America."—Editor Chay Yew

This first major anthology of contemporary Asian American drama in almost two decades showcases plays of the new generation: Julia Cho's *Durango,* Sunil Kuruvilla's *Rice Boy,* Han Ong's *Swoony Planet,* Sung Rno's *Wave,* Diana Son's *Boy,* Alice Tuan's *Last of the Suns,* and Chay Yew's *Question 27, Question 28.* This is work that readily combines the Medea myth with wave-particle physics; it nimbly moves between a field in Kitchener, Canada, and a treetop in Kerala, India. It explores complexities of gender, sexuality, and family as it demonstrates the cultural and aesthetic diversity of Asian American voices writing for today's American theater.

Also included in this volume is *The Square,* a choral piece by sixteen leading playwrights meditating on 120 years of perceptions and relationships between non-Asian Americans and the Asian American community, set in a public square in the Chinatown of an American city.

Chay Yew is a noted playwright and director whose work has been produced Off-Broadway and across the United States. He is the former director of the Asian Theatre Workshop at the Mark Taper Forum, former resident director at East West Players, and an executive board member of The Society of Stage Directors and Choreographers. He lives in Los Angeles.

A major new anthology of contemporary Asian American playwrights.

Also Available

Between Worlds
Contemporary Asian-American Plays
Edited by Misha Berson
Drama
6 x 9 | 272 pp
TP $16.95
978-1-55936-004-3 USA

Theatre Communications Group

The Director's Voice 2
Interviews With Twenty Stage Directors
Edited by Jason Loewith

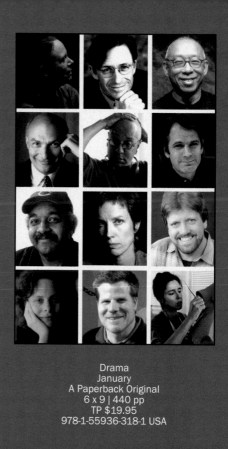

"Directors today are equipped with a larger toolbox than their forerunners, standing on their shoulders as well as those of pioneers in non-Western theater, experimental visual art, community-based theater, and the ever-evolving commercial theater scene."—Editor Jason Loewith

The Director's Voice 2 presents a cross-section of the most diverse and dynamic stage directors defining today's American theater in a conversation with director/producer Jason Loewith. In the twenty years since the debut of the immensely popular first volume of *The Director's Voice,* which has sold over eighteen thousand copies, much has changed. "The nonprofit model was turned on its head in the aftermath of the Reagan years," Loewith notes. "Institution-building is out for these directors; creating a distinctive voice from a multiplicity of influences is in." Taken together, these directors sketch a compelling portrait of the art form in the new century.

Interviews include: Anne Bogart, Mark Brokaw, Peter Brosius, Ping Chong, David Esbjornson, Oskar Eustis, Frank Galati, Michael Kahn, Moisés Kaufman, James Lapine, Elizabeth LeCompte, Emily Mann, Michael Mayer, Marion McClinton, Bill Rauch, Bartlett Sher, Julie Taymor, Theatre de la Jeune Lune (Barbra Berlovitz, Steven Epps, Vincent Gracieux, Robert Rosen, Dominique Serrand), George C. Wolfe, and Mary Zimmerman.

Jason Loewith is an award-winning director and producer who has served since 2002 as artistic director of Next Theatre Company, where his directing credits include the Chicago-area premieres of Lynn Nottage's *Fabulation,* Paula Vogel's *The Long Christmas Ride Home,* as well as *Entertaining Mr. Sloane* and *Measure for Measure.*

Interviews with leading stage directors working in the American theater.

Also Available

The Director's Voice
Twenty-One Interviews
Arthur Bartow
Drama
6 x 9 | 360 pp
TP $18.95
978-0-93045-274-2 USA

Drama
January
A Paperback Original
6 x 9 | 440 pp
TP $19.95
978-1-55936-318-1 USA

Marketing Plans

Co-op available
National advertising:
American Theatre magazine

Theatre Communications Group

413

Universes: The Big Bang
Plays, Poetry and Process
Universes
Introduction by Luis Alfaro

Drama
January
A Paperback Original
5⅜ x 8½ | 300 pp
TP $17.95
978-1-55936-317-4 USA

Marketing Plans

Co-op available
National advertising:
American Theatre magazine

"The troupe always dazzles with its fresh rhymes, varied rhythms, and commitment to keeping it real . . . but the focus always stays where it should: on the language. They blast like jackhammers through the clichés."—Alisa Solomon, *The Village Voice*

"Exuberant, insightful entertainment minted in the urban furnace. . . . Here is Ali and Jack Kerouac and the great Puerto Rican migration and Dr. Seuss; so along with the politics of dislocation and the problems of assimilation come fun and a feverish joy of language."—Lawrence Van Gelder, *The New York Times*

Grown from New York City's spoken word scene, Universes is an ensemble of multi-disciplined writers and performers who fuse poetry, jazz, hip-hop, Spanish boleros, and down-home blues to create their own brand of innovative theatrical pieces. This volume collects the troupe's work created over the past ten years, including *One Shot in Lotus Position, Blue Suite, The Last Word,* and their tour de force *Slanguage,* as well as poetry fueling their works-in-progress. Also included are pieces by directors Jo Bonney, Talvin Wilks, and Chay Yew on working with the ensemble, and a section on the seismic synergy of Universes's collaborative process.

Universes is an ensemble of writers and performers, with a variety of ethnic backgrounds and experiences, based in the Bronx in New York City. The original members are Steven Sapp, Gamal Chasten, Mildred Ruiz, Lemon, and Flaco Navaja, who created the ensemble in 1997. The work now features three of the core members (Sapp, Chasten, and Ruiz), together with rising star Ninja.

The first collection by this unique Bronx-based ensemble.

Theatre Communications Group

Talk Radio

Eric Bogosian

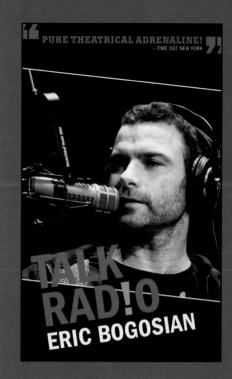

"More timely today than it was twenty years ago . . . *Radio* crackles with intensity."
—Joe Dziemianowicz, *Daily News*

"The most lacerating portrait of a human meltdown this side of a Francis Bacon painting. . . . This revival, like the original production, allows its star to grab an audience by the lapels and shake it into submission."—Ben Brantley, *The New York Times*

Eric Bogosian's *Talk Radio*—his breakthrough 1987 Public Theater hit that was made into a film by Oliver Stone—has been revived in a "mesmerizing" (*Newsday*) production on Broadway, with Liev Schreiber playing the role of the late-night shock jock that Bogosian himself originated. The drama is set in the studio of Cleveland's WTLK Radio over the course of Barry Champlain's two-hour broadcast, being scrutinized that night by producers with an interest in taking the show national, and fueled as always by coffee, cocaine, and Jack Daniel's. Barry's jousts with his unseen callers—ranging from a white supremacist to a woman obsessed with her garbage disposal—are peppered with insights into his character from his ex-deejay pal and his sometime girlfriend/producer, and punctuated with a transformative visit from an embodied voice.

Eric Bogosian is a writer and actor who over the last twenty years has authored five full-length plays and created six full-length solos for himself, including *subUrbia*; *Sex, Drugs, Rock & Roll*; *Pounding Nails in the Floor with My Forehead*; and *Drinking in America*. He is the recipient of three OBIE Awards and a Drama Desk Award, and has toured throughout the United States and Europe.

"Your fear, your own lives, have become your entertainment."
—*Talk Radio*

Drama
September
A Paperback Original
5⅜ x 8½ | 112 pp
TP $13.95
978-1-55936-324-2 USA

Marketing Plans

Co-op available
National advertising:
American Theatre magazine

Author Hometown: New York, NY

Also Available

Humpty Dumpty
and Other Plays
Eric Bogosian
Drama
6 x 9 | 240 pp
TP $16.95
978-1-55936-251-1 USA

Suburbia
Eric Bogosian
Drama
6 x 8 | 112 pp
TP US $12.95 | CAN $15.50
978-1-55936-101-9 CUSA

Theatre Communications Group

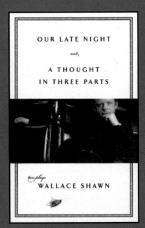

Drama
September
A Paperback Original
5⅜ x 8½ | 120 pp
TP $14.95
978-1-55936-322-8 USA

Two early plays by the noted writer and actor Wallace Shawn.

Our Late Night and A Thought in Three Parts
Two Plays
Wallace Shawn

"[*Our Late Night* is] a short play, but a savage one. . . . Neurosis, panic and sexual surreality underlie Shawn's startling vision of New Yorkers at play."—*Guardian*

Wallace Shawn's OBIE Award-winning, never-before-published *Our Late Night* premiered in New York in 1975 under direction of André Gregory, and was revived in London in 1999 under direction of Caryl Churchill. *A Thought in Three Parts*—currently out of print—created an uproar with its 1977 London premiere, investigated by the vice squad for its allegedly pornographic content.

Wallace Shawn is a noted actor and writer. His politically charged and controversial plays include *Aunt Dan and Lemon, The Designated Mourner,* and *The Fever.*

Marketing Plans
Co-op available
National advertising: American Theatre magazine

Drama
November
A Paperback Original
5⅜ x 8½ | 224 pp
TP $16.95
978-1-55936-321-1 USA

Three plays by acclaimed American playwright Tina Howe.

Birth and After Birth and Other Plays
Tina Howe

"[*Birth and After Birth* is] as appalling as it is perceptive . . . one of the more primal works by this woman who describes herself as a 'well-mannered anarchist.'"—*Newsday*

A revised edition of Tina Howe's early farce *Birth and After Birth,* about overweening parents and their four-year-old child. Also included are *Approaching Zanzibar,* a comedy about mortality, and the "rich, gorgeous and compelling" (*New York Post*) domestic drama *One Shoe Off.*

Tina Howe was born and lives in New York City. Her major honors include an Outer Critics Circle Award, an OBIE Award for Distinguished Playwriting, and a Tony Award nomination for her play *Coastal Disturbances.*

Marketing Plans
Co-op available
National advertising: American Theatre magazine

Theatre Communications Group

Exits and Entrances
Athol Fugard

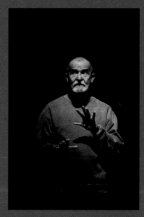

"A rare playwright who could be a primary candidate for either the Nobel Prize in Literature or the Nobel Peace Prize."—*The New Yorker*

This new play about life and art by renowned playwright Athol Fugard is based on his early friendship with actor Andrew Huegonit, considered the finest classical actor of their native South Africa. It is the story of one great artist's exit from the stage and another's beginning theater career.

Athol Fugard's work includes *Blood Knot*, *"Master Harold"* . . . *and the boys*, and *My Children! My Africa!* He has been widely produced in South Africa and London, on Broadway, and across the United States.

Marketing Plans
Co-op available
National advertising: American Theatre magazine

Drama
September
A Paperback Original
5⅜ x 8½ | 96 pp
TP $13.95
978-1-55936-319-8 USA

Playwright Athol Fugard's meditation on life in the theater.

Theatre Directory 2007–2008
35th Annual Edition

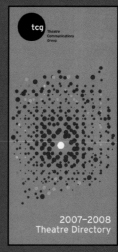

This thirty-fifth annual edition of the pocket guide to the professional theater world contains indispensable reference information on over 420 theaters and related organizations, including:

- Personnel information (artistic directors, managing directors, board chairpersons)
- Theater addresses and fax, business, and box office phone numbers, along with e-mail and website addresses
- Performance seasons
- Regional index listings by state
- Theater index listing by budget size
- Actors' Equity Association contract information
- Special interests listings for all theaters

2007–2008
Theatre Directory

Reference
October
A Paperback Original
4 x 8½ | 280 pp
TP $14.95
978-1-55936-320-4 USA

Theatre Communication Group's annual pocket guide to American theater.

Theatre Communications Group

417

Drama
September
A Paperback Original
Martin E. Segal
Theatre Center
5 x 8 | 226 pp
TP y $20.00
978-0-5954365-6-9
USA

roMANIA After 2000
Five New Romanian Plays
Edited by Saviana Stanescu and Daniel Gerould

The first anthology of new Romanian drama published in the United States, *roMANIA After 2000* introduces American readers to compelling playwrights and plays that address resonant issues of a post-totalitarian society on its way toward democracy and a new European identity. Includes *Stop the Tempo, Romania. Kiss Me!, Vitamins, Romania 21,* and *Waxing West.*

Drama
September
A Paperback Original
Martin E. Segal
Theatre Center
5 x 8 | 226 pp
TP y $20.00
978-0-5954365-7-6
USA

BAiT: Buenos Aires in Translation
Recent Argentinean Plays
Edited and Translated by Jean Graham-Jones

This publication of the four plays presented at Performance Space 122's 2006 festival, brings to US readers cutting-edge work from one of Latin America's most vibrant theatrical scenes. Includes *Women Dreamt Horses; A Kingdom, a Country or a Wasteland, in the Snow; Ex-Antwone;* and *Panic.*

Drama
September
A Paperback Original
Aurora Metro Press
5 x 8 | 96 pp
TP y $18.95
978-0-9551566-5-6
USA

All Talk
Monologues for Young People
Edited by M6 Theatre Company

A series of short, single-voice plays by writers based in the Northwest of England. These powerful, contemporary monologues share the struggles, courage, conflicts, and joys of different characters facing difficult decisions in their lives. Developed through consultation with young people, they offer a range of authentic, memorable voices to stimulate discussion and participatory drama work.

Drama
September
A Paperback Original
Aurora Metro Press
5 x 8 | 300 pp
TP y $18.95
978-0-9551566-1-8
USA

Tina's Web
Alki Zei

Tina's life in Germany had been so happy, it never occurred to her that one day her parents might split and send her back to Greece to live with her grandmother! But Tina doesn't mind anything any more. She's found the answer in a really amazing little blue pill. Sometimes it's as if she's in heaven, sometimes she's crashing back down to earth, and now there's no return.

Theatre Communications Group

The Algebra of Freedom
Raman Mundair

Drama
September
A Paperback Original
Aurora Metro Press
5 x 8 | 76 pp
TP y $18.95
978-0-9551566-6-3
USA

Tony, a policeman, wishes he could turn the clock back; Jack knows that what's done is done; and Parvez, a young Asian man, can't believe that Sara is back from beyond and this time she seems to have all the answers. *The Algebra of Freedom* is a taut political drama that asks questions about identity, redemption, faith, and compassion in a society waging a war against terror.

Coming Back
David Hill

Drama
September
A Paperback Original
Aurora Metro Press
5 x 8 | 200 pp
TP y $18.95
978-0-9542330-2-0
USA

Ryan just got his license. He's in the car with his mates. Tara likes to go running. She's on her way back home. Neither of them is paying much attention. The accident that follows impacts many lives. A moving and compelling story of recovery, told by one of New Zealand's foremost children's writers.

The Reporter
Nicholas Wright

Drama
September
A Paperback Original
Nick Hern Books
5 x 8 | 96 pp
TP y $18.95
978-1-85459-963-6
USA

An enthralling detective story based on the true life story of BBC reporter James Mossman during his last years, from 1963 to 1971, *The Reporter* searches for the truth behind his bewildering suicide. What lies beneath the surface? Or is the surface ultimately all there is? Written by the Laurence Olivier Award-winning author of *Vincent in Brixton*.

The Improvisation Game
Discovering the Secrets of Spontaneous Performance
Chris Johnston

Drama /
Education & Teaching
September
A Paperback Original
Nick Hern Books
6 x 9 | 270 pp
TP y $25.95
978-1-85459-668-0
USA

Packed with exercises and practical techniques, *The Improvisation Game* explores how improvisation can be used both to create performance and as an end in itself. It reveals the techniques, structures, and methods used by key practitioners in the field of improvised drama, music, and dance—among them are Keith Johnstone, Max Stafford-Clark, Phelim McDermott, Tim Etchells, John Wright, and Robert Lepage.

Theatre Communications Group

Drama /
Education & Teaching
September
A Paperback Original
Nick Hern Books
6 x 9 | 270 pp
TP y $25.95
978-1-85459-659-8
USA

Finding Your Voice
A Step-by-Step Guide for Actors
Barbara Houseman
Foreword by Kenneth Branagh

A simple, step-by-step manual, written by a Royal Shakespeare Company voice coach, offers everything that actors need to work on their voices. Suitable for actors at all levels, from students and young professionals to established and experienced actors. Drama teachers in schools and committed amateur actors who want to increase their vocal skills and understanding will also find it invaluable.

Drama /
Education & Teaching
September
A Paperback Original
Nick Hern Books
5 x 8 | 160 pp
TP y $22.95
978-1-85459-160-9
USA

Laban for Actors and Dancers
Jean Newlove

A handbook complete with graded exercises for teachers and students wanting a practical introduction to Laban's famous system of movement. Rudolf Laban is to movement what Stanislavski is to acting. He devised the first wholly successful system for recording human movement, a system which is increasingly influential in the training of actors and dancers.

Drama
September
Oberon Books
6⅜ x 9¼ | 256 pp
TC y US $40.00
CAN $48.00
978-1-84002-710-5
CUSA

The Central Book
Lolly Susi

The Central Book tells the story of the first hundred years in the life of an extraordinary actor-training school founded by the indomitable Elsie Fogerty in 1906. Starting from a single room in the Royal Albert Hall, Fogerty built her small school into a world-famous institution that was to foster the talents not only of performers and other theater practitioners, but also of inspirational teachers and speech therapists.

Drama /
Education & Teaching
September
A Paperback Original
Nick Hern Books
6 x 9 | 270 pp
TP y $25.95
978-1-85459-782-3
USA

Why Is That So Funny?
John Wright

Comedy is recognized as one of the most problematic areas of performances. John Wright brings a wide range of experience of physical comedy to this unique exploration of comedy and comedic techniques. The book opens with an analysis of the different kinds of laughter and is followed by games and exercises devised to demonstrate and investigate the whole range of comic possibilities.

Theatre Communications Group

Against All Gods
Six Polemics on Religion and an Essay on Kindness
AC Grayling

Drama
September
A Paperback Original
Oberon Books
5 x 8 | 116 pp
TP y US $18.95
CAN $23.00
978-1-84002-727-3
CUSA

In a series of bold, unsparing polemics, AC Grayling exposes the dangerous unreason he sees at the heart of religious faith and highlights the urgent need we have to reject it in all its forms, without compromise. In its place he argues for a set of values based on reason, reflection, and sympathy, taking his cue from the great ethical tradition of Western philosophy.

On Religion
Mick Gordon and AC Grayling

Drama
September
A Paperback Original
Oberon Btooks
5 x 8 | 96 pp
TP y US $18.95
CAN $23.00
978-1-84002-714-3
CUSA

Informed by conversations with Britain's leading philosophers, theologians and scientists, *On Religion* is an exploration of the complex issues of faith and religion, presented through a moving, theatrical story. *On Religion* is part of a groundbreaking series of essays that use theater as a way to explore the fundamental preoccupations of modern life.

A Style and its Origins
Howard Barker

Drama
September
A Paperback Original
Oberon Books
5 x 8 | 150 pp
TP y US $21.00
CAN $25.50
978-1-84002-718-1
CUSA

Howard Barker's alter-ego Eduardo Houth first materialized as the photographer of publicity images for Barker's theater company The Wrestling School, one among many fictional identities assumed by him to screen a range of his activities, including set and costume design. Writing about himself in the third person and in the past tense, the result is a unique exercise in self-description.

The Art of the Theatre Workshop
Edited by Murray Melvin

Drama
September
A Paperback Original
Oberon Books
5 x 8 | 256 pp
TP y US $40.00
CAN $48.00
978-1-84002-691-7
CUSA

In 1953 a small company of actors led by Joan Littlewood arrived in London's East End for a six-week season at the vacant Theatre Royal. The company's commitment to theater for all still thrives at Theatre Royal Stratford East over half a century later. *The Art of the Theatre Workshop* is a collection of images by people who worked closely with the company in the early years.

Theatre Communications Group

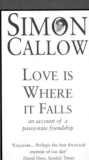

Drama /
Biography &
Autobiography
September
A Paperback Original
Nick Hern Books
5 x 8 | 96 pp
TP y $18.95
978-1-85459-976-6
USA

Love is Where it Falls
Simon Callow

"This extraordinary memoir brilliantly evokes one of the most formidable and influential figures in recent British cultural history, Peggy Ramsay. . . . Those of us who loved her will be astonished by the vivid accuracy of Simon Callow's portrait; but even those ignorant of her existence will surely be touched, fascinated and challenged."—Christopher Hampton, *The Sunday Times*

Drama
September
A Paperback Original
Oberon Books
5 x 8 | 96 pp
TP y US $18.95
CAN $23.00
978-1-84002-716-7
CUSA

Catch
April de Angelis, Stella Feehily, Tanika Gupta, Chloë Moss, and Laura Wade

There is a company that knows who you are and traces every detail of your lifestyle. They know your darkest fears and secret hopes. Claire has created a new identity for herself and promises to do the same for others in crisis. *Catch* is a new collaborative play by five leading writers, which asks timely questions about who we want to become—and at what cost.

Drama
September
A Paperback Original
Oberon Books
5 x 8 | 96 pp
TP y US $18.95
CAN $23.00
978-1-84002-724-2
CUSA

I Like Mine with a Kiss
Georgia Fitch

Celebrating her thirty-ninth birthday with a night on the tiles, Louise and her best friend Annie realize that, despite their best intentions, they're still nowhere near to being like those enviable "modern women who have it all." With a few home truths to face up to, and their friendships teetering on the edge, will the morning after be too tough a pill to swallow?

Drama
September
A Paperback Original
Oberon Books
5 x 8 | 96 pp
TP y US $18.95
CAN $23.00
978-1-84002-745-7
CUSA

Called to Account
The indictment of Anthony Charles Lynton Blair for the crime of aggression against Iraq—a Hearing
Edited by Richard Norton-Taylor

In early 2007, two leading barristers tested the evidence of the grounds for an indictment of the British prime minister for the crime of aggression against Iraq. They examined a number of distinguished witnesses, including MPs, diplomats, international lawyers, civil servants, UN officials, policy advisors, intelligence experts, and journalists. The arguments and testimony gathered here examine the criminal implications of the British government's decision to use force against Iraq.

Theatre Communications Group

Adapt or Die
Plays New and Used
Anton Chekhov, Fyodor Dostoevsky, and Maxim Gorky
Adapted by Jason Sherman

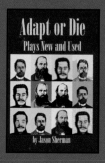

Drama
September
A Paperback Original
Playwrights Canada
Press
6 x 9 | 220 pp
TP y $29.95
978-0-88754-896-3
USA

These four plays by celebrated Canadian dramatist Jason Sherman bring works by three Russian masters kicking and screaming into the twenty-first century. *The Brothers Karamazov* captures the spirit, scope, and dark humor of Dostoevsky's novel. Gorky's unknown gem *Enemies* and Chekhov's bright farce *The Bear* are given vibrant, contemporary language. *After the Orchard,* inspired by Chekhov's *The Cherry Orchard,* is placed in contemporary Ontario cottage country.

Love and Human Remains
Brad Fraser

Drama
September
A Paperback Original
Playwrights Canada
Press
5¼ x 8½ | 112 pp
TP y $18.95
978-0-88754-914-4
USA

David McMillan is a former actor on the verge of turning thirty. Together with his roommate Candy and his best friend Bernie, David encounters a number of seductive strangers in their search for love and sex. However, the games turn ugly when it appears one of the strangers might be a serial killer. A compelling study of young adults groping for meaning in a senseless world.

The Blunt Playwright
An Introduction to Playwriting
Clem Martini

Drama
September
A Paperback Original
Playwrights Canada
Press
6 x 9 | 224 pp
TP y $28.00
978-0-88754-894-9
USA

The Blunt Playwright guides new students of playwriting through the intricacies of writing in a direct, informative, and entertaining fashion. It examines dramatic structure, discusses the creative process, explores the nature of character in dramatic work, provides a number of writing exercises that are useful for generating text, and cites local and international playwrights throughout.

Annie Mae's Movement
Yvette Nolan

Drama
September
A Paperback Original
Playwrights Canada
Press
5 x 8 | 65 pp
TP y $16.95
978-0-88754-904-5
USA

Annie Mae's Movement explores what is must have been like to be Anna Mae Pictou Aquash, a woman in a man's movement, a Canadian in America, an American Indian in a white-dominant culture. This play looks for the truth by examining the life and death of this remarkable woman.

Theatre Communications Group

Drama
September
A Paperback Original
Nick Hern Books
5 x 8 | 64 pp
TP y $18.95
978-1-85459-970-4
USA

Girls and Dolls
Lisa McGee

For Emma and Clare, 1980 was the summer they met at the swings, the summer they built a tree house, and the summer a young mother and her infant daughter moved into number fourteen. Now in their thirties, Emma and Clare struggle to come to terms with the chain of devastating events that began that summer to understand what they did, what they became, and how they were judged.

Drama /
Young Adult Fiction
September
A Paperback Original
Nick Hern Books
5 x 8 | 96 pp
TP y $18.95
978-1-85459-968-1
USA

The Jungle Book
Rudyard Kipling
Adapted by Stuart Paterson

"This exhilarating production ticks all the boxes for families looking for an uplifting treat."—*Time Out*

"Paterson has mastered the art of injecting new zest and color into classic children's stories."—*The London Times*

Rudyard Kipling's classic jungle tales in an acclaimed stage adaptation by Stuart Paterson.

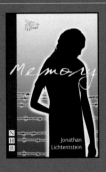

Drama
September
A Paperback Original
Nick Hern Books
5 x 8 | 96 pp
TP y $18.95
978-1-85459-974-2
USA

Memory
Jonathan Lichtenstein

East Berlin, 1990. The Wall has just been pulled down. A man arrives at the flat of his grandmother with awkward questions about the past. Meanwhile, a generation later, in Bethlehem the Israeli security barrier is going up. A play about division, destiny, and the undimmed potency of memory itself from the author of the award-winning *The Pull of Negative Gravity*.

Drama
September
A Paperback Original
Nick Hern Books
5 x 8 | 96 pp
TP y $18.95
978-1-85459-960-5
USA

The Way Home
Chloë Moss

Three people, four walls: the basic recipe for family life. Down the road in Oil Street there are no walls, just wheels, and a fierce sense of belonging that has nothing to do with place. Two ways of life: yards apart and yet worlds apart. A friendship between the sons forces both families to look beyond the walls that divide them.

Theatre Communications Group

Carole Fréchette: Two Plays
Carole Fréchette
Translated by John Murrell

Drama
September
A Paperback Original
Playwrights Canada
Press
5 x 8 | 112 pp
TP y $17.95
978-0-88754-501-6
USA

In *John and Beatrice,* Beatrice waits for the right man to respond to her ad. When John appears, the games begin. It is a play about the difficulty of connection and the meaning of love. In *Helen's Necklace,* Helen wanders through a Middle Eastern city looking for a lost pearl necklace. Helen comes into contact with a series of people, and she is irrevocably changed by her search for a trinket.

Blacks Don't Bowl
Vadney S. Haynes

Drama
September
A Paperback Original
Playwrights Canada
Press
5 x 8 | 96 pp
TP y $14.95
978-0-88754-466-8
USA

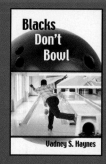

When two black Montreal artists create a show from images of pimps, thugs, and dancehall queens, community leader Frank Simmons is outraged and tries to censor the demeaning images. What Frank does not count on is art's ability to transform as he is forced to confront himself in a way that is both disturbing and revealing. Little will be the same afterwards for Frank, the artists, and perhaps black people everywhere.

RETURN (The Sarajevo Project)
Edited by Theatrefront

Drama
September
A Paperback Original
Playwrights Canada
Press
5 x 8 | 96 pp
TP y $17.95
978-0-88754-725-6
USA

Five years after fleeing Sarajevo and escaping to Canada, Tarik returns to Bosnia to face the family he left behind. Those he left must now reconcile their love for Tarik with their anger at his betrayal. *RETURN (The Sarajevo Project)* is a unique international co-creation developed by an ensemble of Canadian and Bosnian theater artists.

Ten Days on Earth
Ronnie Burkett

Drama
September
A Paperback Original
Playwrights Canada
Press
5 x 8 | 96 pp
TP y $16.95
978-0-88754-737-9
USA

Darrel is a middle-aged mentally challenged man who lives with his mother. When she dies in her sleep, Darrel does not realize she is gone, and, for ten days, he lives alone. Tandem to Darrel's day-to-day routine are the adventures of his favorite children's book characters, Honeydog and Little Burp. The newest play from puppeteer Ronnie Burkett, who garnered critical acclaim for *Provenance.*

Theatre Communications Group

Drama
September
A Paperback Original
Oberon Books
5 x 8 | 96 pp
TP y US $18.95
CAN $23.00
978-1-84002-705-1
CUSA

Woyzeck
Georg Büchner
Adapted by Daniel Kramer

"Explosively powerful . . . thrilling, harrowing, stunning . . . by far the best and most daring account . . . I have ever seen."—*The Sunday Times*

Woyzeck is the heartbreaking story of a young soldier's descent into madness. Inspired by real events, Georg Büchner's unfinished masterpiece remains one of Western drama's most profound and moving explorations of class and morality.

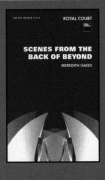

Drama
September
A Paperback Original
Oberon Books
5 x 8 | 96 pp
TP y US $18.95
CAN $23.00
978-1-84002-711-2
CUSA

The Seduction of Almighty God
Howard Barker

The loss of faith and cynical corruption of a few priests is unexpectedly challenged by the arrival of a young man with an unsullied and passionate belief in God. Howard Barker invents a world of shocking and universal metaphor in a place that might be anywhere, struggling with the rise of extreme belief and the dangerous, distorted power it unleashes.

Drama
September
A Paperback Original
Oberon Books
5 x 8 | 96 pp
TP y US $18.95
CAN $23.00
978-1-84002-708-2
CUSA

Scenes from the Back of Beyond
Meredith Oakes

Bill is sustained by his deep sense of a wider culture and an improving world. The only thing the human race needs to do is learn. When he meets people who embody this idea, he naturally likes them—especially if his wife doesn't. A play that explores the comfort, hopes, and fragility of family life in a new Sydney suburb.

Drama
September
A Paperback Original
Oberon Books
5 x 8 | 216 pp
TP y US $29.95
CAN $36.00
978-1-84002-662-7
CUSA

Richard Bean: Plays Two
Toast; Smack Family Robinson; Mr. England; Honeymoon Suite
Richard Bean

These are challenging and exciting plays by an award-winning playwright. In *Toast* seven men come together to bake enough bread to feed the population of Hull, but there's a conflict in the works. *Smack Family Robinson* is about a family of drug dealers and the changes to the business since they began in the 1960s. Also includes *Mr. England* and *Honeymoon Suite*.

Theatre Communications Group

Frobisher's Gold
Fraser Grace

Drama
September
A Paperback Original
Oberon Books
5 x 8 | 96 pp
TP y US $18.95
CAN $23.00
978-1-84002-709-9
CUSA

When pirate-turned-explorer Martin Frobisher discovers a new land in the Arctic filled with riches, Elizabeth I glimpses a golden future of wealth, prestige, and influence. The queen invests heavily to bring civilization to the natives and their assets home to England. *Frobisher's Gold* blends history, comedy, and politics in a tale of imperial desire, improbable coincidences, and bad dentistry.

The War Next Door
Tamsin Oglesby

Drama
September
A Paperback Original
Oberon Books
5 x 8 | 96 pp
TP y US $18.95
CAN $23.00
978-1-84002-729-7
CUSA

Sophie and Max are a thoroughly modern British couple—cosmopolitan and open-minded. Then there's Hana and Ali next door. Though they are neighbors, they are in every other sense a world apart. Tamsin Oglesby's black comedy takes a humorous and subversive look at the world we live in today—one of multiculturalism and blurred boundaries, and one in which violence is right on our own doorstep, no matter where we come from.

Gizmo Love
John Kolvenbach

Drama
September
A Paperback Original
Oberon Books
5 x 8 | 96 pp
TP y US $18.95
CAN $23.00
978-1-84002-685-6
CUSA

Gizmo Love is a hilarious black comedy thriller that delves into the cutthroat world of Tinsel Town—Hollywood at its most ruthless.

Love Song
John Kolvenbach

Drama
September
A Paperback Original
Oberon Books
5 x 8 | 96 pp
TP y US $18.95
CAN $23.00
978-1-84002-715-0
CUSA

Beane is an exile from life—an oddball. His well-meaning sister Joan and brother-in-law Harry try and make time for him in their busy lives, but no one can get through. Following the burglary of his apartment, Joan is baffled to find her brother blissfully happy and tries to unravel the story behind Beane's mysterious new love Molly.

Drama
September
A Paperback Original
Playwrights Canada
Press
5 x 8 | 116 pp
TP y $18.95
978-0-88754-520-7
USA

Mieko Ouchi: Two Plays
The Red Priest and The Blue Light
Mieko Ouchi

Includes *The Red Priest* and Mieko Ouchi's new play, *The Blue Light,* in which one hundred-year-old Leni Riefenstahl is in the office of a young female Hollywood studio executive to make one last desperate pitch to direct her first feature film in fifty years. A thought-provoking contemplation on art, politics, and the seduction of fascism.

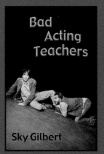

Drama
September
A Paperback Original
Playwrights Canada
Press
5 x 8 | 96 pp
TP y $16.95
978-0-88754-508-5
USA

Bad Acting Teachers
Sky Gilbert

A young actor in search of good training visits three teachers who advertise private lessons. Seeing each of the teachers separately, he is progressively assaulted, insulted, and molested. A meditation on the sadism that so often accompanies power.

Drama
September
A Paperback Original
Playwrights Canada
Press
5 x 8 | 96 pp
TP y $16.95
978-0-88754-516-0
USA

Banana Boys
Leon B. Aureus
Adapted by Terry Woo

A smart, contemporary, and wickedly funny play about five young Asian Canadian men, "Bananas" (read: yellow on the outside, white on the inside), wrestling with issues of race, identity, and the death of a friend. Not quite Chinese and not really Canadian, they stumble through stories, situations, incidents, and interactions that are seemingly mundane, but upon closer examination, ultimately explore the nature of identity.

Drama /
Literature & Essay
September
A Paperback Original
Playwrights Canada
Press
6 x 9 | 220 pp
TP y $40.00
978-0-88754-862-8
USA

The Betty Lambert Reader
Betty Lambert
Edited by Cynthia Zimmerman

A collection of writings by seminal Canadian playwright Betty Lambert. With an introduction by Cynthia Zimmerman, this collection also includes radio plays, stage plays, short stories, and excerpts from a novel.

Theatre Communications Group

The Merry Wives of Windsor
William Shakespeare
Adapted by Gregory Doran; Lyrics by Ranjit Bolt and
Music by Paul Englishby

Drama
September
A Paperback Original
Oberon Books
5 x 8 | 96 pp
TP y US $18.95
CAN $23.00
978-1-84002-722-8
CUSA

When Sir John Falstaff sets out to woo a rich mistress to solve his financial worries, he soon discovers that the wives of Windsor are more than a match for him. Love, song, laughter, and merriment combine in a new musical version of William Shakespeare's popular comedy.

The Bombay Plays
Bombay Black & The Matka King
Anosh Irani

Drama
September
A Paperback Original
Playwrights Canada
Press
5 x 8 | 112 pp
TP y $18.95
978-0-88754-560-3
USA

Bombay Black is a love story between a blind man and a dancer. He is linked to her past and his secret threatens to change each of their lives forever. In a story that pits human nature against love and chance, *The Matka King* reveals a landscape of betrayal and redemption come to life in the red-light district of Bombay, India.

The Real McCoy
Andrew Moodie

Drama
September
A Paperback Original
Playwrights Canada
Press
5 x 8 | 118 pp
TP y $17.95
978-0-88754-902-1
USA

Andrew Moodie's latest play tells the tale of inventor Elijah McCoy (1843–1929), whose name became a byword for quality, as in "the real McCoy." The play explains why we've never heard of McCoy and reclaims a fascinating man's life from undeserved obscurity. No one believed a black man could be an engineer; nevertheless, McCoy devised a solution to one of the greatest problems facing steam locomotion.

Leo
Rosa Laborde

Drama
September
A Paperback Original
Playwrights Canada
Press
5¼ x 8¼ | 55 pp
TP y $15.95
978-0-88754-898-7
USA

Set in Santiago, Chile, three young friends form a bittersweet love triangle during the political upheaval surrounding President Salvador Allende's assassination. Told through Leo's memories, the play travels through childhood, first friends, and first loves. Passion and poetry weave together in this story of innocence lost.

Theatre Communications Group

Company of Angels
Four Plays by John Retallack
John Retallack

Drama
September
A Paperback Original
Oberon Books
5 x 8 | 96 pp
TP y US $19.95 | CAN $24.00
978-1-84002-725-9 CUSA

Paul Sirett: Plays Two
Paul Sirett

Drama
September
A Paperback Original
Oberon Books
5 x 8 | 220 pp
TP y US $29.95 | CAN $36.00
978-1-84002-482-1 CUSA

Torben Betts: Plays Three
Torben Betts

Drama
September
A Paperback Original
Oberon Books
5 x 8 | 224 pp
TP y US $29.95 | CAN $36.00
978-1-84002-412-8 CUSA

The Unconquered
Torben Betts

Drama
September
A Paperback Original
Oberon Books
5 x 8 | 96 pp
TP y US $18.95 | CAN $23.00
978-1-84002-723-5 CUSA

Cymbeline
William Shakespeare
Adapted by Emma Rice

Drama
September
A Paperback Original
Oberon Books
5 x 8 | 96 pp
TP y US $18.95 | CAN $23.00
978-1-84002-721-1 CUSA

Great Expectations
Charles Dickens
Adapted by Neil Bartlett

Drama
September
A Paperback Original
Oberon Books
5 x 8 | 96 pp
TP y US $18.95 | CAN $23.00
978-1-84002-726-6 CUSA

Carrie's War
Nina Bawden
Adapted by Emma Reeves

Drama / Young Adult Fiction
September
A Paperback Original
Oberon Books
5 x 8 | 96 pp
TP y US $18.95 | CAN $23.00
978-1-84002-720-4 CUSA

Don't Look Now
Daphne du Maurier
Adapted by Nell Leyshon

Drama
September
A Paperback Original
Oberon Books
5 x 8 | 96 pp
TP y US $18.95 | CAN $23.00
978-1-84002-730-3 CUSA

Rapunzel
Adapted by Annie Siddons

Drama
September
A Paperback Original
Oberon Books
5 x 8 | 96 pp
TP y US $18.95 | CAN $23.00
978-1-84002-698-6 CUSA

Gilgamesh
Derrek Hines

Drama
September
A Paperback Original
Oberon Books
5 x 8 | 96 pp
TP y US $18.95 | CAN $23.00
978-1-84002-654-2 CUSA

Two Graves
Paul Sellar

Drama
September
A Paperback Original
Oberon Books
5 x 8 | 96 pp
TP y US $18.95 | CAN $23.00
978-1-84002-713-6 CUSA

Tobias and the Angel
A Community Opera
David Lan and Jonathon Dove

Drama
September
A Paperback Original
Oberon Books
5 x 8 | 96 pp
TP y US $18.95 | CAN $23.00
978-1-84002-682-5 CUSA

Sharon Pollock: Collected Works
Volume Three
Sharon Pollock
Edited by Cynthia Zimmerman

Drama
September
A Paperback Original
Playwrights Canada Press
6 x 9 | 224 pp
TP y $39.00
978-0-88754-733-1 USA

Queer Theatre
Critical Perspectives on Canadian Theatre in English Vol. VII
Edited by Rosalind Kerr

September
A Paperback Original
Playwrights Canada Press
6 x 9 | 224 pp
TP y $25.00
978-0-88754-804-8 USA

Environmental and Site Specific Theatre
Critical Perspectives on Canadian Theatre in English Vol. VIII
Edited by Andrew Houston

Drama
September
A Paperback Original
Playwrights Canada Press
6 x 9 | 224 pp
TP y $25.00
978-0-88754-806-2 USA

Space and the Geographies of Theatre
Critical Perspectives on Canadian Theatre in English Vol. IX
Edited by Michael McKinnie

Drama
September
A Paperback Original
Playwrights Canada Press
6 x 9 | 224 pp
TP y $25.00
978-0-88754-808-6 USA

The December Man
Colleen Murphy

Drama
September
A Paperback Original
Playwrights Canada Press
5 x 8 | 96 pp
TP y $16.95
978-0-88754-595-5 USA

Dreary & Izzy
Tara Beagan

Drama
September
A Paperback Original
Playwrights Canada Press
5 x 8 | 96 pp
TP y $16.95
978-0-88754-612-9 USA

The Fly Fisher's Companion
Michael Melski

Drama
September
A Paperback Original
Playwrights Canada Press
5 x 8 | 96 pp
TP y $16.95
978-0-88754-635-8 USA

August
Jean Marc Dalpé

Drama
September
A Paperback Original
Playwrights Canada Press
5 x 8 | 96 pp
TP y $17.95
978-0-88754-506-1 USA

In Gabriel's Kitchen
Salvatore Antonio

Drama
September
A Paperback Original
Playwrights Canada Press
5 x 8 | 96 pp
TP y $16.95
978-0-88754-670-9 USA

Glory Days
Bill Freeman

Drama
September
A Paperback Original
Playwrights Canada Press
5 x 8 | 96 pp
TP y $18.95
978-0-88754-668-6 USA

Oxford Roof Climber's Rebellion
Stephen Massicotte

Drama
September
A Paperback Original
Playwrights Canada Press
5 x 8 | 96 pp
TP y $17.95
978-0-88754-499-6 USA

Powers and Gloria
Keith Roulston

Drama
September
A Paperback Original
Playwrights Canada Press
5 x 8 | 96 pp
TP y $16.95
978-0-88754-721-8 USA

Real Estate
Allana Harkin

Drama
September
A Paperback Original
Playwrights Canada Press
5 x 8 | 96 pp
TP y $16.95
978-0-88754-651-8 USA

Deadeye
Amber Lone

Drama
September
A Paperback Original
Oberon Books
TP y US $18.95 | CAN $23.00
978-1-84002-707-5 CUSA

Washboard Blues
Do Shaw

Drama
September
A Paperback Original
Oberon Books
5 x 8 | 96 pp
TP y US $18.95 | CAN $23.00
978-1-84002-636-8 CUSA

Proving Mr. Jennings
James Walker

Drama
September
A Paperback Original
Oberon Books
5 x 8 | 96 pp
TP y US $16.95 | CAN $20.50
978-1-84002-593-4 CUSA

The Soldiers' Fortune
Thomas Otway

Drama
September
A Paperback Original
Oberon Books
5 x 8 | 96 pp
TP y US $18.95 | CAN $23.00
978-1-84002-687-0 CUSA

Hang Lenny Pope
Chris O'Connell

Drama
September
A Paperback Original
Oberon Books
5 x 8 | 96 pp
TP y US $18.95 | CAN $23.00
978-1-84002-733-4 CUSA

The Glass Room
Ryan Craig

Drama
September
A Paperback Original
Oberon Books
5 x 8 | 96 pp
TP y US $18.95 | CAN $23.00
978-1-84002-712-9 CUSA

The Enchanted Pig
Alasdair Middleton

Drama
September
A Paperback Original
Oberon Books
5 x 8 | 96 pp
TP y US $18.95 | CAN $23.00
978-1-84002-717-4 CUSA

Long Time Dead
Rona Munro

Drama
September
A Paperback Original
Nick Hern Books
5 x 8 | 96 pp
TP y $18.95
978-1-85459-972-8 USA

Bulletproof Soul
Jennifer Farmer

Drama
September
A Paperback Original
Oberon Books
5 x 8 | 96 pp
TP y US $18.95 | CAN $23.00
978-1-84002-731-0 CUSA

The Man of Mode
George Etherege

Drama
September
A Paperback Original
Nick Hern Books
Drama Classics
4 x 6 | 160 pp
TP y $10.99
978-1-85459-965-0 USA

The Indian Boy
Rona Munro

Drama
September
A Paperback Original
Nick Hern Books
5 x 8 | 96 pp
TP y $18.95
978-1-85459-973-5 USA

The Electric Hills
Michael McLean

Drama
September
A Paperback Original
Oberon Books
5 x 8 | 96 pp
TP y US $18.95 | CAN $23.00
978-1-84002-732-7 CUSA

Kensuke's Kingdom
Michael Morpurgo
Adapted by Stuart Paterson

Drama
September
A Paperback Original
Nick Hern Books
5 x 8 | 96 pp
TP y $18.95
978-1-85459-969-8 USA

Dismal Rock
Davis McCombs

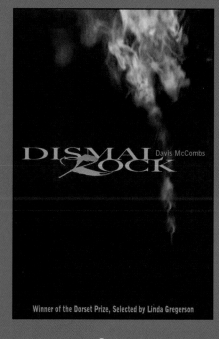

The award-winning poet Davis McCombs revisits the landscape of his youth on the tobacco farms of Kentucky in this insightful collection of verse. Initially chronicling events in local and family history, the poems in this book soon widen in scope until they include subjects as diverse as Dante Gabriel Rossetti, the Elgin Marbles, John Keats, Bob Marley, fatherhood, and fishing.

The author's lens is kaleidoscopic, and yet his poems coalesce around important themes that never lose sight of the specific and the personal. Several poems in this volume explore the grief McCombs feels over the loss of local culture as it resonates within the broader context of ecological destruction, imbuing the global with the undeniably personal. The poems in this collection are intimate and real, visceral and immediate, as if McCombs were haunted by them and had no alternative but to give them voice.

Currently director of the creative writing program at the University of Arkansas, Davis McCombs attended Harvard University and the University of Virginia and was a Wallace Stegner Fellow in poetry at Stanford University. He is the recipient of fellowships from the Ruth Lilly Poetry Foundation, the Kentucky Arts Council, and the National Endowment for the Arts. His poetry has appeared in *The Best American Poetry 1996*, *The Missouri Review*, *Poetry*, *The Kenyon Review*, and *The Virginia Quarterly Review*, and his first book was a finalist for the National Book Critics Circle Award. He was also the winner of the 2005 Dorset Prize.

Dorset Prize winner, Davis McCombs' first book won the Yale Younger Poets Award and was a National Book Critics Circle Award finalist.

Poetry
October
A Paperback Original
6 x 9 | 72 pp
TP US $16.95 | CAN $20.50
978-1-932195-48-4 CUSA

Author Hometown: Fayetteville, AR

Tupelo Press

Poetry
September
A Paperback Original
6 x 9 | 72 pp
TP US $16.95 | CAN $20.50
978-1-932195-47-7 CUSA

Author Hometown: Chapel Hill, NC

Spill
Michael Chitwood

"*Spill* is a book of spiritual yearning, grounded in the here and now of airport terminals, the backyard, a rainy morning, and a broken-down church van."
—Michael Chitwood

With finely honed, vibrant imagery, this poet chisels away at the mundane and unearths the miraculous in his eighth poetry collection. The book is divided into three sections: Chitwood's distinctive vision begins simply, as he evokes an Appalachian upbringing mired in pious certainty and yet haunted by spiritual craving. We follow the pilgrim's path in the following segment, as he attempts to wring holiness from the merely terrestrial, finding only fleeting glimpses of the divine. The final section turns contemplative, as the speaker tries to comprehend the course he has taken and find solace and wisdom in his journey.

Chitwood's verse is sharp, spare, and unpretentious, wonderfully surprising and yet deeply profound. Words are neither wasted nor superfluous; he never forgets that this is an honest conversation with the reader, and he uses the common tongue and humor of a man in thoughtful dialogue with his fellow creatures.

Born and raised in the foothills of the Virginia Blue Ridge, Michael Chitwood received his BA from Emory & Henry College in Emory, Virginia, and then worked as a science writer and editor. He earned his MFA from the University of Virginia. Moving to North Carolina, he began teaching at the University of North Carolina at Chapel Hill, where he remains a full-time visiting lecturer and a commentator on the local NPR station.

Michael Chitwood's eighth book of poetry takes the quotidian— broken tools, airports, animals—and makes it miraculous.

Tupelo Press

Psalm
Carol Ann Davis

Buffeted by grief at the death of her father and joy at the birth of her son, the poet explores and expands the boundaries of language, seeking affirmation in art and music. Her journey is viscerally personal, and yet the reader is beguiled, compelled to join in her vision and share in her enlightenment.

Carol Ann Davis directs the undergraduate creative writing program at the College of Charleston and edits the noted literary journal *Crazyhorse*. She was awarded the W.K. Rose Fellowship at Vassar College and was recently awarded an individual artist's grant in poetry by the National Endowment for the Arts.

Author Hometown: Charleston, SC

Poetry
October
A Paperback Original
6 x 9 | 66 pp
TP US $16.95 | CAN $20.50
978-1-932195-51-4 CUSA

These potent lyrics summon up a dream state, a visionary condition that is beyond language.

Masque
Elena Karina Byrne

In verse simmering with sensuality, Elena Byrne eloquently reveals, then carefully slices away, layer after layer of the masks we wear until our most secret selves are exposed. Pretense is overthrown in her exotic and electric imagery, irresistibly drawing the reader into an unabashedly intimate internal dialogue.

Elena Karina Byrne is poetry moderator for the *Los Angeles Times* Festival of Books and was regional director of the Poetry Society of America for twelve years. Her first book was *The Flammable Bird* (Tupelo Press, 2004). She's recently been published in *The Yale Review, The Paris Review, The American Poetry Review, Poetry, Ploughshares, TriQuarterly*, and *The Best American Poetry 2005*.

Author Hometown: Rancho Palos, CA

Poetry
November
A Paperback Original
6 x 9 | 80 pp
TP US $16.95 | CAN $20.50
978-1-932195-57-6 CUSA

An intensely revealing second book from the former regional director of the Poetry Society of America.

Tupelo Press

Inflorescence
Sarah Hannah

In this fierce, often witty memoir-in-verse, Sarah Hannah confronts her role as caretaker of her dying, mentally ill mother, artist Renee Rothbein. Entwining the lore of wildflowers with richly evocative language, Hannah's stunningly contemporary voice summons truth and love from loss with unflinching honesty and candor. Poems from this collection have been nominated for four Pushcart Prizes.

Sarah Hannah's first book, *Longing Distance* (Tupelo Press, 2004), was a semifinalist for the Yale Younger Poets Prize. Her poems have appeared in many journals, including *Parnassus, The Southern Review, Harvard Review,* and *AGNI.* She grew up in Newton, Massachusetts, and teaches at Emerson College.

Author Hometown: Cambridge, MA

Poetry
September
A Paperback Original
6 x 9 | 72 pp
TP US $16.95 | CAN $20.50
978-1-932195-61-3 CUSA

A cascade of poignant, crackling emotions traces the poet's relationship with her dying mother.

Nutritional Feed
Shin Yu Pai
Art by David Lukowski

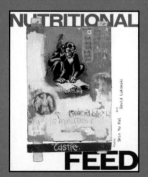

This is an extraordinary collaboration between the mischievous, hip verse of Shin Yu Pai and the abstract paintings of David Lukowski as they explore and critique the education of contemporary popular culture. The two mediums effervesce across the page, ensnaring the reader in a truly unique and memorable conversation.

Shin Yu Pai, an interdisciplinary artist, is a graduate of the School of the Art Institute of Chicago. She has taught at Southern Methodist University and The University of Texas at Dallas, and has completed residencies at The MacDowell Colony, Provincetown Fine Arts Work Center, Taipei Artist Village, and The Ragdale Foundation.

Author Hometown: Dallas, TX

Poetry / Art
September
A Paperback Original
8 x 9 | 72 pp
25 Color plates
TP US $16.95 | CAN $20.50
978-1-932195-44-6 CUSA

An extraordinary artist-writer collaboration, exploring contemporary culture with hip poetry and exciting paintings.

Tupelo Press

Now Voyagers
Some Divisions of the Saga of Mawrdew Czgowchwz, Oltrano, Authenticated by Persons Represented Therein, Book One: The Night Sea Journey
James McCourt

"James McCourt is an ecstatic fabulist, robustly funny and inventive, and touchingly in love with his subject."—*Newsweek*

"James McCourt's *Now Voyagers* is a sustained fugue of inspiration. Scathing wit, gentle ironies, comic pratfalls hurtle by at express speed. Reading it is like holding your breath for several hours. . . . The language that delivers this extraordinary novel shimmers and crackles. Even the longest sentences dance their surefooted way through thickets of references that call up every detail of 1950s New York. . . . Through the book runs a passion for opera, its iconic performances, its grand gestures and green jealousies. *Now Voyagers* is itself a grand opera, a Brobdingnanian masterpiece. . . . This is a big novel—big in size, big in ambition, big in its emotions, big in its capacious reach. There has been nothing like it for many a year." —Brian O'Doherty

Now Voyagers is the long-awaited sequel to James McCourt's first novel, the comic masterpiece *Mawrdew Czgowchwz* (pronounced *mardu gorgeous*). About James McCourt and his earlier work, Susan Sontag wrote, "Bravo, James McCourt, a literary counter-tenor in the exacting tradition of Firbank and Nabokov, who makes his daringly self-assured debut with this intelligent and very funny book."

James McCourt is the author of *Queer Street,* a *Publishers Weekly* Best Book of 2003. He is the author of three novels and two short story collections and has contributed to *The Yale Review, The New Yorker,* and *The Paris Review.*

The long-awaited sequel to James McCourt's first novel, the comic masterpiece about opera fanatics, *Mawrdew Czgowchwz.*

Fiction
October
A Paperback Original
6 x 9 | 800 pp
TP US $17.95 | CAN $21.50
978-1-933527-08-6 CUSA

Marketing Plans

Co-op available
Advance reader copies

Author Events

Washington, DC • New York, NY

Author Hometown: Washington, DC

Turtle Point Press

The Late Show
Poems
David Trinidad

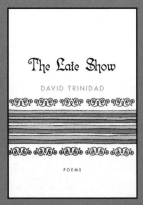

Poetry
September
A Paperback Original
6½ x 9¼ | 96 pp
TP US $16.95 | CAN $20.50
978-1-933527-09-3 CUSA

Pop culture, private memory, and formalist sensibility meet in David Trinidad's long-awaited new collection.

"Deeply personal, yet coolly postmodern, no other writer besides David Trinidad makes the interface between our private memories and our cultural ones seem so seamless. Variously giddy, gossipy, melancholy, obsessive, and euphoric, Trinidad's voice has an amazing plasticity as he slips between genres and forms, tradition and invention, with assurance and grace. *The Late Show* is a unique collection of interlocking facets: part literary memoir, part film encyclopedia, part shrine and *memento mori*—and always undeniably, pure poem."—Elaine Equi

"A beautiful study in detail and devotion. . . . Frame by frame this book is a tremendously engaging, soulful read."—Anselm Berrigan

Marketing Plans
Co-op available • Advance reader copies

Author Events
Los Angeles, CA • San Francisco, CA • Miami, FL • Chicago, IL • New York, NY

Author Hometown: Chicago, IL

Earthquake
Susan Barnes

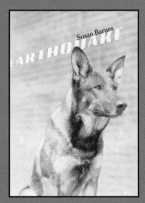

Fiction
September
5 x 7 | 76 pp
TP US $10.00 | CAN $12.00
978-1-933527-11-6 CUSA

Visually acute, roguish, and intimate reflections of a girl's childhood spent in Alaska and Boston.

"The second I finished reading *Earthquake,* without even thinking, I began reading it again. The prose has a lovely tidal pull. It's lyrical, vivid, stark, beautifully contained, dark, unblinking, and lulling. A pure and durable stream of coming-of-age vignettes. *Earthquake* is lush yet gritty, wondrously detailed yet written so cleanly. The book is a gem, and I use the term *gem* almost literally. The prose seems to have found its ideal voice, like a diamond formed at great depths in the earth, under intense pressure, and is fully alive, a sparkling artifact of compressed energy."—Amy Gerstler

Marketing Plans
Co-op available • Advance reader copies

Author Event
Boston, MA • Portland, ME • New York, NY

Author Hometown: Portland, ME

Turtle Point Press

Not Bartlett's
Thoughts on the Pleasures of Life:
People, Gardens, Dogs, and More
Edited by Elise Lufkin

"This delightful collection of quotations is drawn from a wide variety of sources; some of the greatest minds speak to us on topics like gardening, love, politics, and dogs. I plan to keep this book nearby, where I can reach for it at any time."
—Ridley Pearson

"'These few fragments I'll shore against my ruin'—that's what Elise Lufkin has done in her valuable commonplace book, *Not Bartlett's*. The quotations assembled here are like bright shells and stones gathered on a winter beach, souvenirs that both delight and comfort, some familiar, others not—all cause for wonderment and reflection."
—Michael M. Thomas

"There is nothing so special as curling up with a small book that makes you think, laugh, and cry, and this is just what *Not Bartlett's* gives you. This delightful book is a must next to every bed—a perfect gift."—Bunny Williams

This personal collection of quotations by famous writers offers timeless impressions about family, friends, gardening, pets, writing and reading, nature, travel, art, politics, and many of life's other pleasures. *Not Bartlett's* is an absolute treasure imbued with a highly developed sense of intelligence, style, and grace.

Elise Lufkin is the author of *Found Dogs: Tales of Strays Who Landed on Their Feet* and *Second Chances: More Tales of Found Dogs*. She is a lifelong compulsive reader. One of her favorite quotations from *Not Bartlett's* is: "People say that life's the thing, but I prefer reading."

An avid reader's personal collection of quotations about life's pleasures.

Sidelines & Gift Books / Literature & Essay
October
A Paperback Original
Helen Marx Books
5¼ x 7¼ | 95 pp
TP US $11.95 | CAN $14.50
978-1-933527-13-0 CUSA

Marketing Plans

Advance reader copies

Author Events

Salisbury, CT • Sun Valley, ID • New York, NY,

Author Hometown: Sun Valley, ID

Turtle Point Press

The Secret Lives of People in Love
Simon Van Booy

Fiction
6 x 8 | 176 pp
TP US $14.95 | CAN $18.00
978-1-933527-05-5 CUSA

Martian Dawn
Michael Friedman

Fiction
4¾ x 7¼ | 176 pp
TP US $14.95 | CAN $18.00
978-1-885586-44-5 CUSA

Childhood at Oriol
Michael Burn

Fiction
5½ x 8½ | 360 pp
TP US $16.95 | CAN $20.50
978-1-885586-32-2 CUSA

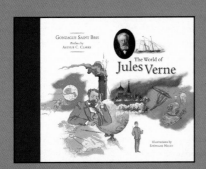

The World of Jules Verne
Gonzague Saint Bris
Illustrated by Stephane Heuet
Translated by Helen Marx

Science Fiction & Fantasy / Biography &
Autobiography
10½ x 8 | 96 pp
67 Color illustrations
TC US $28.00 | CAN $33.95
978-1-885586-42-1 CUSA

Lost Splendor
The Amazing Memoirs of the
Man Who Killed Rasputin
Prince Felix Youssoupoff

Biography & Autobiography / History
5½ x 8½ | 314 pp
TP US $11.95 | CAN $14.50
978-1-933527-12-3 CUSA

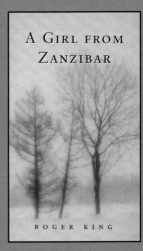

A Girl From Zanzibar
Roger King

Fiction / African Studies
5 x 8½ | 288 pp
TP US $14.95 | CAN $18.00
978-1-885586-60-5 CUSA

Diamond Matters

Kadir van Lohuizen

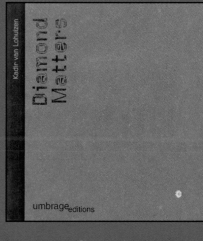

Mirroring the progress of the diamond from the mines of Africa to the world of fashion, *Diamond Matters* records the lifespan of the world's most precious stone. Starting with the mineworkers—many just children—celebrated photographer Kadir van Lohuizen tracks the sparkling ice on its socially upward journey. With interviews from those digging it from hillsides with bare hands to participants in conflicts in Zaire, Sierra Leone, and Angola; to dealers and to wearers, it is a beautiful yet deeply disturbing and thought-provoking book.

The book charts the rising awareness of the blood diamond issue, as pressure and the threat to its image grew in the diamond industry to create a certification system guaranteeing that only conflict-free diamonds came on the market. While new pacts have reduced smuggling and added more transparency, still little of the world's enormous mineral profits flow back to the people. A fair-trade agreement with profits shared by all is the next step. Bound in luxurious suede, with a small diamond on the front cover, and elegantly printed in tritone on five different papers, *Diamond Matters* is an explosive idea in a small package.

Dutch-born **Kadir van Lohuizen** is the recipient of numerous international awards and grants, including prizes from World Press Photo in 1997 and Foundation Vluchteling; the Dick Scherpenzeel Prize in 2000; a 2001 grant from the Foundation for Visual Arts, Design, and Architecture; and more. He is the author of five books and numerous exhibitions.

The lifespan of the world's most precious stone, from miners to mannequins—at a terrible cost.

Photography
September
5¼ x 5¾ | 240 pp
120 B&W photographs
TC US $29.95 | CAN $36.00
978-1-884167-70-6 CUSA

Marketing Plans

Advance reader copies

Torrijos
The Man and The Myth
Photographs by Graciela Iturbide
Text by Gabriel García Márquez

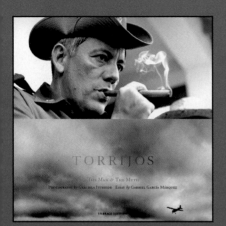

Photography
October
9 x 9 | 112 pp
70 B&W photographs
TC US $39.95 | CAN $48.00
978-1-884167-68-3 CUSA

Marketing Plans

Advance reader copies
National advertising:
Criticas • Latin American Perspectives •
Latin American Politics and Society •
Latin American Research Review •
The Latin American Review of Books •
NACLA Report on the Americas • The Nation

Author Events

Los Angeles, CA • Miami, FL •
New York, NY • Houston, TX

In the annals of Latin American politics, Omar Torrijos of Panama was a David against Goliath, a charismatic leader who challenged the landed oligarchy and redistributed land and wealth. He died tragically in a 1981 plane crash widely rumored to have been the work of the CIA.

This unique, intensely personal homage by two giant talents—the great Mexican photographer Graciela Iturbide and the Nobel Prize-winning Colombian writer Gabriel García Márquez—shows Torrijos as the man behind the story. Never-before-published photographs and never-before-told personal reminiscences offer up candles of memory and understanding and a correction to history. Torrijos' friend describes a moody, lonely president drinking whiskey all night, and in pre-dawn, summoning one of six different women he knew to keep away the demons. In their eyes, Torrijos is understood not as a dictator who silenced opposition, closed the media, ran up debt, and turned a blind eye to corruption, but as a flawed hero in the footsteps of Simón Bolívar: the first leader to advocate for the poor, yet an innovator in schools and jobs who lured foreign investment to create a regional financial center, and a historical giant whose greatest legacy to his people was the Canal Treaty, signed with President Jimmy Carter in 1977. This is a memoir about a man ahead of his time.

Graciela Iturbide has received many honors, including a W. Eugene Smith Grant in 1987 and a Guggenheim Fellowship in 1988, published numerous books, and has held major exhibitions around the world.

One of the world's greatest writers and author of *One Hundred Years of Solitude,* a defining classic of twentieth-century literature, Colombian-born **Gabriel García Márquez** is the winner of the 1982 Nobel Prize in Literature.

A Nobel Prize-winning writer and celebrated photographer reconsider a legendary character in Latin American political history.

Umbrage Editions

It's Complicated: The American Teenager

Photographs and Interviews by Robin Bowman

Essays by Susan Minot
Afterword by Dr. Robert Coles

Robin Bowman's five-year journey into the heart of teenage America created a series of 414 "collaborative portraits," wherein she shares her discoveries of a generation now coming of age. In searing and intimate photographs, presented alongside the young people's voices of passion, pride, embarrassment, lust, pain, bewilderment, anxiety, joy, uncertainty, and rage, the book charts the coming of age of the largest generation in America—77 million strong—in every region of the country and every socioeconomic group: from a Texas debutante to teenage gang members in New York City, from a drag queen in Georgia to a coal miner in West Virginia.

Bowman's intimate photographs ask us to reconcile preconceived ideas and stereotypes of teenagers with the diversity of individuals in the portraits. This book and the traveling exhibition it accompanies are about the inside lives of these kids and how they see their reality in their own voices.

Robin Bowman, a 2005 W. Eugene Smith Memorial fellow, is a photojournalist based in Portland, Maine.

Essayist **Susan Minot** is the award-winning author of *Evening, Lust,* and *Monkeys.*

Dr. Robert Coles is the Pulitzer-Prize winning author of the Children of Crisis series and a Harvard emeritus professor of psychiatry.

Searing, intimate portraits and interviews with America's next generation from small towns and big cities.

Photography
October
9 x 11 | 160 pp
414 B&W photographs
TC US $39.95 | CAN $48.00
978-1-884167-69-0 CUSA

Marketing Plans

Advance reader copies
National advertising:
American Photo • Seventeen •
Teen Vogue • XXL

Author Events

Los Angeles, CA • Washington, DC •
Chicago, IL • Portland, ME • New York, NY

Author Hometown: Portland, ME

Umbrage Editions

The Innocents
Photographs by Taryn Simon

Photography / Current Affairs
12½ x 10 | 128 pp
TC US $34.95 | CAN $42.00
978-1-884167-18-8 CUSA

Speak Truth to Power
Human Rights Defenders Who
are Changing Our World
Kerry Kennedy
Photographs by Eddie Adams

Photography / Current Affairs
11 x 11 | 256 pp
52 B&W photographs
TC US $50.00 | CAN $60.00
978-1-884167-52-2 CUSA

Flesh and Spirit
Claudio Edinger

Photography
9 x 11½ | 217 pp
200 B&W photographs
TC US $40.00 | CAN $48.00
978-1-884167-63-8 CUSA

Inconvenient Stories
Portraits and Interviews
with Vietnam Veterans
Jeffrey Wolin

Photography / Military History
8 x 11½ | 112 pp
50 Color and B&W photographs
TC US $40.00 | CAN $48.00
978-1-884167-61-4 CUSA

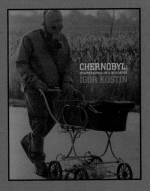

Chernobyl
Confessions of a Reporter
Photographs by Igor Kostin

Photography / History
8 x 10 | 240 pp
100 Color and B&W photographs
TC US $35.00 | CAN $42.00
978-1-884167-57-7 CUSA

Journal
A Mother and Daughter's Recovery
From Breast Cancer
Photographs by Annabel Clark with
Lynn Redgrave

Photography / Health & Fitness
11 x 8 | 112 pp
TC US $29.95 | CAN $36.00
978-1-884167-43-0 CUSA

No Real Light
Joe Wenderoth

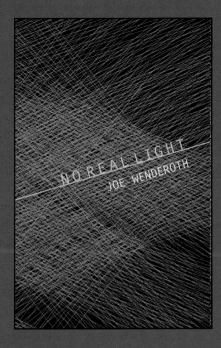

"Joe Wenderoth is a brilliant writer, original and subversive, sensitive and strange. I read his work with awe and admiration."—Ben Marcus

"Joe Wenderoth's brave new poetic talent is like nothing so much as a live wire writing its own epitaph in sparks. . . . He makes quick cuts in the meat of the ordinary, which is the meat of the impossible."—Cal Bedient

This clear-eyed new work from a favorite young poet is searching and solemn, dissatisfied with artificial condolences and pat maxims. Joe Wenderoth's determination in the face of harsh realities is what rescues us, and him, from hopelessness.

Luck

So a screaming woke you
just in time.
An animal's scream, or animals'.
What kind of animal it was
doesn't matter, and cannot,
in any case, be determined.
The point is you are saved.
Your mouth has been opened.

Joe Wenderoth grew up near Baltimore and is the author of five books of prose and poetry. He teaches at the University of California, Davis.

Wave's most popular author presents his first poetry collection since *Letters to Wendy's*.

Also Available

Letters to Wendy's
Joe Wenderoth
Fiction / Poetry
5½ x 6½ | 296 pp
TP US $14.00 | CAN $17.00
978-0-9703672-0-4 CUSA

The Holy Spirit of Life
Essays Written for John Ashcroft's Secret Self
Joe Wenderoth
Poetry / Literature & Essay
5½ x 8 | 160 pp
TP US $14.00 | CAN $17.00
978-0-9746353-7-8 CUSA

Wave Books

Poetry
September
A Paperback Original
5½ x 8½ | 80 pp
TP US $14.00 | CAN $17.00
978-1-933517-22-3 CUSA

Marketing Plans

Co-op available
Advance reader copies
National advertising:
The American Poetry Review •
Boston Review • Poets & Writers • Rain Taxi

Author Events

Los Angeles, CA • San Francisco, CA •
Boston, MA • New York, NY • Seattle, WA

Author Hometown: Davis, CA

Poetry
September
A Paperback Original
6 x 8¾ | 88 pp
TP US $14.00 | CAN $17.00
978-1-933517-24-7 CUSA

An unforgettable debut: Dorothea Lasky is a seductive prophet who delights as well as terrifies.

Awe
Dorothea Lasky

If the book of Revelations had been scribbled in the diary of a precocious fourteen-year-old girl, the prophecies might look something like *Awe*. Dorothea Lasky is a daring truth-teller, naming names and boldly pushing the boundaries of confession. The secrets she tells are truths we recognize in ourselves: "Be scared of yourself / The real self / Is very scary."

Dorothea Lasky was born in St. Louis in 1978. She is the author of several chapbooks and has attended Harvard University and the University of Massachusetts Amherst.

Marketing Plans
Co-op available • Advance reader copies
National advertising: The American Poetry Review • Boston Review • Poets & Writers • Rain Taxi

Author Events
Los Angeles, CA • Washington, DC • Boston, MA • New York, NY • Philadelphia, PA • Seattle, WA

Author Hometown: Philadelphia, PA

Poetry
November
A Paperback Original
National Poetry Series
6 x 8½ | 120 pp
TP US $14.00 | CAN $17.00
978-1-933517-26-1 CUSA

This National Poetry Series-winning collection emerges from half-remembered fairy tales and reconstructed dreams.

The Scented Fox
Laynie Browne

Selected by Alice Notley for the National Poetry Series, Laynie Browne's sixth collection casts a spell. In these fragmented poetic tales, characters disappear and reemerge, their charms reconfigured, their stories unraveling, and their happy endings elusive. The book's coda consists of a fantastical poetic dictionary, asking readers to redefine their sense of meaning.

Laynie Browne was born in 1966 and grew up in Los Angeles. She is the author of six collections of poetry, including *Daily Sonnets* and *Mermaid's Purse*. She has taught creative writing at the University of Washington, Bothell, and Mills College.

Marketing Plans
Co-op available • Advance reader copies
National advertising: The American Poetry Review • Boston Review • Poets & Writers • Rain Taxi

Author Events
Tucson, AZ • San Francisco, CA • New York, NY • Portland, OR • Seattle, WA

Author Hometown: Oakland, CA

Wave Books

Quick Fix
Sudden Fiction
Ana María Shua

Translated by Rhona Dahl Buchanan; Art by Luci Mistratov

"The wink of an eye and we are transported to an unexpected realm. In very few impeccable lines, Shua's micro short stories open new vistas to our perception of dreams, myths, fairy tales, even of our everyday life. To read her is to discover another dimension in fiction: small is absolutely beautiful, and thrilling, and often disquieting."—Luisa Valenzuela

Quick Fix, a bilingual collection, reflects Ana María Shua's ingenious blending of precise language, incisive humor, and incredible imagination into a unique style of sudden fiction.

Ana María Shua was born in Buenos Aires and has published over forty books.

Marketing Plans
Co-op available

Author Hometown: Louisville, KY

Fiction / Latin American Literature
February
A Paperback Original
Secret Weavers Series 21
6 x 9 | 272 pp
30 B&W illustrations
TP US $17.00 | CAN $20.50
978-1-893996-91-5 CUSA

A quick fix of fiction in this age of speed and technology.

Of Whiskey and Winter
Peter Conners
Introduction by Peter Johnson

"Peter Conners' stunning prose poems are packed with keen sensitivity, dreaminess, and wit. I love his time travels, the vibrant layering of image and detail. This is language and vision I want to come home to again and again."—Naomi Shihab Nye

"I don't know what's more remarkable about the poems in *Of Whiskey and Winter,* their exquisite music or their startling, acrobatic leaps. By turns manic and contemplative, zany and wise, his rollicking poems have the power to simultaneously challenge, illuminate and praise the illusive character of the world."—Gary Young

Peter Conners lives in Rochester, New York, and is an editor for BOA Editions, Ltd.

Author Events
Detroit, MI • Buffalo, NY • New York, NY • Rochester, NY • Syracuse, NY • Erie, PA • Providence, RI • Brattleboro, VT

Author Hometown: Rochester, NY

Poetry
September
A Paperback Original
6 x 9 | 88 pp
TP US $15.00 | CAN $18.00
978-1-893996-89-2 CUSA

Rollicking poems that have the power to challenge, illuminate, and praise the illusiveness of the world.

White Pine Press

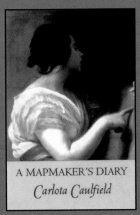

Poetry / Latin American Literature
October
A Paperback Original
Secret Weavers Series 22
6 x 9 | 180 pp
TP US $16.00 | CAN $19.50
978-1-893996-88-5 CUSA

A verbal acrobat, a juggler of words and images, and a magician of memory.

A Mapmaker's Diary
Carlota Caulfield
Translated by Mary G. Berg

"Carlota Caulfield has given us a work of great sensuality and rare luminosity, suffused with an intelligence that is both playful and meditative. Her pleasures and discoveries become ours, her tender, often sly observations are crafted for inheritance. But it is Caulfield's devotion to the daily sacred that helps inspire our own."—Cristina Garcia

A Mapmaker's Diary gathers a selection of poems from both published and unpublished work in a bilingual format by this verbal acrobat, juggler of words, and magician of memory.

Carlota Caulfield is the author of nine books of poetry. She teaches at Mills College in California.

Marketing Plans
Co-op available

Author Events
Los Angeles, CA • Oakland, CA • San Francisco, CA • New York, NY • Portland, OR • Seattle, WA

Author Hometown: Oakland, CA

Poetry / Asian Studies
November
A Paperback Original
White Pine Press Poetry Prize 12
6 x 9 | 96 pp
TP US $15.00 | CAN $18.00
978-1-893996-90-8 CUSA

"An ambitious and brilliant new voice."
—Genie Zeiger

Paper Pavilion
Jennifer Kwon Dobbs

"Dobbs is an astonishing poet. The poetry in *Paper Pavilion* is by turns lyric and incisive, operatic and sweeping. There is a resonant passion that fills every page. With this heartbreaking and exhilarating debut, Dobbs has established herself as one of the most compelling and important poets of her generation."—David St. John

Paper Pavilion captures the theme of transnational adoption and a powerful search for a personal history and identity from Korea to America.

Jennifer Kwon Dobbs is currently an Edwin Mem fellow in literature and creative writing at the University of Southern California.

Marketing Plans
Co-op available

Author Events
Tempe, AZ • Los Angeles, CA • San Francisco, CA • Santa Monica, CA • New York, NY • Stony Brook, NY • Stillwater, OK • Tulsa, OK • Portland, OR • Pittsburgh, PA

Author Hometown: Los Angeles, CA

White Pine Press

Woman on the Terrace
Moon Chung-hee
Translated by Seong Kon Kim and Alec Gordon

Moon Chung-hee's lyrical poems represent poignant self-examination, evoking moments of bewilderment and hopeful resignation to the passage of time and imprisoning conditions of her life. Her work explores the desire to escape the fetters of domesticity as a vehicle for understanding a woman's journey and her negotiations between the desire for freedom and domestic reality.

Moon Chung-hee is one of the most celebrated poets living in South Korea today. Since her debut in 1969, Moon has published eleven books of poems. She is currently the poetry chair at Dongguk University in Seoul, South Korea.

Poetry / Asian Studies
October
A Paperback Original
Korean Voices 11
6 x 9 | 96 pp
TP US $15.00 | CAN $18.00
978-1-893996-86-1 CUSA

Moon Chung-hee is a poet of wild nature, vigorous energy, and sparking passion.

One Human Family and Other Stories
Chung Yeun-hee
Translated by Hyun-jae Yee Sallee

The devastating hold the Korean War still has on the ordinary citizens of South Korea is revealed here in a novella and four short stories. Although the war happened many years ago, old animosities remain, and elderly nursing home residents are traumatized by their belief that the new resident was a collaborator. A child is made a laughing stock when she thinks the condoms tossed aside on the beach by American GIs are balloons.

Chung Yeun-hee has published several novels and numerous short stories and essays.

Hyun-jae Yee Sallee has translated Korean literature for nearly twenty-five years.

Author Hometown: Kissimmee, FL

Fiction / Asian Studies
January
A Paperback Original
Korean Voices 12
6 x 9 | 232 pp
TP US $16.00 | CAN $19.50
978-1-893996-87-8 CUSA

Haunting stories of the aftermath of war.

White Pine Press

449

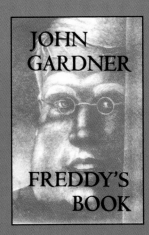

Freddy's Book
John Gardner

Fiction
6 x 9 | 256 pp
TP US $16.00 | CAN $19.50
978-1-893996-84-7 CUSA

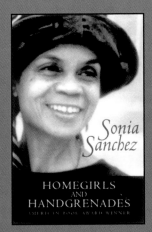

Homegirls
and Handgrenades
Sonia Sanchez

Poetry / African American Studies
6 x 9 | 96 pp
TP US $14.00 | CAN $17.00
978-1-893996-80-9 CUSA

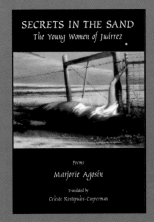

Secrets in the Sand
The Young Women of Juárez
Marjorie Agosin
Translated by Celeste
Kostopulos-Cooperman

Poetry / Latin American Literature
6 x 9 | 96 pp
TP US $15.00 | CAN $18.00
978-1-893996-47-2 CUSA

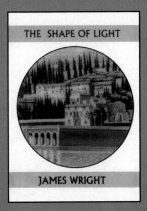

The Shape of Light
James Wright

Poetry / Travel & Travel Guides
5 x 7 | 96 pp
10 B&W illustrations
TP US $14.00 | CAN $17.00
978-1-893996-85-4 CUSA

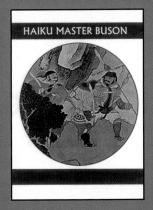

Haiku Master Buson
Buson
Translated by Edith Shiffert
and Yuki Sawa

Poetry / Asian Studies
5 x 7 | 256 pp
TP US $16.00 | CAN $19.50
978-1-893996-81-6 CUSA

The Unswept Path
Contemporary American Haiku
Edited by John Brandi and
Dennis Maloney

Poetry Anthology / Writing
5 x 7 | 192 pp
TP US $15.00 | CAN $18.00
978-1-893996-38-0 CUSA

Hello At Last: Embracing the Koan of Friendship & Meditation
Sara Jenkins

The Buddha actively promoted spiritual friendship, calling it "the whole of the spiritual life," yet much of Buddhist practice is spent meditating in solitude and silence. *Hello at Last* charts one woman's exploration of this apparent contradiction. The author shares practices representing a variety of traditions, all aiming to soften the walls of self and dispel the illusion of separateness. "Offering ourselves as mirrors for each other becomes a breathtaking act of love."

Sara Jenkins is a writer and editor and a student of the Zen teacher Cheri Huber.

Author Hometown: Lake Junaluska, NC

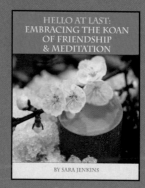

Buddhism
November
A Paperback Original
6½ x 8¼ | 160 pp
TP US $15.95 | CAN $19.50
978-1-899579-79-2 CUSA

Friendship on the way to no-self.

A Guide to the Buddhas
Vessantara (Tony McMahon)

Why does Buddhism refer to many Buddhas? Who are they? What do they communicate? In this beautifully written book, meet the historical and archetypal Buddhas that form part of the rich symbolism of Tibetan Buddhism. An in-depth exploration that is accessible and inspiring, containing detailed and beautiful illustrations, *A Guide to the Buddhas* is an informative primer for those new to Buddhism and a handy reference for experienced practitioners. This is the first of three books examining Buddhist archetypes.

Vessantara, born Tony McMahon in England, is a respected and well-published Buddhist author and teacher who holds a particular love for Tibetan Buddhism.

Marketing Plans
National advertising: Shambhala Sun • Tricycle

Buddhism
February
A Paperback Original
Meeting the Buddhas
6½ x 8¼ | 192 pp
17 Color and B&W illustrations
and photographs
TP US $19.95 | CAN $24.00
978-1-899579-83-9 CUSA

**Meet the Buddhas—
did you know there's more than one?**

The Buddha's Noble Eightfold Path

Sangharakshita

Buddhism
September
A Paperback Original
Buddhist Wisdom for Today
6 x 9¼ | 176 pp
TP US $17.95 | CAN $21.50
978-1-899579-81-5 CUSA

The Buddha's basics: timeless truth.

The Noble Eightfold Path—the Buddha's first teaching—is a timeless truth. One starts with a vision, a moment of insight, then transformation of thoughts and acts follows in the light of that truth.

This teaching is explored in relation to every aspect of life and is a treasury of wisdom and practical guidance. This introduction takes the reader deeper than most while always remaining practical, inspiring, and accessible. This is the first in a new series, Buddhist Wisdom for Today.

Sangharakshita is a leading Western Buddhist teacher and a popular author of more than thirty books on Buddhism.

Marketing Plans
National advertising: Shambhala Sun • Tricycle

Precious Teachers: Indian Memoirs of an English Buddhist

Sangharakshita

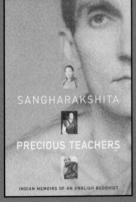

Buddhism / Biography & Autobiography
December
A Paperback Original
6 x 9¼ | 172 pp
TP US $19.95 | CAN $24.00
978-1-899579-78-5 CUSA

**A legacy of enlightenment—
a Buddhist teacher's spiritual lineage.**

Dennis Lingwood, an Englishman and novice Buddhist monk, follows his Indian Buddhist teacher on a pilgrimage to find himself in Kalimpong, a hill station at the foot of the Himalayas. It is 1950, and Tibetan Buddhism has begun its exodus into India, with Kalimpong as a gateway.

In this latest addition to his memoirs, Lingwood, better known as Urgyen Sangharakshita, shares his recollections of those Tibetan gurus and traveling academics who lived in and passed through Kalimpong. Some, like Dudjom Rinpoche and Dilgo Khyentse Rinpoche, formally impart their wisdom; others teach invaluable lessons by just living their lives.

Marketing Plans
National advertising: Shambhala Sun • Tricycle

Windhorse Publications

The Witches' Almanac 2008–2009
Edited by Theitic

The Witches' Almanac has been acclaimed for the quality of its content, art, and design since 1971. It now appears in an excellent updated format. Enlarged to a six-by-nine-inch size, the annual publication offers 136 pages of reading pleasure. The beautifully designed new color cover is laminated to provide a sturdy, "always a keepsake" finish.

This year's article lineup is world-class; articles include: Hsi Wang Mu and peach-tree immortality, the horoscope of Dr. Emoto and a look into his research (positive thought's effect on water crystals), consequences of trance, cryptic Enoch unveiled, women athletes of ancient Greek Olympics, interpreting the Year of the Rat, and a history of Tarot. You will relish sassy Roman shrewdness with Aesop and a Nigerian wisdom tale: both ancient in origin, both full of fun. Plus, we include "Aphrodite and Adonis" from our newest publication, *Greek Gods in Love,* by Barbara Stacy: The flighty goddess of love falls head over heels for the handsomest of mortals.

Along with the new, old favorites still abound: the Moon Calendar, astrology by Dikki-Jo Mullen, and weather forecasts from climatologist Tom Lang. As always, this is a delightful companion for adept, occultist, and those who simply enjoy gleaning lore and legends, ancient rituals, herbal secrets, interviews and biographies, mystic incantations, and many a curious tale of good and evil.

Arcane symbols and intriguing graphic images, including many rare medieval woodcuts, always add to the enjoyment of *The Witches' Almanac.*

The original annual guide for students of magic, divination, mystery, witchcraft, ancient lore, and occult secrets.

Occultism & Parapsychology / Spirituality
October
A Paperback Original
6 x 9 | 136 pp
100 B&W illustrations
TP US $10.95 | CAN $13.50
978-0-9773703-3-7 CUSA

Marketing Plans

50,000-copy print run

Author Hometown: Providence, RI

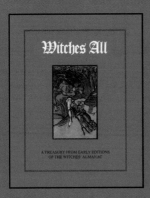

Witches All
Elizabeth Pepper and John Wilcock

Occultism & Parapsychology / Spirituality
8½ x 11 | 112 pp
TP US $13.95 | CAN $17.00
978-1-881098-26-3 CUSA

Magic Spells and Incantations
Elizabeth Pepper

Occultism & Parapsychology / Folklore
5¼ x 8¼ | 96 pp
TP US $12.95 | CAN $15.50
978-1-881098-21-8 CUSA

Magical Creatures
Elizabeth Pepper and Barbara Stacy

Occultism & Parapsychology / Folklore
5¼ x 8¼ | 96 pp
TP US $12.95 | CAN $15.50
978-1-881098-14-0 CUSA

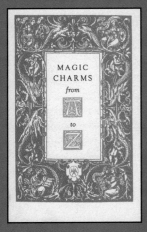

Magic Charms from A to Z

Occultism & Parapsychology / Folklore
5¼ x 8¼ | 96 pp
TP US $12.95 | CAN $15.50
978-0-9773703-2-0 CUSA

Love Charms
Elizabeth Pepper

Occultism & Parapsychology / Folklore
5½ x 7½ | 48 pp
TP US $6.95 | CAN $8.50
978-1-881098-20-1 CUSA

Greek Gods in Love
Barbara Stacy

History / Romance
8½ x 11 | 120 pp
100 B&W illustrations
TP US $15.95 | CAN $19.50
978-0-9773703-1-3 CUSA

Situations, Sings
Collaboratively Composed Poems
Jack Collom and Lyn Hejinian

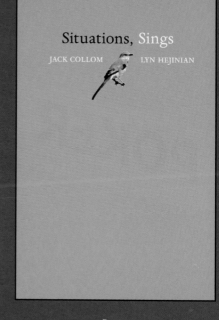

A collection of twelve formally distinct poems collaboratively written by Jack Collom and Lyn Hejinian. The two poets began working together in 1992, and over the years they have developed a repertoire of forms and procedures, all intended to extend the possibilities for invention, play, and the unfolding of unforeseeable meaning. Both poets embrace collaborative authorship as a means of challenging aesthetic preconceptions. In the process, they frequently venture across thematic limits, discovering unexpected coherences. The poems often give themselves over to pleasure, but they are governed by the logic of poetic language and they carry considerable metaphysical depth.

Jack Collom is the author of seventeen small-press books of poetry, including *Red Car Goes By* (Tuumba Press, 2001) and two CDs. He spent the early 1980s in New York, where he taught poetry to children in the Poets In Public Service and Teachers & Writers programs. In 1980 and again in 1990 he was awarded a fellowship in poetry by the National Endowment for the Arts. Collom lives and teaches in Boulder, Colorado.

Published collections of **Lyn Hejinian**'s writing include *Writing Is an Aid to Memory, My Life,* and *The Language of Inquiry.* From 1976 to 1984, Hejinian was the editor of Tuumba Press; she is currently the co-director of Atelos, a literary project commissioning and publishing cross-genre work by poets. In the fall of 2000, she was elected the sixty-sixth fellow of The Academy of American Poets. She teaches at the University of California, Berkeley.

A collection of twelve formally distinct poems collaboratively written by poets Jack Collom and Lyn Hejinian.

Poetry
October
A Paperback Original
Adventures in Poetry
6 x 9 | 160 pp
TP US $15.00 | CAN $18.00
978-0-9761612-4-0 CUSA

Marketing Plans

Advance reader copies
National advertising:
The American Poetry Review •
The Poetry Project Newsletter • Rain Taxi

Author Events

Berkeley, CA • San Diego, CA •
San Francisco, CA • Boulder, CO •
Denver, CO • New York, NY

Author Hometown: Boulder, CO/Berkeley, CA

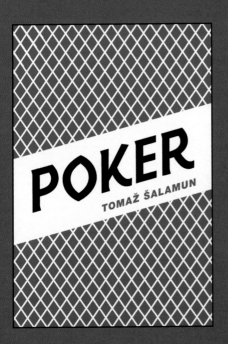

Poetry
November
A Paperback Original
Eastern European Poets Series
5½ x 8 | 88 pp
TP US $15.00 | CAN $18.00
978-0-939010-96-7 CUSA

Marketing Plans

National advertising: Rain Taxi

Author Events

New York, NY

Author Hometown: Seattle, WA

Poker
Tomaž Šalamun
Translated by Joshua Beckman

Poker is Tomaž Šalamun's first book of poetry, originally published in 1966 in Slovenia. This edition, vibrantly translated by award-winning poet Joshua Beckman in collaboration with the author, makes *Poker* available in its entirety in English.

As a young poet Šalamun edited *Perspektive,* a progressive cultural and political journal. Communist authorities eventually banned the journal's publication and arrested Šalamun. His first two books, *Poker* (1966) and *The Purpose of the Cloak* (1968), were released in *samizdat.* Šalamun went on to become one of the most widely respected of European poets and achieved international acclaim, later even serving as the Slovenian cultural attaché in New York City.

Šalamun has had several collections published in English translation, including *The Shepherd, the Hunter* (Pedernal, 1992), *The Four Questions of Melancholy* (White Pine Press, 1997), *The Selected Poems of Tomaž Šalamun* (Ecco Press, 1988), *Feast* (Harcourt Brace, 2000), *A Ballad for Metka Krasovec* (Twisted Spoon Press, 2001), and *The Book For My Brother* (Harvest Books, 2006). Šalamun has won the praise of many poets, including James Tate, Robert Creeley, Robert Hass, who celebrates his "love of the poetics of rebellion," and Jorie Graham, who calls his work "one of Europe's great philosophical wonders."

Joshua Beckman is the author of three books of poetry: *Shake, Your Time Has Come,* and *Something I Expected To Be Different.* He has also authored two books in collaboration with Matthew Rohrer: *Nice Hat. Thanks.* and *Adventures While Preaching the Gospel of Beauty.* Beckman is an editor at Wave Books.

Poker is Tomaž Šalamun's first book of poetry, published in 1966 in Slovenia.

Zephyr Press

consortium book sales & distribution
children's titles
fall | winter 2007–2008

To-Do List
Illustrated by Maya Waldman

Children's Fiction
4N Publishing
7 x 5 | 48 pp
40 B&W illustrations
TC US $12.95 | CAN $15.50
978-0-9741319-5-5 CUSA
Full details on page 1

ABeCedarios
Mexican Folk Art ABCs in
Spanish and English
Cynthia Weill
Photographs by K.B. Basseches
Art by Moisés and Armando Jiménez

Children's Nonfiction
Cinco Puntos Press
7½ x 7½ | 32 pp
30 Color photographs
TC US $14.95 | CAN $18.00
978-1-933-693-13-2 CUSA
Full details on page 124

My Mother Wears Combat Boots
A Parenting Guide for the
Rest of Us
Jessica Mills

Parenting
AK Press
5½ x 8½ | 260 pp
TP US $16.95 | CAN $20.50
978-1-904859-72-7 CUSA
Full details on page 29

Little Zizi
Thierry Lenain
Illustrated by Stéphane Poulin
Translated by Daniel Zolinsky

Children's Fiction
Cinco Puntos Press
8¼ x 10¼ | 32 pp
TC US $ 16.95 | CAN $20.50
978-1-933693-05-7 CUSA
Full details on page 125

Adventure Dad
Rescuing Families from the
Couch One Expedition at a Time
Edited by Joe Kurmaskie

Sports & Recreation /
Family & Parenting
Breakaway Books
6 x 9 | 320 pp
40 B&W illustrations and photographs
TC US $23.95 | CAN $29.00
978-1-891369-71-1 CUSA
Full details on page 95

Double Crossing
Eve Tal

Young Adult Fiction / Jewish Studies
Cinco Puntos Press
5½ x 8½ | 262 pp
TP US $8.95 | CAN $11.00
978-1-933693-15-6 CUSA
Full details on page 126

A Perfect Season for Dreaming / Una temporada perfecta para soñar
Benjamin Alire Sáenz
Art by Esau Andrade

Children's Fiction / Hispanic Studies
Cinco Puntos Press
8½ x 11 | 40 pp
18 Color illustrations
TC US $17.95 | CAN $21.50
978-1-933693-01-9 CUSA
Full details on page 123

Fairy Tale Timpa
Altan
Translated by Michael Reynolds

Children's Fiction
Europa Editions
8¼ x 11½ | 48 pp
42 Color illustrations
TP US $14.95 | CAN $18.00
978-1-933372-38-9 CUSA
Full details on page 185

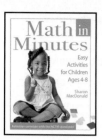

Math in Minutes
Easy Activities
for Children Ages 4–8
Sharon MacDonald

Education & Teaching / Childcare
Gryphon House
8½ x 11 | 224 pp
150 B&W illustrations
TP $19.95
978-0-87659-057-7 USA
Full details on page 207

Julie Black Belt
The Kung Fu Chronicles
Oliver Chin
Illustrated by Charlene Chua

Children's Fiction / Sports & Recreation
Immedium
8½ x 10½ | 36 pp
36 Color illustrations
TC US $15.95 | CAN $19.50
978-1-59702-009-1 CUSA
Full details on page 221

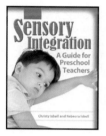

Sensory Integration
A Guide for Preschool Teachers
Christy Isbell and Rebecca Isbell

Childcare / Education & Teaching
Gryphon House
8½ x 11 | 160 pp
63 B&W illustrations and photographs
TP $19.95
978-0-87659-060-7 USA
Full details on page 208

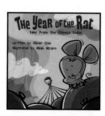

The Octonauts
& the Sea of Shade
Meomi

Children's Fiction / Sidelines & Gift Books
Immedium
11 x 8 | 36 pp
36 Color illustrations
TC US $15.95 | CAN $19.50
978-1-59702-010-7 CUSA
Full details on page 222

Read! Move! Learn!
Active Stories for Active Learning
Carol Totsky Hammett and
Nicki Collins Geigert

Childcare / Education & Teaching
Gryphon House
8½ x 11 | 232 pp
150 B&W illustrations
TP $19.95
978-0-87659-058-4 USA
Full details on page 209

The Year of the Rat
Tales from the Chinese Zodiac
Oliver Chin
Illustrated by Miah Alcorn

Children's Fiction / Asian Studies
Immedium
9⅝ x 10 | 36 pp
36 Color illustrations
TC US $15.95 | CAN $19.50
978-1-59702-011-4 CUSA
Full details on page 222

Are You Ready for Me?
Claire Buchwald
Illustrated by Amelia Hansen

Children's Fiction / Pets & Pet Care
The Gryphon Press
9 x 9¾ | 24 pp
24 Color illustrations
TC US $15.95 | CAN $19.50
978-0-940719-04-0 CUSA
Full details on page 211

The Prosperity Factor for Kids
A comprehensive parent's guide to developing positive saving, spending, and credit habits
Kelley Keehn

Business & Economics / Parenting
Insomniac Press
6 x 9 | 224 pp
24 B&W illustrations
TP $14.95
978-1-897178-42-3 USA
Full details on page 225

Learning Together With Young Children
A Curriculum Framework for Reflective Teachers
Deb Curtis and Margie Carter

Education & Teaching / Childcare
Redleaf Press
8½ x11 | 240 pp
300 Color photographs
TP $39.95
978-1-929610-97-6 USA
Full details on page 323

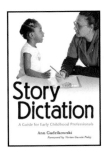

Story Dictation
A Guide for Early Childhood Professionals
Ann Gadzikowski

Education & Teaching / Childcare
Redleaf Press
7 x 10 | 144 pp
15 B&W photographs
TP $24.95
978-1-933653-28-0 USA
Full details on page 324

Early Learning Standards and Staff Development
Best Practices in the Face of Change
Gaye Gronlund and Marlyn James

Education & Teaching / Management
Redleaf Press
8 x 10 | 160 pp
TP with DVD $34.95
978-1-933653-31-0 USA
Full details on page 323

Growing, Growing Strong
A Whole Curriculum for Young Children, 2nd Edition
Connie Jo Smith, Charlotte M. Hendricks, and Becky S. Bennett

Health & Fitness / Childcare
Redleaf Press
8½ x 11 | 240 pp
100 B&W illustrations
TP $25.95
978-1-929610-94-5 USA
Full details on page 324

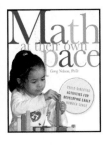

Math at Their Own Pace
Child-Directed Activities for Developing Early Number Sense
Greg Nelson, PhD

Education & Teaching / Mathematics
Redleaf Press
8½ x11 | 184 pp
15 B&W photographs and
20 B&W illustrations
TP $29.95
978-1-933653-29-7 USA
Full details on page 324

Street-Smart College Essays
Personal Statements by Berkeley High Students (for the University of California and Other Select Schools)
Compiled by Janet Huseby

Education & Teaching / Writing
Stone Bridge Press
5⅜ x 7½ | 144 pp
TP US $11.95 | CAN $14.50
978-1-933330-60-0 CUSA
Full details on page 404

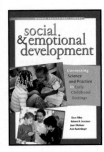

Social & Emotional Development
Connecting Science and Practice in Early Childhood Settings
Dave Riley, Robert San Juan, Joan Klinkner, and Ann Ramminger

Education & Teaching /
Psychology & Psychiatry
Redleaf Press
7 x 10 | 144 pp
15 B&W photographs
TP $24.95
978-1-933653-30-3 USA
Full details on page 324

Catch That Crocodile!
Anushka Ravishankar
Illustrated by Pulak Biswas

Children's Fiction / Art
Tara Publishing
7¼ x 9½ | 40 pp
40 Color illustrations
TC US $14.95 | CAN $18.00
978-81-86211-63-2 CUSA
Handmade Edition
TC 50% NR US $25.00 | Can $30.00
978-81-86211-94-6 CUSA
Full details on page 405

The Sacred Banana Leaf
Nathan Kumar Scott
Art by Radhashyam Raut

Children's Fiction / Art
Tara Publishing
8¼ x 11 | 32 pp
32 Color illustrations
TC US $16.95 | CAN $20.50
978-81-86211-28-1 CUSA
Full details on page 405

The Jungle Book
Rudyard Kipling
Adapted by Stuart Paterson

Drama / Young Adult Fiction
Theatre Communications Group /
Nick Hern Books
5 x 8 | 96 pp
TP y $18.95
978-1-85459-968-1 USA
Full details on page 424

The Book Book
A Journey into Bookmaking
Sophie Benini Pietromarchi

Children's Nonfiction / Crafts & Hobbies
Tara Publishing
6½ x 9½ | 128 pp
128 Color illustrations
TC US $19.95 | CAN $24.00
978-81-86211-24-3 CUSA
Full details on page 406

Carrie's War
Nina Bawden
Adapted by Emma Reeves

Drama / Young Adult Fiction
Theatre Communications Group /
Oberon Books
5 x 8 | 96 pp
TP y US $18.95 | CAN $23.00
978-1-84002-720-4 CUSA
Full details on page 430

4N Publishing

44-73 21st Street, D6
Long Island City, NY 11101
Executives: Erin Canning and L.J. Ruell
ph 718/482-1135
erin@4npublishing.com
www.4npublishing.com
ISBN prefix: 978-0-9741319

Akashic Books

232 Third Street, Suite B404
Brooklyn, NY 11215
Executive: Johnny Temple
ph 718/643-9193
f 718/643-9195
Akashic7@aol.com
www.akashicbooks.com
ISBN prefixes: 978-1-888451, 978-0-9719206,
    978-1-933354, 978-0-9789103

A&C Black

38 Soho Square
London W1D 3HB
UNITED KINGDOM
Sales director: David Wightman
ph 011 44 (0) 207 440 2490
f 011 44 (0) 207 758 0222
salesoffice@acblack.com
www.acblack.com
ISBN prefixes: 978-0-413, 978-0-7136

Alice James Books

238 Main Street
Farmington, ME 04938
Executive: April Ossmann
ph 207/778-7071
ajb@umf.maine.edu
www.alicejamesbooks.org
ISBN prefixes: 978-0-914086, 978-1-882295

Aerialist Press, or Publishing Without a Net

2605 Hennepin Avenue South
Minneapolis, MN 55408
Executive: Dawn Hopkins
ph 612/377-8445
f 612/377-2581
dawn@aerialistpress.com
www.aerialistpress.com
ISBN prefix: 978-0-9762184

Alyson Books

245 West 17th Street, Suite 1200
New York, NY 10011
Executive: Dale Cunningham
ph 212/242-8100
f 212/727-7939
mail@alyson.com
www.alyson.com
ISBN prefixes: 978-1-55583, 978-0-932870,
    978-0-917597, 978-1-59350

AK Press

674-A 23rd Street
Oakland, CA 94612-1163
ph 510/208-1700
f 510/208-1701
publishing@akpress.org
www.akpress.org
ISBN prefixes: 978-1-902593, 978-1-873176,
    978-1-904859, 978-0-972742

Anvil Press Poetry

Neptune House
70 Royal Hill
London SE10 8RF
UNITED KINGDOM
Executive: Peter Jay
ph 011 44 (0) 208 469 3033
f 011 44 (0) 208 469 3363
info@anvilpresspoetry.com
www.anvilpresspoetry.com
ISBN prefixes: 978-0-85646, 978-0-900977

Archipelago Books
25 Jay Street #203
Brooklyn, NY 11201
Executive: Jill Schoolman
ph 718/852-6134
f 718/852-6135
info@archipelagobooks.org
www. archipelagobooks.org
ISBN prefixes: 978-0-9778576,
978-0-9749680, 978-0-9763950,
978-0-97286

Ausable Press
1026 Hurricane Rd
Keene, NY 12942
Executive: Chase Twichell
ph 518/576-9273
f 518/576-9227
editor@ausablepress.org
www.ausablepress.org
ISBN prefixes: 978-0-9672668, 978-1-931337

Arsenal Pulp Press
341 Water Street, Suite 200
Vancouver, BC V6B 1B8
CANADA
Executive: Brian Lam
ph 888/600-7857
f 604/687-4283
info@arsenalpulp.com
www.arsenalpulp.com
ISBN prefixes: 978-0-88978, 978-1-55152

ARSENAL
PULP PRESS

Bellevue Literary Press
Department of Medicine
New York University School of Medicine
550 First Avenue
New York, NY 10016
Executive: Jerome Lowenstein
ph 212/263-7802
f 212/263-7803
egoldman@blreview.org
www.blreview.org
ISBN prefix: 978-1-934137

ArtNetwork
PO Box 1360
Nevada City, CA 95959
Executive: Constance Smith
ph 800/383-0677, 530/470-0862
f 530/470-0256
info@artmarketing.com
http://artmarketing.com
ISBN prefix: 978-0-940899

Bitter Lemon Press
37 Arundel Gardens
London, W11 2LW
UNITED KINGDOM
Executive: François von Hurter
ph 011 44 (0) 207 727 7927
f 011 44 (0) 207 460 2164
fvh@bitterlemonpress.com
www.bitterlemonpress.com
ISBN prefix: 978-1-904738

Aunt Lute Books
P.O. Box 410687
San Francisco, CA 94141
Executive: Joan Pinkvoss
ph 415/826-1300
f 415/826-8300
books@auntlute.com
www.auntlute.com
ISBN prefixes: 978-1-879960,
978-0-933216

Black Rose Books
CP 1258
Succ. Place du Parc
Montréal, QC H2X 4A7
CANADA
Executive: Dimitrios Roussopoulos
ph 514/844-4076
f 514/849-4797
info@blackrosebooks.net
www.blackrosebooks.net
ISBN prefixes: 978-0-919618,
978-0-919619, 978-0-920057,
978-0-921689, 978-1-895431,
978-1-55164, 978-1-551640

BOA Editions, Ltd.
260 East Avenue
Rochester, NY 14604
Executive: Nora A. Jones
ph 585/546-3410
f 585/546-3913
info@boaeditions.org
www.boaeditions.org
ISBN prefixes: 978-0-918526,
    978-1-880238, 978-0-9665639,
    978-1-929918, 978-1-934414

Center for Environmental Structure Publishing
2701 Shasta Road
Berkeley, CA 94708
Executive: Randall Schmidt
ph 510/841-6166
f 510/841-8668
rs@patternlanguage.com
www.patternlanguage.com
ISBN prefix: 978-0-9726529

Breakaway Books
P.O. Box 24
Halcottsville, NY 12438
Executive: Garth Battista
ph 800/548-4348
f 212/898-0408
breakawaybooks@gmail.com
www.breakawaybooks.com
ISBN prefixes: 978-1-891369, 978-1-55821

Central Park Media
250 West 57th Street Suite 1723
New York, New York 10107
Executive: John O'Donnell
ph 646/957-8301
f 646/957-8316
info@teamcpm.com
www.centralparkmedia.com
ISBN prefixes: 978-1-58644, 978-1-56219,
    978-1-933440, 978-1-57800

Bywater Books
P.O. Box 3671
Ann Arbor, MI 48106
Executives: Kelly Smith and Marianne K. Martin
ph 866/390-7426
into@bywaterbooks.com
www.bywaterbooks.com
ISBN prefix: 978-1-932859

Chin Music Press
2621 24th Ave W
Seattle, WA 98199
Executive: Bruce Rutledge
ph 206/784-4700
f 206/784-4700
bruce@chinmusicpress.com
www.chinmusicpress.com
ISBN prefix: 978-0-9741995

CALYX Books
P.O. Box B
Corvallis, OR 97339
Executive: Margarita Donnelly
ph 541/753-9384
f 541/753-0515
calyx@proaxis.com
www.calyxpress.org
ISBN prefix: 978-0-934971

Chris Boot
79 Arbuthnot Road
London, SE14 5NP
UNITED KINGDOM
Executive: Chris Boot
ph 011 44 (0) 207 639 2907
f 011 44 (0) 207 358 0519
info@chrisboot.com
www.chrisboot.com
ISBN prefixes: 978-0-9542813,
    978-0-9546894, 978-0-905712

Cinco Puntos Press
701 Texas Ave
El Paso, TX 79901
Executives: Bobby and Lee Byrd
ph 915/838-1625
f 915/838-1635
info@cincopuntos.com
www.cincopuntos.com
ISBN prefix: 978-0-938317, 978-1-933693

 **contrasto**

Contrasto
Via degli Scialoia, 3
Rome, ITALY 00196
Executive: Roberto Koch
ph 011 39 (0) 632 8281
f 011 39 (0) 632 828 240
rkoch@contrasto.it
www.contrastobooks.com
ISBN prefixes: 978-88-89032,
978-88-86982, 978-88-6965

City Lights Publishers
261 Columbus Avenue
San Francisco, CA 94133
Executive: Elaine Katzenberger
ph 415/362-1901
f 415/362-4921
staff@citylights.com
www.citylights.com
ISBN prefixes: 978-0-87286, 978-0-912516,
978-0-87704, 978-1-931404

Copper Canyon Press
P.O. Box 271
Port Townsend, WA 98368
Executive: Michael Wiegers
ph 360/385-4925
f 360/385-4985
poetry@coppercanyonpress.org
www.coppercanyonpress.org
ISBN prefixes: 978-0-914742, 978-1-55659,
978-0-9663395, 978-0-9718981,
978-0-9776395

Coffee House Press
27 N. Fourth St.
Suite 400
Minneapolis, MN 55401
Executive: Allan Kornblum
ph 612/338-0125
f 612/338-4004
allan@coffeehousepress.org
www.coffeehousepress.org
ISBN prefixes: 978-0-915124,
978-0-918273, 978-1-56689

Curbstone Press
321 Jackson Street
Willimantic, CT 06226
Executives: Sandy Taylor and Judith Doyle
ph 860/423-5110
f 860/423-9242
info@curbstone.org
www.curbstone.org
ISBN prefixes: 978-1-880684,
978-0-915306, 978-1-931896

Common Courage Press
121 Red Barn Road
P.O. Box 702
Monroe, ME 04951
Executive: Greg Bates
ph 207/525-0900
f 207/525-3068
gbates@commoncouragepress.com
www.commoncouragepress.com
ISBN prefixes: 978-0-9628838,
978-1-56751

de.MO

de.MO
123 Nine Partners Lane
Millbrook, NY 12545
Executive: Giorgio Baravalle
ph 845/677-2075
f 845/677-2077
mailbox@de-mo.org
www.de-mo.org
ISBN prefixes: 978-0-9705768,
978-0-9742836, 978-0-9791800

Dewi Lewis Publishing

8 Broomfield Road
Heaton Moor
Stockport, SK4 4ND
UNITED KINGDOM
Executive: Dewi Lewis
ph 011 44 (0) 161 442 9450
f 011 44 (0) 161 442 9450
mail@dewilewispublishing.com
www.dewilewispublishing.com
ISBN prefixes: 978-1-899235,
    978-1-904587, 978-0-948797

Eighth Mountain Press

624 Southeast 29th Ave.
Portland, OR 97214
Executive: Ruth Gundle
ph 503/233-3936
f 503/233-0774
eighthmt@pacifier.com
ISBN prefix: 978-0-933377

The Disinformation Company

220 East 23rd Street
Suite 500
New York, NY 10010
Executive: Gary Baddeley
ph 212/691-1605
f 212/691-1606
books@disinfo.com
www.disinfo.com
ISBN prefixes: 978-0-9713942,
    978-0-9664100, 978-1-932857,
    978-0-9729529

Enigma Books

580 Eighth Avenue, 21st Floor
New York, NY 10018
Executive: Robert L. Miller
ph 212/575-9100
f 212/575-9104
editor@enigmabooks.com
www.enigmabooks.com
ISBN prefix: 978-1-929631

DramaQueen, LLC

11045 Lands Walk Drive Suite 103
Houston, TX 77099
Executives: Tran Nguyen and Isabel Kim
ph 800/883-1518
f 281/498-4723
tranbn@onedramaqueen.com
isabel@onedramaqueen.com
www.onedramaqueen.com
ISBN prefixes: 978-0-9766045,
    978-1-933809, 978-1-60331

Europa Editions

116 East 16th Street, 6th Floor
New York, NY 10003
Executives: Sandro Ferri and Kent Carroll
ph 212/477-8242
f 212/228-4744
info@europaeditions.com
www.europaeditions.com
ISBN prefix: 978-1-933372

Editions Intervalles

80 Boulevard Haussmann
75008 Paris
FRANCE
Executive: Armand de Saint Sauveur
ph 011 33 (0) 153 438 330
f 011 33 (0) 153 430 595
stsauveur@editionsintervalles.com
www.editionsintervalles.com
ISBN prefix: 978-2-916355

The Feminist Press at CUNY

365 Fifth Avenue, Suite 5406
New York, NY 10016
Executive: Gloria Jacobs
ph 212/817-7915
f 212/817-1593
GJacobs@gc.cuny.edu
sales@feministpress.org
www.feministpress.org
ISBN prefixes: 978-0-912670,
    978-0-935312, 978-1-55861

Feral House

2131 Lyric Avenue
Los Angeles, CA 90027
Executive: Adam Parfrey
ph 323/666-3311
f 323/666-3330
ap@feralhouse.com
www.feralhouse.com
ISBN prefixes: 978-0-922915,
   978-1-932595

The Gryphon Press

6808 Margarets Lane
Edina, MN 55439
Executive: Emilie Buchwald
f 952/941-6593
eb6@earthlink.net
ISBN prefix: 978-0-940719

fiveTIES

Five Ties Publishing

396 Twelfth Street, 2L
Brooklyn, NY 11215
Executive: Garrett White
ph 347/529-5077
f 267/501-7658
editor@fiveties.com
www.fiveties.com
ISBN prefix: 978-0-9777193

Haymarket Books

4015 North Rockwell Avenue
Chicago, IL 60618
ph 773/583-7884
f 773/583-6144
info@haymarketbooks.org
www.haymarketbooks.org
ISBN prefix: 978-1-931859

Green Integer

6022 Wilshire Blvd. Suite 202C
Los Angeles, CA 90036
Executive: Douglas Messerli
ph 323/857-1115
f 323/857-0143
info@greeninteger.com
www.greeninteger.com
ISBN prefixes: 978-1-892295, 978-1-55713,
   978-1-931243, 978-1-933382

Headpress

Suite 306, The Colourworks
2a Abbot Street
London, E8 3DP
UNITED KINGDOM
Executive: David Kerekes
ph 011 44 (0) 207 249 1075,
   011 44 (0) 207 275 6001
f 011 44 (0) 207 249 6395
hannah@headpress.com
www.headpress.com
ISBN prefixes: 978-1-900486,
   978-0-9523288

Gryphon House

P.O. Box 207
Beltsville, MD 20704-0207
Executive: Larry Rood
ph 800/638-0928
f 301/595-0051
info@ghbooks.com
www.ghbooks.com
ISBN prefixes: 978-0-87659, 978-1-58904

Helter Skelter Publishing

South Bank House
Black Prince Road
London SE1 7SJ
UNITED KINGDOM
Executive: Sean Body
ph 011 44 (0) 207 463 2204
f 011 44 (0) 207 463 2295
sean@helterskelterbooks.com
www.helterskelterbooks.com
ISBN prefixes: 978-1-900924,
   978-1-902799, 978-1-905139

Holy Cow! Press

P.O. Box 3170
Mt. Royal Station
Duluth, MN 55803
Executive: Jim Perlman
ph 218/724-1653
f 218/724-1653
holycow@holycowpress.org
www.holycowpress.org
ISBN prefix: 978-0-930100, 978-0-9779458

Insomniac Press

192 Spadina Avenue, Suite 403
Toronto, Ontario
CANADA M5T 2C2
Executive: Mike O'Connor
ph 416/504-6270
f 416/504-9313
mike@insomniacpress.com
www.insomniacpress.com
ISBN prefixes: 978-1-894663,
   978-1-895837, 978-1-897178

Ig Publishing

178 Clinton Avenue
Brooklyn, NY 11205
Executives: Robert Lasner and Elizabeth
   Clementson
ph 718/797-0676
f 718/797-0676
igpublishing@earthlink.net
www.igpub.com
ISBN prefixes: 978-0-9703125,
   978-0-9752517, 978-0-9771972,
   978-0-9788431

Joshua Odell Editions

P.O. Box 2158
Santa Barbara, CA 93120
Executive: Joshua Odell
ph 805/966-4606
f 805/966-4627
joshua.odell2@verizon.net
ISBN prefix: 978-1-877741

Image Continuum Press

P.O. Box 51599
Eugene, OR 97405
Executives: David Bayles and Ted Orland
ph 541/344-5955
f 541/344-4493
tno@cruzio.com
www.artandfear.com
ISBN prefix: 978-0-9614547

Kehrer Verlag

Heinsteinwerk Wieblinger Weg 21
69123 Heidelberg, GERMANY
Executive: Klaus Kehrer
ph 011 49 (0) 6221 649 20 18
f 011 49 (0) 6221 649 20 20
contact@kehrerverlag.com
www.kehrerverlag.com
ISBN prefixes: 978-3-933257,
   978-3-936636, 978-3-980444,
   978-3-939583

Immedium, Inc.

P.O. Box 31846
San Francisco, CA 94131-0846
Executive: Oliver Chin
ph 415/452-8546
f 360/937-6272
pr@immedium.com
www.immedium.com
ISBN prefix: 978-1-59702

Leapfrog Press

P.O. Box 1495
95 Commercial St.
Wellfleet, MA 02667
Executive: Ira Wood
ph 508/349-1925
info@leapfrogpress.com
www.leapfrogpress.com
ISBN prefixes: 978-0-9654578,
   978-0-9679520, 978-0-9728984

Long River Press

360 Swift Avenue Suite 48
South San Francisco, CA 94080
Executive: Chris Robyn
ph 650/872-7718 ext. 312
f 650/872-7808
chris@longriverpress.com
www.longriverpress.com
ISBN prefix: 978-1-59265

Marion Boyars Publishers, Ltd.

24 Lacy Road
London, SW15 1NL
UNITED KINGDOM
Executive: Catheryn Kilgarriff
ph 011 44 (0) 208 788 9522
f 011 44 (0) 208 789 8122
catheryn@marionboyars.com
www.marionboyars.co.uk
ISBN prefix: 978-0-7145

Lumen Books

40 Camino Cielo
Santa Fe, NM 87506
Executive: Ronald Christ
ph 505/988-5820
f 505/988-5820
lumenbooks@earthlink.net
www.lumenbooks.org
ISBN prefixes: 978-0-930829, 978-4-7571,
   978-0-936050, 978-84-921103

Melville House Publishing

300 Observer Highway, 3rd Floor
Hoboken, NJ 07030
Executive: Dennis Loy Johnson
ph 201/222-2640
f 201/222-8011
dlj@mhpbooks.com
www.mhpbooks.com
ISBN prefixes: 978-0-9766583,
   978-0-9761407, 978-1-933633

The Magenta Foundation

151 Winchester Street
Toronto, Ontario
CANADA M4X 1B5
Executive: MaryAnn Camilleri
ph 416/925-0310
maryann@magentafoundation.org
www.magentafoundation.org
ISBN prefix: 978-0-9739739

Mercury House

P.O. Box 192850
San Francisco, CA 94119-2850
Director: Jeremy Bigalke
ph 415/626-7874
mercury@mercuryhouse.org
www.mercuryhouse.org
ISBN prefixes: 978-0-916515, 978-1-56279

Manic D Press

P.O. Box 410804
San Francisco, CA 94141
Executive: Jennifer Joseph
ph 415/648-8288
f 415/648-8288
info@manicdpress.com
www.manicdpress.com
ISBN prefixes: 978-1-933149,
   978-0-916397

Methuen Publishing, Ltd.

11-12 Buckingham Gate
London SW1E 6LB
UNITED KINGDOM
Executive: James Stephens
ph 011 44 (0) 207 769 1609
f 011 44 (0) 207 828 2098
www.methuen.co.uk
ISBN prefixes: 978-0-413, 978-0-416,
   978-1-84275, 978-1-902301

Millipede Press
2565 Teller Court
Lakewood, CO 80214
Executive: Jerad Walters
ph 303/231-9720
f 303/231-9720
jerad@millipedepress.com
ISBN prefix: 978-1-933618

New Rivers Press
c/o Minnesota State University
   Moorhead
1104 7th Ave S
Moorhead, MN 56563
Executives: Alan Davis and Wayne
   Gudmundson
ph 218/477-5870
f 218/477-4333
nrp@mnstate.edu
www.newriverspress.com
ISBN prefix: 978-0-89823

Milo Books
The Old Weighbridge
Station Road, Wrea Green
Preston, Lancashire PR4 2PH
UNITED KINGDOM
Executive: Peter Walsh
ph 011 44 (0) 177 267 2900
f 011 44 (0) 177 268 7727
pete@milobooks.com
ISBN prefix: 978-1-903854

New Society Publishers
P.O. Box 189
1680 Peterson Rd.
Gabriola Island, BC, V0R 1X0 CANADA
Executives: Judith Plant and Christopher Plant
ph 250/247-9737
f 250/247-7471
info@newsociety.com
www.newsociety.com
ISBN prefixes: 978-0-86571, 978-1-89804,
   978-1-90217, 978-0-91657, 978-1-88169,
   978-0-97332, 978-0-96641, 978-0-97585,
   978-0-97380, 978-0-97675, 978-0-97733,
   978-0-97719, 978-0-9789257, 978-0-9788848,
   978-0-97390, 978-0-9666783, 978-0-97809

Monkfish Book Publishing
27 Lamoree Rd
Rhinebeck, NY 12572
Executive: Paul Cohen
ph 845/876-4861
Call for fax
bookcohen@aol.com
www.monkfishpublishing.com
ISBN prefixes: 978-0-9726357,
   978-0-9749359, 978-0-9766843

New Village Press
P.O. Box 3049
Oakland, CA 94609
Executive: Lynne Elizabeth
ph 510/420-1361
f 510/420-1361
le@newvillage.net
www.newvillage.net
ISBN prefix: 978-0-9766054

New Internationalist
55 Rectory Road
Oxford OX4 1BW
UNITED KINGDOM
Executive: Daniel Raymond-Barker
ph 011 44 (0) 186 581 1425
f 011 44 (0) 186 579 3152
danrb@newint.org
www.newint.org
ISBN prefixes: 978-1-904456,
   978-1-869847, 978-0-9540499

Ocean Press
GPO Box 3279
Melbourne, Victoria 3001 AUSTRALIA
Executive: David Deutschmann
ph 011 61 (0) 3 9326 4280
f 011 61 (0) 3 9329 5040
info@oceanbooks.com.au
www.oceanbooks.com.au
ISBN prefixes: 978-1-876175, 978-1-875284,
   978-1-920888, 978-1-921235

PARIS
————
PRESS

Paris Press
P.O. Box 487
Ashfield, MA 01330
Executive: Jan Freeman
ph 413/628-0051
f 413/628-0051
info@parispress.org
www.parispress.org
ISBN prefixes: 978-0-9638183,
   978-1-930464

Process
PO Box 39910
Los Angeles, CA 90039
Executives: Jodi Wille and Adam Parfrey
ph 323/666-3377
f 323/666-3330
www.processmediainc.com
ISBN prefixes: 978-0-9760822,
   978-0-9664272, 978-1-934170

Paul Dry Books
117 South 17th Street, Suite 1102
Philadelphia, PA 19103
Executive: Paul Dry
ph 215/231-9939
f 215/231-9942
pdb@pauldrybooks.com
www.pauldrybooks.com
ISBN prefixes: 978-0-9664913,
   978-0-9679675, 978-1-58988

Red Crane Books
P.O. Box 33950
Santa Fe, NM 87594
Executive: Michael O'Shaughnessy
ph 505/988-7070
f 505/989-7476
publish@redcrane.com
www.redcrane.com
ISBN prefix: 978-1-878610

Pegasus Books
45 Wall Street, Suite 1021
New York, NY 10005
Executive: Claiborne Hancock
ph 212/747-6717
f 212/747-6718
claiborne@pegasusbooks.us
www.pegasusbooks.us
ISBN prefix: 978-1-933648

Redleaf Press
10 Yorkton Court
St. Paul, MN 55117
Executive: Linda Hein
ph 800/423-8309
f 800/641-0115
sales@redleafpress.org
www.redleafpress.org
ISBN prefixes: 978-1-929610, 978-1-884834,
   978-0-934140, 978-1-933653

Pond Press
1140 Washington Street
Boston, MA 02118
Executive: Henry Horenstein
ph 617/426-4222
f 617/426-1176
info@pondpress.com
www.pondpress.com
ISBN prefixes: 978-0-9666776,
   978-0-9761955

SAF Publishing, Ltd.
149 Wakeman Road
London, NW10 5BH
UNITED KINGDOM
ph 011 44 (0) 208 969 6099
f 011 44 (0) 208 354 3132
info@safpublishing.com
www.safpublishing.com
ISBN prefix: 978-0-946719

Saqi Books

26 Westbourne Grove
London W2 5RH
UNITED KINGDOM
Executive: Ashley Biles
ph 011 44 (0) 207 221 9347
f 011 44 (0) 207 229 2911
ashley@telegrambooks.com
www.saqibooks.com
ISBN prefixes: 978-0-86356, 978-1-87339

Small Beer Press

176 Prospect Avenue
Northampton, MA 01060
Executives: Gavin J. Grant and Kelly Link
ph 413/584-0299
f 413/584-2662
info@lcrw.net
www.lcrw.net
ISBN prefix: 978-1-931520

Sarabande Books

2234 Dundee Road, Suite 200
Louisville, KY 40205
Executive: Sarah Gorham
ph 502/458-4028
f 502/458-4065
info@sarabandebooks.org
www.sarabandebooks.org
ISBN prefixes: 978-0-9641151,
   978-1-889330, 978-1-932511

Snowbooks Ltd.

120 Pentonville Road
London N1 9JN
UNITED KINGDOM
Executive: Gilly Barnard
ph 011 44 (0) 207 837 6482
f 011 44 (0) 207 837 6348
info@snowbooks.com
www.snowbooks.com
ISBN prefixes: 978-0-9545759,
   978-1-905005

Serpent's Tail

3A Exmouth House
Pine Street
London, EC1R OJH
UNITED KINGDOM
Executive: Peter Ayrton
ph 011 44 (0) 207 841 6300
f 011 44 (0) 207 833 3969
info@serpentstail.com
www.serpentstail.com
ISBN prefixes: 978-1-85242,
   978-0-9631095

Soho Press

853 Broadway
New York, NY 10003
Executives: Juris Jurjevics and Laura Hruska
ph 212/260-1900
f 212/260-1902
www.sohopress.com
soho@sohopress.com
ISBN prefixes: 978-1-56947, 978-0-93914,
   978-9-627160, 978-9-628783

Seven Stories Press

140 Watts Street
New York, NY 10013
Executive: Dan Simon
ph 212/226-8760
f 212/226-1411
www.sevenstories.com
ISBN prefixes: 978-1-58322, 978-1-888363

South End Press

7 Brookline Street #1
Cambridge, MA 02139
ph 617/547-4002
f 617/547-1333
southend@southendpress.org
www.southendpress.org
ISBN prefixes: 978-0-89608, 978-0-8467,
   978-1-878825

Speck Press

P.O. Box 102004
Denver, CO 80250
Executive: Derek Lawrence
ph 800/996-9783
f 800/996-9783
books@speckpress.com
www.speckpress.com
ISBN prefixes: 978-0-9725776, 978-1-933108

Theatre Communications Group

520 Eighth Ave; 24th Floor
New York, NY 10018-4156
Executive: Terry Nemeth
ph 212/609-5900
f 212/609-5901
tcg@tcg.org
www.tcg.org
ISBN prefixes: 978-0-930452, 978-1-55936, 978-1-85459, 978-0-913745, 978-0-9515877, 978-0-88754, 978-1-870259, 978-1-84002, 978-0-9536757, 978-0-8018, 978-0-921368, 978-0-933826, 978-0-952544, 978-0-9542330, 978-0-9546912, 978-0-9630126, 978-0-9666152, 978-1-55554, 978-0-9773074, 978-0-9551566

Stone Bridge Press

P.O. Box 8208
Berkeley, CA 94707
Executive: Peter Goodman
ph 510/524-8732
f 510/524-8711
sbp@stonebridge.com
www.stonebridge.com
ISBN prefixes: 978-1-880656, 978-0-9628137, 978-4-89684, 978-4-925080, 978-1-933330, 978-0-89346

Trellis Publishing

2701 Minnesota Avenue
Duluth, MN 55802
Executive: Mary Koski
ph 800/513-0115
f 218/722-3184
trellis2@aol.com
www.trellispublishing.com
ISBN prefixes: 978-1-930650, 978-0-9663281

Tara Publishing

38/GA Shoreham
5th Avenue, Besant Nagar
Chennai 600 090
INDIA
Executive: Gita Wolf
ph 011 91 44 2440 1696
f 011 91 44 2445 3658
mail@tarabooks.com
www.tarabooks.com
ISBN prefix: 978-81-86211

Tupelo Press

P.O. Box 539
Dorset, VT 05251
Executive: Jeffrey Levine
ph 802/366-8185
f 802/362-1883
publisher@tupelopress.org
www.tupelopress.org
ISBN prefixes: 978-0-9710310, 978-1-932195

Telegram

26 Westbourne Grove
London W2 5RH
UNITED KINGDOM
Executive: Ashley Biles
ph 011 44 (0) 207 229 2911
f 011 44 (0) 207 229 7492
ashley@telegrambooks.com
www.telegrambooks.com
ISBN prefix: 978-1-84659

Turtle Point Press

233 Broadway, Room 946
New York, NY 10279
Executive: Jonathan Rabinowitz
Executive for Helen Marx Books: Helen Marx
ph 212/945-6622
f 212/285-1019
countomega@aol.com
helenmarxbooks@aol.com
www.turtlepointpress.com
ISBN prefixes: 978-0-9627987, 978-1-885983, 978-1-885586, 978-1-933527

Umbrage Editions

515 Canal Street
New York, NY 10013
Executive: Nan Richardson
ph 212/965-0197
f 212/965-0276
nan@umbragebooks.com
www.umbragebooks.com
ISBN prefix: 978-1-884167

Windhorse Publications

11 Park Road, Moseley
Birmingham B13 8AB
UNITED KINGDOM
Executive: Sara Hagel
ph 011 44 (0) 845 458 9514
f 011 44 (0) 121 449 9191
sales@windhorsepublications.com
www.windhorsepublications.com
ISBN prefixes: 978-1-899579, 978-0-904766

Wave Books

WAVE BOOKS

1938 Fairview Avenue East
Seattle, WA 98102
Executives: Joshua Beckman,
  Matthew Zapruder
ph 206/676-5337
info@wavepoetry.com
www.wavepoetry.com, www.versepress.org
ISBN prefixes: 978-1-933517,
  978-0-9703672, 978-0-9723487,
  978-0-9746353

The Witches' Almanac

243 Knight Street
Providence, RI 02909
Executive: Andrew S. Theitic
ph 401/847-3388
f 888/897-3388
theitic@thewitchesalmanac.com
ISBN prefix: 978-1-881098, 978-0-9773703,
  978-0-9709013

White Pine Press

P.O. Box 236
Buffalo, NY 14201
Executive: Dennis Maloney
ph 716/627-4665
f 716/627-4665
wpine@whitepine.org
www.whitepine.org
ISBN prefixes: 978-1-877727, 978-0-934834,
  978-1-877800, 978-1-893996,
  978-0-913089

Zephyr Press

50 Kenwood St.
Brookline, MA 02446
Executives: Cris Mattison, Jim Kates, and
  Leora Zeitlin
ph 617/713-2813
f 617/713-2813
editor@zephyrpress.org
www.zephyrpress.org
ISBN prefixes: 978-0-939010,
  978-0-9533824, 978-0-9706250,
  978-0-9761612, 978-0-9545367

Vice President, Sales

Jim Nichols
Consortium Book Sales & Distribution
1045 Westgate Drive
St. Paul, MN 55114
ph 651/221-9035
f 651/917-6406

Midwest

Stuart Abraham
Abraham Associates
51202 Cedar Lake Road
St. Louis Park, MN 55416
ph 952/927-7920; 800-701-2409
f 952/927-8089

Steven Horwitz
Abraham Associates
2209 Dayton Avenue
St. Paul, MN 55104
ph 651/647-1712
f 651/647-1717
steve@abrahamassociatesinc.com

Roy Schonfeld
Abraham Associates
2084 Miramar Blvd.
South Euclid, OH 44121
ph 216/291-3538
f 216/691-0548

John Mesjak
Abraham Associates
509 Edward Street
Sycamore, IL 60178
ph 815/889-0079
f 845/350-7112

New England & Upstate New York

Melissa Carl
810 Boalsburg Pike
Boalsburg, PA 16827
ph 617/784-0375
f 814/466-2711
melissa.carl@verizon.net

Stephen Williamson
New England Book Reps/Rovers LLC
68 Main Street
Acton, MA 01720-3540
ph 978/263-7723
f 978/263-7721
WWABooks@aol.com

Mid-Atlantic & New York

Dan Fallon
Rovers LLC
184 Thelma Ave.
Merrick, NY 11566
ph 516/868-7826
f 516/868-7826
Fallonbks@aol.com

Bill Jordan
Rovers LLC
2937 Ogden St.
Philadelphia, PA 19130
ph 215/829-1642
f 703/995-0429; 215/243-7319
wejrover@verizon.net

West Coast

Dory Dutton
The Karel/Dutton Group
4911 Morella Avenue
Valley Village, CA 91607
ph 818/762-7170
f 818/508-5608

Bob Harrison
The Karel/Dutton Group
PMB 264
10115 Greenwood Avenue North
Seattle, WA 98133
ph 206/542-1545
f 206/546-5716
bharrison451@earthlink.net

Howard Karel
The Karel/Dutton Group
3145 Geary Blvd. #619
San Francisco, CA 94118
ph 415/668-0829
f 415/668-2463

Lise Solomon
The Karel/Dutton Group
1047 Stannage Ave
Albany, CA 94706
ph 510/528-0579
f 510/528-0254

Ellen Towell
The Karel/Dutton Group
3145 Geary Blvd. #619
San Francisco, CA 94118
ph 415/668-0829
f 415/668-2463

David Waag
The Karel/Dutton Group
749 South Lemay Avenue
Suite A3 PMB 357
Ft. Collins, CO 80524
ph 970/484-5372
f 970/484-3482

Mid-South & Southeast

Bill McClung
Bill McClung & Associates
PMB 607
20475 Highway 46 W # 180
Spring Branch, TX 78070-6147
ph 830/438-8482
f 830/438-8483
bmcclung@ix.netcom.com

Terri McClung
Bill McClung & Associates
PMB 607
20475 Highway 46 W # 180
Spring Branch, TX 78070
ph 830/438-8482
f 830/438-8483
tmcclung@ix.netcom.com

Amanda Armstrong
Bill McClung & Associates
PMB 371
4636 Lebanon Pike
Hermitage, TN 37076
ph 615/874-0400
f 615/871-7072

Patricia Ryan
Bill McClung & Associates
1270 Caroline St. NE, Suite D120-222
Atlanta, GA 30307
ph 337/344-2908

Rachel Carner
Bill McClung & Associates
3904 North Druid Hills Road, Suite 332
Decatur, GA 30033
ph 917/282-4460

Canada

**Sandra Hargreaves/
Colin Fuller/Steve Paton**
Hargreaves, Fuller & Paton
4335 West 10th Ave Ste #13
Vancouver, BC V6R 2H6
ph 604/222-2955
f 604/222-2965
harful@telus.net

Terry Fernihough
Hargreaves, Fuller & Paton
463 East Moodie Drive
Nepean, ON K2H 8T7
ph 613/721-9236
f 613/721-9827
fernihough@storm.ca

Jerry Trainer/Leona Trainer
Hargreaves, Fuller & Paton
16 Bethley Dr.
Scarborough, ON M1E 3M7
ph 416/287-3146
f 416/287-0081

Karen Stacey
Hargreaves, Fuller & Paton
8-4652 Rue Sherbrook Ouest
Montreal, PQ H3Z 1G3
ph 514/704-3626

EDUCATION & TEACHING

ENVIRONMENTAL STUDIES

Building Radar, 259
Fields of Deception, 259

MUSIC

MYSTERY

NEW AGE

OCCULTISM & PARAPSYCHOLOGY

PARENTING

PETS & PET CARE

PHILOSOPHY

PHOTOGRAPHY

POETRY

Consortium Book Sales & Distribution is the exclusive distributor for more than 90 independent publishers from the United States, Canada, the United Kingdom, Europe, India, and Australia. Books are represented by the Consortium sales force in the United States and Canada. In addition to sales and distribution services, we provide marketing, promotional, and event support.

Catalog produced by Stanton Publication Services, Inc., Minneapolis, Minnesota.

Catalog designed by Consortium Book Sales & Distribution and

Stanton Publication Services, Inc.